ICE TRILOGY

VLADIMIR SOROKIN

Translated by
JAMEY GAMBRELL

NEW YORK REVIEW BOOKS

New York

THIS IS A NEW YORK REVIEW BOOK
PUBLISHED BY THE NEW YORK REVIEW OF BOOKS
435 Hudson Street, New York, NY 10014
www.nyrb.com

Originally published in Russian as *Put' Bro*, *Led*, and *23,000*

Library of Congress Cataloging-in-Publication Data
Sorokin, Vladimir, 1955–
[Novels. English. Selections.]
Ice trilogy / by Vladimir Sorokin ; translated by Jamey Gambrell.
    p. cm. — (New York Review Books classics)
ISBN 978-1-59017-386-2 (alk. paper)
1. Brotherhoods—Fiction. 2. Extremists—Fiction. 3. Sorokin, Vladimir,
1955– —Translations into English. I. Gambrell, Jamey. II. Sorokin, Vladimir,
1955– Lëd. English. III. Sorokin, Vladimir, 1955– Put' Bro. English. IV. Sorokin,
Vladimir, 1955– 23 000. English. V. Title.
PG3488.O66A2 2011
891.73—dc22
                        2010044726

ISBN 978-1-59017-386-2

Printed in the United States of America on acid-free paper.
10 9 8 7 6 5 4 3 2 1

NEW YORK REVIEW BOOKS
CLASSICS

ICE TRILOGY

VLADIMIR SOROKIN was born in a small town outside of Moscow in 1955. He trained as an engineer at the Moscow Institute of Oil and Gas, but turned to art and writing, becoming a major presence in the Moscow underground of the 1980s. His work was banned in the Soviet Union, and his first novel, *The Queue*, was published by the famed émigré dissident Andrei Sinyavsky in France in 1983. In 1992, Sorokin's *Collected Stories* was nominated for the Russian Booker Prize; in 1999, the publication of the controversial novel *Blue Lard*, which included a sex scene between clones of Stalin and Khrushchev, led to public demonstrations against the book and to demands that Sorokin be prosecuted as a pornographer; in 2001, he received the Andrei Biely Award for outstanding contributions to Russian literature. Sorokin is also the author of the screenplays for the movies *Moscow*, *The Kopeck*, and *4*, and of the libretto for Leonid Desyatnikov's *Rosenthal's Children*, the first new opera to be commissioned by the Bolshoi Theater since the 1970s. He has written numerous plays and short stories, and his work has been translated throughout the world. Among his most recent books are *Sugar Kremlin* and *Day of the Oprichnik*. He lives in Moscow.

JAMEY GAMBRELL is a writer on Russian art and culture. Her translations include Marina Tsvetaeva's *Earthly Signs: Moscow Diaries, 1917–1922*; a volume of Aleksandr Rodchenko's writings, *Experiments for the Future*; and Tatyana Tolstaya's novel, *The Slynx*. Her translation of Vladimir Sorokin's *Day of the Oprichnik* will be published in 2011.

CONTENTS

Out of whose womb came the ice?
And the hoary frost of heaven, who hath gendered it?

Job 38:29

And so, brethren, let us lay aside works of darkness,
and turn to works of the light.

Saint Gregory Palamas,
Bishop of Thessaloniki (1296–1359)

BRO

Childhood

I WAS BORN June 30, 1908, on the estate of my father, Dmitry Ivanovich Snegirev. By that time my father had made his name as the
largest Russian sugar producer and owned two estates—in Vaskelovo, near Petersburg, where I was born, and in Basantsy, in the
Ukraine, where I was destined to spend my childhood. In addition,
our family had a small but comfortable wooden house in Moscow on
Ostozhenka Street and a huge apartment on Millionnaya Street in
Petersburg.

Father built the estate in Basantsy himself during the "troglodyte
era of the sugar business," when he bought about two thousand hect-
ares of fertile Ukrainian land for sugar beets. He was the first Russian
sugar producer to acquire his own plantations rather than buy up
beetroot from the peasants in the old way. He and Grandfather built
a sugar factory there as well. There wasn't much need for a large house
since the family was already living in the capital. But Grandfather,
cautious as always, insisted it was necessary, repeating that "in hard
times like these, the master should be closer to the beetroots and the
factory."

Father never liked Basantsy. "The land of Ukie flies," he often said.

"Those flies are swarming to your sugar!" Mother would laugh.

There were flies enough for everyone, that's for sure. Summers
were hot. But the winters were wonderful—mild and snowy.

Father acquired the estate in Vaskelovo later, when he had already
become truly wealthy. The house was stern and old-fashioned, with
columns and two wings. It was there I was destined to appear in this
world, prematurely as it turned out: Mother gave birth to me two

weeks early. According to her, the reason was the extraordinary weather that day, June 30. Despite a cloudless sky and no wind, claps of distant thunder sounded. This thunder was unusual: Mama not only heard it, she *felt it* through her fetus, that is, through me.

"It was as though the thunder gave you a push," she would tell me. "You were born easily and weighed as much as a full-term baby."

The following night, July 1, the northern part of the sky was unusually and brightly illuminated, in fact there was not really any night at all; the evening dusk was followed immediately by the dawn. It was very strange—usually the white nights begin to shorten by the end of June.

My mother joked: "The sky lit up in your honor."

She gave birth to me on the hard, always cool leather sofa in Father's office: the labor pains caught her in the middle of "a silly conversation about an old flower bed and a new gardener." Directly across from this sofa there was a floor-to-ceiling wall of oak shelves laden with cones of sugar. Each cone was poured from the sugar of its crop and weighed a pood. Each bore the stamp of its year. These massive white cones of hard sugar were probably the first thing I saw in this world. In any event, they entered my childhood memory on par with images of my mother and father.

I was christened Alexander in honor of the Russian saint and military commander Alexander Nevsky and in memory of my great-grandfather Alexander Savvich, the founder of the Snegirev family's merchant trade. Everyone called me something different: my father called me Alexander; my mother, Shura; my aunt, Sashenka; my sisters, Shurenka; my older brothers Vasily and Vanya called me Sanya; Madame Panaget, the governess, called me Sashá; the horse trainer Frol, Liaxander Dmitrich; the groom Gavrila, the young master.

There were seven children in the family: four sons and three daughters, one of whom, Nastya, was hunchbacked. Another boy died from polio at the age of five.

I was a late child—the oldest of my brothers, Vasily, was seventeen years older than I.

My father was a tall, balding, gloomy man with long, powerful hands. His personality combined great energy, thoroughness, melancholy introspection, crudeness, and ambition. Sometimes he reminded me of a machine that periodically broke down, repaired itself, and once again began working properly. He worshipped progress and sent the managers of four of his plants to study in England. But he didn't like to go abroad himself, saying that "over there you have to walk a tightrope." He had no ear whatsoever for languages and knew only a few dozen memorized phrases in French. Mother said that he became disoriented abroad and felt ill at ease. Father came from an old merchant family of Saratov grain traders who gradually became manufacturers. The large Snegirev family owned four sugar plants, a confectioner's factory, and steam ships. In his youth, Father studied in the Polytechnic Department of Saratov University, but he dropped out after the third year for unknown reasons. He immediately harnessed himself to the family business. Once every two months he would descend into a depressed drinking binge (fortunately, never for more than three days), often smashing furniture and cursing Mother ferociously, but never raising his hand against her. When he sobered up, he would ask her forgiveness, go to the bathhouse and then to church—to repent. But he wasn't particularly religious.

He didn't deal with the children at all. We were in the care of Mother, nurses, governesses, and the endless relatives with which the two estates teemed.

My mother was an example of the self-sacrificing Russian woman who ignores herself in order to take care of the children and see to the family's welfare. Endowed with remarkable beauty (she was half Ossetian, half southern Cossack), an ardent heart, and an open soul, she gave her selfless love first to my father, who fell head over heels in love with her at the Nizhny Novgorod fair, then to us, the children. Moreover, Mother was hospitable to a fault: any guest who happened to drop in was never allowed to simply leave.

Although I grew up as the youngest in the family, I wasn't the most loved: Father favored clever, obedient Ilya, designating him as his successor; Mother adored handsome, gentle Vanyusha, who loved cherry dumplings and books about kings. Father considered the athletic jester Vasily a rake with nothing but "imps in his pea brain," and me a loafer. The personalities of my three sisters were almost indistinguishable:

energetic, life-loving, moderately egocentric, and impressionable, they could shed tears and giggle with equal ease. All three of them were passionately musical, and in this area hunchbacked Nastenka excelled, preparing for a serious career as a pianist. My sisters differed only in their relations with Father. The eldest, Arisha, worshipped him; the middle sister, Vasilisa, was afraid of him; and Nastya hated him.

The family lived in four places: Vasily in Moscow, where he was endlessly struggling with his law studies; Vasilisa and Arisha in Petersburg; Vanya and Ilya in Vaskelovo; and Nastya and I in Basantsy.

I lived and was educated at the country manor until age nine. In addition to the French governess, who taught me foreign languages and music, I had a tutor, Didenko—a homely young man with provincial manners and a soft, ingratiating voice; he taught me everything he knew. He liked to talk about great warriors and the heavenly bodies most of all. Speaking of Hannibal's campaigns and solar eclipses, he was transformed and his eyes shone. By the time I entered the gymnasium I knew a good deal about Attila the Hun and Alexander of Macedonia, and the difference between Jupiter and Saturn. Russian and arithmetic were more problematic.

My pre-gymnasium childhood was quite happy. The warm, abundant nature of the Ukraine rocked me like a cradle: I caught birds and fish with the sons of the estate managers, traveled along the Dnepr on an English launch with Father, collected a herbarium with the French governess, had fun and played music with Nastya, went to the sugar-beet fields and to watch the haymaking with the horse trainer, went to church with Mother and my aunts, learned to horseback ride with the groom, and in the evening observed the stars with Didenko.

In August the whole family would gather in Vaskelovo.

The southern Ukrainian landscape gave way to the Russian north, and instead of chestnut and poplar trees our white house with columns was surrounded by stern, gloomy fir trees, between whose centuries-old trunks the lake glinted. A long stone staircase led from the house to the lake. Sitting on its moss-covered steps and hanging my legs over the water, I loved to toss stones into the lake, watching how a circle is born and, widening swiftly, slips across the glassy surface, heading for the stony banks.

The lake was always cold and calm. But our large family was raucous and vociferous, like a flock of spring birds. Our morose, taciturn father seemed the only ominous crow in the flock. I felt comfortable in this circle of relatives, which, like the circles on the water, widened every day, filling both estates with newly acquired relations and relations of those relations. Father's wealth, Mother's hospitality and tenderheartedness, and our domestic comfort and prosperity all attracted people like honey. Dependents, both men and women, traveling monks and alcoholic actors, merchant widows, and gambling majors down on their luck buzzed about the parlors and outbuildings like a swarm of bees. On weekdays, when we sat down to eat, the table was usually set for about twenty people. On holidays and saints' days, three tables were moved into the dining room at the northern estate, while in Basantsy the tables were taken out into the garden, under the apple trees.

Father didn't object to this. Most likely he enjoyed this style of life. But I never saw any pleasure on his face during these family feasts. He only laughed or cried when he was very drunk. I never heard Father say the word "happiness." Was he happy? I don't know.

My mother was unquestionably happy. Her bright, creative spirit, overflowing with love for mankind, floated and soared above us all, though she often said that "happiness—is when there's so much to do there's no time to think."

I grew up healthy and happy in this human hive.

Like Mother, I didn't think about things much. I was too busy jumping off the groom's dusty two-wheeled cart on a July afternoon and racing through a suite of cool rooms to the sound of Barcaroles with a bouquet of wild strawberries I'd just picked in distant glades and tied with grass to present to Nastya at the piano; at the same time I'd place a snail or a beetle on her hump, which made her scream and spray me with milk while beating me with the score of *The Four Seasons*. Then we would make up and eat berries together on the sunwarmed windowsill.

Only one thing scared and attracted me in childhood.

I had a recurring dream: I saw myself at the foot of a huge mountain, so high and boundless that my legs grew *limp*. The mountain was *frightfully* big. It was so big that I began to sweat and crumble like dried bread. Its summit disappeared into the blue sky. The summit was *very* high. So high that I was entirely bent and fell apart like bread in milk. I couldn't do anything about the mountain. It stood there. And waited for me to look at its summit. That was all it wanted from me. But I *couldn't* raise my head. How could I? I was all stooped and crumbling. But the mountain *really* wanted me to look. I understood that if I didn't look, I'd crumble altogether and turn into bread pudding. I took my head in my hands and began to lift it. It rose, and rose, and rose. And I looked, and looked, and looked at the mountain. But I still couldn't see the top. Because it was high, high, high. And it ran away from me something *terrible*. I began to sob through my teeth and choke. I kept lifting my heavy head. Suddenly my spine broke and I collapsed into wet pieces and fell backward. That's when I saw the summit. It shone WITH LIGHT. The light was so bright that I *disappeared in it*. This felt so *awfully good* that I woke up.

In the morning I remembered the dream in detail and told it to my family at breakfast. But it didn't make any particular impression on them.

With his habitual rough directness Father recommended that I "fantasize less and get more fresh air." Mother simply made the sign of the cross over me that night, sprinkled me with holy water, and placed an image of Saint Panteleimon the Healer under my pillow. My sisters didn't see anything unusual in my dream. My brothers simply hadn't been listening to me.

During the day the mysterious mountain occasionally revealed itself to me alone, here and there—in a snowdrift near the porch, as a wedge of cake on my sister's plate, as a juniper bush the gardener had pruned in the form of a pyramid, as Nastenka's metronome, as a mountain of sugar in Father's factory, as the corner of my pillow.

However, despite all this, I felt quite indifferent to regular mountains. The beautiful atlas titled *Les plus grands fleuves et montagnes du Monde* that Didenko showed me struck no chord of recognition: my mountain was not in there among the Jomolungmas, Jungfraus, and Ararats. They were just ordinary mountains. I had dreamed of the Mountain.

Gradually, my childhood paradise began to show cracks. Russian life seeped in through them. First, in the form of the word "war." I was six years old when I heard it on the terrace of our Ukrainian country estate. We had been waiting some time for Father to return from the factory for dinner, and at Mother's command had already begun the meal, when suddenly the jingle of the droshky bells could be heard, and Father entered somehow more slowly than usual. He was wearing a three-piece nankeen suit and a white hat and holding a newspaper in his hand; he was serious and sternly triumphant. He tossed the paper on the table.

"War!" he said. He pulled a handkerchief out of his pocket and wiped his long, powerful neck. "First it's those Austrian swine, then the Prussians. They want to gobble up Serbia."

The men sitting around the table got up, their voices clamoring as they clustered around Father. Nastya and Arisha turned to Mother in bewilderment. She looked frightened. I had bitten off too big a piece of an egg pasty, so I kept on chewing and stared at the newspaper. It lay close to me, between a carafe of raspberry drink and a dish of cold pork. The big black word WAR was folded in half. Under it I could see a smaller word—SERBIA. It made me think of the *serp*, the sickle women used to reap the wheat and buckwheat growing on our estate fields. Reddish-brown cockroaches were called "Prussians." Imagining a red cloud of them attacking the iron *serp* and gobbling it up, to the horror of the harvester, I shuddered and noisily spat the unchewed piece of pie out on the newspaper.

No one paid any attention to me. The men were making a restrained racket around Father, who stood too straight, as usual, and, thrusting his strong chin forward, was saying something about an ultimatum to Austro-Hungary. The women sat hushed.

I looked at the unchewed piece of pie lying on the black word WAR. I don't know why, but for my whole life that image has been a symbol of war for me.

Later, war became part of everyday life.

News from the front was read out loud at the breakfast table. The names of generals began to seem like those of relatives. For some reason I liked General Kuropatkin best of all. I imagined that he was like Uncle Chernomor in Pushkin's *Ruslan and Liudmila*. I also liked the word "counterattack." We moved to Vaskelovo and went to see our troops off at the station. Mama and my sisters sewed clothes for the wounded, cut bandages, made cotton plugs for wounds, visited sick quarters, and once were photographed with the empress and the wounded. Vasily volunteered, despite Father's protests and Mother's tears.

Soon after the beginning of the war I became acquainted with two other loyal companions of humankind: violence and love.

In the spring, Father traveled to Basantsy and took Nastya and me with him. It was Palm Sunday and we set off for church in three droshkies with our aunts and various hangers-on. It was a pretty, white-and-blue church that father had restored, and it stood at the edge of Kochanovo—the village next to Basantsy. I always felt cozy and calm in the church. I liked everyone crossing themselves, bowing and singing. There was something mysterious about it. During the service I tried to do everything like the grown-ups. When the priest began sprinkling water on the palm branches and drops hit my face, I didn't laugh but stood quietly like everyone else. However, by the end I was always bored and couldn't understand why it had to go on so long.

That day, when the service was over we began to leave the church with the crowd. Right behind us there was a sudden crush of people and several voices began arguing.

"These Ukies are always barging ahead!" one voice said in Russian.

"Those Moscow mosquitoes fly in just to push us around!" said another voice in Ukrainian.

The weather was springlike, the sun was shining, and the remaining patches of snow crunched underfoot. Father and the aunts gave alms to the poor, while Nastya and I sat in the *britzka* and looked at the square in front of the church. It was jammed with people. Some were already drunk. The village people, the Ukies, loitered about here—as did the factory people who worked in Father's plant. The plant was located about a verst from the village, but the factory settlement, built awhile back by my grandfather, lay just beyond the wide ravine. The Ukies shelled pumpkin seeds and made a hubbub; the factory workers smoked and laughed. Suddenly someone in the crowed screamed, we heard the sound of a slap, someone's cap went flying, the crowd surged with excitement, and the men ran to the ravine. The women squealed and ran after them. The square emptied in a second; the only people remaining were the beggars, the cripples, two constables with big sabers, and my relatives.

"Where are they going?" I asked Nastya, who was four years older.

Still chewing on the host, Nastya smacked her palm on the back of the driver's padded coat.

"Mikola, where are they running to?"

The swarthy Ukie with droopy mustaches turned around, smiling. "Well, miss, they's run off like the divil's kin to slug 'em in their mugs."

"Slug whose face?"

"Them own selves, Miss."

"What for?"

"Wouldn't be knowing…"

We stood up in the carriage. In the ravine the men had lined up in two ranks—the plant workers, mostly Russian newcomers, in one; the local Ukrainian villagers in the other. The women, old people, and children stood at the edge of the ravine and watched them from above. A hat flew up again and the fight began. It was accompanied by women's shrieks and encouraging shouts. For the first time in my life I saw people deliberately beating each other. In our family, other than Father's occasional cuffs and Mama's smacks, or a disobedient child ordered to sit in the corner, there were no punishments. Father often yelled at Mother until he was blue in the face, stamped his feet at the servants, and threatened the manager with his fist, but he never touched anyone.

Mesmerized, I watched the fight, not understanding the meaning of what was happening. The people in the ravine were doing something very important. It was *hard* for them to do it. But they were really trying. They tried so hard they almost cried. They groaned, swore, and shouted. It was as though they were *giving* one another something with their fists. It was interesting and frightening. I began to tremble. Nastya noticed and hugged me.

"Don't be scared, Shurochka. They're peasants. Papa says all they do is drink and fight."

I held Nastya's hand. Nastya was watching the fight in a strange way. It was as though she stopped being my sister and became distant and grown-up. And I was left alone. The fight continued. Someone fell on the snow, someone else was pulled by the hair, another guy would move back, spitting red. Nastya's hand was hot and alien to me.

Finally the constables whistled, and the old men and women shouted.

The fight stopped. The brawlers went home cursing—the Ukies to Kochanovo; the factory folk to the settlement. My tenderhearted mother couldn't help herself and cried after them, "Shame on you! Orthodox boys are on the front fighting the Germans, and you fight each other on a holiday!"

The ends of my father's thin-lipped mouth curled in a smile. "It's all right, let them entertain themselves and get it out of their system. It will be quieter that way."

He was afraid of the strikes and walkouts that had shaken Russian factories in 1905. All in all, though, he was content: the mobilization didn't affect his workers since sugar was considered a strategic product during wartime. The war promised great profits for Father.

Mama got in the carriage with us, the coachman tugged on the reins, clucked, and we set off. I let go of Nastya's hand. Two factory fellows passed by in homespun coats. One of them had a black eye, yet he was positively glowing with joy. The other guy touched his broken nose. Mother turned away indignantly.

"There you go, master, sir, we taught those Ukies a lesson!" said the fellow with the black eye, who pulled something from his closed fist and showed it to me, winked, and laughed. "A Ukie tooth got stuck in the mallet."

His friend quickly bent over and blew his nose. Red drops colored the snow. These fellows were *happy*. Both of them had a kind of *invisible* gift. They had received it in the fight. And they took it home with them.

I couldn't understand *what kind* of gift it was. Nastya and the other grown-ups understood, but they wouldn't say. There were *many* things no one would tell me.

I discovered the world's secrets for myself.

At the end of July we moved to Vaskelovo. At noon, after a two-hour lesson with Madame Panaget, I had some baked-milk pudding with bilberries and headed for the garden to play until dinner. The garden had been built a century and a half earlier, but it retained only remnants of its original magnificence—the former owner hadn't taken care of it at all. I loved to launch paper boats in the pond, climb on the willow tree that bent over to the ground, or, hiding behind the juniper bushes, throw pinecones at an old marble faun. But that day I didn't feel like doing any of this. Nastya was practicing her music in the house; Mama and the nanny were making jam; Father had left for Vyborg to buy some kind of machine, taking Ilya and Ivan with him; Arisha and Vasilisa were dozing with their books on chaise longues. I wandered around until I reached the most overgrown corner of the garden, and suddenly saw our maid, Marfusha. Squeezing her body between two iron fence bars pulled slightly apart, she disappeared into the forest that began just beyond the garden. There was something entirely uncharacteristic in her furtive movement; plump and calm, she was usually unhurried and smiling, with silly, wide-open brown eyes. Sensing some mystery in Marfusha's action, I wriggled through the fence and carefully ran after her. Her stern blue dress with its white apron stood out starkly against the background of the wild forest. The girl walked swiftly along the path, without turning around. I followed, walking on the soft, pine-needle-covered ground. A thick grove of old fir trees stood all around. It was dusky in the grove and only the rare birdcall could be heard. After about half a verst the grove ended: a small swamp began here. At the edge of the trees there were three shelters fashioned from fir branches. Every spring Father and his friends came here to hunt black grouse, which mated in the swamp. A whistle sounded from one of the huts. Marfusha stopped. I hid behind a thick fir. Marfusha looked around, and entered the hut.

"I was thinking you'd not come," a man's voice said, and I recognized Klim, a young servant.

"They'll be sitting to dinner soon, the missus is making jam. Lordy, I hope they don't miss me," Marfusha said quickly.

"Don't worry, they won't take notice," Klim muttered, and they fell silent.

I approached the hut stealthily, thinking to give a shout and scare them. On reaching the edge of the hut, I was just about to open my mouth, but I froze on the spot when I caught a glimpse of Klim and Marfusha through the fir branches. A sack was spread out on the ground inside the hut. They were kneeling, embracing, and sucking on each other's mouths. I had never seen people do that. Klim was squeezing Marfusha's breasts with one hand, and she was moaning. This went on and on. Marfusha's arms hung helplessly. Her cheeks were burning. Finally their mouths separated, and curly-headed, skinny Klim started to unbutton Marfusha's dress. This was totally *incomprehensible*. I knew that only a doctor was allowed to take a woman's dress off.

"Wait, I'll take off my apron," said Marfusha, removing the apron, folding it carefully, and hanging it on a branch.

Klim unhooked her dress, bared her young, strong breasts with little nipples, and began to kiss them greedily, murmuring, "Sweetheart, my sweetheart."

"What is he—some kind of a baby?" I thought.

Marfusha shuddered and her breathing was irregular.

"Klimushka . . . my precious . . . Do you really love me?"

He muttered something and unhooked her rustling blue dress even further.

"Not that way," she said, pushing away his hands and lifting the hem of her dress.

There was a white slip under her dress. Marfusha lifted it. And I saw female thighs and the dark triangle of her groin. Marfusha quickly lay down on her back.

"Lordy me, it's a sin . . . Klimushka . . ."

Klim lowered his pants, fell on top of Marfusha, and began to move back and forth.

"Oh, we shouldn't . . . Klimushka . . ."

"Quiet," Klim muttered, moving back and forth.

He began moving faster and growling like an animal. Marfusha moaned and cried out, muttering, "Lord...oy, it's a sin...oh my God..."

Their bodies trembled, their cheeks filled with blood. I understood clearly that they were doing something very shameful and secret, for which they would be punished. I could see that it was very hard for them, and probably hurt. But they *really really* wanted to do it.

Soon Klim grunted, the way men grunt when they're splitting logs, and then he was still. It was as though he fell asleep, lying on Marfusha like a mattress. She kept on moaning softly and stroked his curly head. Finally he rolled over, sat up, and wiped his mouth with his sleeve.

"Lordy...what if there's a baby?" said Marfusha, lifting her head.

Klim looked at her as though seeing her for the first time.

"Yull come tonight?" he asked hoarsely.

"Heavens, who'll let me out?" she said, starting to button her dress.

"Come when it gets dark," Klim sniffed.

"Klimushka, sweetheart, what'll happen now?" she replied, suddenly hugging him close.

"Nothing will happen," he muttered.

"Oh no, I gotta run," she murmured.

"You go, I'll come along after," said Klim gloomily, chewing on a twig.

"It's not wet on the hem is it?"

"Nuh-uh."

I began to back away from the hut, then turned and ran home.

What I had seen in the hut shook me as deeply as the brawl in the ravine. I understood with all my small being that both things were very important for people. Otherwise they wouldn't do them with such passion and effort.

I soon learned about childbirth from my brother Vanya. After that, the scene in the hut acquired another dimension for me: I understood that children are born out of a *secret groaning*, which is carefully hidden from everyone. Vanya informed me that children were only made at night. I began to listen carefully at night. And once, walking by my parents' bedroom, I heard the same moans and growling. Returning to my own bed, I lay there and thought: What a very strange activity this is, making children. Only one thing remained unclear—why is it all hidden?

In the morning at breakfast, when Marfusha, Klim, and Father's old servant Timofei were serving us, and everyone sitting at the table was, as usual, discussing news from the front, I suddenly asked, "But is Marfusha going to have a baby?"

The conversation stopped. Everyone looked at Marfusha. At that moment she was holding a porcelain dish from which the gray-haired, bulbous-nosed Timofei was ladling farina porridge onto our plates with his customary, long-suffering, anxious expression. Klim, standing in the corner of the dining room at the samovars, was filling glasses with tea. Marfusha turned redder than she had in the hut. The dish shook in her hands. Klim looked askance at me and grew pale.

Mother saved everyone. Most likely, she had guessed about the ties between the maid and the servant.

"Shurochka, Marfusha will have five children," she said. Then she added: "Three boys and two girls."

"That's right," Father agreed, frowning as he spooned jam abundantly over his porridge. "And then—another five. So that there's someone to go to war."

Everyone laughed approvingly. Marfusha tried to smile.

She had a hard time of it.

With each month the war intruded into our lives more and more. Vasily arrived home from the front. Not on his own two legs—he was driven from the train station in Father's automobile. The automobile blew its horn three times, and we ran out to meet our war hero, who had written short but memorable letters. Vasily stepped out of the automobile and, leaning on the chauffeur and Timofei, began climbing the steps to meet us. He was wearing an overcoat and a peaked cap, and his face was very yellow. Timofei carefully held his wooden stick. Vasily smiled guiltily. We rushed to kiss him. Mama sobbed. Father walked over and stood nearby, gazing tensely at Vasily and blinking. His strong chin trembled.

In Poland, near Lovich, Vasily had been in a German gas attack.

Although my brother had been poisoned with chlorine, the serpentine words "mustard gas" slithered into me.

Sitting in the parlor by the blazing fireplace, Vasily had tea and pastries and told us how he ran from the chlorine cloud; how he killed eight Germans with a machine gun; how two of his frontline friends were blown to bits by one shell, the warrant officer Nikolaev and the volunteer Gvishiani; how they silently took out the sentries with a horsehair string, "the Gypsy bride"; how to fight lice and tanks; what capital flamethrowers the Germans have; and what a multitude of Russian corpses lay in a huge wheat field after the Brusilov Offensive.

"They lay in even rows as though they'd been deliberately arranged. When they moved to attack the machine-gun nests, they were mowed down like grain."

We listened, holding our breath. The glass of tea shook in Vasily's yellow hand. He kept having to cough; his eyes teared up and were always red now, as though he'd just been crying. Vasily would grow short of breath when walking; to catch his breath he'd stop and lean on his walking stick.

Father sent him to Piatigorsk to take the waters.

Then a year later in Moscow my oldest brother took his own life, firing a revolver at his temple and a ladies' Browning at his heart simultaneously. Vanya said that Vasily shot himself because of a married woman with whom he had been hopelessly in love even before the war.

Father kept growing wealthier and ever more dependent on the war. His business moved up in the world. He acquired many new acquaintances, mostly among the military. He began to drink more, and more often, and was rarely at home, saying that now he "lived on the road." Various thin-eared, energetic young men darted about him; he called them his commissioners. Now he was *involved* not only in sugar but in many other things as well. When he shouted into the telephone, bizarre phrases would reach my ears: "American rubber will grab us by the throat one of these days," "There's a shipment of crackers gone criminally missing in the warehouse," "Those scoundrels from the land committee of the southwestern front are cutting me without a knife," "Six cars of soap shavings have been delayed at the junction," and so on.

My grandmother, who was quietly living out the remainder of her life in the house on Ostozhenka, said one time at Easter, "Our Dimulenka has completely lost his head with this war: he's chasing seven rabbits at one time."

And at the time Father really did remind me of a man in torment, racing hopelessly after something nimble and elusive. He himself grew no livelier for the race; on the contrary, he seemed to ossify, and his immobile face frowned even more. It seemed that he had completely stopped sleeping. His eyes shone feverishly and settled on nothing, roaming constantly when he had tea with us.

Another year passed.

The war had made its way into all the cracks. It had slithered out onto the streets. Columns of soldiers marched in the cities; at the station, cannons and horses were loaded onto the trains. Mama and I stopped visiting Basantsy—it was "restless" there. Our entire family settled in Petersburg. Relatives were left behind on the estates. The wartime capital taught me three new words: unemployment, strike, and boycott. For me they were embodied in the dark crowds of people on the streets of Petersburg who wandered about glumly, and whom we tried to pass by as quickly as possible in the dark, in our automobile.

Petersburg began to be called Petrograd.

In the newspapers people wrote mean poems about the Germans and drew caricatures of them. Vanya and Ilya liked to read them aloud. All Germans were divided into two types for me at that time: one was fat with a meaty, laughing face in a horned helmet, a saber in hand; the other was thin as a stick, in a peaked cap, with a monocle, a riding crop, and a sour, disdainful expression on his narrow face.

My older sister Arisha brought home a patriotic song from school. In her singing lessons, the whole class was composing music to the verses of some provincial teacher:

Arise, Russia, oh great and spacious land,
The mortal fight is now at hand,
With the Germans' dark force,
With the Teutonic knights' horde!

Nastya and Arisha accompanied with four hands, and I sang with pleasure, standing on a chair.

When we moved to the big city, I noticed that everything happened faster than in Basantsy or Vaskelovo: people moved and talked more quickly, drivers raced along and hollered, automobiles honked and rattled, gymnasium students hurried to school, newspaper hawkers shouted about "our losses." Father would enter the apartment, throw off his sheepskin coat, eat hurriedly, close himself in his office with his assistant, and then take off in the automobile with his commissioners and disappear for a week. Mama also moved much faster; she was always going somewhere and buying something. We went visiting often and quickly. I had a lot of new friends—boys and girls.

I was being intensively prepared for the high school: I studied Russian and arithmetic with Didenko, and French and German with Madame Panaget. Lessons progressed much faster than before as well.

Even our two pugs, Kaiser and Shuster, ran faster now, barked louder, and pooped on the rug more often.

We celebrated Christmas 1917 at the large house of Father's new friends. By that time Father had suddenly stopped all his trips and given himself over entirely to a new, menacing word which, like a powerful broom, had swept "trains of chipped lump sugar" and "cars of soap shavings" out of our home. This word was "the Duma." Like fat Patsiuk from Gogol's Christmas story, it had entered our parlor and settled in for the duration. Along with it, Papa's new friends began to come by and sit until late at night. Almost all of them were outwardly identical and entirely different from my tall, gaunt father: they were short, lively, sturdily built, with shaved wide necks, clipped beards, and curled mustaches; they smoked a lot and argued incessantly. Then, once they'd had enough arguing and smoked until they were hoarse, they would write something, dictating to one another at the same time, then father would drink wine with them and they'd go off to dine at Ernest or the new Donon's. Now father was involved only in politics; he would go to meetings of the mighty, mysterious Duma, and in conversations with Mama often talked about some kind of abscess that was "just about to burst" and how "we must seize the moment."

After the beginning of the war, the banker Riabov became Father's best friend in Petrograd. He was also in the Duma.

I fell in love for the first time in my life with the Riabovs' eleven-year-old daughter, Nika. It was Christmas morning and we children were acting out the Christmas story. The Riabovs' older son, Riurik, played Herod; Nastya, the angel of the Lord bringing good tidings; Vanya, Ilya, and Arisha, the three kings; Vasilisa, the Mother Mary; and some overgrown high-school student was Joseph. Children we didn't know well played angels, devils, and slaughtered infants. Nika and I each played two parts: first, Herod's soldiers searching for male children; and then the ass and the ox who warmed the Christ child in the manger with their breath. The Christ child was played by the Riabovs' youngest son, Vanyusha, who was five. When he was successfully born in the second act, and Nika and I fastened on the cow and donkey papier-mâché masks and readily poked our muzzles forward to warm him with our breath, Vanyusha burst into tears. We looked at each other through the cutout eyes and giggled quietly. Nika's brightly sparkling black eyes framed by the donkey's enormous eyelashes, her soft laughter, and the fragrance of some saccharine-sweet perfume elicited an unexpected rush of tenderness in me. I took her moist hand and didn't let go until the end of the act.

I sat next to her at dinner, crowding out a little girl. My feelings for Nika grew with every dish that was served. I chatted with her, talking all kinds of nonsense. While we ate crepes with caviar, I pinched her on the elbow in nervous gaiety; over tea and biscuits, I stuck her finger in my dish of apricot preserves.

Nika laughed.

And there was understanding in her laugh. It seemed she liked me too. After dinner a children's masquerade and dance was held around the Christmas tree. And when the men set off upstairs to smoke and play cards, and the ladies headed to the veranda in the winter garden to trade news, it was proposed that the children play charades. Two lovely English governesses helped us.

"Whaaat to due wiss ziss pepper?" the redheaded, incredibly freckled governess asked, painstakingly pronouncing the Russian words as she pulled little slips of paper with our names out of a box pasted with stars.

"Bark at Nika!" I shouted louder than the others.

We barked at her, sprayed her with water, and carried her around the Christmas tree...

Nika laughed for me with her black eyes. I wanted terribly to do something with her so that everyone else around would disappear. The scene I had witnessed in the hut had nothing to do with this feeling. Nika, being the older of us, understood me. She suddenly decided she wanted to switch her wolf mask for the Baba Yaga witch mask.

"Sasha, let's go, you can help me," she said, running up the stairs to her room.

Once in her room, she ignored me, but her face burned with excitement as she fell on her knees and began to search furiously through a starry violet bag of masks.

"Where is it...? Oh, *mon Dieu*! Here it is!"

I kneeled down next to her, hugged her tightly around the neck, and kissed her cheek.

"Sasha, you're so funny," she muttered, staring at the big-nosed witch mask.

I kissed her again. My heart fluttered. She turned toward me, closed her eyes, and pressed her face to mine. We froze. And for the very first time, I felt that time could stand still.

"Now who do you think could be hiding in here?" came a feigned query, accompanied by the loud rustle of skirts.

Hateful time started up again. And along with it the mistress of the house and a lady with a green fan entered the room. I didn't have time to release Nika from my embrace.

"They're being amorous!" the lady exclaimed rapturously, aiming her lorgnette at us. "Nina Pavlovna, just look at them! How sweet!"

But Nika's homely, taciturn mother was clearly displeased. She looked at us—we were blushing and pressed to each other—attentively.

"Put on the masks. And go downstairs," she said.

We grabbed the tiger and Baba Yaga masks and ran downstairs.

Nina Pavlovna didn't say anything to my parents. But she did everything possible to make sure Nika and I didn't see each other again. My requests to my mother to "definitely visit Nika" came to naught: Nika was either "under the weather," or "visiting relatives," or (despite the Christmas holidays!) "intensively studying arithmetic."

A month and a half of unrequited desire to see my black-eyed love threw me into a feverish state. I lay in bed hallucinating for three days with a high temperature. I would surface from terrifying, colorful dreams into Mother's cool hands placing a towel soaked in water and vinegar on my brow, and bringing me a cup of cranberry *mors* to drink. I never saw my Mountain in any of those dreams. I glimpsed a human sea, a boundless ocean of voices, faces, dresses, and tuxedos, that rolled powerful waves at me. I drowned in them, floundered, attempted to swim out past them, but again and again they covered my head. I knew that somewhere nearby, in the same place, Nika was floundering. But the harder I searched for her in whirlpools rustling with women's dresses, the more furiously I was tossed through endless suites of rooms into smoked-filled parlors and stuffy bedrooms. My head was bursting with voices. Finally I broke through to her and saw my love in her little white dress, wearing a Baba Yaga mask. I ran over to her, grabbed the endlessly long, bumpy nose of the mask, and tore it off. But under the mask I found Nika with a live donkey head. She was chewing on something and stared straight at me with donkey eyes. I awoke with a cry.

I came to on the fourth day.

Neither Mama nor the nanny was anywhere to be seen. I raised my head: the drapes were drawn tight, but through a crack you could see daylight. I got out of bed. My head swam from weakness. Swaying, wearing a nightshirt that went to the floor, I headed for the door, opened it, and frowned: our huge apartment was bathed in sunlight. It issued from the parlor. I headed that way, my bare soles shuffling along the cool parquet floor. In the parlor, all their backs turned to me, stood our family. The windows were open and the spring sun beat blindingly through them. Everyone standing there was looking out the window. I walked over to Mama. She grabbed me, kissed me, hugged me hysterically, and picked me up. I could see our street, Millionnaya Street, out the window. It was usually quiet and almost empty, but now it was flooded with people. The crowd surged, roared, and crawled toward something. Here and there strips of red fabric could be glimpsed.

"What is it, Mama?" I asked.

"It's the Revolution, son," Mother answered.

Later everyone in the family joked: Sasha slept through the Russian Revolution.

Revolution

THEY HAD been talking about it for a long time. For me it didn't happen on that sunny February day, but earlier, on a winter evening. Madame Panaget and I had been coloring pictures in coloring books. Then I had jangled awhile at the piano and drunk a glass of milk with my favorite Ciy biscuits. After that I was supposed to recite my evening prayer to Mama and then go to bed. But Father showed up. Without even taking his coat off he came over to Mama.

"That's it," he said glumly, "there's no more Duma."

Mama stood up quietly.

"Miliukov and Rodzianko got what they wanted," Father said, tossing his fur coat into the maid's waiting arms and lowering himself into an armchair in exhaustion. "They killed off the Duma. The bastards. They managed to murder it after all. Buried it alive."

He pounded his fist on the armrest.

I felt a chill: the Duma, that unseen and powerful Patsiuk who had lived with us for two years, was murdered and buried.

"What will happen now, Dima?" Mama asked.

"Revolution!" Father shook his head darkly, but with a kind of angry pride.

And I, eight years old, suddenly imagined it, this mysteriously menacing Revolution, as the image of the Snow Queen, for some reason holding in her hand that very same "cockroach-eaten" sickle.

If life in Petrograd before the Revolution had moved faster than usual, now everything fairly whizzed by. And immediately there were more people. The streets were almost always full. It became hard to drive, not only in an automobile but in a horse and buggy as well. I learned new words and terms: "sovdep," "revolutionary masses," "interim government," and "queue." The unfamiliar sovdep, in Father's words, sat itself down in the Tauride Palace and, as the first order of business, drank up all the wine and stole the silver spoons from the restaurant. The revolutionary masses often drifted past our windows; everyone, including the cook, was continually talking about the interim government; and the lines for bread grew and grew. I couldn't understand it: Why were people standing in line for bread? The adults' explanations, that there wasn't enough bread for everyone, didn't satisfy me: there was always so much wheat after all; the wheat fields in the Ukraine were endless! I was certain that bread was limitless, like water, like the sky. We always had bread left over after dinner.

And it was strange for me to hear "Give us a bit of bread!" on the streets.

We spent the summer of 1917 in Vaskelovo. It was a surprisingly beautiful, calm, long summer. I had never had such a wonderful, free summer. It was as though I was saying farewell to my former carefree, happy life. And that life, departing forever, said farewell to me, through Vaskelovo's huge, dark fir trees, still lake, forest berries, after-dinner naps on the veranda, my sisters' innocent laughter, the glassy sounds of the piano, and rainbows after the rain.

At the end of the summer I entered the lycée. A chauffeur with the funny surname Kudlach drove me there in a blue automobile. And he drove me every day. It was mostly the children of the rich who attended that school on Kriukov Canal. Many of them were driven in automobiles. But not right up to the school—that was considered "*inappropriate*." The autos stopped a short distance from the school, and we would get out and walk the rest of the way. That was how it was done.

The lessons were interesting for me. At the lycée there were teachers entirely unlike the homely Didenko and the quiet Madame Panaget. They knew how to speak well for a long time. I particularly liked the ever-cheerful mathematician Terenty Valentinovich; the small but incredibly active physical education teacher Monsieur Jacob, nicknamed the Pocket Bonaparte; and the loud Frenchwoman Ekaterina Samuilovna Babitskaya, who always smelled of rose oil. The lycée director, Kazimir Efimovich Krebs, a tall man with a huge head, thick beard, three-fingered left hand, and deep, sonorous bass voice, whom the pupils dubbed Nebuchadnezzar, put me into a state of enraptured fear.

Not three months of my school life had passed when another Revolution struck. Father called it the "Bolshevik distemper" and promised that "this scum won't last long."

He was sorely mistaken.

Everything was different during the second Revolution: only soldiers in overcoats and sailors ran downs the streets, rode on horses, and passed by in trucks. And they all had rifles. Citizens moved about cautiously, trying to keep closer to home. At night you could hear shots.

Then time seemed to *condense*. It flew so fast that everything whisked by and got confused: people, events, seasons.

Despite the "Bolshevik distemper," classes continued in the lycée until the spring of 1918. And they stopped for a very simple reason: a large portion of the pupils and their wealthy parents fled Petersburg. And Russia.

Our family was ripe for flight in July. Things had changed. Ilya, who had taken a fancy to Marxism while still in school, became a Red and went over to the Bolsheviks. He broke ties with Father. He sent Mama a couple of letters through someone, in which he wrote that he was fighting for a free Russia. Then Ilya disappeared forever. Vasilisa quickly married a silent, hook-nosed lieutenant who had been demobilized because of a wound (in his left knee), and just as swiftly left with him for his mother's home in the Crimea.

Father, who had lost everything in Russia, intended to take us to Warsaw at first. There he had "a little something," I never did understand what—a house or a business. Then he planned to go farther— to Zürich, where he had "something." The banker Riabov, who had acquired a house there before both revolutions, made his way to Zürich with his family. In the summer of 1918 the road to Europe lay through Kiev. Dymbinsky, a man with a small mustache, took it upon himself to see Mama and my sisters to Warsaw first, and then Father, Vanya, and me. Father needed another couple of weeks in order to "sort out some business in Peter." Those two weeks turned out to be fateful for the family. Mama, Nastya, and Arisha had barely left when my brother Vanya came down with typhoid fever. He lay in bed for a month, but fortunately recovered, although he had grown very thin and yellow. Then Father was taken by the Cheka. For three months there was no news of him. Our pious aunt Flora, Mother's sister, who took Ivan and me to live at her house on the Moika Canal, prayed every day for our arrested father. And a miracle happened— they let him out. He returned from the Cheka slumped and gray-haired. But he said that in three months in prison no one had once hit him in the face.

As a result, it was winter before we made it to Kiev. We settled in Lipki, a wealthy, well-tended neighborhood, in the large apartment of Papa's brother. The absolute opposite of Father, Uncle Yury, an enthusiastic, whimsical, loud man who had no intention of leaving his native Kiev, received us as though there had been no Revolution or war at all. At home, his table was always groaning with greasy Ukrainian food, a neatly dressed servant served champagne, and Uncle, a bit grayer and thinner, was always talking boisterously and drinking the health of some Hetman I knew nothing about. After stern Petersburg with its bread lines, Uncle's abundant table seemed incredible. But the most incredible thing turned out to be that Mama and my sisters, who had stayed with Uncle Yury, had set off for Warsaw at the beginning of November, and no one knew whether they had arrived or not. However, everyone knew that there was a revolution in Warsaw as well, and that Pilsudski had declared independence. Father was in a frenzy: he screamed at Uncle, calling him a milksop of a bumpkin, and stomped his feet. Uncle Yury tried to calm him as well as he could. He swore up and down that Mama and my sisters were alive and safe.

Uncle Yury was our favorite. He didn't have his own children, he was an incorrigible bachelor. He loved us to death. We loved him in our child's way, like a peer or overgrown child. Long ago, Vanya and Ilya had come up with a complicated nickname for him. The name jumped out of Uncle's mouth every time he visited us in Petersburg. A fancier of restaurants and café chantants, Uncle would invariably demand on the first night of his visit that Father accompany him "somewhere." Father, knowing *how* these excursions "somewhere" ended, would always mutter that "now there's not even anywhere to go." To which Uncle, throwing his handsome head back, would reproachfully spread his hands, which were long like Father's, and flex his fingers.

"Please, Dima! You have Ernest, Cuba, and two Donon's."

These were the names of the four most luxurious restaurants in the city. After which Father and Uncle disappeared until the morning. So for us, Uncle Yury became Ernestcubantwodonons. When his carriage drove into the gates of the northern estate, Nastenka and I would race around the rooms, shouting "Ernestcubantwodonons has arrived!"

While feeding us, Uncle assured everyone that we would be setting out for Warsaw ourselves in a matter of days. Dymbinsky was prowling the city in search of some "devilishly important papers." This dragged on for several weeks: Uncle was waiting for help from his German friends. But the Germans suddenly left Kiev without even informing Uncle. And somehow Petliura with his "barbaric, primitive hordes" suddenly approached Kiev very quickly. People talked about him with horror. Petliura entered the city in order to "hang officers, kikes, and 'Moscvitoes.'" He was Ukrainian. People said he left only Ukrainians alive. I imagined him as the sorcerer in Gogol's "Terrible Revenge," the most terrifying story on earth. As soon as the Germans ran off, Dymbinsky disappeared. And our jolly self-assured uncle became panicked. He shook Father by the shoulders and shouted that "you must run from Lipki as fast as you can." He was certain that Petliura's people would come right straight here to pillage, to the wealthiest neighborhood. Father began to shout back that he knew how to shoot. But he soon dismissed Uncle with a wave of his long hand and began to pack. In the morning we left Lipki in two carriages. Father and I sat in the first one; in the second was Ernestcubantwodonons with a heap of things and his old servant, Savely. There was a slight frost. Despite the fact that it was December, not much snow had fallen. But after a sleepless night of packing and shouting I was chilled and shivering, and *desperate* to sleep. I was dozing in the carriage, slouched against Father and clutching a Ciy biscuit tin in my hands. I had all my treasures in it, a jumble of beloved objects—a collection of pencils, a Swiss penknife, and a tin pistol with a box of percussion caps. Twice we stopped and I woke up: the first time was when a small, plump, very anxious lady with two traveling bags took a seat with Uncle; the second time was on some terribly crooked street when Dymbinsky, holding a briefcase and dressed in a gray summer suit and fuzzy sheepskin hat, his arm bandaged, squeezed in with us. He handed Father the briefcase and kept muttering hoarsely and insistently about a place called Pushche-Voditsu and some barracks. His eyes were red, and the fuzzy hat made me sleepy. I dozed off again. And opened my eyes at the sound of nearby thunder. Both wagons stood on a street with one-story houses surrounded by gardens lightly covered in snow. A fat redheaded woman wearing a nightgown, her braid half undone, was hurriedly closing the shutters. There was another rumble, even closer.

"Six-inch shells. No smaller," said Dymbinsky and tapped the driver's back. "Turn around!"

A large black Mauser suddenly appeared ir his hand. Cussing, the cabby turned into a side alley. Far away, three men in overcoats were running along the lane. Somewhere beyond the houses shots rang out. A machine gun fired. The lady in the second carriage cried out and began to cross herself in a sort of mousy fashion. Dymbinsky swore in Polish. Father shouted at the driver. I felt a sudden, intense chill and moaned as I yawned with my whole mouth. A crack sounded right close by. The window glass in the houses rang. The horse whinnied and jerked. My tin with all my *beloved* things slipped out of my hands and rolled down the icy road.

Both carriages stopped. Father, Uncle, and Dymbinsky screamed at the drivers; the drivers, not understanding where to go, pulled on the reins. The horses snorted and backed up. I watched my tin box rolling. Like a lemon-yellow wheel it rolled, rolled and rolled, rolled until I cried, until there were sharp pains in my eyes. And in it, like a tin drum, was my tin cap gun. Suddenly, as if obeying some unforeseen order, I jumped out of the swaying carriage and rushed after my box.

"Alexander, come back! Come back this min—" Father cried out.

And his voice was *forever* drowned in a terrible crashing sound. This crash swallowed all the voices in the carriages. The crash struck me in the back as though I was a rug hung out for cleaning. And a huge rumble, like a giant, thumped the dust out of me in one blow. I *collapsed*.

Then I opened my eyes. Very close to me I saw ice, soiled by horse manure. The ice was right near my nose. I wanted to get up, but I couldn't. It wasn't clear what stopped me. I couldn't hear *anything*. I pushed against the ice. And with enormous difficulty I raised my head. In front of me was an empty lane. In the middle of it lay my yellow tin. I understood right away that *the most important thing* was behind me. So I began to turn my stiffened neck. It turned *very* badly. But it did turn.

I saw: smoke, overturned carriages, people lying down, and the horse thrashing on its side with its guts sticking out. And black earth on the ice. And something else black that lay quite close to me. I squinted at it. It was a leg in a black boot. And a gray-blue-white-striped wool sock. A fashionable American sock. The sock of Ernest-cubantwodonons. A red leg stuck out of the sock. Sticking out from the leg was . . . something else.

I felt a warm trickle across my lips. I touched them and looked at my hand. It was covered in blood. I understood that I had to get up and go to Papa. Because he had called me. With great difficulty I managed to pull my legs up and rose to my knees. Then a carousel spun around me. Everything—the smoke, the house, the woman in the window, the earth, the leg, the horse and the men, the smoke, men, house, woman in the window—went around, and around, and around. From left to right. Left to right. Left to right.

And I fell back on the ice.

The Road

MY CHILDHOOD ended in Kiev on December 12, 1918. It was blown out of me by an exploding six-inch shell that took the life of my father, my brother Vanya, and Uncle Yury. One of the cabbies died as well. The servant Savely and the other cabby were injured, but they survived. Dymbinsky disappeared. Uncle's mistress, Lidia Vasilevna Belkina, the widow of a staff captain in the czar's army, received a serious concussion, as did I. The very same redheaded woman who had been closing her shutters picked us up and dragged us into her house. I couldn't hear anything for three months. I couldn't walk: my head spun, and I would have to sit down and close my eyes immediately. The most comfortable thing for me was to sit on the floor and stare at it. Over those three months I studied three floors: the clay wattle-and-daub floor covered with brightly colored homemade rugs, a parquet floor covered with huge Persian rugs, and the floor of a train car, covered in spittle and strewn with cigarette butts. The train floor swayed back and forth.

Belkina told me that my relatives had been buried in the Baikov cemetery. She helped arrange to send me with her cousin to Moscow. I set off but I didn't get there. Armed men on horseback stopped the train. And it went off in an entirely different direction. First I ended up in Poltava, then in Kharkov. Then in Kursk. Then Rylsk. Then came the stations Krasnoye, Morshansk; the villages Golubino, Serpukhov; the settlements Pekhterevo, Podolsk.

I finally arrived in Moscow on August 2, 1922. During that time I had grown up. The explosion knocked not only childhood out of me but something else as well. It was as though it cut me off from my past. And along with my past—any love for it. Throughout four years of drifting I never once cried about my dead father. I remembered my mother frequently, I thought about her. But it didn't occur to me to try and find her, to search for her. She had become *inaccessible* not only in the world around me but inside me as well. Only hunchbacked Nastenka, my favorite sister, reached out to me from the past that the explosion had cut off; she would appear at night and live for long periods in my tormented dreams of the familiar and what had been lost. I would awake in tears.

For the entire four years I was constantly on the move, traveling and traveling. One enormous, endless road stretched under my feet and pulled me, tearing me away from every comfortable situation, promising and menacing, scary and calming. I didn't understand *where* I was going or *why*. I was simply led. I was never alone, I never suffered from hunger, and I never once passed the night outdoors under a fence or in a haystack. I was never robbed, never beaten in the face, never stabbed with a knife. People took care of me. I was passed from hand to hand, like some precious thing forever lost by its owner. A thing that *for some reason* definitely had to be preserved. There was a kind of miracle in all of this. Mama's dependents, hopelessly distant relatives, Father's passing acquaintances and business associates, colleagues of my late brother Vasily, a teacher's sisters, and simple strangers turned out to be in the necessary places at the necessary times in order to help "Snegirev's son." Some made sure I got on an overfilled train, others chanced to meet me on the platform, some called to me on the street, and still others arranged places for me to pass the night. Coincidence became the norm. I stopped being surprised by it. I just traveled. But I didn't know where I was going or for what reason. Turning up in some city, town, or village, I knew immediately that I wouldn't stay there forever. The blast had knocked a sense of home out of me. I no longer had any home. There was no longer anywhere I yearned to be. Vaskelovo and Basantsy remained only in memory. And I understood this.

Having lived a month or two in a new place, with new people, I would feel that it was time to move on. So I'd say, "It's time."

Surprisingly, my words had an effect on host after host. Without asking *where* I was heading, they would immediately begin to figure things out, get moving, undertake something, send someone a note, make an agreement with someone else, and a day or two later I would be on the train or catching a ride with some freight to a place where I was expected.

The road led me.

It took me four years to get to Moscow.

During that time a lot of things happened. The Bolsheviks won a definitive victory. The war ended.

Russia became Red.

Petrograd

HAVING ended up in Moscow, I set off for Ostozhenka Street, to find my grandmother's cozy wooden house. But grandmother wasn't there anymore. Nine worker families lived in the house. A woman washing clothes in the courtyard told me that "the old lady died as soon as the authorities 'condensed' the living space." That had happened a year earlier.

I knew no one in Moscow.

Aunt Flora remained in Petrograd. I made it to there on a freight train and found my aunt's apartment on the Moika. Aunt Flora was alive, although she had aged drastically. She didn't recognize me immediately. And she was terribly frightened when I entered. She thought she was seeing my deceased brother Vasily. Then she cried and tried to kiss me on the top of my head as she did when I was a child. But I had grown and she couldn't manage it. I told her everything. She crossed herself and cried. And again tried to kiss me. I bowed my head.

Aunt Flora told me that two of our relatives had been shot, one had left for Paris, and that her sister had disappeared without a trace during the Civil War. The estate in Vaskelovo had become a boarding school for homeless and orphaned children. She had heard that the estate in Basantsy had been burned. I had also heard that in Kharkov. The regional housing department had occupied our apartment on Millionnaya Street in Petrograd.

Aunt Flora's four-room apartment had also been "condensed" and four families had been moved in. My aunt, as a single woman, the widow of a bourgeois, occupied the former pantry. In that dim little room stood an iron bedstead, a mahogany chest of drawers, a Singer sewing machine, and a few icons. From under the bed Aunt pulled out a folded Persian rug that used to lie on the parlor floor, set one of her large embroidered pillows on it, and declared, "It's crowded, Sashulenka, but it's all yours, the more the merrier! Make yourself at home!"

I settled in on that folded rug, next to the door.

Auntie Flora hated the Bolsheviks fiercely, believing them to be the servants of the Antichrist. Her life was closely tied to the church. Childless, widowed early, Auntie had spent most of her time in the church. But she did not want to shave her head and enter a nunnery, as many of her pious friends had done after the Bolshevik victory. She made money to feed herself by sewing clothes and once in a while sold something of the little that remained from her former, prosperous life. The main family valuables had been confiscated from her during a search.

The first thing Auntie did was to sew me a shirt and a pair of trousers. While she worked, she gave me instructions for the future: I must finish high school, enter the university, and receive a higher education.

"While you are young—fill your head!" she would repeat, pumping the pedal of the sewing machine with her small but strong legs.

Arriving at my high school on Kriukov Canal, I noticed that it had been renamed the Herzen School. Of the former teachers there remained only the German woman Violetta Nikolaevna Knorre. Of my classmates only two continued to study there—the fat clodhopper Shtiurmer and the sarcastic, restless, dumpy little fellow Yanovsky. Boris Ivanovich Diakov had become the director; he was a typical member of the Russian intelligentsia who had fallen in love with the Revolution. After an interview with him, I was placed in the fifth class. Studies were to begin on the eighth of September, and the director, who taught history, told us, as he triumphantly polished his pince-nez, how he had spoken to Lenin twice.

I studied three years in that school. At first I enjoyed learning new things and I quickly caught up with what I had missed. It was a progressive school: we didn't take final exams. The teachers whom Diakov invited were genuinely enthusiastic about their profession; they lived for the school, took us on excursions, played lapta and handball with us, set up debates, and in the winter, when the school wasn't heated, they shared their clothes. Almost all of them supported the Bolsheviks. Only the gloomy, pensive drawing teacher was a convinced anarchist and often said that Lenin and Trotsky were restoring the state machine for suppressing individuality.

At the Herzen School I chose a profession. Or, rather, it chose me.

As it happened, after that fateful blast, it turned out that I had a strange and unique ability. Recovering from my concussion in bed and unable to hear anything, I entertained myself by counting the objects around me. At first I simply counted them. Then I began to count their corners. I suddenly noticed that this was very easy. Counting the Japanese shelf of the late Ernestcubantwodonons, which was half hidden by a curtain, I could easily imagine it in space and calculated the number of corners it had: 46. Then I calculated Uncle's desk: 28. A chandelier with octagonal crystal pendants peeking out from the parlor came next: 226. I gradually calculated all the corners in Uncle's apartment. There were 822 of them. After this I was satisfied. When I got better, I entirely forgot this unusual activity.

However, when we began to learn geometry, I remembered it. I was good at geometry. Not just good but, in the words of my teacher Georgy Vladimirovich, "simply extraordinary." I solved problems easily, plotted cross-sections, saw and understood what was difficult for others. Moreover, I could count very fast. After the explosion, mathematics became an intelligible element for me. But I can't say that geometry or mathematics excited or attracted me. The same was true of other subjects: I was indifferent to history, zoology, literature. Drawing and singing seemed meaningless activities to me. Russian was difficult for me. And French—I had just known it since childhood. The only thing that *vaguely* excited me was astronomy. Not exactly astronomy itself but the heavenly bodies, hanging in space. Imagining the Universe, it was as though I *lost myself*. And my heart would begin to throb. However, they didn't teach us astronomy. Mathematics and geometry were quite easy for me. That was what decided my goal.

"Only the exact sciences, Snegirev! Don't even think about anything else!" Georgy Vladimirovich would say, categorically wagging his goatlike beard.

I began to prepare for the entrance exams to the university. The director helped me to get through four external-course exams; at age seventeen I received my high-school diploma and easily gained admission to the physics and mathematics department of the university. But even in the first year, sitting through lectures on higher mathematics, I realized that the world of numbers, theorems, and equations held no interest for me. Nor did physics, for that matter. Descriptive geometry had been clear to me since grade ten; neither it nor analytic geometry held any attractive mysteries for me. I was openly bored in class, absorbed in my own thoughts. But these thoughts were not productive. I fell prey to a sort of *internal stupor*, and plunged into it like a pleasantly warm bath. It should be said that the blast had not only separated me from the past. It had, in effect, *halted my development*. Previously, I had been a lively, social, merry, fidgety boy. I loved to talk to everyone. And I loved movement. It was hard for me to sit still for even a minute. I never thought about anything for very long. After the blast everything changed: I became quiet, closed, sedentary, pensive, and asocial. I had virtually no friends at school. Girls, who were in class with us after separate education was abolished, didn't interest me, either. Rita Reznikov, with her curly black hair and black eyes, sat next to me and loved to poke fun at my introversion and reticence.

"You're so dull, Snegirev, like porridge," she'd say.

I would just answer with a crooked grin. I didn't like to joke and fool around between classes. I would wander the schoolyard, avoiding all my noisy, frolicking classmates.

I was no more social at the university. University life didn't interest me at all. The auditoriums seethed with discussion, lectures grew into debates. There was an ongoing struggle between the "Red" professors and the old, "bourgeois" professors. The Komsomol committee played a significant role in this struggle. The Komsomol could disrupt a professor's lecture with an accusation of "disguised counterrevolution" or "religious obscurantism." Famous Bolsheviks were invited to the university for open debates. Lunacharsky argued with the Metropolitan Vvedensky about the existence of God; Zinoviev gave a lecture on the role of the Komsomol in building the new society; Krupskaya led a debate on the women's question.

I was distant from all of this. After classes I would wander around the city. I wasn't anxious to go home: Auntie's sewing machine chirred away; the neighbor women argued in the communal kitchen. Wandering around Petersburg, I touched the stones. I liked to place my hands on the cold granite. The stones exuded a calm that didn't exist in people. I touched the battered pedestals of building, stroked the smooth columns of St. Isaac's, touched the manes of granite lions, the polished toes of Atlases, the breasts of marble nymphs, and the wings of marble angels. Stone sculptures calmed me.

Arriving home, I would eat the meager dinner that Auntie had left for me, and lose myself in books I took out of the university library. For the most part these were books on astronomy and the story of the Universe. I was excited by the planets and the infinity of the starry world that surrounded the Earth. Sometimes I took out books on mineralogy: I didn't read them, just spent long stretches looking at the color illustrations of stones. I could do this for hours, lying on my rug. I didn't read books on mathematics and physics at all, making do with what I heard in lectures. Literature didn't interest me: the world of people, their passions and ambitions—all that seemed petty, fussy, and ephemeral. You couldn't *rely* on that like you could on stone. The world of Natasha Rostova and Andrei Bolkonsky was really no different from the world of my neighbors who fought and swore in the kitchen over Primus stoves or the slop bucket. The world of planets and stones was richer and more interesting. It was eternal. I tore a picture of Saturn from an astronomy atlas and hung it on the wall. When Auntie sat down to sew, her head was on the same level as Saturn. But could Saturn be compared in any way with Aunt Flora's head, muttering something about the Bolsheviks, Renovationists, and the price of woolen cloth and crepe de chine?

Astronomy was studied only in the third year at university. Nevertheless, I began to race from my physics and mathematics classes to attend the lectures of Professor Karlov, a well-known astronomer and specialist on the spectral analysis of planets. Listening to his rather muffled voice talking about the stellar parallax, the satellites of Mars, sunspots, the orbits of comets, and meteorite showers, I closed my eyes and forgot about everything. I collapsed inward and *hung* in starry space. And this feeling turned out to be stronger than all others. It was *incredibly* pleasurable. I even stopped hearing Karlov himself. And I forgot about astronomy. I simply *hung* amid the planets and stars. It continued this way from month to month. I went to other lectures less and less frequently. I barely passed the first term and just managed to begin the second semester. During the summer all the students worked to make money. I also decided to help Auntie with money. At first I was set up at the Krasny Putilovets factory as a maintenance worker, but on the second day I experienced an extraordinary irritability and feeling of oppression from the machines and mechanisms. The people working with these huge machines irritated me even more: there was something menacing and doomed about them. The plant itself I found *unbearably ugly*. I left Krasny Putilovets and got a job washing dishes in a restaurant at a gambling house on Vladimirsky Prospect. The place was maintained by a typical nepman who looked like he'd come straight out of a Mayakovsky poster—fat and constantly smoking a cigar. I thought about the planets and stars while I washed the dishes. They were always with me: I followed their orbits, delighted in the *fluid* rotation of the heavenly bodies.

In September I again headed for Karlov's lectures. The astronomy course lasted one school year. Karlov always began his course with a new stream of third-year students. I again plunged into the introductory lectures with pleasure. I closed my eyes. And I *hung there* imagining the huge star Betelgeuse. Auditorium No. 8 became my second home. I stopped going to other lectures entirely.

And once, when I was *hanging*, someone touched me on the shoulder.

"Are you all right?" a woman's voice asked me.

I opened my eyes. The auditorium was already empty. A girl sat next to me. She had short black hair and slightly slanted eyes that looked at me with amusement.

"Do you work at night or something? Don't get enough sleep?"

"No . . ." I parted with *my* stupor with displeasure.

"I always watch you, how you doze during the lectures," she grinned.

"I'm not dozing," I answered, looking into her eyes.

She stopped grinning.

"Which . . . class are you in?"

"I'm a second year," I answered.

"Then why do you come to our lectures?"

"I truly love the Universe," I admitted openly.

She looked at me with interest. We got to talking. Her name was Masha Dormidontova. She had been observing me for a whole month. The student who always sat in lectures with closed eyes and an aloof expression interested her. Leaving the physics and mathematics building, we walked along the embankment. Masha asked me questions. I answered absentmindedly. She was animated, with quick reactions and a lively mind. Her father served in the navy. She was studying physics and was enthralled by a fashionable science—meteoritics. Walking around the city with her and listening to her rapid, emotional speech, at first I believed that her only passion was indeed meteorites. Her slanted eyes shining, she spoke enthusiastically about meteorite showers, zodiacal light, iron meteorites with Widmanstätten patterns and stone figures—chondrites and achondrites. But fairly soon it became clear that behind meteoritics there was a specific person, "bold, smart, and decisive," who was presently searching for the largest meteorite in Siberia. She talked about this person with obvious excitement. His name was Leonid Kulik. He was a senior scientific worker at the Mining Institute. Clearly, Masha was far from indifferent to him. I asked about the meteorite that Kulik was searching for. She said that it was an enormous fireball, which had fallen twenty years ago and had caused a sensation throughout Siberia. Still talking, we eventually came to her home on Ligovka Street, near the Moscow station. Masha said goodbye to me affably, adding: "See you tomorrow!"

And I made my way back home to the Moika. The meeting with Masha changed nothing in me. I continued attending Karlov's lectures, collapsing inwardly and *hanging*. This intrigued Masha. She always sat next to me. At first she tried to ask me funny questions in a whisper. But I didn't answer. And she stopped. But after Karlov's last words, she would poke me in the shoulder and say, "*Finita*!" And I would open my eyes.

Karlov's lecture was always last. If Masha didn't stay in the department on Komsomol business or didn't go off to see Kulik at the Mining Institute, I would walk her home. We went on foot or took the tram. I always accompanied her home. She accepted this as a matter of course. She stopped expecting masculine attention from me, deciding, most likely, that I was "a bit touched." Having assigned me the role of confidant of the male sex, she would pour out her soul to me on our walks, telling me her innermost secrets. She enjoyed this. She spoke about Kulik very cautiously, though always with excitement. When Kulik set off for a three-month expedition looking for the mysterious meteorite, Masha begged "desperately" to go with him, but there was an iron rule on expeditions: no women allowed. The expedition didn't find the meteorite. But it did determine the exact time and place of its descent. When Masha showed me a clipping from a newspaper with Kulik's article "The Tungus Meteorite," I immediately saw when it fell to earth: June 30, 1908. I suddenly remembered the unusual *thunder* that Mama had heard during my birth. I closed my eyes. And laughed unexpectedly.

"What is it?" asked Masha.

"I was born that very day. June 30, 1908," I replied.

She was struck by this coincidence. And she promised to tell Kulik about it. But I forgot about the Tungus meteorite (after all, it had *already* fallen) and once again plunged into the dear world of the Universe.

I passed the winter term with two incompletes. But, miraculously, I wasn't expelled; they just made me retake physics and logic during the summer terms. I vaguely followed what was happening not just in the university but in the country as well. Students were discussing Trotsky's exile to Alma-Ata, the struggle in the Party leadership, the peasants' sabotage of state grain procurements. I would pass them by or sit with a remote look. I felt *good*. I had a fulcrum—the planets and the stars. They were always with me. I didn't think about the future at all. I aspired to nothing. What should one strive for when everything *was there already*? I pressed my forehead to the marble lion. And floated in Ganymede's orbit, between Io and Callisto.

But reality soon reminded me of its existence.

In May, returning home from the university, I found Chekists there. They were searching of our closet. Auntie wasn't there. It turned out that in the church where she served, they had conducted a confiscation of church valuables, during which Auntie grabbed a heavy baptismal cross from a Chekist and hit him over the head. She was arrested. I was taken to the GPU on Gorokhovaya Street and interrogated. But they let me go. I tried to find out what happened to Auntie, but only learned that she was imprisoned in Kresty and awaiting trial. A month passed. Auntie was sentenced to five years and sent to Solovki. I never saw her again.

And a few weeks after the trial I was dismissed from the university. There were more than enough reasons: a non-proletarian background, an anti-Soviet aunt, my poor progress. Nor was I a member of the Komsomol. The secretary of our department's Komsomol had long ago christened me an "alien element."

I took my dismissal calmly. I could attend Karlov's lectures without a student card. And I managed to steal two books on astronomy from the library. But Masha was very upset. She went to the dean twice and to the Komsomol committee on my behalf, but without any results. We continued to meet at the lectures and to walk around the city.

Soon I realized that I had nothing to eat: Aunt Flora's stores of barley and flax oil had dried up. I sold her sewing machine. Buying grain, crackers, lard, sunflower oil, carrots, and garlic, I ate my fill and hid the remainder in the chest of drawers. In the morning I set off for the university. But there I found something I had neglected to consider: the lecture course in astronomy was over. Exams were beginning. Disappointed, I headed home. News awaited me there as well: the building manager was sitting in my room. He told me that if I didn't stop my anti-Soviet propaganda, the tenants would petition for my eviction. I listened to him silently. He left, slamming the door. I realized that, taking advantage of my helpless situation, the building manager simply wanted to take my room away from me. I picked up my two books on astronomy and went outside. It was a warm, sunny June day. I wandered aimlessly around the city and felt that it was *pushing me out*. There was no place left for me in it. And nothing tied me to it. I walked as far as Nevsky Prospect, turned, and ambled in the direction of St. Isaac's. I wanted to put my hands on its columns. And press my face to the cold, smooth stone. I took a few steps and ran into Masha. We bumped into each other so hard that my books fell on the pavement. Her portfolio fell open, and her papers tumbled out.

"Lord," Masha muttered, recoiling and pressing her palm to her forehead: her forehead had hit my chin.

I looked at her, crazed. Collecting herself, she started laughing. I helped her put her papers together and picked up my books.

"This is insane!" she said, shaking her head and laughing. "You know, I was talking about you just half an hour ago."

"With whom?" I asked.

"With Kulik. Do you want to go on an expedition? Two of their people have come down with dysentery. And they're leaving the day after tomorrow."

I looked at her silently, rubbing my chin. And suddenly, in one second, just as it happened after the blast, after my head spinning, after Kiev and counting all the corners, I felt that I *was setting out*. I had to move. Farther on.

And I answered, "I want to."

The Expedition

THE NEXT day at 9:00 a.m. Masha and I entered the building housing the Mining Institute. We walked down a dim hallway and soon stopped near a door with a new copper plate that read METEORITE DEPARTMENT. The plate looked unusual. Masha knocked on the door. No one answered. She put her ear to the door.

"Lord, don't tell me he's already in a meeting!"

"Not yet, but he'll definitely be heading there soon," came a slightly haughty, high-pitched voice behind our backs.

We turned around. Before us stood a thin man with glasses and thick, light-brown mustaches à la Nietzsche. He was dressed in an emphatically casual manner.

"Leonid Andreich!" Masha prattled, and I realized that she was deeply in love with Kulik.

"This is your protégé?" asked Kulik, glancing at me with his intelligent, piercing, and somewhat mocking eyes. "He's the one who was born June 30, 1908?"

"Yes . . . this is Snegirev. He's been dismissed from the university, but he's—" Masha muttered, but Kulik interrupted her.

"I don't care about that. Have you been on an expedition before?" "No."

"All right," Kulik's eyes drilled right through me. "Do you know how to dig?"

"Well . . ." I faltered.

"Haul heavy loads?"

"In principle . . . yes."

"In principle! Well, I'll tell you the way it goes." Kulik took out a worn, gilded watch, looked at it, and put it back. "In principle, I'll get rid of you halfway there. And now—follow me."

He turned sharply on his thin legs and took off in a sweeping stride, almost running along the hallway. Masha and I hurried after him. Kulik turned once, twice, ran up a staircase, and disappeared into the open doors of an auditorium. We ran in after him.

"Close the door!" he shouted from the rostrum.

With a habitual movement Masha fastened the hook. I sat at the edge of the room, half turned, and surveyed the place: there were sixteen people sitting in the spacious lecture hall.

Kulik took out a crumpled handkerchief and wiped his glasses. He put them on, immediately took complete control of the rostrum with his long, wiry fingers, and began speaking.

"Hello, comrades. Now then, today we will get acquainted with our greenhorn meteorologists, that is, the newcomers, and we'll correct the vector of our route to the place where the Tungus meteorite fell. Considering that only three of you remain from last year's expedition, since the rest I had to throw out to the dogs, I'll begin by introducing each of you."

He opened a thick, well-thumbed notebook and introduced everyone, naming each person's surname and profession. He didn't mention me. Closing the notebook with a bang, Kulik continued.

"Now I will permit myself to make a short announcement about the so-called Tungus meteorite, because of which so many spades have been broken and so many kilometers traversed. Thus, on June 30, 1908, a huge fireball fell to earth in eastern Siberia. Siberians saw and heard its fall; it created quite a hullabaloo and left incredible traces: a powerful wave of sound carried across all Siberia, forests were felled over hundreds of square kilometers, and there was a huge flash of light and an earthquake, recorded by an impartial seismograph in the basement of the Irkutsk observatory. The meteorite was seen not only by thousands of illiterate and superstitious inhabitants of eastern Siberia but by completely civilized people looking out the window of a train near Kansk—with whom I have had lengthy discussions. To summarize the accounts of eyewitnesses, it can be confidently stated that a huge meteorite fell in Siberia, probably one of the largest that has ever plummeted to earth. But twenty years ago meteorite studies had not yet won irrefutable rights to citizenship as an independent science. Meteorites were studied not only by scientists but by blatant charlatans, who introduced many lies and much confusion into the story of the Tungus meteorite. To the shame of our native science, no one even tried to organize an expedition in the hot traces, literally speaking, of the meteorite: the whole thing ended with a dozen newspaper articles and pseudoscientific publications. And it was only under Soviet power that your humble servant was able to organize the first meteorite expedition, in the difficult year of 1921, thanks to the personal support of People's Commissar Lunacharsky. Comrade Lunacharsky got the necessary sums of money through Narkompros, and NKPS—the Commissariat of Communications—sent a train car for the expedition and provided the necessary equipment. Nikolai Savelevich Trifonov, who is here with us, is the next-to-the-last of the Mohicans of that legendary expedition— en route he will tell you in more detail about the first campaign for the Tungus marvel. The first expedition didn't find the meteorite, but was able to precisely define the area of its fall: the basin of the Stony Tunguska River, or Katanga as the Evenki people call it. Having systematically analyzed the eyewitness evidence of the fall, I came to the conclusion presented in my article for the journal *Earth Science*: a meteorite of colossal size fell in eastern Siberia in 1908. Unfortunately, for a number of objective and subjective reasons, one of which was

NEP, the next expedition was able to leave Leningrad for Siberia only last year. This time we were aided by the academician Vernadsky and by Comrade Bukharin personally. Expedition No. 2 almost made it to the place where the meteorite fell. But 'almost' doesn't count in science, comrade meteorologists. The mistake of the second expedition was in its choice of time. In order to get through the swamps of the taiga, we decided to leave for Katanga in February, when the ice would establish a natural means of access across the bogs. On the one hand, this helped; on the other, it hindered us. The horses couldn't make it from Vanavara along the deer trails to the place where the forest had been felled: there was too much snow. Making an agreement with the Evenki, Trifonov and I traveled on reindeer, sending the whiners and panic-mongers back to Taishet. Alas, not every scientist is prepared to suffer in the name of science! After three days of the most difficult route across the snow-covered taiga, our indefatigable Evenki guide, Vasily Okhchen, brought us to the edge of the collapsed forest. When Nikolai Savelevich and I climbed a hill and saw the felled, broken trees stretching to the very horizon, we felt genuine terror and joy: such a phenomenal destruction of the taiga could have happened only by the volition of an enormous meteorite! What an incredible spectacle! Centuries-old trees had been snapped like pencils! That was the power of a messenger from space that fell to earth! No wonder that the Evenki refused to go farther—the shamans forbade them to enter the 'accursed place.' When the meteorite fell, some of them had deer that perished there and tents that burned. Okhchen will forever remember the terrible rumble and the fire from the sky. Yes! Not only was the forest felled, it burned, was scorched by the fierce fire from the explosion. And so, comrades, the second expedition turned back. Expedition No. 3 is now in this auditorium. And I would verrrry much like to hope that it will not be overtaken by the sad fate of the second expedition! Henceforth, I will be merciless toward whiners and panic-mongers. I am certain that there are none among you. And so! There are more of us this time. There are people here of different professions: astronomers, geophysicists, meteorologists, drillers, and even a cameraman. The student enthusiasts desiring to come with us will, I hope, satisfy their longing for discoveries and adventures. We are taking serious gear with us: equipment for meteorological, hydrological, geological, and photographic work, sets of drills, a water pump, and various other instruments. Now, about the route . . ."

Kulik stepped down from the podium, unrolled a map lying on the table, hung it on a blackboard, and picked up a wooden pointer.

"We leave tomorrow from Moscow station. We will travel by train to Taishet. There we will be met by thirty wagons, which will take us and the equipment four hundred kilometers along the horse route to the village of Kezhma on the Angara River, where we will change horses, saddle up, and ride over the taiga path another two hundred kilometers to the village of Vanavara on the banks of the Stony Tunguska. There is a Gostorg trading station in that settlement that supplies the Evenki with goods, gunpowder, and small shot in exchange for fur pelts. The last outpost of civilization, so to speak. The location of the meteorite's landing is eighty kilometers to the north of Vanavara. We will get there on foot, following the reindeer trail. On passing into the forest blast zone and determining the exact place where the meteorite landed, we will build a barracks from the timber the meteorite has already felled for us, have a housewarming party, and begin our scientific activity. Any questions?"

The plump astronomer Ikhilevich raised his hand. "How long might the expedition last?"

"Colleague, don't pose metaphysical questions," Kulik retorted. "Until we find it!"

"As long as the provisions last," smiled the homely Trifonov.

"Until the cold hits!" the small, fidgety driller Gridiukh added.

A slouching student enthusiast with a barely distinguishable beard stood up. "Comrade Kulik, is it true that smokers . . . well . . . you don't take them?"

"That's the genuine truth, young man! I cannot abide tobacco smoke. And I believe smoking to be a most harmful habit of the old world. You and I are building a new world. So make your choice—tobacco or the Tungus meteorite!"

Everyone laughed. The student scratched his chin. "Well, I guess . . . the meteorite."

"An excellent choice, young man!" Kulik exclaimed.

Everyone laughed even louder.

"Oh, God." Masha shook her head. "How awful that he doesn't take women on expeditions. It's such a mistake! I would keep a journal . . ."

"One more thing, comrades!" said Kulik, growing serious. "The local population that we will be working with—the Evenki and An-gara peoples—prefer goods to money, and most of all gunpowder, shot, and alcohol. We have an abundance of ammunition, but we aren't getting much alcohol. So if each of you could bring a flask of alcohol, it would noticeably hasten our progress across the taiga. Questions? No? Then—to work, comrades! Nikolai Savelevich will instruct you further."

"I'll ask everyone to proceed to packing the baggage," said Trifonov, standing.

The group stood up and people began talking. Kulik took off his glasses and wiped them, squinting shortsightedly.

"Oh, yes! One more thing . . ."

Everyone immediately fell silent. Kulik put his glasses on and looked at me. "Among us there will be a person who was born at the moment the Tungus meteorite fell."

And I realized that Kulik had accepted me on the expedition only because of this. Everyone turned toward me with curiosity.

"Where were you born?" asked Trifonov.

"About thirty versts north of Petersburg," I answered.

"Kilometers, kilometers, young man!" Kulik corrected me. "Your mother heard the thunder during the birth?"

"She did hear it. And she wasn't the only one," I answered.

"It was heard all over Russia that day," the glum geologist Yankovsky spoke up.

"And what else were you told about the day of your birth? Was there anything else unusual?" asked Kulik, staring intently at me.

"Unusual . . ." I thought a minute and suddenly remembered. "Of course. There was something. My family said that there was no night at all. And the sky was lit up."

"Absolutely right!" Kulik raised a long finger. "This phenomenon was noted along the entire coast of the Baltic Sea, in the northern parts of Europe and Russia—from Copenhagen to Yeniseisk! An anomalous luminescence of the atmosphere!"

"Which Torvald Kohl and Herman Seidel wrote about," nodded Ikhilevich. "A bright dawn and dusk, a massive development of silvery clouds…"

"The mass accumulation of silvery clouds…" Kulik repeated in a loud voice. He grew thoughtful and suddenly banged his fist on the rostrum. "This time we are obliged to find the meteorite!"

"We'll find it! It won't get away from us! That's why we're going!" Everyone began talking at once.

"Sasha, Sasha, it's so wonderful!" Masha turned her reddened face toward me. "Find it, find the Tungus meteorite!"

"I'll try," I muttered without much enthusiasm.

I just wanted to travel somewhere. To travel and travel, as I did *back then*.

The next day we left on the Leningrad–Moscow–Irkutsk train, in which we had been assigned an entire car. The four days to Taishet passed in conversations and arguments in which I was a passive listener. In our car, No. 12, they argued about topical questions: Communism, free love, industrialization, world revolution, the structure of the atom, and, of course, the Tungus meteorite. All this was accompanied by what was excellent food for that time, and endless drinking of tea with unlimited sugar, which for me, after my half-starved existence, was particularly pleasant. Having stuffed myself with horse sausage, Baltic herring, boiled eggs, and bread with cow's milk butter, and drunk my fill of strong tea, I climbed onto the top bunk and, half asleep, looked out the window where the endless Vologodsky and Viatsky forests sailed by. After the low Ural Mountains, that view was replaced by the incomparable Siberian landscape. From Chelyabinsk all the way to Novosibirsk the depths of an ancient sea, according to Kulik, stretched in boundless breadth, overgrown with pine and larch. Gazing at these expanses I fell asleep.

Relations among members of the expedition were good, everyone was friendly and well disposed. The mysterious meteorite, which the Soviet newspapers had begun to write about, thanks to Kulik, captivated and excited the imagination. I liked to think about it when I lay on the top bunk. But I always imagined it still gliding through the Universe. That way was even *more pleasurable* for me. Arguments about its composition, velocity, and size went on endlessly. Kulik infected everyone with his enthusiasm, which bordered on fanaticism. For this everyone forgave him his dictatorial manner, his everyday terrorism and intolerance in discussion. On the expedition he called everyone "comrade," as a matter of principle, ignoring names and patronymics. After the victory of the Soviets in Russia, his "scientific Marxism" grew even stronger. Kulik deified "Stalin's iron consistency" and believed in a coming Soviet economic leap capable of "proving to the whole world the dialectical objectivity of our path."

We arrived in Taishet in the morning.

We were met by men driving solid Siberian carts, hot sunny weather, and clouds of mosquitoes. I had never seen such quantities of bloodsucking insects in the air before. Everyone was given a panama hat with cheesecloth netting, manufactured according to Kulik's design, since he had a great deal of experience in dealing with the local mosquitoes. In these identical gray panamas we looked like Chinese peasants. Loading ourselves onto the carts, we set off for our distant destination along a tract that our drivers called "the highway"—a wide but uneven packed-earth road, pocked with ruts and potholes. Fortunately for us, June 1928 turned out dry in eastern Siberia, and the mud puddles on the road were entirely surmountable. The bridges over small rivers, however, were almost all in a sorry state and required repair. Some of them had been almost completely destroyed by the spring floods. We had to go around them and cross at a ford. When, once more pushing our carts over a shaky bridge in a hurry, Kulik would quote a French traveler: "And along the way we came across constructions that had to be circumvented, and which in Russian were called 'Le Most.'"

The road lay through the hilly taiga, where a mixed forest grew. But the summits of these smooth hills, which the locals called mounds, were entirely covered in thick pine growth. These amazing virgin woodlands reminded me of the manes of sleeping monsters. The slender ship timber grew incredibly thick, and when the wind began to toss the trees, they came alive, and with them the whole mound appeared to awaken, and it seemed that a sleeping monster was just about to rise up, straighten himself out, and fill the taiga expanses with a powerful, resounding roar.

Despite the primeval nature of this region, we rarely came across actual animals: someone spotted a marten once, and a moose.

We traveled very slowly, taking almost a week, spending the nights in small villages that looked like northern Russian farmsteads. The endless taiga spread out around five or six isbas made of hundred-year-old pines, enclosed with high pike fences to keep out animals. The locals were always happy to see us. Simple-hearted people, inured to hardship by Siberia's harshness, they lived primarily by hunting, fishing, and income from people passing along the "highway," for whom a separate hut with a stove and bunks always stood ready. We paid them with gunpowder and alcohol. Soviet money was still rare here, and Stalin's program of mass collectivization had not yet reached these wild places. The villagers fed us freshly caught fish, fried mushrooms, dried game, and the customary flour-meal soup, spiced with wild garlic, wild onions, dried carrots, and salted deer or moose. We slept side by side in huts, bathhouses, sheepfolds, and haylofts. But our undemanding drivers would place their carts in a circle at night, bring all the horses inside the circle, light campfires in a circle around them, and sleep on the carts, covering themselves, despite the summer weather, with the ever-present sheepskin.

On the sixth day our wagon train arrived in Kezhma.

A large settlement with a hundred or so houses stood on a high, beautiful bank of the Angara—a wide, powerful river. Dropping off sharply, the banks turned into a small shoal beyond which this mighty river flowed. The water in it, as in all Siberian rivers, was cold and unbelievably pure. The wooded shore on the other side stretched steeply into the distance.

The village was inhabited primarily by Russians, who were called Angars, and the rare, Russianized Evenki. Everyone worked in hunting and fishing. The hunted pelts were handed over to the government for very small sums, and fish, moose, and reindeer fed them reliably all year long. The Angars did not keep domesticated animals.

In Kezhma our expedition's Gostorg credit kicked in: we received eight sacks of dried pike, muksun whitefish, and peled whitefish; three barrels of salted white salmon; a small barrel of lard; and a couple of bags of fish flour. Having bathed and sat in the Siberian steam bath, we gave ourselves over to the hospitality of the local leader, a former chairman of the agricultural soviet and local director of Gostorg. He treated Kulik like an old pal, showed him an article clipped from a Taishet newspaper about last year's expedition. The fellow was most happy that we had "made it all the way here from Petersburg, where Ilyich set up a real carousel for the bourgeois." A former Red partisan who had fought in the Urals, after the Bolsheviks' victory they sent him to distant Kezhma "to carry out the Party line." Arriving here with a cavalry squadron, he "definitively and irreversibly decided the question of Soviet power in Kezhma" over the course of three days: he shot twelve people.

"Now I understand—I should have shot more," he admitted to us candidly over a glass of alcohol diluted with the cold Angara river water.

In Kezhma he had two wives—the old one and a new one—who got along wonderfully and made a real feast for us: the long, crude table in the director's isba was groaning with victuals. Here, for the first time in my life, I tried dumplings with bear lard and *shangi*— little wheat cakes fried on a skillet and covered with sour cream. The boss knew only one thing about the meteorite: "Something crashed there and knocked the forest down." He was categorical in his parting words, advised us not to stand on ceremony with the Evenki, and if necessary to "beat them between their slanted eyes with a rifle butt." He attributed the failure of last year's expedition entirely to the sabotage of the native population and Kulik's "rotten softheartedness." He referred to the Evenki as Tunguses and saw them as hidden enemies of Soviet rule.

"At first I thought: they live in tents in the taiga, eat simple, dress simple, shit in the open—of course they'll support Soviet power. But it turns out they're more kulak than the worst kulaks! All they do is count who has the most reindeer. They need their own revolution! A Tungus Lenin is what they need!"

Kulik tried to object, saying that the main problem of the backward peoples of the USSR was general illiteracy, which had been advantageous to the czarist regime for exploiting them; that the Party had already begun working on this, organizing isba reading rooms and schools for the indigenous people; and that the Evenki, like all the peasants and animal herders, would soon be collectivized. But the headman was unswayable.

"Andreich, if it was my job, I'd collectivize them in my own way: into a cart, to the city with them, do the dirty work, the digging. The shovel will reeducate them! And I'd slaughter all the reindeer and send them off to the starving peasants of the Volga region."

"We conquered famine in the Volga region two years ago," Kulik informed him proudly.

"Really?" smiled the tipsy, red-faced boss. "Well, then, we'll eat the reindeer ourselves."

In the morning we donned our backpacks, having placed in them only the necessary provisions, saddled up the local horses, and set off along a narrow path beaten down by the reindeer. From Kezhma to the Stony Tungus River we had another two hundred kilometers north to travel. The wagon train with the main baggage took off after us.

The tract passed through hills and mounds. Uphill we rode at a walk, going down we drove our slow, broad-chested horses as fast as we could. They got extremely frightened when there was a long descent. Then—up a hill once again, and so on, endlessly.

On the mounds the taiga changed: pine gave way quickly to conifers, and the mixed forest crawled down into a valley; the land gradually became covered with moss and lichen. Animals could be seen frequently. The men met them with cries. Wild birds flew up from the thickets, flapping their heavy wings. I saw Siberian weasels and ermines several times. Scared by us, they shot up the trees in a flash and disappeared in the branches. There were two inveterate hunters among us: the driller Petrenko and the geologist Molik. At the first stop they set off for game and returned fairly quickly with a wood grouse. The large, beautiful bird was plucked, gutted, cut in strips, and boiled with wheat porridge, but its meat turned out to be tough and tasted like pine. During the first expedition Kulik had staked a lot on the local game, hoping to supplement the food with it. But he'd had no luck: during the expedition they had shot only an inedible fox and a few ducks. Our first night in the taiga wasn't easy: we cut off pine branches and constructed beds for ourselves, lay down around the fire, and tried to fall asleep, covering ourselves with our outer clothing. But despite the warm summer weather an eternal cold was exuded by the stony, mossy earth, and it seeped through our clothes. From above, we were harassed by mosquitoes, which didn't diminish in number even at night. Among the tribe of mosquitoes appeared tiny, nimble, furious individuals called midges. With a revolting whine they found their way up sleeves and crawled into the eyes and nostrils. It was impossible to fight them off. We took Kulik's advice and rubbed our wrists and necks with kerosene. Soon the whole expedition began to stink like a kerosene shop. The next three nights were just as hard: people didn't get enough sleep; they cussed and tried to escape the night cold and mosquitoes; during the day they shivered half asleep in their saddles. But Kulik was inflexible. He woke us at exactly six o'clock with the whistle he carried in his breast pocket, keeping the expedition on an iron schedule. He gave the commands for starting up and for stopping with this whistle. His main motto was: For the sake of a great goal you can put up with everything. In people he valued willpower and focus above all, and in the material world—books. Sitting with us at the campfire, he told us how Schopenhauer's *The World as Will and Representation* helped him to stop smoking when he was in exile.

"I had been reading it for days on end, and one morning I left my shack, walked over to the ice hole, and poured out an entire year's supply of tobacco with the words: 'Let the fish smoke. I—am a man of will.'"

Like other social democrats who became Bolshevik, he lived for the future, piously believing in the new Soviet Russia.

"Science should help the Revolution," he would say.

He thought GOELRO, Lenin's plan to bring electricity to the whole country, was brilliant and prophetic, and that Stalin's program of industrialization and collectivization was simply the dictate of the time. But his primary passion was still the Tungus meteorite. When he started talking about it, Kulik completely forgot about Stalin and GOELRO.

"Just imagine, comrades, a piece of another planet, separated from us by millions of kilometers, broke off and is lying somewhere here, not far away." Kulik paused, straightened his glasses, which reflected the flame of the campfire, and raised his head slightly toward the pale Siberian stars. "And in it is the material of other worlds!"

This phrase gave me goose bumps: the familiar, beloved world of the planets surfaced in my memory. Falling asleep on a pile of pine branches, covering myself from the head down to escape the midges, I imagined that mysterious piece of other worlds in black airless space as it flew toward the Earth and shimmered with all the colors of the rainbow. It spun in my head. Plunging into sleep, I counted its corners . . .

Finally, toward the evening of the fourth day, swollen from midge bites and badly bruised from the jolting ride across the mounds, we approached Vanavara.

A dozen new wooden houses clung to the very shores of the Stony Tungus River: a few years earlier the trading station at Vanavara had been rebuilt. The biggest, sturdiest log house had the word GOS-TORG inscribed on it in large white letters, and a faded red flag hung nearby. Around the settlement spread a marvelously beautiful landscape: the very high, sharply descending cliffs of the river's shore were surrounded by thick taiga. The opposite, southern shore, on the contrary, was fairly low, and beyond it, all the way to the horizon itself, blue-green waves of hills scampered endlessly, flooded by the rays of the sunset. Eagles glided in the rosy-blue evening sky where the moon was becoming faintly visible. Their short cries were the only sounds that disturbed the absolute silence.

But then dogs, spying us, began to bark, and people came out of the houses. They greeted Kulik and Trifonov like family. For this trading post isolated in the taiga, our arrival was an event. A bath was fired up in the bathhouse that stood below on the riverbank. They didn't begrudge firewood for it, and the steam filled the room in thick whirls. When we had sat in the steam so long our skin was wrinkled and our eyes dimmed, we ran out on a little wooden dock and jumped into the cold Tungus. It was already getting dark. The northern white nights had passed, and a dark-blue sky scattered with stars hung over our heads. Turning onto my back and feeling the strong current of the river, I gazed at the stars. In Siberia they were higher up and seemed very far away.

They fed us fish stew and *shangi* and put us to bed. In the morning I looked over the trading post. Twenty-eight Russians lived there, along with sixteen Evenki, three Chinese, and two Chechens who had been exiled to Siberia during the czarist regime for a blood feud. Here they were blacksmiths. Gostorg bought up fur pelts from local hunters and the Evenki for a song, as it did everywhere in Siberia, and traded them for what was brought in by wagon train. During the winter, the pelts were taken to Kezhma on reindeer sleds.

Our wagon train arrived a couple of days later. It had had its share of adventures along the way: a horse had broken its leg and they'd had to shoot it, and two drivers had run off, taking three guns and a rucksack of ammunition with them. But Kulik wasn't particularly upset: he was happy that they had brought the equipment and provisions. After our arrival in Vanavara, he had become quite nervous and often grew furious over trivial things. He yelled at me when I dropped a barometer, and he threatened two of the drillers with exile for carelessness with the baggage. Yakov Ikhilevich, the thirty-year-old astronomer, carried on constant professional "meteorological" conversations with Kulik. They almost always ended in arguments with raised voices, and Kulik was the first to explode, reproaching Ikhilevich for "narrow-mindedness and metaphysical thinking." Ikhilevich had been educated as a mathematician; in calculating the fall of meteorites, he had come up with his own universal formula, according to which a meteorite larger than 248.17 tons could not fall to earth without breaking up into very small pieces. He was absolutely convinced that almost nothing remained of the Tungus meteorite and was in the expedition only to confirm his own theory. Kulik, however, longing to find "material from other worlds" fallen to earth in the form of a huge block, or many-ton pieces, had taken "the bore Ikhilevich" with him in order to "laugh at all the cabinet scientist-worms in the person of 'the bore Ikhilevich.'" Falling asleep by the campfire, I could often hear Ikhilevich's dull, nauseatingly detailed muttering and Kulik's sharp, high voice through my sleep.

But in Vanavara the endless discussion with Ikhilevich came to an end. The moment the short Yakov Iosifovich Ikhilevich, resembling an owl in his pince-nez, opened his mouth about the "crumbling of the hyper-meteorite mass on impact," Kulik interrupted him: "Colleague, if you have come with us in order to get in our way, I will send you back."

That was too much. Ikhilevich got mad and stopped talking to Kulik. The falling-out strengthened the general excitement. We were *only* eighty kilometers from the forest collapse zone. The young people were chomping at the bit to go on, but given his past scientific experience Kulik wanted to calculate and prepare everything this time. Farther on we would have to move along a narrow reindeer trail. The wagons couldn't follow. All the baggage was loaded onto horses. It was decided that we'd travel in two groups: the first, with light luggage, would set off on horseback, make camp and pitch tents twenty versts along, prepare food and night quarters; the second group would lead heavily loaded horses on foot and arrive at the camp by evening; everyone would spend the night there, and in the morning the groups would change places—those who led the horses the first day would ride ahead in order to pitch a new camp. Kulik planned to cover the "Okhchen path" in four days. One third of the provisions would remain at the trading post and would have to be brought to us by the Vanavara people.

Vasily Okhchen himself, Kulik's guide from the previous year, showed up in Vanavara the day after our arrival. The fifty-year-old Evenki came from his camp. As he put it: "Okhchen feel big man lord master come." The *lord* Kulik was glad to see him, although it was in part because of Okhchen's fear of the "cursed place" that expedition No. 2 had turned back. Okhchen was a man of few words. But our alcohol untied his tongue. They asked him, of course, about the "fireball."

"Mine then there with reindeer camp at Chamba. Mine brother left Khushma with wife, fishing there. Then all fast it attack. Made very much lotta noise, break forest, dig up earth, finish off reindeers. Brother break arm, lose wife. We run here to Katanga. Now no one people there—no man, no reindeer." He spoke the words through clenched teeth, sucking on his narrow bone pipe.

Okhchen was certain that nothing fell from the sky, but simply that the terrible beast Kholi (a mammoth), who lived in the underground world Khergui, where the shamans used to go to swallow his breath and build up their powers, got angry at the people and shook the earth. And the heavenly birds, the *agdy*, their beaks blazing with flames, went with Kholi's brother Uchir the dust devil to pull down the forest and set fire to it. This happened because the shamans had started drinking firewater (alcohol) too often and had forgotten Kholi. When he was totally drunk, Okhchen told us about hearing Kholi's voice once when he was a boy.

"Winter were very strong, big pine he cracking, reindeer no going. When Elk"—Ursa Major—"stand on back legs"—at midnight—"earth open on Khushma, steam come out, and Kholi yell: 'Ooooo!' Mine fall down lay down no move. Mine very 'fraid Kholi."

Instead of himself, Okhchen offered his eighteen-year-old nephew Fyodor as a guide.

"He know taiga very good."

Fyodor said nothing, merely nodded and smiled. Okhchen gave him a red Berdan rifle and two knives.

Early the next morning the first group left camp, led by Kulik and Fyodor. I was in the second group. We set off at noon. Trifonov led us. The loaded horses walked slowly. We led them by the bridle along the reindeer trail. Each winter the deer trampled down the bushes and saplings, and for this reason the path was never completely overgrown during the summer. In some places even this path was invisible, but the two Vanavarans who walked ahead with axes easily cut a way through. The taiga here was thicker than the Angara taiga. White, gray, and green moss covered the ground underfoot. I noticed for the first time that there are no meadows or grassy clearings in the taiga: empty space is immediately overgrown with bushes and other undergrowth. The sole places that aren't overgrown are ponds and swamps. One can move rapidly only along the animal trails. But we hadn't gone halfway to the camp when a heavy rain shower began. We had to put on our peacoats and move ahead at a goose's pace. We arrived at the camp long after midnight. The first group had also been rained on and had lost an ammunition belt. A wet, angry Kulik shouted at everyone. Having eaten wheat porridge with lard and drunk our tea, we fell asleep in wet tents. Kulik woke us up at six.

Despite all this, we made it to the border of the collapsed forest in four days, just as planned.

But along the road something began to happen to me. The third night I suddenly dreamed my recurring childhood dream, which hadn't happened for at least ten years. Once again I stood at the foot of my great Mountain, lifting my gaze with difficulty along its endless slopes toward the summit. And again I crumbled, like a bread roll in milk. Again I shook before the huge and incomprehensible. Again I had to lift my head with my hands. But the light that poured down on me from the summit was faint and somehow timid, as though the Mountain was fading, was being extinguished like a volcano. I didn't disappear in the Light, as I did in childhood, didn't dissolve into it; I didn't *die* from its immense power. There was a sort of sorrowful doom to the entire dream. Something was dying and departing *forever*. This stunned me: my Mountain was dying. Sobbing, I stood in front of it, holding my head. I gazed at the summit. And nothing happened to me! I saw the Light going out. But I couldn't allow that to happen. I had to help the Mountain, to save it. I had to exert all my strength, I had to do something, do, do, do, do something, in myself. Like in childhood dreams, when you wave your arms, wave, wave, wave, and suddenly you fly off. I mustered all my strength. The Light of the Mountain was going out. I waved my arms, roared, jumped up and down. But I could feel that my muscles, bones, brain, and voice weren't connected to the Mountain. They had no influence on it at all. However, there was something in me that was directly connected to the Mountain. But what? The Light was disappearing! It was melting, going away. I understood that it was leaving FOREVER! Sobbing with helplessness, I leaped, wailed, and kicked the ground. It didn't do any good. I grabbed my body, began to punch it and tear at it, looking for its connection to the Mountain. I looked in my body the way you search for a treasure. My fingers tore at my muscles, pierced the skin. It became painful. Very painful. That didn't stop me. The Mountain was dying. "Don't die!" I sobbed, mangling my body. Suddenly, a finger passed through my ribs and touched my heart. Something in my heart moved, shifted. As though something sleeping had shuddered but didn't awake. *Something else, other* was living in the heart, something other than my heart itself. And it was precisely *this* that was connected to the Mountain. I had to wake this up! But—how? I began to beat my chest with my fists, to scream at my heart. It didn't help. The Light was departing! I thrust my fingers into my chest, grabbed my ribs, and pulled. The ribs cracked. Breaking the ribs and screaming from pain, I stuck my hand into my chest and felt my heart. Warm and resilient, it beat indifferently beneath my fingers. I squeezed it hard. My heart hurt unbearably. But the pain didn't awaken the *something other* that dozed in my heart! It lived on its own! I squeezed my heart as hard as I could. I cried out and woke up.

"What is it, a nightmare?" the unruffled, unflappable cameraman Chistiakov asked me sleepily; he and I shared a tent.

"Yes, yes," I mumbled.

"Take some iodide before bedtime, young man . . ."

I was hot and suffocating. My hands shook in the darkness and my mouth was dry. I touched my chest: it was whole. Somehow managing to get out of my sleeping bag, I crawled from the tent. The taiga was growing light. I sat on the moist, soft moss near the tent. Its coolness calmed me. My shaking fingers nestled in it. Sweat rolled down my face. Growing calm, I drank some water and touched my chest. It hurt, as though I had actually tried to break my breastbone.

When we set off that day, I felt a certain alarm and agitation. These feelings grew with each step the horse took. Everyone made the last crossing together. Kulik hurried us, the guide Fyodor sang something in his own language, Chistiakov took photographs, and Ikhilevich told the students about the Galileo comet. The taiga grew rosy, small swamps came into view, overgrown with tussocks. On rest breaks we gathered blueberries and whortleberries. Our path widened and it became easier to walk. Everyone was anticipating the encounter with the unknown and talked excitedly. I walked along, silent, leading my homely, piebald horse by the reins. My agitation grew, my heart beat more rapidly. This made me remember the glass of spirits and the cocaine brought to me, when I was thirteen, by the porter Samson at the Krasnoye station. At that point I hadn't slept all night; I'd been energetically arguing for a ridiculously long time with half-literate carpetbaggers who were laughing at me. Right now I didn't feel like talking at all. I walked and walked along the mossy path, going around the trees, listening to the beat of my heart.

That evening we entered the forest impact zone. For me it was unexpected. Our expedition caravan had stretched out: the impatient Kulik had gone ahead with Fyodor, and the young people were trying to catch up with them. I wandered along at the end of the caravan with my horse, looking glumly at my feet and remembering the strange dream. Suddenly the sun struck me in the eyes. It was strange and I was unprepared; usually the eternal taiga hid the sun, the rays got stuck in the thick pines. For a moment I thought it was now early morning: the inadequate sleep of the last few nights was making itself felt. Remembering that we were walking northwest, however, I collected myself and raised my head.

There was no eternal forest surrounding me! Instead, all the trees lay on the ground, and a young, low, sparse undergrowth had taken root. In front of us it was as though a curtain had been drawn open. It was possible to see far ahead: the sun was setting between hillocks that stood bare all the way to the horizon, without the taiga growth, just lightly covered in green. I could see our expedition, which had moved far ahead. The tiny figure of Kulik took a gun off his shoulder and shot in the air. All the others cried out victoriously. The path crossed the first prone tree. I walked up to it and squatted down. The powerful fir tree lay in all its thirty-meter length, pulled out by the roots. In places its trunk was touched with rot, the bark had peeled almost everywhere, and the branches had been broken off. Nearby, almost parallel to it, lay a similarly thick, long Angara pine. Its trunk, snapped off midway, was now covered in moss and mushrooms. Farther on, the felled forest began in earnest. All the trees lay with their crowns pointing toward me, and their roots toward the setting sun.

Sticking up here and there were the trunks of broken giants whose roots had held fast in the earth but whose crowns had not been spared by the terrible impact of the air waves. The dead forest impressed one with the scale and force of its sudden demise. I placed my hand on the graying, cracking fir, dappled by timber worms. My heart fluttered, my eyes grew dim. And suddenly I felt wonderful, *terribly* wonderful, as one can only feel in childhood, when everything around you is big and loud and you are really small, but there's a profoundly familiar palm that will warm and protect you, in which you lie as though in a shell. My eyes filled with tears. An involuntary stream of urine flowed with warmth and tenderness down my legs. I began to sob. The horse looked askance at me, stretched its indifferent muzzle, and grabbed a sprig of Saint-John's-wort growing on the rotten side of the pine. I sobbed and urinated, completely forgetting who and where I was. The urine stopped running. I sniffled and stood up. My legs trembled. I wiped the tears away and looked at my black woolen pants. Urine seeped from them. I unbuttoned my pants, took them off, and squeezed them out as well as I could. My head was empty and my heart was beating fast. The horse chewed. I held it by the bridle and led it between two prostrate trees. Their menacing, deracinated root systems almost closed in on one another. The horse, still chewing, loaded down with provisions, snorted as we squeezed between them.

Reaching the others, I stood a ways off with my horse. Everyone was celebrating noisily and their amazement at the fantastical landscape knew no bounds. Kulik was so excited that he was ready to move farther on. But the sun was going down. They set up camp and lit a large campfire from the dry branches of fallen trees. In honor of reaching the site, Kulik allowed everyone to drink some spirits. The group quickly grew jolly and noisy, and began singing songs. Slightly tipsy himself, Kulik sang an old prison-camp song that he had heard while in exile. I kept my distance and remained silent. I had no desire to talk. I just stared into the campfire flames. People handed me a flask with spirits, pushed food at me. I shook my head: I didn't feel like eating, either. I felt *good*. A pleasant stupor engulfed my body. No one paid any attention to me. My heart pounded, I listened to it. Soon I climbed into the tent and fell into a deep, dreamless sleep.

I awoke rested but still uneasy. Looking at the rising sun, I suddenly understood that it was *no accident* that I had ended up in this strange place. I had some strong connection to this lifeless landscape. And something awaited me ahead.

We made the campfire and heated the tea. But again I didn't feel like talking during our quick field breakfast. I still didn't have any appetite. I took a cracker, dunked it in the tea, and sucked on it.

"What do you think, Snegirev, is it iron or stone?" asked the student Anikin.

I shrugged my shoulders.

"For some reason I'm certain that it's stone," said Anikin, his glasses glinting just above the thin stubble that had grown on his face. I shrugged my shoulders again.

We set off.

Kulik determined the route according to the direction of the fallen trees. We had to move from the tops to the roots, that is, in the direction from which the blast had come. Traveling about five kilometers across the dead taiga, I suddenly noticed that the clouds of midges that had constantly pursued us had disappeared. And the birds had stopped singing. Young saplings grew bashfully between fallen giants. There was absolute silence all around. Within it, our steps, voices, and the snorting horses sounded timidly. The silence was much greater than us. The voices gradually fell silent, and people walked along quietly, spellbound and overwhelmed. Every so often we came across reindeer skulls and bones, and a couple of times I saw moose antlers sticking up out of the moss. Not a single crackle of an animal's step disturbed the silence. There was only the dead forest drifting past.

Gradually the hillocks flattened out and there were more swamps. We went around them. In the evening, as usual, we stopped for the night. But the previous gaiety was gone. Everyone around the campfire looked tired, they ate without talking. Even Kulik was subdued. Thin and sharp-nosed, with a thick, bristling mustache, wearing his large, round eyeglasses, he looked like a frightened animal.

At the campfire I once again felt a growing agitation. But it was no longer accompanied by fear and malaise. I was calm. And I was not the least bit tired, although I had walked fifteen kilometers with my horse, skirting swamps, making my way over storm-tossed trees, stepping over mossy tree stumps.

This time Anikin and I were in the same tent. He tossed and turned and pestered me with conversation. I groaned something in reply, lying in the dark with open eyes. I wasn't at all sleepy.

"It's really rather scary here, isn't it, Snegirev? Some kind of vacuum," Anikin muttered as he was falling asleep. "No wonder the Evenki don't come here. Although, of course, superstitions…" He yawned. "But still, damn it, what powerful energy there is in space! That's what man has to conquer…" He yawned again.

He fell asleep.

I lay there, yielding to my feeling. Something pleasantly agonizing was awakening inside me. I didn't understand what it was, but *it* was connected to this place I found myself in. I felt that with certainty. Somehow my heart was beating in a new key. And it froze, stopping. And in this there was a joyous premonition of something enormous and innately and naturally new. It was growing like a *heavy* wave. And approaching implacably. I touched myself and tried to breathe carefully. I didn't fall asleep at all that night. And the night passed quickly. I rose earlier than the others, made the campfire, which had gone out overnight, took our large kettle to the swamp for water, and, hanging it above the fire, sat down nearby. Gazing at the tongues of flame climbing up the dry branches, I remembered my past. It seemed spectral and unstable to me. It stood before me like a frozen picture under glass, like a herbarium in a museum. And the picture didn't elicit any feelings. My happy childhood, the tornado of the Revolution, the loss of my family, the wanderings, studies, loneliness, and orphanhood—it had all hardened under glass *forever*. It all became *the past*. And detached itself from me. The present was only the *new* joy of my heart. It was more powerful than everything.

The kettle boiled and steam escaped from the spout. It looked menacing and silly. And I began to laugh.

"What are you laughing at, Comrade Snegirev?" came Kulik's voice from behind me.

I didn't even turn around. Kulik had also become the past, as had the entire expedition. Over that night I had lost all interest in it. It had become small and helplessly menacing. Like the kettle. Laughing, I threw a branch in the fire.

"Get a move on, wake the others," said Kulik, handing me his whistle.

I stood up silently, took the whistle, and blew it deafeningly. I blew the whistle for a long time. Kulik looked at me attentively.

"Is everything all right?" he asked, when I stopped.

I didn't answer. I *really* didn't want to talk. Every word returned me to the past. To answer Kulik with "Thank you, everything is just fine" would have meant to turn back, *behind the glass*. I was silent again at breakfast. They handed me a piece of dry bread and smoked fish. The food looked beggarly. I didn't touch it, just put it on the cloth. I poured some bilberries into my palm from the elm basket, ate them, and washed them down with tea. Kulik held a short meeting, saying that "the secret is very close." And we set off.

Once again I walked behind. The surrounding landscape hadn't changed. The expedition made its way through felled forest. And the farther into the forest it went, the more exalted and strong I became inside myself. I led my horse without tiring, helping it to step over the trunks lying on the ground, picking my way around obstructions, pulling my horse out of the swamp water. The swampiness of the place made itself apparent: by dinnertime everyone was dirty—the people and the horses. In contrast to me, everyone began to tire quickly and became irritable. Furthermore, the general sense of oppression grew: the dead zone put everyone on his guard. Arguments flared. Yankovsky accused Urnov from Vanavara of stealing sugar. The Vanavaran crossed himself and swore to God he hadn't taken any. Ikhilevich, who had been quiet in recent days, suddenly burst out with a semi-hysterical lecture on the theory of stellar explosions, at the end of which he was almost screaming that "science won't allow fools to joke around." Kulik made fun of him maliciously. Two students continually argued until they were nearly hoarse about who would lead which horse and what to carry on it. They were nicknamed "the Gracchi brothers." The hunters Petrenko and Molik flushed ducks from the swamps four times in one day, but only killed one. Something had broken in Chistiakov's movie camera; he was continually repairing it and swearing up a storm. Trifonov kept criticizing him.

Soon my unwillingness to talk was noticed. People also noticed that I had practically stopped eating. They looked at one another and whispered behind my back. Kulik and Trifonov tried to get me to talk; they asked how I was feeling. I just shrugged my shoulders and smiled. During the camp dinner, when everyone greedily devoured wheat kasha with lard and smoked fish, I ate berries and drank tea. At mealtimes a large oilcloth was usually spread out and the food placed on it; no one would sit there. Crackers, smoked fish, lard, onions, and lumps of sugar lay on the cloth. In the center, on a board, they placed the cauldron with the wheat kasha, flavored with lard and dried carrots. Everyone dug it out with wooden spoons. There were no bowls on the expedition; Kulik said that they would just make a racket on the way and washing up would take time. After the kasha, a thick tea was poured into tin cups. It was drunk holding lumps of sugar between the teeth; Kulik had forbidden drinking tea with sugar dissolved in it. Sitting in the circle, I drank tea from a cup and looked at the people eating. Their food seem abnormal to me. For the first time in my not very long life I suddenly paid attention to *what* people were eating. What they ate was either dead or processed, chopped up, ground, or dried. The smoked wrinkled fish and dried crackers were equally distasteful to me. Of everything that was put out on the oilcloth during dinner, only the onion and berries did not disgust me. They were normal food. Sometimes I would take an onion and eat it, washing it down with tea. Everyone looked askance at me. Anikin, with whom I slept in the tent, became terse and almost stopped talking to me. He no longer theorized about meteorites and comets. Lying in the tent one night, I heard a conversation between Kulik and Trifonov.

"It appears that Snegirev has gone crackers. We have to do something about him."

"What? Isolate him from the group? And how?"

"Hmm, you're right. There's nowhere. Keep an eye on him. After all, he's our talisman."

"Have you become superstitious?"

"While the expedition is going on. Do you disapprove?"

"Not a bit. I'm a dialectician, you know."

"Well, old man, I'm no metaphysician, either!"

They laughed in the darkness.

The second night I spent in a half sleep. I was in wonderful form. Good spirits and energy filled me to the brim. And I was living only in the present: the past was forgotten. I wanted one thing alone: for the *joy* my body felt to go on forever. For that I was ready to do anything...

The morning meeting was anxious. Grumbling began among the members of the expedition: they were thirty kilometers into the felled-forest zone, and there were no traces of the meteorite's fall. Ikhilevich and Potresov tried to convince everyone that the meteorite exploded in the air. Kulik tore them apart rudely, calling them "craven renegades." The geologists proposed going a bit farther and beginning the construction of the barracks. The drillers, who tired more easily than anyone else for some reason, advised that we begin building right in this spot. The students, mesmerized by the strange place and exhausted by the trip, were ready for anything. But Kulik and Trifonov insisted on moving ahead. I listened to the quarrels and arguments, happy that I wasn't like the others, that I had been given something that made my body sing. In contrast to the rest of them, I was happy. And I didn't care whether we went ahead or stopped here.

Finally Kulik couldn't stand it and he blew the whistle, signaling that the day's trek was starting. It was useless to argue with him—he was the leader of the expedition. The baggage was loaded onto the horses, and the expedition set out again. The horses themselves felt pretty good: in the marshes there was enough juicy grass; they grazed there at night and during stops.

About six kilometers along, the felled forest changed: almost all the trunks were broken in half, there were practically no trees torn out by the roots anymore. It was as though the forest had been resurrected, but as tall tree stumps. These stumps began to grow upward with every kilometer. And after another six kilometers the old forest rose up: the trees were whole but were mortally burned. They had all dried out and died. This standing dead forest looked even more unusual than the felled forest. There was hardly any young under-growth here.

The expedition halted. Kulik gave the order to make camp. While we were putting up tents and preparing food, he, Trifonov, and Chistiakov went ahead on horseback. They returned toward evening. Kulik directed everyone to gather and made an important announcement: ahead lay a large swamp. Around it—burned forest. Judging by what they had seen, the meteorite had exploded high above the swamp. If it had fallen to earth, the forest around there would have been completely decimated. The forest directly under the explosion had been burned by the blast but had withstood it, since the direction of the shock wave had been strictly vertical, coming from the sky. Kulik proposed spending the night and heading for the swamp the next day, building a permanent camp there, constructing a barracks, and beginning the search for shards of the meteorite. Concluding his speech, he congratulated the expedition for arriving at the location of the descent. Everyone except me applauded and shouted joyfully. The drillers proposed drinking a toast for the occasion, but Kulik silenced them.

"No drinking! We'll celebrate when we find pieces of it."

Ikhilevich was happier than all the others: his hypothesis on the explosion of hyper-meteorites had proved valid. But Kulik didn't appear disappointed. He was certain that there were large chunks of the meteorite scattered in the swamp. Everyone began arguing again, this time about the pieces. The argument dragged on. I wandered around the campsite in the darkness. Dead forest stood everywhere. The moon illuminated bare, charred tree trunks. I felt *very* good: the joy of belonging to this extraordinary place filled me. Each of my movements, each turn of my body, each breath, each time my finger touched the grass or trunks of the trees elicited an excited burst in my heart. My heart quivered and sang. My blood pounded in my temples, played rainbows in front of my eyes, and sounded in the shells of my ears. Wandering through the tree trunks, I felt that somewhere here, very close now, something was waiting for me, something *enormous and dear*. That's what made my heart sing. I came here because of it. And it was waiting for me. For me and me alone!

That night I was again unable to sleep.

The next morning we set off earlier than usual. Kulik said that it was about eight kilometers to the swamp. This gave the expedition new life. Everyone walked joyfully and talked animatedly, breaking the dead silence. For that matter, it wasn't entirely dead. The scorched forest harbored a real danger: for more than twenty years the trees had been rotting. When there was a strong winter gust, some of them collapsed to the ground. The sound of a falling tree carried a long distance as an echo. Everyone froze, listening to yet another giant toppling. Then they continued moving, looking over their shoulders. The weather was marvelous: it was summery, and the sun warmed.

By about three o'clock in the afternoon we arrived at the swamp. It stretched out ahead for several kilometers. Beyond it, through a light, marshy fog, distant hillocks could be seen. Scorched forest surrounded the swamp. Chistiakov, walking off a ways to answer nature's call, found a spring that gushed from the stony soil and ran toward the swamp in a meandering stream. The water in it was amazingly pure and delicious. Tired of boiled swamp water, everyone drank his fill of spring water for the first time in several days. The spring was immediately named Chistiakov Spring. Kulik walked over to a burned pine with its crown snapped off, pulled his home-made Celtic ax from his belt, and stuck it in the trunk.

"Here a campsite will be founded!"

The travelers all cried "Hurrah!," removed their "Chinese" hats, and threw them in the air. A banquet was announced in celebration. All the victuals that the expedition possessed turned up on the oil-cloth. Buckwheat groats were boiled on the fire, seasoned with lard, onion, and salted white salmon. Flasks of spirits were handed around. I sat eating berries and drinking water. No one paid me any attention. Everyone quickly got tipsy. Toasts were proposed: Kulik was praised for his sagacity and correct choice of route, they drank to the "smart and bold" guide Fyodor, to the inexhaustible Trifonov, the fanatical Ikhilevich, the unbending Chistiakov, the brave Molik and Petrenko, the courageous Yankovsky and Potresov. The students drank toasts to the drillers, the drillers drank to the geologists, the geologists to the astronomers. Okhchen's nephew quickly became very drunk, sang Tungus songs, clicked his tongue, and giggled stupidly. The driller Gridiukh sang along with him in Ukrainian, eliciting general hilarity. In the end, two of the students felt sick. The only ones not to drink were myself, Ikhilevich (who couldn't stand alcohol), and the prudish geologist Voronin. It all ended long after midnight.

When the camp was finally snoring, I again began to walk around. The stars and moon were hidden behind clouds. But the northern sky was light even at night. I wandered among charred trees, touched their trunks, sat down on the mossy earth, then stood up, strolled over to the swamp, to the stream, and touched the water. *The huge and intimate* was somewhere close by. It was waiting for me. It banished sleep from my body, leaving only the excitement of anticipation. It made my heart thrill and tremble.

I met the dawn among dead trees.

In the morning Kulik announced the order of the day to everyone: he and Trifonov, Fyodor, and Chistiakov would head out in search of remnants of the meteorite and draw up a map of the area; all the rest would erect a barracks under the direction of the builder Martynov.

The construction began after breakfast. The stocky, pockmarked, taciturn Martynov finally felt that his time had come: his face reddened from shouting. In a loud voice he ordered everyone around right up until dinnertime. Under his command, the scholars and seasoned geologists looked like pitiful apprentices. First we dug holes for the posts of the barracks, then we knocked down charred trunks, sawed them, and rolled them to the construction site. We chose the deciduous trees because almost all the pines were moldering. The larch trees had been wonderfully preserved over twenty years and sounded like iron when they fell. Only their tops had rotted and broken off. It was difficult to saw them: dried out at the root, they had become harder than the saws we used to cut them. We drove thick-bottomed logs into the pits and crowned them with the first charred crossbeams. The barracks began to grow quickly; the crowns, naturally, were not planed—no ax could manage the hard dry wood. Kulik had given Martynov the directive: build simply, not for posterity.

But the meticulous Martynov forgot this admonition: he shouted and demanded the highest quality from us. Finally, the driller Mishin told Martynov that if he didn't stop bossing them around, he would end up building the whole thing by himself. Martynov quieted down, but not for long. By dinner five rows of logs had been erected. The barracks ended up being spacious.

After the sun went down, the happy explorers returned. Four kilometers to the southwest they had detected three large craters.

The next day three drillers, and Anikin and I as diggers, set off to the site with Kulik. The craters were more or less identical—about twenty meters in diameter and about three meters deep. Water stood at the bottom of them from the melting ice of the permafrost. At first we bailed out pails of it from the largest crater. Then a driller began to drill the sludgy bottom of the crater with a hand drill. Less than a meter down, the bore came up against something hard. Kulik was ecstatic. Everyone grabbed shovels and pails: some dug, others bailed out the water. Kulik worked along with us. I dug, standing up to my knees in swampy ground. I did everything I was asked without thinking about it. I was indifferent: no work could distract me from my inner *rapture*. My heart continued to sing while, splattered with mud, I scooped out the bog. After about three hours something large and formless turned up in the black water. Kulik tapped on it with his shovel. The sound was muffled, obviously not stone and not metal. Kulik hit harder and the shovel sank into a rotten tree: an enormous larch stump turned out to be in the crater. Checking another crater with the drill, the bore also hit a tree. Kulik was depressed, but he tried to keep himself in hand.

"Well, if at first you don't succeed, try, try again," he said, wiping the spattered mud from his face with a handkerchief.

The evening meeting became a kind of scientific advisory council on the tree stumps. The geologists asserted that the craters and the stumps lodged in them were the result of melting permafrost. Kulik didn't argue with them. He was interested in the meteorite.

Another night passed. I spent it inside the tent dozing. My heart's ecstatic state wouldn't let me sleep deeply. I prayed for one thing— that my ecstasy would never end. The expedition members tried not to talk about me and paid me no attention, but they took me on all the jobs. Once I heard Kulik say, "We can thank the stars that Snegirev is a peaceable madman."

In the morning Kulik set off with Fyodor and Molik to reconnoiter; the rest continued building the barracks.

By the evening all ten rows of logs had been laid. The building of charred logs looked ominous. Between the rows of logs you could see large cracks. We decided to lay a shallow-pitch lean-to roof of slender trees, place the tarp we'd brought over it, and cover the whole thing with mossy turf and weigh it down with stones.

Sitting in the evening by the campfire and looking at the flames while the others ate, I suddenly experienced an unusual feeling. It was as though I had lost my body. The only thing remaining was my heart, which was hanging in the emptiness. I felt my heart. It resembled a fetus. Life pulsed evenly in it. But it was sleeping, as yet unborn. And the most striking thing was that I felt the hearts of everyone sitting around the fire. They were exactly the same as mine. They pulsed the same way. And they were asleep as well. Our hearts had not yet been born! This discovery struck me like lightning.

After that I fell into a trance. I not only stopped talking but didn't react to questions and requests. I just sat, hugging my knees, staring into the fire with unseeing eyes. I saw only the not-yet-born hearts. They carried me into a tent and poured opium into my mouth. I fell into a deep sleep.

I awoke three days later to the sound of cries and shots. I was calm. But the joy had deserted me. Making my way out of the tent, I saw the entire expedition standing around the finished barracks. They shouted joyously and shot their guns in the air. I walked over to them. They ran up to me, began to hug me. It turned out that there were three causes for joy: the barrack had been built, a huge crater had been found not far away, and that morning a wagon loaded with provisions had arrived from Vanavara. I listened, but had difficulty understanding. I was drained and indifferent. Kulik approached me.

"So then, Snegirev, are you better now?"

He looked me straight in the eyes, all attention. I answered him with my own look.

"So this is what's going to happen, young man," Kulik said to me, "from now on you are going to eat well, under my supervision. We don't need anyone fasting here. Is that clear?"

I looked him in the eye silently. Kulik took my gaze as agreement. They had already had dinner, so the time for force-feeding me was put off until the evening. After the wagon train was unloaded and its drivers rested, it returned to Vanavara with half our horses, two sick people—the geologist Voronin (he had bad diarrhea and a high fever) and the student Berelovich (who had hurt his eye during the construction)—and the mail. They didn't send me back with the wagon train, feeling that, despite my quiet lunacy, I was capable of being useful. Or perhaps Kulik really did believe that I was a talisman. Soon he gathered everyone and gave an inspired speech. He said that everything was going according to plan, everything was working out in the best possible way: a fifty-meter crater had been found—clearly of meteoritic origin—the bores hadn't located any tree stumps at the bottom of it, therefore something more important would be found; the geologists had panned the local soil in Chistiakov Spring and found microscopic metallic spheres in it, each no more than two millimeters in diameter; these spheres were scattered almost everywhere and provided evidence of the metallic nature of the Tungus meteorite; the barrack had been built and was being equipped for living, all the provisions were being transferred there. Three men would remain in the camp to set up the living quarters, the rest would move to the crater, which was located only three kilometers away, and would work on excavations until evening.

Martynov, Anikin, and I were left in the camp. The barrack was divided into storage and living sections: one for keeping provisions and equipment, the other for sleeping. First we carried over all our supplies and put them into the storage section; then we began to construct bunks from young trees and to caulk the chinks in the walls with moss. Two small windows were cut through the barrack walls. The weather continued to be warm and dry. Martynov and Anikin set off to look for young trees around the edge of the swamp. Sticking white moss into the chinks between the charred, wormhole-ridden beams, I mechanically watched the two receding figures through the cracks. The ax in Martynov's hand sparkled in the sun. And this flash of light suddenly awakened me. My heart quivered, my brain began to work. And I finally understood with my entire being WHY people had come here! They came in order to find *the enormous and intimate. And to take it away from me forever!* I trembled in terror. The clod of moss and the hammer fell from my hands. Why did they take so much time coming here? Why did they put up with such hardships? Why had this barrack been built? In order to find my *joy*! In order to prevent me from meeting it FOREVER!

A cold sweat broke out on my lips. I licked it away. I had to act. I looked around: the barrack. It had been built by people to help them find *the enormous and intimate*. Without it they were helpless in the taiga. I ran out of the barrack. A little ways off stood a barrel of kerosene. Kulik forbade storing it in the barrack. I rolled the barrel over and dragged it inside. I broke the stopper and leaned the barrel over a pail. The kerosene ran into the pail. I grabbed the pail and splashed it on a pile of boxes and sacks. Then I filled a second pail and poured it on the walls. I splashed a third and fourth pail onto the walls from outside. I took some matches and left the barrack. I lit a match and threw it at the black wall. The barrack caught fire.

I turned and walked into the taiga. Choosing a direction opposite from the one where the people had headed, I walked between the blackened trees. My heart quivered again, stronger and more urgently than before. It beat in my chest as though it wanted to break my rib cage and jump out. I understood that I had to hurry and I ran. Time stopped, the black forest jumped around in front of my eyes, sweat poured down my face. I ran and ran and ran. This lasted for an eternity. The sun was setting; the dead taiga was plunged into twilight. The stars sparkled above the charred treetops. My legs began to give way. The breath burst from my dried lips. Suddenly, in front of me, a felled tree appeared—the only one in the entire dead standing forest. An old, thick deciduous tree lay on the ground in its full length, broken in the middle. The huge roots, not completely pulled from the ground, had frozen, raised just above the earth. With my last breath, I fell on the earth, crawled under the hanging roots, and lost consciousness.

The Ice

I OPENED my eyes.

The dark reeked of earth. I moved, stretched out my hand. I touched the ground and roots. The cold soil crumbled. I immediately remembered who I was and where I was. I began to extricate myself from my den. I crawled out from under the root "roof" of the old larch hanging over the ground, which had served as my refuge, and froze: everything around was bathed in bright moonlight. I lifted my head: a huge full moon hung in the blue-black sky surrounded by scatterings of stars. Its light was so bright that I turned away and looked around: everything, all the way to the horizon, was bathed in this incredible light. A fantastical landscape unfolded before me. The illuminated hillocks resembled frozen waves of an unseen ocean. Spilling over, undulating, crisscrossing, and colliding, they receded into the distance toward the horizon, a subtle glow in the eastern sky. The dead forest stood all around in absolute silence: not a sound, not a rustle. And I stood in the midst of this. Alone.

I felt no fear. Just the opposite: the deep sleep under the roots of the ancient tree had calmed me and given me strength. The fever that racked my body abandoned me, as though it had drained into the ground. I raised my arms to the moon and stretched with pleasure.

And moaned.

I was free!

There was no one around. No one laughed at me or gave me orders; no one asked anything of me, drove me on, or gave me idiotic advice; no one talked about Marxism and astronomy. The hated swarm of words that had pursued me like midges the entire month had dispersed and drifted away along with the people. The absolute silence of the world amazed me. The earthly world froze in front of me in the grandest calm. And for the first time in my life I felt distinctly the vile vulgarity of this world. Our world did not come into existence by itself. It was not the result of a chance combination of blind powers. It was created. By willpower. In a single moment.

This discovery shook me profoundly. I cautiously inhaled the cool night air. And froze, afraid to exhale. Books on philosophy and religion, arguments about existence, time, and metaphysics had contributed nothing at all to my understanding of the world in which I existed. But this moment in the midst of a dead, moonlit taiga opened my eyes to a great mystery.

I exhaled.

And took a step.

My heart began to throb in a now familiar way. And I remembered the *huge and intimate*. That which had made me tremble in mute ecstasy, lose sleep at night, walk without tiring, and silently clench my teeth. It was close by. I again felt it with my heart. But calmly now, without tears or shuddering. The huge and intimate was calling me. And I moved in the direction of that call.

I walked between the blackened tree trunks. The moon followed me, clearly illuminating my path. I saw every stone under my feet, every broken bough. The moon played on the charred trunks. They glinted and shimmered like anthracite. The thick moss was springy under my boots. It was easy to walk: there was no longer anything on my shoulders . . . No tins, lard, or crackers. Nothing that connected me to people. This didn't frighten me—I experienced no hunger at all. My inner rapture of the last month had now turned into a staunch, persistent, irrepressible desire: to continue in the direction of the huge and intimate. And to find it.

I walked.

My legs easily overcame the wild, lifeless landscape. I walked for an hour, another, a third. The hillocks drifted slowly by. Finally they gave way and opened up. The moonlight glinted on a thin strip of water.

The swamp!

I approached it.

A slight fog of evaporation hung over it as before. My heart began to pound. I was drawn there by an irresistible force. *The intimate and dear* was close. I stepped forward. The moss beneath me was thicker, completely covering the soil. Swamp tussocks had grown up, and soon a viscous liquid slurped underfoot. With every step my heart beat more intensely. It wasn't the usual palpitations of malaise and excitement. My heart was beating less often, but more powerfully and

strenuously—each beat resounded in my chest, waves spread throughout the body from it. It was as though my heart had begun to live its
own life, separate from the life of my body. Its heavy, even beats
shook me ever so *sweetly*. My body resonated in time to these beats.
My boots plunged deeper and deeper into the swamp, and it became
difficult to walk. The water rose. Soon I was up to my waist. The cold
water rushed into my boots and engulfed my legs. This was the cold
of the permafrost. The moon brightly illuminated my surroundings.
The resonant heartbeats left no room for fear. I wanted only to ad-
vance, I *wanted dreadfully* to go forward. And I hurried forward with
all my might. The icy swamp clutched at my legs. But I was stronger.
Clutching the tussocks with my hands, I forced my way on. One step,
then another. Ten of the hardest steps.

Twenty.

One hundred.

The hummocks ended: ahead lay the smooth duckweed hollow. I
took the one-hundred-and-first step. And sank up to my chest. But
my heartbeat was deafening, and each pulse of blood pushed me
ahead. I grasped at the rotten trunk of an old, broken tree that was
sticking up out of the duckweed. And I understood that ahead, under my feet, would be—a deep quagmire and quicksand. However, I
also realized that there was a strip of water over this quicksand. And
that I could swim in this water. I'd just have to take everything off—
and swim ahead. Grabbing on to the trunk, I pulled my feet out of the
quicksand with a furious movement, pulled myself up, and sat on the
flotsam. I took off the wet clothing clinging to my body. I pulled off
my waterlogged boots. Then, naked, I pushed away from the trunk,
raking aside the water with my hands and pushing with my legs, like
a frog. It was incredible—I was swimming in a bog as though swimming across a lake. The water on top, just below the duckweed, was
clean and cold. I just had to keep on swimming straight ahead without stopping. If I stopped—there was only death, the quicksand
would pull me under. It tickled my stomach with rotten slime, tried
to snag me. But all fear remained behind, in the world of people. I
swam a bit and suddenly understood: the *huge and intimate* was quite
near. Just a little farther—and it would be possible to touch it.

My heart started beating such that rosy-orange rainbows flared in my eyes. I quickly became *very* warm. Then—hot.

Ecstasy seized me.

Sobs burst from my clenched mouth, which had forgotten the language of people. I realized that if I didn't touch *the huge and intimate*, I would die, I'd drown myself. Without *it* there was no reason to live. I had nothing but *it*. I had never desired anything so deeply in my life.

The water that my strokes parted shimmered in the moonlight. The green duckweed played on the surface.

A divine silence reigned all around.

A stroke of the arms, the body slid ahead.

Another stroke.

Another.

Another!

Another!!

Another!!!

My hands touched the Ice.

And I understood *why* I had come here.

I burst into happy sobs.

I had found *the huge and intimate*. My fingers touched the smooth surface. My heart beat deafeningly. I felt like I was losing consciousness. My head cleared in a flash. Divine emptiness resounded in it. While my fingers continued feverishly touching the Ice under the water. Sobbing, I began to choke. The edge of the Ice reached smoothly upward. I pushed through the water desperately. I crawled onto the Ice, like a lizard. There was very little water covering it. Shaking and sobbing, I crawled and crawled farther, along the top surface of the Ice. All around, as far as the farthest hummocks, spread a smooth hollow covered with duckweed. The enormous mass of Ice slept under it, submerged in the swamp. This dear, intimate mass had lain there quietly for twenty years, waiting for me. I'd needed twenty years in order to find the Ice! Sobs racked my body. I burned with heat. My heartbeats shook me. I was choking, swallowing the damp air of the swamp. Ahead the green duckweed gave way a little bit. The Ice glittered over there in the moonlight! A little patch of pure Ice! I pulled myself up and ran toward it, splashing the water, trampling the sleepy, thousand-year-old duckweed. The Ice! The Ice sparkled white and blue! How pure! How powerful! How mine.

Mine, mine forever!

Running up to the patch, I slipped.

And fell, slamming my chest against the shining Ice. I lost consciousness. For a moment.

Then my heart began to resound from the blow of the Ice. And I *immediately* felt the entire MASS of the Ice. It was enormous. And the whole thing was vibrating, resonating in time with my heart. For me alone. My heart, which had been sleeping for all these twenty years inside my rib cage, awoke. It didn't beat harder, but sort of *jolted*—at first it was *painful*, then it was sweet. And then, quivering, *it spoke*.

"Bro-bro-bro . . . Bro-bro-bro. Bro-bro-bro . . .

I understood. This was my real name. My name was Bro. I understood this with my entire being. My arms embraced the Ice.

"Bro! Bro! Bro!" my heart trembled.

And the Ice answered my heart. Its divine vibrations flooded my head. The Ice was vibrating. It was older than everything alive on earth. The Music of Eternal Harmony sang in it. And that music could not be compared to anything. It sounded the Beginning of All Beginnings. Pressing my chest to the Ice, I froze stock-still, listening to the Music of Eternal Harmony. In that moment the entire earthly world paled and became transparent for me. It disappeared. The Ice and I hung alone in the Universe. Amid the stars and wordlessness.

And my awakening heart began to listen closely to the Music of Eternal Harmony:

In the beginning there was only the Primordial Light. And the Light shone in the Absolute Emptiness. And the Light shone for Itself. The Light consisted of 23,000 Light-bearing rays. And one of those rays was you, Bro. Time did not exist. There was only Eternity. And in this Eternal Emptiness we shone, 23,000 Light-bearing rays. And we begat worlds. And the worlds filled the Emptiness. Each time that we, the rays of Light, wanted to create a new world, we formed a Divine Circle of Light consisting of 23,000 Light-bearing rays. All the rays turned toward the inside of the Circle, and after 23 pulses in the center of the

Circle a new world was born. We created the heavenly bodies: stars and planets, meteorites and comets, nebulae and galaxies. Their numbers grew. And their Harmony gave us Joy. The Eternal Music of the Light sang in them. We created the Universe. And it was sublime. And it came about that we created a new world, and one of its planets was covered with water. This was the planet Earth. We had never created these kinds of planets before. And we had never created water. For water is not constant—it is disharmonious. It is capable of creating worlds itself—unstable and disharmonious worlds. This was the Light's great mistake. The water on the planet Earth formed a sphere-shaped mirror. The moment we were reflected in it, we ceased being rays of the Light and were incarnated in living creatures. We became primitive amoebas, inhabitants of the boundless ocean. The water carried our tiny bodies. But the Primordial Light was in us as before, though dampened a bit in the disharmonious, world-spawning water. As before, there were 23,000 of us. We scattered across the expanses of the Earth's ocean. The disharmonious water engendered not only living beings but time as well. We became prisoners of the water and time. Billions of Earth years passed. We evolved along with other beings inhabiting the Earth. Our upper vertebra developed into an enormous tumor called the brain. The brain helped us figure things out better than other animals. So we became humans. Humans multiplied and covered the Earth. Dependent on flesh and time, people began to live by the laws of the brain. They thought that the brain helped them to dominate space and time. In fact, it only enslaved them to disharmonious dependence on the surrounding world. People with well-developed brains were called intelligent. Intelligent people were considered the elite of humankind. They lived by the laws of the mind and taught them to others. People began to live by the mind, enslaving themselves in flesh and time. The developed mind engendered the language of the mind. And humankind began to speak this language. And this language covered the entire visible world in an opaque film. People stopped seeing and feeling things. They began to think them. Blind and heartless, they became more and more cruel. They created weapons and machines. Throughout their entire history people have engaged in three main activities: bearing children, killing other people, and using the surrounding world. People who proposed anything else were crucified and destroyed. Engendered by the unstable and disharmonious water, people gave birth and killed, killed and gave birth. Because humans were a great mistake. Like everything living on Earth. And the Earth turned into the ugliest place in the Universe. This little planet became a genuine hell. And in this hell we lived. We died as old people and were incarnated in newborns, unable to tear away from the Earth, which we ourselves had created. And as before, there were still 23,000 of us. The Primordial Light lived in our hearts. But we didn't know this. Our hearts were sleeping, like billions of other human hearts. What could awaken us, so that we might realize who we were and what we needed to do? All the worlds that we created were harmonious and permanent, dead in the Earth's terms. They hung in the emptiness, giving us joy through the harmony of their peacefulness. The joy of the Primordial Light sang in them. The Earth alone violated the harmony of the Cosmos. For it was alive and developed on its own. The Earth became a dreadful tumor, the cancer of the Universe. The Divine Balance of the Universe was broken. Worlds shifted, deprived of the Divine Symmetry. And the Universe that we created gradually began to scatter in the Emptiness. But a piece of the world of Harmony, which we had previously created, fell to the Earth. This was one of the largest meteorites that had ever fallen to Earth. A huge piece of Heavenly Ice, in which the Harmony of the Primordial Light sang, having traveled for billions of years through the Universe. This was Heavenly Ice, created hard and transparent, according to the laws of Harmony. By its nature it was different from the pitiful earthly ice that formed from impermanent water, although on the outside they could not be distinguished. The dust of the Cosmos had settled on it, forging a thick iron armor. The armor helped it to withstand entry into the Earth's atmosphere and broke off when it hit Earth. This happened on June 30, 1908, here, in Siberia. The Ice fell to Earth and entered its soil. The water of the Siberian swamps hid it from people. The permafrost helped to preserve it. For twenty years the Ice waited for you. It is right beneath you. It is yours. It was sent here by the perishing Universe. Salvation lies in it. It will help you and the rest of Earth's hostages to become rays of Primordial Light once again. It will bring your hearts back to life. They will awaken after a long sleep. They will speak their secret names. And they will begin to speak the language of the Light. The 23,000 brothers and sisters will find one another again. And when the last of 23,000 is found, you will stand in a Circle, join hands, and your hearts will pronounce the 23 words of the Light's language 23 times. And the Primordial Light will awaken in you and will turn to the center of the Circle. There will be a flash. And the Earth, the Light's sole mistake, will dissolve in the Primordial Light. And disappear forever. And your earthly bodies will disappear. And once again you will become rays of Primordial Light. And the Light will shine as before in the Emptiness, for Itself Alone. And it will beget a New Universe—Sublime and Eternal.

I opened my eyes.

And saw the morning sky. The stars had faded. The moon had paled. My face was submerged up to my eyes in warm water. I moved and raised my head. I lay in an indentation formed in the Ice by the contours of my body. This naturally created bath was filled with warm water, with the heat that had left my body. I felt surprisingly calm and well. Calmer and better than I had *ever* felt before.

I sat up. I felt no exhaustion from the previous night. My chest was a little sore, but that was all. I looked at it: a large bruise had appeared in the middle of my chest. This was the place where I had hit myself against the Ice. I smiled. I touched my chest. Then I stood up.

The rising sun illuminated the hillocks in the east: the Siberian day had come. A new day on the planet Earth. The first meaningful day of my existence. I finally understood why I was born and what it was I had to do.

My brain went to work.

The indentation where my body had lain all night resembled the letter Φ: my arms had been resting around my body in half circles. In the center of the half rings, two oblongs of Ice surrounded by water jutted up, formed during the night as the heat of my arms had melted the Ice around them. I kicked the left oblong with all my strength. The base cracked. I grabbed it with my hands and broke it off. I lifted it and held it to my chest. The Ice vibrated. My heart resonated in time with it. The strength of the Ice filled my head. I lifted the massive chunk easily and showed it to the pale morning sky.

I cried aloud.

My cry carried over the swamp, bounced off the distant mounds, and returned to me in the voices of my brothers and sisters who were lost among humans. The first ray of sun hit me in the eyes. The Divine Ice sparkled in the sun. I had to return to the world of people. To search.

I put the piece of Ice on my shoulder and set off along the surface of the Ice in the direction my awakened heart told me to take: westward. Smoothing out, the Ice descended gradually under the water. Submerging along with it, I moved the green duckweed aside. When the water reached my mouth, I swam, clutching the chunk of Ice firmly. And soon my feet touched the silty bottom of the swamp. This wasn't the previous viscous quagmire: you could feel a different sort of ice—the permafrost. Pushing my feet against the earthly ice, I climbed calmly out of the swamp. I looked back. The hollow of duckweed had closed up, hiding the iceberg, as though no one had ever violated its peace. I shut my eyes. My heart felt the *entire* iceberg. It was huge. An eighth of it had lodged in the permafrost; the part underwater was only the top edge, smoothed and melted into the concave form of the surface.

My heart knew: the Ice would wait as long as was needed.

I turned and set off with the chunk of Ice on my shoulder. Naked, smeared with silt, I walked through the sun-flooded, dead taiga. My heart sang, calling to the Ice and remembering my true name: "Bro, Bro, Bro . . ."

I lost all sense of time and didn't feel the weight of the heavy chunk on my shoulder, nor the sharp stones and branches under my feet. The charred, standing forest gave way to toppled trees. The knolls and hummocks, strewn with broken branches and trunks, swam past. The Ice melted a bit on my shoulder, turning to water. Its occasional drops drove me on. I walked along, knowing with certainty where I was headed. My head was clear: during the night it was as though it had been cleansed of everything petty, disturbing, alarming, pointless. My thoughts were surprisingly quick and precise. With every step I discovered anew the world in which I had lived for twenty years. And this filled me with new strength.

Suddenly, descending into a glen, I heard ahead of me snarls, wheezes, and a strange whimpering sound. I walked on, rather than turning away. The snarls grew louder, moans could be heard. The bushes parted ahead of me. And I saw two bears tearing away pieces of a dying, pregnant elk. One of them held her by the throat; the other was ripping open her huge belly. A wheezing moan issued from the elk's mouth, her beautiful long legs thrashed helplessly in the air. The elk's bones cracked under the bears' ferocious paws and fangs. The animal's black belly, dappled with white, gave way, and along with her rosy-yellowish guts the baby elk, not yet born, fell out. Dark, with wet fur and large moist eyes, its gentle rosy-white mouth barely managed to open before bear fangs closed around its head with a crunch. A fountain of the newborn's crimson blood sprayed from the bear's mouth. In the distance another growl could be heard: a large bear cub hurried to join his parents' meal. Rolling up in a brown ball, he dug into the elk's entrails, grumbling with impatience.

This bloody scene in the midst of the dead forest graphically demonstrated to me the essence of earthly life: a creature that had not yet even been born became food for other creatures. The utter absurdity of earthly existence was here in this wheezing elk; in the convulsive, twisted lips of the baby elk, who had never managed to draw breath on Earth; in the furious grumbling of the bear cub; in the invariably good-natured face of the bear smeared with the fresh blood spurting from the torn neck artery.

But the chaos of earthly existence wasn't frightening to me, since I had known the Harmony of the Primordial Light. Without a shudder I walked toward the beasts. They turned their bloody faces to me. Their fangs sparkled.

I approached them, carrying the Ice.

The beasts snarled angrily. Their jaws opened, their brown fur stood up from anger.

I took a step. Another. A third.

The bears roared and ran away. And I could feel that my awakening heart had frightened them. I sensed my power. With an awakened heart in my chest I could do anything. I had nothing to fear.

I went up to the elk. Her body shuddered weakly. There was moisture in her large blue-black eyes. The blood gave off steam in the morning air, spurting from her aorta. I put my bare foot on the animal's shoulder. It was smooth and warm. The pointless and tormented life was leaving the body of the elk. The corpse of the baby elk lay nearby. She died giving birth to him, he destroyed his mother in being born, allowing the bears to overcome her easily. And all the bears wanted was to eat. The law of earthly life. And this had been going on for hundreds of millions of years. And it might go on for billions more.

I clutched the Ice to me. In it lay the destruction of this disharmony.

In it was the Power of Eternity.

It was time to strike a blow.

It was time to correct the mistake.

I would be the one to do it.

Stepping over the elk's body, I continued on my way. I walked for a long time. The Ice melted on my shoulder. But my heart led me calmly. Finally, when the sun began to lean toward sunset, I saw an Evenki camp ahead: two yurts and an empty corral. The reindeer were out to pasture. In the middle of the glade a campfire burned and venison was boiling in a huge cauldron. Here they were waiting for the return of the herd and the herders. Three dogs dozed near the fire. Seeing me they jumped up and joyfully ran to greet me: in these wild places the dogs of herders and hunters barked only at animals. But, running up to me, they recoiled and ran off with their tails between their legs, growling. I went straight to the yurt on the left. My heart led me there. I threw back the dirty strip of tanned deerskin and went inside. The light was dim, entering only through the hole at the top of the cone and through cracks in the walls. In the middle, under the hole, stood a tripod with a copper bowl. Cedar pitch smoked in the bowl, warding off insects. The bluish smoke rose to the top and disappeared through the hole. A girl lay sleeping on deerskins. She was not an Evenka; she had blond hair braided in two plaits, and a broad, high-cheekboned, freckled face. The girl was lying on her back, her arms out to the sides. With my heart I realized that she was very tired and was sleeping deeply. She was wearing a simple but well-made peasant dress with a dirt-stained hem. Next to her lay a fur vest-jacket, a head scarf, a leather belt with a large knife, a carved oak walking stick, and shoulder basket filled with wild strawberries. Farther away stood a pair of filthy boots with puttees hanging off them.

I understood with my heart that I had been walking here all day because of this girl. She was the same as I was. Her heart was also sleeping. It had to be awakened. Kneeling, I took the Ice from my shoulder and only then noticed how small the piece had become. The Ice almost fit in my palms! Most of it had melted along the way. I had to hurry, while the Ice was still with me. The girl slept soundly. Her lips were open, her tired body had given itself over to sleep with pleasure. I brought my hand with the Ice over the girl. Then stopped: no, that wasn't the right way. My arms were strong enough now. I looked around: a bit farther off lay the carefully folded fur clothes of the reindeer herders. Pairs of leather boots stood there—homemade short boots tied with leather laces. I pulled out one lace, took the girl's walking stick, and tied the piece of Ice firmly to the staff. Kneeling at the feet of the sleeping girl, I swung back and with all my strength hit the girl in the chest with the Ice. The Ice shattered against her breastbone and pieces flew about the yurt.

Her sleep was so deep that she only shuddered slightly. Then, suddenly, her whole body jerked, and her blue eyes opened wide. Convulsions seized her young body, she thrashed, as if in an epileptic fit, her eyes glazed over, her mouth began to open soundlessly. And my heart *felt* her awakening heart. The Ice had woken it. It was like a wave that traveled from the girl, from her chest, from her heart. And with great *force* crashed into my heart. And flooded it. And it stood stock-still, frozen in time, joining our hearts like a bridge joins two shores. It was all so new, so powerful and *unusually* pleasant, that I cried out. Our hearts had joined together. And I *understood* who I was. I began to live, joining with another heart. And I stopped being all alone. I ceased to be a two-legged grain of sand. I became *we*! And this was OUR HAPPINESS!

Tossing the staff aside, I grabbed the convulsing girl by the shoulders, lifted her, and pressed her to my chest. She thrashed, her head trembled, foam appeared on her lips. I held her even more tightly.

And suddenly I heard, both with my ears and with my heart, the voice of her awakening heart: "Fer! Fer! Fer!"

My heart spoke in reply: "Bro! Bro! Bro!"

Our hearts began to speak with each other. It was the language of hearts. It brought them together. It was true *bliss*. No earthly love that I had ever experienced before could possibly be compared with this feeling. Our hearts *spoke* in unknown words, words only they understood. The strength of the Light sang in each word. The joy of Eternity sounded in them. They rang out, flowed, poured, and flooded our hearts. And our hearts spoke *themselves*. Independently of our will and our experience. All we had to do was plunge into oblivion, embracing each other. And listen, listen, listen to the conversation of our hearts. Time stopped. We *disappeared* in this conversation. And hung in space, forgetting who and where we were.

Sister Fer

I OPENED my right eye. And saw an enormous ear with a silver earring shaped like a fish. Right beyond the ear I could see the small faces of the Evenki. They looked at me in fright. Some were smoking pipes. My left eye wouldn't open. Something warm and soft was in the way. I wanted to move my arms. But I couldn't: I couldn't feel them. I moved my head. The Evenki, noticing this, began talking to one another with great animation. Someone's head moved next to my face. A deep, greedy breath and moan sounded. The head moved away from my face. The other person's nose stopped pressing on my left eye. I opened it. And I saw a girl's face. She was looking at me. The look in her blue eyes was terrible.

It was Fer. My heart remembered *everything*. I had found Fer. Fer—was my *sister*.

Locked in an embrace, we were kneeling in the middle of the yurt: I was naked, Fer wore her peasant dress. The Evenki people sat around us. They chattered and gesticulated.

I tried to unlock my arms. But I couldn't: they were numb and I couldn't feel them. Fer moaned. A shiver ran through her entire body, her arms moved, and she clutched at me. She whimpered. She pressed herself to me, dug her nails into my back. Her heart *touched* mine. *The wave* rose once again. And struck my heart. And filled it. Heart words *flowed* once more. And the earth swayed underfoot. And Eternity awoke in us. And time stopped.

The Evenki voices grew clamorous. One of them touched my shoulder and looked me in the eyes.

"What you name?" the Evenki asked me.

His heart was dead. I took his wrinkled, windblown, narrow-eyed face for a stone. Fer wailed and cried aloud. She trembled all over. Our hearts were speaking. The unknown words *throbbed and burst*. The Light sang and shone in our hearts. Fer roared, pushed me away, and tore her clothes off. Her chest was cut with a small wound from my blow. Blood had congealed around the wound. Fer grabbed me with her hands. I seized her in return. Our chests pressed against each other. We cried out and moaned. Fer's heart *touched* mine. My heart *touched* hers. The Universe opened wide around us. Fer's urine flowed down both our legs.

The Evenki jumped up with a shout and ran out of the tent. Fer and I began to feel *wonderful*. Because we had *found* each other.

We came to on the evening of the next day.

Unlocking our numb, blue arms, we collapsed onto the pelts that covered the earthen floor. And we fell into a deep sleep.

An elderly Evenka woman woke us. She poked at Fer and me with a bear's shinbone. When we moved, the old woman began to babble in her own language and point to the exit with the bone. The flap was thrown back and through it we could see the same old dead taiga, flooded with the rays of the rising sun.

Fer moaned and began to cry. She looked at me and cried. Because our hearts were silent. I hit Fer in the chest. She screamed and was silent. I seized Fer and pressed her to me. We didn't need to talk: we had known each other for a *very* long time. There was no one closer to me than Fer. Our hearts were exhausted. They required rest.

I took Fer by the shoulders. I opened my lips. And for the first time in the last few days I spoke in the language of people: "We have to go."

She opened her whitened lips: "Where?"

"To look for other brothers and sisters."

"What for?"

"To become the Light once again."

Fer looked me straight in the eyes. She didn't understand *yet*. But she *believed* with her heart.

I helped Fer to rise, and we left the tent. The reindeer stood in their paddock. Two dogs lay near them, and four Evenki pottered about. Seeing us naked, the Evenki laughed and turned away. The dogs sniffed the air and retreated cautiously. Fer's clothes and basket hung near the tent, on a pike stuck in the ground. The basket was still full of berries. We grabbed the basket and quickly ate all the berries. On top of Fer's clothes lay a little bunch of Saint-John's-wort and some sort of root. The old woman had put them there. Fer tossed them aside and began to dress. I helped her. The old woman, without leaving the tent, shouted something at us. Then she stuck her head out and quickly threatened us with the bone. Fer got dressed, looked at me, swiftly took off her leather belt with the knife, took the basket, and walked over to the Evenki. It was *terrifying*: Fer had moved away from me! If she left—I would perish. I stopped breathing. I froze stock-still and waited for her near the pike. She talked fast with the Evenki in their language. She was bargaining. It seemed endless to me. I waited, afraid to budge. Suddenly she ran back to me. Without her belt, basket, and knife. She grabbed me by the hands, cried out joyously, and began to cry. I also held her in my arms and sobbed with joy that she had returned and that she WAS WITH ME AGAIN! It was as though I had found my sister all over again—a minute ago she was gone, I could only hear her voice speaking a language I didn't understand, and now here was Fer, right in front of me! It was a miracle. Fer also began to sob. Embracing and crying we fell on the ground. Sobs overwhelmed us like an avalanche of snow: I had never cried like this in my life. My body shook and writhed, the tears flowed in streams, and I couldn't get enough air—I was suffocating, choking on my sobs, as though they were balls of lead. I opened my mouth and felt I was swallowing myself; I lost consciousness and then immediately awoke in convulsions, sobbing again and again. It was as though I was *vomiting* tears. The same thing was happening to Fer. I heard and *felt* her crying, and that only worked me up more. Finally, we lost consciousness.

We regained consciousness back in the same tent. Fer lay nearby. I was dressed in work boots, pants made of deerskin, and an old sackcloth shirt torn at the elbows—Fer had bartered the basket, belt, and knife for them. The light in the tent was dusky and the Evenki were sleeping. I moved my arm, sat up. My body was tired from the crying and didn't move well. But in my heart all was *very* calm. It had purified itself. I woke Fer cautiously. She looked at me as though seeing me for the first time. Then her heart *remembered* me. And mine *responded*. The Light fluttered in them. And shone *quietly*. It hadn't left our hearts. We didn't even need to embrace and press our chests together. We simply looked in each other's eyes. After lying there a bit longer, we stood up carefully. And, supporting each other, we left the tent.

The sun was rising over the taiga. As though especially for us, the sunrise went on endlessly. The deer and dogs looked at us.

Our hearts had calmed down. I understood that Fer would *never* abandon me. And she, too, understood that I would *never* leave her. I unstuck my lips: "We have to go."

"Where?" asked Fer.

"Where the heart leads us."

My heart was drawing me to the west, to people. And so we slowly walked west.

The sun rose and shone brightly. The dead taiga surrounded us. Here, in this place, there was more toppled forest than burned trees. Over the rotting, mossy trunks you could see young larch and pine. Birds occasionally called out amid the greenery.

We walked for a long time without speaking, without making out the road. Then my lips spoke to Fer.

"Are you from around here?" I asked Fer.

"Uh-huh. From Katanga," she nodded.

"Why are you here, with the Evenki?"

"I ran away."

"From whom?"

"My father."

I had difficulty remembering what a father was. Then I remembered what a mother was. And it felt *very* strange to think that I had had a mother and father. That had all happened to someone else, not me. I recalled the language of people. Then I told Fer about my life. And I told her about the Ice. When I spoke about the Ice, my heart also began *to speak* about it. New words *flowed and glowed*. And Fer's heart listened. And filled. And answered. And sang. And *the words* of the heart were stronger than human words. The lips stammered, the tongue grew stiff. The paltry human words sounded dully. But in our hearts the Primordial Light shone. Fer's face swam nearby against the background of the dead landscape. And it shone with happiness. The sunlight shone radiantly in her blue eyes.

As we walked Fer began to tell me her story. She grew up in Angara in a fishing village, in a large, hardworking family. They were well-off, the men hunted and fished for a living. Then her father had a falling out with his brothers and took the family off to Katanga. There, ten versts from Vanavara, they built a homestead and began to live. Soon afterward her mother died. Her father brought an Evenka woman into the house. Fer was ten years old at the time. The Evenka woman raised her. Her father began to drink. He would get drunk and beat everyone he could get his hands on. Three nights ago her drunken father had beaten Fer because she cried out in her sleep. She had had a very strange dream: she dreamed that her deceased mother sent her to fetch water; Fer took the yoke and two buckets and was walking to the Angara river; it was a hot summer all around; she ran to the river and suddenly saw—the Angara had frozen, not simply like in winter but *entirely*, to the very depths; the whole thing had become ice; Fer descended from the cliff to the river and stepped barefoot onto the ice; it felt good, good as never before; she felt that the icy Angara was moving, that it had its own current and that it was completely *different*; the frozen Angara was flowing backward into a completely different country, and this country was *enormous and all white*. It enticed Fer and frightened her; she was standing on the moving ice and didn't know what to do; fear won out, she left the ice for the shore and watched the ice flow away to a *huge*, *white* country, and she cried from disappointment.

When her father fell asleep, Fer realized that she could no longer live with him. She got on a horse and galloped off. Traveling for a day, she met the Evenki. They were newcomers, outsiders, from Vilyui, otherwise they would never have stopped in the dead forest. She sold them her horse, in order to make it to the Angara and sail to Krasnoyarsk. There Fer planned to get work at the brick factory. She had turned sixteen in May.

She was illiterate—she could read syllable by syllable, but didn't know how to write at all. On the other hand she spoke the Evenki language well. Fer told me that she could do anything if she wanted to—hunt, fish, take care of children. She was tongue-tied by her *new* happiness. Our happiness. I held her firmly by the hand. We walked and walked, paying no attention to the road. Then we again embraced and fell to our knees. And once again our hearts *began to speak*. And again the Light flared. And the Universe opened wide. And time stopped.

This repeated itself many times. Speaking their own language, our hearts learned new words. Our hearts grew stronger. They matured and grew. And they became freer and stronger. Each heart conversation shook us deeply, *tearing us away* from time and earthly life. But afterward we were also stronger, like our hearts. We became calmer and more focused. The joyous madness increased our strength and certainty. We began to understand that together *we could do anything*. And we changed rapidly. We walked, gathering berries and eating them, then we slept, embracing, on the mossy ground, then we spoke with our hearts, then again slept and again walked. We didn't notice the cold of the Siberian earth, which awoke at night. Mosquitoes and midges kept away from us. It took four days for us to reach Katanga. There we found a winter hunting lodge, built on the banks of the river between Vanavara and the farm of Fer's father. The winter lodge was used only during the winter hunting season. Fer was certain that there was no one there. And she was not wrong. In the little log house we slept our fill and recuperated completely. And my heart *told* Fer all about the Ice again. Her face shone with excitement, her heart fluttered, and her lips whispered, "I want to see it."

"You will see it," my lips whispered.

Fer grabbed me fiercely by the shoulders. "I want to see it!"

"You will see it!" I said, shaking her.

Our heart rapture soon became a desire to *search*. It was so strong that it literally pushed us in the back. We had to search for sisters and brothers. And this feeling was stronger than the *excitement* of heart conversations about the Ice. We had become wise in these few days. Our hearts *understood* that the Ice—was simply a bridge to other hearts. The Ice—was an aid. But we needed brothers and sisters.

In the morning we washed in the river, ate our fill of wild strawberries that grew thick on the small grassy glades along the steep riverbank, and set off for the farm of Fer's father. In order to *search* amid the world of people, we had to be *like everyone else*. That meant—having money, clothes, food, arms. Fer's father had all of this. We approached the homestead cautiously and hid in the forest. Fer knew that her father was looking for her and the lost horse. She was counting on him not being home, and her Evenka stepmother wouldn't hinder us. But Fer's heart told her: her father was at home. We sat in the forest and waited for him to leave the homestead. According to Fer, in midafternoon, after dinner, he might go to get alcohol in Vanavara. But her father didn't leave the house then. Finally he came out. And immediately a woman's crying could be heard. Her father was already drunk. He went off along the riverbank in the direction of Vanavara. We waited a bit and entered the hut. The stepmother threw herself at Fer, swearing, but I brandished my walking stick at her, and she crawled under the table with a cry. The same swearing soon sounded from under the table. Then the stepmother looked out timidly. And suddenly, seeing her pretty, slant-eyed face and her small fist threatening us, I felt with my heart that there was no difference between the table and this woman. I was being cursed by a TABLE! I started laughing. Fer also looked at her stepmother attentively. And we *saw together* for the first time, with our hearts. Under the table was a person WITHOUT A HEART! Instead of a heart in the woman's chest there was a pump for the transfer of blood. Besides the Evenka stepmother, two of Fer's younger sisters were in the hut. Blond and blue-eyed like Fer, they looked at us with interest. Their small blood pumps industriously moved their young blood through their bodies. Fer and I looked at each other. And began to laugh. The stepmother stopped swearing and stared at us, frightened, from beneath the table.

"Anfiska, don't worry, I won't say nothing to Pa," said the youngest sister, smiling.

"Pa'll flog ya to death," said the older sister. "Why'd ya take the horse?"

Fer stopped laughing and looked at her sisters intently. She looked at them not only with her eyes. And Fer's heart *didn't see* sisters in them. They were also part of the hut, like the stove or the bench. Fer turned away from them and turned to me. I was her true brother. And she—was my sister. We embraced. Then we began to take everything we needed from the house. We took the hunting knife, a small ax, a fishing spear, clothes, guns, bullets, Fer's birth certificate, an Arctic fox pelt, but of the food—only onions and carrots. The other food seemed inedible to us. There wasn't any money in the house. I took a silver bracelet off the stepmother, and a necklace of jasper beads, and tore the silver and turquoise earrings from her ears. Her wailing didn't stop me. Fer's former sisters cried. Descending along the path to the river, we untied the largest boat and sailed down the Katanga. Fer sat in the prow with an oar, and I sat in the stern with another. We rowed, helped by the current. The river carried us smoothly. The rocky banks, overgrown by the taiga, followed along. The hot sun of the Siberian summer warmed our backs: we were sailing west. Our lips, speaking in the language of people, didn't ask each other: Where are we going? Our heart knew the route. The banks of the Stony Tunguska were completely uninhabited. There was no sign of people. Only birds circled over the shallows, and fish played in the water. Not until evening approached did two lone log cabins appear on the cliff. Smoke came from the chimney of one of them.

"A fugitive village?" said Fer.

The river began to turn smoothly to the right. And on the bank amid the dark taiga greenery some huts appeared. The settlement, as Fer suspected, consisted of former prisoners who had escaped and settled here permanently. They acquired families, hunted, and fished. Boats were moored at wooden docks. Three women were rinsing clothes. They shouted to us. We didn't respond and floated past them. They looked at us, using their hands to shade their eyes from the glare of the setting sun. We passed another turn and saw three large boats ahead moored on the shoals. A campfire burned above on the bank and people sat around it.

"Runners?" Fer said in surprise.

Unexpectedly for ourselves, without discussing it, we began to turn toward the shoals. We *didn't need* to avoid these people. While we rowed over and moored our boat, Fer quickly told me what "runners" were. Each summer nine Angars came to Katanga, acquired three boats, and *ran* them down with the current to the Yenisei River. Along the way they bought pelts from the local people. They always paid in gold dust and paid more than Gostorg. For that reason the locals held back the best pelts until the runners came. On reaching the Yenisei, the runners would abandon the boats and load their take on the steamship that sailed to Krasnoyarsk; there they'd sell their goods and live until spring; when spring came they would buy horses and travel to a gold stream whose whereabouts only they knew; they'd pan for gold, then make their way to Katanga, where, in exchange for the horses, the locals would build them three large boats. Fer said that the runners were tough people, very stern. The locals treated them with caution; they only sold them goods and grub. The Evenki were afraid of them. The runners never stayed over in the villages.

We moored our boat. And approached the campfire. Nine bearded men sat around it eating moose meat boiled with onions from a cauldron. We greeted them. They nodded silently and continued eating, looking at us. There was no threat in their manner, but neither was there any welcome. Then one of them recognized Fer.

"Ain't you that drunk's daughter?"

Fer nodded.

"The drink's got your pa good. He only give us three pelts."

Fer nodded again.

"Drank up the lot, did he?"

Fer nodded again.

She didn't look at the runner speaking to her but at another—a blue-eyed blond with a thick red beard. I also looked at him. My heart *clenched*. Fer's heart did too. The red-bearded fellow held a piece of steaming meat in his left hand and a knife in his right. He bit into the meat with his strong white teeth, cut it off with his knife, chewed, and swallowed. Suddenly he froze and stopped chewing. He looked at me, then at Fer. And paled.

"What now, took a fancy to the young fellow?" a gray-bearded, hook-nosed runner with a broken collarbone asked Fer. "He's a new one. So till we're at the Yenisei—he cain't noway. But aftern that—he's all yours for always, as you please!"

Two of the runners laughed halfheartedly, the rest continued eating. It seemed that the gray-bearded fellow had long since bored them with his jokes.

"Want some chow?" a stocky, strong-armed runner asked us gloomily.

But the cauldron with steaming meat didn't awake any desire in us. We *looked* at the red-bearded young fellow. And we *saw* him. He sighed deeply, straightening out his wide, strong shoulders, threw the uneaten piece back in the cauldron, pulled on the collar of his shirt.

"Okh, ahhhh . . ."

"What is it, youngster?" asked the gray-beard.

"I feel sorta sick . . ." The young man stood up and took a few steps to one side.

He threw up the meat.

"Oh, shit, goddamnit . . ." He spat, walked over to the river, cupped water into his large, strong palms, and drank greedily.

"Ain't you the one now, puking up meat!" a small, flat-faced runner laughed viciously.

"T'ain't yur business, Skunk," the stocky one barked at him. "He ain't in your way. Stuff in as much as yur belly can fit."

We *knew* that the red-bearded fellow was one of us, but we didn't know what to do. Our hearts were tense and quiet. I was seeing this healthy young lad for the first time, but my heart *had known* him for a long time. The most surprising thing was that he moved and behaved like the others, not even suspecting *what* dozed in his chest! He spat it all out, washed his face, and muttered a few words, just like a DOLL! Yet his heart was alive. It was so strange and comic that Fer and I began to laugh. The fellow looked at us sullenly and went to the boats. Our presence obviously made him uncomfortable: his heart was uneasy.

"Real funny-bones, the two a ya," said a runner with metal dentures, squinting at us. "Happy? A good life, is it? Them Sowvyets ain't given ya the what for yet?"

He pulled a large tobacco pouch from his jacket, opened it, and offered it to everyone. Coarse hands reached into the pouch.

"What did you come here for?" a quiet runner with a thin, intelligent face asked us.

"We have an Arctic fox," Fer answered.

"How many?"

"Just one."

"You sailed all the way here for that?"

Fer shrugged her shoulders.

"She left her father," I spoke up. "She's my wife. We're heading to a new place."

The runners didn't display any particular surprise.

"Well, give the fox here," said the intelligent-looking runner, scratching the short beard on his cheek.

I fetched the fox pelt from the boat and handed it to the runner. He shook it, smelled it, then turned it over and examined it.

"One zolotnik," he said quickly.

It was all the same to us. I nodded. The runner untied his purse, took out a copper scale, a weight, and a little bag with gold dust. He quickly weighed out one zolotnik, poured the gold dust into a paper funnel, folded it deftly so that the dust wouldn't spill out, and handed it to me. He stuffed the pelt into a bag filled with skins.

The runners, having finished their meal, began to prepare the boats for departure. This was strange—the sun was already going down.

"You're going to sail at night?" I asked.

"And why not?" the intelligent runner asked, tying up his bag. "The river is smooth here. And it's a whole nuther thousand versts to the Yenisei. There's no time for sleepovers, young man."

"But when do you sleep?"

"During the day when we stop we have a snooze. That does it."

"We'll sleep our fill in the grave!" laughed the hook-nosed runner.

"And you're not afraid to sail past settlements?"

"Settlements! You ain't gonna see no settlements for two days."

As I spoke with them, I followed the red-bearded fellow with my heart. I *felt* his every movement. In comparison to him all the other runners were merely boats on the riverbank. They were no different than Fer's stepmother looking out from under the table. The runners settled into their boats.

A decision had to be made.

"May we sail along with you?" I asked.

"Go ahead, it don't bother us none," the stocky one said, pushing away from the bank with his oar.

"Godspeed," the intelligent one said loudly, and they all crossed themselves.

Their long boats moved out. I put Fer in our boat, pushed off the sandbar, and jumped in. The seagulls sitting on the trees immediately glided down to the smoking campfire and began to peck at the vomit left by the red-bearded fellow.

Fer and I took up our oars.

The runners used their oars rarely but skillfully, helping the current. Their boats traveled in a caravan, one after the other. The red-bearded fellow sat in the last one. Our boat fell in line behind him. Steering the boat, we would glance at the blond nape of his neck. He was tense and behaved uneasily: he smoked a lot, spat in the river, and kept up an irritated mutter. The metal-toothed runner began a long, drawn-out song, which was gradually picked up by the others. They sang of abandoned childhood homes, of a mother's grave, of the wanderer's bitter lot. Their discordant voices carried over the smooth surface of the river.

The sun hid beyond the horizon. The first boat lit a tar torch. The river was submerged in the dim Siberian night. The song finished. And from the banks you could hear the sound of a felled tree. It seemed to urge us on. Our hearts throbbed. We still didn't know *what to do*, but with our hearts we understood *how*. I leaned on my oar, and Fer, sitting closer to the bow, leaned on hers. Our boat pulled up beside the last of the runners' boats. We were getting closer to the red-bearded young fellow. He looked over in our direction. I began to think what I should say to him. But Fer took the lead from me: "Will you show me how to row?"

The red-bearded guy, not realizing that she was talking to him, looked around. But Fer looked straight in his eyes. The two runners sitting in the boat with him laughed, puffing out tobacco smoke. The young fellow laughed spitefully.

"Row…What's there to…?"

It seemed that he was cursing Fer. But then, setting his oar aside, the redheaded fellow grabbed the side of our boat with his strong hands, pulled it over, and jumped in with us. The others, remaining in the boat, laughed.

"Watch out, our Kolyvanets here is on the loose."

"Hey there, youngster, watch out for your wife."

The red-bearded guy sat in the middle of the boat, his back to me, facing Fer. She handed him her oar. He took it, glanced back at me, lowered the oar overboard, and began to row. He was anxious and rowed with too much zeal and strength. We began to pass his partners' boat.

"Don't hurry," I said.

He looked back at me again. In the twilight he seemed bewildered. And I understood—he couldn't escape our hearts. Fer also *understood* this.

"What's your name?" she asked.

"Nikola," he answered.

"Where you rushin' to, Nikola?" asked Fer, and *the way* she said it filled me with such ecstasy that tears came to my eyes.

I adored Fer.

"Whatcha mean, where? There! With them!" The young fellow grinned, trying to get a hold of himself.

"You don't need to go with them," I said.

"Why's that?" A shiver ran through his powerful shoulders.

"You don't need to go with them." Fer spoke.

And our hearts began to speak. Nikola's sleeping heart was between us. It became *agitated*. He froze stock-still with the oar in his hands. I also stopped rowing. Our boat began to fall behind the caravan of runners.

"You need to go with us," I said.

"You need to go with us," Fer said.

The young man fell into a stupor. We froze as well.

The current carried the boat. The caravan sailed on; the flame of the torch grew smaller, disappearing in the twilight. The river began to turn to the right. Our boat was carried to the bank. The bottom scraped against the sand, the bow knocked against the dark bank. The boat stopped.

"Niko-la-a-a-a!" came a weak cry from far off.

The fellow shuddered.

I put my hand on his shoulder. "They won't sail against the current."

"Come on, don't fool around," he muttered, but didn't budge.

Fer took him by the wrist.

"Who ... are you?" Nikola asked.

"I am your brother," I answered.

"And I am your sister," Fer said.

"We came for you," I added.

For a minute he sat in a stupor. Then he let out a sob and began to cry. We embraced him. He wept, his broad shoulders shook. There was much of the child in his weeping. My heart felt that he was *tired of waiting*. And just plain tired. When he calmed down and wiped his face with his sleeve, we helped him out of the boat onto the riverbank, pulled the boat onto the shoal, started a campfire, and sat near the flames. Nikola crossed himself and began to speak incoherently. He hadn't slept for four days, since he'd had a vision. When the runners arrived at the village of Neriunda on the Katanga, three new boats built by the locals awaited them. The runners, as always, paid for the boats with nine horses and began to prepare to sail. The only thing left to do was to tar the boats. They heated the tar in three pails. Nikola picked up one of the pails. He went over to a boat with the pail and a brush, glanced in the pail, and in the hot tar saw his own reflection. It was him, but he was six years old. He was with his father, mother, and uncles at haymaking time; they were sitting on a table-cloth in a field. And suddenly fire flew across the sky. Then there was such a thundering crash that the whole forest swayed. And all the grown-ups fell to the ground in fear. But Nikola wasn't scared by it, just the opposite—he had a *very good feeling in his chest*. He sat and looked at the sky, where a wide trail remained from the fire. When everything quieted down, the grown-ups lifted their heads. And Nikola *didn't recognize* them. His father, mother, and uncles forever ceased to be his family. It was as though they had been pushed aside. Six-year-old Nikola realized that he was *alone*. It scared him so badly that he stopped talking and *instantly* forgot everything that hap-pened. He began talking again only two years later. The hot tar had reminded him of all this. He dropped the bucket. And suddenly he felt that he was once again *alone* among people. This made such an impression on him that he stopped sleeping. He could not drift off, forget himself, and fall asleep.

Neither could he with the runners, not at night while they trav-eled, nor during their daily stops when most of them dozed. People frightened and puzzled him: he didn't understand *who* they were. The runners noticed that he was acting strange and started to make fun of him. But the stocky man from his village stuck up for him. With every passing day of the run, Nikola felt worse. Life among *alien* people seemed horrifying to him. He began to think about sui-cide. When Fer and I appeared he was shocked: he felt that we were *different*. Everything that happened seemed like a dream to him: he didn't know what to do. But he understood it was *no mere coincidence* that we had come.

Having listened to his confused story, Fer and I held his coarse hands, roughened by his toil with the oar. We were happy.

"When were you born?" I asked.

"Three days after Easter in 1902," Nikola answered.

"Where did you live, when you saw the fire in the sky?"

"In Ust-Kut," he replied.

That was about seven hundred kilometers from the place where the Ice fell. I already *knew* with my heart that the Ice had flown from southeast to northwest. It had flown over Ust-Kut. With my heart I *envied* Nikola: he had seen the Ice in the sky. I had only heard it.

"What was it?" Nikola asked.

"Our joy and our salvation," I answered.

He grew thoughtful.

"And how come they call you Kolyvanets, iffen you're from Ust-Kut?" asked Fer.

"I did time in Kolyvan. That's why they give me the nickname . . ."

"What for?"

"Horse rustling. I got two years, but I run away from the convict transport. Joined up with the runners."

He stared at the fire. The flames played in his blue eyes. I squeezed his hand.

"Nikola, what you saw back then—it flew here for us. It fell to the earth. And lies there now, beyond the Katanga. We need to go there."

Nikola stared into the fire silently. He was numb. But Fer was agitated. Her heart *felt* the Ice.

"Oh my, how my heart wants it . . ." She placed her hands on her chest. "And it ain't far?"

"About four days' walk," I estimated. "But—at a fast walk."

"And what will happen?" asked Nikola.

"*Everything* will happen," I answered, helping with my heart.

And Nikola *understood*, even though his heart was sleeping.

The road back to the Ice was a happy one for me, joyous for Fer, and a sore trial for Nikola. Fer and I could walk the taiga day and night without tiring, as though we were being pushed along from behind. Nikola was experiencing much the same thing that I had during Kulik's expedition. He stopped speaking, became furious, and then cried. We led him, holding him up under his arms. Nor could he eat. Fer and I fed off berries and were not troubled by hunger. After my heart began to speak, I forgot hunger forever.

Passing along the riverbed of the Chamba, we found traces of the expedition's campgrounds and set out along the old trail. Four days and nights flew by for me like a single moment. We carried Nikola the last few kilometers: a fever had gripped his body and he mumbled, unconscious. We were *drunk* with delight: every step we took brought us closer to the Ice. The dead taiga parted, admitting us to a miracle. Our hearts *anticipated* with pleasure. Fer sang and roared with joy, her eyes shone like stars.

When we came to the swamp, the sun stood at its zenith. We laid Nikola down on the sun-warmed moss and began to tear off our clothes. Then, taking each other by the hand, we entered the swamp. The icy water seemed as warm to us as milk fresh from the cow. We laughed and cried: the Ice awaited us!

Quicksand grabbed at our feet, branches of trees rotting in the swamp waters scratched us and held on, but what could hinder us? Overcoming the swamp mire, we swam in the strip of water. And soon we touched the Ice. Fer gave a long-winded shout. I pushed her out onto the concave surface of the Ice. And climbed up there myself. The great block of Ice vibrated invisibly under us. Our hearts resounded in reply. Embracing, we collapsed upon the Ice.

We awoke at night. We lay on the Ice in a hollow that had melted under us, in a form shaped like the contour of our bodies. Warm water filled the hollow. We broke our embrace and climbed out onto the top of the iceberg. The moon, obscured by thin clouds, faintly illuminated the watery mirror of the swamp. We stood on the Ice up to our ankles in water. I walked around the lens and discovered my indentation, which recalled the letter Φ. It had been completely preserved, as though I had left it only a minute ago. The spur of Ice still stuck out, slightly melted. The other one I had broken off and taken with me, to people. Fer walked over to me. I took her hand and put it on the place where I'd broken off the icy spur. She *understood* that it was this very Ice that had awakened her heart. Crying and laughing, she began to touch the Ice.

But we had to think about Nikola. His heart was waiting on the bank. I kicked the other spur. It didn't budge. I kicked it again, with all my might. It cracked and broke off. I picked up the piece of Ice and headed back. Fer followed me. My heart remembered the short path to the shore. Climbing out, we went over to Nikola. He lay on his back, his arms outstretched. His eyes were closed, his lips whispered, and his pale face stood out in the darkness. I knelt, lifted the piece of Ice in my hands, and swung back. And froze. And once again, my heart told me: I wasn't doing it right. Not with the hands! For awakening a heart a *hammer* was needed. AN ICE HAMMER!

This is what would help to waken the heart in the name of the Light! This was what we needed! Searching around me, I saw a dried pine branch not far off. Grabbing it, I found my work boots nearby as well, and pulled out the leather laces. Together we tied the Ice to the stick. Fer's small but strong hands tore the shirt covering Nikola's chest. I swung back and with all my strength hit him in the chest with the hammer. The Ice flew apart, smashed to smithereens by the crushing blow, and the stick broke. Nikola's breast missed a beat and jerked. We pressed ourselves to it. Inside his chest a twitching could be heard; his body trembled and he ground his teeth. Our ears and hearts listened to the voice of his awakening heart.

"Ep, Ep, Ep . . ."

The body of our red-bearded brother shook, as though in a seizure. Blood spurted from his nose.

"Ep! Ep! Ep!" his heart pulsated.

His heart was large. And *strong*.

We embraced brother Ep.

Brothers

WE CAME to in the morning.

Ep was weak, his injured chest hurt. But his heart was already speaking timidly with our hearts. Exhaustion and shock had immobilized his strong body: he barely moved. Tears constantly rose to his eyes. Fer and I constructed a hut from the branches of bushes and young trees and placed brother Ep inside it. When he fell asleep again, Fer and I knelt and spoke heart to heart for a long time. In the green, rough hut our hearts learned from each other and from the great Ice lying so close by. The huge block of Ice resonated with our tiny hearts. It was as though they were created for each other. Our hearts were drawn to each other like the opposite poles of magnets. Separately, everything was harder for them. But together they were capable of a great deal. Sensing the awakening power of our hearts, we trembled. Resonating with the Ice, our hearts suggested a solution to us. When we came to and had eaten some berries, our lips gave sound to the Wisdom of the Light. We spoke in the miserly language of the mind, aided by the language of the heart.

We had to go and search for our brothers and sisters. But the Ice should always be with us. It would be more convenient that way, easier. It shouldn't lie here and wait for us to bring a newly acquired brother or sister to it. It should always be with us, among people. We would fashion icy hammers from the Ice. Dozens, hundreds of Ice hammers. They would strike the chests of brothers and sisters. And their hearts would begin to speak.

It took three days for Ep to get back on his feet. His awakening heart helped his body. From a depressed, mortally exhausted being, Ep was transformed into an inexhaustible and bold brother. He kissed our feet from joy, and we taught his inexperienced heart the first words.

Now there were three of us. We were young, strong, and ready to do anything for the Light. In the hut we decided what our plan of action would be: While waiting for the cold autumn, we had to carve out several large pieces of the Ice, haul them on a sleigh to the Khushma, prepare and load the Ice, and sail first along the Khushma, then along the Chamba to the Katanga. There, on the shore, we would dig a hole, place the Ice in the permanently frozen earth, and cover it. From this store we would take a few large pieces of Ice with us and set off on our search.

That was what we did.

Fer, Ep, and I spent two months in the dead taiga near the Ice. We lived in the hut all that time. And we were *absolutely* happy. The Ice was with us; our hearts matured and grew wiser; our bodies filled with a *new* strength. This strength wasn't *only* physical, although our muscles became stronger than before. The new *strength* had forever conquered fear, hunger, and illness in us. The three great enemies had been vanquished, never to be resurrected in our bodies. We fed on berries and the roots of swamp grasses. We slept on the moss, embracing each other, unafraid of the permafrost cold that rose every night from the Tungus earth. Wolves howled and bears roared in the dark, but it didn't scare us: we fell sweetly asleep to the howling of the wolves. Animals avoided our hut. Nor did people bother us: after the fire I started, the expedition left the area. The Evenki continued to be wary of the "accursed" place. Speaking in our new language to our hearts' content, we would light a campfire. Embracing, we stared silently at the fire. It was of this planet, ephemeral, a weak reflection of the Heavenly Fire—the blinding, imperishable fire that had given birth to the worlds of Harmony.

The Siberian summer ended in the middle of August. The leaves of the bushes and the gnarled birches surrounding the swamp turned yellow. A cold northern wind began to blow. And one morning occasional snowflakes spun over our hut—harbingers of the long Siberian winter. The first snow was a sign: the time had come to act. During those two months we not only had spoken with our hearts but had found the shortest passage to the Ice and laid eighteen fallen logs across the swamp. The bog engulfed the logs, but one could lean against them. Undressing, taking an ax and knives, we traversed this log road to the Ice. We cut out eight huge pieces of the Ice and carried them to shore. Each piece weighed about as much as a man. On the shore we built a drag of young trees, and in three trips we hauled the Ice to the Khushma, which ran about a kilometer from the swamp. This river was about twice as narrow as the Katanga and its shores were not so high. We quickly put together a raft as well, and tied the logs with bast fiber torn from young trees. Loading the Ice onto the raft, we attached it to the raft logs with wet bast, took the long oars that Ep had carved, and pushed off from the shore.

The journey by water took three days. Our raft sailed successfully along two rivers and reached the Katanga. We tried very hard to keep the Ice intact. And during the trip we didn't allow ourselves to speak with the heart. The cold water brought us to the place where we had sat that night with Ep by the fire, listening to his incoherent story. Upon landing, we untied the Ice and carried it to the shore. Pieces had melted slightly during the voyage. We dug a hole not far from the shore. It didn't take long to dig it—one and a half meters down the ax struck the icy soil of the permafrost. Gouging out a cavity in it, we put several pieces of the Ice in it, wrapped in moss and leaves; then we covered it all with earth. Ep and I pushed a heavy stone on top of the store of Ice. We dug a hole for the eighth piece of Ice right on the shore. Having hidden the precious Ice, we embraced. Night fell, the stars came out. We built a fire and gave our hearts their will. They spoke all night.

In the morning we dragged the raft, which had been hidden in the bushes, back into the water, and dug up the eighth piece of Ice. We wrapped it in moss, placed it on the raft, and started off. Our hearts told us we had to sail west. That was where the waters of the Katanga carried our boat. None of us knew just *where* we would meet our brothers and sisters, but our hearts helped us to search. Having sailed along the river for two days, we saw a large settlement.

"It's Lakura," Fer told us. "Baptized Tungus live there."

Mooring the boat, we quickly buried the Ice in the sand near the shore and headed to the village. Our hearts were calm. We were met by Evenki, and Fer spoke with them. They told us the latest news: the Russians had gone to the "accursed" place to look for the gold that fell from the sky, but the god of fire, Agdy, burned their dwelling, and they turned back. All of the Evenki in the area already knew this. Despite their Russian Orthodox faith and the old wooden church in the middle of the village, the Evenki remained pagans. They also informed us that the runners who had visited their village not long ago had lost one fellow along the way—he had been kidnapped by the Maiden of the Water. At first it was far from simple for us to socialize with people: I could barely restrain laughter, Ep looked at *ordinary* people with bewilderment, and Fer struggled to utter forgotten words. But here, too, our hearts helped us; they didn't let us down for a second. We had become *wise of heart*. And we knew how to behave with people. Our hearts and the Ice taught us to foresee much.

The local priest, Father Bartholomew, was happy to meet with us. Every Russian who passed through Lakura became a family member for him. First off he had the bathhouse fired up. We washed and steamed our bodies with great pleasure. Then the priest's Evenka wife laid the table for us. Here something unexpected awaited us: the food people normally ate had become for us, brothers of the Light, inedible. We looked at the fish pies, pelmeni with venison, eggs cooked in lard, freshly baked bread, and marinated mushrooms with disgust. In all of this we felt the monstrosity of human life, its lack of freedom. Humans had to *do something* to food before they ate it: fry, boil, chop, marinate, grind, or cure it. For that matter, they always overate tremendously, disfiguring their bodies and willpower. But the most horrendous thing was—that humans devoured living creatures with great pleasure, taking their lives from them only in order to stuff their stomachs with their meat. Meat was digested in their stomachs and fell out of humans in disgusting-smelling excrement. Man's will transformed a living bird into a pile of excrement—and this was completely normal for *Homo sapiens*. Sharing this planet with other living creatures, people gobbled them up. And this great monstrosity was called the law of life.

We could eat only fresh fruits and berries. This was the only food that did not repulse us. In general, after our hearts awoke, we ate *much* less. A handful of fresh berries sufficed for several days. Moreover, we didn't tire, didn't lose our strength like ordinary fasters. Our hearts gave us *tremendous* energy. With such energy we were not afraid of any hunger. Sitting down at the table, I apologized to the hosts and told them that yesterday we had been taken very ill from some fish we ate, and consequently, today we could only keep down raw vegetables and berries. With sighs and groans, the priest's wife brought us turnips and lingonberries. We refused vodka as well. The priest and his wife didn't deny themselves the "pleasure" of drinking to the health of the travelers. Seeing how they poured pure spirits diluted with water into their mouths in order to lose control over their bodies and feelings for a time, we were filled with disgust. The amazing popularity of vodka among humans, and their dependence on it, proved once again that man was incapable of being happy. People drank vodka and wine to "forget," "have a good time," "relax"— that is, to forget themselves and their lives for at least a moment. Drinking until they were drunk, they felt they were happy.

"Where are you going, young folks? Winter is just around the corner!" asked the increasingly drunk Father Bartholomew.

We answered that we were looking for a large construction site where we could make some money.

"Stay with me to build a new church. Weasels have taken over the old one! I'll pay you more than the Soviets," he cajoled.

But we didn't want to stay in the village: our heart *saw none* of our own there. We had to travel farther. We spent the night with Father Bartholomew, bought some carrots and turnips from him, dug up the Ice, loaded it, and sailed off. The Stony Tungus River coursed west toward the Yenisei. We floated past three villages, stopping in each one. And found none of our own. Fortunately, it grew colder, the nights were frosty, and our Ice melted very little. We tried not to touch it, which was *hard*, traveling with it in one boat. Touching the Ice reminded us *acutely* of the Primordial Light. Our hearts felt very *good* at those times.

The taiga grew yellow and red, preparing itself for the long winter. The first snow fell and covered everything. Then came the first cold snap. The river began to freeze at the edges; we traveled down the middle where the water had not yet frozen. Steam hovered above the Tunguska. Two more days passed and the river merged into another—wide and powerful. This was the Yenisei. It carried its lead-colored waters to the north, toward the Arctic Ocean. Its current was so turbulent that ice didn't have time to cover the river—it was carried away. It became harder to navigate—the boat was buffeted, whirlpools spun it around. Our hands never let go of the oars. But our hearts *guided* us. They told us that there were 23,000 of us—a small drop in the ocean of people, but that the Ice, lying here in Siberia these twenty years, was *drawing* many of ours to it. They were intuitively moving toward it, they saw tormenting, sweet dreams about it, they were looking for it. Their sleeping hearts yearned for the blow of the Ice hammer. And so we sailed patiently, fighting the strong Yenisei, warming one another's hands, grown cold in the wind.

We hadn't sailed for more than half a day when the first small landing dock appeared. Near it huddled the huts of a fishing village. A little steam-powered tugboat was moored to the dock, its funnel smoking. We decided to pull up onshore and *have a look* at the village. A little way before reaching the dock, we sailed into the rushes, pulled the boat ashore, rested, and ate some carrots and berries. Then, among the willow clusters, we began to bury the Ice in the sand. We hadn't yet finished our task when three armed, rough-looking fellows emerged from the bushes.

"Now, don't breathe!" a bandit with a black mustache ordered in a hoarse voice, pointing a Mauser at us. "Hands up!"

We raised our hands. The two others approached and searched us. They took away our gold dust and money, as well as the firearms and bullets from the raft.

"What did you bury?" the man with the black mustache asked.

We said nothing. It was an *important* moment. We had to answer these people somehow. As usual, my brain began to give me ideas about how to deceive them, ensnare them with intricate lies in order to save the Ice and ourselves. But my heart cut through the cobwebs of my brain with an order: *Speak the truth!* And this was the best step to take.

"We buried the Ice," I answered calmly.

Fer and Ep *understood* me.

"What kinda ice?" the man with the black mustache asked hoarsely. "Come on, then, dig it up!"

Ep and I dug up the piece of Ice wrapped in moss and buried in a shallow hole. Black Mustache walked over and pushed the moss off with the barrel of his Mauser. He looked at it and touched it.

"Go on, dig deeper."

He thought that we had buried the treasure deeper. With an ax and a knife we dug deeper. Black Mustache waited, then spit in the pit.

"What the hell you want ice for?"

I answered, "In order to awaken the hearts of our brothers and sisters."

The bandits looked at each other. Black Mustache grinned. "And just how you plan on doing that?"

"We will make hammers of the Ice, and strike the breasts of our brothers. Their hearts will awaken and begin to speak in the language of the Light."

The bandits looked at one another again.

"They're cuckoo," said one of them to Black Mustache. "Let's get the fuck out of here." The steamboat whistle sounded. The bandits perked up. "Get rid of them, Semyon, and let's go."

"Wait, Kochura. They ain't locals. Take 'em to the admiral first. You there, pick up that ice. And get your feet moving."

With silent joy I lifted the Ice: it was with us! The bandit led us to the dock. It was empty, and two murdered sailors lay on it. A woman's weeping could be heard from the village. The steamboat sounded again. The bandits pushed us quickly across the gangway and onto the deck. I noticed the name of the tugboat: *Komsomol*. They pulled in the gangway. And the little steamboat set off immediately.

As soon as Fer and I were on the deck of this miserable tugboat that had bent, rusted sides and a soot-covered smokestack, our hearts gave a *jolt. There was one of us* on the ship! I broke into a hot sweat of joy. By myself I didn't *know* that there was one of us nearby. Neither did Fer, when she was alone. But together, Fer and I comprised a unique *heart magnet*, which unerringly detected a brother. With Ep this kind of magnet didn't work.

They took us into the crew's quarters; eight people were crowded in there. They were all armed. Hunting rifles lay on the floor, along with animal pelts, clothes, and simple household tools. The bandits had just finished robbing the village and were sorting out the loot. The boss was a short man in a leather jacket, leather pants, and tall, laced boots. A large pair of binoculars hung around his neck, a holster with a Mauser was at his hip. From underneath a leather cap with a red star blond hair stuck out; his dark-blue eyes, framed by whitish eyelashes, sparkled coldly from underneath white eyebrows. The leader's wide face was remarkable for its intensely severe expression.

Fer and I *saw* him.

"Kozlov, you asshole! I'll shoot you!" he shouted at the fellow with the mustache. "Where were you loafing about, you shit? You want us dead, you provocateur?"

The leader was an obvious psychopath. Cunning and mean.

"Admiral, we caught these three here," Black Mustache said

hoarsely. "We went into the bushes to do our business, and they were burying something in the ground."

The leader directed his angry gaze at us. Fer was standing closest to him. I stood behind her with the Ice in my hands.

"What was it?" the leader replied curtly.

"Some kind of ice," Black Mustache replied.

"What—what's that?" the admiral asked again, squinting angrily.

"Ice," I said clearly and emerged from behind Fer with the piece of Ice in my hands.

The admiral froze. His thin, purplish lips blanched. His tiny eyes settled on the Ice. Then he glanced at us.

"Who...who are you?" he said, speaking with difficulty.

"I am Bro, he's Ep, and this is Fer," I answered. "We've come for you."

His body stiffened.

The din of the bandits stopped. Everyone stood quietly and looked at us. We were *looking* at the admiral. Our *heart magnet* was working. I remembered the runner Nikola sitting in the boat between Fer and me. The situation was repeating itself. But the admiral was a different sort of person. Shaking off the stiffness, he withdrew the Mauser from its holster and pointed the steel-blue barrel at us.

"Come on now, troops, tie them up."

They tied us up. The Ice fell on the floor.

"Now sit them down in the corner. And all of you—back on deck," ordered the admiral. "I'll have a quick parlay with them."

The bandits unwillingly climbed up on deck: it was warmer in the hold.

The admiral stood with his Mauser and look at us. His heart *shuddered*. But he fought it off with all his might.

"Tell me again: who have you come for?"

"For you," I said.

Fer didn't have time *to help* me. The admiral laughed maliciously.

"Admiral, where are we going?" A head with bangs hung down through the hatch.

"To Kolmotorovo."

"Didn't we want to have a look at Yartsevo?"

"The GPU is there, you idiot. I said Kolmotorovo!" he shouted. "Full speed ahead! Three-whistle greetings to oncoming ships! Take the machine gun off the deck! Hide the rifles!"

"Yes, sir!" The head retreated.

The steamboat began to turn around. A flea-bitten fellow brought down the machine gun and set it at the admiral's feet.

"Admiral, the thing is, I wanted . . ." Fleabite mumbled. "I've got two pals in Yartsevo and also—"

"Batten down the hatch!" shouted the admiral, turning white.

Fleabite climbed up the ladder with a sigh and closed the hatch. The admiral walked up to me and squatted. His belt and holster squeaked. He put the muzzle of the Mauser to my forehead. And I *felt* that he wanted to shoot. My heart *froze*.

"Now then, who did you come for?" he asked for the second time. Now Fer helped me.

"We came for you," we *spoke* simultaneously.

His heart throbbed. The Mauser shook in his hand. He exhaled, lowered the Mauser, and leaned on it as the floor of the hold rocked.

"Who are you?" he asked uncertainly.

"Your brothers," I answered.

"I am your sister," said Fer.

The magnet *began to work*. And Ep also *helped*. "I am your brother, too," he said.

The admiral's broad-cheeked, muscular face became distorted: his brain was resisting furiously. I realized that, recently, the admiral had been *suffering*. Just as Nikola had. Just as I had during the expedition. Now he was *very* afraid. His thin lips blanched. Sweat broke out on his pale forehead. The admiral began to shake.

"God . . . damn . . ." he whispered and began to raise the Mauser.

The barrel danced in his trembling, bloodless hands, white with fear. He farted loudly and pointed the Mauser at Fer.

"G-g-god . . . damn . . . shits . . ."

Our hearts *froze*. And I *realized* that we were ALWAYS prepared for death. His shaky finger was already pulling on the trigger. Our hearts *jolted*. And the Ice *answered* them.

The admiral glanced at the Ice in terror. And shot at it. Pieces of

Ice flew about the hold. We cried out. The admiral stood up abruptly. His eyes rolled back in his head. He took one step and collapsed on the floor.

We began to free ourselves from the ropes. The warrior Ep tore his ropes off and untied us. Fer rushed to the Ice. Ep—to the unconscious admiral. I made an *immediate* decision: the machine gun! Equipped with a new cartridge, it shone all oily and new near the fallen admiral. The very same kind lay in the trunk of the porter, Samson, who had sheltered me as an adolescent at the Krasnoye station in the winter of 1920. I grabbed it, released the safety lock, and pulled back the bolt, just as Samson had done that morning, in order to scare away the bullies who wouldn't stop bothering us.

Ep opened the leather jacket covering the admiral's chest, tore the army-issue shirt and striped sailor's skivvies underneath. On his chest was a tattoo of an eagle carrying a dragon in its talons. Fer grabbed a large piece of Ice.

"No!" I whispered. "Tie him up."

They didn't understand. I motioned upward with my eyes. "They'll try to stop us."

They *understood* everything. And immediately tied the admiral's hands and feet with our own ropes.

Ep took the admiral's Mauser. Fer took the rifle. We climbed up the iron ladder and I knocked on the hatch. They had hardly managed to open it when I aimed the fat barrel of the machine gun at the bandit. He was chewing something and took a step backward. We climbed up onto the deck. The bandits saw us.

"Back!" I ordered.

They began shuffling toward the stern. Most of them were still chewing on something. Out of the corner of my eye I noticed some meat wrapped in paper, bread, and a bottle of moonshine on the bench of the stern. After their work, they had decided to have a bite.

"Stop!" I ordered.

They looked at one another cautiously. Their brains had begun *working.*

"Take it easy, brother, we can work this out," Black Mustache said hoarsely. "What is it you want?"

"To awaken the heart of our brother."

I *truly* would have preferred to make a deal with them. To say, "Don't get in our way. If you do this we'll give you everything we have." But my heart told me: they would not keep their word.

"Everyone overboard!" I ordered.

"Whatcher in such a stew about, man?" Black Mustache smiled with yellow teeth and moved toward me. "We'll shower you with gold, as much as you..."

His hand slipped into his pocket.

I aimed the barrel at him and pulled the trigger. The machine gun rumbled and shook in my hands. Bullets pierced Black Mustache's body and flew out the other side with bits of clothes and meat.

I had killed a man for the first time in my life. And I realized: we would NEVER be able to REACH AN AGREEMENT with people. The bandits jumped overboard. But some shot at us from the deck cabin. Ep began to shoot awkwardly with the Mauser; Fer shot skillfully with the rifle. I aimed the smoking barrel of the machine gun at the deck cabin and pulled the trigger. The machine gun once again rumbled and shook in my hands. The bullets ripped through the sheet metal of the cabin, old white paint flaked off and flew in every direction; so did a strange red inscription: LOM O SMOKINGI GNI, KOMSOMOL!, with a red star. Having destroyed the deck cabin, I let go of the trigger, but it was stuck: the machine gun continued to shoot. It pulled to the left, I lowered the barrel; the bullets pierced the deck, splinters flew everywhere, and the machine gun thundered on, it just kept pulling and pulling to the left. Choking from the gunpowder smoke, I lifted the barrel. The machine gun kept firing and tried to pull itself out of my hands. In this fraction of a second I *understood* with my heart what a machine is and *why* it was created by humans: man cannot get along without machines because he is WEAK, he is born an eternal CRIPPLE and needs crutches, supports that help him to live. A machine of *destruction*, created by the human mind, was trying to escape my hands. It was *alive*. Bullets flew toward the sky, shells rained down on the deck.

I didn't have the strength to handle it, so I stepped to the edge and with a desperate movement threw the machine gun overboard. It kept on firing as it fell. But the Yenisei soon swallowed up the machine of destruction.

Gunpowder smoke drifted over the deck. The *Komsomol* was sailing. We broke into the wheelhouse. There the wounded helmsman in a sailor's uniform writhed on the floor, and Fleabite lay dead with his mouth open. Ep stood at the helm.

"Who else is on the ship?" I asked the helmsman.

"Stokers...two...They locked them...Don't shoot," he moaned.

"How do I get there?"

"Behind the galley...the hatch..."

We found the hatch. It was closed with a bayonet. The stokers were working in the furnace room like *a piece* of the steam engine. We returned to the deckhouse.

"Hold the wheel," I told Ep.

"I've never steered a ship," he said, squinting at the Yenisei.

"And I've never shot a machine gun," I answered.

Fer and I descended into the captain's quarters. The bound admiral had come to and was rolling around furiously on the floor, trying to free himself. We seized him and held him to the floor. He moaned and bit. He smelled of excrement: he had soiled himself when he *felt* the Ice with his unawakened heart. We tied him to the handrail of the ladder. Fer grabbed a piece of the Ice. My eyes scanned the place; there were no sticks or hammers to be seen. Next to a heap of animal skins lay some weapons. I grabbed a sawed-off rifle from the pile and tore a shoulder strap from the admiral's jacket. With the thin belt we attached the Ice to the rifle. Fer held the head of the moaning, howling admiral against the handrail. I ripped off his skivvies, swung the Ice hammer back, and struck his tattooed chest with all my might. His breastbone cracked. The Ice shattered in all directions. The admiral jerked and then hung helplessly from the ropes. We froze: we heard nothing at all. His heart was silent. This *couldn't* be happening. Just beyond the bulkhead, the iron heart of the steamboat beat faintly. "Hit him again! It can't awaken!" Fer cried out.

But the Ice hammer was destroyed. I looked at the floor: as it pitched, pieces of Ice slipped in and out of puddles. Fer grabbed the largest of them. We began to tie it to the rifle again. Suddenly the admiral twitched. We pressed against his chest, now red from the blow.

"Rubu . . . Rubu . . . Rubu . . ." his heart spoke, awakening.

We cried out joyously. Our hearts caught up the newly born heart. The admiral moaned and opened his eyes. We untied him and placed him on the ancient leather couch. Rubu again lapsed into oblivion. His heart was small and *weak*. In comparison to his, Fer's heart seemed a mighty giant.

I climbed onto the deck. Standing at the helm, Ep cried out. His heart *knew* what had happened in the captain's quarters. I ran to the deckhouse and took the helm. Shaking and sobbing, he rushed below. And from the captain's quarters came his joyous howl.

Rubu was with us.

He turned out to be a former sailor and Red Commander. For his thirty-seven years, Rubu, known in the world of men as Kazimir Skoblo, had had an extremely colorful biography. Before the Revolution, as a boy, he had run away from his prosperous family to join the navy. He did his naval service in the Baltics, working his way up from ship's boy to bosun. Then he went underground, joined the Russian Social-Democratic Workers' Party, and carried out propaganda work; in Odessa, he married the bomber Marina Yezvovich, was arrested and sent to Siberia; his wife died in Kiev during a terrorist action, and he ran away from his exile to St. Petersburg. There he lived illegally and threw two bombs; during the October coup he was a commissar of the naval regiment, then worked in the Cheka; during the Civil War he fought in the Ukraine, where he was Commissar of the Proletarian Sword Division; in an argument he shot the commander of the division, for which Trotsky condemned him to execution. He ran away to join the anarchists, commanded a machine-gun platoon for Makhno, suffered a severe concussion, and spent three months lying in the attic of a small house under another name. He returned to the Reds, up beyond the Urals, joined the partisans, and was the political leader of the detachment; after the war he ran river steamboats on the Tobol, then on the Irtysh, and became a family man. Three months ago, a former division soldier recognized him; not waiting to be arrested, Kazimir Skoblo ran, taking the money from the steamboat with him, along with weapons and documents; while in hiding, he organized a small band of thugs, made it to the Yenisei, stole the tugboat *Komsomol*, and managed to plunder five villages and two cargo ships.

About two months earlier Kazimir Skoblo had had a dream: he was a seventeen-year-old sailor on leave in Vyborg, in the small room of a prostitute; they were sitting on the bed, in front of which there was a small table; a bottle of New Bavaria beer stood on it, as did a bottle of the sweet water Fruit Honey; there was a pound of Crawfish Tail candies, a pound of French cookies, and a pack of Vazhnyia cigarettes—all that he could buy with the money he had. Kazimir had never had a woman before; the prostitute's name was Lyalya, and she had already slept with his friends—the sailors Naumov, Sokhnenko, and Grach. Kazimir was nervous, he tried to behave roughly, he was embarrassed that his member had been standing up like a stick for quite some time now, pushing against his black bell-bottoms; the prostitute noticed this and laughed at him; she shoved him with her chubby shoulder and blew cigarette smoke into his ear; he blushed, laughed stupidly, and poured the beer into glasses. They drank and smoked; the prostitute asked him to pour some Fruit Honey into her beer; Kazimir poured it nervously, in a hurry; the prostitute's glass was full to the brim. She giggled and gave Kazimir one condition: if he could bring the glass to her lips without spilling it, she'd sleep with him; if he spilled it, she'd kick him out. Kazimir didn't know whether she was joking or speaking the truth; he carefully lifted the glass, carried it to Lyalya's red, laughing lips; suddenly, outside, there was a distant but *very* powerful clap of thunder; Kazimir froze with the glass in hand; he looked at the curve of the overfilled glass and saw barely noticeable waves running along it. He *felt* that they came from that far-off, powerful thunder. He couldn't tear his eyes away from the miniature, sweeping waves and kept on staring and staring at the glass; suddenly, in the liquid he saw a blind pilgrim who came to their house on occasion to drink water when he was eight years old: she had been born blind, she didn't have any eyes at all, but she could heal all sorts of illness and foretell fates. To the young Kazimir she said, "When you grow up and become utterly confused about yourself and life, two brothers and a sister will come to you and they'll show you something that will change you forever." She left, and Kazimir forgot her prophecy; he remembered it only now, when he heard the distant thunder; he dropped the glass, the prostitute laughed, and when he looked at her—she had no eyes. At this point he woke up.

On awakening, Kazimir remembered: this dream was what happened to him in reality, when, as a seventeen-year-old sailor in Vyborg, he had gone ashore from the mine cruiser *Watch Guard*. That time he dropped the glass. But the prostitute let him have her anyway. And he immediately forgot about his vision.

He began to have the same dream frequently. At night, tortured, he tried to fight off the dream, he wanted to see something else in his sleep, but to no avail. During the day he felt a growing agitation, as though *something enormous* were moving inexorably toward him.

Speaking with his heart, Rubu understood the meaning of the prophecy and sobbed. His past life seemed like a nightmare to him. As it did to all of us.

We sailed down the Yenisei for two days and nights. On the third, the stokers locked in the boiler room informed us: all the coal had been used up. About twelve kilometers shy of Krasnoyarsk we ran the *Komsomol* up on a shoal and debarked onto the forest-rimmed shore. We took a pouch of money from the steamboat, gold dust, and some revolvers. We changed clothes as well: the bandits, having plundered five villages, had quite a lot of quality clothing. Rubu was weak, we held him by the arms. But we didn't have to walk for long: a road ran along the shore of the Yenisei. The first cart that came by had been ordered to take a sick Red Commander to Krasnoyarsk. Riding into the city, we immediately rented a house on the edge of town and hid there: Rubu needed time to recover, his broken sternum hurt. But his *new* heart helped his body: our wounds healed more quickly than humans' did. Four days later brother Rubu was already on his feet. We embraced him. Standing together on the small porch, the four of us silently *rejoiced* in one another. We didn't need lightweight, short-lived human words. We had *our own* language. I opened the window onto the veranda: a golden autumn still held in Krasnoyarsk, the first snow hadn't stuck to the ground. Silently, we gazed at the street with its wooden fences, birch trees, and one-story houses. It was evening. Watchdogs barked back and forth, somewhere an accordion played its wheezing notes. A drunken carter drove an empty dray down the street. His old horse plodded along unwillingly. The carter lashed her with the reins, cussed, and, noticing us, gave a drunken laugh, nodding at the horse.

"There's a heartless nag, the old cunt!"

Rubu *winced*. And we *winced* as well. The heartless carter reproached the horse for heartlessness, beating her and exploiting her. This was a living picture of earthly life, an example of the "harmony" of being. Rubu let out a sob and clutched at his chest. A shiver ran through his body, tears burst from his eyes. We *understood*: his *weeping-heart* time had come. Sobbing, he fell into our arms. Sobs wracked him for a week. When he emerged from them he was entirely *different*.

We didn't know what to do in Krasnoyarsk: the Ice was far from us, our hearts were silent, and we needed to be cautious with Rubu— the GPU was looking for him. But the help of the Light came to us. And a few days later, we understood the reason we had ended up in Krasnoyarsk.

That morning we decided *to take a look* at the town. I was certain that the heart magnet Fer and I possessed could find others like us if the pull of the Ice had brought them to this old Siberian town. We hired a cabbie, sat in the carriage, and drove around as slowly as possible. Wandering the streets, we moved toward the center. Our hearts were silent. Finally we turned onto Voskresenskaya, the main street, and rode down it. Mourning flags hung near a large building that looked like a theater, and a crowd of people had gathered. It was impossible to go any farther: cavalry stood in front of us and a brass band waited. I ordered the driver to turn around. And suddenly out of the crowd a young man in glasses, wearing a Chekist's uniform and a black ribbon tied round his arm, ran toward us.

"Are you from Achinsk? Comrade Kudrin?" he asked Rubu anxiously.

"Yes," Rubu answered unexpectedly.

"Well, what are you waiting for then, comrades?" The fellow in glasses waved his hands reproachfully. "They're already about to bring the body out, and you still haven't arrived! Let's go, come on …"

We descended from the carriage and followed him through the crowd. The guards standing at the entrance with black bands on their bayonets let us into the building. In the spacious hall it was quiet and calm. There was a coffin, covered in flowers and wreaths. In the coffin lay a balding, middle-aged man with a mustache in the uniform of a Chekist, with a medal. Around him stood an honor guard of the local top brass. At some distance was a crowd of mourners. Almost all of them were military or Chekists in leather coats and jackets. As in an Orthodox church, the women stood apart from the men. Fer went to stand with the women; Ep, Rubu, and I with the men. People approached the coffin single file to bid the deceased farewell: first the men, then the women. Then there was a modest, quiet command; the coffin was lifted and carried from the hall. People began to sort through the wreaths.

"Comrade Kudrin! This one's yours …" the same young man said, handing Rubu a wreath.

Rubu took the wreath and nodded at me. I walked over to him and we carried the wreath. On the black band in gold letters were the words REST IN PEACE, OUR VALIANT FRIEND! FROM THE CHEKISTS OF ACHINSK. The most astonishing thing was that no one but us claimed this wreath. The rest of the people took their own wreaths. As soon as we were outside, the brass band thundered. The coffin was carried along Voskresenskaya Street. Behind it came the wreaths, then the authorities, strolling at a leisurely pace; the band marched, the cavalry rode carrying a flag, and then a huge crowd followed. Fer and Ep ended up in the first rows of the crowd. Walking in step with Rubu, I suddenly felt a slight excitement *in my heart*. Looking back, my eye met Fer's. But she shrugged her shoulders. I had *felt* that we weren't here by accident. Judging by the situation, they were burying the head Chekist of Krasnoyarsk.

The funeral march played as we walked to the cemetery; we stood around the freshly dug grave. The coffin was set upon a wooden podium covered in red satin and black crepe. Next to the grave they placed a plywood cube painted a dark red. The crowd moved aside and a middle-aged Chekist in a uniform decorated with two medals stood on the cube. I hadn't seen him in the auditorium during the farewell proceedings. Probably he had only just arrived. His face—resolute, intelligent, and rough—was framed by a small, light-chestnut beard and hair of the same color that was combed back unevenly. His grayish-blue eyes were stern. He scanned the crowed, rolled back his sloping shoulders, grabbed his belt with his left hand in a practiced gesture, and closed his right into a fist. Then he spoke.

"Comrades! Death has torn a valiant friend from our ranks, a comrade-in-arms, and an indefatigable warrior for the proletariat and world revolution, Comrade Valuev. The ardent heart of this faithful soldier of the Revolution gave out. A brilliant Communist, iron-hard Chekist, a man with an expansive soul and true Leninist-Stalinist temperament burned up in battle and the work of the Party. The fiery heart of this Chekist has stopped beating—"

He suddenly stopped speaking. And my heart *beat faster*.

He paused, took a deep breath, and continued.

"Today, Communist Pyotr Valuev, we are all distressed to be burying you in the damp earth. But for me, your old comrade, it is especially painful. We met, Pyotr Frolovich, in the era of bloody czarism. The czar exiled us to the same small town, to Obdorsk, for our underground revolutionary work. They wanted us to sit there quietly, cease our campaign, stop drilling into the oppressed people. But then you and I up and showed those vermin—*bam*!" Here he shot his fist forward sharply and fiercely. His sunken cheeks filled with blood for a moment.

My heart could feel how Fer's heart was throbbing. Our *magnet* had begun to work: we recognized a brother! There was no sweeter moment for our hearts. I closed my eyes. This resolute Chekist was one of *us*. That was why we had ended up in Krasnoyarsk.

I opened my eyes. The Chekist spoke passionately, aided by his fist. His face burned with indignation. He *truly* did not want to believe in death. I looked at Rubu. His inexperienced heart did not yet *know*. But his brain recognized the speaker.

"Who is that?" I asked.

"Deribas. The head of the OGPU for the Far East."

I squeezed the fingers with which Rubu held the wreath. He looked me in the eyes. My face shone with joy.

"Yes!" I whispered.

And Rubu's heart *understood*. Rubu began to shake, and tears poured from his eyes. We moved our excited gaze to our new brother. Who as yet had no clue. "It was not in battle that you fell, dear comrade, not near Kherson from a White Guard saber, not in Pavlodar from a counterrevolutionary bullet. You died on another front, Pyotr Frolovich. On the most difficult and most necessary battle with counterrevolution, with the hidden scum, vermin, and enemies of the people. To our bright future, to the great ideas of Lenin-Stalin! Our Party, our people, our Chekists will not forget you, Communist and Chekist Pyotr Valuev. Rest in peace, dear comrade!"

He stepped off the red cube.

Then the secretary of the oblast Party committee and coworkers of the deceased spoke in turn.

They placed a cover on the coffin and nailed it shut. They lowered it and swiftly began to fill in the grave. Some Chekist waved his hand, and the hurried cavalry shot their weapons. He waved it again—and the band played "The Internationale." Everyone standing around the grave began to sing.

They stuck a red star in the fresh hillock and covered it with wreaths. Fer and I, without saying anything, made our way through the crowd to Deribas. He stood with the secretary of the oblast committee, smoking. Chekists milled around them.

"Comrade Deribas!" I said in a loud voice.

The Chekists turned toward us. And the bodyguards immediately blocked our way. Deribas lifted his stern gray-blue eyes to look at us.

"We have very important business with you," I said.

"Who are you?" Deribas asked abruptly.

"Your brother."

He looked at me carefully. His heart was absolutely calm.

"What's your name?"

"Bro."

At that moment his heart *winced*. Fer and I *felt* his heart.

"What?" he asked again, frowning.

"Bro!" I repeated loudly and grasped Fer by the shoulders. "And this is your sister, Fer."

Deribas's sunken cheeks blanched. His heart flared up. But a *very* strong will struggled with his heart. *Restrained* it. And his heart yielded. Trying not to show this inner *struggle*, he finished his cigarette. He tossed the butt, stepped on it, and said, "Mikhalchuk, arrest them."

The Chekists aimed their revolvers. We were searched, they took my Walter and Fer's Browning.

"Put them on the train," Deribas ordered. "We'll have a chat along the way."

We were led through the crowd. I saw Ep and Rubu out of the corner of my eye. Standing stock-still, they looked at us. But we walked along calmly, without giving any signs: as usual, we *didn't know* what to do, but we *believed* in our hearts. The Chekists took us to the station. There was a train with two cars surrounded by a chain of guards. We were led to the second car and locked in a compartment. We embraced joyfully: we had found another brother! Our hearts began to speak. They already knew each other well and knew how to gain strength from conversations of the heart. We didn't notice the train setting off. Some time passed, and our heart conversation was interrupted: the door was opened by the sentry. Next to him stood a Chekist.

"Out!" he ordered.

We left the compartment and moved along the corridor. The car was half empty. The few soldiers of the guard sat in compartments. We passed between the train cars and found ourselves in a first-class car that had been refurbished for the trains of high-level personnel. Many of the partitions had been torn out and sofas placed along the shuttered windows; rugs lay on the floor, and in the corner near a window were a machine gun and a gunner dozing on his feet. Deribas sat, in charge, surrounded by four Chekists in uniform and two Party workers in typical tunics. They had just eaten: a soldier and a woman in a white apron were removing the dirty dishes. On the table stood two empty bottles of Shustovsky prerevolutionary cognac. Deribas opened a pack of Cannon *papirosy* and put them in the center of the table. He looked tired. His heart *was not on guard* against strong emotional experiences. But his brain suppressed them. Judging by his haggard face, even though it was rosy from alcohol, he had buried a very dear friend today.

Everyone seated lit cigarettes.

"Let me introduce you, comrades," Deribas spoke, drawing hard on his cigarette. "Before you stand my brother and my sister."

Everyone around the table looked at us. He continued.

"Here you have the life of a Chekist—we bury friends and find relatives. And each of these relatives has a pistol in a pocket. Not bad, eh?"

The Party functionaries laughed. The Chekists smoked calmly.

"Who are you?" Deribas asked me.

"I am Bro," I answered honestly.

"And you?" His gaze pierced Fer.

"And I am Fer."

"Who sent you?"

Fer was silent: she didn't know *how* to express our truth in the language of humans.

I answered. "The Primordial Light. Which exists in you, in me, and in her. The Light. It lives in your heart, it wants to awaken. You have been asleep all your life and lived like everyone else. We have come to awaken your heart. It will wake up and will speak in the language of the Light. And you will become happy. And you will realize who you are and why you came into this world. Your heart yearns for awakening. But your reason fears and hinders the heart. Your past, meaningless life will not let go of you. It wants you to keep on sleeping, and for your heart to sleep with you. It hangs on your heart like a sack of stones. Throw it off. Trust in us. And your heart will awaken."

Deribas glanced at his companions. He winked at them.

"So that's the way the cookie crumbles! I shall soon awaken, comrade Communists."

The Party functionaries laughed. The Chekists looked at me angrily. But our *magnet* was working: Fer helped me *a great deal*. Deribas's heart quivered. But he was fighting until the last: *mortally* pale, he continued to joke.

"And exactly how are you going to awaken it? With bullets?"

"No. With an Ice hammer. We will make it from the Ice sent to the Earth in order to awaken our Brotherhood. This is the Ice of Eternal Harmony, the Ice that we all created together when we were rays of Light. We committed a Great Mistake and fell into a trap. The Ice returned to us in order to save us. So that we can again become Light, so that this ugly planet will disappear forever. The Ice hammer will strike you in the chest. And you will call out your true name."

He listened, his body rigid. His nerves were stretched to the limit. We *felt* his heart, like a little wild animal that has been cornered.

"Hmmm . . ." Deribas opened his whitened lips and grinned awkwardly. "These are the kinds of lunatics we have here in Siberia . . . this, uh . . . nowadays there are many, quite a few."

His joke didn't work.

"No, there are very few of us," said Fer.

"Altogether there are 23,000. And you—are one of us," I added.

He glanced at me furiously, tore open the collar of his tunic, and began to rise. His hand shook, his beard trembled.

"You . . . you . . . you're an enemy." he hissed.

His eyes rolled back and he collapsed in a faint. The Chekists caught him.

The Party people jumped up.

"He's tired . . . heart problems," muttered one of them.

"Is there a doctor on board?" another worried.

"He doesn't need a doctor," I answered.

The Party boss gave a nod to the Chekists. "Take away those . . ."

And we were led back to our compartment. But not for long. An hour later I was again take to Deribas. He lay on the sofa in his spacious compartment. Near him sat a Party functionary and a Chekist. They had opened the window and the wind fluttered the curtains. The wheels of the train clacked loudly. Deribas was pale. He made a sign to me. I sat down.

"Go out, I'll talk to him," said Deribas.

"Terenty Dmitrich, you'd do better to rest," objected the Party functionary.

"Go on out, go on, Pyotr."

They left. I remained seated. Deribas stared at me for a long time. But now it was without fear and anger.

"You knew my grandfather?" he finally asked.

"No," I answered.

"Then who told you about the ice?"

"The Ice."

He paused for a moment. "Is that a nickname?"

"No. It's the Ice that flew through space and fell to Earth near the Stony Tungus River."

"And it knows how to speak? It has a mouth?"

"It doesn't have a mouth. But there is the memory of the Primordial Light. I hear it with my heart."

Deribas looked at me attentively. Fer wasn't with me, and our heart *magnet* wasn't working. Reason once again enchained Deribas's heart in armor.

"You have three days until Khabarovsk. If you won't tell me who sent you and where you heard about the ice, you won't leave this train on your own. You'll be thrown off it. Got it?"

"I have already told you the truth," I answered.

He called the guards and I was taken back to Fer.

It took us almost four days to make it to Khabarovsk. During this time no one asked us about anything anymore. When the guards brought us food—boiled potatoes—we refused them. Then a young Chekist showed up to ask why we weren't eating. We told him about our preferences. We were brought four carrots. We ate them. And spoke with our hearts in the half-lit compartment with gated windows. And we hung in the abyss. Amid the stars and the Eternity. The Light shone in our hearts. They became stronger. We learned more and more new words of the Light. We perfected ourselves. And we forgot about the *difficult* world of humans. As soon as we arrived in Khabarovsk, we were reminded of it.

As soon as the train stopped, we were brought to Deribas.

He stood in his compartment, dressed in a leather coat.

"Well, then?" he asked, lighting a cigarette. "There are two ways for you to go: on the ground or under it. If you tell me who sent you and who told you about the ice, you will go the first way. If you don't talk, you'll go the second. *Tercium non datur*," he added with a terrible accent.

We remained silent. But our *magnet* began speaking.

"Made up your mind?" he continued, but he could *feel us*.

His armor had cracked, ever so slightly.

"We will go the first way," I said. "And you will go with us. After the Ice awakens your heart. The Ice, which awaits you."

He blanched. His reason began to fight his heart once again. It grabbed on to laughter.

Deribas laughed nervously.

"Seryozha!" he called.

A young Chekist entered the compartment.

"Listen, what should I do with these Pinocchios?" he asked with a grin, trying not to look at us.

"Comrade Deribas, let me interrogate them. I can make the deaf and dumb talk."

"Maybe they really are crackers? Ice, for fucking sake . . . Where is this ice of yours?"

"Four days' walk from the Stony Tungus. And part of it is buried on the shore."

His heart *trembled*. Reason yielded, but slowly. Deribas tossed his unfinished *papirosa* on the rug.

"To hell with all of them! My friend died, the counterrevs are on the move, and now—ice, goddamnit! Seryozha, to the cellar with them. And question them so they'll start talking."

He left the compartment in irritation, but also with *obvious relief*. The young Chekist was puzzled: something was happening to his iron chief. The steamroller of willpower with which Deribas so skillfully crushed and shattered people didn't seem to work against us.

From the train station we were sent to the OGPU building, located on Volochaevskaya Street, and placed in different cells. They were in the cellar and were crowded. For the most part, my cell contained formerly affluent people who had lost everything after the Revolution. In Fer's cell were their wives. Now the ruthless Soviet authorities had taken the last thing these people had—their freedom and life. They were accused of counterrevolutionary plots, concealing gold, and anti-Soviet propaganda. The men were exhausted from the interrogations and the crowdedness of the gloomy cell; some of them had been ferociously beaten. Fear paralyzed these people; they conversed in whispers, prayed, and cried secretly. Beyond the wall of my cell were criminals who cursed loudly and often sang: the new authorities were softer on them than the old regime, as they considered them socially close to the proletariat, but having gone astray.

Ending up in the cellar of the OGPU, I listened carefully to the quiet conversations between the prisoners. From them I learned that in the city and the entire Far East region there were two all-powerful men—Deribas, the head of the OGPU; and Kartevelishvili, the secretary of the Party Regional Committee. They were the sovereign bosses of the Far East. But recently they hadn't been getting along very well. Deribas, according to the prisoners, was the soul of evil, who had descended upon Khabarovsk from Moscow. He was stern and merciless to all the "formers," and arrests went on continuously. One of the imprisoned, who had fought with the Whites during the Civil War, said that Deribas had the staunch belief, which had become his rule of action, that all the "formers" should either dig ditches for Stalinist construction projects or feed the worms. Articulating this maxim during interrogations and witness confrontations, Deribas usually added his awkwardly pronounced "*Tercium non datur.*" Accordingly, the arrested "enemies of the people" were either condemned to long sentences in the camps or to execution.

I spent the night half dozing, trying to *reach* Fer's heart. And at dawn I was successful. Our hearts *touched* each other through the brick walls of the underground. It was a miracle given to us by the Light. Now things were much easier for us: I could speak with Fer's heart at any moment, and she also felt me. We could *help* each other, using our heart *magnet.* The next morning I used *the magnet* for the first time.

As soon as the prisoners had eaten their breakfast of fried dough, I was taken to interrogation with that same young Chekist from Deribas's train. Sitting behind a table, he introduced himself as Investigator Smirnov and demanded that I name the "participants in my counterrevolutionary conspiracy." If I refused, he promised to disembowel me.

My heart told me: it was time to act. I answered that I was ready to name the people who had sent us, but only personally to Deribas and in a face-to-face encounter including Fer. An hour later, Fer and I were brought to Deribas's office. He was alone, sitting behind a table and writing something. Above him hung two portraits: Stalin and Karl Marx. While he was writing, Fer and I tuned our *magnet*. Deribas raised his eyes to look at us. And immediately turned them away. And I felt that we were the first people in his life whom he *didn't understand*...Which meant—he didn't know *how* to treat us. He couldn't simply execute us: *something* torturous prevented him from doing that. Serving in the penal system, he had come across all sorts of prisoners. He'd seen courageous White Guards ready to die, who spat in his face; uncompromising priests, who saw the Communists as the demons of hell; violent monarchist-plotters, who prayed for the murdered czar; fanatical SRs, who thought the Bolsheviks had betrayed the Revolution; anarchists, who placed no value on their own lives; and people who simply had strong spirits. The machine of the OGPU ground them all up, and for each of them Deribas had his approach. He understood each of them; each of them had a shelf in his mind. Us, he failed to understand. Because he was the same as us.

I told him everything I *knew* about the Ice.

He listened with a stony face, his eyes lowered.

"This is what I've decided," he said, his fingers trembling as he retrieved a cigarette. "Today I will send my people to the Stony Tungus, to the place where you buried your ice. They will bring it here in good condition. If there isn't any ice there—I will personally shoot you."

We were taken away.

In the cell I moaned and growled with excitement, frightening the "formers." We had *broken through* the iron armor of Deribas! In the logic of the OGPU his order to make the expedition to the Katanga seemed complete madness. Any other Chekist of his rank would have had us tortured long ago, and then executed. The next day he would have forgotten about the madmen who talked about Ice flying in from outer space. And our bullet-pierced hearts would have happily allowed the worms inside.

But our hearts had not awoken in order to make the worms happy.

Their job was to awaken the sleeping. Our heart *magnet* was drawing in the "iron" Deribas, slowly but surely. The Chekist expedition returned in about two weeks. And the Chekists brought the Ice! The hearts in our bodies, locked in the underground, were overjoyed.

We saw our Ice in Deribas's office. One of the seven pieces lay on a silver tray. Deribas sat behind his desk. Over the last two weeks he had grown pinched and lost weight. In his light-chestnut hair and his slightly reddish beard, streaks of gray had appeared. Two bodyguards stood next to him: he was *afraid*.

"You spoke the truth," he said, lighting up and blowing out the smoke as though trying to shield himself from us. "They found the ice you buried. Seven pieces of it."

We approached the Ice and placed our hands on it.

Deribas didn't interfere. He sat with his eyes closed. He had lost himself *completely*. We were in bliss, *speaking* with the Ice.

"And what . . . now?" Deribas muttered, as though asking himself.

"Now order a simple stick and a strip of leather be brought here," I said.

Deribas lifted the telephone receiver. "Pospelov, bring me a simple stick and a strip of leather."

When the order had been carried out, I asked Deribas to remove the guards and lock the door. The guards didn't look at us or him like madmen: the office of the head Chekist of the Far East had seen stranger things.

Deribas ordered the guards to leave. Then he stood with difficulty and walked to the door. It was only about eight meters, but for him the distance became eight kilometers. I will never forget *how* this man walked, this man we had broken. Slumping, he could barely drag his legs in his squeaky boots. His head trembled, his mouth was half open, his strong peasant hands hung loose. He was literally dragging himself to the door. In order to lock it forever. And leave behind it the terrible world of people.

Reaching the door, Deribas turned the key in the lock and leaned his forehead against the door.

"I will . . . shoot you," he whispered.

But his weak hand couldn't even reach his holster. His sluggish fingers clenched and unclenched. I turned him around sharply, his back to the door, unbuttoned his tunic, and ripped open his undershirt. There was no cross on his neck.

Fer and I lifted the Ice and threw it on the floor. It cracked. We grabbed an appropriate piece, tied it with the leather to the stick. And approached Deribas. He passively *waited* for us. His heart waited.

I swung back and struck him in the chest with the Ice hammer. He cried out briefly and, losing consciousness, began to fall on us. We caught him and laid him flat on his back on the floor. The blow had been strong: blood flowed from the broken breastbone. Deribas's eyes rolled back, his body quivered and jerked, as though he were having an epileptic fit.

We waited for the awakening of the heart.

It trembled. And suddenly stopped.

Deribas stopped jerking. We froze. His face had turned *deathly* pale. His heart wasn't beating.

There was a knock at the door, and the voice of his secretary asked, "Comrade Deribas?"

He felt that something had happened in the office. And immediately the phone on the table rang. Deribas lay before us, lifeless.

"Comrade Deribas!" the secretary cried and knocked on the door.

But Deribas answered neither us nor the humans.

"Break down the door!" cried the secretary.

The guards threw themselves at the door. I froze. Because I didn't know *what* to do. And suddenly Fer clutched at his shoulders, shaking him.

"Brother, speak with your heart! Little brother, our dear, sweet little brother, speak with your heart!"

His heart didn't answer.

The door cracked.

Fer lay on top of Deribas, embracing him. A piercing cry escaped her mouth. And I *felt* how her heart *stirred* our brother's stopped heart.

And his heart came to life.

"Ig, Ig, Ig," it spoke.

We cried out for joy.

The door flew open and the Chekists rushed into the office. But we didn't notice them: our faces were pressed to the bloody chest, our heart *caught* the voice of the awoken heart, and our lips repeated the name of our brother.

"Ig, Ig, Ig!"

Someone hit me on the head with the handle of a revolver, and I lost consciousness.

I came to in an isolation cell.

It was almost dark: light pushed through the iron "muzzle" on the tiny cellar window. I lay on a wet floor. It smelled of human urine. I raised my head and touched it: there was a large lump on the back of my head, and my hair was sticky with dried blood. I rose carefully, holding on to the wall. My head spun slightly. But my heart beat evenly: as if it *had been resting* while I lay without consciousness. I looked around: there was nothing in the cell. I walked around carefully. My head hurt. I pressed it to the cool "muzzle." And suddenly remembered everything.

My heart trembled joyously: I had another brother, Ig!

I moaned with joy, closed my eyes, and smiled in the darkness. My heart began to *search* for Fer. The thick brick walls were no impediment: Fer was nearby, in the cell. We began to talk. And we felt *very* good...

A few days passed.

I was woken by the scraping of the locks. The door opened and the warden jerked his head: "Out."

I left the cell. And soon I stood in the office of the director of investigations, Kagan. Small, swarthy, with a cruel and intelligent face, he started asking me questions about what happened. I realized that I shouldn't tell *him* the truth. Therefore I said that Deribas was interrogating us, then he had an epileptic fit, he fell and hit his chest on the table. And we tried to help him. This answer, strange as it seemed, satisfied Kagan. Turning a sharpened pencil in his hands, he pressed a button, ringing a bell.

I was sent to the general cell.

And a few days later Fer and I were taken to the hospital where Ig lay. At the entrance to a separate ward sat a guard wearing a white doctor's robe over his tunic. He opened the door and let us into the spacious, light room. Ig lay on the only bed in the room. He had turned almost completely gray. His face shone with *inexpressible* joy. We ran to him, embraced him. And he began to sob from happiness. Our hearts began to *touch* his awakening heart. It was so *young*! Ig quivered and cried.

We spoke the first words to the awakening heart.

A large, red-cheeked woman doctor came in.

Seeing us embracing the crying Ig, she broke into a smile.

"So these are your relatives, Comrade Deribas?"

Ig nodded.

She placed a glass of medicine on the stool and sighed, her large breasts heaving.

"What great happiness it is to find your dear kin on earth."

We *completely* agreed with her.

We were freed the same day, and Ig's assistant, the Chekist Zapadny, congratulated us: in the department everyone already knew that Deribas, who had lost his family in the Civil War, had found a sister and brother. The witnesses of our talk about the Ice and a secret mission were told that, trying to get to Krasnoyarsk, we had eaten virtually nothing (this was true!), which meant that we were slightly "touched in the head" by the time we arrived. Congratulating us, the broad-faced Chekist Zapadny apologized for the "laying on of hands" and the "forced lack of hospitality."

"Gracious, you really do look a lot like our Terenty Dmitrich!" he admitted to us quite sincerely.

"Well, of course: blue eyes!" I thought *secretly and joyously*.

They gave us quarters in the OGPU dormitory.

Ig left the hospital three days later. The doctors diagnosed him with "extreme exhaustion and stress, causing a deep loss of consciousness with features of a quasi-epileptic seizure." From Moscow came Yagoda's directive: send Deribas on vacation to regain his health. The chairman of the OGPU of the USSR loved and valued "the ferocious Deribas, whose iron hand had brought order to the Far East."

In Khabarovsk, Ig occupied a lovely house on Amursky Boulevard. His former wife and son stayed in Moscow, and here he was living with an actress of the Dramatic Theater. In Ig's home we once again met alone, just the three of us. Ig had recovered, his chest was healing, and his heart had begun to *live*. In the small but cozy living room we started a fire in the fireplace, drew the drapes, threw off our pitiful human clothes, lowered ourselves onto the rug, and froze in an embrace.

Time stopped for us.

When we awoke, for the first time since we met, Fer and I were able to eat our fill of fruit, which was plentiful in Ig's house. The head of the regional OGPU sent Crimean grapes and peaches, Astrakhan watermelons and plums, pears and mandarin oranges from the Caucasus. Ig enjoyed watching how, our naked bodies illuminated by the flames from the fireplace, we enjoyed the fruit, us. He resembled an infant learning to walk. Once cruel and implacable, seeing life as an unending, ruthless struggle, it was as though he had crawled out of his old, steel armor, riddled with bloody spikes, and now, soft and defenseless, was taking his first *step*.

Our hearts gently touched his.

Fer and I told our newly acquired brother about our lives. And he told us about his. The life of forty-five-year-old Terenty Deribas had followed a path marked by the sign of Eternal Struggle: a peasant childhood in a remote village, then the town trade school, a working-class factory milieu, an illegal group of the Russian Social-Democratic Workers' Party, the romanticism of the revolutionary underground, belief in a bright future, leaflets and proselytizing, Russian Marxism, arrest, exile, escape, again arrest, again exile, Revolution, workers' brigades, an inborn ability to lead, to infect people with his own anger and bend them to his will, the Civil War, becoming commissar first of a regiment, then a division, afterward came the army, victory over the Whites, experience and authority, a position in the All-Russian Cheka, ruthlessness toward remaining enemies, Lenin's personal gratitude, steadfastness and cruelty, absolute loyalty to the Party, the position of director of the OGPU's Secret Department, member of the collegiums of the OGPU, and then—ambassador plenipotentiary of the OGPU for the Far East.

During the war and later, Deribas had personally shot dozens of people; thousands were executed on his orders. For the Bolsheviks he was an ideal machine of suppression and destruction.

When the Ice hammer struck him in the chest, Deribas died.

And Ig appeared on earth. And became our brother.

He told us an amazing story. In 1908 he was living in exile again in western Siberia, in a little village on the banks of the great Irtysh River. He was waiting for winter, when the Irtysh would freeze and it would be possible to make a deal with a driver and escape over the ice to Omsk on a sleigh. At the end of June he had a dream: he dreamed about his grandfather, Yerofei Deribas. In his dream his grandfather's entire body was made of ice—his head, his crooked cavalry legs, and the stump of his right arm, lost during the war with the Turks. His grandfather was sitting at a new table that still smelled of freshly planed wood, in a newly built cottage of the Deribases', in the very same settlement, Uspensk, where Terenty had been born and grown up. In the middle of the table lay a roasted pig head. Seven-year-old Teresha sat across from his grandfather. Grandfather cut off pieces of the hot, steaming pork with his only, and extremely deft, left hand, and offered a piece to each member of the family, along with a humorous remark. Everyone was laughing and eating the pork with a good appetite. Terenty felt how delicious the meat smelled, he was *very* hungry; he drooled, he couldn't wait any longer—he was *terribly* hungry. However, Grandfather was taking his time: the ice hand, armed with a knife, cut off another piece, handed it out, but again it was not for Terenty. While Grandfather told his joke, he held the warm pork in his hand; grease dripped from it in large drops. Finally everyone except little Terenty had received his piece and was eating the warm pork with relish. Grandfather himself was eating as well.

"Grandpa, what about me?" Terenty asked.

Grandfather ate and looked at Terenty with icy eyes.

"Grandpa, what about me?" Terenty asked again, on the verge of tears.

Quickly swallowing the last of his piece, Grandfather wiped his icy beard with his ice hand, burped, and said, "It ain't needful for you."

Terenty's face was contorted with hurt.

"And what do I need?"

"This is what," Grandfather answered, and suddenly his icy fist slugged Terenty sharply and *very* painfully in the chest.

After that blow, Terenty's entire being understood that he needed the Ice.

That night in Siberia, sleeping on the tile stove in his hut, Terenty was awakened by an enormous clap of thunder. The hut swayed. His chest hurt as though someone had actually hit him. And he *sensed* that his grandfather had died at that very moment. It was true: Grandfather Yerofei passed away the morning of June 30, 1908.

Hearing the first story about the Ice from me on the train, he remembered his grandfather and the fantastical dream. At the same time he began to have the feeling that I *had known* his grandfather. That was why he had asked me about him so obsessively.

Ig's dream strengthened our faith in the power of the Ice. Each of *our people* had had dreams related to the Ice. And in this was the Great Wisdom of the Light.

After catching up on sleep, we got ready to travel. The Chekist Deribas was supposed to go to a sanatorium on the Crimean shore of the Black Sea in order to regain his health. We traveled with him. We were given new documents with the celebrated surname Deribas: I became Alexander Dmitrievich, Fer was Anfisa Dmitrievna. We had to stop in Krasnoyarsk and find Rubu and Ep, so as to take them with us. We were worried about them—the OGPU was looking for Rubu. Furthermore, we had to preserve the remaining six pieces of Ice. Ig hid four pieces in his attic: it was cold there, and winters in Khabarovsk were very cold. He packed two pieces in wooden chests, closed them with the lead seals of the OGPU, and ordered that they be loaded onto the train. They were placed in the unheated space between the cars.

At the end of October the train set off. Traveling in it were guards, a cook, a doctor, Deribas's secretary, and us. It was already winter in eastern Siberia—the snow lay on the hillocks that swam past the windows and it swirled around the cars. The train with a red star on the nose of the locomotive rushed toward the west. The wheels clacked along the frozen rails of the Trans-Siberian. The three of us sat in Deribas's compartment and talked about the future. A *very* significant endeavor awaited us. The endeavor of our lives. We stood at the beginning of the great road to the Light. It was important not to make any mistakes, not to act in haste. Neither did we have the right to move too slowly.

There were only five of us, five awakened hearts. There remained 22,995 brothers and sisters scattered about the complex world of this planet. They lived in different countries and spoke different languages, unaware of the Great Kinship, knowing nothing about their true nature. Their hearts slept, pumping blood like wordless machines in the corporeal darkness. Then they wore out, grew old, and stopped. And they were buried in the earth. But the Light, on leaving the dying heart, immediately passed to the heart of a newborn person, making him our brother. And this tiny heart began to pump blood again in the darkness of an infant body.

We had to break this vicious cycle. By means of the Ice hammer we had to separate the Divine Light from vile, short-lived flesh.

Our hearts burned with passion.

But passion alone was not much. We had to begin a long, persistent war against humankind for our brothers and sisters. This required huge resources. In order to sift through the human race, searching for the golden grain of our Brotherhood, we had to control this race.

Money provided power in the world of people. But in Soviet Russia money didn't play the same role as in the rest of the world. In a country living under the red flag with the hammer and sickle, only the state wielded absolute power. In order to achieve success in Russia, we would have to become part of the state machine, take cover under it, and, wearing the uniforms of officialdom, go about achieving our goal. There was no other way. Any secret society existing outside of the totalitarian state was doomed. We couldn't allow ourselves to become underground members of a secret order, hiding in the dark corners under the hierarchical ladder of power. That road led only to the torture chambers of the OGPU and the Stalinist camps. We had to clamber up this ladder and stand solidly on it. Then the difficult and painstaking process of searching for *our people* would possess the necessary protection. The fellowship had to enter the power structure. We had to make our way through its thick skin. In order to search for *our brothers and sisters.*

That was what our heads decided.

That was what our *wise* hearts prompted us to do.

So we began the search. We decided to stop in every large town. And we did. The train stopped in Chita. Ig called his secretary and right before our eyes climbed easily back into the steel armor of the Far East's top Chekist. With others he again became Deribas, ruthless and principled, the guard dog of the Revolution. He ordered his secretary to bring the head of the local OGPU. When the boss, perplexed, climbed into the car, Deribas ordered him to provide us with a car, a driver, and a Chekist escort. Fer and I drove around the city in the car. Our heart *magnet* began to work. We were *looking.* Stopping on the streets, we went into markets and stores, into Soviet organizations and barracks. All day we moved around the cozy, two-story town of Chita, surrounded by mountains, white with snow. But our hearts were silent: there were none of *us* in Chita. Exhausted and despairing from the heart's anticipation, I decided that we should return to the train station. On the way back I realized *just how* widely we were scattered among humans: in a town with a population of forty thousand, there wasn't a single one of us! Fer's heart, and mine, appreciated the miraculous and rapid acquisition of three brothers. The Light living in our hearts helped us.

Arriving at the small square in front of the station, strewn with cigarette butts and pine-nut shells, we began to get out of the car. And suddenly our hearts felt a *jolt.* Somewhere nearby a flute sounded plaintively. Fer looked around. Her heart *felt* our presence more powerfully than mine. Like a sleepwalker, she moved across the square, bumping into idlers and passengers waiting for the trains. I followed her. The Chekist, not understanding whom we had been searching for so intensely all day, stood by the car and smoked. As I walked, my heart began to tremble. The feeling got stronger and stronger. My eyes, watching Fer's back, clouded with tears. How I *loved* my sister at such fateful moments! She led me. And our hearts *called out to each other.*

Fer stopped short. I almost ran into her.

On a wooden box, there sat an intelligent-looking, middle-aged man dressed in a once-expensive but now tattered dirty coat with a soiled Arctic-fox fur collar. He was playing the flute. A cracked pince-nez trembled on his long, hooked nose. His reddish mustache was covered in frost. His light-blue eyes looked vacantly doomed: this man no longer had anything to lose. There were holes in his old gray felt boots. He was playing something plaintive and mournful.

We stood stock-still in front of him.

Our hearts *trembled*: he was our brother!

His sleeping heart could feel the power of the Light, which flared in our hearts, for the first time. The melody stopped abruptly. Our brother raised his eyes. They met with ours. His pince-nez trembled, his eyes widened in horror. He raised his flute to fend us off, and fell from the box. He cried out hoarsely, "Nooooooo!"

We lifted him under his arms. He wailed in a raspy, congested voice and tried weakly to break loose. His terror wasn't a sham: his delicate, emaciated face paled, and a spasm ran through the muscles of his mouth.

"Noooo! No! Noooo!" he wailed, writhing in our hands.

People looked at us with curiosity. The Chekist ran over.

"We were looking *for him*!" I informed the Chekist with a voice breaking with joy.

"I know this guy, the rat!" the Chekist grabbed the station musician by his collar. "White scum! Come on then, you, enough pretending!"

The three of us dragged the struggling musician to the platform where our red-nosed train stood. Along the way the musician lost consciousness. The flute fell from his stiff fingers. But we didn't pick it up. What would he need a flute for now? Joy burst from our hearts. We wanted to laugh, squeal, and roar from happiness.

"This cockroach here played in the White's orchestra," the Chekist muttered. "They didn't knock him off, felt sorry for the turd: after all, he's a musician . . . Comrade Babich told him to stay away from Chita—'Don't let me hear there's a trace of you in town, you piece of

White shit'—but no, he had to crawl back, the scoundrel. Were you looking for him for the old stuff?"

"For *new things*!" I answered joyously.

The Chekist remained silent.

We carried the unconscious flautist into the main compartment; Deribas gave the command. And the train began to move. The local Chekists standing on the platform saluted. The city of Chita, which had presented us with a brother, swam past the window, away from us forever: there were no more of *us* there. Evening fell, in the two-story houses the windows lit up dimly. The snow-covered mountains hid the town.

The guards brought the box with the Ice into the compartment. Then they left. Ig locked the door. His hand trembled with impatience. We opened the crate. We took the Ice and placed it on the floor. And, unable to restrain ourselves, grabbed it with our hands. Our hearts *resonated* with the Ice. Moans and cries burst from our lips.

The musician moved and opened his eyes. He looked at us in terror. It was time to awaken our brother.

"Don't be afraid of anything," I told him. "You are among *the people closest* to you."

He screamed like a wounded hare. Ig covered his mouth, tied it with a handkerchief. We began to undress the wandering musician. Under his coat was a woman's old top, torn at the elbows; under that, a dirty tunic. It teemed with lice. His body was thin and hadn't been washed for a long time, like a truly homeless man. He writhed in our hands and moaned weakly. Ig broke off the necessary piece of Ice with the handle of a revolver. Fer pulled the laces from her boots and looked around: in the corner of Deribas's compartment stood a red flag. On Soviet holidays it was attached to the locomotive. Fer grabbed the flag and tore the faded red cloth from it. We tied the Ice to the stick; Ig lifted the moaning musician and pressed the man's back to his own chest. I aimed at the thin, dirty chest bone, drew back, and struck it with the Ice hammer. The blow was so powerful that the musician and Ig toppled backward, tripped on the sofa, and fell. The stick broke, pieces of the Ice skittered all around. One of them cut Fer on the forehead above her eyebrow. The musician lost consciousness. Ig rushed to him and removed the gag from his mouth. He wasn't breathing.

"You killed him!" Ig exclaimed.

But Ig's heart was still very *young* compared to ours. We *knew* that the brother was alive. Blood began to run from his nose. Fer pressed her ear to the flautist's chest. His heart remained silent.

"Speak with your heart," she whispered passionately.

"Speak with your heart." I gave his heart a little push.

"Speak with your heart," Ig growled.

And our brother began to speak with his heart.

"Kta, Kta, Kta."

Our exclamations of joy were so loud that Deribas's secretary knocked on the door.

Ig shouted out happily.

Brother Kta moved and let out a moan. He was in pain: the force of the hammer had cracked his chest bone. But his awakened heart beat and spoke, beat and spoke.

"Kta! Kta! Kta!"

We cried for joy. Kta moaned. Blood dripped from the wound and flowed down his thin ribs. Ig pressed a kerchief to the wound and, tears pouring out of his eyes, shouted so loud that his face turned purple.

"Furman, get the doctor!"

"Yes, sir!" came the answer on the other side of the door.

I rushed to collect the precious Ice. But my heart suddenly *let me know*: I should not pick up these pieces; the Ice hammer strikes ONLY one heart. There was the Wisdom of the Light in this. I froze, squatting over the pieces lying on the rug. A louse crawled across one of them. It shook me out of my stupor. Lifting the main piece, I placed it back in the crate, closed the top, and nailed it shut with the handle of a revolver. Ig grabbed the splinters of wood from the stick and pushed them and the red material under the sofa.

There was a knock at the door. Ig opened it. The doctor entered, followed by the secretary Furman.

"His sternum is broken," said Ig, pointing to Kta. "Do what you need to, Semyonov. You are responsible for his life."

The doctor touched the chest. Kta cried out.

"A crack," muttered the doctor. "We need a soft splint."

"Do it . . . do what you have to! Or I'll shoot you!" Ig shouted, losing control of himself.

The doctor turned pale: Deribas had never spoken to him that way.

I put my hand on his back and nudged him with my heart: "Calm down."

Unlike Fer and me, Ig had not yet *cried* with his heart. And he had not yet discovered the Wisdom of the Light.

The doctor placed a soft bandage on Kta's chest and gave him a shot of morphine. Kta fell into a deep sleep. We covered him with a blanket and left him on a sofa in the compartment. The guards carried the crate with the Ice back to the cold space between cars. We sat around Kta as he slept. Night fell. I turned off the light in the compartment. The car rocked. Outside stretched a black, impenetrable forest; occasionally we caught sight of the starry sky. We held hands in the dark. Our hearts beat *regularly*. They protected our *newborn's* sleep.

The next morning Kta came to. Fear had not yet left his emaciated body. But we did everything to make sure that he *understood* who we were.

The next day was spent along the shore of the Baikal, the huge Siberian lake. Suddenly we stopped. Deribas was informed that two trains had collided up ahead. Fixing the rails took four days. Over this time, Kta finally returned to his old self. We saw the design of the Light in this: the trains collided to allow an awakening heart some rest.

Kta told us about himself: he, Iosif Tseitlin, came from a moderately well-off Jewish family. He graduated from the Moscow Conservatory in flute, played in the Bolshoi Theater orchestra, during the Civil War escaped from the capital to the area beyond the Urals, was captured by the Whites, played the trumpet in a military band, was then imprisoned by the Reds, miraculously escaped execution, lived four years in Chita giving private music lessons, then was arrested as a "former person," again miraculously escaped the repressions, was exiled from the town, wandered here and there, playing at stations, then *for some reason* returned to Chita, although the head of the OGPU there, Artyom Babich, had threatened him with the firing squad.

Tseitlin had also had a *strange* dream: June 29, 1908, outside of Moscow at the dacha of the pianist Maria Kerzina, there was a musical evening in honor of her husband's birthday; he was a well-known industrialist, a patron of the musical arts, the chairman of the Moscow Circle of Russian Music Lovers; chamber music was played at the party, Tseitlin also performed, playing with a string quartet; everything ended with a traditional dacha table and a noisy nocturnal swim in the Kliazma River. That evening Iosif drank more than usual and early in the morning he awoke thirsty, with a headache; descending from the attic so as not to bother the sleeping guests, he went out into the small garden, found the well, opened its wooden top. The bucket on the rope had already been lowered, he had only to lift it; Iosif grabbed the iron handle of the drum and began to turn it, pulling up a full bucket. The well was deep, *very deep*; Iosif turned and turned the iron handle, raising the bucket and thinking about the healing, teeth-chattering cold of the well water; but the bucket wouldn't appear; tortured by thirst and impatience, Tseitlin looked in the well; it was *incredibly* deep: you couldn't see the bottom! The well walls narrowed to a black point over which a small bucket hung—it was still very far away; Iosif began to turn it with all his might; the rope wrapped around the drum, making it fatter and fatter, until it turned into a thick skein; Iosif grew tired and began turning with both hands; they trembled from tension. Finally the bucket appeared, and Iosif looked at it: it was cubic in form; the unexpectedness of this caused him to stop turning and stare at the unusual bucket; the purest well water splashed in it; at this moment the sun rose, and its rays touched the water in the bucket; the surface of the water instantly shone with light and it was as though it had become a *light-bearing* icon; the picture on this icon was of a blue-eyed, blond youth and a young woman with a large chunk of ice in her hands;

from them a *new* strength arose, and shook Tseitlin so profoundly that he let go of the handle. He woke up on a bed in the dacha's attic, very thirsty. He went out into the garden, as in his dream, found the well in the same place, and opened it; a full bucket of water stood on the edge of the well chamber; he began to drink greedily from the bucket; having drunk his full, he stepped back, saw his reflection in the water, and *understood* that someday a young man and a girl with a piece of ice would come for him.

When Fer and I approached him on the square in front of the train station, he recognized us and cried out because his dream had come true.

We *spoke* with Kta.

Then the train moved.

The next stop was Irkutsk. We did the same thing as in Chita: sat in a Chekist car and rode around the city. It was more civilized then Chita, here there were not only one- and two-story homes, but we came across fairly beautiful buildings as well. And again we spent the whole day driving through the city, taking a look at busy places. And again no one noticed our heart *magnet*. Evening fell quickly. Arriving at the station, Fer and I got out of the car. The train station was bigger than in Chita. But the square in front of it was smaller. It was also strewn with cigarette butts, the shells of seeds and pine nuts. We stopped in the middle. But here *no one* was playing the flute.

Irkutsk was empty.

We returned to our train and it departed. After *illuminating* Irkutsk with our hearts, Fer and I felt an enormous exhaustion: it was as though we had run the gauntlet, like soldiers who had committed some offense in the czarist army. Our hearts had been squeezed and were empty. We didn't even have the strength to cry. Barely making it to our beds, we collapsed and fell asleep.

When we awoke, we were already in Krasnoyarsk.

Here we had to look for Ep and Rubu—and for new brothers and sisters. We were met at the station: the Irkutsk Chekists had informed Krasnoyarsk about Deribas's train; a car took Ig and me to the municipal directorate of the OGPU. Fer remained in the train with Kta. The first order of business was to drive to our old address.

The little house, on whose terrace I had heard the drunken carter talk to his horse, was empty. Our brothers had left. The neighbors knew nothing. Returning to the directorate, Ig demanded the operational summaries for the last month. In one of them there was a report about the theft of a truck belonging to the city bakery. Three days later this car had been found abandoned in Kansk. There the thieves got on the train; the ticket seller at the station recognized them. They bought tickets to Khabarovsk. That meant that they were already there! Ep and Rubu were struggling to come to our aid, not knowing that we had already *been helped*. Now we had to find them in Khabarovsk. Or in some other Siberian town? But we were heading for the Crimea! It was impossible to return: we had taken the Ice westward in order to find and awaken other hearts. Ep and Rubu waited for us somewhere in the east. Russia's huge distances were oppressive: people could get lost like grains of sand in such expanses. *But* brothers all the more so. Ig sent a telephonogram to Khabarovsk: to detain the two dangerous criminals *alive*; anyone who dared to shoot them would be tried. The sinister wheels of the OGPU began to turn: the search for Ep and Rubu took on new life.

We began *our* search: the black Ford drove through the gates of the OGPU building on Lenin Street. Fer and I were seated in the back. Krasnoyarsk brought us no joy, either: for two days the Black Maria rolled through the city, reminding its inhabitants of nighttime arrests; for two days the doors of the university, the barracks, three dormitories, four schools, and a hospital were opened to us. The faces of people swam past the heart *magnet* in an endless stream. But there were none of *us* among them.

On the third day we left Krasnoyarsk.

Fer and I *became accustomed* to our work. We no longer became so exhausted from the heart *illumination* of whole cities.

Next was Novosibirsk.

There we were lucky. We had hardly x-rayed the market when Fer's sensitive heart began to throb: there was someone. At first I didn't feel anything. Then—I did feel it, but *together* with my amazing sister. We circled around the market, but *didn't see* our brother, though we could feel him keenly. This continued for more than an hour. Fer began to despair: she screamed and beat her chest, as though trying to force her heart *to see* more clearly. And suddenly it became clear where the *source* was: just a little way from the market stood a small church. The Bolsheviks hadn't touched it, and a service was being held. The doors opened and closed, letting the believers enter and leave. This was precisely what had *distracted* us. *The source* was inside. We entered the church. And closed our eyes in rapture: *he* was leading the service! Tall and stately, about forty-five years old, with a mane of blond hair, a broad beard, a courageous, noble face, and close-set blue eyes, he stood at the gates of the altar wearing the gold-flecked garments of a priest; waving a smoking censer, he called to the believers in a strong, deep voice.

"Let us pray for the Lord's world."

They prayed, crossing themselves and bowing. Fer grabbed my hand and squeezed it until it cracked. Our hearts rejoiced. The service went on *too* long. But we were enjoying the anticipation. We understood that this service was our brother's last. Occasionally he glanced at us, picking us out of the crowd. But his heart was calm. Finally the whole thing was over. Those who took Communion lined up in front of the priest. As soon as he was finished administering the Sacrament, he was arrested and brought to our train. He turned out to be courageous not only on the outside: he resisted, threatened us with the tortures of hell, and began chanting the psalms. The Ice hammer interrupted his singing. He lost consciousness, and when he came to he was already a *different man*.

"Oa! Oa! Oa!" his heart said.

We cried for joy, embracing him.

Oa brought us happiness: after him in each large city on our route we acquired more brothers. Not only brothers. There was more than one sister. That was how the will of the Light was accomplished.

In Omsk we found Kti.

In Chelyabinsk—Edlap.

In Ufa—Em.

In Saratov—Ache.

In Rostov-on-Don—Bidugo.

It's possible that there were other brothers in these cities, but when we found one, we could no longer search for others: we didn't have the strength. The newly acquired were immediately taken to the station, to the train. Then the search would be interrupted and the divine process of *awakening* would begin. It amazed not only the new brothers, but everyone who held the newly found in their trembling hands, gagged the wailing mouths, swung back, and with all their might struck the chests with the Ice hammer; everyone who greedily listened to the flutter of awakening hearts, and then, sobbing with ecstasy, repeated the sacred names of the brothers in the impoverished language of humans.

"Kti! Edlap! Em! Ache! Bidugo!"

After this exertion, we could not get back into a Chekist Black Maria and set off on our search again: our hearts demanded rest. So the train with the red star moved on. The newly acquired were placed in the second car, where there were separate guest compartments. The doctor took care of them. All of them were blue-eyed and blond. Like Fer and me, and Ig. Like Rubu and Ep. And we understood definitively that this was an identifying sign of the Light: the dark-haired and gray-eyed could not be *one of us*. Our search needed to be *only* among the blue-eyed and light-haired.

Our hearts made us wise. So that his assistant and the local Chekists didn't start asking questions about our not quite ordinary search, Ig told them that we were looking for a secret spy network along the Trans-Siberian, organized by a certain religious sect. This story dismissed all questions. The Chekist doctor Semyonov had stopped caring long ago whom he treated and for what. The guard and Deribas's assistant, hearing cries and blows from the compartment of the boss, were certain that we were torturing the arrested.

We were *awakening* them from a dead dream.

But we understood that soon we would not have the means to do this: after Saratov the weather warmed considerably, the outside thermometer showed ten degrees Celsius. The Ice in the crates began to melt. We had to do something. Ig and Fer and I made a decision: to leave the crates of Ice in Rostov-on-Don, placing them in special refrigerators. In 1928 the only place in town where there were large industrial freezers was at the sausage factory. The Ice was placed in iron crates, closed with locks, and put in the freezer. By Deribas's decree, the director of the refrigeration guild had personal responsibility for them.

We decided to continue the search, but without the Ice. Ig proposed simply arresting our brothers and keeping them in the same prison car where Fer and I had been kept on the way to Khabarovsk.

But after we parted with the Ice, luck turned its back on us: our magnet found no one in either dusty, fruit-filled Simferopol or in the seaside city of Sevastopol. Emptied by our *hearts* and distressed, Fer and I fell into a deep sleep.

When we awoke we were already in a car: we were being driven along a serpentine mountainous road. Between us sat Ig, who had changed into a white tunic without any marks of rank and white trousers. His face shone with joy, he held us by the hand. We raised our heads and looked outside: it was a sunny, warm autumn day in the Crimea; mountains of yellow and red vegetation floated past us. I looked around. There was another car behind us: four of our newly acquired brothers rode in it—Oa, Kta, Kti, and Bidugo. Ig had directed that the rest be placed in the Simferopol military hospital. In the early-morning Crimean air, just in front of us, was a splash of bright red—the automobile in which the local bosses rode: the secretary of the Crimean oblast Party committee, Veger, had decided to personally accompany the legendary Deribas to the RKKA sanatorium. They had known each other well since the Civil War.

Passing through Yalta, that most beautiful Crimean city, we arrived at the sanatorium, drowning in yellowed chestnut trees and acacia. There we stopped. What we had long *expected* happened to brother Ig here. First, the director of the sanatorium descended the marble staircase—a smiling, fat Georgian with Stalinist mustaches, dressed in the same white tunic Ig was wearing and greasy gray trousers.

"To your health, dear guests!" He threw his pudgy hands up and with a clap placed them on his chest, bowing to the new arrivals.

"Hello there, Georgy," said the ugly, large-faced secretary of the obkom, extending him a hand. "Just look who I've brought you." Veger nodded at Ig, who was getting out of the car.

"Comraid Deribass!" The fat Georgian minced along to our car. "We're worn out waiting for you, I swear on my honest, is autumn already, the warmth, he is going, and you all the time are not coming and not coming! Vy you don't have enough respect for your health, you don't take care, I swear on my honest, please, Comrade Stalin is standing on you!"

The secretary laughed. Ig smiled, as Deribas *was meant to*, and shook hands with the large man. They were acquainted.

"Good. We traveled and traveled, and now we've arrived. Haven't been here for two years, is that right?"

"That's very bad, very bad, Comraid Deribass, I swear on my honest!"

"But this time—I've come with relatives! How are things here with you? Can we rest?"

The fat man pressed his pudgy palms to his pudgy chest.

"Comraid Deribass, I always sed, that Red commanders rest with their heart."

Ig grew pale.

"What's that . . . you said?"

"With their heart! With their very heart, I swear on my honest!" said the director, patting himself on the chest.

Ig's heart shuddered. And Fer and I understood what would happen now. With a sob, Ig drew air into his lungs, threw his head back, and began to fall backward. We caught him.

"Epilepsy!" I told everyone.

In truth it was Ig's *heart crying*. And he cried along with it.

There was a lot of hustle and bustle, the doctor on call ran over. Ig sobbed and beat himself. He was carried off to the ward and given an injection of morphine. Our room was nearby, in the next ward.

"So you see, my friends." The secretary of the obkom patted Fer and me on the shoulders. "Suppressing enemies in the Far East—it's not like shucking sunflower seeds. Comrade Deribas is tired, he's overworked. He needs calm. Take care of your brother's heart. The Party has great need of it."

"And so do *we*," Fer replied.

The Power of the Heart

IT TOOK Ig five days to cry out all the tears. Emptied and cleansed by the *heart crying*, he lay on the sofa in a three-person ward and ate Crimean grapes with the caution of a weak old man. I sat in the armchair across from him; Fer, on the windowsill of the open window; Kta on a chair in the middle of the ward; Oa stood, leaning against the doorframe. Although it was the end of October, the weather was still warm, and a breeze lightly stirred the window curtain and Fer's hair. An enormous floor clock had just struck four in the afternoon. The weary autumn sun warmed Fer, the putty-filled parquet, and the yellowing leaves of the acacia outside the window.

We had met in Ig's room in order to talk about the future. Kti and Bidugo weren't with us: the heart awakening had shaken them harder than others; Ig had ordered that they be placed in a hospital ward while he recovered.

We needed to understand just *how* we would live henceforth among people. And not just live but search for *others like us*. Myriad questions arose: where to live, who to be in this Bolshevist country, how and where to carry on our search, where to hide those we found, how to transport the Ice, where to keep it, and most important— what to do so that no one arrested us as conspirators, tortured us, and then shot us in the cellars of the OGPU.

Everything that had happened was nothing short of a *miracle*. We realized that we had been *incredibly* lucky these last two months. But it would be extremely dangerous to place our hope on luck in the future. We had to *calculate* our future life. And come up with a plan of action.

At that quiet hour of the fading autumn day our hearts were silent. But we didn't feel like speaking in the language of humans, either. We sat looking out the window at the fading sun. No one moved; only Ig ate grapes slowly. His fingers tore off the violet fruit and put it in his mouth.

Finally, I broke the silence.

"How are we going to live?"

Everyone turned to face me. Only Fer, sitting on the windowsill, remained immobile. Her lithe young figure was lit by sunlight. It was as though she were holding on to the light, refusing to let it be extinguished.

"How are we going to live?" I asked again.

Ig stopped swallowing grapes. The brothers remained silent. Their hearts as well. And suddenly for the first time since my heart had awoken I felt a sense of *helplessness*. As soon as my heart grew quiet, I became an ordinary person. And I began to look for protection in reason. From the moment of my awakening, when I hit my chest on the huge mound of Ice, it was as though I had been set on wheels, and had rolled and rolled along on them, not stopping, not doubting anything. Now my "train" had stopped. Something had happened in me and in us. I *felt* that it was no accident that the brothers were so quiet. They had *nothing* to reply. They had also *stopped*. Ahead of us lay the world of people. And no one had laid down the rails for our wheels. That world was stern and merciless.

And for the first time, signs of earthly fear stirred in my head. My brothers' faces grew pale: they felt the same thing. Ig's hand holding the bunch of grapes convulsed into a fist. Reddish juice spattered through his fingers. His lips turned white.

The Wisdom of the Light had abandoned our hearts.

We felt loneliness. And we became AFRAID. It was terrible: the fear that I had conquered lying on the mound of Ice suddenly returned. I was afraid of fear. But far more frightening was the very *possibility* of fear. Its return scared and shook me more than the immediate fear itself.

Suddenly Fer moved and *with the greatest difficulty* turned to us. Her face was petrified with terror. I had never seen her like that. She looked at us as though we were dying. The hair stood up on my head. In an instant I realized that we would never tear the block of Divine Ice from the Tungus swamp, never find all of *us*, would never become the Light. We were doomed to perish in this alien and ruthless world, which pulverized living creatures. In a world that had opened its funereal jaws to us.

Human Death silently entered the sun-drenched room.

We grew stiff and cold. Only motes of dust whirled in the rays of the sun.

But suddenly Fer, who had been sitting in a stupor on the windowsill, began to raise her hands. It was *impossibly* difficult for her to do this. That mortal fear impeded her movement. But she fought. Her arms rose and stretched out toward us.

And we *understood*.

Kta, who was sitting to Fer's right, began to stretch his hand out to her. From the left, sitting in my chair, I stretched mine. From his bed, Ig reached for me, and Oa, standing in the doorway, reached out for Ig. Never in my life had it been so hard for me to stretch out my arms. My arms were *heavy* and wouldn't obey. It was *very* difficult for the others as well. Shaking and straining, we reached out to one another. We accomplished *the most intensely challenging* work.

For a moment I felt that the sunlight flooding the room was a viscous substance that we were trying to part with our hands. Our hands and arms stretched, stretched, stretched. Kta fell off his chair; I tumbled from my armchair; Oa and Ig collapsed and crawled along the floor. We all crawled toward the windowsill *in torment*, toward Fer who was sitting there. Our bodies were drenched in an icy sweat. Sweat flowed into my eyes. I could see only the blurry contour of Fer's hand. Salvation lay in that hand. And I made it there. Kta made it to her right hand.

We clutched one another's hands. With our last bit of strength we formed a Circle. A Lesser Circle of Light. As soon as we had done this, our hearts shuddered. And came to life.

The Light once again *began to speak* in them—with such force that cries of rapture burst from our lips. Fer had saved us! The Wisdom of the Light had not abandoned her. Our only sister had become the Great Savior of the Brotherhood of the Primordial Light.

We crawled over to her and embraced her, crying from the rapture of salvation. She was still sitting on the windowsill. We *loved* our only sister. And she *loved* us. Squeezing our hands and laying them on her breast, she looked down at us. Tears of joy flowed from her eyes and dripped on our faces. The sunlight played in Fer's tears.

Our hearts *began to speak* with new strength.

This continued all night.

In the morning we *knew* what we had to do. An alien world surrounded us on all sides as before. But roads and tracks had now been laid down upon it. The strength of the heart had laid these roads. It was as though that strength had opened the world. And we could see the deep crevices that awaited us. We had to move along these roads without fear and trepidation, crawl into the crevices of the world, imitate it. And accomplish our great goal.

In the language of people Fer said, "The Light will always be with us. It *will teach* us. And we will do everything that is necessary."

We *never* again trusted our reason alone. Any idea, any endeavor, any job, each of us checked first and foremost with the heart. The strength of the heart would show *the way*. Reason facilitated *movement* along this path. The strength of the heart nudged reason, backed it up. And reason moved, overcoming the world, taking everything we needed from it and tossing aside anything superfluous, anything that hindered us. False fears, uncertainty about the future, worry about the life of our brothers—everything flew away.

In this sun-drenched ward we acquired *complete* freedom. Because we put our trust in our hearts *fully forevermore*. And we knew their might.

The number of heart words increased, acquired in our hearts. The language of the heart became richer with every conversation. When we embraced, we learned from one another. Our hearts grew more certain.

And the power of the heart was with us.

Sisters

ONCE IG was completely back on his feet, it was decided to make use of his vacation to begin the search for *our people* in nearby towns. Getting in touch with the local OGPU, Ig obtained a car and driver. Fer and I were supposed to set off in the car on a search mission. According to the plan, we had an escort—a Chekist from the operations department of the Simferopol OGPU. Ig informed him in the iron voice of Deribas that he was sending Fer and me in search of a secret counterrevolutionary organization, which had escaped from Siberia to the Crimea for the winter, and whose members we knew by sight. Accordingly, the Chekist should cooperate with us in capturing the "masked enemies of the people." As soon as the heart *magnet* found one of *ours*, we should point him out to the Chekist so that he could arrest him. It was decided not to take any of the newly acquired with us but to dispatch them immediately to the local jails. After Deribas's vacation was over, it would be necessary to convey them to our train. On the way back we would have to collect the crates with the Ice in Rostov-on-Don, and on the long voyage to Khabarovsk we would hammer *ours* with the Ice hammer.

In the early Crimean morning the automobile fetched Fer and me from the sanatorium. We set off on a three-day trip: Sevastopol, Simferopol, Melitopol, Berdyansk, Rostov-on-Don. The search was easier for us now: we knew for *certain* that brothers and sisters of the Light were blue-eyed and light-haired. An endless line of people, faces and bodies, passed before us. We floated on a sea of people, parted it, plunged headfirst into it, and swam up again. We breathed the crowd. It smelled of the sweat of life and muttered about its own affairs. The crowd was always in a hurry. Our magnet saw straight through it. And the deeper we immersed ourselves in the process of searching in the human sea, the harder it became for us. The crowd grew thicker. Our hearts trembled from the tension.

In Sevastopol we found two sisters.

In Melitopol—one.

In Simferopol—no one.

And no one in the big city of Rostov-on-Don. We spent an entire day there. After a lengthy and difficult search, Fer vomited bile from the extreme tension. She became hysterical, and she frightened the Chekist who was escorting us. I collapsed from exhaustion and blood flowed from my nose. The automobile took us to the dormitory of the OGPU, and the chauffeur and the Chekist helped Fer to climb the steps of the porch. I followed, trying not to fall. The young, tan Rostov Chekists who met us were worried.

"What's happened, comrades?" they asked.

Fer and I didn't have the strength to move our tongues. We walked, holding on to the wall, to our room. And we heard the escort Chekist answer the locals: "There you go, guys, see how those Siberians sniff out enemies of the people. Nonstop. Learn from them!"

We fell onto the beds. The sea of people whirled in my head. And in it there wasn't *a single* dear, familiar face! We embraced and sobbed.

In small, cozy Berdyansk, however, our heart *magnet* found six of us! And they were all sisters! This affected Fer and me like a flash of the Light. But physically it completely crushed us: after the searches and arrests of the sisters we found, we fainted on the dusty pavement of Berdyansk. When we regained consciousness we were already on the backseat of the car: Fer and I were being taken to Yalta. I raised my head with great difficulty, and pushed myself up on weak arms. Outside the window, pyramid-shaped poplars flew by.

"Has everyone we found been arrested?" I asked, though it was *enormously* difficult to remember the words.

"And how!" replied the Chekist sitting in the front. "You can rest in peace on that one."

Relieved, I rested my spinning head on the leather seat back. Fer was sleeping.

"What I wanted to ask," said the Chekist, lighting a cigarette, "is why's they all birds?"

"Their husbands have already been arrested," I muttered.

"Gotcha," said the Chekist, shaking his dark head seriously, and then asking, "Lots more to go?"

"Lots," I answered, stroking Fer's sleeping lips.

"That's the ticket!" the Chekist agreed brightly. "Enemies ain't gonna just go and disappear on their own. Well, all right then. We'll clear the weeds out of the field."

On returning to the sanatorium, we lay in bed for a day, renewing our strength. The brothers were continually with us, helping our bodies and hearts. We were fed fruit by hand, like little children. All of *ours* were excited: they couldn't maintain their calm, thinking of the nine sisters we'd found. The brothers asked for *stories*, stroked our hands, which had touched the sisters; they tried to *feel* them. But what could our lips tell them? Could the paltry language of humans possibly convey the *rapture* of discovery? We spoke with our hearts, holding the brothers by their hands. And they *understood* us.

A week passed.

Kta and Oa had gone through the cleansing by tears. They had been kept in the hospital wing. All the brothers coming to the sanatorium were under the patronage of Deribas, which meant—the OGPU.

"Their nerves need to heal," Ig told the head doctor of the sanatorium. "You know what our work is like."

The head doctor—a Jew from Yalta and a member of the intelligentsia who had lived through the horrors of the Civil War and by some miracle survived the Red Terror—nodded with understanding.

Ig had fully recovered after his *crying* and with quadrupled strength set about furthering our great endeavor. For regular people he was one and the same Iron Deribas, tough and decisive, quick and merciless, energetic and straightforward. The nearly old man who lay quietly on the sofa on that memorable sunny day, with a bunch of grapes in his hand, had disappeared forever. The voice of Ig-Deribas rang through the hallways of the sanatorium, his boots squeaked triumphantly, his eyes glittered. He exuded the unseen energy of *overcoming* life, which people took as an absolute love of life. Short, quick, and forceful, he became the "soul" of the sanatorium. Everyone adored him: the military men in the dining hall, with whom he discussed fanatically the "arch importance of the Party-line gradient in overcoming the kulaks' sabotage of grain procurements," shared military reminiscences and dreams of world revolution; the director, with whom he played raucous games of billiards and argued about "local excesses in the ethnic question"; the female personnel, who laughed at his frivolous, crude jokes. He slept no more than three hours a day, swam in the autumn sea for a long time, played noisy games of skittles, sang louder than everyone during evenings of military songs.

"Now there's a real bon vivant!" thought the frail head doctor as he straightened his pince-nez and watched Deribas laughing.

But we *knew* the true nature of this "lover of life." Brother Ig was *preparing* himself for the eternal struggle in the name of the Light. And he didn't spare his human nature, pulling it back like a bow in order to deliver a smashing blow with his arrow. A telegram came from Khabarovsk: Ep and Rubu had been found and arrested. During their capture, they shot two Chekists, but they themselves weren't hurt. We rejoiced.

Ig's vacation was coming to an end. It was time to continue our Great Endeavor. Three days before departure we gathered at dawn on the rocks of a cliff not far from the sanatorium's beach. The sun had not yet risen, a weak tide rolled in over yellow-gray stones, and the cool air was bracing. Ig, Fer, Kta, Kti, Oa, and I climbed up the largest cliff, whose summit actually extended over the sea like the keel of a dreadnought. We sat down, forming a Circle, and held one another's hands. Our hearts began to speak. They spoke of *what was to come*. A ray of sun sparkled on the horizon of the sea and stretched as far as us, illuminating the immobile faces with half-closed eyes. But we didn't notice it. The sun dimmed beside the Light shining in our hearts.

At the beginning of November, Deribas's train set off from the station at Sebastopol. We didn't leave any of the brothers in the Crimea, even those who hadn't yet *cried* with the heart. The simple local leaders and tanned Pioneers saw us off. Veger, the obkom secretary, sent three enormous baskets of fruit; the local OGPU sent a huge pumpkin with the inscription TO THE CHEKISTS OF THE RED EAST FROM THE CHEKISTS OF THE RED SOUTH. Deribas, now dressed in the uniform of the OGPU plenipotentiary, with three red rhombuses and two medals on his lapel, stood, as he was expected to, on the back platform of the train car and waved. When the train moved out, the director of the sanatorium moved with it along the platform. Placing his hands on his plump chest as always, he spoke with his Georgian accent: "Comraid Deribass, faraway there in the Far East, you try to ketch all zee enemies in the vinter, I swear on my honest, so they doesn't stop your coming back to us summertime!"

Deribas saluted, wiped the smile from his face, and entered his compartment.

In Rostov-on-Don we collected the Ice. And our nine sisters.

When the soldiers with rifles brought them to the train and gave the order "Get in!," the women cried and wailed; someone said that they were being sent to Siberia. Crying, they climbed into the car. But our hearts *burned* with joy. Fer and I were ready to kiss the feet of each of them. Light-haired and blue-eyed, the sisters differed considerably in age: from fourteen to fifty-six. Three of them, in the earthly sense, were real beauties.

The sisters were locked into the guard's car.

As soon as the train moved, we began. The guards brought us the first sister—a pretty, rotund Melitopol Jewess with a reddish shock of hair and huge forget-me-not blue eyes. Strong and loud, she sobbed, calling out to her mama in Ukrainian, or muttering in Yiddish: "*Gotyniu toirer! O gotyniu toirer!*"

Gagging her, we stretched her arms out on the door. Ig tore her dress, Fer and Oa moved the huge white breasts with light-pink nipples aside, I firmly held her fat knees, and Ig, trembling from *heart* rapture, whacked her tender chest with the Ice hammer, using all his strength.

Her name was Nir.

The next was a plump, sturdy Ukrainian. A merchant from the Sevastopol market with straight platinum hair and a tanned, round face, she tried to buy her way out, offering "nine tenners hidden under the floor." When we started to undress her, she helped us, muttering in Ukrainian, "Whatever you want, just don't shoot me."

I struck her. It took four blows for her heart to call its name: "At!"

She flooded us with her urine—as we howled with the joy of *discovery*.

Sister Orti—a Komsomol beauty from Berdyansk—fought us furiously, threatening to complain to "Veger himself," whose nephew was her fiancé. Oa, strong and broad-shouldered, took the Ice hammer in his hands for the first time; with the first shattering but imprecise blow, he broke her collarbone and beat the sacred name out of her heart: "Orti!"

She lost consciousness from the pain and the *awakening*.

We had a lot of trouble with the small, frail beggar girl taken from the front of the Sevastopol church. Her thin, dirty chest, covered with pus-filled pimples, withstood six blows; her heart only shook and then stood still for long periods, scaring us that it would stop. The impatient Bidugo finally grabbed the lifeless girl and pressed her against his body; then Ig hit her for the seventh time so hard that a shard of Ice flew across the room and almost put out Kta's eye. Blood spurted from the beggar's lips. But her heart came to life.

"Nedre!"

The tow-headed, angular, modestly dressed workers from a Berdyansk tannery, Zina Prikhnenko and Olesya Soroka, had been born twin sisters, it turned out. It was incredible, but they even worked in the same guild: that was how the Light's craft brought them together. There was no doubt they had been waiting for us. Standing stock-still, they submissively entered Deribas's compartment, obediently stood at the door, and allowed themselves to be tied by the hands. They stood, their pale blue eyes not blinking, while we unbuttoned their shirts, tore the underclothes covering their chests, and turned their crosses to their backs. But as soon as the Ice hammer was raised, their legs gave way and they lost consciousness: they had dreamed of the hammer, the Ice sparkled in forgotten childhood dreams, where shining and powerful people *plucked* at their child hearts sweetly, pursued them, giving them no peace. Bidugo struck them.

"Pilo!"

"Ju!"

Klavdiya Bordovskaya, arrested in her fashionable atelier, which had survived NEP's demise, largely owing to the beauty and amorousness of its mistress, had decided that she had been arrested for connections with the director of the regional trade association, a thieving morphine addict who had committed suicide. As soon as she was brought to us, she threw herself on her knees before Ig and, embracing his boots, shouted that she would "sign everything." Noticing that Fer and I were tying the Ice to a stick, she decided that she was going to be "tortured with potassium chlorate salts," and screamed so loudly that we had to gag her immediately. With a powerful and biting blow to her sleek breast, I ended the career of the fashion designer.

"Khortim!"

A well-bred lady of noble blood, a stately widow of a White Guard captain, with unfathomable ultramarine eyes, crossed herself furiously, as though we were demons, and cursed us with damnation of everything imaginable. While she was being tied to the door, malicious hissing and curses burst from her delicate lips. She burned with hatred, writhing in our hands. Once tied, however, she froze and grew silent, preparing for death. For her we were the "Bolshevist scum that ruined Russia." The Ice hammer split the skin on her chest quite forcefully. She stood, grown pale, as though a marble sculpture, looking *through* us with her amazing eyes. Pressing my ear to her bloody, proud breast, I heard: "Epof!"

The last one turned out to be the mother of seven children, a housewifely woman, all hustle and bustle, simple and kind, like the warm dough that her children so loved to eat, washing it down with cold milk. Invoking her children and her Red Army husband, she begged us to let her go. Born for the re-creation of life, to continue the race, she couldn't allow herself to die. For her it was equal to a great sin. Brother Edlap, a former blacksmith, awoke her heart with one blow, forcing her to forget her children forever and to *remember* her name: "Ugolep!"

And so, we acquired nine sisters.

All the Ice we had taken with us was used up in striking their breasts. Pieces of it were strewn across the floor of Deribas's compartment. They were melting, mixing with the urine of the awakened sisters. Pieces of the Ice-hammer sticks lay at our feet. Part of the Great Work had been successfully accomplished.

There were now twenty-one of us.

We rejoiced.

And took care of the newly acquired in every possible way.

We placed the sisters as well as we could—in the guest compartments, in the compartments for the arrested, in the dining room. They were shaken: moaning from pain, they cried tears of *farewell* to the life of humans; their bodies reset themselves; their hearts *pronounced* the first words. We *helped* them. And they were already crying with the joy of *overcoming* the old. The doctor put a splint on

Orti's broken collarbone. He didn't understand what was happening on this train, going full steam from the south to the east of this vast country in which these strange and ruthless Bolsheviks had taken power. Deribas's assistant didn't understand anything, either. But the tradition of not asking the bosses superfluous questions had already taken root: all across the country the punitive apparatus of the OGPU had turned into a large machine that worked according to its own laws, hidden to the view of outsiders. If the Bolshevik Party still breathed with hot discussions, the OGPU grew increasingly *mute*, hiding from outside eyes. Chekists learned to work silently. Orders that came from higher-ups hadn't been discussed for some time. Ig understood this and used it to achieve our own goals.

Purposes grew like bushes. Our hearts swiftly defined the direction, our heads barely managed to figure out the opportunities. The Power of the Light carried us. In Saratov the train stopped. The Brotherhood made a decision: Fer, Oa, Bidugo, and I would go to Moscow. The rest would continue with Ig to Khabarovsk. Ig-Deribas sent a telegram to the capital: his influential friends in the OGPU should help us, find us jobs, provide us with living quarters. That way, the heart *magnet* would begin to work in the largest Russian city. And newly acquired brothers could speak with the heart.

We said *heartfelt* farewells to our brothers and sisters. It was a *powerful* farewell: forming a Circle, we all held hands. And spoke in the language of the Light. The compartment disappeared. We hung in the void, among the stars. Our hearts *lit up*. Shining words flowed. Experienced hearts taught weak, recently awakened hearts. Time stopped.

After several hours our hands parted.

And we descended from Deribas's train onto a wood platform. A Volga blizzard blew across it, caught up in snowy whirls. Huddled in clumps, passengers wrapped tightly for winter sat on their belongings in anticipation of the train. In the shivering crowd the fear of getting lost in the endless expanses of this cold and unpredictable country could be felt. But more than cold and hunger, they were afraid of one another. Their numb hands clutched their trunks, suitcases, and wooden chests with locks hanging from them. They waited for the train. In truth, they had *nowhere* to go.

But we did have *a destination*.

We walked *past* them.

With the permit issued by Deribas, we were given seats on the arriving train.

And we traveled to Moscow.

Moscow

ON NOVEMBER 12 we arrived at Kursk station. I had not been in the capital of Russia for almost four years. It greeted us with freezing weather, sun, snow that was soot-gray, and crowds of people. The platform was flooded: some people rushed to a departing train; others exited arriving trains in throngs. We instantly found ourselves in a crowd of muzhiks who had come to the capital to make money. In rough sheepskin coats, felt boots, and fuzzy hats, they plodded along in a herd, carrying saws wrapped in sackcloth under their arms and on their shoulders—trunks from which ax handles protruded. The muzhiks smelled like the village. Moscow *struck* Fer's sensitive heart: hundreds of thousands of people, *ours* among them, here, in this city!

Fer immediately *jolted* me with her heart: we've begun! But I squeezed her hand: now wasn't the time. She pulled her hand away from me, gritting her teeth, and cried out angrily. I seized her by the shoulders, shook her, stopping her.

"This city will be ours," I said.

"Brothers are perishing every minute! We have to hurry!" she answered furiously.

"No. We have to *enter* this city correctly. Then we will take it," I replied.

"There's no time! No time, Bro!"

"Fer, this city could destroy us. And then we will never find our own."

And I *added* to the statement with my heart. She *replied*.

Oa and Bidugo *listened* to us. The Wisdom of the Light at this moment spoke through my heart: in Moscow it was imperative to act discreetly.

Though furious, Fer *understood*. She embraced me in tears.

Hiring a carriage, we rode through Moscow. Almost everywhere was the smell of food. Food was carried along the streets on trays, the store windows were bursting with rolls and sausage. Many passersby were chewing something as they walked. NEP was breathing its last, and it was as though people felt the coming of severe Stalinist social-ism and were storing up food.

Arriving at Lubyanskaya Square, we entered the large building where the OGPU was located. It was from here, from this yellowish-gray, many-storied mansion that the threads of this mighty organiza-tion stretched to all ends of the USSR. Deribas's bosses sat here, his close friends worked here. I showed our pass. They took our luggage, weapons, and outer clothing. Soon Fer and I were walking along the squeaky parquet behind our escort. Oa and Bidugo remained outside in the waiting room. Our escort took us to the office of the assistant head of the Special Department of the OGPU, Yakov Arganov. We entered the secretary's room, occupied by a handsome desk and a typ-ist. The secretary announced our arrival by telephone, then threw open the leather-covered door; we entered. Arganov was sitting at his desk and scribbling something rapidly; he had a lively, cunning face, black hair, thick eyebrows, and an owlish nose. The secretary closed the door after us. Arganov raised his head and squinted. Then he smiled.

"Aha! Deribas's foundlings. So you made it to White-Stoned Moscow after all."

He adroitly extricated himself from behind the desk and came up to us; he was short and narrow-shouldered.

"Now, let's see, let's see . . ."

He fixed his black, birdlike eyes on us.

"And you look like him! Well, come now, let's introduce ourselves. Arganov."

He extended his small but tenacious hand. We shook it.

"Alexander Deribas, Anfisa Deribas."

"Yes, yes. You're straight from the train? Hungry?"

"No, thank you, Comrade Arganov, we're fine."

"How's Terenty? Gotten his health back? What befell my combative friend?"

"The doctors say it was exhaustion," I answered.

"Yeah, yeah! Devilish nonsense!" Arganov waved his short hand dismissively, turned sharply, walked over to the desk, and picked up a box of Cannon cigarettes. "Deribas could take on three of me. He's called me the last three days in a row—his voice is normal. He sent a telegram off to Batrakov. Epilepsy, I ask you! What goddamn epilepsy? I've known Terenty since 1917. Epilepsy!" He offered us the open pack of cigarettes, but we shook our heads; he lit up quickly and with a whistle exhaled smoke from his large, thin-lipped mouth. "There's idiots everywhere you look."

The telephone rang. He picked up the receiver.

"Arganov here! Well? What do I care about your Kishkin? More nonsense! There's Pauker's order: sixteen special cars by four tomorrow morning! And you don't need a lot of guards: these are nepmen, where they gonna run? Hell, it's not 1920. No, you call yourself. You keep harping on that Kishkin, Kishkin..."

He hung up the phone. Irritated, he took a drag on his cigarette.

"Kishkin! Kishkin!"

His unseeing gaze ran over us and he picked up the receiver again.

"Anton, come in here."

The secretary entered.

"Listen, I remembered the name of that Polish guy, you know... Gorbanya's case. It wasn't Kislevich, it was Kishlevski."

"Kishlevski?"

"Kishlevski, that was it!" Arganov grew even livelier. "Give Borisov a call; tell him to free those Kisleviches. He got the wrong ones, Pinkerton! Nonsense..."

"That's why they're not talking!"

"Of course! As soon as Somov hanged himself, everything got mixed up! Good that I remembered. Kishlevski! Exactly! Go on, Anton, before someone tells Yagoda."

The secretary nodded and turned, but Arganov hadn't finished.

"Wait a minute. And there are these young people."

He could see us again.

"Are you educated?"

"I studied at the university," I answered.

"I can read and write," Fer answered.

"All right then, we'll set you up in the archive. Take them to Genkin . . . no, better straight to Tsessarsky! And they should put them in the dormitory, in the old one on Solyanka. Got it? But first—Kishlevski! Understand? And no nonsense!"

"Yes, Comrade Arganov, sir!"

"There are two more with us," I added.

"Anton, figure it out . . . That's it for now!" Arganov hurriedly shook our hands.

A little while later we were sitting in the department of cadres. Arganov's patronage turned out to be considerable. His secretary helped us with the registration of Oa and Bidugo's documents: we said that our friends had been robbed, and their documents as well, in the train. Oa introduced himself as a former artist (he actually did draw beautifully and painted icons); Bidugo (a carpenter from Rostov-on-Don) didn't change his profession, calling himself a carpenter and cabinetmaker. Fer and I were set up in the archive department of OGPU: I was to help the archivist organize dossiers; she was to glue the folders and envelopes for these cases. Oa was sent to work in the department of visual propaganda at the OGPU's House of Culture; Bidugo, to the warehouse as a carpenter. Fer and I were assigned to the OGPU dormitory; Oa and Bidugo were housed in a huge communal apartment densely packed with single workers.

Thus began our Moscow life. At the OGPU we received grocery cards, tickets to the cafeteria, and a very tiny salary. But Deribas had given us a bit of money to take with us. We bought apples, carrots, cabbage, and grain with it. This is what we ate. In the dormitory we were called "derirabbits": in the evenings we chewed on vegetables. We carried grain around in our pockets, trying to chew it on the street, where no one disturbed us with conversations. Soon our two main problems were identified: food and close contact with people. In the OGPU, as in all Soviet organizations, the expectation was that everyone went "to lunch" in the cafeteria together during the lunch break. It took an enormous amount of work for us to avoid this. It was almost unbelievable, but our hearts *gave hints* about what to do and how. We successfully *avoided* it. As "blood relatives" of Deribas, the Chekists tried to take care of us; they kept inviting us to dinner. We refused in a panic, using any excuse, even going as far as various illnesses: visiting people meant you had to drink wine and eat people's food. The head of the archive accounting department, Genkin, wishing to "fatten us up," gave us a ticket to the "good" cafeteria (normally we would have been expected to dine in the cafeteria for workers). We pretended that we went there, shuddering from the smell of the cafeteria alone: it was a place where they boiled and fried the corpses of rabbits. One time I couldn't refuse and I swallowed a piece of fried baby rabbit. I vomited immediately. Fer drank some wine, which was literally poured down her throat on Stalin's birthday, celebrated in the archive department. She was in *terribly* bad shape. In the department everyone decided that Anfisa Deribas had alcohol intolerance. But we could calmly inhale tobacco smoke into our lungs. Smoking helped us "be one of the group" in the Soviet collective. Naturally, we had no dependence on tobacco like genuine smokers. In the workers' dining hall people were fed various kashas, but we couldn't eat them, either: our organisms could accept only *whole* food, untouched by decay and flame, not boiled, not frozen, not ground, not marinated. The corpses of living creatures were entirely indigestible for us, but neither could we eat still-living creatures: our hearts wouldn't accept blood. Neither living nor dead. Only grain, fruits, and vegetables could be digested in our stomachs and give us strength. We only took that which was *whole* into our bodies, what had not been destroyed by humans. Smoke was whole. As was water.

When the archivist, returning from the "good" cafeteria, picking at his teeth, muttered that "the baby rabbit today was to die for," I nodded and muttered, "Of course."

On weekdays we worked, trying to merge into the mass of Soviet people, *remembering* their habits, life values, moral principles, humor, and fears. We penetrated alien skin, in order to *be one of them*. It was *surprisingly* easy for us to do this: the power of the heart helped. The Light speaking in us fortified our inner strength and multiplied our opportunities. After the awakening of our hearts each of *us* had become a genuine Proteus: each discovered within not only a capacity for transformation but also an incredible *flexibility* in dealing with the stern, unpredictable world. Having thrown off the stone armor of our past, dead life and broken kinship ties, it was as though we had become boneless and were able to easily bend and penetrate the *crevices* of the world. Nothing restrained us, only the Light shone ahead, led us to our secret goal. Our ability to mimic had no analogy in the world of people. It was the highest artistry, an artistry that no professional actor had ever dreamed of. No one could appreciate it because this theater had no audience: only a stage on all four sides.

Furthermore, we were possessed of amazing endurance; we slept no more than four hours a day. At the end of the workday we didn't feel tired and "voluntarily" took on new jobs, trying to seem "selfless and conscientious." Soon Fer and I were called the "twin Deribases." The bosses and co-workers were pleased with us. Oa and Bidugo also exhibited a "labor ethic and enthusiasm" at their work.

On the weekends the four of us went to Sokolniki Park, secluded ourselves in the forest, and, holding hands, spoke with our hearts for hours. Fer and I taught Oa and Bidugo and learned from them. The wisdom of our hearts grew.

We were waiting for the Ice.

It arrived in Moscow on January 2, 1929, at the Kazan station, in the baggage section of the Khabarovsk–Moscow train. Brothers Ep and Rubu arrived on the same train. We embraced on the filthy, phlegm-smeared platform. Our hearts flared: Ep and Rubu! Our first brothers, sent to us by the Light, discovered on the rivers of severe Tungusia, then lost. We shouted and wailed with ecstasy, frightening the Soviet passengers. Ep was wearing the uniform of the OGPU; Rubu, civilian clothes. His outer look had changed; he had grown a beard, wore glasses, and outwardly looked like a Soviet engineer. The brothers accompanied four crates with Ice, the very same ones that we had hidden in Deribas's attic.

When the querulous porters hauled the first crate from the baggage car and placed it on the sleigh, a fog descended in front of my eyes—the Ice! I approached it, fell on my knees, and pressed my body to the crate. With a yelp, Fer pressed against the crate from the other side. Our hearts *jolted* from the presence of the Ice. And the Ice vibrated in response. The ephemeral earthbound world swayed beneath our feet. It was powerful.

The porters stood waiting, sniffing their frost-blue noses in bewilderment. A passing policeman stopped.

"What is that?"

Fer and I didn't move, kneeling before the Ice.

"Very important equipment," Rubu answered.

"All right, then." The policeman looked askance at Ep's *icy* blue eyes, saluted, and moved on.

In our theater there was no audience.

Two crates of the Ice were brought to Lubyanka by order of Deribas and placed in the warehouse under protective covering. There the Ice could be safely kept until spring. The other two crates we hid in the basement of a burned-out house on Solyanka Street, not far from the dormitory.

Deribas got Ep a job in the transport department of the OGPU, which allowed him to move around a lot and be *nearby*, with a means of transport at hand. With new documents and a new name, Rubu was made an agent in the procurement department of the Peat Institute, whose Party committee secretary had served in the same regiment with Deribas. Several weeks later our brothers Edlap and Em, and our sisters Orti, Pilo, and Ju, who had undergone the *heart sobbing*, made it to Moscow as well. They were young, energetic Komsomol activists according to their documents; all of them matriculated at Rabfak because of their proletarian origins and recommendations from the Komsomol organization of the Far East OGPU. The Bolsheviks' idea was that this new educational institution would prepare cadres of young Red professors loyal to the Party's goals, who would gradually replace the old "ideologically putrefied and petit bourgeois" intelligentsia.

Now there were eleven of us in Moscow.

The Ice was nearby. Everything was ready to begin the search.

But our hearts *restrained* us: we still did not have the last link in the chain. We already *knew* how to search for our brothers. We had the *means* to awaken their hearts.

However, we had to understand, once and for all, the *correct* way of doing this. So that *all of us* could do it correctly and safely.

The Ice Hammer

AT THE beginning of February the temperature dropped. Moscow's women wrapped up in scarves; sparrows and pigeons hid under roofs; carriage drivers covered their horses with double blankets. Only the peddlers were happy: buns and loaves of *kalachi* froze quickly, so no one could check their freshness. The water pipes froze. People and animals were afraid of the cold, they kept close to houses and stores.

But we weren't afraid of the frost: the fire of the heart warmed us.

One morning on our day off from the Stalinist five-day workweek, we all met at the Sokolniki tram stop. Silently, we headed for the park. In the minus-forty-degrees-Celsius weather it was completely empty: neither skiers, nor skaters, nor loud-voiced Soviet athletes, nor peddlers with cigarettes were there. Even the crows had hidden. There were only the trees in a web of hoarfrost, immobile, cracking occasionally. We walked past them along the promenade, our feet squeaking on the packed snow. The promenade ended and we stepped into the deep snow and waded through it until we found ourselves in a large glade surrounded by trees.

Forming a Circle and taking one another by the hand, we sat down in the snow.

Our hearts felt a *jolt*. And began to speak.

We needed an Ice hammer. We wanted *to know* everything about it: what it was like, how to make it, how to strike with it, what to say with our lips while striking, and what to say with our hearts. In our Great Endeavor everything was clear as the Light and transparent as the Ice. Except for the *instrument* for awakening the hearts. What should it be like? We had struck the chests of *our own* nineteen times, and each time the hammer was different. Each time it was made in a hurry, using whatever there was at hand. The Ice was tied with strips of rawhide to a staff, with rope to a sawn-off rifle, with a shoulder strap to the pole of a Soviet flag, with a handkerchief to a stick, with a piece of wire to an iron pipe. Furthermore, the pieces of Ice were completely arbitrary in size and shape. We didn't make the Ice hammers according to a single *image*. This was *wrong*. Our hearts warned us.

And gave us ideas.

We wanted *to see* a correct Ice hammer.

Our heart *created* it.

We became hot. Steam rose from our faces and clutching hands. Our faces were covered in sweat.

And our hearts *saw* the Ice hammer as it should be. It hovered in the center of the Circle, like the arrow on a sundial, turning against the sun.

We *understood* how we had to make a proper Ice hammer. The piece of Ice should be a cylinder with a round slot cut out in the middle of the side. The handle of the hammer should be placed in the slot, and it should made from a branch or piece of wood that had died its own death. The handle should be tied to the Ice with two strips of animal hide, taken from an animal that had also died naturally. The size of the Ice cylinder should be such that, Fer and I, as the first two acquired, could cover its surface with our palms. The hammer's handle should correspond to the length of our forearms. The thickness of the handle should correspond to the thickness of our middle fingers. The width of each strip of hide for attaching the cylinder should correspond to the width of the middle fingers of two of the first-discovered.

The image of the Ice hammer imprinted itself in our hearts. Now we *knew* how it should be made.

The Ice hammer hovered in the center of our Circle.

In order to awaken the heart of a brother, it was necessary to strike with the Ice hammer in the middle of his bare chest, while pronouncing in the language of people: "Speak with the heart!"

At the same time we were to *speak* heart to heart with the brother as well as we could.

Each hammer was destined for one brother. It could be used only once. The stick and strips remaining from the used hammer were to be thrown away. They could not be used again.

That was all that we learned about the Ice hammer.

The winter sun rose.

And the revolving hammer disappeared.

Warmed by hearts and faces, we sat in the snow, holding hands. Joy filled us. We cried out loudly. The echo carried our voices across the snowy forest.

That very day we began preparing the first *proper* Ice hammer. In Sokolniki Park we found a dried-up maple tree and broke off branches from it. Near the tram stop we saw the corpse of a stray dog, frozen to death, in a gully. Ep cut off a strip of skin from its back with a knife.

In the evening we gathered in the cellar of the burned-out house. Lighting a candle, we retrieved the crate with the Ice. And carefully sawed off the necessary piece of Ice. We filed it into the proper form, and carved out a rounded slot. Then Fer and I—the first-discovered brother and sister—grasped the piece with our palms. It turned out to be a little big. Brothers Ep and Bidugo filed it down. We again checked the size of the piece. Our palms hid it completely. The head of the Ice hammer was ready. Fer and I bent our arms at the elbow and stretched our right forearms end to end in a straight line. Rubu placed our arms against the maple branch, checked the size, and sawed the branch flush. The handle was slightly filed down and inserted into the opening in the piece of Ice. According to the size of Fer's and my middle fingers, Pilo and Ju cut out two bands from the dog skin and cleaned them of fur. Brother Oa tied them tightly to the handle.

The Ice hammer was ready.

Under the wretched light of earthly fire we held the Ice hammer in our hands, like a firstborn child. I took it and placed it to my chest, causing my heart to throb. With a moan I handed it to Fer. She placed the Ice to her breast and cried out. She gave the hammer to Ep. He grabbed the hammer, embraced it, and gave it to Rubu.

In this way the hammer passed from hand to hand, until it returned to me. I squeezed it in my hands, swung back, and struck at the dark air surrounding us in the cellar. The hammer sliced through it with a whistle.

We *froze*.

The weapon of struggle against the hell of this earth was in our hands. But there was only one. To attain victory we required dozens, hundreds, thousands of such hammers. We needed an ARSENAL. We couldn't start a war for the liberation of our brothers and sisters without having a mighty arsenal.

And so we began the meticulous task of making the Ice hammers. We had to work at night. The lifeless cellar of the burned-down house was an ideal place for this: even the rats didn't bother us. All through the night, by the light of candles, we filed down the Ice caps, sawed and adjusted handles, cut strips from the corpses of dead animals, set the Ice caps on the handles, and screwed them on. We worked silently. Cold and exhaustion didn't hinder us: the Divine Ice was right there in our hands. Our fingers touched it, our hearts trembled. With our own hands we were creating our history. The history of the Brotherhood of the Primordial Light. Each hammer we created was handed around the Circle. It was pressed to chests, like an infant. It was *spoken* to. And reverently placed in crates—to sleep until the Main Battle.

Before the end of February we had made sixty-four Ice hammers, completely using up two of the four pieces of Ice that had been brought to Moscow.

Meat Machines

HAVING created a store of Ice hammers, we began to think about where we could shelter the newly discovered. This was extremely important. None of *our people* had individual living quarters, we all lived in the Soviet collective, without the opportunity to be alone. But newly discovered brothers required peace, care, and isolation. Moreover, after being *struck*, many of them would have need of medical help. This created a serious problem. And it demanded a solution. We went to Sokolniki again, sat in a Circle in the snow, and spoke with the heart. The heart gave us an idea: *a house out of town*. Sitting in the Circle, we *saw* it. The house *took form* behind thick spruce—wooden, prerevolutionary, with an old attic and a weathervane in the form of Pegasus.

The heart could not deceive: two days later we saw the actual house. It had belonged to a Moscow University professor, Golovin, whose son, a former White Guard officer, had been arrested and accused of being part of an "anti-Soviet plot." Such an arrest at that time could have only one outcome: a bullet in the back of the head in the cellar of Lubyanka. Soon the old professor was arrested as well. His wife couldn't bear the double loss and died suddenly of a heart attack. The Golovins' Moscow apartment and dacha in the Moscow suburb of Liubertsy were confiscated by the OGPU. Some bureaucrat from the first department moved into the apartment with his family, but the dacha was officially transferred to the property directorate, to be given to some Chekist boss during the summer. Until then, it was closed and sealed. The Wisdom of the Heart suggested the necessary solution to Ig: a call from Khabarovsk to Arganov, beginning as a cheery chat about current events between two old friends, and ending with Arganov discussing the Golovin case and *himself* offering to let Deribas's brother and sister live in the Liubertsy dacha until summer.

The Power of the Light was present in this: our will parted the *thickness* of the surrounding world, taking what was necessary from it.

Fer and I moved into the dacha, in order to "guard OGPU property." The dacha was behind a fence, and the woody plot hid the house from outside eyes. A better place for sheltering the newly discovered could not be hoped for. With money we had saved, we purchased and brought to the dacha vegetables, bedclothes, and medications. We also brought thirty Ice hammers and hid them in the woodshed. We traveled to work in Moscow on the early trains.

Everything was ready for the beginning of the search. Fer and I chose the day: March 6. It was a day off, so the other brothers could keep near our *magnet*. Without them we would be helpless.

The Brotherhood prepared: when we met, we spoke with our

hearts, marked *the way*, safeguarded ourselves. Ig *was* with us: from far-off Khabarovsk came the help of his heart. The tear-off pages of the Soviet calendar fell speedily, like autumn leaves: March 2, 3, 4. We *readied ourselves.*

But on March 5 something *very* important happened to me. That morning, when I arrived at work, I was given an unexpected task: to go to the public library, pick up a file of information collected from the bourgeois press, and bring it back to Lubyanka. The colleague who usually did this in the archive department was out sick. Discovering that I knew two foreign languages, the head of the department entrusted me with the job. Arriving at the library by tram, I showed my identification and went to the restricted reading section. The library worker who gathered the information from Western newspapers for the OGPU said that he needed another half hour to look through the papers that had just arrived. He suggested that I wait in the reading room. I picked up several Soviet newspapers, went out into the general reading room, and sat down at a free table. Despite the fact that it was early morning, the room was almost full. Everyone was silently reading and writing, their heads lowered. On the blind wall of the reading room hung four enormous old portraits: Pushkin, Gogol, Tolstoy, and Chernyshevsky, which had replaced the portrait of Dostoyevsky that had hung there formerly, since by then even Dostoyevsky had been denounced as a "reactionary writer." The portrait of Chernyshevsky had been painted recently, and the liveliness of its colors stood in stark contrast to the aged depictions of the three Russian classics. Looking at the portraits of the writers, I vaguely remembered them, their presence in my former life. And I thought of how there was *no* difference for me now between Dostoyevsky and Chernyshevsky. Then I suddenly felt a *very* deep exhaustion. The last three days I hadn't slept at all: at night we fixed up the dacha, which had been destroyed by the Chekists when they searched it; we prepared ourselves for the beginning of our search, and spoke *intensively* with our hearts. Lowering my eyes, I began to look through the new issue of *Pravda*. But exhaustion suddenly overwhelmed me: my arms stiffened, my eyes kept closing. I hadn't felt so *helpless* for quite some time. My heart grew numb. The stuffy air of the reading room smelled like old books and furniture, and was quickly putting me to sleep, like ether. Blinking my closing eyes, I began to read a collective letter from the workers of the Red Vyborger factory, who were calling for a Socialist competition in all the factories and plants of the USSR. I dozed off, dropping my head on the table.

I fell into a vivid and deep sleep: I dreamed I was in literature class at my gymnasium; I was sitting, as usual, at the desk with Shtiurmer; the classroom was flooded with rays of sunlight; outside the clean windows it was the beginning of summer; utter silence reigned in the classroom; the only thing audible was the scratching of pens and the measured steps of our literature teacher Vikenty Semyonovich, walking slowly between the rows as we wrote a final composition. I understood that this dream was from my old life, long forgotten by me; for that reason it seemed funny and pitiful, but I *was watching* it because I was very tired; everyone is sitting, leaning over their desks; before me is a sheet of lined paper with the blue insignia of our school in the corner; my hand writes the title of the composition on it, "Fyodor Mikhailovich Dostoyevsky"; I dip the pen into the inkwell, hold it over the paper, and suddenly realize that I have *completely* forgotten who Dostoyevsky is; I raise my head and see the large portrait of Dostoyevsky leaning against the classroom blackboard; I look at it intently; but the more intently I look, the more clearly I realize—before me is the depiction of a bearded, gloomy man with a massive forehead, who is entirely unknown to me; he gazes at me seriously. I look around: everyone is writing compositions about Dostoyevsky; I try to remember and *understand*: What did this gloomy gentleman do? Why are we writing an essay about him? Who is he? But my memory is silent; not knowing what to do, I glance at my classmates: they are all industriously scratching their pens, all writing. I realize that I'm wasting time, I nudge Shtiurmer with my elbow; he turns unwillingly: "Who is that?" I ask, pointing at the portrait with my eyes; he retrieves a thick book from his desk—the collected works of Dostoyevsky—and hands it to me; I take it, open it, and suddenly realize *clearly* that this book, the sum of the life of the bearded man with the serious gaze, is only paper covered with combinations of letters: it is about this book, this paper covered with letters, that we are writing our final exam essay. Only about paper—and nothing else! Everything becomes *incredibly* funny to me, now that I have to describe this paper in an essay; I start laughing and *interrupt* the dream.

Lifting my head, I opened my eyes: I was in the reading room. But in actuality, I was sleeping. And was already in another dream. All around sat the same people and the quiet rustle of paper. I raised my eyes. Four large portraits hung in their places. But instead of the writers in frames, there were *strange* machines. They were created for writing books, that is, for covering thousands of pages of paper with combinations of letters. I realized that this was the dream that I *wanted* to see. The machines in the frames produced paper covered with letters, that was their work. The people sitting at these tables were engaged in another kind of work: they believed in this paper *with all their might, they measured their life* and learned how to live from this paper—learned how to feel, love, worry, calculate, create, solve problems, and build, in order to teach others later how to live according to this paper.

I *understood* this dream as well. And interrupted it. I raised my head. I was sitting on the Ice in that very same hollow melted by my body the night when my heart first spoke. There were only stars around me. There was no Earth: the mound of Ice floated in black space. This was no longer a dream, but something *absolutely necessary* for me. I placed my hands upon the Ice. And immediately *touched* its heart. The Ice *answered* me instantly. Forcefully and abruptly. It *shuddered*. And I took this unexpected blow with my heart. My heart trembled in response and discovered something *new*. I *could see* with my heart. The Earth appeared all around. I saw our entire planet with my heart. All of it, from the stones, to the water and plants, to the animals and people on it, consisted of atoms—our building material, engendered by the Light. All of it was the same—there *wasn't any* difference between a stone and a man, a tree and a bird. And amid this uniform mass of *erroneous*, *blundering* combinations of atoms, there shone twenty points of Light. They shone in the hearts of my brothers and sisters. I *saw* each of them. They were complete, perfect amid this gloomy world.

I *woke up* and opened my eyes. Once again I raised my head. I was sitting in the reading room at a table. People were sitting all around me. Four portraits hung on the wall. But instead of the writers' faces, something congealed and trembled. That happens sometimes when you look at an object through eyes that have been crying. But there weren't any tears in my eyes. I rubbed them. No pictures appeared. I began to look at the portraits intensely: instead of faces, pinkish-brown flashes swirled. I turned my eyes to the people sitting around me. *Something* had changed in their outward appearance. I had stopped seeing them only with my eyes. A *new* vision was revealed to me. I saw humans with my heart. In their entirety.

I stood up *cautiously* and approached the window. Beyond was a city of people.

And time stopped.

With my *heart* I saw the history of humankind. A many-million swarm of voices surrounded me: millions of beds squeaked, sweet moans sounded, sperm flooded into millions of vaginas, eggs were fertilized, wombs swelled, fetuses pushed and kicked, cries of birth-giving could be heard, millions of bloody newborns were squeezed into the world and cried out weakly; they were washed, their umbilical cords cut, they were swaddled, placed at breasts, they greedily sucked their mothers' milk, began to grow, crawl, sit up, stand, began to walk, reach for toys, speak, and run; they went to the first day of school with book bags and flowers, began to write letters on paper, read books, learn the rules of life, love and hate, play and sing, wonder and deride, torture and idolize, hope and despair, embrace tenderly and beat viciously until blood flowed, betray and sacrifice. They finished school, became adults, went to work, began to earn money, fell in love, embraced, flung themselves on beds, carried out millions of sexual acts, conceived, gave birth to infants, grew old, died.

And I saw: armies many thousands strong attacking one another to the beat of a drum, holding in their hands *well*-made weapons of murder; I saw volleys of guns and cannons, smashed skulls, eyes poked out, battles; I heard the whistle of hot lead, the moans of the wounded, the joyous roar of the victors—those who were able to kill *better*; I saw the power of one group of people over others, monstrous humiliations, cringing toadyism, the ruthless suppression of other people's will, overfilled prisons, barbaric torture, skin flayed from the living, people burned alive on a slow fire; mass demonstrations, show trials and executions carried out to the crowd's approving roar, workers manufacturing the perfect *weapons* for the destruction of people; I saw the sale of slaves and women; the poor, people dying on the street, children swollen with hunger.

And I saw: helpless old men dying in their beds, young people drowning in rivers, people being burned by flames, people writhing from terrible diseases, going mad, women taking their own lives from unhappy love, dying while giving birth, infants born dead.

And I saw: thieves killing for money, rapists forcing women at knifepoint to spread their legs, con artists deftly bankrupting others, liars of genius who turned deceit into a great art, calculating poisoners, executioners calmly taking a meal after their work, inquisitioners sending people to the flames in the name of good, mass murder carried out against those belonging to another nation.

And I saw: people locking their houses with *complicated* locks so that other people could not enter.

And I saw: hunters murdering animals for pleasure, exquisite meals prepared from the corpses of beasts, fish, and birds, human mouths devouring meat juicy with blood, animal farms breeding animals in order to skin them and make *beautiful* clothes from their pelts, women flaunting these clothes and flattering men.

And I saw: maggots devouring carrion, a beetle eating the maggot, a bird pecking at the beetle, a ferret chewing the bird's head off, an eagle tearing the ferret apart with its talons, a lynx pouncing on the eagle, wolves gnawing at the lynx, a bear breaking the wolf's spine, a falling tree killing the bear, flies laying eggs in the rotting bear carcass, maggots breaking out of their eggs and devouring the carrion.

And I understood the very essence of human beings.

Man was a MEAT MACHINE.

I returned my gaze to the portraits: paint swirled, trembled, blended. There were no faces. I looked about the room. An old man sat behind the nearest table with some magazines. I walked over to him and stared at the open magazine. Instead of images, I saw the same swirling colored and gray dots. I took my identification card out of my pocket and looked at it. In the place of the photograph a gray blot swirled. As soon as I had discovered the essence of man, I stopped being able to see images of people. I walked through the hall cautiously, as though afraid to *spill* what I had discovered. People sat still, concentrating. They were meat machines. And each of them existed by himself. They sat there, immersing themselves in *paper*. Each was interested only in this paper and completely uninterested in his neighbor. Between them there was and could be no fellowship. They were *our* mistake. We created them billions of years ago, when we were Light-bearing rays. Meat machines consisted of the same atoms as other worlds we had created. But the combination of these atoms was ERRONEOUS. For this reason the meat machines were mortal. They could not be in harmony, either with the surrounding world or with themselves. They were born in suffering, and in suffering they left this life. Their entire life boiled down to the struggle for comfort, the continuation of the existence of bodies that needed food and clothing. But their bodies, appearing on Earth suddenly, like an explosion, disappeared just as rapidly. They aged quickly, got sick, writhed, became motionless, rotted, and dissolved into atoms. That was the path of the meat machines.

And I saw the Earth. It floated and spun in the Cosmos, between the worlds of Peace and Harmony, which we had created. And only the Earth was restless and disharmonic. And we alone were to blame for this.

And we alone could correct the mistake.

"Everything's ready, you can take it," said a voice.

I looked around.

Behind me stood a meat machine in a gray Russian peasant shirt with blue oversleeves and small round glasses on an unremarkable mustachioed face. He was waiting for an answer. I tried to remember, preparing an answer in his language. And suddenly *I saw* his life: a fairly difficult birth, a painful childhood, a miserly, rough father, a quiet, submissive mother, fear of heights, love of dogs, a broken finger, the lycée, the death of his sister, the fear of catching diphtheria, successful studies, an unsuccessful sexual act with a prostitute, fear of women, the university, a sex act with an upperclassman, the Revolution, the death of his father, life in a commune, the death of his lover, war, concussion, an unsuccessful marriage, an unsuccessful suicide attempt, the library. He loved: cheese, pocket watches, the Bolshevik Party, the orders of silent, strong men, the fantastical novels of Wells, Trotsky's slogan about the liquidation of the family, bicycles, chess, cinematography, his work, clear dishes, the smell of sperm, long conversations. He didn't like: heights, swamps, spiders, flour gruel, dreams about a slow fat man, loud women, children, hangnails, priests, squeaky boots; more than anything on earth he feared torture by fire.

"Are you ill?" he asked.

"*I* am quite healthy," I answered, and, slowing down, asked him, "Where does your slow fat man live?"

He froze. I couldn't distinguish the expression on his face, but I *saw* how taken aback he was.

"I . . . I don't know," he answered.

"But I do. In your late sister's room, near the cabinet with the crack. In a wet corner."

He stood stock-still. I took the package from him, returned to my table, placed the packet in a case, and left the room. Putting on my coat, I left the library and went out into a city of meat machines. They walked along the street, rode on sleighs and in automobiles, jumped onto the trams, crowded the stores. Some of them were rushing to work, others—home. Waiting for the meat machines at work were only machines or paper covered with letters; at home—other meat machines and food prepared for them. The entire city consisted of tiny stone caves. In each cave lived a family of meat machines. The caves were firmly locked against other meat machines, although none of them differed *structurally* from one another. But the meat machines were afraid of one another because some of them had big caves and others had small ones. At work the meat machines earned money in order to buy food and clothes. They ate in the caves, slept there, and produced new meat machines. This happened at night: the meat machines lay on each other and moved. Then in one of them a tiny meat machine began to grow. Nine months later it was born and began its life in the cave. It grew and gradually became a normal meat machine. That was how the meat machines lived in their city.

It was possible to ride the tram to Lubyanka, but I walked. The passersby floated past me. And I could *find out* everything about each of them. My heart saw them. The faces of the passersby merged into one *indistinguishable* face. The face of a meat machine. At the corner of Tverskaya and Mokhovaya streets someone grabbed me by the sleeve. I stopped.

"Hey, Komsomol buddy, where's Glavpromsbyt around here?"

A stocky, warmly dressed meat machine stood in front of me. He had come to Moscow from Podolsk. He was born in a train, grew up in a bourgeois family with a father who drank and a mother who worked; he always worked, first as a hauler on the river, then as a porter in town; he served in the cavalry, ended up in the war, cracked three peoples' heads open, shot one in battle, executed sixteen prisoners, served in the Cheka, was fired for rape, got married, worked at a factory, at the ports, on the railroad, speculated on different things, forged documents, went into business, became a procurer, traded in sugar, buckwheat, and morphine. He loved: meatballs in tomato sauce, airplanes, bosses, the revolver under his pillow, forcing his wife to resist him before the sex act, the smell of pharmacies, monetary deception, thinking about the bright future as he fell asleep, velvety black lamb's wool, women's gloves, horse parades. He feared: bosses, snakes, dying in his sleep, thoughts about the endlessness of the universe, sudden artillery bombardment, syphilis, and arrest.

"Don't hide morphine. You'd do better to hide sugar," I said. Leaving him to stand there in bewildered shock, I walked on.

Meat machines kept on walking past me. Each carried the swarm of personal history. Each buzzed and whirled. I moved among these swirling zones. They were energetic holes. Their energy was inimical to the energy of the Light in my heart. I felt that each penetration into someone else's life drained energy from my heart. I tired *very quickly*. I walked on, trying to touch the meat machines only very *lightly* with my heart.

Not far from the OGPU building a beggar crawled along the sidewalk. I walked up to her. I couldn't restrain myself—I entered her swarm: a successful birth in a white-and-blue bedroom, a father strewing the mother and newly born daughter with rose petals from a golden dish, a wealthy family, a happy childhood, singing with piano accompaniment, hide-and-seek, horses, jam, croquet, a poodle named Arto, love of her father's strong hands, a doll named Brunhilde, fear of her strict mother, the death of a brother, a pillow with "a secret," a herbarium, a parrot who could say the word "locomotive," a formal ball, a boy who kissed her on the cheek, love for this boy, tears, fever, the desire to always be with this boy, with this boy named Sasha, with this golden-haired boy with blue eyes, a dream about the boy removing her Baba Yaga mask, which refused to come off, anyway, anyhow. The mask of Baba Yaga, Baba Yaga with a *very* long nose.

The beggar woman stopped crawling.

She raised her face. It was dark with years of dirt. Instead of a left eye there was a dark yawning depression. The eyebrow above it was split by a deep scar from the blow of a saber: heat, dust, a long trip on a cart, straw, watermelons, diamonds in a left boot, night, a campfire, people, people coming out of the forest, a murdered horse, swarthy people, swift people, stinking people tearing dresses, quick people lying down on her one after the other and then again lying down on her, and again lying down on her, the coming of the dawn, saber blows.

I recognized Nika Riabova. And I, too, stopped.

She looked at me with a cloudy, teary eye. Her lips separated, revealing yellowed teeth.

"Immer mimmer Jean Valjean . . ." she muttered. Then she passed gas, laughed, and crawled farther down the sidewalk.

I *watched* her go. Nika crawled away. With her, everything human crawled away from me. And I DIDN'T WANT to stop her.

She crawled like a machine. She too was a meat machine. One of hundreds of millions.

I turned around. And went on my way.

I walked to Lubyanka. Passing through the entrance I climbed to the second floor and handed the parcel to the boss. He was displeased by the delay. His mouth pulsed gloomily. I had to explain something to this meat machine. I recalled the words of meat machines.

"Comrade director, it was the library's fault. They were still working on fresh material."

"All right, Deribas, go and eat," he answered. "Twenty minutes. And then back to it."

The director loved: being a director, fried chicken, carving wooden picture frames, duck hunting, thin, hysterical women, the smell of gasoline, and military parades.

I went to the cafeteria to take a couple of apples to eat. The place smelled of food for meat machines. The large cafeteria was full of meat machines. They energetically ate borscht, barley porridge, and drank tea with sugar. I looked at them. Their faces swirled. They sweated. They felt fine. They reminded me of the guild at the machine factory. The meat machines sat and swallowed food. Spoons clinked, teeth chewed. This was a guild for the processing of food. Suddenly I *noticed* sister Fer. She entered the cafeteria. And the gloomy world of the meat machines *parted*. Fer was DIFFERENT! I went to her. My heart *spoke* with her. And I *saw* all of her. Her entire life. Fer *understood* what I saw. She picked an apple up off the tray and put it in my hand. Our fingers squeezed the apple. It split.

We left the cafeteria.

The Circus

THE BROTHERLY Circle of Light helped me to understand *what was new* in me. At night I held the Ice hammer in my hands and pressed it to my breast. My heart *calmed itself*. It healed with every new blow of the Light. Now it *saw* the world of the Earth.

The next day off, Fer, Rubu, Ep, and I set out to search. Our *magnet* illuminated the Moscow crowd. We took the tram down to the National Hotel and walked up Tverskaya Street. Our hearts *exerted themselves*. We went into stores, *looked* at the lines of people, glanced into the entrances of buildings. Meat machines moved all around us. They were busy with their affairs. Their faces whirled with worry. Their hearts pumped blood. Their muscles moved their bones. And around every meat machine was a *swarm*. I walked through dozens of these swarms, protecting my heart from them. It was *searching*. Fer was close by. She moaned from the tension. We *were trying*.

Having walked all the way up Tverskaya to Lesnaya Street, we stopped. Our hearts grew *heavy*. They beat hard, pulsing with the Light. The Moscow crowd was *heavy*. It hung in a dense *din*, which had to be *moved aside*. We crumpled in this din. Our faces covered with sweat. Our legs swayed beneath us. Rubu and Ep held our backs up. They pushed against us from behind. We threw our heads back and leaned against our brothers. We looked at the sky. We breathed heavily. We *remembered* the Ice. And *lay down* on it. And gathered new strength. The huge mass lying in Siberia *answered* us.

Resting a bit, we crossed to the other side of Tverskaya. And moved down underground. The *din* of the meat machines seized us. We *illuminated* and *parted it*. Ep and Rubu held us up by our backs. *They helped* us with their hearts. Our legs moved with difficulty. We arrived at Strastnoi Boulevard. We stopped and rested. We turned around and our hearts *flared*: one of ours! A tall, skinny man in an expensive coat was getting into an automobile. There were two others with him. While he slowly settled himself on the seat, I *saw* him: a foreigner, from a good family, an old father, eighteen columns of a university courtyard, a rapier, two scars, a new home, war, shrapnel, seven shards, the small breasts of his wife, coffee rings on a blueprint, two daughters, fear of blood disease, fear of safety pins, fear of getting lost in the forest, underground work, cement, water and machines, milk chocolate, shaving a woman's pubis, a great deal of money, hemorrhoids, a labyrinth of trimmed hedges, an orderly desk, his favorite horse Nereid, a lake in the mountains, an airplane, the circus. The circus. The Circus.

The car growled loudly and took off.

"Stop!" Fer screeched, running after the car. Her legs swayed and she fell into Rubu's arms.

Her heart *was exhausted*. She gulped at the air. Her face grew pale. I kneeled. I gathered wet snow from the sidewalk and sucked on it. Ep held me by the shoulders.

"The circus," I said. "They're going to the circus."

Fer began to vomit. Then she came to herself.

The Moscow circus was located on Tsvetnoi Boulevard. We bought tickets. That evening we sat in a circular hall. Fer and I immediately noticed *our own*. He was sitting next to the minder who was with him in the automobile. The four of us sat *calmly*. The hall was filled with meat machines. A brass band started to play a march. The curtains opened and the show began. Clowns and acrobats came into the arena. Meat machines applauded them. One clown hit another on the head with a large hammer made of papier-mâché. From each blow the other's head rang loudly and streams of fake tears flowed. And the meat machines were happy that they weren't as stupid as the clowns. The acrobats risked their lives, flying on trapezes right up under the cupola. They received money for this. The meat machines enjoyed the agility of the acrobats. And were afraid that the acrobats would fall. Then muscular meat machines came out into the arena. They lifted weights, tore apart chains, held three women on one arm. Then they began to fight. The ordinary meat machines followed the fight of the strong meat machines with great interest. Many in the auditorium envied their strength. After the strong men, little meat machines ran out into the arena. They began to goof around, dance the Charleston, and giggle in thin, high voices, depicting nepmen. Suddenly from behind the curtains a bear ran out. He was in a muzzle, in a large jacket with a red star on it, and wearing the apron of a yard keeper. A large red broom was attached to his paws. The bear ran at the little meat machines. And they ran away from him with a yelp, hiding behind the curtains. The audience whistled and laughed. The trainer ran over to the bear and discreetly stuck a piece of meat in his mouth. A loud voice announced that "a red broom would soon sweep the garbage out of the Soviet capital." The audience applauded. *Our brother* sat and watched everything with interest. We *calmly* observed him. A female trainer in a bright dress ran into the arena. An elephant came out. In the trainer's hand was a baton wound with a gold ribbon. On the end of the baton was a fuzzy ball. Inside the ball a sharp steel point was hidden. The trainer stuck the elephant so that it would follow her commands. The audience saw her touching the elephant with a fuzzy ball. The huge elephant was afraid of the little trainer. He climbed onto a barrel and raised his front legs. Then he stood on his front feet and lifted his back ones. He wanted this to end as quickly as possible so they would take him back to his cage where there was food. The meat machines clapped. They liked the trainer. The elephant was taken away. And three monkeys ran into the arena. They were dressed in tuxedos. They depicted Chamberlain, Curzon, and Poincaré. The monkeys scrambled up on a large drum with the inscription IMPERIALISM and began to jump. The audience laughed and clapped. The Soviet meat machines were happy that the monkeys resembled the foreign meat machines that criticized the Soviet newspapers. Then came a magician. He began to deftly deceive the meat machines. And they were in awe of his skills. He pretended that he pulled a rabbit and baby chicks out of his hat, pretended that he was sawing a woman in half. Pretended that he became invisible. The meat machines liked it that the magician could deceive them so deftly and discreetly. The trainer came out with a dog. He told the audience that the dog knew how to count to ten. But he was also deceiving them; in fact, the dog did not know how to count. It simply barked on time, in order to receive a piece of sugar from the hand of the trainer. But the meat machines clapped for the dog and believed that it knew arithmetic. After the dog came a meat machine in the costume of a knife thrower with his knives stuck in his belt. A wooden circle was placed in front of him. He asked for a volunteer from the audience. The volunteer turned out to be a woman who had been in the front row. In fact, she also worked in the circus. The knife thrower tied her to the circle, walked away, and then began to throw knives at the circle. The knives landed near the woman's body. Then he gave a command and the circle began to spin. He was brought four knives with torch handles. The lights in the circus went out. A drumroll sounded. The knife thrower lit the knives and threw them at the circle. The meat machines enjoyed the knife thrower's agility. But they didn't know that most of his life he'd been throwing knives at the circles. The woman had been working with him for the last year. He had caused serious wounds to four women. This woman had nine scars from his knives. She was given money for this. At the end of the show came the gymnasts with the Soviet flag, sickle, and hammer. They played around, and then began to make a pyramid on the summit of which was a flag, and on its sides a hammer and sickle. The meat machines applauded for a very long time. They rose and began to move toward the exit. We had been waiting for this moment. We immediately pushed our way through to *ours*. He was accompanied by a thickset meat machine. I quickly *looked through* the minder and realized that he was a Chekist. And that he had been attached to the foreigner as a guard. The foreigner was important to Soviet meat machines. We followed him along the path. They exited onto the street. Near a church stood nine carriages with drivers and six automobiles. One of the cars was waiting for him. He walked over to the car, retrieved a cigarette case, and lit a cigarette. I stood close by and *looked through* him. He was connected with something underground: cement, earth, water, dirt, liquid, workers, hoses. He smoked. The minder also smoked, something cheap and unfiltered. A *papirosa*. He despised the foreigner. But he did his job. Fer, Ep, and Rubu stood a ways off. I *waited*, to see what to do. The foreigner laughed, finished smoking, and tossed the cigarette butt on the ground. The minder opened the door of the automobile for him.

"No. Valk. Breaze," the foreigner said in broken Russian; he turned and headed down the boulevard.

The minder set off after him. The automobile turned around and drove behind them, keeping close.

I took Fer by the arm. And we followed him. Ep and Rubu moved off. The foreigner walked along the boulevard ring toward Tverskaya. An occasional passerby walked down the boulevard. The foreigner walked to Petrovka and turned in the direction of the city center. Near the Petrovsky Monastery he stopped and shivered.

"Sergie. Is cooled. Go home."

The minder made a sign to the driver of the automobile. The car drove up. The minder walked over to the car and opened the back door. I looked around: ahead a carriage moved off and a pair of meat machines laughed drunkenly. Here and there lampposts illuminated the street. A dog barked. I jolted the brothers' hearts. They *understood*. The brothers grabbed their weapons. Ep hit the minder on the head with the butt of his gun. He fell. I aimed a pistol at the foreigner.

"*Ne bouge pas!*"

Rubu placed the butt to the windshield of the automobile. The driver froze.

"*Montez dans la voiture!*" I ordered the foreigner.

He began to sit down slowly in the automobile. I pushed him. Rubu sat on the front seat next to the driver. The Chekist who'd fallen moaned. Ep and Fer lifted and pushed him into the car. Fer squeezed in behind him.

"Stay," I told Ep. "Call Pilo and Ju."

And he moved away from the car into the dark.

The foreigner was frightened. I sat next to him, pushing the pistol into his stomach. The cracked head of the minder was on my knees.

"Sit still," I told him in Russian.

"Turn around," Rubu ordered the driver, searching him.

The driver obediently began to turn the wheel. He didn't have any weapons.

"Drive to Liubertsy," Rubu said, putting the barrel of the gun to the driver's temple.

"There's not enough gas," muttered the driver.

I *saw* that he was deceiving us. And quickly *looked through* him. "There's enough gasoline. Remember your dead wife. Don't be afraid of bees. They won't sting you a third time."

The driver froze.

"Take a swallow from your mother-in-law's flask. And let's go."

The driver, not understanding, glanced at me. Then, with a trembling hand, he opened the glove compartment and removed the flask of buffalo-grass vodka. He took a big swallow. He closed the flask and put it away.

And we sped off.

Along the way the foreigner began to ask me in French who we were and what we wanted. I answered that we wouldn't hurt him.

The minder moaned weakly the whole way, then grew quiet: his heart had stopped. Ep's blow proved too powerful. Arriving at our location, we drove on to the territory of the dacha. We tied up the driver and locked him in the cellar. We took the foreigner into the house. As soon as we closed the door, we jumped on him, trembling from impatience. Rubu grabbed him from behind and pressed against him. Squealing, Fer tore the clothes from his chest and grabbed him by the knees. He was extremely frightened because he didn't understand our actions. He offered us money. Retrieving an Ice hammer from the attic, I hit him on the chest so hard that he immediately lost consciousness and blood flowed from his ears and nose. We *fell* on him.

"Kovro, Kovro, Kovro," he answered with his heart.

We cried from joy. Our hearts *rejoiced*. Undressing brother Kovro, we washed him, rubbed him down, bandaged his chest, and put him to bed. His awakened heart brought him out of the swoon. Powerless, he lay in the light of the kerosene lamp and looked straight ahead with wide-open greenish-blue eyes. We sat nearby. And carefully *touched* his heart. We *calmed* him. We already had experience dealing with awakening hearts.

Kovro began to mutter weakly in German. He lost consciousness, and again came to himself. The awakened heart made him completely powerless—he couldn't move a finger. Fer stroked his hands, licked and warmed his pale face with her breath. We stroked his body.

He was a German. In the world of meat machines he was called Sebastian Wolf. He had just turned thirty-five. He came from a prominent manufacturing dynasty: his father and uncle owned coal mines in Bochum and a copper-melting plant in Düsseldorf. As soon as he finished the gymnasium, he volunteered to go to the front, was wounded by shrapnel, and demobilized. Studying in Hannover and Oxford, he received two diplomas—architecture and electronics degrees. Turning down a position as director of his father's mines, Wolf began to make his own career. The architectural bureau he founded began to work on projects with great prospects—underground communications. At the age of thirty, Sebastian Wolf had become well known in Europe as an engineer and architect. He constructed underground factories and citadels, tunnels through mountains, and mines for building metro systems. The firm S. Wolf and Company became fashionable in underground construction. The Bolsheviks offered him an enormous sum for the project of laying down communications for the Moscow metro. Wolf agreed. Arriving six months earlier in Moscow, he signed a contract. His name didn't show up officially in the press: Soviet propaganda could not allow anyone to know that a bourgeois engineer was taking part in the construction of the Moscow metro. He agreed to this as well: what was important to him was the project itself and the money. The project was almost ready; in Germany Wolf's wife and children were waiting for him.

But his main passion was conquering the underground.

For entertainment he loved horse racing, sword fighting, and the circus. The circus was connected with a childhood dream. The family lived on an estate near Düsseldorf. One time, his older brother took eight-year-old Sebastian into town to show him the French traveling circus that had come to the city on tour. The boy really loved the circus. He was particularly struck by the blue girl on the pink elephant. The girl danced on the elephant, and it bowed to the audience and doffed its hat. People threw money into the hat. Sebastian fell in love with the blue girl. The next day he demanded that he be taken to the circus again. But the circus had already left Düsseldorf. Sebastian became hysterical. His temperature went up that night. He had a dream: he was in an empty circus ring, in the middle of which was an elephant made of ice. The blue girl sat on the elephant. She invited Sebastian to ride on the elephant. He walked over, the elephant picked him up with its trunk and placed him on its back. Sebastian sat on the elephant. The girl hugged him by the shoulders. And commanded the elephant: "Olé." The ice elephant walked in a circle. And squeaked. The squeak of the ice elephant made Sebastian cry *sweetly*. Because the elephant was very cold but *very* kind. And *unbearably* intimate.

The blue girl embraced Sebastian from behind with her warm hands and whispered into his ear, "*Un enfant ne peut pas pleurer!*"

After that Sebastian fell in love with the circus forever, although his father's family considered the circus a vulgar spectacle. Sebastian went to the circus when he was in high school, before the war, and as a student, and after that. He went to the famous circuses of Paris, Lisbon, London, and Hamburg. But he never again saw the blue girl on the pink elephant.

The ice elephant came to him in feverish dreams each time he hallucinated with a high temperature. And each time, Sebastian cried *sweet* tears in his dream, hearing the icy squeak.

We *protected* the calm of brother Kovro.

In the morning sisters Pilo and Ju came. They relieved us. They sat down near the bed of the newly acquired brother. Before the sun rose, we again got in the car with the chauffeur and rode farther from Moscow. We turned from the highway into a dense forest, shot the chauffeur, poured the remainder of the gasoline over the car and both corpses, and lit it. After that we walked for a long time to a railway station. We got on the train and traveled to Kazansk station. Fer and I were late to work by forty-four minutes. To make up for it, the boss required us to wash the floors after work. And he also "signaled the irresponsibility of the Deribases" to the Komsomol secretary, so that we would be "raked over the coals" at the Komsomol meeting. The boss's face swirled powerfully.

"Did you forget where you work? Forget whose name you carry? Discipline above all! The OGPU—is no circus!"

The Search

IT TOOK Kovro four days to recover. The blow of the Ice hammer had injured his chest muscles, which swelled up and hurt. But his awakening heart helped. We took turns on watch at the dacha, protecting brother Kovro. He was in shock and disturbed. His condition changed swiftly: sometimes he kissed us rapturously, pressing us to his broken chest, at others he would sob hysterically, calling on his mother and all the saints in German. His delicate fingers trembled, his eyes burned. And his heart quivered.

Fer and I *knew* that his heart had to go through the crying. For this reason it was dangerous to let Kovro out. When he woke up, he rushed for the door. We seized him, pressed him to us, *spoke* with his heart. He shouted furiously, thrashed about in our arms, then calmed down.

We knew that the OGPU was looking for him. And we tried to be extremely careful.

Finally, on the fifth day, Kovro collapsed into the *crying*. He sobbed, submerged himself in sleep, awoke, and sobbed again. Sisters Pilo, Ju, and Orti took turns sitting near him. Brothers Edlap and Bidugo guarded them.

Fer and I began the search again.

At first we had luck: as soon as we entered the unemployment office, where there were crowds of unemployed meat machines, our *magnet* detected a sister. But she turned out to be a tiny infant. Her unemployed mother held her in her arms, standing in line. Waiting until the mother was turned down yet again and went home, we followed her. It cost us a *great deal* of restraint not to take the baby from her. But we couldn't preserve the life of our sister. We simply had to keep track of her, once we found the address. Thus we found out that our nameless sister was growing up in Krivokolenny Lane, in a communal apartment on the first floor of house No. 6. The meat machine who had squeezed our sister out into the world from her vagina was feeding her with her milk. We had to wait until the breast of *our sister* was strong enough to withstand the blow of the Ice hammer. And it was necessary to help this meat machine. That evening we gathered all the money that we had, placed it in an envelope, and left it with the nursing meat machine. She was very happy with the find, thinking the help came to her *from on high*. And in this she was correct.

Continuing our search, we quickly *understood*: walks through the street at rush hour were much too *difficult* for Fer and me. Moving through the crowd, our hearts were torn apart. To illuminate with our *magnet* a crowd of hurrying meat machines, as opposed to sitting or standing ones, was immeasurably harder. The moving crowd *oppressed* us, it *hummed and swirled*, as though it intended to carry us off with it, back into that terrible and lightless life. It yearned to swallow us. The crowd knocked us off our feet, it forced us to hold on to our brothers. Our knees trembled. As soon as we began to illuminate the crowd, we grew instantly exhausted, and after a few minutes our legs literally collapsed. Then days were required for our hearts and bodies to get back to normal.

We *decided* not to work anymore with moving crowds: it had become dangerous. We would instead *illuminate* meat machines in places where they worked, gathered, ate, watched shows, prayed, listened to speakers, and read books. Such places included plants and factories, theaters and movie houses, libraries, meeting rooms, churches, restaurants, and cafeterias.

The first two outings brought no results. There were none of *ours* at the evening of proletarian poetry in the Polytechnic Institute or at the Komsomol meeting of the OGPU.

However, we were very lucky on the third outing: we were able to acquire two free passes to the opera *The Queen of Spades* at the Bolshoi Theater. Squeezing through the cackling crowd into the vestibule, we sat in the gallery, high up amid the university students and Workers' Faculty students. The brightly illuminated hall was full. The meat machines gradually calmed down and sat in their seats. The lights went out. The orchestra began to play. Meat machines in costumes from the beginning of the previous century came onstage and began singing in unison. All of them, thanks to their inborn characteristics and many years of training, could produce lengthy sounds of different frequencies and tones. The meat machines sitting in the audience weren't able to produce those kinds of sounds. For that reason they came to hear the singing meat machines. The meat machines were pretending to be cardplayers. Then women appeared, dressed in crinolines. They began to sing in higher voices. The audience burst into applause; melomanes and students in the gallery shouted "Bravo!" The subject of the opera boiled down to two main themes—love and money, the merger of which, in the opinion of the meat machines, guaranteed complete earthly happiness. The orchestra played to the singers. The musicians tried hard to follow a particular harmony that meat machines had worked out over thousands of years. In these pitiful sounds, merging with the voices of the singer, you could feel an unconscious longing for a world of Higher Harmony, unattainable for meat machines.

Fer and I began to meticulously *examine* the hall. The meat machines sat immobile, enchanted by what was happening onstage. We could see them *well*. In the parterre where the Soviet higher-ups sat with their wives, we could see gymnasts and military uniforms; foreigners sat there as well; bureaucrats occupied the dress circle, the intelligentsia and music lovers sat farther up. We didn't discover anyone in the parterre. But as soon as the *magnet* touched the dress circle, our hearts *jolted*: there was someone! We shivered: Fer squealed and ground her teeth; a loud moan escaped from me. The meat machines sitting nearby shushed us, taking us for half-mad music lovers. We were in ecstasy not over a German's aria, however, but over a young woman in evening dress and a fur wrap in the third row of the dress circle. She was looking at the stage, frequently looking through a mother-of-pearl opera glass on a collapsible handle. Next to her sat a meat machine in a navy uniform. I didn't try to *see through* her life—we were sitting too far away. During the intermission we came close to her. She was one of the "formers": a private home on Piatnitskaya Street, a happy childhood with dolls, a dog named Rhett, a pony called Tsora, the gold epaulettes of her father, the plump hands of her mother, sisters, a brother, heavy periods, fear of losing all her blood, love for Antosha, marriage in Elokhovsky Cathedral, a miscarriage, Italy, another miscarriage, the Revolution, the death of her father, the flight of her mother, poverty, fainting from hunger, a second marriage, the heavy odor of her husband.

After the intermission we began to *watch* the balconies and the gallery. But then a murmur went through the audience, and everyone turned their heads. In the former royal box Stalin appeared with his wife. This was unexpected for *us*. But not for the meat machines: Stalin often attended the Moscow theaters. The figures of bodyguards appeared in the aisles. Fer and I *stopped*. We *ignored* the crowd of whispering meat machines for a moment and turned our *magnet* on the new ruler of Russia. He sat in a shadowy box. We *watched* him intently. He was not one of *ours*. His heart was a simple pump for moving blood. He himself—was a powerful meat machine. From afar I dimly *saw* his heavily swirling life: there was nothing in particular to distinguish him from the other meat machines sitting in the audience and looking at him. He was like many of them. He had an *enormous* love of power. But many in the audience loved power just as much. The meat machines continued looking back at their leader for a long time. Stalin calmly watched the stage. There a corpulent meat machine was singing that life was only a game in which he who "catches a moment of success" is happy, and the loser is doomed to cry, cursing his fate. He finished the aria, eliciting a stormy ovation in the hall. And then we *saw a new brother*: an old man in the second level of the balcony. He clapped, shouted "Bravo!," and was as joyous as a child. As a genuine music lover, he had come to the opera with binoculars. They lay in front of him on the velvet parapet of the balcony.

Fer and I squeezed each other's hands until they cracked, so we wouldn't shout out from *excitement*. In the dark hall sat two of *ours*.

Having calmed down, we *examined* the upper balconies and the gallery. There was no *third* to be found. When the opera finished, flowers flew out onto the stage, the singers were called back for bows and ovations. Stalin also applauded and disappeared with his bodyguards. We rose and realized that we were having difficulty moving. We were extremely tired. Holding on to each other, we descended to the cloakroom before the crowd, dressed, and began to wait for *ours*. First the woman appeared. The sailor led her by the arm. They dressed and began to leave. We followed and I *looked* at both of them: the sailor was her uncle and lived with her as with a wife. Ep and Rubu were keeping watch at the exit. I *showed* them the woman with the sailor. And they followed them. We waited for the old man. Fortunately, he walked rather slowly and lived close by. We were able to follow him to his apartment in Stoleshnikov Lane. I also *looked* at him: he had worked as a waiter at the Slavic Bazaar restaurant his entire life, but at the same time remained a passionate music lover; four times he had applied to the vocal department of the conservatory and four times he had failed; he was alone, loved cats, and was afraid of bandits, who had once mugged him, cracking his head open; he prayed to his deceased mother, inventing his own prayer.

Ep and Rubu followed the woman. She lived near Kursk station.

As we fell asleep that night, we *decided* how best to kidnap the woman and the old man and where to strike them with the hammer.

But the new day changed our plans: Ig arrived in Moscow from Khabarovsk. We met him at Lubyanka. Embracing him, I felt how *strong his heart had grown*. That evening we *all* went to the dacha in Liubertsy and sat on the floor, taking one another by the hand. Kerosene lamps illuminated our faces. In the center of the Circle sat brother Kovro. He had gone through the *heart crying*. We *spoke* to our brother's heart. It timidly *answered*.

That night we devised a strategy for searching: Fer and I would look for *ours*, and then the brothers would follow them, kidnap them, bring them to the dacha, strike them with a hammer, and give them aid; if kidnapping were impossible—the hammering would be carried out on the spot. Ig found a car to transport the newly acquired. Its owner, Solomatin, a relative of Deribas's wife, who'd had an auto-repair shop during NEP, had gone bankrupt, spent some time in the cellar of the OGPU, and was released thanks to the intervention of Deribas. He owed him his life. After the collapse of NEP, the automobile lover not only had no fuel for the car but had nothing to live on: he was barely making ends meet in the carpenter's shop, and the Moscow automobile shops wouldn't take him because he was a former nepman and member of the White Army. Solomatin would do anything for a piece of bread.

Above all, our Brotherhood needed money, which played a huge role in the world of meat machines. And we decided to rob several wealthy Muscovites. In order to take their valuables, we didn't even have to kill them. In the beginning I *saw* them in the crowd; Rubu and Bidugo followed them. Making use of my ability to see the secret of any meat machine with my heart, I found out where they kept their savings. One of them, a former court jeweler, was hiding his treasure in a brick safe in the attic of a neighboring house. Another, the son of a banker who had escaped to Paris, had buried a little box with gold coins in Neskuchny Park. A third kept several large diamonds hidden under his windowsill.

As soon as this all became ours, we had solved the problem of money: the gold coins were sold on the black market, the other gold items were taken to a secondhand shop where they were sold for a low price. The price didn't interest us much: I could find a lot more gold hidden by meat machines. We kept the diamonds: to reach its goal, the Brotherhood of Light had a long road ahead.

Having hired Solomatin and his car, we began working. First we kidnapped the woman found in the Bolshoi Theater, and on the next day, the old man. Both of them were taken to the dacha in Liubertsy and hammered.

Her name was Atlu.

His was—Pcho.

Brother Kovro was driven to the nearby Moscow suburb of Odintsovo, where, unshaven and wearing dirty clothes, he appeared at a police station. Giving his name, he demanded in his broken Russian that they inform the OGPU about him. The Chekists, who had been looking for the missing Wolf for two weeks, arrived immediately. Kovro told them that he had been kidnapped by bandits, taken somewhere blindfolded, and held in a trunk; the bandits tried to get money out of him, then he was taken to a new place. Along the way he managed to escape. The OGPU was very happy that he had turned up: the Bolsheviks needed Wolf badly for the construction of the metro, and they did not want any scandal with German businesses over "the disappearance of a well-known architect in wild Soviet Russia." Brother Kovro returned to his deluxe room at the Hotel Metropol, where Sebastian Wolf had been living, and a few days later was again working on his drawings. His heart *strengthened* with every day. For us Kovro was the first hope of searching in Europe.

Having an automobile with a chauffeur, we became freer in our search. Solomatin was paid pretty good money. He was told no details. I knew that he thought us some kind of Chekist born-agains, kidnapping people to rob them, so as not to share with the upper echelons. The cover of Deribas calmed him. In truth, Solomatin feared only dead children (his older brother had drowned as a boy) and hunger.

On Easter, Fer and I *looked through* the crowd at four Moscow churches. But we found only one. Brother Tsfo was a large, filthy, illiterate peasant, who had escaped to Moscow from a remote village in the Tambov region. The peasant men of his village, brought to a state of desperation by Soviet power, used axes to hack up government expropriators who had come once again on requisition outings for grain and potatoes. The head of the Agricultural Soviet and three local Communists were locked up in a bathhouse, which was burned down. Then the peasants, with their families and cattle, disappeared in the Tambov forests. The punitive organs of the OGPU burned their village in response and followed their trail—to catch and execute the rebels. Brother Tsfo, who had lost his family as far back as the Civil War, while running from authorities, made his way to the railroad and rode to Moscow on the roof of one of the cars. Here he asked for alms and ate bits and pieces of whatever people threw away. Hirsute and strong as a bear, he resisted us furiously. Edlap broke four of his ribs before his warrior's heart began to speak.

Soon after this, what had happened to me in the library happened to Fer: she could no longer see pictures of MEAT MACHINES. The transformation came over her in the women's bathhouse, where there was a large poster hanging in the dressing room: SOVIET WOMEN, STRUGGLE AGAINST BOURGEOIS PREJUDICE! On the poster these prejudices were named: manicures, pedicures, lipstick, rouge for the cheeks, removing moles and the hair on one's legs, shaving one's underarms, plucking one's eyebrows, wearing corsets. The poster depicted two women: a tall, thin, corseted, made-up, manicured bourgeois lady, and a simply dressed Soviet Komsomol girl. Fer couldn't distinguish one from the other: the pictures grew blurry. She looked at herself in the mirror and couldn't see her face. However, she saw a woman sitting nearby. At the age of eighteen this woman had abandoned her newborn child. In order to check herself, Fer reminded the woman where and how it happened. The woman fainted. Fer shouted for joy: "A Gift of the Light!"

Now Fer and I saw the surrounding world of brothers and meat machines *identically*. This *vision* opened new possibilities for us. Looking through yet another meat machine together, our hearts *glanced* at each other. Whatever slipped past me was noted by Fer; what she didn't notice, I saw.

Together Fer and I penetrated the *hidden* worlds of meat machines. Their secrets and thoughts became *entirely* transparent. We discovered that the essence of earthly life WAS OPEN TO US.

A new Wisdom awoke in our hearts.

And it brought in *new* corrections to the process of searching.

One night Fer and I went up to the roof of the dormitory, sat down, and held hands.

We *saw* the world.

And we saw it in time. Meat machines moved around. Previously, each of them lived life in isolation. Now they joined together. The idea of a general brotherhood made them unify. In the past it had not had such power among meat machines. Now it would gather them in crowds. And make them forget about their former earthly goal: personal comfort. This *new* idea made meat machines suddenly feel a *new* kinship: the kinship of belief in collective happiness. It unified them. It pulled them out of their stone coffins onto the town squares! Forced them to forget about their families. It demanded self-sacrifice.

This unification of the meat machines had never occurred before: only war could tear them away from their families, from the stone graves they called "houses," from money and personal property. But wars were soon over. The meat machines, having killed others like themselves, again returned to their former values: comfort, family, money, personal happiness. Now they often declared war on these values and learned to live life only through the idea of all-around equality and brotherhood. Deprived of harmony in themselves, they furiously sought it in the crowd. The crowd *swirled* with collective life. Each meat machine tried as soon as possible to dissolve into the crowd. And acquire collective happiness. They experienced this *new* happiness. For this, meat machines were ready to kill those who didn't share their idea of collective happiness. To kill those who didn't want to unify, who didn't share, and who lived according to their former interests. This was a *new* war, unlike the previous. It was coming closer. Quickly.

And we understood *why* the Ice fell to the Earth at this moment, in the century of the unification of meat machines. Because in the crowd it was easier to search! In this lay the Highest Wisdom of the Light. When the meat machines were together, we could quickly find *ours* among them. We wouldn't have to travel all over the Earth: the century of the unification of meat machines would gather crowds in large cities. And Fer and I would *look through them*. And we would find the 23,000 brother and sisters.

Meeting in Sokolniki Park for a Small Circle, we *reported* to the brothers and sisters what we had realized that night on the rusty roof of the OGPU dormitory.

The next day we continued the search.

Over the course of 1929 Fer and I *looked through* dozens of Party, Komsomol, and union meetings. We sat through political classes, stood at demonstrations and sports holidays. Many times we searched in almost all the Moscow theaters and at the hippodrome. We weren't able to get into the Fifth Congress of the USSR Soviets, but in one week we *looked through* the First All-Union Congress of Communal Farm Women. We *watched* the crowd at the opening of the first planetarium in the USSR, at the launch of the first electric train engine at the Dynamo factory, at Red Square during the festivities honoring the pilot Gromov, who had flown from Moscow to the European capitals in the airplane *Wings of the Soviets*.

Altogether, sixty-two brothers and thirty-two sisters were found. But not all of *ours* survived. We were not yet *prepared* for certain eventualities. For the first time we experienced the loss of our brothers: Ache and Bidugo perished during the kidnapping of brother Sa, a Party functionary; sister Khortim, who suffered from hemophilia, died from loss of blood. At first this *shook* us. Fer and I held sister Khortim in our arms as she died. When I *saw* that the Light was abandoning Khortim's halted heart and there was NO WAY I could help, everything in me *shifted* backward. Each cell of my body reached *back* to the Ice. I stopped breathing. And grew blind. The surrounding world disappeared. Only the DARK remained. And the hearts shining in it. They hung in the dark and shone. Then the Light left one of the hearts. And I *understood* that neither my heart, nor the hearts of my brothers and sisters, could help the Light remain in Khortim's heart. These last moments of the heart's flame dying were the most *excruciating*.

It was extinguished. Forever.

But Fer and I *immediately* felt that the Light that had left Khortim was incarnated in a newly born heart. Somewhere in the DARKNESS surrounding us. And that heart *began to beat* in a new way. It was no longer the heart of a meat machine. It had become *ours*. It was waiting for us.

And I could see the world once again. The world we were in.

We weren't subject to earthly death. The Light that left one heart was reincarnated in another. But our bodies were mortal. They didn't live long. We had to search. And search QUICKLY. So that the search didn't turn into a vicious circle; in order to conquer Time.

So that sister Khortim and brothers Ache and Bidugo would be with us again.

So we searched.

Among the newly acquired were soldiers, Soviet bureaucrats, engineers, Party workers, factory workers, "formers," speculators, homeless, housewives, criminals, and one underground millionaire. They all passed through our hands; each of them Fer and I *saw* with the heart, the Ice hammer had struck each of their breasts.

We had to give up the dacha in Liubertsy: it was occupied by a high-placed Chekist. But we rented two other dachas—not too far from Moscow, with large, forested plots surrounded by tall fences. In these places we could calmly hammer *ours*. Their cries and moans didn't reach alien ears. No one hindered our care for the wounded, no one was alarmed by the *heart crying*. On being awoken and going through the purifying crying, brothers and sisters returned to Soviet life, merged into it as though nothing had happened. But the Primordial Light burned in their hearts. They were part of the Brotherhood of the Light. And they did all they could toward achieving our goals.

The search continued intensively.

Many of *ours* also stopped seeing faces and images and beheld the world with their hearts. The secrets of meat machines opened to them. This helped to keep the Brotherhood secure, to know *where* danger awaited us, *where* we shouldn't tread. Knowing the secrets of the cities gave us the opportunity to be economically free. Money became easily available to us. Because we *knew* where it was kept.

But in Soviet society, where there was total control, by no means was everything decided by money. Only power granted absolute freedom. And we *were moving* up. But very, very cautiously. Sister Morod, whom we acquired during a Communist "volunteer" workday, occupied a high position in one of the Moscow regional committees. Brother Sa was Party secretary of a weaving mill. We found two in the OGPU. But they didn't occupy high positions.

The search continued.

But by the end of the year, Fer and I realized that we were aging *rapidly*. There was a reason that our hair turned gray early, that we experienced a *horrible* exhaustion after each search in a crowd. Fer and I were the only ones who had a heart *magnet*. No one else in the Brotherhood, not a single pair, possessed such unerring and precise vision as we did. Only Fer and I, together, staying close to each other, possessed this powerful Gift of the Light. We were the only ones who could *search*. And *see* with certainty. The Wisdom of the Light told me: we were the first acquired. A man and a woman. We were the first to touch the Ice. And we were *given* more than others. But more was *taken away* from us as well: we were aging swiftly.

Our early graying, wrinkles, and unhealthy pallor were immediately noticed at work. Our hands began to shake. Climbing the stairs, we rested on each landing, like old people. The director sent us to the doctor. We went, although *we knew* the reason. The doctor didn't find any illnesses, other than "catastrophic aging." Soon we had to leave work. The Brotherhood guarded us. We settled in the large apartment of brother Londu, a well-known Moscow doctor who treated the Soviet nomenklatura. We felt calm and comfortable in his home. We took care of ourselves: during the day we slept, ate fruit, drank an infusion of plants grown in the mountains far from the world of meat machines. In the late afternoon we took a bath in warm cow's milk. This restored us, made our blood run faster. In the evening the brothers drove us on the search. Ending up in yet another hall, where made-up actors pranced and grimaced onstage, or a meat machine read a paper about the advent of Communism, we *looked through* the entire hall. Each search *shook* our bodies. Fer and I sat, our fingers locked, *helping* each other. It was exhausting and difficult work. The nature of meat machines resisted the search. Our *magnet* destroyed the resistance. For all the brothers we *discovered*, we paid with our cells. Our cells perished. Our bodies aged and weakened.

But no one except Fer and I could *search and find*. This was our work. And we had to hurry.

The Brotherhood grew with each day.

It became a powerful organism living by its own laws. The laws of the Light. It penetrated the world of the meat machines, insinuating itself into their structures, occupying important positions.

Brother Kovro, finishing his work in Moscow, returned to Germany. His father died, leaving him half of his fortune. Thus, the Brotherhood acquired a large villa in the Bavarian Alps and a house near Düsseldorf.

But before moving west, we had to grow stronger in Russia.

Fer and I took care of ourselves. We tried to live cautiously, not waste our strength. We conserved energy, closing our eyes. We dozed in chairs. The brothers massaged our feet. They brought us fresh fruits. We swallowed them. We touched each other's bodies, taking care of our bones and muscles. We needed our bodies to carry our hearts on the search. And we searched.

The meat machines were furiously whirling and swirling. They were gathering. They dug up the ground, welded metal, piled rocks. They built iron machines. Machines to kill other meat machines. Thousands of iron machines formed rows and chains. They crawled over the Earth. They amassed in stone spaces. They were rubbed with a special oil. From the bowels of the Earth they sucked out heavy blood and poured it into the iron machines. The machines fed on the heavy blood of the Earth. They growled and roared. And prepared to crush and kill.

Other iron machines could fly. And throw large iron eggs on the cities of meat machines. The eggs exploded violently and destroyed cities. Meat machines perished in their stone caves. Cities burned.

These flying machines also formed rows. They were painted in dark and light colors. They also fed on the heavy blood of the Earth.

Other steel machines for the destruction of meat machines were also built. Some of them could float on the surface of the water and swim, even though they were very heavy. They would float up to cities and furiously spit iron eggs at them. Which exploded and destroyed the cities.

There were machines that could swim under the water. And drown other machines floating on the water's surface.

There were more and more of these machines. The meat machines were working hard. They built the iron machines day and night.

The meat machines were preparing for a huge war. In order to kill meat machines that spoke different languages and destroy their cities. And then occupy these destroyed cities and restore them. And live in them. And give birth to new meat machines.

The war was drawing near. It was necessary to millions of meat machines. They were expecting it. During this war tens of millions of meat machines were supposed to die. And with them, many of *ours*. We had to search more rapidly. While the meat machines hadn't yet begun to fight.

We continued to search among meat machines who spoke Russian. We searched for *ours* in the two main cities of Russian-speaking meat machines. The search was conducted systematically and cautiously. Fer and I were dressed in various uniforms and brought to large gatherings of meat machines. These gatherings would go on for several days. The meat machines sat in spacious auditoriums. Some of them got up on a tribune and spoke about what had to be done to make all meat machines happy. Fer and I held each other's hands. And *looked through everyone* sitting in the room. And we found *ours*. Their hearts contained the Light. We *saw* this Light. And *removed* the brothers and sisters from the crowd of meat machines. Then the Ice hammer woke their hearts.

Three Earth years passed.

Altogether, in the country where the Ice lay, there were 186 of us.

The Brotherhood had strengthened in that country. Brothers Rek, Avu, Orzhe, Tnola, and Sa, and sisters Morod and Fiu joined the leadership elite. Brothers Ig, Kha, Zchap, and Shoror occupied important positions in the penal system. Brothers Gba and De commanded large military divisions of meat machines. Brother Pep invented new types of iron machines. Sister Chekh headed up a hospital where high-placed meat machines were treated.

Now it was possible to move westward.

On March 7, 1931, with the help of brothers Ig and Shoror, Fer and

I crossed the border of the country where the Ice lay. We were transported in an iron machine that used fire and water, and moved along iron tracks. Fer and I wore clothes that important meat machines in the government wore. Brothers Gzem and Tu were nearby. The iron machines brought us two days later to the main city of meat machines who spoke German. We began to live in this city. We had a spacious stone cave in a part of the town that the local meat machines called Marvelous Mountain. This part of the city was considered very pretty. Rich and famous meat machines lived here. They had a lot of money. Their stone caves were arranged with objects that other meat machines had made, working meticulously for a long period of time.

Brother Kovro and the brothers in Moscow helped us. Three months and twelve days later eighteen brothers and eighteen sisters arrived. They began to live in Kovro's large stone cave, built in the mountains in the south of the country of German-speaking meat machines. Two months and eight days later, nine brothers came to Kovro. He helped them get settled in the main city of this western country.

The search in this western country began slowly. During the winter the Ice was brought to us, 1.5 metric tons of Ice. Brothers Ig, Zchap, and Avu knew how to send it to the country where we had settled. The Ice was sent to the south of the country, to brother Kovro. There the brothers and sisters began to make Ice hammers. They were kept in cold places.

Fer and I carefully *searched* for ways to continue the search in this country. And we *understood* where we had to penetrate and where to begin. In this country the meat machines especially loved one particular entertainment. It had been invented recently but it became popular very quickly. Like most of the entertainments of meat machines, it was fairly simple: the meat machines gathered in an auditorium, the lights went out, and on white material shadows resembling meat machines were projected from a special box. These shadows accomplished unusual feats on this white material: they jested, murdered, robbed, traveled to exotic countries, married queens, grew much smaller in size, flew to the nearest planet, fought with nonexistent beasts, lived in palaces. The meat machines sitting in the auditorium followed the shadows intently and forgot about their real lives. The lives of the shadows concerned them much more deeply. They dreamed of extraordinary deeds and adventures. And received immense pleasure from observing the shadows. Sitting in the dark hall, they laughed and cried. Some fainted from emotion. The lives of the shadows helped them to forget about the misery of their own lives. The majority of them had absolutely no idea how these shadows ended up on the white material. They were created by special groups of meat machines. They used a combination of substances and light. And also the special meat machines, the ones that grimaced in the theaters. These meat machines were very well known. Their faces were multiplied on sheets of paper. These sheets hung in crowded places. And in the stone caves of meat machines. Simple meat machines wanted to be like these shadows in every way. They dressed like the shadows, imitated the shadows' gait, their gestures and mannerisms. The shadows on white quickly began to overtake old entertainments—the theater and the circus. They became fashionable.

The Brotherhood decided to make use of this new fashion. With the help of brother Kovro, in the main city of the German-speaking meat machines an organization was founded that looked for meat machines to become shadows on white material. Many meat machines dreamed of becoming shadows, so that other meat machines would look at them with delight in dark auditoriums. Moreover, in this city there were many meat machines who didn't have any work. They were not paid any money, therefore they had no means of buying food and clothing. Becoming a shadow on white material would be salvation for them. Because meat machines that became shadows on white material received a great deal of money.

The meat machines called the shadows on white "stars," even though they were only gray shadows on white. But the Brotherhood decided to use the delusions of meat machines. It called the new organization Rising Stars in order to attract the meat machines. For money, the meat machines who specialized in the combination of letters on a page wrote a lot of letters about Rising Stars. These letters were multiplied on thousands of sheets of paper. The meat machines bought the sheets of paper and read about the Rising Stars. They thought that Rising Stars was waiting for them. And that that each of them could become a "rising star," that is—a gray shadow on white.

The Brotherhood rented a large stone cave in the center of the city. Meat machines desiring to become shadows on white were supposed to come there. Sheets of paper announced that the organization Rising Stars was looking for blue-eyed and light-haired meat machines. Meat machines with different colors of hair and eyes would not be seen.

On the appointed day a long line of blue-eyed, light-haired meat machines formed at the entrance to the cave with the sign RISING STARS. Bright lamplights stood in the cave. And machines that could print images of meat machines on paper. These machines were run by brothers Gzem and Tu. Fer and I sat in armchairs. The meat machines came in one at a time. They told us about themselves. And they showed what they knew how to do: some could make various sounds with their throats, others depicted feelings, and yet others danced. We *looked through* them. If we found one of *ours*, Gzem told them that there was a possibility of becoming a "new star." And that they were very talented. A contract was signed with them. Then the newly acquired were taken to the mountains, to brother Kovro. There the Ice hammer woke their hearts.

This continued for eight months and twelve days. During this time 10,309 meat machines passed through our cave. Among them there was one hunchbacked meat machine in whom I recognized my sister from the world of the past. The same one with whom I parted when I was a small meat machine. Fate had carried her to this big city. She had been born blue-eyed and light-haired like I had. And she also came to try her earthly luck. She didn't recognize me. Standing before Fer and me, her fingers plucked strings on an empty wooden object, and with her throat she gave off high sounds. She tried her very hardest to make us like her. Her clothes, according to the standards of meat machines, were poor. Her heart was dead. She was an ordinary meat machine. Fer *understood* that I had grown up with this hunchback. And she held my hand. Fer was my sister.

Looking at the "rising stars," we found forty-five brothers and fifty-seven sisters. They were kept in several caves belonging to the Brotherhood. We healed their wounds. They cried with their hearts.

And merged into the Brotherhood of the Light. The majority of these newly acquired didn't occupy important positions in the government of meat machines. We needed money for their well-being. And the brothers robbed a stone cave where meat machines kept money and gold. Fer and I helped. We were housed in the neighboring cave. And every morning, like weak old people, we were taken outdoors in our wheelchairs. We *looked through* the lives of the meat machines who worked with money and guarded it. Four days later we knew the life of each of them. On the fifth day the brothers penetrated the cave belonging to the main guard of the money. They took away his wife and three children. Then it was proposed that he exchange the money and gold for his children and wife. He *really* did not want to do this. Because money and gold were very important to him. But the strength of the love for his wife and children was a little stronger. For that reason, he brought out of the cave a bag of money and half a bag of gold. We returned the children to him, but we had to kill his wife because she remembered the faces of the brothers.

After that we had no problem setting up the newly acquired brothers and sisters. The Brotherhood bought stone caves in the cities and their outskirts, iron machines to travel in, objects and substances, weapons, and clothes worn by military meat machines.

Changes soon happened in the country of German-speaking meat machines. A meat machine that spoke loudly and furiously came to power. It loved to speak in front of crowds of meat machines. The crowd listened to it and believed it. This meat machine called on all German-speaking meat machines to unite in order to fight against meat machines that spoke different languages. It said that German-speaking meat machines were the best in the world. They were the smartest, the most honest, and the most responsible. Therefore they should rule over all the other meat machines. But the German-speaking meat machines had very little room for living. That's why their stone caves were crowded, they had little food, and their children grew up weak and unhealthy. This meat machine said that German-speaking meat machines had to make many military machines and go to different countries to conquer new space for themselves. In these other countries there would be much food. And it would be possible to build new, spacious stone caves. In them the children of German-speaking meat machines would grow up healthy and happy.

Most of the German-speaking meat machines responded to the appeal of this meat machine. They liked its decisiveness. They called this meat machine their leader. It became the ruler of this country and instructed everyone what to do, when, and how. And the meat machines followed orders. But whoever didn't believe this meat machine and didn't want to follow its orders could not live peacefully in this country. The leader passed new laws to guide the country's life and created a strong organization. The organization made sure that German-speaking meat machines lived according to the new laws.

We *understood* that without support in this organization, it was dangerous to continue the search.

And the Brotherhood decided to wait a bit and gather strength, in order to acquire support in various ways from the new authorities.

The Brotherhood *compared* the two countries where we began our search: the Russian-speaking and the German-speaking. They differed not only in size and the number of meat machines living there. The crowds of meat machines in these countries had their own distinct *inner drone*. In the German-speaking crowd this *inner sound raged* about Order. The crowd *yearned* for Order. But only in the world of meat machines. It believed the world of the Earth to represent Absolute Order. In the Russian-speaking crowd there was an entirely different *inner drone*. It also raged about Order, but not in the world of meat machines—in the surrounding world. The Russian-speaking crowd was *vaguely disturbed* about the absence of Absolute Order in the world. It wanted to fix many things in this world. It considered the nature of meat machines perfection. But, raging about Absolute Order for the surrounding world and fiercely striving for it, it involuntarily introduced Disorder into the lives of meat machines. The *drone* of the Russian-speaking crowd destroyed the nature of the meat machines. Whereas the *drone* of the German-speaking crowd attempted to improve it.

In our search we had to take both *drones* into account. We *named* these countries in our own way. Although the big one was in *essence* the country of Disorder, we named it the Country of Ice, because the

Ice that lay in it was the most important thing for us. The smaller country we called the Country of Order.

But the most important thing was that we *felt* that these countries were moving toward each other *in agony*. Their *inner drones* were in essence quite distinct, but when they combined, they merged into a certain very particular *drone*, one that was indispensable for both of them, though they didn't have a clue about this. They considered each other enemies. We *understood* that between them a huge war would soon begin.

And the Brotherhood had to prepare for it.

Fer and I moved to the mountains, to the large stone cave that once belonged to the family of brother Kovro. Now it belonged to the Brotherhood. There was a forest around the cave. It grew on the mountains. Twenty-nine brothers and forty-four sisters lived in this cave. The rest of the brothers and sisters lived in other places in this country. Fer and I spoke with the brothers and sisters through our hearts. We *were anxious*. Because we were aging *very* rapidly. Of the entire Brotherhood, only Fer and I could see the hearts of *ours*. We could only do this *together*. Separately, neither Fer nor I possessed the Gift of the Light. We could only search together. And immediately find ours. Each search shook our hearts and destroyed our bodies. We could barely walk. The brothers drove us in iron machines and moved us in wheelchairs. Our arms and legs trembled. Our bodies were weakening and drying up. Wrinkles covered our faces. Most of our free time we slept, gathering strength. The brothers fed us fruits, bathed us in milk, rubbed oils on our bodies. They took care of us. Fer and I didn't participate in any of the Brotherhood's work other than the search. For this was the Most Important Work.

But we *were anxious*.

Because we felt the rapid aging of our bodies. After aging, earthly death would follow. And we would be unable to search. Or help the Brotherhood. We had to find two successors who could also *see* together, like we did. We *tested* the hearts of the newly acquired. We searched for others like us. We tried replacing Fer or me with another of the brothers or sisters. But no one could replace us. And that was the hidden *threat* to the Brotherhood.

We asked our hearts. But they stayed silent. The only thing we could do was search for *ours*. And search among *ours*.

There was no other way.

Embracing, Fer and I fell asleep. Our hearts searched even in our sleep. They *recalled* the hearts of the others. And *tested* them.

This continued endlessly.

For two Earth years we prepared for the continuation of the search. Finally the long-awaited day arrived. That summer in a southern city of the Country of Order an important event had occurred. The whole country had waited for it with impatience. In that city tens of thousands of the strongest meat machines, those most devoted to the leader, gathered. Along with them gathered the most important meat machines of the country, the ones who helped the leader rule over millions of meat machines. Over a period of six days all those gathered were supposed to be convinced how strong, united, devoted to the ideas of the leader, and prepared to go to war for new lands they were. The entire country prepared for this event.

The Brotherhood prepared for it too. For us, such a gathering of meat machines offered the possibility of finding some of *ours*. And not only among the simple meat machines. But among the authorities as well.

By order of the leader each meat machine in his country was supposed to know everything about this meeting of the strongest meat machines. To achieve this, hundreds of meat machines were hired who knew how to write letters on paper so that all who read these letters in other cities would have a good idea of what was happening at the gathering in the southern city. But in addition to meat machines who could write letters rapidly, the leader hired one meat machine who could produce shadows on white using various substances and light. And produce them so that any meat machines who watched these shadows would immediately understand what had happened at that very same large gathering. The Brotherhood decided to use this meat machine. Fer and I *found out about* her life. She loved not only to be a shadow on white but to create other shadows. More than anything she was afraid of dying in her sleep. For this reason she slept very little and lightly. She also really loved the leader. Not as a leader but as a vivid, strong meat machine. She thought of him as a fountain of hot water illuminated by a blue light. And she dreamed of making his shadow on white. To realize her dream she hired one hundred and seventy meat machines connected with the production of shadows on white.

The Brotherhood had already been working in the world of meat machines for several years, producing shadows on white. Therefore the brothers made an effort to work in her group. Twenty-nine meat machines were supposed to watch the gathering of meat machines through special iron boxes from different angles. In these boxes, with the aid of substances and light, shadows on white gradually added up. Of the twenty-nine who worked with the iron boxes, six were our brothers and another seven meat machines worked for the Brotherhood. Of the remaining one hundred and forty-one of ours there were two brothers, two sisters, and twelve meat machines who also worked for the Brotherhood.

Everything began with the arrival of the ruler. He flew in on an iron machine, got into another iron machine, and drove to the center of the city. The meat machines stood on the street and welcomed the leader. But Fer and I didn't *look through* the crowd. Because it was moving.

Fer and I stood near the large stone cave where the leader was supposed to stay. The cave was decorated with red-and-black material. The leader drove up to the cave, entered it, and stood at an open window. The crowds of meat machines shouted for joy. The leader raised his right arm and showed the crowd his palm. At this moment Fer and I *saw* him. He wasn't one of us. We *looked* into his life. It writhed with a furious violence. Like the ruler of the Country of Ice, the leader *adored* his power over millions of meat machines. But even more strongly, he *adored* the possibility of losing power over millions of people. He sought power in order to lose it in the most agonizing way possible. This was the main passion of his life, although he himself *wasn't aware of it.*

The ruler of the Country of Ice wanted power simply in order to rule. Power was the only thing he *adored.*

Over those six days, Fer and I attended all the gatherings of meat machines. At the first gathering the Brotherhood dressed us in the clothes of meat machines who tilled the earth and grew crops. We greeted the leader along with the other earth-tillers. We were the oldest of them. At another gathering the brothers dressed me in the clothes of a fighting meat machine. On my chest they hung metallic articles that meat machines are awarded for knowing how to kill well. I was seated in a wheelchair, Fer stood behind me. At that gathering there were many meat machines who had fought. The leader spoke to them, as did other high-placed meat machines. At the gathering of meat machines who built roads and stone caves, Fer and I were seated in a box with two windows. While the leader greeted the crowd, we *watched* the crowd through these windows. And we *remembered* ours. The next was the gathering of young meat machines. We were brought to that one in two large suitcases. They were set up next to each other. We *looked through* the huge crowd of rapturously shouting young meat machines. Finding *ours* in it, we *remembered* them. The next day the meat machine that produced shadows on white worked with her group in a place where the young meat machines who had come to the gathering lived temporarily. We were in this group. And we easily *recalled* the newly acquired. The brothers found out their earthly names. At the gathering of meat machines that gave birth to meat machines, Fer sat in a wheelchair, and I stood behind her. She greeted the leader along with all the other meat machines and listened to his speech. He said that meat machines should give birth to healthy, strong meat machines. During his speech we *looked through* the crowd. There were also gatherings of smaller groups of meat machines. We attended several of those as well.

On the sixth day the leader gave a short speech. After that the meat machines organized themselves into even rows and began to leave the city. Other meat machines shouted after them. Meat machines that knew how to extract various sounds from objects blew forcefully into them and banged on them loudly. These sounds accompanied the even rows of meat machines that were leaving the city.

The leader flew off aboard a flying machine. His assistants left the city in machines that moved by water and fire. And only the meat machines that lived in the city remained.

The search had ended. It was *very* important.

Seventy-six brothers and sisters merged into our Brotherhood. And we were strengthened in the Country of Order. Brothers Pot, Iya, Men, and Ofka occupied high positions among the ruling meat machines. Brothers Zel, Yapor, Ili, and An had power in the leader's herd of guards. Brother Nieg and sister Vafu had a great deal of money, many stone caves, and expensive objects. Many strong and healthy young people, were now in the Brotherhood, and they were ready to do anything for the Primordial Light.

But this search in the southern city turned out to be *far from simple* for Fer and me.

Our bodies had lost weight, our muscles had grown weak, our arms hung limply. We stopped taking in food and only drank water. Water that fell from the sky. And we breathed. Our hearts beat rarely. The sisters warmed us with their bodies, held us in their arms, placed us in fresh cow's milk. Then they wrapped us in thick material and placed us in the sun. We slept.

This continued for a long time. The Earth turned around the sun. The planets and stars, which we had created, followed their own orbits.

Life did not abandon our bodies. They began to accept food once again and to move.

When Fer and I had grown stronger, the sisters taught us to walk. Holding on to each other, we walked near the stone cave in the mountains. Then we would sit on the grass. We touched each other's bodies. And hearts, which were capable of *noticing* and rescuing thousands of kin among the hearts in the crowds of meat machines.

In the Country of Order a new meeting of meat machines took place. This time they gathered not to listen to the speeches of the leader and prepare themselves to conquer nearby countries. Instead, the meat machines put on a competition of strong, agile bodies. The meat machines with the strongest and most agile bodies from different countries came to the main city of the Country of Order to compete with one another. To show strength and agility, they ran, jumped in length and height, threw pieces of iron, lifted heavy objects, swam, chased leather balloons with their feet, wrestled, fought with iron rods, beat on one another with leather gloves, spat metal at sheets of paper with iron pipes. This took place in view of tens of thousands of simple meat machines, who were not as strong and agile. They followed the doings of the strong meat machines and applauded them joyfully. The strong bodies elicited excitement and envy in them.

The meat machine that knew how to create shadows on white was also at this gathering. With her group of assistants she followed the competition of strong and agile meat machines through iron boxes in which shadows on white added up. Then the whole country was supposed to see these shadows. And the Brotherhood again made use of this. We penetrated the crowd of meat machines that followed the competition and *looked through* it. In the course of twelve days we found eighty-seven brothers and one hundred and one sisters.

Once again Fer and I *replenished* our strength in the mountains.

We were bathed in fresh milk, wrapped in cloth dipped in mountain herbs, and placed in baskets hung between trees for a long time. Rocked by the mountain wind, we slept, *observing* the hearts of the newly acquired. This gave us joy and calmed us.

The brothers started preparations for yet another search. But something *unexpected* happened. The ruler of the Country of Ice began the *energetic* destruction of high-placed meat machines. He did this in order to retain his power. Thousands of strong meat machines, who had been ruling over and directing millions of simple meat machines, were seized and locked up in stone caves. The Brotherhood *was unable* to elude this. We weren't able to *understand* everything in the world of meat machines. We *understood* each meat machine. But the crowd of meat machines was *not entirely* transparent to us. Its drone *suppressed* our hearts. And we didn't *see* everything in a crowd. For this reason we weren't able to warn *ours* in time. And one day brothers Ig, Zchap, and Shoror were seized and placed in a cellar. The meat machines locked them in. They began to beat the brothers and torture their bodies. Confessions were demanded from them for things they had not done. The Brotherhood could not help them. And the meat machines murdered our brothers.

We *saw* the Light leaving their hearts.

Across the entire Country of Ice, experienced and powerful meat machines were seized and locked up. Their bodies were tortured and they were forced to confess to things they had not done. Some of them did not confess. And they died from torture. Others confessed. They were either murdered or taken off to a cold region far from the cities. There they were forced to cut down trees and dig up the earth, and at night they were locked in woodsheds. They were fed very meagerly. The meat machines died quickly in this cold region.

In place of the destroyed meat machines, the ruler of the Country of Ice appointed other meat machines, younger and less experienced. They satisfied the ruler. The Brotherhood *understood* that in a few years these meat machines would suffer the same fate—they would be seized and destroyed. And this would continue as long as the ruler was alive.

We *understood* that in the Country of Ice it was *dangerous* to penetrate the echelons of power. As long as *this* ruler was alive, the risk of losing brothers was too great. As soon as he died and another took his place, the Brotherhood would again strive to infiltrate the leadership of the country. For this reason the Brotherhood made an important decision: the brothers and sisters occupying high positions in the leadership of this country must leave it as soon as possible.

A month later, thirty-eight brothers and eight sisters left the Country of Ice and made their way to the Country of Order. Three brothers perished at the hands of the border guards during the move. A large number of the brothers and sisters who arrived remained in the Country of Order. The rest were sent to two small northern countries. There the Brotherhood acquired a few stone caves. The brothers and sisters arriving from the Country of Ice began living in them. They began to prepare for the possibility of a search in these countries, where many blue-eyed, blond-haired meat machines lived.

Fer and I had finally recovered our strength.

And were ready for a new search.

But a war began between the meat machines. We *knew* about this a long time ago. Its beginning, however, like much in the world of meat machines, happened rapidly and unpredictably. The Brotherhood *expected* a big war between the countries of Order and Ice. But a small war began in a different place. The ruler of the Country of Order commanded his meat machines to attack a small country to the east. The meat machines of the Country of Order quickly occupied half the country. The other half was occupied by meat machines of the Country of Ice. Then the ruler of the Country of Order sent his meat machines into other bordering countries. The meat machines of the Country of Order seethed with desire to kill in the name of Order. For this they used iron machines and iron pipes, which spat pieces of hot metal. These pieces hit the bodies of meat machines and killed them. A country was thought to be strong if it had many meat machines, iron machines, and iron pipes that could spit hot metal. The Country of Order had a lot of them.

The Brotherhood was prepared for the war.

We began the search among those meat machines who were preparing to fight. They gathered in even rows, moved around learning how to work with the iron pipes that spat hot metal. The Brotherhood began to use Fer and me again. Two boxes were prepared for us, resembling the boxes in which meat machines put their clothes when they moved from town to town. Before the search Fer and I would take off our clothes, lie down in these boxes, and press our legs to our chests. The boxes were closed. And our brothers took them to the place where the meat machines clustered. By that time Fer and I had become very thin by the standards of meat machines. We ate very rarely. We drank water only every three days. Our bodies became very light, and our legs and arms thin. A delicate wrinkled skin stretched over our bodies. We could not be shown to meat machines —they would have been scared and put on guard. Even in comparison to very old meat machines we looked unusual. Our faces resembled skulls. The hair on our heads had become completely white.

Therefore we could *look through* meat machines only from boxes. The Brotherhood carried us in boxes all around the Country of Order and the countries it had conquered. Fer and I lived in the boxes. And we grew accustomed to them. We slept in the boxes and spoke to each other with the heart. When the search began we *looked through* the crowds of meat machines. This mostly took place during their meetings, when they stood immobile or sat and listened to some meat machines speaking loudly to them about the war in the name of a beautiful future. Upon finding *ours* in a crowd, we *looked into their* lives, found out their names in the world of meat machines. Through a gap in the box I whispered these names to the brothers. By various means they found the newly acquired. And Ice hammers awoke their hearts.

The Brotherhood grew.

But soon the big war began too. Its beginning was equally unexpected for us. We *were expecting* the Country of Ice to be the first to attack the Country of Order. But the Country of Order took the lead over the Country of Ice. The attack took the meat machines of the Country of Ice and its leaders unawares: they didn't believe that the Country of Order, which had fewer meat machines and iron machines, would attack the large, strong Country of Ice. The unexpectedness helped the attacker. The meat machines of the Country of Order, sitting in their iron machines and armed with powerful pipes, moved quickly to the east through the Country of Ice, destroying meat machines and iron ones. The meat machines of the Country of Ice retreated, dropping their metal-spitting pipes. Many of those retreating ended up being taken prisoner by the attackers. The imprisoned meat machines were kept in fenced-off, guarded places. They were supposed to work without pay for the Country of Order.

The Brotherhood *could feel* that the search should begin among the imprisoned meat machines. The brothers did everything possible to penetrate those places where the imprisoned meat machines of the Country of Ice were held. There were hundreds of thousands of them. Fer and I were placed in our boxes and transported to these locations. We *looked through* the crowds of imprisoned meat machines. And we found *ours*.

In one crowd I *saw* the meat machines who had led me to the Ice. The very same strong, single-minded meat machine who had led us through the impassable forest to the place the Ice fell. Now this was a weak, sick meat machine. Its body was emaciated from lack of food, its leg was swollen. The authorities of the Country of Ice had forced it to take a hot-metal-spitting pipe in hand and go off to fight. It had been captured and was dying, without ever finding out *what* had fallen from the sky to Earth in 1908. It didn't know what the Ice was. And it didn't know that I *was looking* at its life from my box.

Fer and I searched. Not only among the meat machines. As before, we searched among the newly acquired. We searched intensively for those who were capable of replacing us and of seeing with the heart just as we did.

But we had not yet found any like us.

We *worried*, lying in our boxes. We were *the eyes* of the Brotherhood. If these *eyes* were to close, it would be very difficult to search. And the search for the 23,000 would be drawn out for decades. Our hearts moaned from the insurmountable but long-awaited. We *loved* the Brotherhood. We wanted so *badly* to become the Light again. We hated the Earth.

But we were aging and weakening. Life was fading in our bodies. Only our hearts *lived*, as before. They *worked*.

The war spread.

The meat machines of the Country of Order moved east, to the two main cities of the Country of Ice. They laid siege to these cities. The meat machines of the Country of Order penetrated the south and west as well. New countries were drawn into the war. Gradually there were forty-seven of them. Millions of meat machines, sitting in iron machines, pushed their way into enemy countries, spit hot metal from wide pipes, killed other meat machines that spoke different languages, destroying their cities.

Millions of meat machines died in combat, in destroyed cities and villages. Among them our not-yet-found brothers and sisters. Fer and I *could feel* their deaths. And we hurried the Brotherhood. In the mountains we formed a Small Circle, closed our eyes, and *spoke* in the language of the Light. Younger brothers and sisters *learned* from us. Fer and I were *happy* to give them everything we could and knew. Our shriveled hands touched their faces. Our hearts *jolted* their hearts: we must hurry! We *showed them* where to search and for whom. Our mouths opened, we whispered in the language of the Earth the names of newly acquired brothers and sisters. They looked for them. But they weren't able to find and awaken all of the newly acquired *in time*. Not all of them lived to feel the saving blow of the Ice hammer. Many were lost in the chaos of war. Many perished in bombed cities and in battles. Their hearts died without awakening.

The war dragged on for several years. Meat machines of the Country of Ice, gathering strength, manufacturing many iron machines and pipes that spat hot metal, began to crowd out the meat machines of the Country of Order. They resisted and the others began to retreat. Gradually they retreated to their own borders. A large and powerful country, separated by an ocean, entered the war. In the war it was on the side of the Country of Ice. The meat machines living in it called it the Country of Freedom, since it did not have a single, all-powerful ruler as the countries of Ice and Order did. Thousands of meat machines from the Country of Freedom boarded floating and flying machines and arrived at the shores of countries enslaved by the Country of Order. The meat machines of the Country of Freedom began to spit hot metal from their powerful iron pipes at the meat machines of the Country of Order and to drop iron eggs on their cities. The meat machines of the Country of Order resisted furiously, but soon they began to retreat under the onslaught of meat machines that floated over the ocean.

For the Brotherhood it was clear that the war would end in victory for the countries of Ice and Freedom over the Country of Order. But we also *realized* the leader of the Country of Order would pursue his main passion DURING the tormented loss of power. And that in pursuing this passion he would try to destroy as many meat machines as possible. We had to find our new brothers and sisters in time, and save them from the death of those found earlier. The leader of the Country of Order and his assistants had organized several secret places for the destruction of meat machines. They thought that these meat machines were alien to the idea of Order. According to the leader's convictions, these meat machines hindered the establishment of complete order in the country by their very existence. Although they were no different from the rest of the meat machines of the Country of Order either outwardly or inwardly. They did the same thing as all meat machines: they worked, gave birth, battled, built, grew old, and died. They weren't the enemies of the Country of Order, like the meat machines of the countries of Ice and Freedom. The only thing different about them was that their ancestors had not lived in the Country of Order. These meat machines came to the Country of Order from the east. Therefore, the ruler and his assistants thought of them as aliens. The Brotherhood immediately *took an interest* in the places where the meat machines were destroyed. We used these fenced-in and well-guarded places to search for *ours*. Brothers wearing the clothes of the military meat machines were able to fix things so that the blue-eyed and light-haired meat machines weren't destroyed but were kept in a large wood barn. When enough had been put there, they were taken to a secret place where Fer and I *looked through* them. This took place three times. We found forty-eight brothers and twenty-nine sisters. But toward the end of the war the destruction of meat machines began to increase. A great number of them were destroyed in one place located in a country that had been seized by the Country of Order. In this place were many blue-eyed, blond meat machines. And they were selected and set apart for us. They were supposed to be taken off, but the Country of Ice strengthened its attack and the Brotherhood found that it was impossible to export them. They were supposed to be destroyed, like others before them. It was imperative to immediately reach this place and *look through* the prisoners. The brothers, making use of military meat machines, traveled to this place. We were put in our boxes and taken with them. At first we traveled in an iron machine along the usual road, then the brothers transferred to a long iron machine that carried us along an iron track. The place we were heading was fairly large. It was located in a field and fenced off with iron strings with thorns. It was guarded by meat machines with iron pipes that spat out hot metal. This was done so that the meat machines that had been prepared for annihilation wouldn't run off. Our long iron machine drove into this place. And the gates were locked after it immediately. When the brothers took Fer and me out of the machines and placed us on the ground, we instantly sensed a *seeing* heart. One of the two we were looking for to replace us. This heart *was beating* somewhere nearby. We became *joyously* excited in our boxes. The place where we were *whirled* with thousands of lives. Meat machines from several countries had been placed in wooden barns. They awaited annihilation. In this place there were five large ovens. Near each oven there was a stone cave. The meat machines chosen for destruction were brought to this cave. They were told that it was a bathhouse where they would wash themselves. The meat machines took their clothes off. But instead of water, poisonous air flowed down on them, air created by the intelligent meat machines to kill other meat machines. This poisonous air asphyxiated the meat machines. When they were all dead, the stone cave was opened and aired out. Then other meat machines threw the bodies of the asphyxiated meat machines into the ovens. In the ovens the bodies burned and turned into ash. Ash lay in a thick layer everywhere in this place. The majority of the meat machines awaiting annihilation knew that poisonous air, and not a bath, awaited them inside the stone caves. But they submissively waited for death. Although they were far more numerous than the guards, the meat machines didn't try to unite and attack those who destroyed their meat machines. They awaited their fate. Many hoped that they would survive. We heard the swirling *drone* of their lives. And among them we *distinguished ours*. The brothers talked to the head meat machine of this place, who directed the destruction of meat machines. The head meat machine did not want to give us the chosen blue-eyed, light-haired meat machines for some time. The head meat machine had many questions for the brothers who had arrived. The brothers gave the meat machines several stones, very expensive ones in the world of meat machines. And the head meat machine of the place permitted us to take the chosen ones. They were in two large barns. The guards gave them an order and they walked from the barn to our long iron machine. Many of them were extremely emaciated from hunger and moved slowly. The *seeing* but unwoken heart moved along with them. Fer and I *realized* that it was among those who had been picked out. When they all got into the long iron machine, they were locked up. And our long iron machine pulled out of the place for the destruction of meat machines. Fer and I *trembled*: our hearts could feel the presence of many of *ours* among these meat machines. And we felt the presence of a *seeing* heart. We began to hurry the brothers. The iron machine traveled along iron rails for a quarter of a day, and they stopped it on the edge of a forest. There was a large ravine there. The brothers ordered the meat machines to get out of the long machine and gather in the ravine. The meat machines submissively fulfilled the order.

They descended into the ravine and stood there. The brothers ordered them to sit down. The meat machines sat on the ground. The brothers carried Fer and me out of the train, set the boxes on the edge of the ravine, opened them, and took us out of our boxes. We were set down on the edge of the ravine. We began to *look through* the meat machines. They stared at us silently. They were not at all afraid of how we looked because they themselves were very similar. But they didn't understand what we were doing. We began to find *ours*. The brothers immediately took them out of the gully and put them on the long machine. We found the *seeing* heart almost immediately. It was a brother who possessed it. He was put on the machine. We found seventeen brothers and thirty sisters. They were all put on the long machine and locked up. When the search was finished, the brothers picked us up and carried us into the long iron machine. The brothers, who were using the clothing of military meat machines and guarding the meat machines in the ravine, also got on the long iron machine. The machine slowly moved away. The meat machines who remained in the ravine watched us. They didn't understand why we were leaving. They were certain we had gathered them in the gully in order to destroy them with pipes that spit hot metal. But we went on our way with the newly acquired. On board the brothers retrieved the store of Ice hammers and prepared to strike those we had found. Fer and I pointed out the brother with the *seeing* heart. We were longing for him to awake first. He was thin, with a gaunt, young face. He was twenty-three years old. When the brothers undressed him and began to tie him to the wall, he made absolutely no effort to resist. He only prayed. And clutched in his right hand a piece of crumpled gray paper. Fer and I *saw* his life and understood what this piece of paper was. When he was taken to the place of destruction, a certain meat machine had given him this paper. This meat machine knew many prayers, and in its former, peacetime life, meat machines would come to it so that it could tell them how to live correctly. When it gave him the crumpled paper, the meat machine said that this paper—was him. And what he would be depended on him—whether he would be all crumpled up or straightened out. And in the place of destruction he smoothed out the paper on his palm every night. And in the morning he crumpled it up. Tied to the wall, he squeezed the paper in his fist. As soon as the Ice hammer struck his emaciated chest, the crumpled paper fell out of his hand. And his *seeing* heart spoke.

"Ub! Ub! Ub!"

And Fer and I *realized* that Ub was one of our two successors. He could *see* the world just as we did. If he were paired with another *seeing* heart. We would find this heart as well. The war would end, the meat machines would begin to restore the damage and give birth to children. The Brotherhood would strengthen itself even more firmly in this world. Our mortally exhausted bodies would die, our hearts would stop, the Light would leave them. But the hearts of Ub and his partner would beat and search. They would find EVERYONE. And the acquired hearts would form a Large Circle and pronounce the 23 words with their hearts. And the Light would begin to shine. And the Earth would disappear. And Time would stop. And Eternity would arrive.

But we had to continue to *live* in the present.

The brothers unhooked the parts of the iron machine that were empty. Without them the machine was shorter, but the brothers and the newly acquired all fit. The machines traveled faster. We had to get the newly acquired to a secluded place as soon as possible, a place where they could receive treatment. Many of them could not even stand because of constant hunger. But no one died from the blow of the Ice hammer: their woken hearts helped them. Fer and I sat next to Ub. He had lost consciousness and his breathing was shallow. We held his hands. They were almost as thin as ours. We touched his face. We *took care* of his heart.

After the sun went down the iron machine turned north. We had to bring those we found to a prearranged place where the brothers were waiting for them. By morning we had reached this place. It was a place where iron machines that traveled along iron tracks stopped. Many of them stood there. During the trip the newly acquired had been dressed in normal clothes. When our machine began to stop, Fer and I were again put in our boxes. We had a *hard* time letting go of Ub's hand. The machine stopped. But something was moving over it. High above. In the sky.

Fer and I cried out in our boxes: our hearts *could see* the four flying machines above. The flying machines opened their bellies. And dropped huge iron eggs filled with a fierce substance. Iron eggs flew down from above. There were forty of them. We *saw* them over us. And *realized* that one of us would perish. The iron eggs began to fall. As soon as they struck the ground, the fierce substance tore them apart. And with them—everything else around. The shells of the iron eggs flew forcefully in all directions. The iron eggs exploded near our machine. The shells of the iron eggs pierced the walls of our machine and passed through the bodies of eighteen brothers and twelve sisters. The shells of the iron eggs passed through the head of brother Ub. The shells of the iron eggs passed through Fer's torso.

It passed all the way through Fer's body.

Through Fer's heart.

And Fer's heart stopped.

Time

THE EARTH'S Time is many-colored. Each object, each living being, lives in its time. In its color. The time of stones and mountains is dark crimson. The time of sand is purple. The time of the black soil is orange. The time of rivers and lakes is apricot. The time of trees and grasses is gray. The time of insects is brown. The time of fish is emerald. The time of cold-blooded animals is olive. The time of warm-blooded animals is sky-blue. The time of meat machines is violet.

And only we, the brothers of the Light, have no earthly color. We are colorless, as long as the Primordial Light is in our heart. For the Light—is our time. And it is in this time that we live. When our hearts stop and the Light leaves us, we acquire a color. Violet. But not for very long: as soon as the body grows cold, its time becomes dark yellow. The time of corpses of living creatures on Earth is dark yellow.

Sister Khram

SEVEN years have passed since Fer's death.

My hands move slowly. My fingers stir with difficulty. They rarely touch things. Things of the Earth. Ephemeral things. Which rot and fall apart. The brothers and sisters love my hands. Because they *know* them. They place them on their faces. And stop stock-still. And I *take care* of my brothers and sisters.

My eyes no longer see the world of things. The darkness of the Earth's world stands before me. But my heart *sees*. My heart *knows* many things.

The war of the meat machines ended. The countries of Ice and Freedom were victorious. The Country of Order lost. Its meat machines seethed with exhaustion and desperation. They killed and perished. Their leader fulfilled the tormented desire of his life: he heroically lost a great war. Fleeing deep into the Earth, he killed himself with metal from an iron pipe. The victorious meat machines put the leader's assistants on trial. They were hanged by the neck with ropes so that they couldn't breathe. And the leader's assistants suffocated. The victorious meat machines began to rebuild what had been destroyed. In the place of burned cities they erected new ones. The meat machines gave birth to meat machines. Newborn meat machines were growing. And inhabited the new cities.

I *see* this.

New iron machines, even more powerful than the ones that were crushed, are being built. Thousands of new pipes that spit metal are created every day. Millions of iron eggs that destroy cities again await their hour.

I *see* this.

At the end of the war the meat machines created a powerful, fierce substance that had never before existed. When exploded, this substance could destroy entire cities. The most intelligent meat machines created it. This substance was packed into two large iron eggs and dropped on two cities. In exploding, the eggs entirely destroyed both cities. In these cities, 223,418 meat machines perished instantly.

But there were none of *ours* among them. *Ours* perished in other places.

And I *saw* this.

In four years of war the Brotherhood lost forty-nine brothers and seventy sisters. They died in different countries. From hot metal, in crashes of iron machines, in burning cities, from illnesses and wounds.

These losses did not deplete us. The foundation of the Brotherhood had been laid before the war. It was *correctly* laid. And remained firm.

After the war the Brotherhood strengthened in six countries. We stood firmly amid the work of meat machines. We owned stone caves, complex machines, expensive objects. We possessed places that produced things that meat machines could not do without: clothes, footwear, objects for stone caves.

The Brotherhood came to have a lot of money. This helped us to search.

But the main difficulty remained: after the death of Fer, the Brotherhood had been deprived of an All-Seeing Eye. Alone I could not differentiate *ours* in the crowd. My heart couldn't manage it. It *choked* in the drone of the crowd. I could only sense *ours*. I could only guide the search.

My heart needed Fer's heart. Fer and Ub, our hope, perished together. My box was no longer needed by the Brotherhood. It was burned.

I am *alive*.

And as long as *I am alive*, I *know* where to search.

I guide the brothers as well as I can. But all the same, for the moment they are searching blind. Kidnapping blue-eyed, light-haired people, they strike each with the Ice hammer. This is complicated and laborious. But there's no other way. And so we search.

After the war, a great deal of Ice was needed for striking.

The Ice lay in the Country of Ice.

It needed to be brought to countries where the Brotherhood had based itself. Where the search was being carried on. The brothers took on the procurement and delivery of the Ice. They were able to arrange things so that the meat machines began to mine the Ice. Near the place where the Ice lay, settlements of meat machines that had committed offenses in the eyes of the law of the Country of Ice had been established. For this they were usually forced to cut down trees and mine rare metals from the earth. But the brothers were able to persuade the authorities of the Country of Ice that the Ice was crucial to strengthening the might of that country. Intelligent meat machines helped us in this. The Ice began to be extracted and shipped to the main city of this country. From there the Brotherhood secretly transported it to the necessary countries. The brothers sawed it into hundreds of pieces. And manufactured hundreds of Ice hammers.

The search continued.

In the course of another year we found no more than fifty of *ours*. Many hundreds of blue-eyed and light-haired meat machines died under the blows of the Ice hammers. The brothers had to strike everyone kidnapped. This was *extremely* slow in comparison to earlier times when Fer and I found dozens of brothers in one day. When we *parted* the whirling crowd. When we passed through its drone. When we immediately *saw* 199 of *ours* in that ravine. When the brothers, having trouble keeping up with the newly acquired, gave them their own clothes. When Fer and I fell from exhaustion of the *heart*, and bile ran from our mouths and blood from our ears. But we *moaned* from happiness.

Gathering in the mountains in a Large Circle, we *asked* our hearts, we asked the Light: Is there any hope at all of returning to the previous search? Is there any hope of *quickly* obtaining all 23,000? Is there any hope that in a few dozen Earth years all of us will stand in the Grand Circle? That we will pronounce the 23 heart words and once again become the Primordial Light?

There was hope.

Rather—there was half of a hope.

The brothers carried her in to me one winter night.

This happened at the end of the war, six months after Fer died. They had found her among the meat machines taken prisoner and driven from the Country of Ice into the Country of Order. They were intended to be used as workers. The brothers searched in such places. Her heart called her name: "Khram!"

And I *heard*. Although I was in the mountains, far from her. Her name *resounded* in me. I sensed a *seeing* heart. Khram was *half*. The other *half* was Ub, who died along with Fer. If a piece of the iron egg's shell had not passed through Ub's head, he and Khram would have become a pair of *seers*. They would have become the Eye of the Brotherhood. The same kind of Eye that Fer and I had been. And the search would have continued rapidly. And we would have found EVERYONE.

But the Earth took Fer and Ub away from us.

And the Light brought us Khram as a gift.

They carried her into our stone cave. Khram was still weak. Her heart had just awoken. Khram looked at us only with her eyes. But I could *see* her with my heart. I knew just *who* it was they were bringing into the cave. Many in the cave knew this. Khram was placed on a large stone in the middle of the cave. And all of us, brothers and sisters, *gently* welcomed her heart. *Her seeing* heart. So she would understand *who* she was in the Brotherhood.

Then she went through the *heart crying*.

Her heart was ready for everything. The Wisdom and the Power of the Light sang in it.

And I *was at rest*. For the first time since the deaths of Fer and Ub.

If the Light had sent us Khram, it meant that it would send us yet another *seeing* heart. It would come. We simply had to wait. To search and prepare Khram for the Last Search.

She settled in with us in the mountains. I *protected* her young heart. I spoke with it carefully. I gently *touched* it. In a Lesser Circle we *supported* Khram. Her heart strengthened each day. And for ninety-four nights in the Lesser Circle we *spoke* the 23 words. She stood with us on the snow. With twenty-two who were wise of heart. We *spoke* the words. And the words of the Light *shone* in our hearts. And Khram's heart *shone* along with ours. It was powerful. It could accomplish many things.

We *supported* Khram.

She was walking in Fer's footsteps. I made her path simpler. Because I *knew* Fer, I *helped* Khram.

The time came when we stood in a Great Circle. On a hill one moonlit night, 230 of us, brothers and sisters, stood holding hands. And Khram stood with us. The world of the Earth slept. But our hearts were not sleeping. Much was *revealed* to the Great Circle. We *understood* that which had been hidden. What could not be revealed to each of us separately.

We *understood* which direction to take. Where the Brotherhood should focus its labors.

An important day arrived for Khram.

It was July 6, 1950, in the time of meat machines. In a little northern country where the Brotherhood had based itself. On that day Khram awoke, like the other brothers and sisters, with the rising of the sun. She spoke to all of us with her heart. And that was my last heart talk with her. The brothers carried me to her. With my weak hands I held her young, strong hands. The Brotherhood of the Light surrounded us.

I *began to speak*.

"Khram, today you will be leaving our Brotherhood. You have mastered the language of the heart. You have learned all 23 heart words. You are ready for great deeds in the name of the Light. You will travel east, to the country where the Ice lies. And you will search for brothers and sisters. You will awaken their hearts. And take them away from meat machines. In the Country of Ice only three of *ours* remain: sister Yus, and brothers Kha and Adr. They are awaiting our help. And yours."

I did not *speak* with her about the most important thing. She knew it without me. She *knew* what had been revealed to everyone during the Great Circle: she would have to find her other half. The one who would help her to complete the search.

The half for which all of us were waiting. Standing in the Great Circle, we *knew* that the Ice must draw out this half. But we didn't know in what part of the huge Country of Ice to search for a second *seeing* heart.

Khram *understood* this.

With my weakening fingers I squeezed her hands.

She gently squeezed mine.

Our hearts *flared*, in saying goodbye. To meet again. Forever. In the Greatest and Last Circle. In order to become Light.

Khram's fingers let go. And left my trembling hands. Khram began to move away from me. She was overcoming space. She was prevailing over time. She was speeding toward the east. To the land where the Ice lay. Where brothers were waiting for her. Where the second *seeing* heart was waiting to be found.

I *saw Khram off.*

My heart sank.

My heart grew weak.

My heart stopped.

My heart has done its work.

And the Light leaves it.

ICE

PART I

Brother Ural

23:42, Moscow Suburbs, Mytishchi, 4 Silikatnaya Street, building 2

THE NEW warehouse of Mosregionteletrust.

A dark blue Lincoln Navigator drove into the building. Stopped. The headlights illuminated: a concrete floor, brick walls, boxes of transformers, reels of underground cable, a diesel compressor, sacks of cement, a barrel of tar, broken wheelbarrows, three milk cartons, a scrap heap, cigarette butts, a dead rat, and two piles of dried excrement.

Gorbovets leaned on the gates. Pulled. The steel sections aligned. Clanged. He slid the bolt shut. Spat. Walked to the car.

Uranov and Rutman climbed out of the car. Opened the trunk. Two men in handcuffs lay on the floor of the SUV, mouths taped.

Gorbovets came over.

"The light turns on somewhere here." Uranov caught the string.

"Can't you see?" Rutman pulled on a pair of gloves.

"Not too well." Uranov squinted.

"The main thing is we hear it!" Gorbovets smiled.

"The acoustics are good here." Tired, Uranov wiped his face. "Come on."

They dragged the captives out of the car. Moved them over to two steel columns. Tied them tight with rope. Took up positions around them. Silently stared at the bound men.

Five people were visible in the headlights. All of them were blond and had blue eyes.

Uranov: 30 years old, tall, narrow shoulders, a thin intelligent face, a beige raincoat.

Rutman: 21, medium height, skinny, flat-chested, lithe, a pale unremarkable face, a dark blue jacket, black leather pants.

Gorbovets: 54, bearded, not very tall, stocky, sinewy peasant hands, barrel-chested, crude features, a dark yellow sheepskin coat.

The bound captives:

1st: around 50, stout, ruddy, well-groomed, wearing an expensive suit;

2nd: young, puny, hook-nosed and pimply, black jeans and a leather jacket.

Their mouths were taped with semitransparent packing tape.

"Let's start with this one." Uranov nodded toward the heavy guy.

Rutman took an oblong metal case out of the car. She placed it on the cement floor in front of Uranov and opened the metal locks. The case turned out to be a mini refrigerator.

Ice hammers, two of them, placed head to tail, lay inside: long, rough wooden shafts, attached to cylindrical ice heads with strips of rawhide. Frost covered the shafts.

Uranov put on gloves. He picked up a hammer. He stepped toward one of the bound men. Gorbovets unbuttoned the fat man's jacket. He removed his tie and yanked his shirt. The buttons popped and scattered, exposing a plump white chest with small nipples and a gold cross on a chain. Gorbovets's coarse fingers grabbed the cross and jerked. The fat man gave a low moan. He began to make signs with his eyes. Rolled his head back and forth.

"Respond!" Uranov cried aloud.

He swung the hammer back and hit him in the middle of the chest. The fat man moaned louder.

The three stood still and listened.

"Respond!" Uranov commanded again after a pause. And again he hit him hard.

The fat man's insides growled. The three froze and listened.

"Respond!" Uranov hit him again, harder.

The man moaned and wailed inside. His body shook. Three round bruises appeared on his chest.

"Lemme whack the fucker." Gorbovets took the hammer. He spit on his hands. Swung it back.

"Respond!" The hammer crashed into the chest with a juicy thud. Splinters of ice scattered.

And again the three stood stock-still. They listened. The fat man moaned and shuddered. His face grew pale. His chest began to sweat and turned purple.

"Orsa? Orus?" Rutman touched her lips uncertainly.

"That's his guts grumbling." Gorbovets shook his head.

"Lower, lower down." Uranov nodded in agreement. "He's empty."

"Speak!" Gorbovets roared and hit him. The man's body jerked. It hung feebly from the ropes.

The three moved very close. Turned their ears to the purple chest. Listened carefully.

"Guts growlin'..." Gorbovets exhaled sadly. He swung back.

"Reee-spooond! Reee-spond! Reee-spoond!"

Bang. Bang. Chips of ice flew out from the hammer. Bones cracked. Blood began dripping from the fat man's nose.

"He's empty." Uranov straightened up.

"Empty..." Rutman bit her lip.

"Empty, the motherfucker..." Gorbovets leaned on the hammer. He was out of breath. "Oof...goddamn...how many of you empty ding-dongs they gone and multiplied?"

"It's just a bad streak," Rutman sighed.

Gorbovets slammed the hammer on the floor with all his strength. The ice head shattered, shards of ice flying everywhere. The torn straps of rawhide fluttered. Gorbovets threw the handle into the refrigerator. He picked up the other hammer and passed it to Uranov.

Uranov wiped the frost from the handle, staring gloomily at the fat man's breathless body. He turned a heavy gaze to the young man. The two pairs of blue eyes met. The captive thrashed and began to wail.

"Don't be scared, kid." Gorbovets wiped drops of blood off his cheeks. He held one nostril, leaned over, and blew his nose on the floor. He wiped his hand on his sheepskin coat. "Sheesh, Iray, it's the thicksteenth thumper we've bashed, and it's another beanbag! What kinda friggin' luck is this? It's a regular evacuation, I tell you. The thicksteenth! Another empty dingaling."

"Could be the hundred and sixteenth." Uranov unbuttoned the jacket of the second captive.

The young man whined. His rickety knees knocked together.

Rutman began to help Uranov. They tore open the black T-shirt with the red inscription WWW.FUCK.RU. Shivering under the shirt was a white bony chest covered with spotty freckles.

Uranov thought a moment. He handed the hammer to Gorbovets. "Rom, you do it. I haven't had any luck for a while."

"Okeydoke..." Gorbovets spat on his palms. Pulled himself up. Swung back.

"Re-SPOND!"

The icy cylinder hit the frail chest with a whistle. The captive's body jerked from the blow. The three listened closely. The young man's thin nostrils flared. Sobs broke from them.

Gorbovets sadly shook his shaggy head. He drew the hammer back slowly.

"Respond!"

The whistle of air splitting. A sonorous blow. A spray of ice splinters. Weakening moans.

"Something...something..." Rutman listened closely to the black-and-blue chest.

"Just the upper part, the upper..." Uranov shook his head.

"It's thumbsing...I don't know...maybe it's in the throat?" Gorbovets scratched his reddish beard.

"Rom, again, but more precise," Uranov ordered.

"How mush more precise can ya get..." Gorbovets swung back. "Ree-spond!"

The chest cracked. Ice scattered on the ground. A bit of blood spattered from the broken skin. The young man hung limp from the ropes. His blue eyes rolled back. The black eyelashes fluttered.

The three listened. A weak staccato grumble sounded in the boy's chest.

"It's there!" Uranov twitched.

"Lord almighty, bless the Light!" Gorbovets tossed the hammer aside.

"I was sure of it!" Rutman laughed joyfully. She blew on her fingers.

The three pressed against the young man's chest.

"Speak with your heart! Speak with your heart! Speak with your heart!" Uranov spoke in a loud voice.

"Speak, speak, speak, come on little man!" Gorbovets mumbled.

"Speak with your heart, with your heart; speak, with the heart..." Rutman whispered joyfully.

A strange, faint sound came and went from the bloody, bruised chest.

"Speak your name! Speak your name! Speak your name!" Uranov repeated.

"Your name, little fella, tell us your name, your name!" Gorbovets stroked the young man's fair hair.

"Your name, say your name, speak your name, name, name..." Rutman whispered to the pale pink nipple.

They froze, transfixed. They listened closely.

"Ural," said Uranov.

"Ur...Hurrah, Ural!" Gorbovets pulled on his beard.

"Urrraaaal...Uraaaaal..." Rutman's eyelids closed in joy.

They began fussing about happily.

"Quick, quick!" Uranov pulled out a coarse knife with a wooden handle.

They cut the ropes. Tore the bandage from his mouth. Placed the young man on the cement floor. Rutman dragged a first aid kit over. He found the smelling salts and brought them over. Uranov placed a wet towel on the battered chest. Gorbovets supported the young man's back. He shook him carefully.

"Come on now, little guy, come on now, little one..."

The boy's whole puny body jerked. His thick-soled boots thudded against the floor. He opened his eyes. Inhaled with difficulty. He passed gas and whimpered.

"Now—there, there. Go ahead and fart, little one, go ahead and fart..." In a single swoop, Gorbovets lifted him off the floor. He carried him to the car on his sturdy, crooked legs.

Uranov picked up the hammer and knocked the ice onto the floor. He tossed the shaft in the mini refrigerator, closed the top, and picked it up.

They settled the young man on the backseat. Gorbovets and Rutman sat on either side, propping him up. Uranov opened the gates. He drove out into the dank darkness. He climbed out and closed the gates, got back in behind the wheel, and steered the car along the narrow, uneven road.

The headlights illuminated the roadside and remaining patches of dirty snow. The glowing clock face showed 00.20.

"Your name—is Yury?" Uranov glanced at the young man in the rearview mirror.

"Yu...ry...Lapin," he said with difficulty.

"Remember, your true name—is Ural. Your heart spoke that name. Up until today you were not living, just existing. Now you are going to live. You will have everything you want. And you will have a great purpose in life. How old are you?"

"Twenty..."

"You've been sleeping for twenty years. Now you've awoken. We, your brothers, awakened your heart. I'm Iray."

"I'm Rom." Gorbovets stroked the boy's cheek.

"And I'm Okam." Rutman winked at him. She pushed back a lock of hair from Lapin's sweaty brow.

"We'll take you to a clinic where they'll help you and where you can rest."

The young man cast an exhausted glance at Rutman. Then at Gorbovets and his beard.

"But...I...but when will I...when...I have to—"

"Don't ask any questions," Uranov interrupted. "You're in shock. And you have to get used to it."

"You're still just a weakling." Gorbovets patted his head. "Get yourself some shut-eye, and then we'll have a talk."

"Then you'll find out everything. Does it hurt?" Rutman carefully placed the wet towel on the round bruises.

"It…hurts…" The young man sniffled. He closed his eyes.

"Finally that towel came in handy. I keep wetting it and wetting it before every hit. Then—it turns out that it's just one more empty. So you have to go and wring the water out!" Rutman laughed. She embraced Lapin carefully. "Listen…it's so cool that you're one of us. I'm so glad…"

The SUV banged over the potholes. The young man shrieked.

"Slower…don't gun it…" Gorbovets fiddled nervously with his beard.

"Is it very painful, Ural?" Rutman spoke the new name with pleasure.

"Very…Oooowww!" The young man groaned and cried out.

"That's all, that's it. No more bumps from here on," said Uranov. He drove on, carefully.

The car emerged onto Yaroslav Highway. It turned and took off toward Moscow.

"You're a student," said Rutman affirmatively. "Moscow University, the journalism school."

The young man moaned in response.

"I studied too. In the economics department of the Pedagogical Institute."

"Whoa, man alive!" Gorbovets pulled on his nose. "Messed yourself didja! Got scared, little one!"

A slight smell of excrement came from Lapin.

"That's completely normal." Uranov squinted at the road.

"When they hit me, I squeezed out some brown cheese, too." Rutman looked straight at the young man's thin face. "And I let go a stream of hot water, quietly. It was great. But you…" She touched him between the legs. "You're dry in front. Are you Armenian?"

The boy shook his head.

"But there is something from the Caucasus?" She ran her finger down Lapin's hook nose. "Maybe from the Baltics—no? You have a beautiful nose."

"Don't come on to him, you horny she-goat, he don't care about his nose right now," Gorbovets grumbled.

"Okam, call the clinic," Uranov ordered.

Rutman took out a cell phone and dialed.

"It's us. We have a brother. Twenty. Yes. Yes. How long? Well, in about…"

"Twenty-five minutes," Uranov said.

"We'll be there in half an hour. Yes."

She put the cell phone away.

Lapin leaned his head against her shoulder. Closed his eyes. He sank into oblivion.

They drove up to the clinic: **7 Novoluzhnetsky Prospect.**

They stopped at the guard booth. Uranov showed his pass, then drove up to a three-story building. Behind the glass doors stood two hefty orderlies in blue robes…

Uranov opened the car door. The assistants ran over with a gurney. They lifted Lapin out of the car. He woke up and moaned feebly. They placed him on the stretcher. Strapped him down. Rolled him inside the clinic door.

Rutman and Gorbovets remained by the car. Uranov followed the stretcher.

A doctor was waiting for them at reception: a plump, stooped man with thick graying hair, gold-rimmed glasses, a meticulously trimmed beard, and a blue robe.

He stood next to the wall, smoking. He held an ashtray.

The orderlies rolled the bed up to him.

"The usual?" asked the doctor.

"Yes," said Uranov, looking down at his own beard.

"Complications?"

"It appears the chest bone cracked."

"How long ago?" The doctor took the towel off Lapin's chest.

"About… forty minutes ago."

A female assistant ran in: medium height, chestnut hair, a serious, high-cheekboned face.

"Excuse me, Semyon Ilich."

"Okay, then…" The doctor stubbed out his butt and set the ashtray on the windowsill. He leaned over Lapin, touching the swollen, bright purple chest. "Right, first of all: our cocktail here is glowing in the fog. Take care of him. Then do an X-ray. And then bring him to me."

He turned sharply and headed for the doors.

"Should I stay?" asked Uranov.

"No need to. Come back in the morning." The doctor left.

The assistant tore open a hypodermic. She attached the needle, broke two ampoules, and drew the liquid into the hypodermic.

Uranov ran his hand over Lapin's cheek. Lapin opened his eyes. He raised his head, looked around, and coughed. Then he jerked away from the stretcher.

The orderlies fell on him.

"Nnnnooo! Nnnnno! Nnnooo!" he cried hoarsely.

They held him down to the bed. Began to undress him. The odor of fresh excrement rose from him. Uranov exhaled.

Lapin wheezed and cried.

One orderly wound a tourniquet around Lapin's thin forearm. The assistant leaned over it with the needle.

"There's no need to suffer ..."

"I want to call hooooome ..." Lapin whined.

"You're already home, brother," said Uranov, smiling.

The needle entered the vein.

Mair

LAPIN awoke at three in the afternoon. He lay in a small twin bed. The ceiling was white. The walls were white. There were semitransparent white curtains on the window. On a white bedside table with bent legs was a vase with a spray of white lilies and a white fan, turned off.

Next to the window, sitting on a white chair, was **a nurse**: 24 years old, slim, fair hair cut short, blue eyes, large glasses with silver frames, a short white jacket, pretty legs.

The nurse was reading the magazine *OM*.

Lapin squinted to look at his chest. It was bound in a white elastic bandage. Smooth. You could see a gauze bandage under it.

Lapin took his hand out from under the blanket. He touched the bandage.

The nurse noticed. She placed the magazine on the windowsill, stood up, and walked over to him.

"Good day, Ural."

She was tall. Her blue eyes looked at him attentively through her glasses. Her full lips smiled.

"I'm Kharo," she said.

"What?" Lapin unstuck his cracked lips.

"I'm Kharo." She sat down carefully on the edge of the bed. "How do you feel? Are you dizzy?"

Lapin looked at her hair. He remembered everything.

"I'm, I'm still here?" he asked in a hoarse voice.

"You're in the clinic." She took his hand. She pressed her warm, soft finger to his wrist and took his pulse.

Lapin breathed in cautiously. Breathed out. There was a dull, weak ache in his chest, but no pain. He swallowed some saliva. Frowned. His throat burned. It hurt to swallow.

"Do you want something to drink?"

"Yes, something."

"Juice, water?"

"Orange . . . juice . . . Is there orange juice?"

"Of course."

She reached over Lapin. Her snow-white robe rustled and Lapin smelled her perfume. He looked at the open collar of the robe. A smooth, pretty neck. A birthmark just above the collarbone. A thin gold chain.

He turned his eyes to the right. There was a narrow table with drinks. She filled a glass with yellow juice, wrapped it in a napkin, and offered it to Lapin.

He turned over.

With her left hand the nurse helped him to sit up. His head touched the white headboard. He took the glass from her hands and drank.

"You aren't cold, are you?" She smiled. She looked straight at him.

"No. What time is it?"

"Three," the nurse said, glancing at her thin watch.

"I have to call home."

"Of course."

She took a cell phone out of her pocket.

"Drink up. Then you can call."

Lapin drank half a cup greedily. He exhaled, licked his lips.

"You're thirsty now."

"That's for sure. And you …" he said, using the formal form.

"Use the familiar with me."

"And you … you've been here a long time?"

"In what sense?"

"Well, I mean, working?"

"This is my second year."

"Who are you?"

"Me?" She smiled even more broadly. "I'm a nurse."

"And what is this … a hospital or something?"

"A rehabilitation center."

"Who's it for?" He looked at her birthmark.

"For us."

"Who's … us?"

"The awakened people."

Lapin grew silent. He finished off the juice.

"Some more?"

"A little." He held out the glass.

She filled it up, and he drank half.

"I don't want any more."

She took away the glass and put it on the little table. Lapin nodded at the cell phone.

"May I?"

"Of course." She handed it to him. "Go on and talk. I'll go out."

She stood and left immediately.

Lapin dialed his parents' number, coughed. His father picked up.

"Yes."

"Pop, it's me."

"Where'd you disappear to?"

"Well, um …" He touched the bandage on his chest. "You see …"

"What do I see? Did something happen?"

"Well…um…"

"In trouble again? In the slammer?"

"No, not that…"

"Where are you?"

"Well, me and Golovastik went to a concert yesterday. At Gor-bushka. Well, um, and I ended up staying at his place."

"And you couldn't call?"

"Um, well, we…got busy…his place is a mess…"

"Drinking again?"

"No, no, we just had a little beer."

"Dumbbells. We're about to have dinner. Are you coming?"

"I…well, we want to go for a walk."

"Where?"

"In the park…near him. He wants to take the dog out."

"Your choice. We've got chicken with garlic. We'll eat it all up."

"I'll try."

"Don't get stuck there."

"I won't…"

Lapin turned the cell off. He touched his neck and threw back the blanket. He was naked.

"Shii…where's my underwear?" He touched his penis.

He felt a sharp pain in his chest and gritted his teeth. Pressed his hand against the bandage.

"Goddamn…"

The nurse opened the door cautiously.

"Are you finished?"

"Yes…" He hurriedly pulled the covers back over him.

She entered.

"Where's my clothes?" Lapin frowned. He rubbed the splint.

"Does it hurt?" She sat down on the edge of the bed again.

"I got a twinge…"

"You have a small fracture in your chest bone. You'll have to keep it strapped. You may get a sharp pain from lifting or turning. Until it heals. That's normal. They don't put casts on the chest."

"Why not?" He sniffed.

"Because people need to breathe," she smiled.

"Where're my clothes?" he asked again.

"Are you cold?"

"No...it's just, I...I don't like to sleep naked."

"Really?" She looked at him sincerely. "I'm the opposite. I can't go to sleep if I have something on. Even a chain."

"A chain?"

"Uh-huh. See..." She stuck her hand behind the lapel of her robe and pulled out a chain with a tiny gold comet. "I always take it off at night."

"Interesting." Lapin grinned. "You're so sensitive."

"People should sleep naked."

"Why?"

"Because they're born naked and die naked."

"But they don't end up naked. They're in a suit. And a coffin."

She put the chain back.

"People don't put the suit on themselves. And they don't lie down in the coffin on their own."

Lapin said nothing. He looked to the side.

"Do you want to eat?"

"I want...I have to...I need my clothes—and to go to the bathroom."

"Urinate?"

"Yeah..."

"There's no problem with that." She leaned over. Pulled a white plastic bedpan out from under the bed.

"No way...I don't..." Lapin gave a crooked smile.

"Relax." She moved the bedpan under the covers with a quick, professional gesture.

The cool plastic touched Lapin's ribs. Her hand took his penis, directed it into the opening.

"Listen..." He pulled his knees up. "I'm not paralyzed or anything..."

Her free hand stopped his knees. Pressed. Pushed them down on the bed.

"There's no problem here," she said softly and emphatically.

Lapin laughed, embarrassed. He looked at the copy of *OM*, then at the lily in the vase.

Half a minute passed.

"Ural? Do you want to go or not?" she asked with soft reproach.

Lapin's face grew serious. He blushed slightly. His penis jerked. Urine silently flowed into the bedpan. The nurse held his penis in place.

"There you go. So simple. You've never urinated into a bedpan?"

Lapin shook his head. The urine flowed.

The nurse reached over with her free hand. Took a napkin from the drinks table.

Lapin bit his lip and inhaled carefully.

The stream stopped. The nurse wrapped his penis in the napkin. She carefully removed the warm bedpan from under the blanket, placed it under the bed, and wiped off his penis.

"Were you born with blue eyes?" she asked.

"Yes." He looked up at her from under his brow.

"Well, I was born with gray eyes. And till the age of six I was gray-eyed. Then my father took me to his factory. To show me some marvelous machine that assembled clocks. And when I saw it, I froze in delight. The way it worked was so amazing! I don't know how long I stood there: an hour, two . . . I came home, fell sound asleep. And the next morning my eyes had turned blue."

Lapin's penis began to tense.

"Black eyelashes. And eyebrows," she said, examining him. "You probably like gentle things."

"Gentle?"

"Gentle, tender things. Do you?"

"I . . . well . . ." He swallowed.

"Have you had women?"

He laughed nervously. "Girls. Have you had women?"

"No. I've only had men," she answered calmly, letting go of his penis. "Before. Before I woke up."

"Before?"

"Yes. Before. Now I don't need men. I need brothers."

"What does that mean?" He pulled his knees up, hiding his hardening penis.

"Sex—is an illness. Fatal. And all humankind is infected with it." She put the napkin in the pocket of her robe.

"Really? That's interesting..." Lapin grinned. "And what about—gentle things? You were just talking about it?"

"You know, Ural, there's tenderness of the body. But that is nothing compared to tenderness of the heart. The awakened heart. And you are going to feel this now."

The door opened.

A woman came in dressed in a white terry-cloth robe: 38 years old, medium height, plump, light brown hair, blue eyes, her face round, not pretty, smiling, calm.

Lapin pressed his shaking knees to his chest. Reached out for the blanket. But the blanket was down at his feet.

The nurse stood up. Walked over to the woman. They kissed each other on the cheek solicitously.

"I see that you've already met." The woman who had entered looked at Lapin with a smile. "Now it's my turn."

The nurse left. She pulled the door closed silently after her.

The woman looked at Lapin.

"Hello, Ural," she said.

"Hello..." He glanced aside.

"I'm Mair."

"Mayor? Of what?"

"Of nothing." She smiled. "Mair is my name."

She threw off her robe. Naked, she walked over to Lapin and stretched out her plump hand.

"Stand up, please."

"Why?" Lapin looked up at her large, pendulous breasts.

"I beg of you. Don't be embarrassed by me."

"Hey, I could care less. Only...give me my clothes back."

Lapin stood up. He placed his hands on his rickety hips.

She stepped toward him. Carefully embraced him and pressed her chest to his.

Lapin laughed nervously, turning his face away.

"Hey lady, I'm not gonna screw you."

"And I'm not proposing you do," she said. She stood motionless.

Lapin let out a bored sigh.

"Are you gonna give me my clothes back, huh?"

And suddenly he shuddered. His entire body twitched. He stood stock-still.

They were both transfixed. They stood, embracing. Their eyes were closed.

They stood motionless for forty-two minutes.

Mair shuddered and sobbed. She released her hands. Lapin fell powerlessly out of her embrace onto the floor. He jerked convulsively. Clenched and unclenched his teeth. With a sob he greedily gulped the air. He sat up and opened his eyes. He stared vacantly at the leg of the bed. His cheeks were aflame.

Mair picked up her robe and put it on. She placed her small plump palm on Lapin's head.

"Ural."

She turned and left the room.

The nurse entered holding Lapin's clothes. She squatted down next to Lapin.

"How are you?"

"Okay." He ran a trembling hand down his face. "I really want . . . um . . . to . . . I want . . ."

"Does your chest hurt?"

"A little . . . kind of . . . I . . . um . . ."

"Get dressed." The nurse stroked his shoulder.

Lapin reached to pull his jeans over. A pair of underwear was underneath. New. Not his.

He felt them.

"Ma'am . . . I mean, did you . . ."

"What?" asked the nurse. "Should I turn around?"

"Did you . . . what?" He sniffed.

He looked at her, as though seeing her for the first time. His fingers trembled slightly.

The nurse stood up and moved away to the window. She drew back the curtain. She gazed at the bare branches outside.

Lapin stood up with some difficulty. Stumbling and stepping back, he put on the underwear. Then the jeans. He took the black T-shirt. It was new, too. Instead of WWW.FUCK.RU, this one said BASIC. Also in red.

"But why…this?" His fingers scrunched the new T-shirt.

The nurse looked around.

"Put it on. It's all yours."

He looked at the T-shirt. Then he put it on. He went for the jacket. His things were lying on it: keys, student ID, wallet. The wallet was unusually thick.

Lapin picked it up. He opened it. It was stuffed with money: five-hundred-ruble notes, dollars, too.

"But this…isn't mine," he said, looking at the wallet.

"It's yours." The nurse turned around and approached him.

"I had…seventy rubles. Seventy-five."

"This is your money."

"It's someone else's…" He looked at the wallet. Touched his chest. She took him by the shoulders.

"Listen, Ural. You don't really understand what happened to you yet. I'd say—you don't understand at all. Last night you woke up. But you still haven't shaken off the sleep. Your life will change direction completely now. We will help you."

"Who is—we?"

"People. Who've awoken."

"And…what?"

"Nothing."

"And what will happen to me?"

"Everything that happens to people who've awoken."

Lapin looked at her pretty face with glassy eyes.

"What is—everything?"

"Ural"—her fingers squeezed his bony shoulders—"be patient. You've only just gotten out of bed. A bed you've been sleeping in for twenty years. You haven't even taken the first step. So put the wallet in your pocket and follow me."

She opened the door. Went out into the hallway.

Lapin put on his jacket and stuck the wallet in the inside pocket.

He put the keys and his student card in the side pockets. He went out into the hallway.

The nurse walked briskly. He followed her cautiously. He touched the bandage on his chest.

Near reception, the doctor and Mair were waiting for them. Mair wore a dark purple coat with large buttons. She stood with her hands in her pockets. She looked at Lapin just as warmly and affably as earlier. She smiled.

"So then, young man, we have a little crack in the breastbone," began the doctor.

"I've already been told," muttered Lapin, his eyes glued to Mair.

"Repetition is the mother of instruction," the doctor continued impassively. "Don't take the bandage off for ten days. No lifting cinder blocks. No world records, please. No making love to giants. And take this," he said, holding out two packets of medicine. "Two times a day. And if it hurts—a painkiller. Or seven glasses of vodka. Do I make myself clear?"

"What?" Lapin turned toward the doctor with a heavy gaze.

"It's a joke. Take this," said the doctor, handing over the two packets.

Lapin stared at him. He took the packets and put them into different pockets.

"The young man doesn't understand jokes," the doctor explained to the women with a smile.

"He understands everything perfectly well. Thank you." Mair pressed her cheek against the doctor's cheek.

"Be happy, Ural," said the nurse in a loud voice.

Lapin turned to her abruptly. He stared at her: pretty, slim, a warm expression. Large glasses. Large lips.

Mair nodded to them. She stepped out into the glass lobby and onto the street. It was overcast. Chilly. Wet bare trees. Leftover snow. Gray grass.

Lapin followed her out. He took careful steps.

Mair walked over to a large dark blue Mercedes. She opened the back door and turned to Lapin. "Take a seat, Ural."

Lapin stepped in. He sat on the springy seat. Blue leather. Soft music. The pleasant aroma of sandalwood. The blond nape of the driver's neck.

Mair sat in the front.

"Let me introduce you, Frop. This is Ural."

The driver turned: 52 years old, a round simple face, small cloudy blue eyes, fleshy hands, and a dark blue suit that matched the car.

"Frop." He smiled at Lapin.

"Yuri . . . I mean . . . Ural." Lapin grinned awkwardly. Suddenly he laughed.

The driver turned back. He took the wheel and the car set off smoothly. They drove out onto Luzhnetsky Embankment.

Lapin couldn't stop laughing. He touched his chest with his hand.

"Where do you live?" Mair spoke.

"In Medvedkovo," Lapin managed to say as he licked his lips.

"In Medvedkovo? We'll take you home. What street?"

"Near the Metro . . . around there. I'll show you. . . . Near the Metro. I'll get out there."

"Fine. But before that we'll drop in somewhere. There you'll meet three brothers. People your age. They will just say a few words to you. And they'll help you. You need help now."

"And . . . where is it?"

"In the center. On Tsvetnoi Boulevard. It won't take more than half an hour at the most. Then we'll drive you home."

Lapin looked out the window.

"The most important thing for you now—is to try not to be surprised by anything," Mair spoke up. "Don't be scared. We aren't a totalitarian sect. We're simply free people."

"Free?" Lapin muttered.

"Free."

"Why?"

"Because we've awoken. And those who have awoken—are free."

Lapin looked at her ear.

"It hurt me."

"Yesterday?"

"Yes."

"That's natural."

"Why?"

Mair turned to him.

"Because you were born anew. And birth—is always painful. For the woman giving birth, and for the newborn. When your mother pushed you out of her uterus, bloody and blue, don't you think it was painful for you? What did you do then? You started crying."

Lapin looked into her blue eyes, which seemed to squint because of slightly puffy eyelids. Around the edges of the pupil a haze of yellow-green was barely observable.

"So that means I . . . that yesterday I was born again?"

"Yes. We say: you awoke."

Lapin looked at her carefully cut dark blond hair. The ends trembled slightly. In time with the movement of the car.

"I awoke."

"Yes."

"And . . . who is sleeping?"

"Ninety-nine percent of humanity."

"Why?"

"It's hard to explain in a few words."

"And who . . . isn't sleeping?"

"You, me, Frop, Kharo. The brothers who wakened you yesterday."

They turned onto the Garden Ring Road. Ahead of them was a huge traffic jam.

"There you go," sighed the driver. "Soon the only way to get around the center will be on foot . . ."

A dirty, Russian-made car, a Zero Nine hatchback, was driving next to the Mercedes. There was a fat guy at the wheel, eating a cheeseburger. The paper wrapper grazed his flat nose.

"What about the one . . . who stayed there?" Lapin asked.

"Where?"

"I mean . . . yesterday . . . what about him? Did he wake up too?"

"No. He died."

"Why?"

"Because he was empty. Like a nutshell."

"What . . . but he wasn't a human being?"

"He was a human being. But empty. Sleeping."

"And I'm.... not empty?"

"You are not empty." Mair pulled a pack of gum out of her purse, opened it, and took a piece. She offered some to the driver. He shook his head. She offered it to Lapin.

He took the gum automatically. Unwrapped it. He looked at the pink rectangle. He touched it to his lower lip.

"I ... um ..."

"What is it, Ural?"

"I ... I'll go now."

"As you like." Mair nodded to the driver.

The Mercedes braked. Lapin yawned nervously. He touched the smooth, cool handle of the lock. He pulled on it. He opened the door with difficulty and climbed out. He walked between the cars.

The driver and Mair watched him for a long time.

"Why do they all run away at first?" asked the driver. "I did, too."

"It's a normal reaction," said Mair, chewing again. "I thought he'd try earlier."

"A patient one ... Where to now?"

"To Zharo."

"At the office?"

"Yes." She glanced back at the backseat.

On the smooth dark blue leather lay the dull pink rectangle of gum, folded in half.

Swiss Cheese

LAPIN walked along. Then, with effort, he started to run. He could hardly lift his legs. He grimaced, pressing his hand to his chest. He crossed the street.

All of a sudden.

Pain.

His chest.

Like an electric shock.

He screamed. He felt it in his elbow, his ribs, his temples. He moaned and bent over. He fell on his knees:

"Son of a bitch..."

A well-dressed man stopped.

"What's wrong?"

"Bitch..." Lapin repeated.

"Life, you mean? That's for sure."

Lapin barely managed to stand up. He hobbled toward Patriarch Ponds. There hadn't been any snow here for a long time. Wet sidewalks. The city mud of spring around the pond.

He wandered down Bolshaya Bronnaya Street and turned onto the boulevard. He sat on a bench, leaning on its damp hard back.

"Fuckin'... nonsense..."

A grimy old woman rambled over. She looked in the trash can and moved on.

Lapin got out his wallet. He extracted the dollars and counted: 900.

He counted the rubles: 4,500. Plus his own seventy. And a five-ruble coin.

He looked around. People walked by at a clip. Others were in no hurry. A guy and a girl drank beer as they walked.

"That's the right idea..." Lapin took out a five-hundred ruble note, put the wallet back.

He stood up carefully. The pain had receded.

He limped over to a kiosk and bought a bottle of Baltic. He asked for it to be opened, drank half straight down, and took a breather. He wiped away the tears that came to his eyes and headed for the Metro. Pushkin Square was crowded. He finished off the beer and placed the bottle carefully on the marble parapet. He started down the stairs, then stopped: "What the fuck?"

He turned back. Standing on Tverskaya Street, he stuck out his hand. Two cars stopped right away: a dirty red one and a green one that was cleaner.

"Chertanovo," Lapin said to the driver of the dirty red car.

"And..."

"And what?"

"A hundred fifty, that's what!"

Lapin nodded. He sat down in the seat next to the driver.

"Where exactly?"

"Sumskoi Passage."

The driver's mustache nodded sullenly. He turned on some music: lousy, but loud.

After an hour of heavy traffic the car pulled up to Lapin's seven-story building. Lapin paid and got out. He rode up to the fifth floor, unlocked the door, and entered a crowded foyer. The apartment smelled like cats and fried onion.

"Ahhhh . . . the appearance of Christ to the people," said his father, glancing out of the kitchen, chewing.

"Goodness!" His mother looked out. "And here we were already hoping that you'd moved in with Golovastik."

"Hi," Lapin barked. He took off his jacket. Touched the bandage: Could you see it through the T-shirt? He looked in the oval mirror: you could see it. He went into his room.

"We already ate everything, don't hurry!" his mother shouted. She and his father laughed.

Lapin kicked open a door with a sign FUCK OFF FOREVER! The room was dark: bookshelves, a table with a computer, a stereo set, a mountain of CDs. There were posters on the wall: *The Matrix*, Lara Croft naked with two pistols, Marilyn Manson as Christ rotting on the cross. An unmade bed. The Siamese cat Nero dozed on a pillow.

Three shirts hung on the back of a chair. Lapin took the black one. He put it on over the T-shirt and lay down gingerly on the bed. He yawned, then cried out, "Aaah—ooooh—shiiiiit!"

Nero rose reluctantly and sauntered over to him. Lapin blew in his ear. Nero turned away. He jumped down onto the old carpet and left the room.

Lapin looked at Lara Croft's large lips. He remembered the nurse. Khar . . . Khara? Lara. Klara.

He grinned. He shook his head, exhaling sharply through crooked teeth.

Lapin's mother looked in the half-open door: 43 years old, plump, chestnut hair, a young face, tight gray pants, a black-and-white sweater, a cigarette.

"Are you really full?"

"I'll eat." Lapin buttoned up his shirt.

"Tied one on yesterday?"

"Uh-huh…"

"Too much trouble to make a phone call?"

"Yeah." Lapin nodded seriously.

"Jerk." His mother left.

Lapin lay there looking at the ceiling. He fidgeted with the steel tip of his belt.

"I'm not heating things up twice!" his mother yelled from the kitchen.

"Who cares…" he said, brushing her off. Then he got up. He winced. With difficulty, he pushed himself off the bed, stood up, and shuffled into the kitchen. His mother was washing dishes.

A plate with a piece of fried chicken was on the table. And boiled potatoes. A bowl of sauerkraut stood nearby. A plate of pickles, too.

Lapin gobbled down the chicken. He didn't finish the potatoes. He washed it all down with water.

He went into the living room. He picked up the phone and dialed a number.

"Kela, hi. It's Yurka Lapin. Can I talk to Genka? Gen? It's me. Listen, I need…ummm…to talk to you. No, nothing…Just advice. No, it's not that. It's…uhhh. Something else. Now? Sure. Okay."

He replaced the receiver and went to the foyer. He started to pull on his jacket—and almost screamed with pain.

"Oy…shhhiii…"

"What, you're going out again?" his mother asked, clattering the dishes.

"I'm going over to Genka's, not for long…"

"Will you buy bread?"

"Uh-huh."

"Need money?"

"I have some."

"You mean you didn't drink everything up?"

"Not everything."

Lapin left the apartment, slamming the door. He walked to the elevator, then stopped. He stood there. He turned around and walked down the stairs to the fourth floor. On the landing, he stopped and squatted. He began to cry. Tears ran down his cheeks. At first he cried silently. His shoulders shook. He pressed his thin hands to his face. Then he began to whine. Grudging sobs broke from his mouth and nose. He began to sob out loud. He wept a long time.

He had a hard time calming down. He rummaged in his jacket pockets. No handkerchief. He blew his nose on the broken, yellowish-brown floor tile. He wiped his hand on the wall next to the words VITYA IS A SHITHEAD.

He started to laugh. He wiped away the tears.

"Mair, Mair, Mair . . . Mair, Mair, Mair . . ."

He began sobbing again. His finger picked at the blue wall. He touched his breastbone.

Gradually he calmed down.

He stood up, walked down the stairs, and went out on the street. He walked past three buildings, entered the fourth. He climbed to the second floor and rang the bell of apartment 47.

The green steel door opened almost immediately.

Kela stood at the threshold: 28 years old, medium height, stocky, muscular, a flat face, reddish mustache, a small shaved head.

"Hey." Kela turned on his heel and left.

Lapin entered the hallway of a two-room apartment: four tires, a box of audio equipment, a coat stand with clothing, mountain skis, and boots.

The sound of loud music came from Kela's room. Lapin went in to Gena's room: boxes with videotapes, a bed, a chest of drawers with a hutch, photographs.

Gena was sitting at the computer: 21 years old, disheveled; he looked like Kela, but was heavier.

"Greetings." Lapin stood behind him.

"Hi," Gena said without turning around. "Where'd you disappear to?"

"Everywhere."

"Mean you dissolved?"

"Yeah."

"Well, I dug up this cool site yesterday. Take a look..."

He typed in www.stalin.ru. A pale photograph with Stalin's image appeared. Under it was the caption COLLECT STONE BOUQUET FOR COMRADE STALIN!

Under the caption were seven stone flowers. Gena moved the cursor over one of them. Clicked. A picture came up: a cow, tattooed with Stalin's picture, grazing in a meadow of stone flowers. A slogan floated over the cow: FIGHT THE UNCONSCIOUS, EVERYBODY!

"Cool, huh?" Gena poked him in the thigh with his chubby elbow, directed the cursor to another of the flowers, and clicked.

A picture came up: two Stalins pointing threateningly at each other. The slogan floating over them read GOT A MAN—GOT A PROBLEM; GET RID OF A MAN, GET RID OF A PROBLEM!

"Way to go, someone's having a blast!" Gena grinned.

"Listen, Gen. You know anything about secret sects?"

"Which ones? Aum Shinrikyo?"

"No, well...others...like an order..."

"Like the Freemasons?"

"Sort of. Can you dig up something on the Web?"

"You can dig up anything you want. What do you need Masons for?"

"I need the ones we have here."

"Kela's up on that stuff. All he does is go on about Freemasons, Masonic lodges..."

"Kela..." said Lapin, touching his chest. "He's obsessed with black asses. And Jews."

"So? He knows about all different kinds. What do you care?"

"Some assholes attacked me. A fuckin' brotherhood. Of 'awakened' people."

"Awakened?"

"Yeah."

"And what do they want?" Gena moved the mouse around quickly, looking at the screen.

"I don't know."

"Then to hell with them...Hey, look! Cool, huh? They're really into that Stalin!"

"I need to talk to someone. Someone who knows who they are."

"So go and ask him. He knows everything."

Lapin went into Kela's room: wood shelving with books, a large stereo with huge speakers, a small television, portraits of Alfred Rosenberg, Pyotr Stolypin, a Russian National Unity poster: SUPPORT THE NEW RUSSIAN ORDER!, three sets of nunchaku, laced boots with thick soles, sixty-kilo weights, three-kilo dumbbells, twelve-kilo dumbbells, two baseball bats, a mattress, and a brown bearskin on the floor.

Kela was sitting on the mattress drinking beer and listening to the band Halloween.

Lapin sat down next to him. He waited until the song was over.

"Kel, I have a problem."

"What?"

"Some kind of sect...or maybe order...sort of...hassled me, got right up in my face."

"How?"

"Well, they go on and on, and talk about, like 'We're—the awakened people. Brothers. Everyone else is asleep.' They promise money. Kinda like Masons."

Kela turned the music off. He placed the remote on the floor.

"Remember, once and for all: there's no such thing as Masons by themselves. There's only kike Masons. You heard about B'nai B'rith?"

"What's that?"

"The official kike Masonic lodge in Moscow."

"Kel, you know, these, the ones that...well, that visited me, they're not Jews. They're all blond, like me. Even got blue eyes. That's right! Hey, listen," he suddenly remembered, "I only just realized! They've all got blue eyes!"

"Doesn't matter. All the Masonic lodges are controlled by the kike oligarchy."

"They said stuff like, everybody is asleep, like hibernating, and we have to wake up, kinda like being born again, and the whole thing started outside, they came up to me near the student union and asked me for—"

Kela interrupted. "Even three hundred years ago all the Masons were either pure kikes or mixed blood. Before that, fuck, I mean the kikes used the Masons like puppets, but now—it's the politicians. All politicians are whores. Man, fuckin' bastards. And our kikes"— Kela locked his sinewy fingers together and cracked his knuckles— "they've all got a Star of David and 666 tattooed on the end of their pricks."

Lapin sighed impatiently.

"Kel, but I . . ."

"Just fuckin' listen . . ." Kela stretched out a brawny arm and took a book off the shelf. He opened it at the bookmark.

"Franz Liszt. A great composer. He writes about the kikes: 'There will come a moment when all Christian nations in which Jews live will raise the question of whether or not to suffer them further, or to deport them. The significance of this question is as important as the question of whether we want life or death, health or sickness, social peace or continual unrest.' Get it!"

The doorbell rang.

"Genka, open it," Kela shouted.

"Why is it . . ." Gena shuffled angrily toward the door. He opened it.

A huge guy entered Kela's room: 23 years old, shaved head, wide shoulders, leather jacket and pants, big hands, on the side of his palm a tattoo: FOR THE AIRBORNE FORCES.

"Hey! Wazup, my man?" said Kela, getting up from the mattress.

"Wazup, Kel."

They swung their arms back and slapped their right palms together hard.

"They say the iron's rusting over here!" The guy smiled, showing strong teeth.

"Fuckin' rusting away, man. Over there." Kela nodded at the weights.

"Yeah." The guy went over, took hold of them, and lifted. "Got it."

"But only for a coupla weeks, Vitya, max."

"No prob." The guy took the weights in his right hand. Looked at Lapin. At the beer. "Hittin' the foamy?"

"Nah." Kela flopped on the mattress. "Just shootin' the breeze with the young folks."

"You're a good guy, Kel." The guy nodded and left with the weights.

"You heard about the Union of Satan and the Antichrist?" Kela asked Lapin.

"What's that?"

"How about B'nai Moishe?"

"No."

Kela sighed.

"Jesus fuckin' Christ. I don't know what the fuck makes you guys tick."

"Compooters," said Gena, glancing into the room.

"Fuck compooters." Kela gave a nod. "Do you know who invented the Internet and where? And what he did it for?"

"You already said a million times," said Gena, scratching his cheek. "So what?... So the Jews and Chinese invented everything in the world."

"You read *My Name Is Legion*?" Kela stared at Lapin.

Someone rang the doorbell.

"Open it." Kela nodded at Gena.

The guy in leather came in again. Holding the weights.

"Kel, listen, I forgot: Vovan said to come over on Friday. To have a few. You in?"

"Sure."

"I'll come by."

"Good. Hey, Vityok, these guys ain't read *My Name Is Legion* and they don't do any damn sports."

"Each to his own." The guy smiled, showing his teeth. He held the weights out to Gena. "Hold this a sec, youngster."

"Get outta here!" said Gena, laughing. "I have kidney stones."

"For real?"

"For real!" Kela answered for Gena. "How ya fuckin' like that, Vitya? The kid's only twenty—and he's got kidney stones!"

"Wooow..." The guy leaned against the doorjamb, still holding the weights. "I ain't heard of that. So young. Stones. We used to... uhhh. In our battalion the sergeant cured a first lieutenant. He couldn't sleep in the cold."

"How come?"

"Kidney stones. He got him soused, on beer. Four liters. Then he says, 'Let's go take a leak.' So they get up. The first lieutenant's pissing. And the sergeant whacks him on the side of the kidneys—*wham-bam*! He's like—ooooowwww, shit! His piss is all bloody. But all the stones came out. So there you go. Field medicine."

The guy turned around and left.

The phone rang. Kela picked it up.

"Yeah. Hey, my man. Ah! Fucking shit man, what's the story with you? That's fuckin' it! I'm going to pick it up tomorrow. Tell me about it! Today I'm walking down the street thinking—am I really gonna trade in that rotten '04 for a normal fuckin' set of wheels? Uh-huh! Yeah...yeah...That's for fuckin' sure. Uh-huh!"

"Are you buying a new car?" asked Lapin.

"Not new. A '93 Golf." Gena yawned.

"Got rich?"

"The folks laid a coupla thou on us."

"Great."

"Let's go to a chat and bullshit. There're lots of film buffs."

"I wanted to talk over stuff with Kela."

"That's Voronin. It's gonna be a long one. Come on, let's go."

"All right..."

They returned to Gena's room. They sat down side by side at the computer. Gena quickly entered a chat room under the name **KillaBee :/**).

Zkhus /:
I bought argento's "Phantom of the Opera" yesterday, too. I was counting on Julian Sands, who's not usually in shitty films. I think he's the coolest actor since Mickey Rourke. Fanfuckintastic flick!!!—

De Scriptor /:
Yeah and "Darkness" is crapola.

Natasha /:
Julian Sands sucks. He was only good in "Black Book 2," but "Phantom of the Opera" is total bullshit.

KillaBee /:
Ur all floppy-dicked cuntsuckers! And Julian Sands is Filipp Kirkorov's nephew :)

Old As A Mammoth /:
Scuzzy! Where the DZTVZ are u coming from?

KillaBee /:
A mammoth's cunt, Fuzzy Wuzzy. How come u r jacking off on Sands when there's Chuuuuulpan Kamyyyytovaaaaa and Keanu Reeves!!! Guys, I'm in love with them!

De Scriptor /:
Dumbfuckism is incurable :/(. But it can be used for peaceful causes.

Mole /:
that wet slit will piss on everything again.

KillaBee /:
Definitely, boys :/—

Zkhus /:
Here's a suggestion—fuck off to your own chain link.

Old As A Mammoth /:
killabeeby, can it, will ya. Check out: www.clas.ru. u can order rare films. Home delivery. I got my favorite, Cronenberg :)))

Mole /:
anyone seen Argento's "Demons"?

Vino /:
Argento didn't make "Demons." It was either G. Romero or Lucio Fulci. RenTV showed "Phenomena" by your vapid Argento—what trash. With a heavy metal soundtrack.

KillaBee /:
Woooow, look who's here! The vin-o-dictive nightingale is singing sweetly. r u still hard? I'm always ready, motherfucker!!!! :/)

Vino /:
KillaBee, if you want someone to screw you till you're blue in the
clit, then.... ///!

"Gen, I'm going home." Lapin got up. Touched his chest.

"What's wrong, Lap? Let's write something. Come on, something
cool, no kids' stuff."

"Yeah, well...to hell with it. I wanted to talk to Kela, but he got
onto his kikes again."

"Why'd the fuck you work him up? You shoulda talked about something else. Freemasons, Masonic lodges...That's all he's gonna talk
about now. I never bring up ethnic stuff with him anymore. He drives
me fucking crazy."

Lapin waved his hand. He stood there a minute.

"Gen."

"What?" said Gena, typing.

"Let's grab a beer."

"Where?" asked Gena, turning around in surprise.

"Anywhere. I have...that is...I've got tons of money."

"From where?"

"Thin air."

Kela came in with a new bottle of beer.

"And I'll tell you what else, Genka. I'm gonna say it for the last goddamned time: you keep on sucking that hash—I'll send you to the
progenitors. Go smoke that fucking shit there, in the can."

"I haven't had a toke for ages, what do you mean?"

"The day before yesterday? Huh? When I brought in the smokes.
And your gang of assholes was here? Don't tell me you weren't."

"What're you talking about? Kel? We were listening to the new
Air Force CD."

"Don't bullshit the boss. Fuckin' idiots. You don't understand shit." He took a swig from the bottle. "You know what dead Chechens' brains look like? Swiss cheese. With holes. This big. From what? From hashish. Got it?"

"You already told me." Gena popped a piece of gum in his mouth. "Kel, you know beer makes the liver get all covered in fat."

"Just fuckin' think about it. I warned you. For the last time."

Kela left.

"Jeez, shit…" Gena sighed. "I'm so sick of this. Christ, why are they so psyched about pumping iron? Vityok, Shpala, Bomber—they're dunces, it figures—they've only got a few gray cells to start, why not pump? But Kela—he's smart. He's read more books than all of them put together. And it's the same thing—a healthy body, shit, a healthy spirit. And every morning he sticks those lousy friggin' dumbbells in my bed! Think about it. I'm sleeping, and he goes and sticks those fuckin' dumbbells under my ass! What a loony bin…"

Lapin looked at the screen. Got up. "I'm off."

"What's wrong?"

"I've still got something to do…"

"Lap, why are you so…today?"

"So what?"

"Well, kind of…beat up?"

Lapin looked at him and laughed out loud. A sudden attack of hysterical laughter forced him to bend over.

"What's with you?" Gena said, confused.

Lapin laughed. Gena looked at him.

Lapin had a hard time calming down. He wiped away the tears that had come to his eyes. Sighed deeply.

"That's it…I'm off."

"What about the beer?"

"What beer?"

"You were the one who wanted to have a beer, no?"

"I was joking."

"Some kinda joke, leetle boy…"

Lapin left.

It had grown dark outside and was beginning to freeze. The puddles cracked underfoot.

Lapin limped to his door and walked in. He pressed the elevator button, looked at the wall. He saw the familiar graffiti. Two tags— ACID ORTHODOX and DESTRUCTION-97—were Lapin's work. He noticed a new inscription: URAL, DON'T BE AFRAID OF AWAKENING.

Black marker. Neat handwriting.

Diar

07:08, The Kiev Highway, Kilometer 12

A WHITE Volga automobile turned onto a forest road. Drove about three hundred meters. Turned again. Stopped in the glade.

A birch grove. Leftover snow. Morning sun.

Two people got out of the car.

Botvin: 39 years old, heavy, blond, blue eyes, a kind face, a blue-green athletic jacket, blue-green pants with a white stripe, black sneakers.

Neilands: 25, tall, thin, blond, decisively stern, blue eyes, sharp facial features, a brown raincoat.

They opened the trunk.

Nikolaeva lay inside: 22, a cute blond, blue eyes, a short fox-fur coat, high black suede boots, her mouth taped with a white bandage, handcuffs.

They pulled Nikolaeva out of the trunk. She kicked and whined.

Neilands took out a knife. He sliced through the back of the coat. And the sleeves. The coat fell to the ground. Under the coat was a red dress. Neilands cut it. He cut the bra.

Medium-size breasts. Small nipples.

They led her to a birch tree and began tying her to it.

Nikolaeva let out a muffled wail. She struggled. Her neck and face turned red.

"Not tight. Let her breathe freely." Botvin pressed her writhing shoulders against the birch.

"I don't make it tight." Neilands worked with intense concentration.

They finished. Botvin took a longish white refrigerator case out of the car. He opened it. Inside lay the ice hammer: the neat weighty head, the wooden handle, the rawhide straps.

Neilands pulled a one-ruble coin out of this pocket.

"Heads."

"Tails," said Botvin, trying out the hammer.

Neilands tossed the coin. It landed upright on its edge in the snow.

"Well how do you like that?" Botvin laughed. "So what do we do, try it again?"

"Go ahead and hit," Neilands said with a wave of his hand.

Botvin stood in front of Nikolaeva.

"Now listen, sweetheart. We aren't robbers or sadists. Not even rapists. Relax. There's nothing to be afraid of."

Nikolaeva whimpered. Tears ran from her eyes. So did her mascara.

Botvin swung back.

"Speak!"

The hammer struck her sternum.

Nikolaeva grunted.

"That's not it, hon," said Botvin, shaking his head.

He drew back. The sun sparkled on the side of the hammer.

"Speak!"

Another blow. The half-naked body shuddered.

Botvin and Neilands listened.

Nikolaeva's shoulders and head trembled. She hiccuped rapidly.

"Close, but no cigar." Neilands frowned.

"Let the Light's Will be done, Dor."

"You said it, Ycha."

Two birds called each other in the forest.

Botvin slowly drew the hammer to one side.

"Come on, luv . . . spea-ea-k!"

The powerful blow shook Nikolaeva. She lost consciousness. Her head hung limp. Her long blond hair covered her breast.

Botvin and Neilands listened.

A sound awoke in the bruised chest. A faint rasp. Once. Twice. A third time.

"Speak with the heart!" Botvin said. He held his breath.

"Speak with the heart!" Neilands whispered.

The sound broke off.

"It was definitely there . . . Lift her head," said Botvin, raising the hammer.

"One hundred percent . . ." Neilands moved behind the birch. He lifted Nikolaeva's head and pressed it to the rough, cold trunk. "Just—take it easy, now . . ."

"You bet . . ." Botvin drew back. "Speeeak!"

The hammer smashed into the chest. A spray of ice splinters flew out in all directions.

Botvin pressed his ear to the chest. Neilands looked out from behind the birch.

"Khor, khor, khor . . ." could be heard from the breastbone.

"We've got it!" Botvin shouted, tossing the hammer aside. "Speak, little sister, speak with the heart, talk to us!"

"Speak with the heart, speak with the heart, speak with the heart!" muttered Neilands. He began hurriedly searching in his pockets: "Where is it? Where? Where did I . . . where is it?"

"Wait a sec . . ." Botvin patted all his pockets.

"Jeez, damn . . . it's in the car! In the glove compartment!"

"Damnit . . ."

Botvin lunged toward the Volga. He slipped on the wet snow and fell—onto the dirty brown grass. He crawled quickly to the car, opened the door, and pulled a stethoscope from the glove compartment.

The sound didn't stop.

"Hurry!" Neilands cried in a falsetto.

"Damnit all . . ." Botvin ran back. He stretched out a dirty hand holding a stethoscope.

Neilands stuck the ends in his ears. He held the stethoscope to the violet-colored chest.

Both of them froze. An airplane flew by in the distance. Birds called to each other. The sun went behind a cloud.

There was a raspy sputtering sound in Nikolaeva's chest—faint but regular.

"Di...ro...aro...ara..." whispered Neilands.

"Don't be in such a hurry!" said Botvin, exhaling.

"Di...di...ar. Diar. Diar. Diar!" Neilands sighed in relief. He took the stethoscope off and handed it to Botvin.

Botvin put it clumsily in his ears. His plump, dirty hand pressed the black circle to the chest.

"Di...et...di...ero....Diar. Diar. Diar. Diar."

"Diar!" Neilands nodded his narrow head.

"Diar." Botvin smiled. He wiped his face with his muddied hand. He laughed. "Diar!"

"Diar!" said Neilands, slapping him on the shoulder.

"Diar!" Botvin replied, tapping on his chest.

They embraced, swayed, pushed away from each other. Neilands began to cut the rope. Botvin tossed the hammer in the case. He took off his jacket.

They freed the unconscious Nikolaeva from the ropes and handcuffs. They wrapped her in the jacket and lifted her. They carried her to the car.

"Don't forget the hammer," wheezed Botvin.

They laid Nikolaeva on the backseat.

Neilands grabbed the case with the hammer. He tossed it in the trunk.

Botvin got in the driver's seat. He started the engine.

"Wait." Neilands strode over to the birch tree. He unzipped his trousers, spread his legs.

Nikolaeva moaned weakly.

"She's coming to. Diar!" Neilands smiled.

A stream of urine hit the birch.

Con

NIKOLAEVA woke up from a touch.

Someone naked and warm was pressed to her.

She opened her eyes: a white ceiling, an opaque light fixture, the edge of a window behind a semitransparent white curtain, curly blond hair. A smell. Aftershave lotion. A male ear with an attached earlobe. A male cheek. Well shaven.

Nikolaeva moved. She glanced down: the edge of a sheet. Under the sheet her naked body. An enormous bruise on her chest. Her legs. A dark, muscular male body. Pressing to her. Entwining her in its arms. Turning her on her side. Powerfully pressing her chest to his.

"Listen . . ." she said hoarsely. "I don't like it that way . . ."

And suddenly she froze, stupefied. Her body shuddered. Her eyes closed halfway and rolled to the side. The man also froze. He shuddered and his head jerked. Pressed to her, he too was stupefied.

Thirty-seven minutes passed.

The man's mouth opened. A faint, hoarse moan escaped him. The man moved. He flexed his hands. Turned over. Rolled off the bed onto the floor. He stretched feebly and let out a sob. His breathing was heavy.

Nikolaeva shuddered. She rolled her legs over, sat up, and let out a cry. She held her hands to her chest and opened her eyes. Her face was crimson. Saliva drooled from her open mouth. She whimpered and began to cry. Her shoulders heaved. Her legs trembled restlessly on the sheet.

The man exhaled with a moan. He sat up and looked at Nikolaeva.

She was crying hard, her body shaking helplessly.

"Want some juice?" the man asked quietly.

She didn't answer. She looked at him fearfully.

The man stood up: 34 years old, a slim muscular blond, with big blue eyes and a delicate face, handsome and sensitive.

He walked around the bed. He took a bottle of mineral water from a nightstand and opened it. He poured it into a glass.

Nikolaeva watched: his tanned body, golden hair on the legs and chest.

The man caught her look. He smiled.

"Hello, Diar."

She didn't answer. He drank from the glass. She unstuck her lips, swollen and scarlet with blood.

"I'm thirsty . . ."

He sat down next to her on the bed and embraced her. He put the glass to her lips. She drank greedily. Her teeth chattered against the glass.

She drank it down. She exhaled with a moan.

"More."

He rose. He filled the glass to the brim and brought it to her. She gulped it down.

"Diar..." he said, stroking her hair.

"I'm... Alya," she said. She wiped her tears away with the sheet.

"You're Alya for ordinary people. But for the awakened, you are Diar."

"Diar?"

"Diar," he said, looking at her warmly.

Suddenly she coughed. She clutched her chest.

"Careful." He held her sweaty shoulders.

"Ow... it hurts..." She moaned.

The man took a towel from the nightstand. He placed it on her shoulders and began to dry her off carefully.

She examined her bruise and whimpered.

"Oy... but... why did they..."

"It will pass. It's just a bruise. But the bone is intact."

"Jeezus... and that... what was that you were doing... jeezus... why the fuck were you doing that? Huh? What the fuck was that for?" She shook her head. Held her knees to her chin.

He embraced her shoulders.

"I'm Con."

"What?" she said, looking at him with confusion. "A Con?... Artist?"

"You didn't understand, Diar. I'm not *a* con, I am Con."

"An ex?... The regular kind?"

"No," he laughed. "C O N—three letters. It's my name. I'm not a con artist, and I've never been a convict of any kind."

"Really?" She looked around, bewildered. "What's this? A hotel?"

"Not exactly." He pressed against her back. "Something like a rest home."

"Who for?"

"For the brothers. And sisters."

"Which ones?"

"Ones like you."

"Like me?" She wiped her lips against her knees. "You mean, I'm a sister?"

"Yes, a sister."

"Whose?"

"Mine."

"Yours?" Her lips trembled and grimaced.

"Mine. And not only mine. Now you have lots of brothers."

"Bro-thers?" She sniffled. She grabbed his hand. Suddenly she screamed at the top of her lungs—hysterically and for some time. The scream turned into sobs.

He embraced her, held her close. Nikolaeva wept, burying her face in his muscular chest. He began to rock her like a baby.

"Everything's okay."

"Why . . . again . . . why . . . oooo!" She sobbed.

"Everything, everything will be all right for you now."

"Ooooo!! How could . . . oy, what did you do to me . . . Christ . . ." Gradually she calmed down.

"You need to rest," he said. "How old are you?"

"Twenty-two . . ." she whimpered.

"All these years you've been sleeping. And now you've awoken. It's a very strong shock. It's not only joyful. It's frightening as well. You need time to get used to it."

She nodded. And sobbed.

"Is there . . . a . . . handkerchief?"

He handed her a tissue. She blew her nose loudly, crumpled the tissue, and threw it on the floor.

"Jeezus . . . I sure cried my eyes out."

"You can take a bath. They'll help you to collect yourself . . ."

"Uh-huh . . ." She looked fearfully at the window. "But where . . ."

"Is the bathroom? They'll take you in a minute."

Nikolaeva nodded distractedly. She glanced over at the lily in the vase. At the window. At the lily again. She took a deep breath, jumped up off the bed, and ran for the door. Con didn't move. She threw the door open wide and flew out into the hall. Ran. Bumped into a nurse smoking a cigarette next to a tall brass ashtray. She smiled at Nikolaeva with her blue eyes.

"Good morning, Diar."

Nikolaeva ran toward the exit. Her bare feet slapped along the new, wide parquet of the hall. She ran up to the glass doors, pushed the first one, and leaped into the entryway. She pushed the second one. She ran across the wet asphalt.

The doctor looked at her through the glass. He folded his arms on his chest and smiled.

A fair-haired chauffeur in a parked silver BMW gazed after her. He was eating an apple.

Nikolaeva ran naked through Sparrow Hills. Bare trees stood all around. Dirty snow lay on the ground.

She tired quickly. Stopped. Squatted. She sat for a while, breathing heavily. Then she got up. She touched her chest and frowned.

"The bastards..."

She walked on. Her bare feet splashed through puddles.

A big road was visible ahead. Now and then a car drove by. A wet spring wind blew. Nikolaeva stepped out on the road. Immediately she felt the intense cold. She shivered and hugged herself tight.

A car went past. The middle-aged driver smiled at Nikolaeva.

She raised her hand. A Volkswagen passed her. The driver and the passenger opened their windows. They looked out and whistled.

"Assholes," muttered Nikolaeva. Her teeth were chattering.

A Zhiguli came into view and stopped.

"Are you one of those polar bears or something?"

The driver opened the door: 40 years old, bearded, with glasses, a large silver earring, and a black-and-yellow bandana on his head. "The ice has broken up already!"

"Lis-s-s...sten...t-take...meee...they...s-s-stole..." Nikolava's teeth chattered.

"You got mugged?" He noticed the large bruise between her breasts. "They beat you?"

"They b-b-b-eat the sh-sh-shit outta...m-m-m-e...bas-s-s-tards."

"Get in."

She climbed in and sat down. Closed the door.

"Oy, shit…it's sooo cold…"

The driver took off a light white jacket. He threw it over Niko-laeva's shoulders.

"So, where to, the police?"

"No way…" She frowned. She wrapped herself in the jacket. Shaking. "I d-d-don't deal with thos-se j-jerks…take me home. I'll pay you."

"Where?"

"Strogino."

"Strogino…?" he said, in an anxious voice. "I have to get to work."

"Oy, it's so cold…" She trembled. "Turn-n-n the heat up…"

He slid the heat up to high.

"Why don't I take you as far as Leninsky Prospect, and you can catch another ride there."

"Come on, how am I gonna…again, I mean…oy…damnit… take me home, I'm begging you," she said, trembling.

"Strogino…that's completely out of my way."

"How much do you want?"

"Hey…that's not the point, luv."

"That's always the point. A hundred, one fifty? Two? Let's go for two hundred. That's it."

He thought a minute. Changed gears. The car took off.

"Gotta smoke?"

He offered her a pack of Camels. Nikolaeva took one. He held the lighter for her.

"Why did they…they took your clothes and left you in the woods?"

"Uh-huh." She took a deep drag.

"All your clothes?"

"As you can see."

"Wow. That's hardcore. Shouldn't you report it?"

"I'll handle it myself."

"What do you mean, you know them?"

"Something like that."

"That's a different story."

He was quiet for a while, then asked, "Are you one of those, um, er, 'butterflies of the Moscow night'?"

"More like…daytime…" She yawned sleepily, exhaling smoke. "A Cabbage White."

He nodded and grinned.

Semisweet

12:17, Strogino, 25 Katukova Street

THE ZHIGULI drove up to a sixteen-story apartment building.

"Come with me," Nikolaeva said, getting out of the car. She walked up to the front door and dialed an apartment number on the intercom: 266.

"Who is it?"

"It's me, Natashka."

The door beeped. Nikolaeva and the driver entered. They took the elevator to the twelfth floor.

"Wait here." She handed him his jacket. Rang the doorbell.

Natasha, sleepy, opened the door: 18 years old, a plump face, black hair cut short, a red terry-cloth robe.

"Give me two hundred rubles." Nikolaeva walked past the girl into her room. She got the same kind of red robe out of the closet and put it on.

"Jeezus fucking…What's up?" Natasha followed her.

"Two hundred rubles! To pay the driver."

"I only have dollars—two one-hundred-dollar bills."

"Aren't there any rubles? Do you have any rubles?!" Nikolaeva shouted.

"Hey, no, what are you screaming for…?"

"Or small bills?"

"Two one-hundred dollar bills. What is that, what happened to you?" Natasha noticed the bruise on her chest.

"None of your business. Does Lenka have any?"

"What?"

"Rubles."

"I don't know. She's still asleep."

Nikolaeva went into another room. Two women were sleeping on the floor.

"What, Sula came over too?" said Nikolaeva looking at them.

"Uh-huh," said Natasha, looking out from behind her. "They crawled in late last night."

"Then—fuck 'em . . ." Nikolaeva said, annoyed.

"So, what's up?" The driver stood at the open front door.

"Come in," Nikolaeva said.

He entered. She closed the door behind him.

"Listen, we gotta big problem with rubles. How about I give you a blow job?"

He looked at her, then at Natasha. Natasha grinned. She went back to her room.

"Come on." Nikolaeva took him by the hand.

"Well, actually, um . . ." He stared straight at her.

"Come on, come on . . . in the bathroom. What can I do, we're flat out of dough, you can see for yourself. And if I wake those bitches up—I'll never hear the end of their shit . . ." She tugged at his arm.

"I can go and change money," he said, stopping.

"Don't be ridiculous." She turned on the light in the bathroom. Pulled him by the hand. Locked the door. Squatted. Began unbuttoning his pants.

"Uh . . . how long have you . . . um?" he said, looking up at the ceiling.

"You ask a lot of questions young man . . . Oho! We're quick on the uptake . . ." She touched his stiffening member through his pants.

She unfastened his belt and unzipped the zipper. She pulled his gray trousers and his black underwear down.

The driver had a small, crooked penis.

She sucked him quickly, grasping his lilac testicles in her hand. She began moving rapidly.

The driver stuck his backside out. He leaned over slightly and rested his hands on the washing machine. He snuffled. His earring swung as he moved.

"Wait...hon..." He put his hand on her head.

"It hurts?" she asked spitting out his penis.

"No...It's just that...I'll never come that way...let's...uh... the normal way..."

"I won't do it without a condom."

"But I...I...don't carry them with me..." He laughed.

"This is not a problem..." She went out and came back with a pack of condoms. She unwrapped one and slipped it on him quickly and deftly. She threw off her robe, turned her backside to him, and set her elbows on the sink.

"Go ahead..."

He entered her quickly, grabbing her with his long arms. He moved back and forth rapidly, wheezing.

"That's good...oy, good..." she repeated calmly. She examined her bruise in the mirror.

He came.

She winked at him in the mirror.

"You rascal, you!"

She looked at him attentively. Suddenly her lips began to tremble. She covered her mouth with her palm.

He breathed hard through his nose, his eyes closed. He put his head on her shoulder.

She stretched out her arm and closed the drain on the bathtub. She turned on the water, barely able to restrain her sobs.

"Okay. That's it. I...I...I need to get warm."

He had a hard time turning her around. He opened his eyes. His penis slipped out of her vagina. The driver looked at it.

"In...in the loo," she suggested. She grabbed a half bottle of shampoo off a shelf and dumped it in the bathtub. She sobbed out loud.

He glanced at her glumly.

"What's wrong? You feel bad?"

She shook her head—then grasped his hand. She went down on her knees, pressing his hand to her chest. Her sobs grew stronger, and she squeezed her mouth shut.

"What is it?" he said, looking down at her. "They mistreated you, is that it? How come you're..."

"No, no, no…" She sniffed. "Wait a sec… wait…"

She pressed his hand to her chest. She wept.

He looked sideways at himself in the mirror. He stood there patiently. The sperm-filled condom hung from his shrinking penis. It swayed in time to her sobs.

It took her a while to calm down.

"It's… It's all… so… that's all… go…"

The driver pulled up his trousers and left.

Nikolaeva got into the bath and sat down. She hugged her knees and rested her head on them.

The sound of flushing water came from the loo.

The driver glanced into the bathroom.

"Is everything all right?" asked Nikolaeva without raising her head.

He nodded. He looked at her curiously.

"If you want, come by again sometime."

He nodded.

She sat motionless. He wiped his nose.

"What's your name?"

"Alya."

"Mine's Vadim."

She nodded into her knees.

"Are you… in big trouble?"

"No, no." She stubbornly shook her head. "It's just… just… that's it… bye."

"Well, bye."

The driver took off. The front door slammed.

The bath filled with water. It reached Nikolaeva's armpits. She turned the faucet off and lay down.

"Lord… CON, Con, Con, Con, Con…"

Bubbles fizzled around her tear-stained face.

Nikolaeva dozed off.

Twenty-two minutes later Natasha stuck her head into the bathroom.

"Alya, get up."

"What?" Nikolaeva opened her eyes, annoyed.

"Parvazik's here."

Nikolaeva sat up quickly.

"Fuck! You ratted on me?"

"He just showed up on his own."

"On his own! You viper! Well, just try and ask me for more sheets!"

"Go to—"

Natasha slammed the door.

Nikolaeva ran her wet hands over her face. She swayed.

"Oh, shit ... What a little cockroach ..."

She stood up with difficulty. She took a shower, wrapped her head in a towel, and dried off. She put on a robe and went out into the hallway.

"Have a good soak?" she heard from the kitchen.

Nikolaeva went in.

Two men were sitting there.

Parvaz: 41 years old, small, black hair, swarthy, unshaven, with small facial features, dressed in a gray silk jacket, black shirt, narrow gray trousers, and boots with buckles.

Pasha: 33, heavyset, light-haired, pale skin, a meaty face, dressed in a silvery-lilac-colored Puma leisure suit and light blue sneakers.

"Hello there, beautiful," Parvaz said, lighting a cigarette with a match.

Nikolaeva leaned against the doorjamb.

"I thought you and me, we made an agreement together." He took a drag on the cigarette. "In, what is it called—good faith? You promised me something. Isn't that right? You said lots of words. Crossed your heart. Isn't that right? Or do I have a problem with my memory?"

"Parvazik, I have a problem."

"What kind of problem?"

"Someone came after me, big-time."

"And who it was?" Parvaz sent a long stream of smoke pouring out of his small, thin lips.

Nikolaeva opened her robe.

"Here, take a look."

The men looked at her bruise silently.

"You see, it's really, I mean . . . I still haven't come to . . . Give me a smoke."

Parvaz handed her a pack of Dunhills and some matches.

She lit up. She put the cigarettes and the matches on the table.

"So yesterday I did my gig on the pole, and then I went around the club—to rustle up a trick. It wasn't very crowded. There were two guys sitting there, one of them called me over. So I went, did the belly wave, shook my tits. He says, 'Sit down, sit for a while.' I sat. They ordered champagne. We drank and started bullshitting. They were regular johns, they sold some kind of humidifiers or something. One was from the Baltics, gorgeous guy, tall, with a complicated name . . . Reetus-fetus . . . I couldn't remember it, and the other guy, Valera, was fat. 'Well,' I said, 'I'm cold, I'll go get dressed.' 'Yeah, yeah, of course. And come back to us.' So I put on a dress and went back to their table. 'What do you want?' I say, 'Something to eat.' They ordered me some grilled sturgeon. 'You been dancing striptease for a long time?' they asked. I say—not long. 'Where are you from?' 'Krasnodar.' Stuff like that. And then the Baltic guy says, 'Let's go to my place?' I said, 'Three hundred bucks a night.' 'No problem.' So they pay the bill, and split. With me. They had a Volga, a white one, brand new. I got in with them. We drove away from the club, and then one of them—*bam!*—sticks this mask on me with some kinda shit. Right on . . . like this . . . right on my face. And that's it. Then I came to: it was dark, I'm lying on my side, my hands are cuffed in back, it stinks of gas. I'm in the trunk. I'm lying down. There's some shit near me. The car keeps on driving and driving till it stops. They open the trunk, drag me out. We're in some woods. It's already morning. They rip my clothes off and tie me up to a birch tree. They really did! They taped my mouth before that with some kind of bandage . . . So. And then—then the shit really hit the fan! They had this . . . this kind of case. And there was a sort of ax in it, like a stone ax. On a crooked stick. Only it wasn't stone, it was ice. A sort of ice ax. So then, one of these bastards take this ax, swings it back, and *wh-a-a-m*—he whacks me right in the chest! Right here. And the other one says, 'Tell us everything.' But, I mean, my mouth was taped shut! I'm groaning, but I can't talk, can I?

And those shits just stand there waiting. Then they did it again: whacked me right on the chest! And they're still saying, 'Talk.' I got all dizzy, it hurt like hell, jeez, damnit. Then they go and do it a third time. *Wham-bam*! And I fainted. Yeah. Then I came to in some kind of hospital. And some guy is screwing me. I tried to resist, but he pulls a knife and holds it to my throat. Right. So he gets his rocks off and starts drinking. I'm lying there—didn't have the strength to move a finger. And he says, 'Now you're gonna live here.' I say, 'What the fuck for?' He says, 'We're gonna fuck you.' I say, 'You're gonna have problems, I'm with Parvaz Sloeny.' And he says, 'I don't give a shit about your Parvaz.' So then he gets drunk fast ... and I say, 'I need to go to the pot.' He calls some sort of attendant, a strong guy. He took me there. I'm walking down the hall naked, and I see his dick is stiff. I go in the john, and he follows me. 'Turn around and bend over!' So I bent over, what else could I do? He screwed me, and split for the hallway. But in the john there was this window, kinda like a double-glazed one. And no bars, that's the main thing! So I opened the window and crawled out into some woods. I took off for the woods! I ran and ran. Then I realized—it's Sparrow Hills. I went out on the road and flagged a car, and then—well, Natashka saw me come in. I could find that place again easy, that hospital."

Parvaz and Pasha looked at each other.

"And you, brother, you always being surprised—how come we come up with losses ... " Parvaz stubbed out his cigarette. He laughed. "Ice's ax—holy shit! Maybe it's twenty-four-carats gold ax? Huh? Or diamonds? Huh? You made mistake, it wasn't water ice—it was real ice. Diamond. Diamond's ax—right on the chest, on the chest. Huh? It's good. For your healthy. Good for you."

"Parvazik, I swear, it's ..." Nikolaeva raised her hand.

"An ice's ax ... fuckin' A!" He laughed. Rocked back and forth.

"Shit, Pash. Ice's ax! I tell you, brother, we gotta get in a different business. *Basta*. Let's go to the markets and sell oranges!"

"Parvazik, Parvazik!" Nikolaeva cried out, crossing herself.

Pasha hooked his powerful hands and twiddled his two short thumbs rapidly. He muttered in a female falsetto, "You shitsucker, how come you're getting so disrespectful? You don't wanna work like normal people? You tired of normal life? You want things to go bad? Wanna get tough? Get slapped around?"

"I swear, Parvazik, by everything on earth, I swear!" Nikolaeva crossed herself. She kneeled down. "By my mother I swear! I swear on the memory of my dead father! Parvazik! I'm religious! I swear by the Virgin Mary!"

"You're religious? Where's your cruss?" Pasha asked.

"Those bastards tore my cross off too!"

"Your cruss, too? Such bad guys they were?" Parvaz shook his head sadly.

"They almost wasted me! I'm still shaking all over! If you don't believe me—let's go to Sparrow Hills, I'll find the place, the place, my cross will be there!"

"What cruss? What fuckin' cruss? You as bad as they come, that's what you are. Cruss!"

"If you don't believe me—call Natashka! She saw! She saw me limp in naked with the fucking bejeezus beat out of me!"

"Natash!" Pasha shouted.

Natasha appeared immediately.

"When did she get here?"

"About an hour ago."

"Naked?"

"Naked."

"Alone?"

"With some dick."

"Pash, that was the driver, he brought me back when I..."

"Shut up, cunt. And what kind of dick was he?"

"With an earring, a beard...She owed him money. And she blew him in the bathroom."

"But that was for driving me home! For the fare! I ran off without a stitch on me!"

"Shut up you moldy wad of prick cum. What did they talk about?"

"Nothing special. She blew him real fast and said, 'Come by again if you want.'"

"You little piece of shit!" Nikolaeva stared angrily at Natasha.

"Parvazik, she said she wouldn't give me any more sheets and stuff." Natasha ignored Nikolaeva.

Parvaz and Pasha looked at each other.

"Parvazik…" Nikolaeva shook her head. "Parvazik…she's lying, the bitch, I…she keeps wearing all my dresses! I did everything for her!!"

"Who's at home?" Parvaz asked Natasha.

"Lenka and Sula. They're sleeping."

"Get them in here."

Natasha left.

"Parvazik…"

Nikolaeva was kneeling. Her face was distorted. Tears welled up and splattered.

"Parvazik…I…I…told you the whole truth…I didn't lie the teensiest bit, I swear…I swear…I swear…"

She shook her head. The towel came unwound. The edge covered her face.

Parvaz stood up. He walked over to the sink. He leaned toward the trash can.

"I believe you that time. I forgive you that time. I was helping you that time."

"Parvazik…Parvazik…"

"I gave you back your passport that time."

"I swear, I swear…"

"I thought to myself that time, I thought, 'Parvaz, Alya, she is a woman.' But now I understood: Alya is not a woman."

"Parvazik…"

"Alya—is a garbage rat."

He pulled an empty champagne bottle out of the trash can. He held it squeamishly with two fingers.

"Semisweet." He pushed the table to one side with a sudden jerk. He placed the bottle on the floor in the middle of the kitchen.

Sula entered the kitchen: 23 years old, small, chestnut hair, olive skin, an unattractive face, large breasts, a slim figure, colorful robe.

Lena followed right behind: 16, tall, a good figure, a pretty face, long blond hair, pink pajamas.

They both stopped at the door. Natasha could be seen in the rear.

"Girls, I got some bad news," said Parvaz. "Very bad news."

He thrust his hand in his slim pockets. Stood up on his toes. Rocked back and forth.

"Last night Alya did something very lowlife, very bad. She behaved herself like a garbage rat. She cut off a piece in a very bad way, very lowlife. She spit on everyone. She shitted on everyone."

He was silent. Nikolaeva kneeled. She sobbed.

"Clothes off," ordered Parvaz.

Nikolaeva untied the belt of her robe. She shrugged her shoulders. The robe slipped off of her naked body. Parvaz yanked the towel off her head.

"Sit on it."

She got up. Stopped crying. She went over to the bottle. Aimed and started to sit down on the bottle with her vagina.

"Not your cunt! Sit on it with your ass! You're gonna work for me with that cunt!"

Everyone watched silently.

Nikolaeva placed her anus over the bottle and sat. She balanced carefully.

"Sit!" Parvaz shouted at her.

She sat down more freely. Cried out. She propped her hands on the floor. "No hands, cunt! No hands!" Parvaz kicked her hand and pushed down sharply on her shoulders.

"Sit!"

Nikolaeva screamed.

Mokho

19:22, 6 Tverskaya Street

A DARK blue Peugeot 607 drove into the courtyard. It stopped.

Borenboim sat in the backseat, reading a newspaper: 44 years old, medium height, thinning blond hair, an intelligent face, blue eyes, thin glasses in gold frames, a dark green three-piece suit. He finished reading, threw the paper on the front seat, and picked up a slender black briefcase.

"Tomorrow at 9:30."

"Okay," nodded **the chauffeur**: 52, a longish head, ash-gray hair, a big nose, fat lips, a brown jacket, a light blue turtleneck.

Borenboim got out. He headed for entrance 2. His cell phone rang in his pocket. He took it out and stopped. He put the phone to his ear.

"Yes. Well? That's what we already agreed on. Nine o'clock. There. No, let's go upstairs, the food's better and it's quieter. What? Why didn't he call me at the office? Huh? Lyosh, what is all this? . . . It's like a game of telephone or something! How can I consult in absentia? He should just come over like normal. Bonds are in good shape now all around, they've been going up for two months, there's nothing to talk about on that score. What? All right. That's it . . . Oh, yeah, Lyosh, have you heard about Volodka? They brought an excavator up at night and dug out two bathhouses. That's right! Savva told me. Ask him, he knows the details. That's the scoop. Okay, that's it."

Borenboim stepped into the entryway.

The door attendant: 66 years old, thin, a wig, glasses, a grayish-pink sweater, brown skirt, and felt boots.

Borenboim gave her a nod.

He entered the elevator, took it to the third floor, and got out. He retrieved his keys and began unlocking the door.

Suddenly he felt something sticking into his back. He started to turn around, but someone grabbed him hard by the left shoulder.

"Don't look around. Straight ahead."

Borenboim looked at his door. It was made of steel. Painted gray.

"Open it," ordered a low, male voice.

Borenboim turned the key twice.

"Go in. Make a move, I beat the shit out of you."

Borenboim didn't move. The butt of a silencer was pressed against his cheek. It smelled of gun oil.

"You didn't get it? I'll count to one."

Borenboim pushed the door with his hand. He entered the dark foyer.

A hand in a brown glove extracted the key from the door. The man followed Borenboim in, immediately closing the door behind them.

"Turn on the light," he ordered.

Borenboim groped for the wide button of the switch. He pressed it. The lights in the whole five-room apartment lit up at once. Music could be heard: Leonard Cohen's "Suzanne."

"On your knees," said the man, poking the gun between Borenboim's shoulder blades.

Borenboim lowered himself onto the beige area-rug.

"Hands behind you."

He let go of the briefcase and stretched his hands behind him. Handcuffs clicked shut over his wrists. The man began searching Borenboim's pockets.

"There's money in the desk in the study. About two thousand. That's it," Borenboim muttered.

The man went on searching him. Took his wallet out of his pocket, his cell phone, a gold Gucci lighter.

He put everything on the floor.

He opened the briefcase: business papers, two pipes in a leather case, a tin of tobacco, a collection of stories by Borges.

"Get up." The man took Borenboim by the elbow.

Borenboim stood up. He glanced at the man.

The man: 36 years old, short, strongly built, blond, blue eyes, short hair, a heavy face, a thin light-colored mustache, a steel-colored raincoat, a light gray scarf, a black leather backpack on his back.

"Forward," the man said, poking Borenboim with the gun.

Borenboim moved forward. They passed the first living room with the round aquarium and soft furniture. They entered the second. This one had low Japanese furniture. Three scrolls and a flat-screen television hung on the walls. The stereo system stood in a corner—a dark black-and-blue pyramid.

The man walked over to the pyramid. He looked at it.

"How do you turn it off?"

"There's the remote." Borenboim nodded toward a low square table. A black-and-blue remote control lay on the edge.

The man picked it up. He hit the "power" button and the music stopped.

"Sit." He pushed on Borenboim's shoulder. Sat him down on a narrow chair with a red pillow.

He put the pistol back in his pocket and removed his backpack. He opened it up. Took out a hammer and two steel mountain-climbing spikes.

"What are the walls in the building?"

"What do you mean?" Borenboim, grown pale, blinked tensely.

"Brick, concrete?"

"Brick."

The man yanked two of the scrolls off the wall. He took aim and, level with his shoulders, hammered the spike into the wall with three blows. He moved over a couple of meters, hammered in the second spike. On the same level. Then he took out a cell phone. He punched in a number.

"Everything's okay. All right. It's open."

Dibich soon entered the apartment: 32 years old, a tall, thin, broad-shouldered blond, blue-gray eyes, a cruel bony face, grayish-blue coat, dark blue beret, dark blue gloves, a dark blue-and-yellow scarf, an oblong sports bag.

She looked around. Barely glanced at Borenboim.

"Good."

The man took a rope out of his pack. He cut it in half with a knife.

They lifted Borenboim. They removed his handcuffs and began to strip off his jacket.

"Can you tell me what you want—like human beings?" asked Borenboim.

"Not yet." Dibich took his right hand and tied the rope around it.

"I don't keep money at home."

"We don't want money. We're not robbers."

"Then who are you? Insurance agents?" Borenboim grinned nervously. He licked his dry lips.

"We're not insurance agents," Dibich answered seriously. "But we need you."

"For what?"

"Relax. And don't be afraid of anything."

She tied his hand to the spikes in the wall.

"Are you sadists?" Borenboim stood with his hands out to his sides.

"No." Dibich took off her coat. Under it she wore a dark blue suit with delicate stripes.

"What do you want? What the fuck do you want?" Borenboim's voice cracked.

The man taped his mouth shut. Dibich unfastened the bag. An oblong, mini refrigerator lay in it. She opened it. Took out an ice hammer.

The man unbuttoned Borenboim's vest and shirt, ripped open his undershirt. Suddenly Borenboim kicked him in the groin. The man bent over. Hissed. Fell to his knees.

"Asshole . . ."

Dibich waited. She leaned on the handle of the hammer.

"Goddamn . . ." The man frowned.

Dibich waited a bit. She looked at the scroll hanging on the wall.

"The ice is melting, Obu."

The man stood up. They approached Borenboim; he tried to kick Dibich.

"Hold his legs," she said.

The man grabbed Borenboim's knees. Held them tight. Froze.

"Speak with the heart!" Dibich swung back gracefully. The hammer made a half circle through the air and whistled. It slammed into Borenboim's chest.

Borenboim growled. Dibich placed her ear to his chest.

"Speak, speak, speak . . ."

Borenboim groaned. He jerked.

Dibich stepped back. Swung back. Hit him—with all her might.

The hammer cracked. Pieces of ice flew all around.

Borenboim moaned. He hung limp on the rope. His head slumped down on his chest.

Dibich pressed close.

"Speak, speak, speak . . ."

A sound arose in his chest.
Dibich listened carefully.
The man listened, too.
"Mo…kho…" Dibich said.
She straightened up with a satisfied look.
"His name is Mokho."
"Mokho," the man spoke. He frowned—then he smiled.

Brothers and Sisters

BORENBOIM opened his eyes.

He was sitting in a triangular bathtub. Warm streams of water flowed pleasantly around his body. Two naked women sat opposite him.

Ar: 31 years old, plump, blond, blue eyes, large breasts, round fleshy shoulders, a simple smiling peasant face.

Ekos: 48, small, slender, blond, blue eyes, an attentive intelligent face.

The light in the spacious bathroom was dim. Just three fat blue candles burned on the edges of the tub.

"Hello, Mokho," smiled the plump woman. "I'm Ar, your sister."

Borenboim wiped the moisture from his face. He looked around. He gazed at the candle.

"And I'm Borenboim, Boris Borisovich. My only sister, Anna Borisovna Borenboim-Vikers, died in a car accident in 1992. Near the city of Los Angeles."

"Now you will have many sisters and brothers," said Ekos.

"I doubt it." Borenboim touched the large bruise on his chest. "My mother is in the other world as well. My father is in the hospital following a stroke. The likelihood that he will gladden me with a brother or sister is about zero."

"Blood isn't the only form of brotherhood."

"Of course. There are also brothers in misfortune." Borenboim nodded. "When they put you in a common grave together alive."

"There is a brotherhood of the heart," Ar said softly.

"Is that when a person sells one of his heart valves? And has an artificial one put in its place? I've heard about that. Not a bad business."

"Mokho, your cynicism is boring." Ekos took his left hand in hers. Ar took the right one.

"I'm really a very boring person. That's why I live alone. As for cynicism—it's the only thing that saves me. Rather, that saved me. Up until March 2nd."

"Why only until March 2nd?" Ekos asked, stroking his wrist under the water.

"Because I made a bad decision on March 2nd. I decided to drive only with the driver, and not to take my bodyguard. To loan him to Rita Soloukhina. Who needed a driver. Why? She burned her hand. When? She was making fondue. With soft cheese, with—"

"Do you regret helping her?" asked Ar, stroking his other hand.

"I regret that I betrayed my cynicism for a moment."

"You felt sorry for her?"

"Not exactly . . . I just like her legs. And she's a good worker."

"Mokho, that's a rather cynical argument."

"No it isn't. If it were truly cynical, I wouldn't have ended up as a chump who gets taken with bare hands."

"Weren't they wearing gloves?" asked Ekos, raising her slender eyebrows. She and Ar laughed.

"Yes," said Borenboim seriously, biting his lips, "the bastards were wearing gloves. By the way, girls, where are my glasses?"

"Do you take a bath in your glasses?"

"Sometimes."

"They fog up."

"That doesn't get in the way."

"Of seeing?"

"Of thinking. Where are they?"

"Behind you."

He turned around. Next to his head on a marble stand lay his glasses and his watch. On the watch: **23:55**.

He put on his glasses. He began putting on his watch.

A naked girl walked through the open door: 12 years old, a thin angular body, hairless pubis, short strawberry-blond hair, large blue eyes, a calm kind face.

"Hi, Mokho."

Borenboim looked at her darkly.

"I'm Ip."

Borenboim was about to say something, but he noticed a large white scar on the girl's chest. He looked at his bruise.

"May I put my hand on your chest?" the girl asked.

Borenboim looked at her scar, then he looked at the women. Each of them had scars in the center of her chest.

"They...you, too?" He straightened his glasses.

The women nodded, smiling.

"They hit me on the chest with the ice ax sixteen times." Ar rose to her knees. "Look."

He saw the scars of healed welts on her chest.

"I lost consciousness three times. Until my heart spoke and pronounced my true name: Ar. After that they carried me to the bathhouse, washed me, and bandaged my wounds. And then one of the brothers pressed his chest to mine. And his heart spoke with my heart. And I cried. For the first time in my life, I cried from happiness."

"I was hit seven times," Ekos spoke up. "Here...you see...there's one big scar and two small ones. I was completely covered with blood. They took me at the dacha. Tied me to an oak. And hit me with the ice ax. But my heart was silent. It didn't want to speak. It didn't want to awake. It wanted to sleep until death. To rot in the grave, asleep, like billions of people...My skin is very delicate. The ice broke it right away. There was a lot of blood. The hammer was soaked in blood. But when my heart finally spoke and pronounced my true name—Ekos—the man who wielded the ax kissed me. On the lips. That was my first brotherly kiss."

"Kissed you?"

"Yes."

"The one who struck you?"

"The one who struck me."

"You mean the guy who set you up and knocked you out?" Borenboim laughed nervously, looking into the girl's big eyes.

"Put it that way, if you like," Ekos answered calmly.

"Your cynicism—is a kind of armor. Your only defense against sincerity. Which has always frightened you," said Ar, stroking his hand.

"As soon as that defense crumbles, not only will you be happy, you will understand what genuine freedom is," added Ekos.

The girl was still on her knees. She looked at Borenboim with a childlike, questioning look.

"Hmm, yeah... probably..." He had trouble tearing his eyes from the girl. "But the one who knocked me out didn't kiss me. Too bad."

He straightened his glasses decisively and, without warning, stood up. Water splashed on the women.

"Here's the thing, girls. I'm not in the mood for underwater massage right now. So we're not going to relax. I don't have the time. Call in your muscle. Let them tell me in plain Russian: how much, where, and when."

"There isn't any 'muscle' here," said Ekos, wiping her face with her palm.

"There's only us and a servant." Ar smiled.

"And the cat," said the girl. "But she's asleep in the basket right now. She's going to have kittens soon. May I put my hand on your chest?"

"What for?" asked Borenboim.

"To speak with your heart."

Borenboim got out of the bath. He took a towel and wiped his glasses. He began drying himself. He winced from the pain.

"So the muscle is outside. Got it."

"Outside?" Ekos stroked her shoulder. "There isn't anyone there either. Only birch trees."

"And snow. But it's already dirty," added the girl.

Borenboim glanced at her sullenly. He tied the towel around his thin torso.

"Where are my clothes?"

"In the bedroom."

He left the bathroom. He found himself in a spacious house with many rooms. It was richly decorated: rugs, expensive furniture, crystal chandeliers, old-master paintings. Mozart playing softly somewhere.

He walked over to a window. Pulled back the green velvet drapes. Looked out on the birch forest at night, white patches of leftover snow glowing in the half dark. A dog barked somewhere in the distance.

"What you like to chink?" It was a woman's voice, heavily accented.

He turned around.

A Thai woman stood a ways off: 42 years old, short, rather ugly, heavy, in a gray leisure suit, blue flip-flops with sequins on swarthy bare feet with lilac toenails.

"Where is the bedroom?" Borenboim looked at her feet squeamishly.

"Heyah it is." She turned around and walked off.

He followed her.

She led him to a room. Pointed with a wrinkled hand.

The bedroom was small, its walls covered in Indian linen in a yellow-green pattern. There was a mirror with a small table under it, an Indian brocade hassock, two large bronze vases in the corners, a double bed covered with an Indian bedspread. On the bed lay Borenboim's clothes in a neat pile.

He went over to them and picked them up. He checked the pockets: his wallet, keys. The cell phone was in his briefcase.

He put on his underwear and trousers. His torn undershirt had been replaced with a new one.

"Efficient . . ." He grinned.

He put on the undershirt, his shirt, the vest. He began tying his tie.

"May I speak to your heart?" came the sound of the girl's voice.

He looked around: Ip stood naked in the door of the bedroom. Drops of water shone on her child's body.

He knotted his tie, put on his boots and his jacket. He buttoned the two bottom buttons of his jacket.

He glanced at himself in the mirror. He walked out of the room, brushing against Ip's wet shoulder.

"What you like to chink?" The Thai woman stood in the middle of the living room.

"Chink," he grimaced. "Aspen tree juice?"

"Apsen tea what?" she said, not understanding.

"Aspen juice. Or birch milk, at least?"

"Burr-uch?" she said, her small forehead creasing.

"Forget it," Borenboim said, dismissing her with a wave of his hand. "Where's the exit?"

"Ovah heyah." The woman obediently set off.

She went into the foyer. She opened a white door into a covered entrance. She put on a large pair of felt boots with galoshes, right over her flip-flops. She wrapped a gray wool scarf around her head, opened the front door, and walked down the marble steps.

Borenboim walked out of the house. The yard, and the house itself, were brightly lit. A thick birch forest surrounded the house.

The servant walked down a wide paved road toward steel gates set in a high brick wall. The felt boots shuffled along.

Borenboim looked around. He raised the collar of his jacket and inhaled the raw night air. He followed the servant tensely.

She walked up to the gates, put the key in the lock, and turned it.

The gates slid back.

"May I talk to your heart?" said the voice behind him.

Borenboim looked back at the house. Two stories, white walls, gray roof tiling, two chimneys, decorative grates on the windows, a copper sun over the door. Against the illuminated background of the house stood a barely distinguishable naked figure. She approached silently. In the gloom Ip's eyes seemed even larger.

There was no one in the half-dark windows of the house.

"May I?" Ip took his hand in her damp hands.

Borenboim looked through the open gates: beyond them was an empty night street. Puddles. A post. A chipped fence. A normal dacha village.

"You'll catch cold," he said.

"No," Ip answered seriously. "Please, may I? Then you can go home."

"Okay," he said with a businesslike nod. "Only make it quick."

She looked around, looked at the swings near a gazebo, and pulled him by the hand.

"Let's go over there."

Borenboim went. Then he stopped.

"No. We're not going there."

He looked at the gates.

"We'll go over there."

"All right," she said, pulling him toward the gates.

They walked outside the gates. Ip pulled Borenboim to an icy snowbank on the side of the road. He followed her. Ice crunched under his boots. Ip moved silently and easily on her bare feet.

"An angel, damnit…" Borenboim thought. He said, "Only quickly, half a minute. I'm serious."

The small Thai woman in the felt boots stood orphaned at the open gates. The suburban Moscow wind fluttered the ends of her wool scarf.

Ip led Borenboim to the snowbank. She climbed up on him. Her face was on the same level as Borenboim's face. His glasses gleamed in the dark.

The girl carefully embraced him with thin but long arms and pressed her chest to his. He didn't resist. Their cheeks touched.

"Okay." He turned slightly, moving his face away.

He looked at the illuminated house. He sang out in a low voice in English, "'Darling, stop confusing me with your'…"

Suddenly, his entire body shuddered. He was rooted to the spot.

Ip was, too.

They stood motionless.

The Thai woman watched them.

Twenty-three minutes passed. The girl released her hands. Borenboim fell weakly on the icy road. Ip slid onto the snowbank. She sniffled, pulling air through her clenched teeth, gulping for air. The streetlamp faintly lit her fragile white body.

Borenboim moved. He cried out feebly. He sat up. Moaned. Then fell again, stretching out. He breathed greedily. Opened his eyes. In the black sky, between the flocked clouds, stars twinkled dimly.

The girl got up off the snowbank, barely causing the snow to crack. She walked to the gates and went inside. A faint hum could be heard, and the gates closed.

Borenboim turned over. The snow made a crunching sound. He got up on all fours. Crawled. He pushed his hands against the earth and rose to his feet slowly. Unsteady, he straightened up.

"Ooooo...no."

He looked at the street. At the snowbank.

"Not...oh, my god..." He shook his head.

He went up to the gates. He began banging them with his dirty hands.

"Hey, hey...come on...hey..."

He listened. Everything was quiet on the other side.

Borenboim threw himself at the gates. He beat on them with his hands and feet. His glasses flew off.

He listened. Silence.

He wailed, pressing himself against the gates. He slipped to the ground and began to cry. Then he got up, took several steps back, and with his legs bent, took a running leap, kicking the gates.

He listened. No answer.

He inhaled more air and cried out as loud as he could.

An echo carried the cry all around.

A dog began to bark somewhere far away. Then another.

"Please, I beg of you...I'm begging you!" Borenboim shouted, banging on the gates. "I'm begging you! I'm begging you! I'm begging!!! Damnit, I'm begging!!!"

His heartrending cry broke off in a wheeze. He fell silent. He licked his lips.

The moon sailed out from behind the clouds. Two dogs barked reluctantly.

"No...you can't do this..." Borenboim stepped back from the fence, his glasses crunching under his feet. He leaned over and picked them up. The left lens was cracked, but it hadn't fallen out.

He took out a handkerchief and wiped his glasses. Put them on. He threw the handkerchief in a puddle. Sniffling, he sighed. He wandered along the street.

He made it to an intersection, turned, reached another intersection, almost ran into a car. A red Niva jeep braked sharply. The puddle splashed him.

The driver opened the door: 47 years old, a thin wrinkled face, sunken cheeks, steel teeth, a leather cap.

"You outta your fuckin' mind?"

"Sorry, pal." Borenboim leaned his arms against the hood. He exhaled with exhaustion. "Take me to the police. I was attacked."

"What?" The driver screwed up his eyes nastily.

"Take me there, I'll pay…" Borenboim wiped the drops of water from his face. He dug in his inside pocket. Took out his wallet and opened it. Held it up to the dirty headlight: all four credit cards were in place. But, as always, not a single ruble. And? Another card: a Visa Electron. In his name. He'd never had one of those. He had a Visa Gold. He turned the new card over.

"What the fuck?" he said in English.

In the corner of the card he made out a handwritten PIN code: 6969.

"Well, are we gonna stand around a long time?" the driver asked.

"Just a minute, just a minute… Listen… what station are we at?"

"Kratovo."

"Kratovo?" Borenboim looked at the driver's hat. "Novoriazansk Highway… Take me into Moscow, pal. A hundred bucks."

"That's it. Get away from the car," the driver replied angrily.

"Or to the police… I mean, to the highway… to Riazanka!"

The driver slammed the door. The Niva zoomed off. Borenboim jumped back.

The jeep turned the corner.

Borenboim looked at the card.

"Shit… gifts of the magi… with a PIN code, no less! Nonsense, utter nonsense."

He returned the card to his wallet and stuck the wallet in his pocket. He walked down the street past the fences and darkened dachas. He shivered. He put his hands in his trouser pockets.

There was a light on in the window of one dacha.

Right next to the solid gates in the wall was a little wicket gate. Borenboim went over to it and tugged. The gate was locked.

"Anyone home?" he shouted.

A dog began barking in the house.

Borenboim waited. No one responded. He shouted again. And again. The dog barked.

He dug out a handful of wet snow and made a snowball. He threw it at the window of the porch.

The dog kept on barking. No one came out.

"'And neither wake the prince...nor the dinosaur,' as the poet said...shit." Borenboim spat. He walked along the dark street, which narrowed to a muddy path. Green and gray fences squeezed in on either side.

Borenboim walked along. A thin layer of ice crunched under his feet.

Suddenly the path broke off. Ahead was a steep descent, muddy with melted water and snow. He could dimly make out a small river. Black. Occasional chunks of ice.

"'The ball is over, the candle is out, I'll fuck you slowly'..."

Borenboim stood there for a minute. He shivered and turned around. Walked back. He came to the house with the light in the window and made a snowball. He threw it in the air. He kicked it. Suddenly, he sobbed out loud like a child, defenselessly. He ran down the street, sobbing. He screamed. Then he stopped.

"No...not like that...Oooo. Mama...! You asshole...fucking asshole...oooo! It's just...just...you asshole..."

He blew his nose in his palm. Sniffling, he walked on. Turning right, then left. He came out on a wide street. A truck was driving by.

"Hey, chief! Hey!!" Borenboim cried out hoarsely in desperation. He ran after the truck.

The truck stopped.

"Chief, give me a ride!" Borenboim yelled as he ran up.

The driver looked out drunkenly through the window: 50 years old, a crude yellowish-brown face, a rabbit-fur hat, a gray padded jacket, a cigarette.

"To Moscow."

"To Moscow," laughed the driver. "Holy shit, man, I'm going home to sleep."

"Then to the station?"

"To the station? It's right here, why drive there?"

"Right here?"

"Sure."

"How far?"

"Ten minutes on foot, for Christ's sake. Go that way..." He waved a dirty hand out the window.

Borenboim turned around. He headed down the road. The truck drove off.

Headlights appeared ahead of him. Borenboim lifted his right hand. He waved it.

The car drove by.

He arrived at the station. A white Zhiguli was parked next to a twenty-four-hour kiosk selling drinks. The driver was buying beer.

"Hey pal, listen," said Borenboim walking over to him. "I have a big problem."

The driver looked at him suspiciously: 42 years old, tall, stout, round-faced, in a brown jacket.

"What is it?"

"I...need to find a house around here...I can't remember the number..."

"Where?"

"Here...right nearby."

"How much?"

"Fifty bucks."

The driver squinted his puffy, piglike eyes.

"Money up front."

Borenboim automatically took out his wallet, then remembered.

"I don't have any cash...I'll pay, I'll pay later."

"No go," said the driver, shaking his massive head.

"Wait a minute..." Borenboim touched his cheek with a dirty hand. Then he took his watch off his left wrist.

"Here, take my watch...it's Swiss...it's worth a thousand bucks...I was attacked, you understand? Let's go, let's find them."

"I don't play other people's games," said the driver, shaking his head.

"Hey, friend, you won't come out a loser!"

"If you was attacked, go to the cops. They're right here."

"What the fuck do I need the police for?...What's the goddamn problem, it's worth a thousand bucks! Maurice Lacroix!" Borenboim shook the watch in front of him.

The driver thought a moment, then sniffed.

"No. No go."

"Jeez, shit…" Borenboim exhaled tiredly. "Why are you so fucking law abiding all of a sudden?"

He looked around. There weren't any other cars.

"All right, all right. I'll find them later. Can you at least take me into Moscow? I'll give you rubles or dollars when I get home. Whatever you want."

"Where in Moscow?"

"Tverskaya, the center. Or wait… better to Leninsky. Leninsky Prospect."

The driver squinted.

"Two hundred bucks."

"Okay."

"Money up front."

"Christ! I just told you—I was robbed, mugged! Here's the security deposit—the watch! I can show you my credit cards!"

"Watch?" The driver looked at it, as though he'd never seen it. "How much does it go for?"

"A thousand bucks."

He looked bored, then he sniffed and sighed. Took the watch. Examined it. Stuck it in his pocket.

"All right, get in."

Rat Droppings

35 Leninsky Prospect

THE ZHIGULI drove into a courtyard.

"Wait just a minute." Borenboim got out of the car. He walked over to the door of entrance 4. Punched in an apartment number on the intercom.

For a long time no one answered. Then a sleepy male voice asked, "Yeah?"

"Savva, it's Boris. I have a problem."

"Borya?"

"Yes, yes, open up, please."

The door beeped.

Borenboim walked in. He ran up the steps to the elevator and took it to the third floor. He approached a big door with a video camera. The door opened slowly.

Savva looked out of it: 47 years old, big, heavyset, balding, a sleepy face, wearing a dark red robe.

"Borya, what's up?" he said, squinting sleepily. "Good lord, you look like something the cat dragged in."

"Hi." Borenboim straightened his glasses. "Give me two hundred bucks to pay the taxi."

"Are you on a binge? Did someone beat you up?"

"No, no. It's a lot more serious. Come on, come on, hurry up!"

They entered a spacious foyer. Savva slid back the door of a semi-transparent wardrobe. He reached in the pocket of a dark blue coat, retrieved his wallet, and took out two hundred-dollar bills. Borenboim grabbed them and rushed downstairs. But the Zhiguli wasn't there.

"Damn!" Borenboim spit on the ground. He went to the corner of the building. The car was nowhere to be seen.

"Sometimes these people are incredibly sharp." He laughed angrily. Crumpled the bills. Stuck them in his pocket. "Fuck you," he said in English.

He went back to Savva's.

"Was it enough?" Savva went into the kitchen. He turned on the light.

"Quite."

"Your glasses are broken. You're all muddy…what happened, were you attacked or something? Come on, why don't you…take this off, put on…you want something else to put on? Or want to go straight into the shower?"

"I want a drink." Borenboim took off his filthy jacket and threw it in a corner.

He sat down at a round glass table with a wide border of stainless steel.

"Maybe take a shower first? Were you beaten?"

"A drink, a drink." Borenboim rested his chin on his fist and closed his eyes. "And something strong to smoke."

"Vodka? Wine? There's . . . beer, too."

"Whiskey? Or don't you have any?"

"You insult me, boss." Savva left the room with a sweeping gesture. He returned with a bottle of Tullamore Dew and a pack of Bogatyr cigarettes. "Ain't nothin' stronger."

Borenboim quickly lit up. He took off his glasses. Rubbed his forehead above the eyebrows with his fingertips.

"On the rocks?" Savva took out a glass.

"Straight."

Savva poured the whiskey.

"What happened?"

Borenboim drank silently, emptying the glass.

"Hooooowever, my father in heaven!" Savva sang in a church chant. He poured some more.

Borenboim downed it. He turned the glass back and forth.

"I was attacked."

"Right." Savva sat down opposite him.

"But I don't know who they are or what they want."

"Ich bin ne undershtandt." Savva slapped his palms on his pudgy cheeks.

"Me neither. Nicht undershtandt. Yet."

"And . . . when?"

"Yesterday evening. I went home. Right by my door some prick stuck a pistol in my side. And then . . ."

Sabina entered the kitchen sleepily: 38 years old, tall and strapping, athletic.

"Zum Gottes willen! Borya? Are you having a man's drinking bout already?" she said, speaking with a light German accent.

"Binosh, Borya has a problem."

"Did something happen?" She stroked his messy hair. She leaned over and embraced Borenboim. "Oy, you're all muddy. What's this?"

"Just … men's business." He kissed her on the cheek.

"Serious?"

"So-so. Not very."

"Do you want to eat? We have some salad."

"No, no. I don't need anything."

"Then I'll go to bed." She yawned.

"Schlaf wohl, Schätzchen." Savva embraced her.

"Trink wohl, Schweinchen." She patted him on his bald spot. She left.

Borenboim took another cigarette. He lit it from the butt of the first and continued.

"Then this guy followed me into the apartment. Handcuffed me. A woman came in. They hammered two spike things into the wall. And strung me up with a rope. They crucified me, goddamnit, on the wall, like Christ. So. And then … it was … very strange … they opened a sort of … it was like a safe … and there was this weird hammer in it … an odd, archaic sort of form … with a handle made from a branch … very crude. But the hammerhead wasn't steel or wood, it was ice. Ice. I don't know whether it was artificial or real, but it was ice. And then—picture this—the broad starts slamming my chest with this hammer. She keeps saying, 'Talk to me with your heart, tell me with your heart.' But … it was so strange! They taped my mouth shut! With packing tape. I'm mooing, she's bashing me. With all her fucking strength, man. So, this ice splinters and flies around the room. She's pounding me and talking all this bullshit. It hurt like hell, went straight through me. I've never felt pain like that. Even when my meniscus went out. So. They're banging and banging me. Then I just lost consciousness."

He took a swallow from the glass.

Savva listened.

"Sav, this all sounds like nonsense. Or a dream. But—here, take a look …" He unbuttoned his shirt to show the huge bruise on his chest. "That's not a dream."

Savva stretched out a pudgy hand. He touched it.

"Does it hurt?"

"A bit … when you press it. My head hurts. And my neck."

"Drink, Borya, relax."

"And you?"

"I . . . I have to go in early tomorrow, that is, today."

Borenboim emptied the glass of whiskey. Savva poured some more right away.

"But the most interesting part was after. I wake up and I'm sitting in a Jacuzzi. There are two women with me. The water's bubbling. And these women start patting me gently and telling me some non-sense about a brotherhood, that we're all brothers and sisters—talk-ing about sincerity, frankness, and so on. It turns out that they'd been hit in the chest with the same kind of hammer, they showed me the scars. Actual scars. And they were pounded until they spoke with their hearts. They said all of us in this fucking brotherhood have our own names. Their names were Var, Mar, I don't remember. And my name—is Mokho. You get it?"

"What?"

"Mokho!"

"Mokho?" Savva looked at him with small, weak-sighted eyes.

"My name is Mokho!" Borenboim shouted and began laughing. He leaned against the back of the stainless-steel chair. Clutched at his chest. Winced. Swayed.

Savva watched him intently.

Borenboim giggled nervously. He rocked back and forth on the chair. He took a new handkerchief out of his pocket. Wiped his eyes. Blew his nose. Rubbed his chest.

"It hurts when I laugh. So you see, Savochka. But that's not all ei-ther. We're sitting there, sitting in that Jacuzzi. And suddenly a girl comes in. Really young . . . probably about eleven. Blondish, with huge blue eyes. And with the same sorts of scars on her chest. She comes in and sits down next to me. I'm thinking: Okay, now I get it, they're gonna try and pin rape of a minor on my prick. But she just sits there. And suddenly I notice—they're all blue-eyed blonds. The two who bashed me with the hammer were also blue-eyed and blond. Like I am! You get it?"

Savva nodded.

"And I realized this wasn't the usual kind of attack. I say to them,

'Girls, that's enough splashing, call over your heavies. I'll ask what they want.' And they say, 'We don't have any muscle here.' And you know, I believed them. Uh-huh. And this little girl, this blue-eyed Thumbelina, she kept on saying, kept repeating the same thing over and over like she was a doll: 'Let me talk to your heart, let me ...' So I just got up. My clothes were there. I got dressed. Looked around. Nobody else around. There's no one. It turned out to be a real New Russian house, real fat cats. There's no one there, only the servant. And this naked girl. I walked out into the yard, headed for the gates. And the naked girl followed me. The servant opened the gate, no problem, so I left. There was a street, a normal dacha kind of street, this was all in Kratovo. And the naked girl—followed me out the gate! She started with the 'Let me talk to your heart' stuff again. Well, I think, what the hell—go on, talk! She comes up to me, hugs me, and glues herself to my chest like a leech. And you know, Savva"—here Borenboim's voice trembled—"I ... well, you've known me twelve years. ... I'm a grown-up guy, all business, pragmatic—shit, man, I know what's what, it's hard to pull anything over on me, but ... you know ... what happened then was ..." Borenboim's delicate nostrils began to flutter. "I ... it ... I still don't know what it was ... and what the whole thing was ..."

He fell silent and blew his nose in his handkerchief. He drank a little bit.

Savva poured some more.

"And ... ?"

"Just a minute ..." Borenboim exhaled, licked his lips. He sighed and continued. "You see, she hugged me. So, big deal, she hugged me. But then suddenly I got this funny feeling ... like ... everything in me became ... sort of slower, slower. My thoughts, and everything ... everything. And I could feel my heart really clearly, fucking unbelievably clearly ... very sort of ... acute ... sharp and gentle at the same time. It's hard to explain ... but it's kind of like the body, it's just some kind of senseless meat, and there's a heart in it, and this heart ... it's ... well it's not meat at all, but something else. And it started beating really unevenly, like I had an arrhythmia ... or something. And this little girl ... this ... she froze and didn't move. And suddenly I could feel her with my heart. Just like I could feel someone's hand with my hand. And her heart started talking to mine. But not in words, in... sort of like...spurts or waves or something...and my heart was trying to answer. In the same kind of bursts..."

He poured himself some more whiskey and drank it. Took a cigarette from the pack and rolled it in his hands. Sighed. Put it back in the box.

"And when it started, everything all around, everything, the whole world, it kind of stopped. And everything was sort of...so good and clear, right away...so good..." He sobbed. "I've...never, like that... never, never ever...felt...anything like...that."

Borenboim let out a sob. He pressed his hand against his mouth. A wave of silent sobs rolled over him.

"Listen, maybe, you..." Savva began to get up.

"No, no...no..." Borenboim shook his head. "Just sit there...Sit awhile..."

Savva sat back down.

Raising his glasses, Borenboim rubbed his eyes. He sniffed.

"And that's not all. When it was all over, she went back into the house. I...was...I stood there and knocked. Banged on the gates. I really wanted her to be with me again. Not her. But her heart. So. But no one opened them. Those are the rules of the game, damnit. So I left. I walked to the station. Hired some stiff to drive me in. Oh! And when I reached in my pocket, I found this in my wallet..."

Borenboim took out his wallet. He extracted the Visa Electron card. Threw it on the table.

Savva picked it up.

"And now, that's it..." Borenboim drank some whiskey. "I have a premonition that this isn't just a piece of plastic. There's something there. You see, in the corner there?"

"A PIN code?"

"What else could it be?"

"It could be." Savva gave him back the card.

"Yugrabank. Do you know it?"

"I've heard of it. A Gazprom outfit. In Yugorsk. Kind of far away."

"Do you know anyone there?"

"No. But that's not a problem—to find someone. But what exactly do you want to know?"

"Well, like who deposited it? I'm sure there's money in the account."

"Why guess? Wait till the morning. Listen, those . . . the ones that hammered you?"

"I didn't see them again."

Savva sat there quietly. He chewed on his lip. Touched his small nose.

"Borya, how could they stick a gun in your side if you've got a bodyguard?"

"That's the whole thing! Yesterday I gave my bodyguard to an employee. She burned her hand and can't drive. So I, well . . . helped a girl out by giving her my guy. Fucking human-loving asshole that I am . . ."

Savva nodded.

"Well, what do you think?"

"Right now—nothing."

"Why?"

"Listen, Bor. But . . . just don't get mad. Are you . . . snorting very much?"

"Not a speck in the last month."

"You sure?"

"I swear."

Savva frowned.

"Well, what should I do?" Borenboim took a cigarette. Lit it.

Savva shrugged his meaty shoulder.

"Call Platov. Or your own guys."

Tipsy by now, Borenboim grinned.

"That's exactly what I'll do! In about three hours. But I want to understand . . . I want to hear your opinion. What do you think about all this?"

Savva didn't reply. He looked at Borenboim's pointed beard. Beads of sweat appeared on it.

"Sav?"

"Yes."

"What do you think about this?"

"Well, somehow . . . nothing."

"Why?"

"I don't know."

"What do you mean, you don't believe me?"

"I believe, I believe," said Savva, nodding his head. "Bor, I believe anything and everything nowadays. Three days ago the health inspectors showed up at the bank. In the basement next door they were spraying for cockroaches. And they did us at the same time, too. They began with the cockroaches, and then found mountains of rat droppings. And you know where? In the ventilation system. Mountains of it, huge deposits. Fucking unbelievable! And the most incredible thing was that no one had ever heard any rats. Not the employees, not the guards, not the cleaning ladies. And there wasn't anything for them to eat in our place. Why would they be shitting so much? Or what—they're eating in one place and crawling into my bank to take a shit? A real mystery! I thought and thought about it. I called a meeting of the directors' council and said, 'Gentlemen, it seems we have a provocation on our hands. There's no goddamn rats anywhere! But there's shit. Therefore, someone put it there on purpose. Is this a hint? About what?' No one said anything. You know that we only recently managed to get Zhorik off our case. And then Grisha Sinaiko, he's a smart guy, he spent four years at Creditanstalt, he looked at me with this intense look and said, 'Savva, this is not a hint. If it was human shit—that would be an obvious hint. Then it'd be time to sweat. But rat droppings—aren't a hint. They're just r-a-t droppings! And if there's rat shit, then that means that rats were shitting. Ordinary Moscow rats. Believe my experience.' You know what, Bor? I thought about it. And I believed him."

Borenboim stood up sharply. He picked up his jacket from the floor. Went into the foyer.

"Give me some rubles for a taxi."

Savva rose with difficulty. He followed him.

"Listen, Bor," he said, placing a heavy hand on Borenboim's thin shoulder, "I really recommend that you—"

"Give me some rubles for a taxi!" Borenboim interrupted.

"Bor. If you want, I'll call Mishkarik at the FSB, okay? They'll definitely be able to tell you something—"

"Give me some rubles for a taxi!"

Savva sighed. He disappeared into darkened rooms.

Borenboim put on his jacket and hit the wall with his palm. He clenched his fists and exhaled with a hiss.

Savva returned with a packet of hundred-ruble notes.

"Put my coat on. You'll be cold like that."

Borenboim pulled two hundred-ruble notes out of the pack. He fished the two crumpled hundred-dollar bills out of his pocket and forced them into Savva's hand.

"Thanks a lot, honey child," he said in English.

He opened the door. He left.

Rat Heart

6 Tverskaya Street

BORENBOIM unlocked the door of his apartment. He entered and turned on the light.

The music started up: Leonard Cohen as usual.

Borenboim stood at the half-open door.

He looked into the apartment. Everything was as it had been.

He closed the door. He walked through the rooms, looked into the bathroom, the kitchen.

No one.

His briefcase, cell phone, and lighter were lying on the low table in the Japanese living room.

He looked at the walls. All three scrolls hung in their previous places. He walked over to them. He moved the left scroll aside. The hole from the spike had been carefully filled. The water-based paint hadn't dried yet. The second hole under the other scroll had also been repaired.

"Holy shit…" Borenboim muttered, shaking his head. "No-waste production. This is a serious outfit."

He chuckled.

He opened his briefcase and leafed through the papers: everything was in place. He got out his pipe. He filled it with tobacco, lit up, and began to smoke. He walked over to the aquarium shaped like a half circle. He whistled. The fish grew excited. They swam up to the surface.

He retrieved a covered Chinese cup from a niche in the wall. Opened it. The cup contained fish food. He tapped bits of food into the aquarium.

"My poor starving…"

The fish gobbled the food.

Borenboim closed the cup. He put it back in the niche.

He turned off the music. Taking a bottle of Famous Grouse whiskey from the Japanese cabinet, he poured half a glass and drank it. He sat down. He picked up his cell phone, put it back on the table, stood up, and went to the kitchen. He opened the refrigerator.

It was empty except for four identical containers of salad on the second shelf. Wrapped in plastic.

He took out a container of beet salad. He put it on the table, got out a spoon, and sat down. He began to devour the salad.

He ate everything.

He put the empty container in the sink and wiped his lips with a napkin.

Back into the Japanese room: he picked up the telephone and punched in a number. He listened, then changed his mind.

"Shut the fuck up!" he exclaimed in English.

He tossed the phone on the table. Poured some more whiskey. Drank. He knocked the ashes out of the extinguished pipe and started to fill it again. He stopped. Got up. Walked back to the aquarium.

"'Darling, stop confusing me with your wishful thinking…'" he sang. He sighed. His thin lips contorted in a sad grimace. He tapped the thick glass.

The fish swam toward him.

He went into the bathroom and turned on the tap. He placed the glass of whiskey on the edge of the tub. Undressed. Looked at himself in the mirror. Touched the bruise on his chest.

"Speak, heart…speak, mitral valve.…Bastards!"

He laughed a worn-out laugh.

He got into the bath.

He drank the rest of the whiskey.

He turned off the water.

He leaned his head back against the cold depression of the headrest.

He sighed in relief.

He slept.

He dreamed a dream: he was a teenager, at his stepfather's dacha in Sosenki, standing at the gate and looking out at the street. Vitka, Karas, and Gera were walking down the street toward him. They were supposed to go together to the Salarevsky dump. The guys were approaching. They held sticks for poking around in the garbage. His stick stood next to the fence. He picked it up and walked toward them. They walked quickly and happily down the street. It was early in the morning, midsummer, the weather dry and cool. He was enjoying himself and his step was light. They came to the dump. It was enormous, stretching to the very horizon.

"We're going to go through and turn it up from south to north," said Karas. "There are turbines in there."

They picked through the garbage. Borenboim sank in to his waist. Sank even lower. There was an underground vault. An intolerable stench. The heavy, sticky trash quivered like quicksand. Borenboim cried out in fear.

"Don't be chicken," Gera giggled, grabbing him by the feet.

"These are positive catacombs," Vitka explained. "This is where the parent accelerators live."

People walked through the catacombs. Odd, fearsome machines passed by.

"I have to find the computer dough, then at home I'll make traveling boots for super-powered diesel locomotives," Borenboim thought to himself. He kept picking through the trash.

All sorts of objects turned up. Suddenly Karas and Gera broke through a wall with their sticks. A gloomy din emerged from the opening. "It's the turbines," Borenboim realized. He looked into the opening and saw a huge cave with bluish turbines rising in the center. They produced a dismal roar: smoke spread from them, stinging the eyes.

"Let's get out of here before we're squashed!" Vitka advised.

They ran along a twisting path, getting bogged down in sticky, squelching garbage. Borenboim bumped into a piece of computer dough. A silvery-lilac color, it smelled like gasoline and lilac. He pulled the dough from the heaps of trash.

"Mold it in the form, or else it will come unsoldered," said Karas.

Suddenly, a rat jumped out of the computer dough.

"Bastard, he ate the computer program!" Vitka shouted.

Vitka, Gera, and Karas began to beat the rat with their sticks. Its gray body shook with the blows, and it squeaked pitifully. Borenboim looked at the rat. He felt its palpitating heart. It was a tender little bundle which sent waves of the subtlest vibrations across the whole world, sublime waves of love. And the most remarkable thing—they were in no way connected to the death throes and horror of the dying rat, they existed all by themselves. They penetrated Borenboim's body. His heart contracted from a powerful attack of tenderness, joy, and delight. He pushed the guys aside and lifted the bloody rat. He bent over it and sobbed. The rat's moist eyes closed. Its heart quivered, sending its last farewell waves of love. Borenboim caught them with his heart. He understood the language of hearts. It was untranslatable. Sublime. Borenboim sobbed from happiness and pity. The rat's heart shuddered for the last time. And stopped: FOREVER! The horror of losing this tiny heart seized Borenboim. He pressed the bloody little body to his chest. He sobbed aloud, as he had in childhood. Sobbed helplessly on and on.

Borenboim woke up.

His naked body shuddered in the water. Tears poured down his cheeks. He lifted his head with great difficulty and winced: his chest and neck hurt even more. He sat up in the cold water. Wiped away his tears. Sighed. He looked at his watch: he had slept for one hour and twenty-one minutes.

"Ooo la la . . ." He got out of the bath painfully and pulled a towel from the snake-shaped towel hanger. He wiped himself off, hung the towel in place, and turned toward the mirror. He moved closer, studying his blue eyes. The black pupils reminded him of the rat's moist eyes.

"It ate computer dough…" he muttered. A sob escaped him. "It ate…ate and ate…The bastards…"

His face was distorted by a spasm. Tears burst from his eyes.

Smithereens

00:44, Point Club

THE GROUP Leningrad was wrapping up its concert. The singer, Shnur, sang:

> In the black-black city on black-black nights,
> Doctors and ambulances blackened by the lights,
> Drive merrily along while they sing a song of lies,
> In the black-black city, people die like flies!
> But I don't give a flying…fuck!…

Shnur sent the microphone into the audience. About three hundred young people were standing around and dancing. The audience shouted: "…I'm made—of meat!!!"

Everyone jumped and sang.

Lapin jumped and sang with them.

Ilona, nearby, was doing the same: 17 years old, tall, thin, with a lively laughing face, leather pants, platform shoes, a white top.

"Farewell, Point!" Shnur shouted. The audience whistled.

"Awesome, right?" Ilona nudged Lapin in the side with her fist.

"Let's get drinks before everyone lines up!" he shouted in her ear.

"Okay."

They went over to the bar.

"A bottle of champagne," said Lapin, handing the barman some money.

The barman opened the bottle and gave him two glasses.

"Let's go over there, in the corner." Ilona tugged on Lapin.

In the corner, the edge of a rough, wooden table was free. They sat down at the table. Lapin poured the champagne into the glasses. Two guys and a girl sat nearby.

"Well, then, master?" Ilona raised her glass. "What should we drink to?"

"Let's drink—to being together." They clinked glasses.

"Maybe to Shnur?"

"Let's drink to Shnur."

They drank.

"Is this the first time you've heard them?" Ilona asked, lighting a cigarette.

"Live—yeah."

"A recording's not the same. You don't get the high. Wow!" she wailed. "Awesome, man, awesome. Aargh . . . Wish I had a joint."

"You want one?" asked Lapin, emptying his glass.

"Uh-huh. I always want weed when I'm having a blast."

"Well . . . can't . . . we get some here?" Lapin looked around.

"It's only the second time I've been here. I don't know anyone."

"It's my first time."

"Really? So you really came just for Leningrad, right?"

"Uh-huh. I found out by accident that they had a gig here. So I came."

Lapin lit a cigarette.

"Not a bad place, is it?" said Ilona, looking around. She was quickly getting tipsy.

"It's a big space." Lapin rubbed his chest.

"Really cool, huh? Damn, I really want some weed. Listen, you have any dough?"

"Sort of."

"Let's go to this place I know. They've always got it. Lots of things. Only it's not close."

"Where?"

"In Sokolniki."

"What is it?"

"Just a rented crash pad. Some friends live there."

"Well, why not, let's go."

"Fare thee well to our fair ... Olympic Teddy Bear."

Ilona stood up and stretched. Lapin took the half-drunk bottle. They headed for the exit through the dancing crowd.

They got their coats at the coat check and stepped out into a dimly lit passageway with walls welded together from sheets of steel. Occasional figures appeared in the distance.

"Whoa! It's cold ..." Ilona shivered. Lapin embraced her. He pulled her to him roughly and awkwardly.

"Cuddles?" Ilona asked.

Lapin began to kiss her thin, cold lips. She responded. With his free hand he squeezed her breast. The bottle slipped out of his other hand. It shattered at their feet.

"Damn ..." Lapin flinched.

"Ouch!" Ilona looked down.

Lapin laughed.

"Glass in the plural ... not just smashed, but smashed to smithereens—Russian style."

"Out on the town, are we?" some guy asked. He was squatting next to the wall. Smoking.

"Let's get another one, okay?" Lapin breathed into her ear.

"*Basta*!" Ilona smashed the shards with her dark blue platform shoe. The glass crunched.

She took Lapin by the hand. Pulled him toward the exit.

"Champagne is—great. But there'll be stronger stuff there."

Lapin held her back.

"Wait ... "

"What is it?" She stopped.

He embraced her. He froze, holding her to him. They stood for a minute.

"It's cold." Ilona giggled quietly.

"Wait ..." Lapin's voice trembled.

She grew quiet. Lapin pressed against her and shuddered.

"What's wrong?" She licked a tear from his cheek.

"Just ..." he whispered.

"What is it, are you crashing?"

He shook his head. Sniffed.

"It's just … things are fucked up."

"Then let's go." She took his hand decisively.

Liubka

23:59, Andrei's apartment, 17 Kutuzov Prospect

A BEDROOM with pale lilac walls. A wide, low bed. Muted music. Dim lighting.

A naked Nikolaeva was sitting on top of a naked Andrei. She rocked rhythmically. Nikolaeva's upper chest was wrapped in a silk scarf, with both of her breasts left free.

Andrei was smoking: 52 years old, heavy, round-faced, bald spots, a hairy chest, a tattooed shoulder, and short pudgy fingers.

"Don't rush, don't rush …" he murmured.

"The boss is king," said Nikolaeva, slowing down.

"You have fabulous breasts."

"Like them?"

"You didn't do anything to them?"

"They're all mine. Ooooo … what a sweet dick …"

"Does it reach your guts?"

"Oof … and how … oy … Too bad we can't do it in the bottom today …"

"Why?"

"A boo-boo."

"Hemorrhoids?"

"Uh, not exactly … oy … the, uh, consequences … oy … of an accident …"

"How did you manage to aim like that? To get run over by a car … oy, shit … that was smart … I look both ways four times before I … oy … cross … not so fast …"

"Ohhhh...wow...great...ooo...Andriusha...ooooo...
aaahhh!"

"Not so fast, I said."

Nikolaeva held her hips. She lowered her head. Shook her hair.
Cautiously moved her rear end. Then some more. And some more.

Andrei frowned.

"Oy, oh, shit...I'm already...Alka, you bitch...I said...don't...
rush! It's gonna spray! No! Push, push right there! Damnit! Get off!
Come on, why the fuck did you go and ruin it like that?"

Nikolaeva jumped off him immediately. With one hand she
grabbed his condom-covered penis. With the other she pushed on
the space between his anus and his testicles.

"I'm sorry, Sash...I mean...Andriush..."

"Harder, push harder!"

She pushed harder. He moaned. Jerked his head.

"Now distract me, goddamnit..."

"What, how Andriushenka?"

"Come on, tell me something..."

"What?"

"Umm, something funny...come on, come on, come on..."

"Like a joke?"

"Something...oy, shit...come on, come on..."

"I can't remember jokes..." Nikolaeva scratched her shaved pubis.
"Oh, I know! Here's an unfuckingbelievable story Sula told me.
When she was fifteen, some guy took her home with him, wanted to
screw her, but she wouldn't let him, like—she was a virgin and all that
stuff. The guy messes around with her in bed, spends all this time with
her, like almost two hours, his dick is smoking, and she still won't
spread her legs. Then he says, 'Let me screw you in the butt.' 'Well,
okay,' she says. She sticks it up for him. As soon as he gets it in he
comes—couldn't wait anymore. And like there was so much fucking
sperm! It just poured inside like they were giving her an enema. He
rolls off her. And Sula, can you believe it? She gets up, squats, and takes
a dump right on his Persian rug! While he's sitting there with his
mouth open, can't believe his eyes, she gets dressed and off she goes!"

"Oy, shit…Alya, come on…I can't stand it anymore anyway…"

"Right away, hon," she said, and sat on him. She directed his penis into her vagina. Began moving quickly. Took his balls in her hand.

"Yeah…yeah…that's it…" Andrei murmured. He froze. Squeezed his fists. Cried out. Began pounding Nikolaeva's sides with his fists. "Yes, yes, yes!"

She covered herself with her arms. Moved up and down. Squealed.

Andrei stopped hitting. His arms fell helplessly on the bed.

"Oh, shit…" He reached for the ashtray. Picked up a stubbed-out cigarette.

"How was it?" Nikolaeva licked his pink, hairy nipple.

"Oy…" He stretched. "Like sparks were coming out of my eyes…"

"You're so great…" She stroked his shoulder. "So round…like Winnie the Pooh. And your penis is awesome. I come right away."

He grinned. "Cut the bullshit. Pour some wine."

"Seel vous play." She reached over. Pulled a bottle of white wine, Pinot Grigio, out of a bucket of ice. Poured two glasses.

Andrei took his wine, lifted his sweaty head, and drained the glass. He lay back on the bed.

"Jeez…you're one cool babe."

"Pleased to hear it."

He looked at the empty pack of cigarettes.

"Run into the kitchen, there's some cigarettes on the shelf."

"Where?"

"Next to the vent. There's a glass shelf."

"Andriush, can I take a shower first?"

"Sure. I'll go and get them."

Nikolaeva got up. She held her vagina with her palm. She ran into the bathroom. In the bath she stood under the shower. Turned on the water. Rinsed her whole body quickly. Washed her vagina for a long time. Turned off the water. Shouted: "Petya! Sheesh, I mean… Andriush! May I take a bath?"

"You may…" came the reply from the bedroom.

Nikolaeva sat down in the cold tub. She turned on the faucet, took some shampoo from the shelf, and squirted it into the stream of water. Bubbles spread across the bath. She started singing. The water rose to her armpits. Nikolaeva turned off the water. She drew her knees up and slept.

She dreamed about Liubka Kobzeva, who'd had her throat cut in the Solnechny Motel. They were in the kitchen of that very apartment on Sretenka in Moscow that Liubka rented and shared with Billy-Goat-Gruff. Nikolaeva was sitting at the window, smoking. Outside the window it was winter, snow was falling. It was cold in the kitchen. Nikolaeva was dressed lightly, for summer, though she wore high gray felt boots. But Liubka was barefoot and wearing a blue robe. She was fussing about the stove and making her favorite dish, Uzbek meat pies.

"What a stupid idiot I am, really," she muttered, kneading the dough. "I went and let myself be stabbed! I mean, really . . ."

"Did it hurt?" Nikolaeva asked.

"No, not too much. It was just scary when that SOB came at me with a knife. I completely froze. I should have jumped out the window, but me, idiot that I am, I just stared at him. He goes and gives it to me, first in the stomach, I didn't even notice, and then in the neck . . . and then it was like, there's blood all over everything, tons of it . . . Hey, Al, where did I put the pepper?"

Nikolaeva looks at the table. All the objects can be seen quite clearly: two plates, two forks, a knife with a cracked handle, a grater, a salt cellar, a rolling pin, a packet of flour, nine round medallions of dough. But no pepper shaker.

"That's always the way it goes when you need something—it disappears into thin air," said Liubka, continuing to look around. She bent down. Looked under the table.

Through the open collar of her robe Nikolaeva saw the crudely sewn incision reaching from her neck to her pubis.

"There it is . . ." Liubka said.

Nikolaeva saw the pepper shaker under the table. She leaned over, picked it up, and handed it to Liubka. Suddenly, she felt quite intensely that Liubka's HEART WASN'T BEATING in her chest. Liubka was talking, muttering, moving around, but her heart was motionless. It was standing still, like a broken alarm clock. Nikolaeva was seized by a terrible sorrow. Not because of Liubka being dead but from this stopped heart. She felt an overwhelming pity that Liubka's heart was dead and would NEVER beat again. She realized that she was about to cry.

"Liub . . . do you . . . put onion in the stuffing?" she asked with incredible difficulty, standing up.

"Why the hell do you need it when there's garlic?" Liubka looked at her attentively with dead eyes.

Nikolaeva began to cry.

"What's wrong?" Liubka asked.

"I need to piss," Nikolaeva's disobedient lips babbled.

"Piss here," said Liubka with a smile.

Sobs overwhelmed Nikolaeva. She cried for the GREAT LOSS.

"Liub . . . ka . . . Liub . . . ka . . ." escaped her lips.

She grabbed Liubka, pressed her to her breast. Liubka moved her aside with her cold hands, covered in flour and dough.

"What's wrong with you?"

Liubka's icy chest was HEARTLESS. Nikolaeva sobbed. She understood that this could NEVER be fixed. She heard the beat of her own heart. It was alive, warm, and TERRIBLY dear to her. This feeling only made things even more painful and bitter. She suddenly understood how SIMPLE it was to be dead. Horror and grief filled her. Warm urine flowed down her legs.

Nikolaeva woke up.

Her face was covered in tears. Her mascara was running.

Andrei stood next to the bath in a red-and-white terry-cloth robe.

"What's wrong?" he asked impatiently.

"Huh?" She sniffled. She began to sob again.

"What happened?" he asked, frowning sleepily.

"I . . . ummm . . ." She cried. "I dreamed about my girlfriend . . . her . . . she . . . was murdered six months ago . . ."

"Who did it?"

"Oh . . . some guys from the market . . . some Azeris . . ."

"Ah . . ." he said, scratching his chest. "Listen, I want to get some sleep. I have an important meeting tomorrow. The money is on the kitchen table . . ."

He left.

Nikolaeva wiped away her tears. She got out of the bath. She glanced at the mirror.

"Jesus…"

She spent a long time washing her face. She dried off, wrapped herself in a big towel, and left the bathroom.

The apartment was dark. The sound of Andrei snoring came from the bedroom.

Nikolaeva crossed the bedroom on tiptoe. She found her things and went into the kitchen. The light on the vent above the stove was the only one on. Two hundred dollars lay on the table.

Nikolaeva got dressed. She put the money away in her wallet. She drank a glass of apple juice. She went into the foyer, put on her overcoat, and left the apartment, carefully closing the door behind her.

Upper Lip

02:02, Komar and Vika's Rented Apartment, 1 Olenii Bank

"Work your fist a little." Komar tied a tourniquet around Lapin's forearm.

"There's nothing to work—you can see everything," laughed Vika. "Wish I had veins like that!"

"Komar, you fucker, you could do me first!" said Ilona, watching angrily.

"Guests first, jeezus fucking Christ. Specially 'cause he's bankrolling…." Komar inserted the needle into the vein. "Shit, I ain't seen such spotless ropes in a blue moon."

"So Ilona, did you really see Leningrad?" asked Vika.

"Uh-huh…" Ilona looked at Lapin's arm.

"Was it hot?"

"Uh-huh."

"What did they play? Old stuff?"

"Old stuff! Old! Old!" said Ilona, shaking her wrists crossly.

Komar pulled the plunger toward himself: 27 years old, shaved head, big ears, skinny, stooped, long arms, sharp facial features, wearing a torn blue T-shirt and wide black pants.

Blood appeared in the hypodermic. Komar tugged on the end of the tourniquet. He smoothly injected the contents of the hypodermic into Lapin's vein.

"There we go."

Vika held out a piece of cotton: 18 years old, small, dark, plump, long-haired, purple polyester pants, a light blue top.

Lapin pressed the cotton to his vein. He bent his elbow. Flopped back on a filthy pillow.

"Oh, shit . . ."

"Well?" said Komar, smiling.

"Yeah . . ." said Lapin and smiled, parting his lips with difficulty. He looked at the rusty water stains on the ceiling.

"You fucker, are you gonna hit me or not, for heaven's sake, Komar?" Ilona shouted.

"No problem, Madam." Komar unwrapped a new hypodermic.

Vika poured the white powder from the packet into a tablespoon, added water, and boiled the spoon over a candle. Komar sucked the semitransparent liquid in the spoon into the hypodermic.

Ilona tied the tourniquet around her upper arm herself. She sat down opposite Komar. Stretched out her arm. In the bend a few tracks could be seen.

"Ilon, I didn't get it, did they just play old stuff?" asked Vika, lighting up a cigarette.

"No, not only," Ilona answered irritably, pumping her fist.

"'When summertime comes, we'll go to the dacha and leave the town / A shovel in hand, we'll mess around, mess around . . .' They did that one?"

"Yeah, yeah, yeah," Ilona muttered crossly.

"I really like the one they do: 'Ta-ta-ta . . . some people shoot up / me, I do booze / but I could speed up, after a snooze . . .'"

Komar took his time and found a place for the needle.

"Hmm, it's good you don't overdo things, sweetheart."

"You think I'm an idiot or something?" Ilona laughed nervously.

"Women! Go figure!" The needle entered her vein.

Lapin smiled. Stretched. Rolled his shoulders around. "Yeah...now...this is...totally different..."

"What's different?" asked Vika. "Speedball? Of course it is. It's heavier than plain old smack."

"Heavier. But I don't like all this bullshitting: speedball, speedball, and they haven't really tried a fuckin' thing...There are so...so many...ummm...mediocre people around here...hacks...no talent..."

"Why?" asked Vika with a happy smile.

"Because every asshole wants to be smarter than he really is. Smarter and more authoritative. Everybody's all buzzed about their authority, that's all they think about. As if a human being's main purpose on earth were to achieve a position in society at any price, even at the price of other people's suffering."

Vika and Komar exchanged glances.

"Yeah. Well, one thing's for sure, if we got a lot of anything, it's suffering...leaking right outta our assholes..." Smiling, Komar injected the dose into Ilona's vein.

"Oy..." She closed her eyes. Bent her arm at the elbow. Coughed.

Vika stretched her arm out for Komar. It was riddled with needle tracks. "There's still another little place here."

"Just don't breathe on my forehead."

"Sorry, Kom."

Ilona stretched.

"Awesome!"

She kissed Lapin. He embraced her awkwardly.

"Only don't go too fast, Kom." Vika looked at the needle.

"Are my pupils big?" Ilona leaned over Lapin.

"Yes," he replied seriously.

"Are they pretty? What color?"

"Something...like...you know..." Sweating, Lapin looked at them carefully, straight on. "Here's the thing...it's those balls...you know, those Chinese equilibrium balls...you have to roll them around in one hand, they're made of different precious stones, like, maybe jasper or something, and when a ball like that...the yin or the yang, I think it's the yin...so...and one ball lies there, that is, there's this energy, this bioenergy that flows from it, and there's also all these electrical accumulations, and all this stuff together...the energy of the stones, too, we hardly know anything about the energy of stones, I mean stones are so fucking ancient...but you know they used to be soft like sponges, and then over time they petrified and became real stones and there's all this...this unfuckingbelievable information stored up in them, so it's kind of like a super memory chip, there's all this stuff written down there, so mucking fuch that...I mean, so fucking much of everything, about everything, different events, people, everything that happened...It's all in stones, man...And who needs computers, you just have to know how to use the stones, find the right approach...a normal, competent approach...and then the shit'll hit the fan, I mean, human beings will become the fucking lords of the world."

"Your upper lip is really incredible," said Ilona happily, touching his lip with her finger.

Sand

12:09, Warehouse of the Cargo Trading Company, 2 Novoyasenevsky Prospect

A LARGE semicircular hangar, a multitude of boxes and packages containing food products. A one-meter-square sheet of thick plywood lay on top of four cases of canned vegetables. Around the plywood several people sat and smoked.

Volodya Straw: 32 years old, medium height, a thickset body, brown hair, a sullen disposition, a motionless face with a small broken nose, a short sheepskin jacket.

Dato: 52, pudgy, small, bald, with a round face in a permanent grin, an unbuttoned white raincoat, delicately knit white sweater, beige silk shirt with a high collar, white leather trousers, a gold Tissot watch, a gold bracelet, and a gold ring with a ruby.

Khmelev: 42, medium height, thin, dark brown hair, a thin, narrow, calmly worried face, steel-gray jacket, a dark blue three-piece suit, white shirt, and a light-blue-and-red tie.

Khmelev's cell phone rang.

"Yes," he said, putting it to his ear.

"They're here," a voice informed him.

"How many?"

"Six…seven guys in two cars."

"Okay, just let Blindeye and a couple of bodyguards through."

"Got it."

Dato tossed a cigarette butt on the cement floor. Crushed it with his black patent-leather boot.

"Two of them won't be able to carry it in."

"That's their problem," muttered Khmelev.

"So, like usual?" said Straw, sniffing as he stood up.

"Like usual, Vova," said Dato, slapping his fleshy knees.

The door opened.

Gasan Blindeye entered the hangar: 43 years old, short, puny, swarthy, balding, hook-nosed, wearing a black leather coat. Two strongmen carrying a heavy metal coffer followed him in with some difficulty.

Dato stood up. He stepped forward to greet Gasan. They embraced, touched cheeks twice.

"Hello, Dato."

"Hello, my friend."

The two guys set the coffer on the floor.

"Put it here," Dato pointed to the plywood with his small, pudgy hand.

The two lifted the coffer. They carried it over and set it down. The plywood cracked, but held.

"Sit down, my friend." Dato nodded.

Straw moved a case of macaroni toward Blindeye.

"Dato, let everyone leave us alone." Blindeye unbuttoned his coat.

"Why?"

"We need to talk."

"These are my people, Gasan. You know them."

"I know them, Dato. But let them leave."

Dato glanced at Khmelev. Khmelev nodded.

"All right then, my friend. We'll do it the way you say. Go on, go out for some air."

Khmelev, Straw, and the other two went out. Gasan sat down on the box. He rubbed his cheeks in exhaustion. Dato waited silently.

"I've changed my mind, Dato," Gasan said.

"I don't understand. What did you change your mind about?"

"I'm not selling."

"Why?"

Gasan clenched his hands. He touched the tip of his sharp, crooked nose with his thumbs.

"Just because . . . I'm not selling. That's all."

Dato chuckled louder than usual.

"I don't understand you, Gasan. Why aren't you selling? The price doesn't suit you? You want more?"

"No. The price is the old one. It always suited me."

"So then what's the deal?"

"No deal. Just—I don't want to."

Dato looked at him attentively.

"What's with you, brother? Are you sick or something? You got problems?"

"I'm not sick, brother. And I don't have problems. But I'm not selling the product."

Dato didn't say anything. He took out a gold cigarette case, removed a cigarette, and took his time lighting it. He walked around, then turned to Gasan.

"But why did you bring the product if you don't want to sell?"

"To show you, brother."

"I saw it before. More than once."

"You take another look at it. Look carefully."

Gasan stood up. He opened the locks on the coffer and pushed back the metal lid. Under it was a white plastic lid. Gasan pulled it. It opened. Under it was a refrigerator—completely filled with sand.

Dato froze for a minute with the cigarette in his lips.

"Now you understand, Dato, why Gasan does not want to sell you the product."

"Now I understand."

Gasan went up close to him.

"We have rats, brother. Fat goddamn rats."

"Does Tractor know?" asked Dato.

"Not yet. Why the hell should he know?"

Dato stuck his hand in the sand, felt around, scooped up a handful. He threw it forcefully on the floor:

"Crooks!"

"But it's definitely not the ice cutters."

"Then who? Your guys?"

"I know my own. And they know me. I would cut off my hand, that's how I trust them."

"Hand...foot..." Dato spat angrily. "Your own guys could also turn into rats. Fuckers! Crooks! Gasan, look for them yourself. I'm not going to those blonds. I'll give the money back. And that's it."

"Just wait a minute, brother."

"What's to wait? One of your people skimmed some off the top, it's your problem. You go talk to them."

"Don't get all overheated, my friend. It's not my problem. It's our problem."

"No fucking way! They pinched it from your place, what've I got to do with it? I'm not involved."

"You're involved because the rat lives in your house."

"What? What fucking rat?"

"A fat one. And it sleeps in your house. It eats your bread."

Dato stared hard at him.

Gasan rummaged in his pockets. He took out a round wooden tobacco box, opened it. It contained cocaine. He shook a little onto the lid. He took out an ivory straw and a plastic card.

"Let's have a snort, brother. I haven't slept for three days."

"And what about...the rat? In my place? You ready to answer for what you're saying?"

"I'll answer."

"So who is it?"

"Don't rush."

"What the fuck do you mean, don't rush? Who is it?"

Gasan quickly cut the powder with the card. He split it into two thick lines. Handed Dato the straw.

"Come on, brother."

Dato took the tube. He leaned over and quickly snorted his line. He returned the tube to Gasan, who placed it in his hooked nose. Slowly he drew half of the line into one nostril, then he drew the rest into the other.

"But how did you find out?" Dato sniffed. "You never talked to my people. How did you find out? What is it, I have a stool pigeon in the house?"

"Your boys are all right, Dato."

"Well then, who, goddamnit?!"

"Just wait a minute." Gasan made two more lines. "Let's finish it off. And I will tell you how to handle this."

"Handle … handle … There you go!" Dato kicked the box. Buckwheat spilled out of the hole.

Gasan snorted his line. Dato brushed him away.

"I don't want any more."

Gasan snorted the second line. He put away the tobacco box and the straw. He wiped his nose with a handkerchief.

"All right, let's do it this way. We'll close this. And you'll take it to your place."

"What the fuckin' hell I want sand for?"

"Let your people think that everything's okay"

"And the dough?"

"You give me the briefcase. But you'll take the dough out."

"And?"

"You take the trunk to your place. And then we start hunting rats."

"So you know who it is—or not?"

Gasan came closer, whispering in his ear.

"And does he have the ice?"

"No."

"But where's the ice? The blonds got it already?"

"No. No, Dato. The ice is at your house."

Dato looked straight at him.

"What? Where?"

"In the freezer."

"At my place?"

"At your place, at your place, Dato."

"And who did this?"

"Your Natasha."

Bosch

21:00, Dato's Apartment, 7 Malaya Bronnaya

A SPACIOUS kitchen. White furniture. Expensive utensils. A gold-plated saucepan full of water on the lit burner.

Orange lay on the marble floor, tied up: 29 years old, red hair, with the massive body of a former athlete.

Natasha sat in the corner: 26 years old, pretty, long-legged, in a torn red dress. Her hand was handcuffed to the radiator.

Dato and Gasan Blindeye sat at the table.

Crowbar and **Boiler** stood nearby: broad-shouldered, muscular, with small shaved heads and thick necks.

A half-drunk bottle of Yury Dolgoruky vodka stood on the table in front of Dato. Gasan was cutting cocaine on a plate.

Dato poured himself some vodka. Drank it. Took his time lighting a cigarette. Looked at Natasha.

"There's one fucking thing I can't understand. Not for the life of me. What was it you didn't have?"

Natasha didn't say anything. She looked at the leg of the chair.

"I picked you up out of the shit pile, I helped your brother, I helped your mother. I took you to the Caribbean, dressed you like goddamned Princess Diana. Fucked you every day. What else did you need?"

Natasha said nothing.

"Yeah. Women—they're a mystery." Dato blew smoke out. "Huh, Gasan? Third time I run into a rat. What's going on?! Shit. Is it fate?"

"I don't know, brother." Gasan snorted his line. "Might be fate."

"And then I can't get my head around the fucking thing: so, say you skimmed some ice on the sly, I dunno, knocked off fifty thou. Then what? What're you gonna do then? Where would you go? Dig a hole underground or somethin'? Or what, fifty thou is such big bucks for you?"

Natasha didn't answer.

"Dato, leave her alone," said Gasan, wiping his nose. "Women's roles are always secondary."

"Live and learn, live and learn . . ." Dato knocked the ash off his cigarette. He looked at the pan. "Well, is it boiling?"

Boiler glanced in the saucepan.

"It's about to boil."

Orange tossed and turned on the floor. Crowbar pushed him down with his foot.

"Lie down."

"Dato, I swear to God or I'm a skunk, it wasn't my idea. I swear, I swear," Orange muttered.

"You're already a fuckin' skunk." Dato glanced at his sweaty red head. "A stinking rat."

"Shakro put a piece to my head two times. In Dagomys that time, and after the wedding. He heard about the blonds from Avera."

"From Avera?" Gasan grinned. "Avera is in the ground."

"He hit on Shakro, Shakro owed him from the Tibet pyramid," said Orange, raising his head a bit. "And then he sold him this stuff about the blonds and the ice. He said, 'Here's a nice piece of action, take it. If you get yourself a slice, you'll pay me back.'"

"And what, Shakro ordered you to pinch it from Gasan?" Gasan asked.

"Shakro wants to take over the ice . . ."

"What?" Dato grinned. "What kinda bullshit're you shoveling, asshole? Avera was taken down. What fucking debt, what Tibet?"

"Even without Avera he wants to. I swear to God, Dato. His boys are saying he's totally naked now, he and Ryba are on the outs, and they'll jump you."

"And take over the deal?" Dato smiled.

"They want to."

"So rough and rude? No parlay?"

"He told me, 'Go on, grab a piece of it, I'll see. If you don't —we'll take him down.' "

"And just what does he wanna see?"

"Well, he wants to watch you stew."

Dato stubbed out the butt, got up, and walked over to Orange. He thrust his hands in his pockets. He rocked on his feet.

"Hmm. Yeah. You fuckin' mutt. You're a mad dog, stark raving mad. Strayed from the code."

He nodded to Boiler. Boiler took the pan off the stove. Crowbar held Orange's head down to the light blue marble floor with his boot.

"I swear, Dato . . . Gasan . . . I swear . . ." Orange mumbled.

Boiler sat on Orange's legs. He started pouring boiling water on his back.

Orange howled and jerked.

Crowbar and Boiler flattened him.

"The truth, dog, give us the truth," said Dato, rocking on his feet.

"I swear! I swear!" bellowed Orange.

Boiler splashed water on his back. Orange thrashed.

"The truth, the truth."

"Dato! Don't!" Natasha shouted.

"The truth, dog."

"I swear, I swear!"

"Splash some on his face," Gasan suggested.

Boiler splashed water on Orange's head. He moaned.

"Don't, Dato! Leave him alone!" Natasha cried.

"You'll get your turn, rat!" said Dato, kicking her.

"Talk, otherwise we'll boil you like a crab," said Gasan, calmly watching Orange's shuddering body.

"Shakro wants to take over the ice!" Orange roared.

"Don't bullshit me, you little crook! Don't bullshit me! Don't bullshit! Don't bullshit!" Dato began to kick him in the face.

"A little rat . . ." Gasan spat. "Pour some on his balls!"

Boiler and Crowbar began to pull down Orange's pants.

"Dato! Dato! Dato!" Natasha cried.

"Quiet, rat!"

"Dato, don't, don't! I'll tell you everything!" Natasha screamed.

"Shut up, rat!"

"Let her tell, Dato." Gasan went over to Natasha. "Tell us the truth."

"I'll tell you everything, just don't!"

Dato made a sign to Boiler. He stopped splashing boiling water on Orange.

"Go on bitch: talk."

Natasha wiped her nose with her free hand. She sobbed.

"He's lying about everything. It wasn't Shakro. It was me."

Dato looked at her.

"What the fuck for?"

"You'll dump me at some point. Like Zhenka. I know about your...that...ballerina. And I...I'm...I don't really have anything. My mother's about to die."

"And so?"

"Well...I wanted to skim off some dough...just..."

"And you put him up to it?"

She nodded.

"For how much?"

"Fifty-fifty."

Dato turned his gaze to Gasan. Gasan remained silent. Natasha let out a sob. Orange moaned on the floor.

Dato looked at Orange.

"Turn him over."

Boiler and Crowbar turned him over on his back. Dato squatted down. He looked into Orange's gray eyes.

"It's true."

He stood up. Gasan proffered his hand. Dato slapped his palm. He exhaled in relief.

"Let's go talk."

They went into the next room: dim light, a lot of expensive furniture.

"That's what I thought, that it wasn't Shakro." Gasan stretched and then shivered, as though chilled. He locked his thin fingers together. Cracked his knuckles.

"Take over...shit!" Dato grinned nervously. He opened the bar, took out a bottle of cognac, and poured some. He drained his glass.

"Every fucking punk crook is just waiting to set me on Shakro. Fucking jackals, alla'them!"

"He just heard about it...maybe from Avera, from his boys... maybe from Dyriavy..."

"But why does everyone know, Gasan? Why does every goddamn cockroach know about the fucking ice?"

"You're asking me?"

"Who should I ask? Avera? Zhorik? They're fucking worm food. But you're alive."

"You're alive, too, my brother," Gasan looked at him seriously. "We're both alive. So far."

"So far as what?"

"So far as we understand that there's no pockets six feet under."

Dato turned away. He walked to the window. He rocked on his toes. Gasan went up to him. He placed a hand on his shoulder.

"You know me, my friend. I don't need anybody's share. Mine is plenty for my powder."

Dato look out the window at nighttime Moscow.

"Little shits!"

"We have to do something about them, friend."

"Something..." Dato repeated, rocking on his stocking feet. "Somefuckingthing."

He turned abruptly. Went into the kitchen. Gasan followed him slowly.

In the corner of the kitchen stood a massive white Bosch refrigerator. Dato opened the freezer section. It was filled with frozen food. He began to throw the packages on the floor. They hit the marble floor with dry clunks. Under the food lay a large cube of ice. Dato looked at it angrily.

"Because I never eat anything frozen...right, bitch?"

He approached Natasha.

She whimpered and turned away.

"A safe place, right?" Gasan stared glumly.

"Why're all these fucking broads so smart all of a sudden?" Dato slapped himself on his thighs. "I don't get what's going on."

"Liberation," Boiler spoke out unexpectedly.

"Huh?" Dato turned to him.

"Yeah...that's when chicks got equal rights with guys," Boiler muttered.

Dato looked at him attentively. Turned to Gasan. "Let's have the box."

Gasan took out his cell phone. He dialed. "Drive on over."

A few minutes later two guys entered the apartment with the coffer. They put on rubber gloves. They took the cube of ice out of the freezer, put it in the coffer, and carefully took the coffer away.

Dato poured himself some vodka, downing it in a gulp.

"Okay. Orange—goes in the garbage."

Orange jerked as hard as he could. He shouted something inarticulate. Boiler and Crowbar fell on him. Crowbar threw a noose around Orange's thick, freckled neck.

Natasha vomited. Her head hung down impotently.

Orange wheezed and tossed a long time. He passed gas.

Finally he was still.

Boiler rolled in a large blue plastic suitcase from the coat closet. He put Orange's corpse in it. They wheeled it out of the kitchen. Out of the apartment.

The door closed behind them.

Gasan sat down at the table. He took out his tobacco box and sprinkled some cocaine on a plate. He began cutting it with a plastic card.

Dato took a key out of his pocket. He un-handcuffed Natasha from the radiator. She slumped weakly to the floor. Her breathing was shallow. She was shaking.

Dato opened the door of the freezer.

"Get in."

Natasha lifted her head.

"Get in, rat!"

She obediently crawled into the freezer. Dato slammed the door. Leaned his back against it.

"I'll fuckin' freeze her. That's it."

Gasan grinned. Snorted a line of cocaine. Then some more.

Dato took out a cigarette. Lit it.

Natasha could barely be heard whimpering in the freezer.

Dato smoked. Gasan rubbed cocaine on his gums.

"I'll get myself a new whore," Dato mumbled.

Gasan stood up. Went over to him.

"Send her to Turkey. To Rustam."

"What fucking Rustam?!" Dato shook his head angrily. "She going to the fucking morgue. Turkey!"

"Friend, don't do this."

"Go fuck yourself. She's my broad."

"The woman is yours. The business is ours."

Natasha whined and banged on the door.

"I'll fuckin' waste her." Dato shook his head stubbornly. "Shameless cunt."

"Don't do this, Dato."

"Get outta here!"

"Don't do this, brother."

"Back off, Gasan, don't bug me, goddamnit."

"Don't do this! You'll bring us all down, you pig head!" Gasan grabbed Dato.

"What the hell ... get your paws off ..." Dato struggled.

"Pig head ..."

"Get ... your ... paws off ... asshole ..."

They fought next to the huge white refrigerator.

"I'm pregnant!" could suddenly be heard out of the freezer.

The struggle stopped.

Dato pushed Gasan away. He opened the door.

"What?"

Natasha sat there, bent over.

"What did you say?"

"I'm pregnant," she said quietly.

"By who?" growled Dato.

"By you."

Dato looked at her vacantly. At her bare knees. Then at her toes with their dark blue nail polish. A frost-covered dumpling lay next to her feet.

Dato stared at the dumpling.

Natasha fell out of the freezer onto the floor. She crawled across the marble.

"When ... how long?" asked Dato.

"Second month ..." She crawled out of the kitchen. Crawled into the bathroom.

Dato rubbed the bridge of his nose in exhaustion. Gasan slapped him on the back.

"So there, you see, brother ... and you wanted to freeze her!"

Blockade

04:15, Komar and Vika's Rented Apartment

A DILAPIDATED bathroom, light blue tile cracked and chipped off in places, rust stains in the bathtub and sink, the dim light of an old lightbulb, dirty underwear soaking in a basin.

Lapin and Ilona lay naked in the overfilled tub. Ilona was sitting on Lapin and smoking. His penis was in her vagina. She moved slowly. In a state of semi-oblivion, Lapin opened and closed his eyes.

"But the main thing ... is, I mean ... He doesn't understand anything about craft ... the actor's craft ..." Ilona mumbled rapidly through dry lips. "Keanu Reeves is fabulous, too, I get off on him because he can do a love scene honestly, but he seems so hot and cool and all ... and I really, you know ... well I just don't believe him ... not even a smidgen ... and I mean what the fuck should I pay money for if I don't believe the actor, I mean, if there's no belief ... Oy, your balls are so hard!"

She moved sharply. Water splashed over the edge of the bathtub.

The peeling door opened. Komar entered, naked. His penis was erect.

"Let's switch, you cool Texas Ranger dudes."

"Okay." Ilona climbed out of the bath.

"Oh, shit man, you've flooded the place ... " Komar looked at the floor. "The neighbors are gonna be banging on the door again ... "

"You two are just about the same." Ilona grabbed Komar by the penis.

"Size makes a difference?" he asked hoarsely, grinning.

"You bet."

"Then let's go."

"What about shooting up?"

"As soon as I come—we'll do it."

They went out. Lapin took his hand out of the water. Looked at his nails: they were blue—like the tile.

Vika walked in, naked.

"So, then, right in the water?"

Lapin opened his eyes. Vika crawled in with him. Took his penis and placed it in her vagina.

"It's cold ... " said Lapin, unsticking his lips.

"We can let this out and run a new bath," said Vika, beginning to move.

"Okay, let's ... "

She reach over to the drain and pulled the plug. The water began to flow out.

"I had this boyfriend, he was a junkie too, he like to stick his balls in that hole when the water was draining, that is, when he was a little boy."

"What?"

"We used to tell each other how we got off when we were kids ... I ... umm ... Oy, what a great penis you've got ... I ... liked to sit on the corner of the table and cross my legs like this ... and he would squat in the bathtub, fill it, and then pull out the plug and stick his balls in there. Then he'd jack off. And think about Communism."

"What for?"

"Well, I mean, not exactly about Communism itself, who the fuck needs Communism ... It's not too hot?" She turned on the hot water.

"It's fine."

"But, you know, about how in Communism there would be communal women…and…he…Oy, oy, oy…he…ummm. Oy, oy, oy…I mean…Oy, oy…oy…"

"Fucked all of them." Lapin held Vika's breasts.

"Oy, oy, oy…" She frowned. "Oy, I'm coming…O-o-o-o-oy…"

"For some reason, ummm, I mean, I can't seem to come…"

"Oy…oy…" She stopped moving. "Koma will give us a hit—and you'll come."

"I want to now," said Lapin, moving.

"If you want, stick it in my ass. Koma does that sometimes too, when he can't come, he sticks it in my ass—and it spurts out right away. Want to?"

"I don't know…I've never tried…umm…there's shit in there."

"You jerk-off. There's no shit in there! So are you going to or not…Then let me masturbate you."

"You?"

"I'm really good at it. Come on, turn on your side…and I'll lie down behind you. It's hot already."

She turned the faucet off. Put the plug in.

Lapin turned on his side. Vika laid down behind him. Her right hand took his penis. She stuck the left one between his legs and squeezed his balls.

"Oh, poor guy, we're so tense here."

She began masturbating his member.

Lapin let his eyes shut. He dropped off into a dream.

He was an old man. Eighty-two years old, thin and dried up. He was descending the dark, cold staircase of a large apartment building. Pieces of plaster and broken glass lay on the stairs. He was wearing a heavy winter coat, felt boots, and heavy mittens. It was very cold. He shivered down to his very bone marrow. A slight steam escaped from his dried lips. His right arm was half bent. He held the handle of a copper teakettle in the bend of his elbow. The empty kettle knocked against his hip. Descending, he held on to a wooden banister. Each step was difficult. The cold air burned his throat. His head trembled slightly, and as a result, everything he saw also trembled and swayed. He stopped on the landing of the second floor and fell back against the gray, cracked wall. He held the kettle with his left hand. He stood there, breathing heavily. He looked at the space between two doors. The words THE KUZOLEVS ARE KULAKS! *and* SLONIK IS A TICK *had been scratched on the wall. One of the doors had been pulled out. The black space of a burned apartment yawned beyond it. The insignia of the Zenith soccer team was drawn in ink on the door of the other. He stood there, his eyes half open. He breathed. Below, someone was climbing the stairs. He opened his eyes. A hunched figure in a gray padded jacket appeared before him. The man placed an icy bucket of water on the dirty cement floor. He straightened up with a faint moan. He wore a black navy-issue winter hat with earflaps, tied with a torn gray scarf, and huge mittens; his soiled padded pants were tucked into felt boots. A thin, yellowish-gray, ageless face with an over- grown beard arose in front of him. The whitish eyes looked at him.*

"Building 2 has been completely cordoned off. Half of it collapsed."

"And . . . this one?" he asked.

"Now you have to go through 12."

The bearded man glanced through the door of the burned-out apart- ment.

"While we were standing around with our mouths open, the stoker and Yanko took everything out. I dropped in yesterday—not a splinter left. The SOBs. They could've at least shared. Shut themselves up in the boiler room—and that's it. Can't get through to them. That's who should be shot. They're worse than the Fascists."

The bearded man picked up his bucket and moaned as he lifted it. He suddenly really wanted to ask the bearded man something important. But then he immediately forgot what, exactly. Worried, he pushed him- self away from the wall.

"Umm and . . . Andrei Samoilovich . . . I'm, you know . . . not a Party member. You don't have any plywood, do you?"

But the bearded man was already lugging the bucket upstairs, hold- ing out his left arm for balance.

His eyes followed the man for a long time. Then he continued down. Exiting the half-dark entryway, he was immediately blinded: every- thing around was bathed in bright sunlight. Standing for a bit, he opened his eyes. The courtyard was still the same: enormous snowdrifts, the stumps of two poplars that were cut down, the carcass of a burned-out truck. A narrow path led through the snowdrifts to the street. He moved cautiously along it. A black arch swam over his head. This is the gateway. Dangerous. Very dangerous! He moved along the wall, leaning on it with his left hand. But there's light ahead: the street. He took longer steps—and he was suddenly on the avenue. In this place it was wide open. The middle of the avenue had been cleared, but near the houses there were still mountainous snowdrifts. People moved along the avenue. There weren't many of them. He moved slowly. Someone was pulling something on a sled. A sled! He had had one. But the Borisovs stole it. They burned the wooden seat in their makeshift stove; they hauled water on the iron frame. But he carries it in his teakettle. It's a long way to the Neva. You can melt snow, of course. But you need a lot of it. And it's heavy too…

He readied himself to go out into the middle of the avenue. A ways away, the groundskeeper was talking to Lidia Konstantinovna from building 8. They stood next to a corpse lying facedown in the snow. The corpse's buttocks had been cut off.

"Just look, all the dead have their asses sliced off!" croaked the groundskeeper, who was wrapped up in some kind of rags. "And why is that, I wonder? A gang! They make croquettes and meatballs from corpses and fry them up in axle grease! Then they barter them for bread at the market!"

Lidia Konstantinovna crossed herself. "We should show the patrols."

He walked over to them. "You wouldn't have a splinter or two?"

They turn away and plod off.

"How does the earth stand these goddamned White Guard bastards?" he hears.

Chewing his lips, he walks out onto the prospect. What were they talking about? Croquettes! He remembered the pork croquettes at the Vienna restaurant on Bolshoi Morskoi, and at Testova's Moscow pub. And at the Yar restaurant. At the Yar! They were served with potato croutons, red cabbage, and green peas. The Yar had truffles, too, a divine six-layered kulebiaka pasty, sterlet soup, crème brûlée, and Lizanka made a fuss, she wanted to go visit those… that… oh… the one with the mustache who couldn't say his r*'s . . . poems, poems, lord, how the frost goes right through you . . . croquettes. . . . Meatballs.*

A truck suddenly passed him, almost hitting him. Red Army soldiers with rifles sat in it, wrapped in overcoats. The chains on the truck's wheels clanked. He stopped. His eyes teared as they followed the truck. What's this? On the side of the truck instead of a number there was a large white sign: CROQUETTES. *Croquettes!! There were croquettes in there! He suddenly understood this keenly and clearly, with every cell of his weak body.*

Throwing down the kettle and waving his hands, he began to run after the truck. His large kneecaps jolted forward, the mittens flew off of his bony black hands and hung on their elastic. He ran after the truck. It was crawling along slowly. He could catch up with it. There are croquettes in there! He could see them, skewered on Red Army bayonets. Hundreds, thousands of them!

"Let me have a croquette, too!" he screeched like a rooster.

"Cr . . . cro . . . quette . . . too!"

"And . . . let me . . . croque . . . too!"

"Cr . . . cro. . . croque . . . ettooo . . . !"

His heart was beating, beating, beating. Broad and wide. Like building 6. Like the Irtysh River in May 1918. Like Big Bertha. Like the siege itself. Like God.

His feet became tangled. He careened. Creaked. Cracked. And split in pieces like a rotten tree, on the snow the truck had tamped down. A whitish haze swallowed up the truck. His heart beat.

Pdum.

P-dum.

Pa-dum.

And stopped. Forever.

Lapin opened his eyes. He was crying. Clots of sperm spurted from his penis into the water. Vika's hand helped. Lapin's legs jerked convulsively.

"Like thick sour cream." Vika's huge, wet lips moved near Lapin's ear. "Don't get laid much, huh?"

A Girl Is Crying

14:11, The Balaganchik, 10 Tryokhprudny Lane

A HALF-EMPTY restaurant. Nikolaeva came out of the restroom, approached a table.

Lida was sitting at it and smoking: 23 years old, a slender model's figure in a tight leather outfit, mid-size breasts, a long neck, a small head with a very short haircut, a pretty face.

"The john is downstairs." Nikolaeva sat down opposite Lida. "It's not very convenient."

"But the food is fabulous," said Lida, chewing.

"The cook is French," said Nikolaeva, pouring red wine into their wineglasses. "So, where did I stop?"

"Cheers," said Lida, raising her glass. "At the naked blond with blue eyes."

"Cheers," said Nikolaeva, clinking glasses with her.

They drank. Nikolaeva took an olive, chewed it, spit out the pit.

"It didn't even matter, naked—or not. You know, the thing is that I've never felt anything like it, nothing has ever gotten to me that way. I just . . . sort of like fell into it . . . and my heart felt so . . . sweet . . . sort of . . . as if . . . I don't know . . . it was like . . . I don't know. Like being with Mama in childhood. I cried my eyes out later. You get it?"

"And you're sure he didn't screw you?"

"Absolutely."

Lida shook her head.

"Hmmm. One of two things: it's either some kind of druggies, or Satanists."

"They didn't shoot me up with anything."

"But you lost consciousness. You said you fainted."

"Yeah, but there's no tracks! My veins are intact."

"Well, maybe it wasn't in a vein. I had one client and he stuck cocaine up his ass. Got high. He said that that way his septum wouldn't get ruined."

Nikolaeva shook her head in disagreement.

"No, Lidka, they definitely weren't druggies. There's something else going on there. You know what kind of assets they have? This is a serious company. You can tell."

"So that means Satanists. Talk to Birutia. The Satanists fucked her once."

"And? Was it hardcore?"

"Nah, but they smeared so much chicken blood on her that she kept on washing and washing—"

"Yeah but this was my blood, not chicken blood."

Lida stubbed out her cigarette.

"Well, I just don't get it."

"Me neither."

"Alya, you weren't soused, were you?"

"Come on!"

"Yeah, well... And your heart, you said... well... it was really intense? Like if you fall in love with someone?"

"Stronger... it... how the hell to explain it... well... like when you really really feel sorry for someone and it's someone really really close to you. So close, so close that you're ready to give him everything, everything... I mean... well, it's..."

Nikolaeva sniffled. Her lips trembled. And suddenly she began sobbing, readily and intensely, as though she'd vomited. The sobs overwhelmed her.

Lida grabbed her by the shoulders.

"Alya, sweetie, calm down..."

But Nikolaeva sobbed harder and harder.

The few customers in the restaurant looked at her. Her head was shaking. Her fingers clutched her mouth and she began to slide off the chair.

"Alechka, Alya!" said Lida, holding her up.

Nikolaeva's body writhed and shuddered. Her face turned red. The waiter came over.

Sobs burst from Nikolaeva's mouth along with saliva, her head shook and tears spurted on all sides. Powerless, she sank to the floor. Lida leaned over and began to slap her on the cheeks. Then she took a swallow from a bottle of mineral water and sprayed it on the ugly red face and distorted features.

Nikolaeva sobbed. Until she was hoarse. Until she began hiccuping. She arched on the floor, twitching like an epileptic.

"Oh my God, what's wrong with her?" Frightened, Lida tried to help her.

"Give her ammonia salts!" a portly man advised loudly. "It's a typical case of hysteria."

The waiter leaned over and stroked Nikolaeva. She passed a violent stream of gas and began sobbing with renewed force.

A woman came up.

"Did something happen to her?"

"She was mistreated," said Lida, looking at her in fright. "Oh my God, this is awful! I've never seen her like this…Alya, sweetie, come on, Alya! Oy, call a doctor!"

The woman got out her cell phone and dialed 03.

"What should I say?"

"It doesn't matter!" said Lida, brushing her aside. "I can't stand this!"

"Well…I have to say something…"

"Just say…" The waiter chewed on his small lips worriedly. "Say that a girl is crying."

Suite of Diamonds

21:40, Empty lot near Karamzin Passage

A SILVER Audi-A8 stood with dimmed headlights. Inside were Dato, Volodya Straw, and Crowbar. A dark blue Lincoln Navigator turned off from the road and approached them. It stopped twenty meters away. Uranov and Frop got out. Uranov held a briefcase in his hand.

Dato, Straw, and Crowbar got out of the car. Dato raised his hand. Uranov raised his in response. Uranov and Frop approached Dato.

"Hey, man." Dato proffered his stubby fingers.

"Hello, Dato." Uranov offered his long, slender hand.

They shook hands.

"Why the delay?" asked Uranov. "Are there problems?"

"There was one problem. But we disposed of it. Now everything's in order."

"Something having to do with delivery?"

"No, no. Internal affairs."

Uranov nodded. He looked around. "Well, then, shall we touch it?"

"Touch it, my friend."

Uranov raised his hand. Frop opened the back door of the vehicle. Mair got out and walked over to Dato's car.

Crowbar opened the trunk. A refrigerated coffer lay in it. Crowbar opened it. Ice shone in the coffer.

Mair took her blue leather gloves off and put them in her pocket. She stood, looking at the ice. Then she put her hands on it. Her eyes closed.

Everyone froze.

Two minutes and sixteen seconds passed.

Mair's lips opened. A moan escaped her mouth when she exhaled. She took her hands off the ice and pressed them to her red cheeks. "Fine."

The men began moving around with relief. Uranov gave Dato the briefcase. Dato opened it, looked at the packets of dollars. He nodded and closed it. Mair turned and went back to her car. Crowbar closed the coffer, removed it from the trunk, and gave it to Frop. Frop carried it to the car. Crowbar slammed the trunk.

"When's the next?" Dato asked.

"In about two weeks. I'll call you." Uranov stuck his hands in the pockets of his beige overcoat.

"All right, pal."

Uranov quickly shook his hand, turned, and strode over to the automobile.

Dato, Crowbar, and Straw got into their car.

"Count it." Dato handed the briefcase to Straw. He opened it and began counting the money.

The off-road vehicle turned around sharply and took off.

Crowbar gazed at it as it disappeared.

"I swear, I just don't get it, Dato."

"What?" said Dato, lighting a cigarette.

"I mean, those blonds...what sort of ice is it?"

"What do you care? You hand over the goods—and that's it. Let's go."

Crowbar started the car and turned onto the highway.

"Yeah, sure, of course. But what, can't we pass off some other ice? I mean, it's a waste. Just some piece of ice and so much bullshit around it: the ice, the ice, the ice. What kind of ice is it? No one knows. And it costs a hundred thou. What's the big fucking deal, man?"

"I don't even want to know," said Dato, blowing smoke out. "Everybody gets their rocks off how they want. The main thing is it's not radioactive. And not toxic."

"You checked?"

"Damn straight."

"Then all the more reason to slip them a phony. Hey, we can freeze a couple of buckets of water. And fuck it!" chuckled Crowbar.

"You're green. Even though you done time." Dato yawned.

"They've already been double-crossed," murmured Straw, counting the dollars.

"Who?" asked Crowbar.

"Vovik Shatursky. He was found later. In the fuckin' garbage. With his throat slit."

"Shit, man," Crowbar exclaimed in surprise. "But that's...wait a minute! You mean he ran the ice too?"

"Yeah, he did. Before Gasan and us. He and Zhorik shipped it together."

"And now they're in the underground business together." Straw slammed the briefcase shut and handed it to Dato.

"In the shareholder's society Mother Earth-Worm. Heard about it?" Dato smiled. "It's a business with a lotta prospects. Want the phone number?"

Dato and Straw laughed.

"Shit." Crowbar shook his head in surprise, without taking his eyes off the road. "And here I thought the Chechens or somebody offed him."

"No, brother." Dato placed the briefcase on his knees and drummed on it with his short fingers. "It wasn't the spades. It was the diamonds."

"But how? And this . . . Dato, tell me, this ice here, is it—" Crowbar continued.

Dato interrupted. "What fucking ice! What are you talking to me about, boy? Ice! Spades! Zhorik! I got more serious things on my mind!"

"What?" asked Crowbar quietly. "The mayor's office again?"

"What fucking mayor's office!"

"Shishka pull some kinda shit again?"

"What goddamned Shishka!"

"Taras making trouble, then?"

"Whaaaat fucking Taras?!" said Dato, rolling his eyes angrily. "Baby food, you fuckin' asshole! That's the most goddamn important thing in the world!"

For a moment they all rode in silence.

Then Straw began to laugh. Crowbar stared at Dato in the rearview mirror, not understanding.

Dato leaned back and was overcome by a high-pitched, Asiatic giggle.

They passed the Teply Stan metro station.

Then the Konkovo station.

Crowbar started laughing too.

Tracks

22.20, The office of the ICE Corporation, 7 Malaya Ordynka St.

THE LINCOLN Navigator drove into the gates of the attached courtyard and stopped. Ire, Mer, and Frop got out of the car. Frop and Ire carried a refrigerator case with the Ice. Mer went to the door and press a button. The door was opened by a guard in a dark blue uniform. Mer, Frop, and Ire entered, took an elevator upward, and moved down the hallway. At the far end, two armed guards sat next to a massive door. Catching sight of the group, they stood up from their plastic chairs, grabbed their sawed-off automatics, and stood stiffly next to the door. Mer moved toward the doors, looked straight at the security cameras, and said:

"Mer."

The door opened. The three entered a large office decorated in a high-tech style. In the middle of the office, standing on a large light-blue-and-white rug with a picture of two crossed blue hammers and a flaming crimson heart, were: brother **Lavu**: 33 years old, tall, blue-eyes, dressed in a dark blue suit; sister **Tse**: 41 years old, medium height, blue-eyes, dark blonde hair, wearing a black-and-white three-piece suit; and brother **Bork**: 48, tall, thin, with thinning light-chestnut hair and dark blue eyes, wearing large glasses, an ash-colored sweater, and light trousers.

As soon as the door closed behind the new arrivals, Frop and Ire placed the case on the rug.

"Mer!" Tse exclaimed, taking a step to meet her.

"Tse!" Mer stepped toward her.

They embraced with a moan, tightly, then swayed and grew still.

Frop opened the case.

Lavu and Bork approached, placed their hands on the Ice, and closed their eyes. Ire walked over to the glass bar counter, poured himself some water, and opened the refrigerator. The refrigerator's transparent doors were full of fresh fruits. Ire took a tomato and a large fig and closed the refrigerator. He drank the water in one gulp and began eating the tomato and fig greedily. Frop sat down on a low, frosted stainless-steel armchair upholstered in black leather, stretched his legs out, and with a sigh of exhaustion leaned back on the headrest.

Lavu and Bork opened their eyes and sighed deeply.

"The next to the last," Frop said, closing his eyes.

"There's still another cube?" Lavu asked.

"Left over from what the meat machines stole, there was another one," answered Ire, chomping on his food.

"Who was in charge?"

"Mer."

"Mer..." Ire opened the refrigerator and took out another tomato and fig.

Lavu glanced at Mer standing immobile with Tse.

"And who *knew*?" he asked.

"Ma and Nu *knew*. The meat machines don't have any more Ice. We bought up everything they stole back then in Ust-Ilinsk."

"The eighteenth cube." Lavu closed the case.

"The eighteenth," Ire confirmed and plunged his teeth into the fig. "In a couple of weeks the meat machines will bring the last one."

"And we'll close." Bork said.

"We'll close," Lavu nodded.

"What should be done with *those other* meat machines after all this?" Ire asked.

"We don't need Dato." Lavu walked over to the steel table and pressed a button on the control panel. "But Gasan, he'll come in handy. For *covering tracks*."

"*Covering tracks* requires calculation." Bork moved toward the half-closed blinds, glancing at the evening street.

"This doesn't need calculation, brother Bork." Lavu sat down at his desk, opening a folder of documents. "*Covering tracks* is superficial. All the possibilities are obvious."

Bork thought awhile, running his finger down the blinds.

"That's right, Lavu," Ire agreed, eating the last of his tomato. "Superficial tracks don't require any expenditure. Certainly not the powers of the Mighty. The meat are always ready to kill one another."

"But their rage has to be *correctly* directed, Ire," said Bork.

"Bork, this isn't the first time the brotherhood has used the meat." Wiping his hands with a handkerchief, Ire went up to Bork. "Their rage is totally predictable."

"The meat is unpredictable in one circumstance only," Lavu interjected, sorting through his papers. "When it *coagulates*."

"Right now the meat is peaceful." Ire sighed, placing his hand on Bork's chest. "There's no reason for the Mighty to help."

"It's always better to be prepared," Bork place his hand on Ire's chest in reply.

"The energy of the Mighty isn't endless."

"The energy of the Mighty is needed for the Circle," Frop spoke up from the armchair.

"The energy of the Mighty is needed for the Circle," Lavu nodded.

The door opened and two guards entered the office; they lifted the case and carried it out. The door closed after them.

Mer and Tse, who had been frozen in an embrace, shuddered, untwined their arms, and sighed deeply.

"The energy of the Mighty is needed not only for the Circle," Mer spoke. "The brotherhood doesn't hide what is primary from the meat. It's only the *veil* that requires secret layers. The energy of the Mighty supports the veil."

"*Covering tracks* can be done by a Lesser Circle as well," Tse finished the thought.

The brothers stood still. They were trying to *understand* this new thought.

"*Covering tracks* can be done by a Lesser Circle as well," Mer *repeated*, looking into Tse's eyes. "And afterward, ask for help from the Circle of the Mighty."

The brothers *understood* the new thought. Tse's heart was stronger than all of theirs. She was able to *know*. The new thought flowed from her strong heart.

Mer was the first to shake off the stupor, and she knelt down, holding out her hands. Tse kneeled next to her and took her by the hand. Lavu came around the table, kneeled next to Tse, and squeezed her fingers. Bork kneeled next to Lavu, Ire next to Bork. Frop rose from the armchair and took his place in the circle.

Everyone's eyes closed. Their hearts *began to speak*.

Peace

10:02, Office of the Vice President of Tako-Bank, 18 Mosfilmovskaya Street

THE LONG, narrow space of the office, gray-brown walls, Italian furniture.

Matvei Vinogradov sat behind a Spanish cherrywood table bent like a wave: 50 years old, small, black-haired, narrow-shouldered, sharp-nosed, thin, a well-tailored suit of lilac-gray silk.

Borenboim sat opposite.

"Mot, for heavens' sake, forgive me for pestering you so early in the morning." Borenboim stretched. "But you can understand."

"Don't worry about it," said Vinogradov, sipping his coffee. He picked up that very same Visa Electron card.

"69,000, is that right?"

"69." Borenboim nodded.

"And the PIN code is written down. Heavy. This is serious business, Borya. Presents like this smell bad."

"Very."

"Listen . . . and no one's done anything, called you, threatened you, right?"

"Absolutely."

Vinogradov nodded.

Sokolova entered with a piece of paper: 24 years old, slim, in a light green suit, unremarkable face. She handed over the piece of paper. Vinogradov took it and began reading.

"That's what I thought. You're free, Natashenka."

She left.

"And . . . ?" Borenboim frowned.

"They did it the simple way. Completely legal, in accordance with the Central Bank and the Civil Code. Here's how it goes: the donor applies for the main card using the passport of some front guy, and in the application form indicates he wants to have an additional card issued. In your name. When the cards are received, the primary card in the name of the front guy is confiscated and destroyed. Only yours remains. Finding the front, in your case—Kurbashakh, Radii Avtandilovich, born August 7, 1953, in the town of Tuimaz—would be almost impossible. Only Allah knows where this Kurbashakh abides at present. All in all, it's smart. Although . . ."

"What?"

"I would have made it even simpler. There's a completely anonymous product: Visa Travel Money. There's no owner's name at all. Have you used them?"

"No…" said Borenboim grumpily, averting his eyes.

"Any Petrov can get one of these cards and give it to Sidorov. I've seen it done. One woman sold six apartments in Kiev, and in order to avoid taking the money through Ukrainian customs, she asked for this Visa Travel Money. But there's one problem: the limit on individual operations in Russian ATMs is three hundred and forty bucks a day. In a nutshell, this woman milked the ATMs like goats for almost five months, and then it all ended when one of them swallowed her card, and she—"

"Motya, what should I do?" Borenboim interrupted, impatiently.

"You know what, Borya"—Vinogradov scratched his forehead with an ivory knife—"you need to talk to Tolyan."

"Is he at home?" asked Borenboim, rocking nervously in the armchair.

"No. He's swimming right now."

"Where?"

"At the Olympic."

"Early morning? Good for him."

"Unlike you and me, Tolya does everything right." Vinogradov laughed. "He swims in the morning, works during the day, snorts and screws in the evening, and sleeps at night. And I do everything the other way around! Go on over there. You won't be able to find him during the day. No way."

"I don't know… whether it's okay. I've met him a couple of times. But we aren't very well acquainted."

"It doesn't matter. He's a businesslike guy. Mention my name if you want, or Savka."

"You think?"

"Go on, go right this minute. Don't lose any time. Your FSB agents don't know shit. And he'll explain the whole thing."

Borenboim got up suddenly, frowned, and clutched his chest.

"What's wrong?" Vinogradov's handsome eyebrows knit in a frown.

"Oh… it's just something… like arthritis," said Borenboim, straightening his thin shoulders.

"You need to swim, Borya," Vinogradov advised seriously. "At least two times a week. I used to be falling apart. And now I've even stopped smoking."

"You're strong."

"Not stronger than you." Vinogradov stood up, stretched out his hand. "Give me a call afterward, okay?"

"Of course." Borenboim shook Vinogradov's thin, firm fingers.

"And anyway, Bor, how come we hardly ever see each other? It's like we're some kind of hard-hearted workaholics."

"What?" Borenboim asked cautiously.

"We never drink together, Bor. You and I've become totally heart-less!"

Borenboim paled abruptly. His lips began to tremble. He clutched at his chest.

"No. I…have…a heart," he enunciated firmly. And burst out sobbing.

"Borya, Bor…" Vinogradov rose halfway.

"I…h-have…a…a…a…h-h-heart!" Sobbing, Borenboim got the words out and then collapsed on his knees. "I haaaave…I haa…aaa…aaaa…veeee…aaaa!!"

Sobs wracked his body, tears sprang from his eyes. He bent over. Fell on the rug. Thrashed about in hysterics.

Vinogradov pressed a button on his phone.

"Tanya, quick, come here! Quick!"

Walking around the ornate table, Vinogradov leaned over Borenboim.

"Borka, hey pal, what's going on…come on, we'll find these assholes, don't be afraid…"

Borenboim sobbed. Intermittent sobs merged into a hoarse wail. His face turned crimson. His legs jerked.

The secretary entered.

"Give me some water!" Vinogradov shouted at her.

She ran out. She returned with a bottle of mineral water. Vinogradov swigged a mouthful and sprayed it on the wailing Borenboim, who continued to wail.

"Do we have any tranquilizers?" Vinogradov held Borenboim's head.

"Just aspirin," muttered the secretary.

"No valerian drops?"

"No, Matvei Anatolich."

"You don't have anything…" Vinogradov wet a handkerchief and tried to place it on Borenboim's forehead.

Borenboim howled and writhed.

"Jesus fucking…what the hell is this…?" Bewildered, Vinogradov smacked his lips, got down on his knees.

He began to pour the water from the bottle onto Borenboim's red face.

It didn't help. Convulsions shook the thin body.

"Something's wrong here," said Vinogradov, shaking his head.

"Did something bad happen to him?"

"Yeah, something real bad. He got sixty-nine thousand dollars transferred to him, and he doesn't know who did it! A big disaster, shit!" said Vinogradov, smiling bitterly, losing his patience. "Borka! Come on, that's enough, really! Enough!! Borya!! Stop! Quiet!!"

He began to slap Borenboim on the cheeks. Borenboim wailed even louder.

"Jeez, what the hell's going on here?" Vinogradov stood up and stuck his hands in his pockets.

"Maybe some cognac?" the secretary proposed.

"Damn, everyone's gonna come running now! Tanya, call an ambulance right now. They'll give him a shot of something in the ass…I can't stand this. I can't listen anymore!"

He sat on the edge of the desk. He looked around, searching for a cigarette. Then remembered that he quit. He shook his hands in the air.

"What a way to begin the fuckin' day…"

The secretary picked up the receiver. "What should I say, Matvei Anatolich?"

"Say that…the man has lost…"

"What?"

"His peace of mind!" Vinogradov shouted irritably.

Boy Is Crying

14:55, Central Moscow, Mokhovaya Street

LAPIN strolled from the Lenin Library metro station to the old Moscow University building. A backpack hung on his shoulder. Fine-grained snow sifted down from an overcast sky.

Lapin entered the cast-iron gates, looked in the direction of the "psychodrome"—a small square near the monument to Lomonosov. A group of students with bottles of beer stood there.

Skinny, stooping **Tvorogov** and small, long-haired **Filshtein** noticed Lapin.

"Lapa, come over here!" Filshtein waved.

Lapin walked over.

"How come you're so early?" asked Tvorogov.

Filshtein laughed. "Lapa lives on New York time! Mr. Radlov was asking about you."

"Yeah. Like: Where does my pet hang out?" Tvorogov butted in.

"What?" Lapin asked in a gloomy voice.

"Got a hangover, Lap? Bring your paper? Gonna hand it in?"

"No."

"We didn't either!"

Filshtein and Tvorogov laughed.

"Gimme a swig." Lapin took Tvorogov's bottle and drank. "Is Rudik here?"

"Don't know," said Tvorogov, lighting a cigarette.

"Take a look in 'Santa Barbara.'"*

"Listen, is it true that his ancestors were in some kind of sect?"

"Hari Krishnas, I think," said Tvorogov, blowing out smoke.

"No, not Hari Krishnas." Filshtein shook his curly head. "Brahma Kumaris."

"What's that?" Lapin returned the bottle to Tvorogov.

"Brahma is one of the gods of the Hindu pantheon," Filshtein

---

*Bathroom on the second floor of the university building.

explained. "You can ask Rudik what Kumaris is. They go to the Himalayas every year."

"Him too?"

"Are you nuts?! He's not into that stuff. He gets off on heavy metal. Hangs out with Spider. Why? You interested?"

"Just a little."

"What were you up to yesterday, Lap, you get drunk or get laid?"

"I shot up too." Lapin headed for the entrance.

He entered. Went up to the second floor. Walked through the empty smoking room. Walked through the open door of the men's toilet. It was empty except for a hunchbacked cleaning woman of uncertain age. An overturned urn lay on the dirty floor in a puddle of urine. Cigarette butts, cans of beer, and other garbage were piled up nearby. The cleaning woman was moving the trash toward the trash bin with her mop. Lapin clucked in dissatisfaction. Noticing him, the hunchbacked woman shook her head accusingly.

"A lot of pigs. Trash and trash. No heart in you."

Lapin winced. The hand that held the strap of the backpack unclenched. The backpack slipped from his shoulder and fell on the floor. Lapin let out a sob. His eyes quickly filled with tears.

"No!" he hissed.

He opened his mouth and let out a long, plaintive cry that rang in the empty toilet and burst into the hallway. Lapin's legs gave way. He clutched his chest and fell backward.

"Ooooo! Oooo! Oooooo!" He gave a drawn-out wail.

The cleaning woman stared at him angrily. She set her mop in the corner. She walked around Lapin and limped into the hallway. Three students were heading for the bathroom, drawn by the cries.

"Granny, what's going on?" asked one.

"Another drug addict!" The cleaning woman looked at them indignantly. "Who studies here these days? Fairies and drug addicts!"

The students stepped over Lapin. He moaned and sobbed, and every so often let out a lengthy scream.

"Shit, man. Typical withdrawal," one of the students concluded. "Vova, call 03."

"Forgot my cell." Another was chewing gum. "Hey, who has a cell around here?"

"Oy, what's wrong with him?" squealed a girl who had just come out of the women's room and looked in.

"You got a cell phone?"

"Yes."

"Dial 03, he's in withdrawal."

"Zhenia, maybe we shouldn't?" One of the students began to doubt.

"Call, you idiot, he'll croak here!" the cleaning lady screamed.

"Go fuck yourself…" The girl dialed 03. "What should I say?" The student spit out his gum.

"Like in the song. Say: 'Boy is crying'…"

Eight Days Later

12:00, Private Clinic, 7 Novoluzhnetsky Prospect

A SPACIOUS white ward with a wide white bed. White venetian blinds on the windows. A bouquet of white lilies on a low white table. A white television. White chairs.

Lapin, Nikolaeva, and Borenboim were asleep in the bed. Their faces were haggard and gaunt: there were circles under their eyes, their sunken cheeks had a yellowish tinge.

The door opened silently. The same plump, stooped doctor entered. He began to open the blinds. Mair and Uranov followed him in. They stood near the bed.

Daylight flooded the ward.

"But they're still sleeping soundly," said Mair.

"They'll wake up soon," the doctor said with certainty. "The cycle, the cycle. Tears, sleep. Sleep and tears."

"There was a problem with the kid?" asked Uranov.

"Yes." The doctor stuck his hands in the pockets of his blue robe.

"The other two were sent to hospital 15, as usual. But they initially thought he was a drug addict. So we had a bit of a hassle with the transfer."

"Did he really shoot up?"

"There's a needle track on his left arm. But no, he's not a drug addict."

They stood silently.

"Tears…" said Mair.

"So what—tears?" The doctor straightened the blanket over Borenboim's chest.

"They change faces."

"Well, if you cry for an entire week!" chuckled the doctor.

"I still don't understand why people always call the ambulance when someone starts sobbing uncontrollably. Why don't they try to calm them down themselves…" said Uranov thoughtfully.

"It's frightening," the doctor explained.

"How…wonderful it is." Mair smiled. "The first weeping of the heart. It's like…the first spring."

"You remember yourself?" The doctor shook his massive head. "Yes, you blubbered like a Beluga whale."

"You remember?"

"Now, now, my dear, it was only some nine years ago. I remember your graybeard, too. And the girl with the dried-up hand. And the twins from Noginsky. Doctors have a good memory. Don't we?" He winked and laughed.

Mair embraced him.

Borenboim stirred. He moaned.

Lapin's pale hand flinched. His fingers closed. And opened.

"Perfect." The doctor glanced at the white clock. "When they're together, the cycle evens out. All right, then! Hurry up, ladies and gentlemen!"

Mair and Uranov left quickly.

The doctor stood for a minute, turned, and followed after them.

The nurse, Kharo, silently pushed a wheelchair into the room.

A skinny old lady sat in the wheelchair.

She wore an old-fashioned, light blue dress. Her head was covered by a pillbox hat with a blue veil. Blue stockings stretched over unbelievably thin legs ending in blue patent-leather boots.

The old woman unclasped the wrinkled, dried-up hands on her knees and lifted her veil.

Her narrow, thin, wrinkled face was filled with extraordinary bliss. Her large blue eyes shone young, smart, and strong.

Kharo left the room.

The old woman looked at the three, who were awakening.

When all three had awoken and noticed her, she spoke in a quiet, even, calm voice.

"Ural, Diar, Mokho. I am Khram. I welcome you."

Ural, Diar, and Mokho looked at her.

"Your hearts wept for seven days. This weeping is in grief and shame for your previous, dead life. Now your hearts are cleansed. They will no longer sob. They are ready to love and speak. Now my heart will speak the first word of the most important language to your hearts. The language of the heart."

She stopped speaking. Her large eyes closed halfway. Her sunken cheeks turned slightly rosy.

The three in the bed shuddered. Their eyes also closed halfway. A slight convulsion crossed their haggard faces. The features of these faces came to life, blurred, and shifted, abandoning their usual expressions, which had been conditioned by the experience of their former life.

In agony, their faces began to be revealed.

Just like the buds of wild plants, dormant for decades in cold and timelessness.

Several moments of transformation passed.

Ural, Diar, and Mokho opened their eyes.

Their faces shone with a rapturous peace.

Their eyes sparkled with understanding.

Their lips smiled.

They were born.

PART II

I HAD JUST turned twelve when the war began.

Mama and I lived in Koliubakino, a small village with only forty-six houses.

Our family wasn't very big: Mama, Grandma, Gerka, and me. My father left for the war right away on June 24. No one knew where he went, where he ended up, or whether he was even alive. There were no letters from him.

The war went on and on somewhere. Sometimes at night it thundered and boomed.

But we lived in the country.

Our house was on the outskirts. Our family name was Samsikov, but in the village manner we were called the Outskirts, because we had lived forever at the edge of town, my great-grandfather and grandfather, everyone had always lived at the edge of the village; that's where they built their huts.

I grew up a sensible girl, I did everything around the house, helped my elders if something had to be cleaned or made. Back then, everyone in the village worked, from the tiniest to the oldest. That's the way things were done, there weren't any shirkers.

I understood that it was hard for Mama with Father gone. Although things had been even harder with him: he drank a lot. Before the war began, he worked in timber for a while. He and the forest warden sold timber on the sly, and drank up the proceeds. He was a binger. And he had a mistress in the next village. She was fat, with a large mouth. Polina.

The Germans arrived in our village in September '41, and they set themselves up. They stayed there until October of '43. They stayed for two years.

The soldiers were rear-line forces, not battle troops. The fighting ones went farther on—to capture Moscow. But they never did.

Our Germans were mostly about forty years old; they seemed like old men to me, since I was just a girl. They stayed in the peasant houses, all over the village. Their officers lived in the village council building. Things were all right with these Germans around, in two years they didn't kill anyone, but when they retreated they did burn our village. Well, that was the order they were given, it wasn't their own idea.

They were intelligent men, and practical.

The day after they came they started building a privy. Our village had never ever had any privies before this. Everyone went "out in the yard"—you'd squat somewhere and that was it. Grandma would go in the cowshed, where the cow stood. Mama—in the garden. Us kids—wherever we needed to. You'd squat by a bush—and that was that! No one in the village had any privies, it never occurred to anyone to build one special. The Germans kept on building, and Grandma laughed: Why waste all that hard work, the shit ends up in the ground anyway!

But Germans are Germans: they like order.

As soon as they arrived they started building privies and benches. Next to the houses, like they were planning on living with us for a long time.

They would throw some food our way—that helped. They had corn, flour, and tins of meat. They even baked their own bread—they didn't trust us. Were they afraid we'd poison them?

They had schnapps. I didn't try it, I was just a girl. But I did try beer for the first time in my life that winter.

They had their own Christmas; they all gathered in the village council. Mama and some of the other women cooked pork, chickens for them; they fried potatoes in lard, and baked white rolls from their flour. They put everything on the table. The other girls and I crawled up on the stove and watched. Then the Germans rolled out a small barrel, stuck a sort of copper faucet in it, and began pouring beer into mugs and glasses. It was yellowish and foamy. They drank, then they sang and swayed back and forth. It went on and on till nighttime.

They drank schnapps too. I watched from above. One German gave me a mug: Drink! I tried the beer. It had a strange taste. But I remembered it. So there you go.

All in all, life was cheery with the Germans. It was kind of interesting: Germans! They were completely different, and they were funny. Three of them lived with us: Erich, Otto, and Peter. The settled in the house and we moved into the bathhouse. The bathhouse was brand new; father had built it of thick logs, it would warm up good and hot.

The Germans occupied the house. They were an odd bunch! They were all about forty. Otto was fat, Erich was small and had a hook nose, and Peter was a beanpole, wore glasses, and had flaxen hair. Erich was the shittiest: he was always displeased. Do this for him, bring that. He'd say nothing or mumble something. He loved to fart. He'd fart, mumble, and head off into the village.

Otto was the kindest and funniest. Mama and I would make them breakfast in the morning, and he'd wake up, stretch, look at me and say, "*Nun, was gibt's neues*, Varka?"

At first I just smiled. But then Peter-with-the-glasses taught me some words, and I always answered, "*Überhaupt nichts*!"

Otto would roar with laughter and go take a leak.

Peter was always lost in thought, he had "his head under a pillow," as Grandma would say. He'd go out, sit on the new bench, and smoke his long pipe. He'd sit, smoke, and swing his leg. He'd stare at something, just sitting there like a bump on a log, and then suddenly sigh and say, "*Scheiss der Hund drauf!*"

He also loved to shoot crows. He'd go out into the orchard with a gun—and bang away, until the glass shuddered.

The Germans made three things in our village: ropes, sleigh runners, and wooden plows.

That is, our village people did all the work, and the Germans kept an eye on things and sent the stuff off somewhere. Mama and the other women went out to collect the bast, weave the ropes, and the old men and young fellows bent the sleigh runners and cut the plows. Iliukha Kuznetsov, an armless deserter, explained: This is so the bombs in the boxes don't bump around and blow up.

Our three Germans really loved milk. They went crazy over it: as soon as Mother or Grandma milked the cow, before it was even strained, the Germans would be pushing into the cowshed.

"*Ein Schluk*, Masha!"

They called Mama Gasha. They called me Varka. But they called all our other girls Mashas. They were just crazy about their milk...! They'd almost get up under the cow with their cups. There wasn't any hurry—they drank all the milk anyway! But they were in a rush so the fresh milk wouldn't cool down, they liked to drink it warm. They'd make a big fuss. We laughed.

So that year passed, and then the Red Army began to attack. The Germans ran off.

They had two orders: burn all the villages, and take all the young people with them to work in Germany. They only gathered up twenty-three people from the whole village. The rest ran off or hid. I didn't bother for some reason. I don't know why, but somehow I just didn't want to run anywhere. And where could you run to anyway? There were Germans everywhere. We didn't have any partisans. And it was scary in the forest.

Mama didn't say anything to me, either. She didn't even cry: she was used to everything. She wailed when they burned our house. But she wasn't very afraid for the children. And we were sort of numb, too, we didn't know what was happening, where they'd take us and why. No one cried. Grandma kept on praying and praying that we wouldn't be killed. They let me go. But Gerka stayed with them, he wasn't even seven yet.

They quickly gathered us in a column. Mother handed me father's padded coat and managed to slip me a chunk of lard. But I lost the lard on the road! What a laugh!

I can't figure out how it fell out of my pocket! That piece weighed about three pounds...

Later I dreamed about that lard. Dreamed I grabbed hold of it, but it was like the oat pudding they boil up for wakes—it slipped between my fingers!

We walked on foot with the Germans to Lompadi, where the railroad was. There they put us in this big farm building where they used to keep the collective farm cattle, but the Germans had also taken the cattle back to Germany. There were about three hundred of us from the entire region crowded in that place, all young guys and girls. They stationed guards so we wouldn't run off. Took us out only when we had to go. We stayed there for three whole days.

The Germans were waiting for a train to load us up and send us off. This train was coming from Yukhnov and collecting all the others like us. It was a special train, just for young people.

It was pretty cold at that farm—it was late autumn, there was already a ton of snow, the roof had holes in it, and the windows were covered with boards. There wasn't any stove. They fed us baked potatoes. They'd bring in a tub, set it in the middle; we'd grab the potatoes, laugh and eat, all of us grimy! And somehow everyone was happy: we were all young! We weren't afraid of anything, we never even thought about death.

The front wasn't far away. At night when we lay down, we could hear the guns firing: *boom, boom, boom*!

Then the train came. It was huge, with thirty-two cars. It had been going for a long time and was already full. So they started pushing us into the cars: girls separate, boys separate. There were already plenty of our people there. Then it finally hit us. Everyone was suddenly afraid, and the girls started crying: What will happen to us? Maybe they'll murder us all!

I began to cry too though I rarely cried.

They shoved us in and slid the doors shut. The train headed west. There were about fifty of us girls in the car, but no benches, no bunks. The straw on the floor was soaked in piss; the corner was piled with shit. There was one tiny little window with a grate. It stank. Thank god, at least it was freezing cold; the shit in the corner froze solid. In the summer we'd have all suffocated from the stench.

The train crawled along slowly, stopping often. Some of us sat, some stood, like herrings in a barrel.

We began to talk. That made things easier. Some older girls nearby told me about their lives. They were from Medyn, city folk. Their fathers had died in the war; one had deserted, then worked as a *polizei* and blown himself up with a grenade: he touched the wrong part of it and that was that. He took out a couple of people's eyes along with him.

One girl, she was eighteen, had lived with a German. Her mother lived with a German too, so they lived all right. This Tanya fell in love with the German, and when his division was moved and went on to Belorussia, she ran six versts alongside and kept howling: Martin! Martin! Then some officer got tired of her, took out his pistol, and shot at her feet. Three times. Then she left them alone.

Two women in our village also lived with Germans. They liked it fine. One of them always had tins and corn flour. She got pregnant after a while.

The girls in the car said that we'd be taken to work in Poland or Germany. Half the girls wanted to go to Germany, and half to Poland. The ones who wanted to go to Germany thought that there was no front there and a lot of food. And the ones who wanted to go to Poland said that the Germans would be defeated anyway and there would be war everywhere, so it was better to go to Poland, it would be easier to escape. They had big arguments.

There were four girls from Maloyaroslavets, committed Komsomol members; they had wanted to join the partisans but didn't make it in time. Now all they could think of was how to get out of here, away from the train. But the Germans didn't take us out for nature's calls, and they didn't feed us at all: How could you feed such a crowd?

We pissed right on the floor, on the straw. It all ran out through the cracks. And we made our way to the corner, to the pile, to take a shit. Everyone stood with their back to it, crowding away from it. They threw straw on the shit. One girl, a half-wit, sat nearby. She sang all kinds of songs. She was a village idiot, but the Germans took her, too, since she was young. She wasn't afraid of the smell of shit. She sat next to that pile, picking lice out of her hair and singing.

The worst part was when the train stood still for a long time at substations, or in the middle of a field. We're moving, moving, and then—screech! We stop. And stand there—for an hour, then maybe another. Then we'd creep on along.

We crawled across all of Belorussia that way.

We slept sitting up. We'd lean against one another and fall asleep . . .

Then the girls woke us up and said: We've entered Poland. It was early, early in the morning. I made my way to the little window and looked out: it was kind of cleaner there, prettier. There were fewer troops. Neat little houses. Very few burned ones.

Everyone started talking about how near Katowice there was a big camp for workers. There were only Russians, and from there they sent everyone all over Europe. Europe was very big, and in every corner there were Germans, in all the countries. At the time I didn't know anything about Europe: I had only managed to finish four years of school. I just knew that Berlin was the capital of Germany.

But the girls from Medyn knew everything about Europe and talked about different cities, though they'd never been to them, either. That Tanya, the one who ran after Martin, said that Paris was the best of all. Her Martin had fought there. He told her how beautiful it was and what delicious wine they had. He gave her schnapps to drink. And he gave her a scarf. But she left him, it was all so stupid.

One girl said that we would all be herded into an underground factory where they sewed clothes for the Germans. Right now all across Germany there was an emergency secret order to sew a million padded jackets for the eastern front. Because they were getting ready to attack Moscow, and the Germans' overcoats weren't very warm. That's why they were retreating. As soon as there were a million padded coats they would put them on the best divisions and those troops would jump into new tanks and make for Moscow. A *polizei* she knew had told her all about it.

Then the Komsomol girls started screaming that she was a rat and a traitor, that the Germans hadn't been able to take Moscow in '41, they'd frozen in their overcoats—and rightly so. And when the Red Army finally smashed the Germans, they'd bring Hitler to Moscow, straight to Red Square, and they'd hang him by his feet across from the Mausoleum; they'd hang traitors like her right next to him. They said Comrade Stalin would demand an account from everyone: people who had surrendered, people who'd licked the Germans boots, and women who'd laid down under Germans.

Tanya shouted at them to shut up with their Stalin. Because two of her uncles had been attacked as kulaks, and her father had rotted who knows where, and she and her mother had to live from hand to mouth, and with the Germans they could at least eat normally for the first time, and she'd even fallen so deep in love that she'd almost gone mad.

The Komsomol girls shouted: "Fascist whore!"

She shouted at them: "Stalinist dogs!"

They jumped on one another and started fighting. Then other girls got involved: some for Tanya, some for the Komsomols.

What a scene! Everyone all around was fighting. I wanted to get through to the wall, but I didn't have the strength. They all began fighting in bunches, then the train started suddenly and tossed us around. Gracious! Where did all that strength come from—we hadn't eaten in two days!

A couple of times I got slugged in the kisser, and sparks filled my eyes. People rarely fought in our village. Only in the spring, during the planting. Or at a wedding. In springtime—it was over fields. Someone would always get their head cracked open with a coupling bolt. At weddings—it was because of moonshine. They'd distill it from potatoes, set it on the table, drink—and start fighting.

My late grandpa told us stories: once there was a wedding, the guests sat down, drank, everything was calm, people were eating, the young people were kissing. But everyone was bored. One guy sat and sat, then sighed and said, "Well, someone has to start!"

He hauled back and slugged the guy sitting across from him right in the face. The guy fell head over heels, and the fight started.

Well, I don't know what would have happened if not for that half-wit idiot. She was sitting there near her pile and dozing, but as soon as the girls started fighting—she woke up. And oh did she howl! She was probably scared out of her wits, being half asleep. She scooped up some shit from the pile—and flung it straight at one of the girls! Again! And again!

They all squealed bloody murder! But they stopped fighting.

Then we came to a halt somewhere before Kraców. We stood and stood and stood. We stood there almost the whole night. It was stifling. Some cried, while others slept. Some laughed.

The four of us made it over to a corner and sat down. It was dark, and somewhere far away outside we could hear someone playing on a harmonica. Right away I began remembering home, Mama, Grandma, and Gerka. The tears came all by themselves. But I didn't cry out loud.

Our life hadn't been bad: Father earned money from selling timber, and not from a workday salary like on the collective farms. Not because he wasn't from the village—he just got lucky. One time he pulled Matvei Fedotovich, the forest warden, out of the bog. When he worked as a ranger he learned to hunt. What would you expect? After all, he spent all his time on a horse with a gun. When something jumped out—*bang*! Our forest warden loved to hunt, too. So they would go out and hunt together. Once, when they were duck hunting in the Butchinsky swamp, the forest warden stepped into quicksand and was pulled down. Father pulled him out. The old forester, Kuzma Kuzmich, had been murdered by Gypsies, so there was a job open. And the forest warden just up and appointed father! He became a forester. He got paid 620 rubles salary every month.

When you have money you can get by. Other men, as soon as winter hit—they'd be off to the city to earn money and buy something. You can't buy anything with workday credits. They'll give you potatoes or maybe rye. Sometimes it was oats. They'd boil and boil the oats in a cauldron all winter and eat them. Like horses.

But we ate well. We kept a horse, a cow, two pigs, geese, and chickens. We always had lard. Once in a while Mama would fry eggs in the morning on the big frying pan—they swam in lard! You'd take a piece of bread and dunk it—glorious! And afterward—buckwheat blini with cottage cheese.... You'd dunk them, and wash them down with baked milk—oh it was delicious! We had honey too, we bought it at the market. Father bought me boots at the market, too, and a princess doll, and four books so I could learn to read.

The other girls only had alphabet books, but I had real books with pictures: *The Magic Horse*, *Soviet Moscow*, *The Gingerbread Man*, and *The Wolf and the Seven Kids*.

The market was amazing, wonderful! Some mornings father would say: "So, then, Varyusha, what about going to the market today?"

I would fly out ahead of mother to harness the horses! Oh how I loved to harness horses! Father taught me when I was a small child: there weren't any grown boys in the family! And I rode horses well— what else do you expect? I was always around horses: first there was Frisky, then Zoya, who was stolen, and then Boy.

I'd take them out, brush them down, and hitch them to the cart with the painted backboard. Father would put on his calf boots, fill a new powder bag, and sit down in front. Mama and I always sat in the back. The whip went *crack*!, and off we'd go. It was thirty-six versts from our place to the market. It's in Zhizdra. What didn't they have there! All kinds of dishes, and rugs, and yokes. I loved the toys. One man sold little painted whistles. Another one sold toys: a peasant and a bear working in the forge. And there were all kinds of dolls. Good ones.

Everything would have been fine if father hadn't been a drinker. Mama said that's why there weren't any more children . . .

On the other hand—why remember the past? The Germans burned the village anyway.

So I bawled quietly.

That's right. We stood there and stood there. Then in the morning the train jerked. We moved along awhile and stopped: Kraców. Girls started standing up—we're here! Then someone slid the door back— and there were the Germans. They were looking at us, saying something. One of them held his nose and turned away. They started laughing: the stench in our car was strong. Then a Pole came over with a bucket of water. The Germans said, "*Trinken!*"

The Pole handed us the bucket. We began drinking one at a time. We drank up one bucket, and he brought another. We drank up the second as well. He gave us a third! I wasn't really very thirsty, but when my turn came, I started and couldn't stop, like I was in a trance. They barely got it away from me.

Altogether, our car drank four whole buckets of water.

Then two Poles drove a cart over. It had chopped-up pieces of raw horse meat on it. And one of them began shoveling the pieces into our car. He tossed them. The German shouted: "*Essen!*"

And they closed the door again. We stood there, and then—what else could we do? We all tried to sort it out: if they're feeding us, then that means that we're going on farther, to Germany itself. And how far is it? No one knew. Maybe two weeks or more? Maybe a month? Europe is big. Maybe even bigger than Russia.

We were hungry. We tore that raw horse meat into smaller pieces and chewed on it.

The train kept on going. We didn't stop for long anymore. Probably the railroads were better in Poland, so our train moved at a clip.

I chewed on the horse meat and fell asleep for a long time. I slept and slept, like a corpse. I was exhausted, of course. And it was scary. Whenever I was scared—I got sleepy. As soon as Father started beating Mother—I'd start yawning from fear. My head would hurt. I felt like lying down on the floor and not getting up, like sleeping until it was all over.

One time, Avdotia Kupriyanova and I got lost in the forest. We were sent to gather mushrooms, and she said: "Var, I know a secret mushroom glade, there are only white mushrooms growing—let's go." So she took me to that field. She walked on and on, and led me into such a thicket that I got scared: the trees were huge, you couldn't see the sun, it was dark as night.

We were lost. It was terrifying! There were wolves in our parts, and in '30 a bear ripped two cows to shreds. As soon as Avdotia saw that we were lost she began howling like a total idiot! What could I do? We went on, and I pulled her by the hand. Then I got so scared that I lay down under a bush and fell asleep. She fell asleep next to me. When I woke up—we'd been found. The road was nearby, some peasants were heading for the fields, we heard them. We shouted. They came over. Mother said it was a miracle . . .

I woke up when they slid the door back and shouted: "*Stehen auf! Aussteigen! Schnell! Schnell!*"

We got up little by little and crawled out of the car.

We crawled out onto an enormous public square. Not exactly a train station, but the sort of place where trains park, drive up, and drive off. I'd never seen anything like it: lots and lots of tracks, and freight trains standing idle. Whole trains with timber, and empty cars. And cisterns. There were soldiers everywhere.

They made us line up next to the train. Four people had died along the way, who knows from what. They were immediately taken away.

A German stood on a box and began speaking in Russian. He said that now we were in the great country of Germany. This was a huge honor for us. For that reason we should all work hard for the good of Greater Germany. He told us that we would go to a filtration camp where we would be given good, good clothes, and our documents for living in Germany would be processed. And then we would go to different factories and plants where we would live and work. All of us would be fine. And the most important thing for us to understand was that Germany was a cultured country, and that everyone in it lived happily. And that young people were even happier than others.

Then we were formed into columns and led off.

We walked from that place. We walked about seven versts. We arrived at a large camp with a barbed-wire fence and guard towers. Germans walked around with German shepherd dogs, and there were cars.

We were divided into barracks: girls separately, boys separately. There were bunks in our barracks. And there were other girls too—from Poland, Belorussia, and the Ukraine. But there weren't very many of them. They told us that no one stayed here more than three days: they put us through the camp and then took us to our workplace.

We asked them—where will you send us? They said, "Different places." No one could know for sure. And if someone got sick—they'd go to the work camp. That was the worst of all. They beat you with bricks there.

We stayed put awhile and then we were taken to the hygiene processing center.

It was an enormous bathhouse—gracious! I'd never seen anything like it. It was a huge sort of barracks—all brand new, and smelling like fresh boards. As soon as I entered and smelled that smell, I remembered our saw mill at Kordon. How I would ride behind the board when Uncle Misha's place was being built. We built him such a beautiful house, father got the best lumber. Then Uncle Misha went and hung himself. These things happen.

First thing they did in the barracks was line us up. Then they began taking us off three at a time.

I went with two other girls. There were tables, and German women in army uniform were sitting there writing something. But one stood holding a kind of crop. And she talked in Russian: "Take your clothes off."

We undressed. Stark naked. She looked at us front and back. Then she looked at our hair. Everybody had lice. I had lice too, what do you expect? She pointed her crop at two of the girls, and gestured toward a pile of hair: "Haircut!"

One girl began sobbing. The German lady snapped the crop across her bottom. She laughed. The girls sat down on the chairs, and women with clipping machines descended on them. She didn't tell me to cut my hair. She pointed the crop at the door of the bath: "Go in there."

I went in. It was sort of like a steam room. But there weren't any basins, just iron pipes with holes in them up above. Lukewarm water sprayed out of the holes. I looked at those pipes—what was I supposed to do? I stood there awhile, then I went on. Then there was a kind of dressing room. Again there were German army ladies. And tables with different kinds of clothes. The German lady gave me a clean undershirt and a blue scarf. She nodded at the exit. I went out and found another dressing room. Our clothes were there. But they smelled funny. It turned out that this was the place where we'd undressed. The barracks were built in a kind of circle, like the carousel at the fair. The same German lady with the crop said, "Get dressed."

I pulled on the new underclothes, then the wool stockings, and my green dress. Then a sweater. Then my padded coat. My old head scarf wasn't there. They took it. My old undershirt wasn't there either. I tied the new scarf around my head. And the other girls, their hair already cut, went to wash.

The German lady said, "Sit down at the table."

I sat down. There was another German woman across from me too. She also spoke Russian: "What's your name?"

I said, "Samsikova, Varya."

"How old?"

"Fourteen."

She wrote everything down. Then she said, "Stretch out your arm."
I didn't understand at first. She repeated, "Give me your arm!"

I stretched it out. She put a stamp on my arm—*bam*! It was a number in ink: 32-126.

Then she said, "Go over there."

There was a door. I opened it. I was in the yard. A soldier with a machine gun pointed me to another barracks. As I approached it I started to smell food. Lord, I thought, are they really going to feed us? I thought I was walking, but my legs ran all by themselves. Behind me some more girls came out. They ran, too.

We went inside. It wasn't a barracks, but a lean-to made of planks. Under it there were these huge cauldrons, about ten of them, and there was food cooking. There were Germans with bowls and ladles, and some of our people, who'd already come out. The Germans gave everyone an empty bowl. They gave me one, too—and we got in line. I waited my turn, and a German put a ladleful in my bowl—*plash*! It was pea soup. Thick, like porridge. But nobody had a spoon. Everyone sucked it over the rim.

I sipped it up quickly, wiped up the bowl with my hand, and licked the soup off.

A German was watching me. "*Willst du noch?*"

And I said, "*Ja, ja. Bitte!*"

And he gave me some more—*plop*! I sipped the second bowl more slowly. I looked around me: our people were chatting, there were Germans everywhere. Everything was different; a totally different life had begun.

I ate the second portion—and felt drunk. I rested next to the cauldron. It was warm and shiny. The German laughed. "*Also, noch einmal, Mädl?*"

I remembered what Otto said when he'd drunk enough milk. So I answered, "*Ich bin satt, ich markt kein Blatt.*"

The German roared with laughter, and asked me something. But I didn't understand.

I went back to the barracks.

By evening, everyone on our train had been processed and fed. But for some reason they didn't cut everyone's hair. Me and three other girls from our barracks hadn't had their hair cut. Tanya explained: "It's because you don't have lice."

I said, "What do you mean? Just take a look!"

She parted my hair.

"You do have them! Well, then they forgot. Hide your hair under a head scarf, or else they'll remember and lop it off till you're bald."

That's what I did: I tied the scarf tighter, to hide my hair.

When it got dark, that same German lady with the crop came in and said, "Now you all go to sleep. In the morning you'll be taken to your workplaces. You'll live and work there."

And they locked the barracks doors with a chain.

Some fell asleep right away, some didn't. I settled down close to Tanya and Natasha from Briansk and we kept on talking about what would happen. They were older than me, they'd heard a lot about Europe, and about Germans.

Natashka told us that in Briansk the Germans had showed films for their people. And two times a German invited her and a girlfriend. And she saw a film of Hitler and a naked woman who sang and danced and laughed. There were Germans dressed in white wandering around the woman. They looked at her and smiled. Hitler, she said, looked like he was so nice, with his little mustache. He was cultured, you could tell right away. And he talked very loud.

I'd been to the movies six times in all. Our closest club was in Kirov, twenty-five versts away. My father took me two times on Boy. Then Stepan Sotnikov took me with their children. I saw *Chapaev* twice, then *Volga-Volga*, *We Are from Kronshtadt*, *Seven Brave Hearts*, and one other picture, I forgot what it was called. It was about Lenin, how a woman took a shot at him. And he ran away in his cap. Then he fell. But he didn't die.

Down below on the bunks girls kept on trying to figure out who would win the war, us or the Germans.

Tanya and Natashka didn't care who, as long as they didn't bomb anything.

We'd been bombed three times. But all the bombs hit the orchards, not the village. But they did break the glass and slash the cows. One village woman stepped on a mine and it blew up. They brought her to the village. They brought her in on a mat, no leg, her guts spilling out. And she kept saying over and over, "Mamochka, my beloved, my sweet mama. My sweet mama. Mama, Mama, Mama." Then she died.

Then I fell asleep.

When I woke up—everyone had already risen. The girls and I ran to piss. There was a big privy, nice and clean. We pissed, and some even took a shit. Then we went to eat, to those cauldrons. Again there was pea soup. But watery, not like yesterday. And they didn't give seconds. I sipped the soup. I'd just finished licking the bowl when they shouted: "Line up!"

And we all went out to the big square.

They lined us up—fellows separate, us girls separate. The Germans stood around watching. They were silent. One kept looking at his watch. So, we stood there, the Germans not saying anything. We stood there for an hour, until our legs went numb. Natashka said, "They're waiting for trucks, to take us."

Suddenly we heard cars coming. And they drove straight into the camp. But not trucks, light passenger cars. Three cars. Shiny black, beautiful. They drove up and Germans got out of them. Just like the cars, all dressed in black. One of them, the most important—was very tall; he wore a black leather coat and gloves. All the other Germans saluted him.

He saluted too, walked over to us, crossed his arms on his stomach, and looked. He was handsome, fair-haired. He looked and said, "*Gut. Sehr gut.*"

Then he said something to the Germans. The lady who spoke Russian said, "Remove all headgear."

I didn't understand at first. I understood when the fellows took off their caps and hats and the girls started untying their scarves.

I thought: Here we go, now they're going to shave my head. And sure enough, the German lady said, "Whoever has hair—step forward."

There was nothing to be done—I took a step. Another fifteen or so people stepped forward: boys and girls. All of us they hadn't shaved.

The strange thing was that everyone was tow-headed, like me! It was even funny.

The German lady said, "Line up!"

So everyone stood side by side.

That German, the important one, walked over and looked at us. His look was sort of...I don't know how to say it. Long and slow. And then he came up to each of us. He'd come close, lift our chins with two fingers, and stare. Then he'd move on. He didn't speak.

He came up to me. He lifted my chin and stared at my eyes. He had a face that was...well, I'd never seen anything like it. Like Christ on an icon. Skinny, tow-headed, with blue blue eyes. Very clean, not a speck of dust or dirt. He wore a black peaked cap, and on the top of it—was a skull.

He looked at me, then at the rest. And he pointed to three of us.

"*Dieses, dieses, dieses.*"

Then he touched his nose with his glove, as if he was thinking. He pointed at me.

"*Und dieses.*"

He turned and went back to the cars.

And the German lady said, "Those who were chosen by his honor the Oberfürher—follow him immediately!"

So we went, the four of us.

The German went to the first car; the door was opened for him and he got in. Another German nodded for us to go to the second car. He opened the door. We walked over and climbed in. He closed the door and sat down in the front with the driver.

We took off.

I had never ridden in a passenger car. Only in trucks, when we transported the grain. And when we had the cattle plague in Koliubakino, they brought us calves in two cars for breeding. The Party *raikom* provided the cars. And Mamanya and I rode after those calves with the cattle worker Pyotr Abramych, all the way to Lompadi. I saw a passenger car in Kirov once. When we went to the movies. That car just stood there, because it had driven into the mud and gotten stuck. And everyone was standing around thinking how to get it out. The fat man who arrived in the car swore at the other one, from the *raikom*. The fat man yelled real loud: "Up your ass, Borisov, you have to go and drive in the ice."

Borisov stood there, silent, staring at the car.

Well, then. I looked around the Germans' car. It was all so beautiful! The driver sat in front with the German, we sat in the back. Everything was shiny and clean, the seats were made from leather, there were all sorts of handles. And it smelled like airplanes—the way it does in the city.

That car ran real easy. You didn't feel it driving, it just rocked over the potholes, you coulda thought you're in a cradle. That's when I understood why they call those cars "light" passenger cars.

There were two other girls with me and one young fellow. We drove and drove. Who knows where.

We drove about two versts, then turned into the forest and stopped. The German jumped up, opened the door and said, "*Aussteigen!*"

We got out. We looked and saw the two other cars nearby. There was new forest all around.

The important German stepped out of his car. He said something to the other Germans. They tied our hands behind our backs. So quick and crafty that I didn't understand what was happening, and—*poof*—they'd already got me! They pulled us along with a rope and led us over to four trees. They tied us to the trees.

The girls began to whimper. So did I. It was clear as day—we wouldn't get out of this forest. We're wailing, one girl started praying, and the boy, who was older than us, he shouted: "Sir, sir, I'm not a lousy Yid! Please, sir!"

But they just tied us up to the trees. And then they gagged us so we couldn't shout. Then they waited. The important one looked at us—and pointed to the boy. Two of the Germans went to the car.

I realized that they were going to kill us here and now. For what—I didn't know. Lord almighty, could it really be because we hadn't had our heads shaved?! Was that really our fault? It was those horrible Germans who forgot to shave our heads, not me who refused! I didn't care! Was I really going to end up underground because of my hair?!

Mama, Mama mine. So this is how everything would end! I was going into the wet earth here, and no one would ever know where the grave of Varka Samsikova was!

I stood there thinking. Tears filled my eyes.

The Germans were getting something out of the car. They carried an iron trunk toward us. They set it down, opened it, and took out a sort of ax or sledgehammer—I couldn't tell at first. So, they weren't going to shoot us, just chop us to bits alive. Oh, how evil!

They went over to the young man. He struggled against his ropes, poor dear guy, like a little bird. The German pulled open the fellow's coat—*whap*! Then his shirt—*rrrip*! He tore it open. His undershirt, too—*rip*! They bared his chest.

The important one nodded. "*Gut.*"

He reached out his gloved hand. The other German handed him the sledgehammer. I looked at it—it wasn't exactly a sledgehammer, it wasn't clear what it was. It looked as though it was made of ice. Or salt, like the kind they give cows to lick on the farm. No metal. The important German swung the sledgehammer back and hit the young fellow in the chest with all his might—*bam*! His whole body shuddered.

Another German put a kind of pipe to the fellow's chest, like a doctor, and listened. The important one stood by with the sledgehammer. The German shook his head. "*Nichts.*"

Again, the important one swung back, and—*bam*! The other German listened again. Once again he said, "*Nichts.*"

The important one smashed the fellow's chest again. They had beaten him to death. He just hung there on the rope. The Germans tossed the sledgehammer, took a new one from the box—and went over to the girl who was tied to a birch tree next to me. She sobbed wordlessly and trembled all over. They unbuttoned her plush jacket, slashed her sweater with a knife, and tore her undershirt. I looked— she had a little cross around her neck. My grandma put one on me, too, but the schoolteacher Nina Sergeevna took it off. "You are Pioneers," she said, "and there's no God. So we're going to tear up religious prejudice by the roots." She pulled the crosses off every student who had one and threw them into the weeds. Grandma said: "Unbelievers never die." I think that's the truth.

The important German again picked up the sledgehammer that wasn't made of metal, swung back easily, and slammed the girl on the chest—crack! Her bones seemed to crunch. The fiend stood back, while the other one put the tube on her and listened. He listened to the girl dying. After the first blow, she just hung unconscious on the ropes, her head all floppy. Then the third German lifted her head and held it, so it wasn't in the way. Again—*crack! crack! crack!* They beat her so hard that her blood splattered on my cheek.

The beasts.

Then they beat the other girl. She was only about fifteen, I think, like me. And the same height as me. But her breasts were already big, nothing like what I had. They beat her, beat her until blood spurted from her nose. She had a gag in her mouth.

I was the only one left.

When they'd finished beating the busty girl they threw down the sledgehammer. They took out cigarettes, stood in a circle, and lit up to take a break. They talked. The most important German wasn't happy. He said nothing. Then he shook his head and said, "*Schon wieder taube Nuss...*"

The other Germans nodded.

I stood there, I could see them smoking. I was thinking: any minute now, any minute, these fiends will finish their smoke—and that'll be it. I didn't feel afraid or sad, deep down. It was more like everything was as clear as the blue sky when there aren't any clouds. Like in a dream and I wasn't alive at all. Like everything had been a dream: Mama, the village, and the war. And these Germans.

They finished smoking and tossed their butts. They crowded around me.

They unbuttoned my jacket and took a knife to my sweater, the one that Grandma knit out of goat's wool. They pulled it back. I had my green dress on under my sweater. Father bought it for me at the county store in Lompadi. They slashed my dress with the knife, and then the German undershirt I'd been given at the camp. One German rolled the ripped edges of my dress and sweater back, sticking them under the rope, so that my chest was bared.

The important man stood with the sledgehammer and looked at

me. He mumbled something, and handed the sledgehammer to another German. Then he took his cap off his head and gave it to the one behind him. He stood just to my right.

The other German hauled back, grunted like he was splitting firewood, and bashed me right in the chest! I saw sparks. It took my breath away.

The important man suddenly dropped to his knees in front of me and put his ear to my chest.

His ear was cold, but his cheek was warm. His head was very, very close, fair and smooth, like it had been rubbed with cooking oil. His hair laid straight and flat, and stank of perfume.

I looked at his head from above, looked, and looked, and looked. Like it was a dream. Here I was dying, and I felt so calm. I even stopped bellowing.

He called to the German with the sledgehammer. "*Noch einmal*, Willi!"

Willi heaved once more—*wham!*

The important German pressed his ear to me again, listening.

"*Noch einmal!*"

Oof! He hit me so hard that chips flew off of the sledgehammer. I realized that it really was made of ice.

Everything swam before my eyes.

The important guy pressed his ear to me again. His ear was already covered with my blood. And suddenly he shouted, "*Ja! Ja! Herr Laube, sofort!*"

And the German with the doctor's tube rushed over to me. He stuck the tube to my chest and listened. He mumbled something, squinching his sour face.

The important German pushed him away.

"*Noch einmal!*"

And they slammed me again. I felt as though I was falling asleep: my lips filled with lead, and my mouth grew numb and heavy, like it was someone else's; it felt fuzzy, like the inside of a stove. Then I was so, so light, like a cloud, and the only thing in my chest was my heart and that was all. No stomach—I wasn't breathing, or swallowing. This heart in me seemed to *move*. That is, it was just . . . I couldn't tell what.

Like some little creature. It stirred, fluttered. It muttered something sweet as honey: khrr, khrr, khrr. Not the way it used to—from fear, you know, or joy. This was completely different, as though it had just awoken and before it was really deep, deep asleep. Here they were, killing me, and my heart woke up. There wasn't any fear in it, not the tiniest smidgen. There was only this sweet muttering. Just everything good, honest, and so tender that I felt petrified. The hair on my head moved: that's how good I felt. All the fear drained away: *What is there to be afraid of, if my heart is with me!*

Nothing of the sort had ever happened to me.

I froze stiff and didn't breathe.

The German with the tube started listening to me again. He spoke very loud, "Khra...Khra...Khram!"

The important one grabbed the tube from him and put it on my chest himself.

"Khram! Genau! Khram!"

And he began to shake with joy.

"*Herrschaften*, Khram! Khram! *Sie ist* Khram! *Hören Sie! Hören Sie! Hören Sie!*"

They all started blabbering and fussing around me. They cut the ropes off. But suddenly everything about them was disgusting to me—their horrible nasty voices, and hands, and faces, and their vehicles, and this drooling forest, everything all around. I stiffened so as not to scare off my heart, so that it would keep on muttering so sweet, so that the heart sweetness would take all of me in through my guts. But they started pulling me out of the ropes like a doll, grabbing me. My heart suddenly fell quiet.

I fainted dead away.

I don't know how much time passed.

I came to.

I hadn't even opened my eyelids, and I could feel—everything was rocking. They were taking me somewhere.

I opened my eyes: I saw that the room was small. It swayed slightly. I looked around—there was a window next to me, with a curtain on it. There was a little gap in the curtain and I could see the forest going by.

I realized I was on a train.

As soon as I realized this, my head became sort of empty. As though it wasn't a head, but a hay barn in spring—not a stick of straw, not a blade of grass. The cattle had gobbled everything up over the winter.

Emptiness. Enormous, no end to it. In all directions. But this emptiness didn't scare me or anything, it was sort of good. It was—*whoosh!* Like racing down an icy hill on a sled—*whoosh!* You start and you're already at the bottom. This emptiness was the same—*whoosh!* It rode into my head. And my head was empty, completely empty, though I understood everything and acted the right way.

I freed my hand from under the blanket. I looked at it—my left hand. I'd seen it thousands of times. But I looked at it—as though seeing it for the first time. Even though I knew everything about it! I remembered all the little scars, the one where I cut myself on the sickle, and where I hit a nail. I remembered so well, like someone was showing me a movie. That blue spot on my pinkie over there: Where did it come from? Well, it was from the time that Uncle Semyon returned from the army, he'd made himself a badge he pinned on his chest: a heart with an arrow. And he was teaching the boys how to make them: you had to nail a picture to a bit of wood, then burn a boot heel, take the soot, and rub it on the nails. That was it! You pinned the wood on your chest. Our neighbor Kolka made one, but father scolded him and threw the wood out, and then I pricked my pinkie on that wood with the nails. On one nail.

That's what.

The little room I was in was so lovely, all wood. And the screws in the wall were shiny. Two beds, a little table in the middle, a yellow ceiling. Warm. And it smelled clean, like in the hospital.

Someone was lying on the other bed. In a uniform. Turned toward the wall.

I freed my hand from under the blanket and sat up. I saw that I was only wearing my underclothes. And my chest was bandaged.

Then I suddenly remembered everything. At first, it was like my memory was lost: who I was, where I was—I couldn't understand anything: I was just riding and riding.

I looked around: there was an iron box on the table. A book.

I lifted the curtain: woods, woods, and more woods. Trees were the only things flashing by.

I sat up and hung my legs over the edge of the bed. I looked down—my cowhide boots weren't there. There were no clothes to be seen. I hung my head down, looking in the corners. Then my throat got scratchy and I started coughing. It made my chest hurt terribly.

I moaned and grabbed my chest.

The guy who was dozing jumped up and rushed to me. It was the same German who had brought the ice sledgehammers. He fussed about, embraced me by the shoulders and mumbled, "*Ruhe, ganz Ruhe, Schwesterchen...*"

He laid me down on the bed and covered me with the blanket. He leaped up, buttoned his collar, straightened his tunic, unlocked the door, and ran out, closing the door. I had barely managed to think a thought when the important German came in.

He was still the same—tall and fair. But not wearing black anymore. He wore a blue robe.

He sat on my bed and smiled. He took my hand, lifted it to his lips, and kissed it.

Then he took off his robe. Under the robe he had on a shirt and pants. He took off the shirt. His skin was so white. Then he started taking off his pants. I turned away.

Now he's going to go and make a woman of me, I thought. I lay there, listening to his trousers rustling, and wasn't even afraid. I lay there senseless. What did I care? I'd just lived through so much in that grove that nothing mattered anymore.

He got undressed. He threw the blanket off me and started taking off my underclothes.

I looked at the wall, at the new screws.

He undressed me all the way. And then he lay down next to me. He patted my head. And turned me toward him. I closed my eyes.

He turned me to him carefully, wrapping his long arms around me. He pressed his whole body to mine, pressed his chest to mine.

And that was it! He lay there, that's all. I thought, that's the way the Germans do it, they're careful with girls, first they calm them down, and then—*bam!* In our village they do it right off, I'd been told.

I lay there. Suddenly I felt a shock, a jolt through my whole body, as though I'd been hit by lightning. My heart stirred once again. Like some little creature. At first I felt strange, anxious, as if I'd been hung upside down like a piece of meat in the cellar. Then it felt good. I felt I was floating down a stream, riding a wave that carried me, faster and faster. Suddenly I could feel his heart as if it were my own. His heart began to tug at my heart. It was so incredibly sweet. So dear and familiar.

It burned clear through me.

Even my mama hadn't ever been so close to me. No one had.

I stopped breathing, and plunged into the feeling as into a well.

He kept on plucking and pulling at my heart with his heart. Like it was a hand. He'd squeeze it, or open it up. I grew numb. I completely stopped thinking. I wanted only one thing—for it to never stop.

Lord, how sweet it was. He'd start plucking at my heart, I'd just go numb, go numb like I was dying. My heart would flutter and stop. It would just stand there, like a horse sleeping. Then—*bing!* It would come alive again, quiver, and he'd start plucking at it again.

But everything on earth comes to an end eventually.

He stopped. We both sort of died. We lay there in two big lumps. Neither of us could lift a finger.

The train kept on going—chug-a-chug, chug-a-chug.

Then he loosened his hands. And collapsed on the floor.

I lay there and lay there. Then I sat up and I looked around. He was on the floor, as still as a corpse. Then he moved, suddenly embracing my legs. It was so dear and sweet!

I didn't even have the strength to cry.

He got up and dressed. Laid me down in bed and covered me with a blanket. Then he left.

I couldn't lie still. I got up. I pulled back the curtains from the window and looked out. I saw forest, fields, and villages. I looked at them as though I was seeing all this for the first time. I felt no fear. There was such joyous peace in my chest. Everything was clear!

Then he returned. This time he was dressed in his black uniform. He brought me some clothes: a pretty dress, all sorts of underclothes, boots, a coat, scarf, and beret. And he started dressing me. I watched him. On the one hand, I was embarrassed, but on the other, my soul was singing!

He dressed me and sat down next to me. He looked at me with his blue eyes. And I looked at him.

I felt so good!

It wasn't that I'd fallen in love with him. It was good in a totally different way. You can't say it in words. I felt I'd been given in marriage. To something great and good. Something that was forever and eternally my own, very dear, very beloved.

It wasn't love, the thing you have between girls and fellows. I knew about love.

I'd fallen in love twice before. First with Goshka the shepherd. Then with Kolya Malakhov, an already married man. Goshka and me kissed, and he squeezed my breasts. We'd go up in the hayloft to do it. He wanted to paw me lower down—but I didn't let him.

I fell in love with Kolya Malakhov myself. He didn't know anything and still doesn't, if he's alive. Like Father, he was sent to the war on June 24.

Before the war he was married off to Nastenka Pluyanova. He was seventeen and she was sixteen. We worked at the haymaking together. He cut, I dried and raked. I got stuck on him. He had curly hair, he was handsome and merry. When I caught sight of him—my heart would freeze. I'd be soaked to the bone in embarrassment. I'd go beet red. I even stopped eating for two days. Then it would pass somehow. Later—it happened again. I could think only of him. I cried and cried: dumb old Nastenka was so lucky! Then it sort of let go of me. Just as well. Why should I pine after someone else's fellow? That's love for you.

But this—was something else.

We rode the whole day in silence. We sat side by side.

Then the train stopped. The German got up, put the coat on me. And took me by the hand through the entire car. It was full of German officers. We got off the train at the station. I looked around—

what a station, I'd never seen anything of the sort! It was all iron and so high, no beginning or end to it. There were trains everywhere! People everywhere! And they all had things with them, and were well dressed. Everything was clean. Like in the movies.

He took me across the station. The other Germans followed him. Behind them a peasant with a mustache wheeled the suitcases on a cart.

I walked behind him. Everything was different. It all smelled different. A city smell.

Suddenly the station came to an end. We walked straight out into the city. It was so beautiful! All the houses were beautiful. There wasn't any war here at all—all the buildings were whole, people strolled down the streets calmly. Some even had dogs. They sat on benches and read newspapers.

We came to some automobiles. Just as black as the other one I'd ridden in, and just as shiny. Everyone got in. The important German and I got in the first car, and it drove off. Through the whole city.

I looked out the window and suddenly said, "*Was ist das?*"

He laughed. "*Oh, du sprichst Deutsch, Khram! Das ist schöne Wien.*"

Then he started talking fast, but I didn't understand anything. Over the two years that the Germans stayed with us, I learned some German words. I even knew swear words. But I never studied German in school.

I just smiled. Then he made a sign to the German who sat in front. He had met us at the station. And he was fair and blue-eyed, too. But he wasn't wearing a black uniform, he was in regular clothes. And a hat.

He spoke to me in Russian, and I thought he must be Polish. He said, "This city is called Vienna. It's one of the most beautiful cities in the world."

He told me all about the city: when it was built and what marvelous things there were to see. But I didn't remember anything.

Suddenly the important German ordered the chauffeur, "Stop!"

We stopped. The important one said something. And the Germans nodded.

"*Eine gute Idee!*"

The important one got out, opened the door, and signaled to me. I got out. I looked around: just a street. And a store with a pretty sign was right in front of us. Such a wonderful aroma came from that store! I felt faint!

The important German and I went inside. There were mirrors all around, and thousands of candies, cakes, pies, and other sweets. Very pretty girls in white aprons stood around. Behind me the Pole said, "What do you want?"

I said, "I don't even know."

The important man pointed to something behind the glass. The girl began to do something like mixing dough, and then—*whoop!* She handed me a little funnel with a pink ball on it. I took it. The ball smelled sweet. I tried it—but it was cold. It made my teeth ache. I looked at the German.

He nodded as if to say, go ahead and eat it.

And I ate it. It resembled sweet snow, but thicker. Delicious, but strange.

I ate and ate. And stopped.

Really, after everything that had happened, I didn't much want to eat. But the smells were good. I said, "It's cold. You can't eat much. May I wait for it to thaw?"

The Germans laughed. And that Pole said, "It's ice cream. You have to eat it cold. A little at a time. You don't have to hurry, you can finish it in the car."

I nodded. And we got back in and drove off down those beautiful streets. I looked out the window and ate slowly.

But honestly, I didn't really like the ice cream. The caramel roosters that Papa brought from the market were tastier. I could have sucked on them day and night.

We left the city and drove into the hills. The hills got higher and higher, till they were as high as the sky! I'd never seen anything like it in my life. We had two hills between Koliubakino and Pospelovka. When the girls and I walked to the Pospelovka village store we walked across the hills. You'd climb up to the tippy-top, stand there—oh, you could see so far! You could see our house like it was on the palm of your hand. Sometimes I could even see our rooster.

These hills took your breath away. The road became a narrow, twisty snake, and when you looked down you saw enormous pits! There were fir trees growing everywhere.

I asked, "What is this?"

"These are the mountains called the Alps," the Pole answered.

We drove through those Alps. Higher and higher.

We were so high that we reached the clouds, and drove on into them!

I kept looking down, but I couldn't see anything—that's how high it was!

We kept on driving and driving, there was no end to it. I was rocked from side to side, and my chest began to smart. I dozed off.

I woke up.

It was already dusk and I was being carried in someone's arms! The important German was carrying me. It was so embarrassing! No one had carried me for a long time.

I didn't say anything. He carried me along a road. The woods all around were covered in snow. The stars shone in the sky. The other Germans walked behind us. I looked to the right: Where was he taking me? And there was a large house! All made of stone, with light in the windows, and towers and everything, how beautiful!

He walked up the steps to a sort of porch. They were expecting him—the doors clanked open. The doors were incredibly heavy, all strapped with iron.

He walked in carrying me; everything was made of stone, the ceiling swam before my eyes. The lamps were lit. His boots made a sound—*clok, clok, clok*.

He walked and walked.

Suddenly some other doors flew open and there was a lot of light all at once.

The German stopped. He set me down carefully, like a doll. But not on the floor. He put me on a white stone, as big as a trunk. In Zhizdra an iron Lenin stood on that kind of stone before the war. Then the Germans knocked him down.

I lay on that stone. I looked around—there were lots of people, maybe forty. Men, women. And they were all looking at me silently.

The German said something to them in German. And they approached me from all sides. They came, like sheep, smiling. And they all came over to me! I was kind of dumbstruck. They walked up to that stone and suddenly all of them got down on their knees and bowed to me.

I looked around for my German—what should I do? But he had also bowed down to the floor in his black uniform. So did all the Germans who came with us. And the Polish man.

Everyone was bowing to me!

Then they lifted their heads and looked at me.

I saw that they were all blond. And they all had blue eyes.

They got up from their knees one by one. An old man came over to me and stretched out his hands. He spoke in plain Russian.

"Come down and be with us, Sister."

And so I got off the stone.

He said, "Khram! We are happy to have found you among the dead. You are our sister forever. We are your brothers and sisters. Each one of us will now greet you heartily.

He hugged me and said, "I am Bro."

A jolt passed to me from his heart. As though his heart was saying good day to my heart. Once again I felt the sweetness I'd felt in the train. But he soon unclasped his hands and moved aside.

All the others began to approach me. They took turns. Spoke their names and hugged me. Each time something pulsed and tugged at my heart. In all different ways: from one person it was like this, from another—like that.

It was all so sweet, it went right through me. Like glasses of wine were being poured onto my heart. One! Two! Three!

I stood there in a dream. My eyes closed. I wanted only one thing—for it continue an eternity.

Finally the last one walked up, said his name, hugged me, tugged at my heart—and stepped back. Suddenly it was empty around me— they all stood a ways off, warm and friendly, smiling at me.

The old man took me by the hand and led me off through room after room filled with expensive things. Then up a staircase. He brought me to a big room, entirely done in wood. In the middle was a bed. White, clean, fluffy, airy. He led me over to the bed and began to undress me. He shone all over. He had such an amazing smile, like his whole life he'd only seen kind things and had dealings with kind people.

He undressed me naked and put me in bed. He covered me with a blanket and sat down next to me.

He sat there and looked at me, holding my hand. His eyes were blue, oh so blue, like water.

He held my hand, then he put it under the covers and said, "Khram, my sister. You must rest."

But I felt so good. My whole body was singing. I said, "What do you mean? I slept the whole way, like a broody hen! I'm not the least bit sleepy now."

He said, "You have used a good deal of energy. You have a new life ahead of you. You must prepare for it."

I wanted to argue with him, to say, I'm not at all tired. But then exhaustion suddenly overwhelmed me, as though I'd been hauling sacks or something. I fell into a deep sleep straightaway.

I came to: Where was I?

It was the same room, the same bed. The sun was blazing in through a crack in the curtains.

I slid off the bed and went to the window. I pulled back the curtain: oh my goodness gracious, what a beautiful sight! There were mountains all around. They didn't have any forest covering them, they were naked, covered only in snow. And they reached to the sky. They were all blue. And the sky, it was right up close.

And there wasn't a soul in these mountains.

I suddenly needed to piss bad. Then I remembered what woke me up! I dreamed that I was a baby wrapped in diapers. And some strange person was holding me on his knees. I want to piss so bad. I have to ask, so I don't wet him. But I don't know any words yet! And there I am in my diapers, squirming and thinking, how do you say, "I want to piss?" That's when I woke up.

And I needed to go so bad it was as if I'd done nothing but drink water for days. But I didn't know where to go. I went and opened the door. There was a hallway. I walked out and along it, thinking maybe there's a bucket around somewhere. Then I saw a staircase going down, a pretty wood one with carved pinecones. I walked a few steps down and looked around—there were all sorts of doors. I pushed against one of them—it wasn't locked. I entered.

There were three couples on their knees, embracing. Naked. And silent.

No one even glanced at me.

As soon as I saw them I remembered everything that had happened in the train. I suddenly felt so good that I couldn't hold it anymore and pissed all over myself. It flooded out of me onto the floor. There was so much—it poured and poured! I just stood there and watched them, and everything went kind of blurry. And the puddle reached all the way over to them! I wasn't ashamed at all—I froze there as if I was made of stone, it was good, no energy to move. I stared at them like they were sweets in a candy shop, that was all. They were standing in my urine! And they didn't budge!

Then someone called out behind me.

"Khram!"

I came to my senses—it was a woman. She spoke to me, but the language was strange—I sort of understood the words separately, but together it was hard. It wasn't Ukrainian or Belarusian. And it wasn't Polish. In the camps I understood Polish.

The woman took me by the hand and led me somewhere. Naked, I walked behind her, the wet soles of my feet slip-slapping along.

She brought me to a huge room that was covered with sparkling stones. In the middle of the room was a tub—all white—filled with water. The woman unwound the bandage from my chest and took the cotton off the wound. Then she pulled me toward the tub. I got in and lay down. The water was warm and pleasant.

Then another woman came in. They began to wash me as they would an infant. They washed me all over, then told me to stand up. I stood up. There was this metal plate above my head. And this plate suddenly began to pour water on me, like a little rain shower. It was so wonderful! I just stood there laughing.

Then they dried me off. They put a new bandage on my wound. They sat me down on a stool with a cushion and rubbed sweet-smelling stuff all over me. When I was rubbed down, they combed my hair and wrapped me up in a soft robe. They picked me up like a sack and carried me off.

They brought me to an enormous room. There were all kinds of wardrobes and cabinets, and in the middle there were three mirrors, and a little table right next to them that was covered with little bottles. It smelled of perfume. They sat me down at that table, and I could see myself in three mirrors at once. Good lord! Was that really me? I'd turned into someone completely different over the last weeks. I don't know what happened—either I'd gotten older, or smarter, but the only thing left of the old me was my hair and eyes. It was even kind of scary...But what could I do about it? At times like these my late grandfather used to say, "Live and don't be afraid of anything."

First they cut my hair. They gave me a pretty hairdo, and put some smelly stuff on it. Then they trimmed the nails on my hands and feet. Then they evened my nails out with this little file. Just like you do with horses' hooves, when you shoe them! I could barely keep from laughing, but I realized: this is Germany!

Afterward the women began dressing me: they slipped off the robe and started pulling all kinds of clothes out of the wardrobes and chests of drawers: dresses, underclothes, and brassieres. They laid them out. Everything was so pretty, clean, white!

First they measured me for the brassiere. My titties were still little. They chose the smallest bra and put it on me. Lord almighty! In our village even the grown women never wore brassieres, never mind the girls! I'd only seen these brassiere things in Zhizdra and in Khliupin in the village store where they sell dresses and bolts of dress fabric.

Then they put white drawers on me. Short, pretty ones, like on a doll. Then they hooked stockings onto the drawers. And right over it all—a short white slip. Oh, what a slip. Covered in lace and smelling of sweet perfumes! Everything was beautiful—no doubt about it. Over that they put on a blue dress with a white collar. Then they started picking out shoes. When they opened the boxes I took a look. Oh my goodness! Not ankle boots, not boots at all, but honest-to-god shoes, all patent-leather shiny! They brought me three boxes to choose from. My head almost began spinning. I pointed with my finger—and they put the shoes on my feet. Shoes with heels!

They painted my lips and powdered my cheeks. They hung a string of pearls around my neck. I stood up and looked at myself in the mirror—I even squeezed my eyes shut! A real beauty stood there in front of me, not Varka Samsikova!

They took me by the hand and led me on. We went downstairs.

Downstairs there was another enormous room, made of stone. It had a huge table. The people who met me the night before were sitting around it. Only they weren't in uniform, they were in regular clothes. Everyone was eating. The food was pretty, all kinds.

They sat me down at my place. Everyone smiled at me, like family. That old man, Bro, said, "Khram, you are our sister, share our repast with us. The rules of our family are to eat nothing living, neither boil nor fry food, neither cut nor pierce it. For all of these things violate its Cosmos."

He took a pear and handed it to me. I took it and began eating. So did everyone at the table.

I looked at the table: there was no meat, no fish, no eggs, no milk. No bread. But there were different fruits—tons of them. Not only pears—watermelon, cantaloupes and other melons, tomatoes, different kinds of cucumbers, apples, even cherries! And many, many more fruits that I had never seen.

Everyone ate with their hands. No knives, forks, or spoons were to be seen.

I looked at the cantaloupe—I'd never eaten it, only seen it at the market. One man noticed me looking at it, so he took the largest melon. He pulled over a sort of sharp rock. He swung back and—*crack* went the stone against the cantaloupe! It spurted all over and pieces went flying all around! Everyone smiled. He picked a piece out and handed it to me. Then he gave the rest to the others. I tasted cantaloupe for the first time. It was scrumptious!

Then I ate strawberries, sweet peppers, and three other kinds of fruits. I stuffed myself with cherries.

They all ate, rose, and each went his own way.

The old man Bro came over to me. He took me by the elbow and led me to a little room. It was full of books. He sat me down at a small table and took a seat across from me. He said, "Khram, what are you feeling?"

I said, "My chest aches a little bit."

"And what else?"

"Well," I said, "I don't know … it's hard to say …"

"Do you feel good with us?"

"Yes," I said.

"Has your heart felt good?"

"Very," I answered. "I have never felt this good."

He looked at me with a smile and said, "There are very few people like us. Only one hundred fifty-three on earth."

I said, "Why is that?"

"Because," he said, "we aren't like everyone else. We know how to speak not only with our mouths but with our hearts. Other humans speak only with the mouth. Their hearts will never speak."

"Why?"

"Because they are living corpses. The absolute majority of people on this earth are walking dead. They are born dead, they marry the dead, they give birth to the dead, and die; their dead children give birth to new dead—and so on, from century to century. That is the circle of their dead lives. There is no way out. But we are alive, we are the chosen. We know what the language of the heart is, the language we have already spoken to you. And we know what love is. Genuine Divine Love."

"What is love?"

"For hundreds of millions of dead people, love—is nothing but lust, the thirst to possess another's body. For them, it all boils down to one thing: a man sees a woman, she pleases him. He doesn't know her heart at all, but her face, figure, walk, and laughter attract him. He wants to see this woman, be with her, touch her. And that's when the illness called 'earthly love' begins: the man seeks to acquire the woman, he gives her gifts, courts her, swears his love, promises to love her and no one else. She begins to take some interest in him, then she feels sympathy for him, then she starts to think that this is the very person she's been waiting for. Finally they become so close that they are ready to commit the so-called 'act of love.' Hiding away in a bedroom, they undress and lie down on the bed. The man kisses the woman, plays with her breasts; he falls on top of her, thrusts his member in her, pants and groans. She moans, at first from pain, then from lust. The man ejects his seed into the woman's womb. And they fall asleep in sweat, emptied and exhausted. Then they begin to live together, they have children. The passion gradually leaves them. They turn into machines: he makes money, she cooks and cleans. Sometimes they live like this until their very death. Or they fall in love with others. They separate and recall the past with anger. They swear loyalty to their newly chosen man or woman. They start a new family, have new children. And again they become machines. This disease is called earthly love. For us this is the greatest evil. Because we, the chosen ones, know an entirely different love. It is as large as the sky, and as sublime as the Primordial Light. It is not based on external attraction. It is deep and strong. You, Khram, have felt a small dose of this love. You have barely touched it. It was but the first ray of the great Sun that touched your heart. The Sun called the Divine Love of Light."

I wanted to ask him something, but he suddenly reached his hand out to me and took my hands in his. I didn't even have time to speak; he closed his eyes. He seemed to be asleep.

Suddenly, my heart felt—*ping*.

And just like that time on the train, everything swam. Only this was stronger. Like I dove headfirst into a whirlpool—I saw stars. It was as though he'd shot me in the heart.

Then something entirely different began. I felt that he was leading my heart step by step up a staircase. It beat against every step. But each time it beat in a different way, each step was completely different, made of some entirely different material.

It was so sweet and terrifying that I just died of happiness.

He kept dragging my little heart along.

Higher and higher.

It was sweeter and sweeter.

And then—that was it! The last step. The sweetest of all.

And I suddenly understood with my heart that there were only 23 of these steps.

But I hadn't counted them. I just understood with my heart.

Then he stopped. And I—was just sitting there, as I had been. Everything was swimming around me, but my heart was burning like a flame. I couldn't talk.

Then he said to me, "Just now I spoke to you in the language of the heart. Previously, everyone spoke only a few words to you with the heart. There are only twenty-three heart words in all. I spoke them all to you. Now you know them all."

I just sat there—I felt so good, I couldn't move. I'd never felt so wonderful in my life. I suddenly understood everything, I began to sob so hard that I was convulsed; I fell down on the floor and howled and wailed and sobbed. Bro got up, patted my head, and said, "Cry, Sister."

I wept. I wept like I'd never wept in my life: my whole insides were turned out.

He called some others over to carry me into the bedroom. I was writhing like an eel in their arms, and tears were spurting out of my eyes!

In the bedroom they undressed me and put me in bed. But I was sobbing so hard I couldn't stop. I'd go numb, numb all over until I couldn't feel anything, as though I was just about to die. And then I'd come to—where was I? I'd lie flat on my back in bed. As soon as I'd come around just a little—the tears would start again. And I'd work myself up till I was writhing again. Then I'd howl and weep until I lost consciousness.

I wept this way for seven days.

Then I came to. I lay there a bit. I no longer felt like crying. My heart was at peace. It was glorious! So calm and wonderful. But I was so weak that I couldn't move a finger. I lay there looking out the window. Outside I could see fir trees in the snow. Those firs were so glorious and well proportioned. The snow lay on them and sparkled in the sunshine.

I don't know how long I lay there.

Then a woman came in. She brought me something to drink. I drank.

The old man, Bro, came in. He sat on my bed and held my hand.

He said, "Everything's behind you, Khram. Your heart cried from shame at your past life. That is normal. It has happened to each one of us. Henceforth, you will never cry again. You will delight and be joyful. Joyful that you are alive."

And my new life began.

Can I tell the whole story? Of course not. Memory captures only bright and dear moments. But my new life consisted entirely of bright, dear moments.

I spent three years in our Home in the Austrian Alps. Then, when the war came to the mountains as well, we left our Home and made our way to Finland. There, in the forest, on a lake, another Home awaited us. I spent another four years there.

I remember everything: the faces of sisters and brothers, their voices, their eyes, and their hearts, which taught my heart the sacred words.

I remember...

New blue-eyed, fair-haired people appeared, people whose hearts had been awakened by the ax of Ice; they merged into our brotherhood, came to know the joy of awakening, wept tears of heartfelt remorse, discovered the divine language of hearts, and replaced the experienced and mature, those who had already learned all 23 words.

Finally a fateful day arrived for me: July 6, 1950.

I rose with the sun, like the other brothers and sisters. Walking out into the meadow in front of the house, we stood in pairs, as always; we embraced and fell to our knees. Our hearts began to speak the sacred language. This continued for several hours. Then we released our embraces. We returned to the house, readied ourselves, and shared our meal.

After our repast, Bro took me aside. He said, "Khram, today you will leave our brotherhood. You will go to Russia. And you will search for the living among the dead. In order to awaken them and return them to life. You have traveled a long road with us. You have mastered the language of the heart. You have learned all 23 three heart words. You are ready to serve our greater goal. I will tell you what you need to know. This tradition lives only on the lips, it does not exist on paper. Listen carefully: In the beginning there was only the Light. And the Light shone in Absolute Emptiness. The Light shone for Itself Alone. The Light consisted of 23,000 Light-bearing rays. And we were those rays. Time did not exist. There was only Eternity. In this Eternal Emptiness we shone. And we birthed whole worlds. The worlds filled the Emptiness. Thus was the Universe born. Each time we wanted to create a new world, we formed a Divine Circle of Light from 23,000 rays. All the rays were directed inside the circle, and after 23 impulses in the center of the circle a new world would be born. These were the stars, planets, and galaxies. Once, when we created a new world, one of its seven planets was covered with water. This was the planet Earth. We had never created such planets before. This was the Light's Great Mistake. For the water on the planet Earth formed a sphere-shaped mirror. As soon as we were reflected in it, we ceased being rays of light and were incarnated in living creatures. We became primitive amoebas that inhabited the boundless ocean. The water carried our tiny, semitransparent bodies, but as before, the Primordial Light lived in us. And as before there were 23,000 of us. But we were scattered across the ocean expanses. Billions of earthly years passed. We evolved together with the other creatures that inhabit the Earth. We became human beings. People multiplied and covered the Earth. They began to live by their minds, enslaving themselves to their flesh. Their lips spoke in the language of the mind, and this language covered the entire visible world like a membrane. People ceased seeing things. They began to think them. Blind and heartless, they became more and more cruel. They created weapons and machines. They killed and birthed, birthed and killed. They turned into walking corpses. Because human beings were our mistake. As was everything living on Earth. And Earth became hell. And we, the dispersed, lived in this hell. We died and were incarnated again, without the strength to tear ourselves away from the Earth that we ourselves had created. As ever, there were 23,000 of us. The Primordial Light lived in our hearts. But our hearts slept, as do billions of human hearts. What could awake them, so that we might understand who we were and what we should do? All the worlds we created before Earth were dead. They hung in the Emptiness like Christmas ornaments, to give us joy. The joy of the Primordial Light sang in them. Only the Earth violated this Cosmic Harmony. For it was alive and developing on its own. It developed like an ugly, cancerous tumor. But the Cosmic Harmony cannot be violated for long. A piece of one of the tree ornaments we created fell to the Earth. This was one of the largest meteors ever. And it happened in 1908, in Siberia, near the river. The meteorite was called the Tungus Event. In 1927 a group of learned people formed an expedition to locate it. They arrived at the place, saw the destroyed forests, but they did not find the meteorite. There were fifteen people on this expedition. Among them was one twenty-year-old student, a tow-headed lad with blue eyes. Arriving at the site of the meteorite's landing, he experienced a strange feeling, one that he had never felt before: his heart began to tremble and quiver. As soon as this happened, he fell silent. He stopped conversing with the other members of the expedition. He felt with his heart that the meteorite was somewhere nearby. The energy exuding from the meteorite stunned the youth. In two days that energy turned his life around. The members of the expedition thought that he had gone mad. The expedition left empty-handed. He fell behind. Then he returned to the place where it fell. And he found the meteorite. It was a huge chunk of Ice. It had sunk into swampy soil, the putrid water had closed over it, hiding it from humans. The youth plunged into the swamp, slipped, and hit his chest hard against the Ice. Suddenly, his heart began to speak. He understood everything. He broke off a piece of the Ice, put it in his rucksack, and went out among people. The Ice was heavy, it was difficult to walk. The Ice melted. When he arrived at the nearest village, only a small piece of the Ice remained, one that fit in the palm of his hand. In the village, he found a girl sleeping in a yurt. She was tow-headed, and her blue eyes were half open. He picked up a stick from the ground, tied the piece of Ice to it with a shoelace, and struck the girl with the Ice hammer in the chest with all his might. The girl cried out and lost consciousness. He lay down near her and fell asleep. When he woke up, she was sitting nearby and looking at him like a brother. They embraced. Their hearts began speaking to each other. They understood everything. They set off to look for more of their kind."

He was silent for a moment and then added: "I was that youth."

Then Bro continued.

"I have never spoken with you about the goals of our brotherhood. Each of us who fully commands the language of the heart feels them. You are close to this. But we don't have time to wait, for you must leave for Russia as soon as possible, to search for our brothers and sisters there, for those who don't belong to the hellish world, for those in whose hearts the memory of the Light still lives."

He fell silent, and gazed at me.

"What must I do?" I asked.

"You must sift through the human race. Look for the gold in the sand. There are 23,000 of us. No more and no fewer. We are blue-eyed and fair-haired. As soon as all 23,000 are found, as soon as all know the language of the heart, we will stand in a ring and our hearts will pronounce the 23 heart words in unison. And in the center of the ring the Primordial Light will arise, the very light that created the worlds. And the mistake will be corrected: Earth will disappear, dissolve in the Light. Our earthly bodies will dissolve together with the world of the Earth. Once again we will become rays of the Primordial Light. We will return to Eternity."

Bro had barely finished speaking when there was a movement in my heart. I FELT everything that he had told me in earthly language. I saw us standing in a circle, holding hands and speaking the heart words.

Bro felt this and he smiled.

"Now, Khram, you know everything."

I was stunned. But one question tormented me.

"What is the Ice?"

"It is an ideal Cosmic substance generated by the Primordial Light. Outwardly it resembles earthly ice. In fact, however, its structure is entirely different. If it is shaken, the Music of the Light sings in it. In striking our breastbone, the Ice vibrates. These vibrations awaken our hearts."

He said it, and I immediately felt what he was saying. And I understood what ICE was.

"Three of our brothers are in Russia," Bro continued. "They will
help you. And together you will accomplish great feats. Commence,
Khram."

Thus began the return to my homeland.

The next morning near Lake Inari I crossed the border into the USSR.
A passenger car was waiting for me in the forest. Two men in KGB
officer uniforms sat in it. One of them silently opened the door of the
car, and I got in. We drove off, first along a forest road, then a highway. We traveled in silence. We were stopped by military patrols
three times. My companions presented documents to them and they
immediately let us pass.

Four hours later we entered Leningrad.

We stopped near a building on Morskoi. One of the officers invited me to follow him. He and I entered the building and climbed to
the fourth floor. The officer rang apartment 15, turned, and went back
downstairs.

The door opened. On the threshold stood a blond man of medium
height in the uniform of a lieutenant colonel of the state security. He
was extremely anxious, but restrained himself with all his might.
Keeping his eyes fixed on me, he stepped back into the depths of the
apartment. I trembled as well: my heart felt a brother. I closed the
door and went to him. The apartment was almost dark because of
the closed drapes. Nonetheless, I could make out the blue of his
straining eyes.

We embraced and fell to our knees. Our hearts began to speak.
This continued until evening. His heart had longed wearily for the
sacred, and it trembled violently. But it was fairly inexperienced and
knew only six heart words.

Finally we broke our embrace.

Coming to, he said, "My earthly name is Aleksei Ilich Korobov."

His heart name was Adr.

He was silent again, and simply looked at me for a long time. But I
was used to it. In our Home the brothers and sisters spoke in earthly

language only when absolutely necessary. Then he picked up the telephone receiver and said, "The car."

We went out onto the street. It was already dark.

A chauffeured automobile and guard were waiting next to the entrance. We were taken to Moscow Station. There we boarded the Leningrad–Moscow train and locked ourselves in a sleeping car. Adr placed fruits on the table. But he couldn't eat; he just continued looking at me as before.

I was already hungry and ate a few fruits with pleasure. Then he told me his story. He was a regular officer of the MGB, and in 1947 the Ministry of State Security sent him to Germany on business for GUSIMZ, the Main Directorate of Soviet Property Abroad.

In Dresden, at a holiday banquet honoring the second anniversary of the victory over Germany, he became closely acquainted with his direct superior, General Lieutenant Vlodzimirsky, who headed the GUSIMZ office. Previously, they had met only in the line of duty. Vlodzimirsky, who was considered a tough, unsociable man at Lubianka, suddenly displayed a great deal of sympathy for Korobov, introducing him to his wife, inviting him to the private house where he usually stayed.

In the town house, he and his wife tied Korobov to a column and hit him with the Ice hammer. He lost consciousness. Then they placed him in a hospital where he came to in a separate, guarded ward. On the third day, Vlodzimirsky came to him, lay down in bed, embraced him, and spoke to him with the heart.

Thus did Korobov become Adr.

He asked me about the brotherhood, and I told him everything I knew. From time to time he cried from a feeling of tenderness, embraced me, and pressed my palms to his chest. But I restrained my heart so as not to shake Adr too strongly.

I understood my strength.

In the morning we arrived in Moscow at Leningrad Station. An automobile was waiting for us there.

We drove out of town and a while later arrived at Vlodzimirsky's dacha.

It was a warm, sunny day.

Adr took me by the hand and led me into a large wooden house. Curtains covered the windows. Vlodzimirsky stood in the middle of the living room. He, too, was of medium height and had a compact body; a pair of gold silk pajamas clung to his stocky figure; his thinning dark-blond hair was combed back, and tears of rapture filled his greenish-blue eyes. Even at a distance I could feel his large, warm heart. I quivered in anticipation.

Vlodzimirsky's wife stood a ways off—a thin, lovely woman. But she wasn't one of us, and for this reason I didn't notice her at first.

Vlodzimirsky approached me. His head jerked, his strong hands shook. Making a guttural sound, he lowered himself to his knees and pressed against me.

Adr came up behind me and also pressed against me.

They both began to sob.

Vlodzimirsky's wife also began to cry.

Then Vlodzimirsky swept me up in his arms and carried me to the second floor. There, in the bedroom, he laid me down on a wide couch and began to undress me. Adr and his wife helped him. Then he undressed himself. Vlodzimirsky was truly built like an athlete. He pressed his wide white chest to mine. And our hearts merged. He wasn't a newcomer to the language of the heart and he knew fourteen words.

My small, young, girl's heart immersed itself in his powerful heart. It breathed and throbbed, burned and shuddered.

I had never felt so much with anyone, not even with Bro, the old man.

Our hearts had long been searching for each other. They raged. Time stopped for us . . .

We released our embrace two days later. Our arms were numb and would not obey us, we were so weak we could barely move. But our faces shone with happiness. My new brother was named Kha.

Adr and Vlodzimirsky's wife led us to a bathroom and put us in a hot bath. Massaging my numb hands, his wife introduced herself.

"My name is Nastya."

I responded with a warm look.

When we were finally feeling like ourselves, Kha began to speak.

"Khram, there are only four of us in Russia: you, me, Adr, and Yus. Adr and I are high-placed officers of the MGB, the most powerful organization in Russia. Yus is a typist in the Ministry of Machine Construction. I was pounded in 1931 in Baku by brothers who then left with Bro. We found Yus. You know that the Ice is the only thing that helps us to find our brothers. All of our efforts are currently directed at procuring a regular supply of the Ice, and secretly transporting it abroad where the most active search for our brothers and sisters is being carried out. The Scandinavian countries are the most active of all. In Sweden, one hundred and nineteen of our brothers live in three houses. In Norway there are about fifty. In Finland—almost seventy. Before the war, we had forty-four in Germany. Some of them occupied important positions in the NSDAP and the SS. Unfortunately, everything was more difficult in Russia. Four brothers, employees of the NKVD, perished at the end of the thirties during the 'great purges.' One sister from the Moscow City Committee of the Party was arrested and executed because of a denunciation. Two others died in the siege of Leningrad. I wasn't able to help them. Another one, my closest brother, Umeh, whom we found in 1934, was a colonel general of the tank troops. He died on the front. Thank the Light that this had no effect on the supply of Ice. But it is very difficult for us to look for new brothers. You must help us."

"How do they get the Ice?" I asked.

"Before 1936 we organized different expeditions. They were carried out in secret. Each time we hired Siberians, local hunters who crossed the swamps to the place where the meteor fell, and sawed off pieces of the Ice under terribly difficult conditions, bringing it to a secret place. There they were met by officers of the NKVD. The Ice was taken to the train station; it was sent to Moscow in a refrigerator, like valuable cargo. Getting it abroad was much easier. But this method was extremely risky and unreliable. Two expeditions simply disappeared, and another time plain ice was palmed off on us. I decided to radically change the way we acquired the Ice. At my initiative and with the help of influential brothers in the Siberian NKVD, a directorate was created with special authority for the raising of the

Tungus meteorite. Two brothers, the ones who died in Leningrad, were prominent people in the Academy of Sciences. They established the scientific importance of the project, proving that Ice from the meteorite contained unknown chemical compounds capable of revolutionizing chemical weapons. Seven kilometers from the place where it landed we organized a corrective labor camp. The inmates of this small camp retrieve our Ice. This is only done in winter, when it is easy to cross the swamps."

"But how do they distinguish our Ice from ordinary ice in the winter?"

"We distinguish it, not they." Kha smiled. "Here, in Moscow. They break it up with crowbars where it fell, cut out metric cubes of ice, and drag them back to the camp. There the pieces of ice are loaded onto sleds, and horses carry them across the tundra to Ust-Ilimsk, where they are loaded onto railway cars and taken to Moscow. Here Adr and I enter the cars and put our hands on the ice. Only about forty percent of it turns out to be our Ice."

"And how much ice is there in the meteorite?"

"According to external estimates—about seventy thousand tons."

"Glory to the Light!" I smiled. "And it doesn't melt?"

"When it fell, the block lodged in the permafrost. The tip is hidden by the swamp. Of course, the upper part of the block melts a bit in summer. But the Siberian summer is short: snap—and it's gone!" Kha smiled in response.

"Thank the Light, there's enough Ice to achieve our great goal," added Adr, as he massaged us.

"And who makes the Ice hammers?" I asked.

"At first we did it ourselves, but then I realized that each person should do his own job." Kha stuck his strong, handsome head under a stream of water with obvious pleasure. "In one of the *sharashkas*—the closed scientific laboratories where imprisoned scientists work—we established a small department for making the Ice hammers. Only three people. They produce five or six hammers a day. We don't need more."

"Don't they ask what the hammers are for?"

"My dear Khram, these are engineers who are serving twenty-five-year sentences for 'wrecking.' They are enemies of the people; they don't have anyone to ask, or any reason to ask. They just have instructions for making the hammers. They have to follow these instructions rigorously if they want to receive their camp rations. The boss of the *sharashka* told them that the Ice hammers are needed to strengthen the defensive power of the Soviet state. That's enough for them."

The old scars from the Ice hammer could be seen on Kha's wide white chest. I touched them cautiously.

"It's time to go, Khram," he sighed resolutely. "You'll come with me."

We got out of the bath. Adr and Nastya rubbed us down and helped us dress. Kha arrayed himself in his general's uniform, and they put me in the uniform of a State Security lieutenant. Adr handed me my documents.

"According to your passport you are Varvara Korobova. You are my wife, you live in Leningrad, you and I came here on a work trip. You are employed by the foreign department of the Leningrad GB."

A black automobile waited at the dacha gates. The three of us got in and drove to Moscow. Nastya remained at home.

"Is it hard to live—with one of the empties?" I asked Kha.

"Yes." He nodded, seriously. "But that's the way it has to be."

"Does she know everything?"

"Not everything. But she senses the greatness of our enterprise."

In Moscow we arrived at the massive headquarters of the MGB on Lubianskaya Square. We entered, showed our documents, and proceeded to the third floor. In the hallway, several officers saluted Kha as we passed. He responded listlessly. Soon we entered his huge office where three secretaries stood waiting to greet us. Kha walked past them and threw open the double doors of the office. We followed him, and Adr closed the doors.

Kha tossed a leather dossier on his large desk, turned, and embraced me.

"There are no eavesdropping devices here. How happy I am, Sister! You and I will accomplish great things. You are the only one of us who knows all 23 heart words. Your heart is wise, strong, and young. We will tell you what needs to be done."

"I'll do everything, Kha," I said, stroking his athletic shoulders.

Adr approached me from behind, embraced me, and pressed against me.

"My heart wants yours so dreadfully," he whispered at the nape of my neck, his voice trembling.

"And mine as well, and mine..." Kha muttered warmly.

One of the four black phones rang.

Growling with displeasure, Kha loosed his embrace, walked over to the table, and picked up the receiver.

"Vlodzimirsky here. What? No, Bor, I'm busy. Yes. Well? What do you mean you can't? Bor, why are you fucking around with mummies? He's ready to drop, damnit. As soon as I leave the department, everything falls apart. Inform Serov. Well? So? He actually said that? Jeezus..." He sighed with displeasure, scratched his heavy chin, and chuckled. "You're a bunch of no-goodniks. Viktor Semyonich is right to write about you. All right, bring him over here. You have twenty minutes."

He replaced the receiver and looked at me with his blue-green eyes.

"It's my work, Khram. Forgive me."

I nodded with a smile.

The oak door of the office opened timidly and a balding head poked through.

"Excuse me, Lev Emelianovich?"

"Come on now. Carry on!" said Kha settling at his desk.

A small, thin colonel with an ugly face and a thin black mustache entered the office. Behind him, two hefty lieutenants were dragging a plump man in a tattered, bloody uniform with the epaulettes torn off. The man's face was swelling from the beatings and turning blue. He collapsed helplessly on the rug.

"The best of health to you, Lev Emelianovich." The bald man approached the desk in a half-bow.

"Greetings, Borya." Kha stretched out his hand in a lazy gesture. "What are you doing violating the rules of subordination? You're shaming us in front of the Leningraders!"

"Lev Emelianovich!" The colonel smiled guiltily, as he noticed Adr and me. "Ah! Hello there, Comrade Korobov!"

They shook hands.

"Now, then, Borya, follow Korobov's example." Kha pulled a cigarette out of a cigarette holder and stuck it in his mouth without lighting it. "He got married. And you're still entangled with actresses."

"Congratulations," the colonel said, offering me his small hand.

"Varvara Korobova," I said, giving him my hand to shake.

"You see what sumptuous young maids they have wandering around 4 Liteiny Prospect? Not like the dried-up vertebrates we have here." Kha directed his gaze to the injured fat man.

"So what's going on?"

"The viper has gone stubborn over Shakhnazarov," the colonel said angrily, looking at the fat man. "He gave evidence on Alexeev, he gave evidence on Furman. But with Shakhnazarov—I don't know… that was it. The bastard's forgotten how they sold the motherland to the Japanese together."

Kha nodded and placed the cigarette in an ashtray.

"Emelianov. Why are you holding back?"

The fat man sniffed, but said nothing.

"Answer, you bloody wrecker, you saboteur!" shouted the colonel. "I'll rip your liver out, you Japanese spy!"

"Now, now, Borya," Kha spoke up calmly. "Sit down over there. In the corner. And hold your tongue."

The colonel quieted down and sat on the chair.

"Pick the general up. And sit him in the armchair," Kha ordered.

The lieutenants lifted the fat man and sat him down in the chair.

Kha's face suddenly grew sad. He looked at his nails. Then he directed his eyes to the window. There, against the background of a sunny Moscow day, stood the black monument to Dzerzhinsky.

Silence fell in the office.

"Do you remember the Crimea in '40? June, Yalta, the resort?" Kha asked quietly.

The fat man raised his glassy eyes to Kha.

"Your wife, Sasha, isn't that right? She liked to swim in the early morning. So did Nastya and I. One time, the three of us swam out so far that Sasha got a cramp in her leg. She was frightened. But Nastya and I are sea folk. I held her under her back, and Nastya dove down and bit your wife on the calf. And we helped her swim back. As she swam she talked about your son. Pavlik, I think it was, no? He had made a steam locomotive himself from a samovar. The steam engine moved. And Pavlik heated it with pencils. He burned two boxes of colored pencils that you had brought him from Leningrad. Isn't that the way it was?"

The fat man remained stubbornly silent.

Kha stuck the cigarette in his mouth again, but didn't light it.

"At that time I was just a plain old major in the NKVD. They gave me a bonus—a trip to the resort. And you were commander of a whole corps. The legendary Com corps, Emelianov! I looked at you in the dining room and thought: He's as far away from me as the sky itself. And now here you are protecting Shakhnazarov. That louse isn't worth your little finger."

The fat man's chin began to twitch, his round head swayed. Tears suddenly burst from his eyes. He grabbed his head in his hands and began to weep loudly.

"Take the general to 301. Let him get some sleep, give him a good meal. Then he'll write it. The way it should be," said Kha, looking out the window.

The colonel, who had grown quiet, nodded to the lieutenants. They grabbed the sobbing Emelianov and led him out of the office. The telephone rang.

"Vlodzimirsky," said Kha, picking up the receiver. "Hello there, Began! Listen, I opened *Pravda* yesterday and couldn't believe my eyes! That's right! Good for you! Those are the kind of cadres Lavrenty Pavlovich has! Our lads! Merkurov should sculpt a bust of you and Amayak now!"

Kha let out a booming laugh.

"Be well, Korobov," said the colonel, stretching out his hand and, glancing at Kha, shaking his head. "There's no one else like our Lev Emelianovich."

"He's got an absolute memory, what do you want?" smiled Adr.

"That's the least of it. He's a genius..." sighed the colonel enviously as he left.

Kha finished his conversation and hung up the phone.

"You have to complete the documents for a work trip. With Radzevsky on the sixth floor. Then we'll go to see Sister Yus."

Adr and I went up to the sixth floor, and a business trip to Magadan was arranged for us. We received our per diem money and documents. We left the building with Kha, got into an automobile, and drove along Vorovskaya Street. Leaving the automobile and driver on the street, we walked through courtyards and ended up at a shabby doorway and then went up to the third floor. Adr knocked on the door. It immediately opened wide, and a tall, elderly woman wearing a pince-nez threw herself on us with a cry. She was literally wailing and shaking with joy.

Adr held her mouth. We entered the apartment. It was large, with four bedrooms, but it was a communal apartment. However, four of the rooms were sealed. As Kha later explained to me, he had Yus's neighbors arrested. That made it easier to meet.

Seeing me, Yus immediately wound her long, gouty, arthritic arms around my shoulders, pressed her large, flaccid breasts to me, and we collapsed on the floor. Adr and Kha embraced in turn, and lowered themselves to their knees.

Despite her age, Yus's heart was childishly inexperienced. It knew only two words. But it imbued them with such strength and desire that I was taken aback. Her heart pined, like a traveler lost in the desert. It drank in my heart desperately, without stop.

Nearly nine hours passed.

Yus's arms parted, and she lay flat on the old parquet.

I felt emptied, but satisfied: I had taught Yus's heart new words.

Yus looked terrible: pale and thin, she lay unmoving, her lilac eyes glassily staring at the ceiling; her dentures stuck out of her slightly open mouth.

But she was alive: I could clearly feel her heavily beating heart.

Kha brought her an oxygen pillow from her room, and placed the rubber tube with its funnel-shaped opening to her grayish lips. Adr opened the valve.

The oxygen gradually brought her around. She sighed with a moan.

They lifted her up and carried her into the room. Adr sprayed water on her face.

"Maaar-ve-lous," she said, exhausted, and stretched her shaking hand to me.

I took it in mine. Her old fingers were soft and cool. Yus pressed my hand to her chest.

"My child. How I needed you!" she said, and smiled with difficulty.

Adr brought us all water and apricots.

We ate the apricots, washing them down with water.

"Tell me about the House," Yus asked me.

I told her. She listened with an expression of almost childlike amazement. When I got to the conversation with Bro and to his travels, tears poured down Yus's wrinkled cheeks.

"What happiness," she said, pressing my hand to her chest. "What happiness to obtain another living heart."

We all embraced.

Then Kha told her about the current plans. A complex task lay ahead of us. Adr and I listened to Kha, holding our breath. But Yus couldn't listen for more than ten seconds: she jumped up, threw herself on me, embraced my legs, pressed against me, muttering tender words, then ran back to the window and stood there, sniffling and shaking her head.

Her room was a chaotic mess of books and objects, and a German typewriter with a sheet of paper in it rose out of them like a cliff. In her former life, Yus had earned money at home by typing, and during the day she typed at the ministry where she worked. Like all of us, she had no financial problems.

Yus begged Kha to take her on the work trip, but he forbade her. She began to sob.

"I want to speak with you..." she whimpered, kissing my knees.

"We need you here," said Kha, embracing her.

Yus shivered violently. Her dentures clattered and her knees trembled. We calmed her with valerian drops, put her in bed, covered her with a down blanket, and placed a hot water bottle at her feet. Her face shone with bliss.

"I found you, I found you..." her old lips kept whispering. "I just hope my heart doesn't burst."

I kissed her hand.

She looked at me with profound affection and immediately fell into a deep sleep.

We left, got in the car, and in an hour we were at the military aerodrome in Zhukovskoe. An airplane was waiting for us there.

We settled down in the small cabin. The pilot reported to Kha on our state of readiness, and we took off.

It took almost twenty-four hours to reach Magadan: twice we stopped to fuel up, and we spent the night in Krasnoyarsk.

When I flew over Siberia and saw the endless forests sliced by the ribbons of Siberia's great rivers, I thought about the thousands of blue-eyed, fair-haired brothers and sisters living within Russia's unembraceable expanses, daily enacting the mechanical rituals imposed upon them by civilization, unaware of the miracle hiding inside their chests. Their hearts slept. Would they awake? Or, like millions of other hearts, having beaten their allotted time, would they rot in the Russian earth, never knowing the intoxicating might of the heart's language?

In my head I pictured thousands of coffins disappearing into graves scattered with earth; I felt the intolerable immobility of these stopped hearts, the decay of divine heart muscles in the dark, the nimble worms that devoured the powerless flesh. My living heart shuddered and fluttered.

"I must awaken them!" I whispered, looking out upon the ocean of forest swimming below me . . .

We landed in Magadan early in the morning.

The sun had not yet risen. At the airport, two automobiles and two MGB officers were waiting for us. Four long zinc cases were loaded into one car, and we got into the second.

After driving through the city, which seemed to me no better but no worse than other cities, we turned onto a highway, and after a rather bumpy half-hour ride, we rolled up to the gates of a large corrective labor camp.

The gates opened immediately, and we entered the territory of the camp. There were wood barracks and, in the corner, shining white, stood the sole brick building. We drove up to it. We were met by the camp's administrators—three MGB officers. The camp director,

Major Gorbach, gave us a hearty welcome and invited us into the administrative building. But Kha told him that we were extremely pressed for time. Then he fluttered around and gave the order: "Sotnikov, bring them here!"

A dozen or so exhausted, filthy prisoners were soon brought to us. Despite the warm summer weather, they all wore tattered padded coats, felt boots, and hats with earflaps.

"Your people wear felt boots in the summer?" Kha asked Gorbach.

"No, Comrade General. I was holding these in the hard-regime barracks. So I issued winter clothes to them."

"Why did you put them in hard regime?"

"Well...it's...more reliable."

"You're an asshole," replied the comrade general. Turning to the prisoners, he said, "Take off your hats."

They took off their hats. All of them looked like old men. Four were blonds, one an albino, and two had completely gray hair. Only four had blue eyes, including one of the gray-haired ones.

"Listen, Major, is your head screwed on right? Haven't had any concussions lately, have you?" Kha asked Gorbach.

"I wasn't at the front, Comrade General," answered Gorbach, turning pale.

"Who were you ordered to find?"

"Blonds with light eyes."

"Are you color-blind?"

"No, sir, I can see colors normally."

"What the hell kind of normal is this?" Kha shouted, pointing at one prisoner's gray head. "This one is blond in your opinion?"

"In his testimony he wrote that prior to 1944 he was blond, Comrade General," Gorbach answered, standing at attention.

"You're playing with death, Major," Kha said, throwing a piercing gaze his way. "Where is the place?"

"This way...over here, please." Gorbach pointed at another building.

Kha took a cigarette out of his cigarette case, rolled it between his fingers, and sniffed it.

"Take these four here, and follow the instructions."

"And where should the others go?" Gorbach asked timidly.

"To hell." Kha tossed the cigarette on the ground.

Presently we entered the building. The biggest room had been designated for the hammering. The windows were shuttered, three bright lamps burned, and handcuffs were attached to the walls. The four prisoners were pinned to the wall, naked to the waist, their mouths and eyes bound.

One of the zinc cases was brought in. Kha ordered everyone out of the building.

Adr opened the case. It had thick walls and was filled with the dry ice that ice cream is stored in. The Ice hammers protruded slightly from under the steaming dry ice. I placed my hands on them. I immediately felt the unseen vibration of the heavenly Ice. It was divine! My hands trembled, my heart beat greedily: ICE! I hadn't seen it for so long!

Adr put on a pair of gloves, pulled one hammer out, and began his work. He struck the gray-haired man. He turned out to be empty, and quickly died from the blows. Then Kha took the hammer. However, that day we were out of luck: the others were also empties.

Tossing aside the broken hammer, Kha took out a pistol and shot the crippled empties.

"It's not so easy to find our people," said Adr with a tired smile, wiping the sweat from his brow.

"Yet what happiness when we do find them!" I smiled.

We embraced, pieces of ice crunching under our feet. My heart felt every single sliver of Ice.

Leaving the building, we heard shots nearby.

"What was that?" Kha asked the major.

"Comrade General, you gave orders that the others were to receive the highest penalty," the major answered.

"You idiot, I said—to hell with them."

"My fault, Comrade General, I didn't understand." Gorbach blinked hard.

Kha waved him away, and went over to the car.

"All of you slobs need to be purged."

In the course of two weeks we traveled to eight camps and hammered ninety-two people. We found only one living one. He turned out to be a forty-year-old recidivist-thief from Nalchik named Savely Mamonov, known by the nickname "Blast Furnace." The nickname had been given to him for the tattoo on his buttocks: two devils holding shovels of coal. When he walked the devils seemed to be shoveling coal into his anus. But this was not the only tattoo on Blast's chubby, hairy, short-legged body: his torso and arms were covered with mermaids, hearts pierced by knives, spiders, and kissing doves. In the middle of his chest was a tattoo of Stalin. From the blows of the Ice hammer the leader's face began to spout profuse amounts of blood. I pressed my ear to that bloodied Stalin and heard, "Shro…Shro… Shro…"

My heart felt the awakening of another heart.

This experience is comparable to nothing else.

Tears of ecstasy spurted from my eyes, and I pressed my bloodied lips to the ugly, coarse, heavily scarred face of our newly acquired brother.

"Hello, Shro."

We cut his fetters and removed the bandage from his mouth. His body slid powerlessly to the floor, his eyes rolled back, and from his lips could be heard a weak but angry whisper: "Fuckin' cunts."

Then he lost consciousness. Kha and Adr kissed his hands. I cried, touching his gnarly body, which had carried the locked vessel of the Primordial Light inside it. Henceforth this body was destined to live.

A month later, Shro and I were sitting in a restaurant atop the Moscow Hotel near the Kremlin. It was a warm, dry August day. A soft wind rippled the striped tent. We were eating grapes and peaches. Below, the great Russian city stretched out before us. But we weren't looking at it. Shro held my hand in his rough, tattooed hands. Our blue eyes could not part for a second. Even when I placed a grape between Shro's lips, he continued looking at me. We spoke almost no words in earthly language. Yet our hearts trembled. We were prepared to entwine our arms and fall down anywhere—here over Moscow, in the Metro, on the sidewalk, in an entryway, or on a garbage heap. Our feelings were so elevated, however, that self-preservation was part of them.

We took care of ourselves.

And our hearts.

For this reason we allowed them to speak only in secluded places where there were no living dead.

"Can we still croak?" Shro asked suddenly after a silence of many hours.

"Death doesn't matter anymore," I answered.

"Why?"

"Because we met."

He squinted. Grew ponderous. Then he smiled. His steel teeth sparkled in the sunlight.

"I got it, Sis!" he wheezed. "I got the whole fucking shebang!"

We all understood everything: my young self, awkward Shro, wise Kha, ruthless Adr, and ancient Yus.

We were engaged in a great undertaking.

Time made way for eternity. We passed through time like rays of light through an icy thickness. And we reached the depths...

In September and October we visited eighteen camps in Mordovia, Kazakhstan, and western Siberia. Almost two hundred Ice hammers were broken on the emaciated breastbones of prisoners, but only two hearts began to speak, pronouncing their names.

"Mir."

"Sofre."

There were now seven of us.

We continued our search among the lower echelons of society. Kha's new arrangements were dictated largely by the times: the repressive state structure was destroying the Soviet elite too quickly and too unpredictably. It was difficult for high-placed people to survive the Stalinist meat grinder. No one was certain of his safety; no one was protected from arrest. Even those who drank and sang Georgian songs with Stalin.

For that reason we made no attempt to find our own among the Party and military bosses. The losses of the '30s and '40s had sobered Kha forever.

But the camps did not resolve the problem of our quest. The few brothers found among them were a paltry reward for the huge risk and painstaking preparations.

Kha and Adr worked out a new search plan: we had to travel to the north of Russia, to Karelia, and the White Sea, to lands rich in fair-haired blue-eyed people.

With the support of his patron, the all-powerful Lavrenty Beria, Kha created a special division within the MGB called "Karelia," purportedly to seek out deserters and German accomplices who had taken refuge in the forests of Karelia. It was a small but mobile subdivision consisting of former SMERSH operatives called upon during the war to fight against German spies and saboteurs. However, in line with traditional NKVD practices, the SMERSH people were largely in the business of fabricating false cases, arresting innocent Red Army soldiers, and beating the necessary evidence out of them—after which the newly minted "German spies" were safely shot.

The sixty-two cutthroat SMERSH operatives Kha chose for the Karelia Special Forces—which reported directly to Beria himself—were prepared to carry out any order. These truly merciless individuals viewed the human race as garbage and received great satisfaction from discharging large numbers of bullets into the backs of heads. Adr led the group.

In April 1951 the division began a secret operation called "Dragnet": arriving in Karelia, in the small town of Loukhi, the operatives set about arresting blue-eyed blonds, both men and women. They were taken to Leningrad, where, in the basements of the Big House, Kha, Shro, Sofre, and I hammered them.

It was hard work. Sometimes we had to hammer up to forty people a day. By evening we would collapse from exhaustion. The laboratory where, in the past, three imprisoned engineers prepared the hammers, couldn't handle the volume. Five more workers were added, tripling the production; they worked as much as sixteen hours a day, making thirty hammers daily. The hammers were brought to Leningrad by airplane so that we could pound the white-skinned Karelian breasts in the dusky cellar of the MGB.

Our hands and faces were scarred by shards of flying Ice, our hands and arms became iron though our muscles ached and hurt, our nails sometimes bled, and our feet would be swollen from hours of standing still. Kha's wife helped us. She wiped our faces, spattered with Karelian blood, gave us warm water to drink, and massaged our arms and legs. We worked as though possessed: the Ice hammers whistled, bones cracked, people moaned and wailed. One floor below us shots rang out incessantly—the empties were being finished off. As always, they comprised ninety-nine percent. Only one percent remained alive. But how much joy we received from each one of a hundred!

Each time I pressed my head against a bloody, quivering chest and heard the flutter of a wakening heart, I forgot about everything else, I cried and shouted with joy, repeating the heart name of the newborn.

"Zu!"

"O!"

"Karf!"

"Yk!"

"Owb!"

"Yach!"

"Nom!"

They were few and far between. Like nuggets of gold in the earth. But they existed! And they glittered in our work-weary, bloody hands.

The living were immediately taken to the MGB prison hospital, where the doctor, following Kha's instructions, provided the necessary care.

Gradually, their numbers grew.

The special division completed the operation in Loukhi and moved south along the railroad—through Kem, Belomorsk, and Segezh, to Petrozavodsk. While the agents were combing each city, a special train stood at the station, earmarked for the transport of prisoners. After the town had been searched, the train full of fair-haired people departed for Leningrad.

In the course of two and a half months of incessant work, we found twenty-two brothers and seventeen sisters.

This was a great Victory for the Light! Russia had turned toward Light-Bearing Eternity.

The Karelia special division was nearing the old Russian port of

Petrozavodsk, the capital of Karelia, a large city with a population of 150,000, teeming with blue-eyed, fair-haired residents.

To implement the Dragnet-Petrozavodsk operation, the special division was reinforced with twenty officer agents and fifteen wardens from the Lubianka prison.

Dozens of Ice hammers awaited their hour in refrigerators.

But the ominous month of July 1951 approached. The "Doctors' Plot" being fabricated in the bowels of the Lubianka—an alleged plot of doctor-murderers planning to poison Stalin and other Party bigwigs—had turned against the MGB. Abakumov, the minister of state security, was arrested. The threat of a new purge hung over the Lubianka.

Beria's old enemies in the Central Committee and the Ministry of Defense acquired new life. Denunciations of Abakumov's deputies, of whom Kha was one, flooded the Politburo.

Kha decided to halt the Karelian operation.

The special division was called back; an empty train returned to Leningrad.

We had to wait things out, to "sink to the bottom," as Kha said. Adr and I received a month-long vacation and set off for one of the MGB's resorts on the Crimean coast, not far from Evpatoria. Kha and his wife flew to Hungary to vacation on Lake Balaton. Shro lived with Yus. Mir and Sofre spent the summer working at one of the MGB's Young Pioneers camps.

After the cellars of the Big House, it was hard for me to adjust to the hot, indolent Crimea, where everything is designed for primitive Soviet "rest," which involves an almost vegetative existence. Our thirty-nine newly acquired brothers and sisters would not leave me in peace. Hundreds of kilometers away from them I felt their hearts, I remembered each and every name, and I spoke with them.

Adr, understanding my state of mind, tried to help. Early in the morning, before sunrise, we would swim out to the wild cliffs, entwining there and lying still for many hours like ancient lizards.

But Adr's heart wasn't enough for me. I yearned for the prison hospital where all of my brothers and sisters lay. I wanted them. I begged and pleaded, crying.

"It's not possible Khram," Adr whispered to me.

And I beat my useless hands against the cliffs.

Adr ground his teeth in futility.

Soon something began to happen to me. It started on a Sunday evening, when Adr, who tried in every way possible to help me fight off boredom, decided to take me to the movies. They showed movies on Sundays in a simple summer theater. Instead of the promised new comedy, they began showing *Chapaev* that night. Someone shouted out that they'd already seen *Chapaev* twenty times. An old corpse countered, "No matter, you can watch it for the twenty-first time!"

I had seen *Chapaev* as a girl. At the time the film shook me. I remembered it very well. But this time, when the first scenes began and people appeared on the sheet they used as a screen, I couldn't see them clearly. They were just gray spots, flickering appearances, sputters of light and shadow. At first I thought that the projectionist had made some mistake. But I was able to read the list of captions and names. Everything else swam in front of me. I looked at the audience: everyone watched silently, no one cried out "Focus!" or "Murder the projectionist!"

Adr watched it too.

"Can you see the screen clearly?" I asked him.

"Yes. And you?"

"I can't see anything."

"We're probably sitting too close," he decided. "Let's move farther away."

We got up and moved to the last bench. But for me nothing changed: I still could read the captions, but I couldn't make out anything else. Adr thought that I simply had bad eyesight. When another caption appeared on the screen, he asked, "What does it say?"

"In the White Guard headquarters," I read.

He grew thoughtful. Next to us a tipsy couple sat kissing. I began watching them. The lust of those corpses seemed so bizarre to me. Watching them kiss was like watching two mechanical dolls. The woman noticed my look.

"Whadderya gawkin' at? Look thata way!" She pointed to the screen, and the man groping her pudgy body laughed.

I turned my eyes toward the screen. Petka was telling Anka how a machine gun worked. All I could see was two quivering dark spots.

"What's this?" Anka asked.

"Those are stocks," the invisible Petka answered.

And the two spots merged.

The audience laughed.

"Let's get out of here," I said, standing up.

Adr and I left. It was a dark southern night. The cicadas chirped. Under the heavy darkness of the acacias and chestnut trees, the odd light shone out of the resort building. We entered the lobby.

Two concierges dozed behind the counter. On the wall above them hung a large picture of Stalin. I had never noticed it before, but something made me look at the portrait. Instead of Stalin in his white tunic, a white-and-brown splotch flecked with gold floated inside the frame.

I stared at the portrait and moved closer. The splotch shimmered and swam.

I squinted, shook my head, and opened my eyes again: it was still the same.

"What's the matter?" asked Adr.

"I don't know." I shook my head.

The concierges had woken up and were watching me with curiosity.

"Who is that?" I asked, staring at the portrait.

"Stalin," Adr answered tensely.

The concierges exchanged glances.

"Varya, let's go to sleep, you're tired." Adr took my arm.

"Wait a minute." I leaned on the counter and fixed my eyes on the portrait.

Then I turned my gaze to the concierges. They looked at me apprehensively. I noticed a pile of postcards lying on the counter. I picked one up. At the bottom of the postcard "Greetings from the Crimea!" was written in dark blue. Above the caption there was a clump of something greenish red.

"What is this?" I asked Adr.

"Roses," he said as he took me forcefully by the elbow. "Let's go. I beg of you."

I put the postcard down and obeyed.

Climbing the stairs with Adr, I heard the concierges whispering.

"They come here to get drunk."

"What do you expect—the bosses are in Moscow, there's no one to keep them in line."

In the room, Adr embraced me. "Tell me what's happening to you?"

Instead of answering, I got out our passports. I opened them. In the place where the photographs were glued on I could see only gray ripples. But I could read all the words normally.

I took a little mirror out of my purse and looked at myself. The features of my face swam and merged in the reflection. I directed the mirror toward Adr's face: it was the same. I couldn't see his face in the mirror.

"I can't see pictures. Or reflections," I said, tossing the mirror aside. "I don't know what's happening…"

"You're just tired," said Adr, embracing me. "The last two months have been very hard."

"They were wonderful." I flopped down on the bed. "It's much harder for me to wait and do nothing."

"Khram, you understand that we can't take the risk."

"I understand everything," I said, and closed my eyes. "That's why I'm putting up with it."

I fell quickly into a deep sleep.

From the moment my heart had been awakened, I hadn't had any dreams. The last vivid, though short, dreams I had had were in the train when we were being transported like cattle from Russia: I dreamed about Mama, Father, the village, and noisy village holidays when we were all together and happy. But everything always broke off in the middle of what was closest and dearest to me, and I would awake in the same terrible train car.

My very last dream had been one night in the filtration camp: I dreamed of a fire—a huge, terrifying fire. Everything was burning all around, people ran hither and thither like shadows. I was looking for our dog Leska. I loved her a great deal. The longer I looked for her, the more clearly I understood that she had burned alive because none of the adults had thought to untie her. They were saving all kinds of sacks, trunks, and horse yokes. The most awful thing in that dream was the feeling of impotence, the impossibility of turning things back. I awoke in tears, crying out, "Leska! Leska!"

Then, that night in the sanatorium, I dreamed again for the first time in eight years. Or, not exactly dreamed, because I didn't see the dream in my head; instead *I felt the dream.*

I was sitting in the garden near the House and touching sister Zher, who was sleeping. It was summer, and the weather was warm and windless. We had just finished speaking with our hearts. I loved Zher's heart. It was agile and active, and it was quicker than mine. After two hours of heart conversation my mouth was dry, as always, and my arms were numb and ached a bit. Zher was sleeping like a baby—spread out on her back with her mouth slightly open. Her face exuded a tired bliss. I began touching her small chin. It was covered in tiny freckles. There were even more of them on the bridge of her nose. I touched her nose. Zher's strawberry-blond eyelashes didn't even flicker: her sleep was deep. Suddenly I heard a weak whimper behind me. With my heart I felt that my dog Leska stood behind me. I looked around. Furry gray-and-black Leska stood there, panting joyfully, her pink tongue hanging out. Her greenish eyes were bright with joy. My heart trembled with happiness: my beloved Leska was alive, she didn't perish in the fire! A piece of the rope hung around Leska's neck, and the fur on her right side was singed.

"Leska, you're alive!" I exclaimed and stretched toward her.

But the dog suddenly cringed and ran toward the House. I jumped up and followed her at a run, calling her name. Leska ran up the steps, darted into a partly opened door on the south porch, which was entwined with wild grapevines. I ran after her. The porch was empty. It was dim and cool there, as it always was in summer. In the middle there was an armchair, and the old man Bro sat in it. Leska sat nearby. She looked at me attentively. Bro pointed his finger; I turned my head and saw my full-length reflection on the opposite side of the terrace. It was neither a painting nor a photograph, but something striking in its perfectedness: an absolute copy of me. I walked toward my double. But the closer I came, the more strongly I felt the EMPTINESS inside the copy of me. It was pure image, a surface that copied my form. There was nothing at all inside the image. I went closer. The copy of Varka Samsikova was absolute in its exactitude. I examined the smallest pores on the face, the little scar over the eyebrows, the moisture at the corners of the blue eyes, the golden fuzz under the cheekbones, the cracks in the lips, and the birthmark on the neck. My copy also studied me closely. Finally we both turned to Bro. Leska stood up; she whimpered excitedly and her ears perked up as she looked at us.

"Call the dog," Bro said.

"Leska!" I called.

"Leska!" called my copy.

The dog ran first to the copy, sniffed it, yelped, and, growling, shrank back and came to me. I sat down and ran my fingers through her fur with pleasure. My copy stood there, smiling, watching us. Leska growled at her again. The copy disappeared.

"Why did the dog recognize you?" Bro asked.

"She felt me," I answered.

"Yes. The dog is alive, as are all animals. She saw you with her heart, not her eyes. But the living dead see the world with their eyes, and only with their eyes. The world that the heart sees is different. Khram, you are ready to see the world with the heart."

I awoke. I opened my eyes.

It was morning.

The world was the same as yesterday. I lay in our bed. Adr wasn't in the room. I rubbed my eyes and sat up. Then I took a shower, pulled myself together, dressed, and left the room.

I went downstairs and walked into the cafeteria where visitors ate breakfast, and froze in astonishment: instead of people, MACHINES MADE OF MEAT sat at the tables! They were ABSOLUTELY dead! There was not a drop of life in their ugly, gloomily worried bodies. They devoured food: some in glum concentration, others in an energetic flurry, some with mechanical indifference.

A couple sat at our table. They were eating living fruits: pears, cherries, and peaches.

But these marvelous peaches could not confer even the teensiest bit of life to their bodies!

Why were they eating them? It was so amusing!

I began to laugh.

Everyone stopped eating and stared. Their faces turned toward me. For the first time in my life I didn't see human faces. These were the muzzles and snouts of meat machines.

Suddenly the mass of dead meat was pierced by a ray of light: Adr was crossing the cafeteria, heading toward me. He was COMPLETELY DIFFERENT! He was alive. He was not a machine. He was my BROTHER. He had a HEART. It shone with the Primordial Light.

I moved to meet him. And we embraced amid the world of monsters.

Snickers crawled across the bodies of the meat machines like worms. One of the machines that was chewing opened her mouth and spoke in a loud voice: "And they say that no one in the MGB knows how to love!"

The cafeteria filled with the greasy laughter of meat machines...

From that day on, I began to see with the heart.

A veil fell from the world, a veil stretched over it by meat machines. I no longer saw only the surface of things. I could now see their essence.

This doesn't mean that I was blind. I saw objects and was perfectly well oriented in space. But images of any kind—paintings, photographs, movies, sculpture—disappeared from my life forever. Paintings became merely canvases covered with paint; on the movie screen all I saw was the play of splotches of light.

I could see a person or a thing from the inside with my heart. I knew their history.

This revelation was equal only to the awakening of my heart from the blows of the Ice hammer.

After those blows, however, my heart simply awoke and began to feel; but now I knew how to KNOW.

I calmed down.

There was no reason for me to worry.

The month of vacation passed.

In Moscow, Ignatiev was appointed to replace the arrested security minister Abakumov. He was a Party functionary completely new to Lubianka and therefore he was very unpredictable. But his first deputy was Golidze—one of Beria's protégés and an old friend of Kha's. That reassured us. Under Golidze's cover we would be able to complete the search operation for the living in Karelia.

Kha recalled us from the Crimea. We flew into a wet, September capital, ready to accomplish new feats in the name of the Light...

But the unforeseen happened.

Ignatiev, who began investigating "Abakumov's criminal activity," received a denunciation from the deputy director of the camp where the precious Tungus Ice was extracted. MGB Lieutenant Voloshin wrote that Abakumov established "Camp No. 312/500 for the extraction of ice no one needs, under inhumanly hard conditions of permafrost, in order to provide for Japanese spies who made their way into the territory of the USSR and caused harm to our toiling people."

Most likely, Voloshin simply decided to use another purge to receive a new appointment or promotion for his "vigilance."

Despite its obvious absurdity, the denunciation had its effect: work in the camp was directed to cease. Fortunately, Ignatiev appointed an investigatory commission headed by Colonel Ivanov from the Interior Ministry's Main Financial Directorate. Ivanov was indebted to Kha, who had saved him from arrest in 1939.

Kha made Ivanov include Adr and me in the commission, as secretaries.

Just before the trip, Kha called Ivanov and us into his office.

We stood before his massive desk.

"Fly, eagles, fly," he directed us, thrusting an unlit cigarette between his stern, handsome lips. "Sort it out—the what and how of it. You are meticulous guys. Dig down deep into the earth, like wild boars."

"But Comrade Lieutenant General, it's the permafrost zone," said Adr, smiling tactfully.

"What a fucking joker." Kha pierced him with a quick glance, and struck the table with his finger. "I want everything turned inside out! Is that clear?"

"Yes sir!" we answered in unison.

"I have a suspicion"—Kha looked out the window, squinting, holding the pause—"that this Lieutenant Voloshin is himself a Japanese spy."

"Do you ... really think so, Comrade Lieutenant General?" asked Ivanov cautiously.

"Just a hunch. He's muddying the waters, the fiend. While he himself is up to his dirty old tricks. There's a shitload of them out there in the tundra. That samurai breed is entrenched. So many agents, even a lazy SOB could rack them in. In the '40s we arrested so many, and they just kept crawling over from the Far East, the bastards. So keep your eyes open, Ivanov. Don't make a mistake."

Kha gave Ivanov a significant look. And Ivanov made no mistake.

He knew that Vlodzimirsky was Beria's man, and not the fallen Abakumov's. And Beria was closest of all to Stalin. That meant it was worth obeying the hint.

As soon as we arrived at Camp No. 312/500, buried in snow and strafed by icy winds, Ivanov ordered Lieutenant Voloshin arrested.

In the middle of the deep polar night, under the light of three kerosene lamps in a log barracks, Voloshin was placed naked on his back on a bench and tied down. Ivanov, a thorough man, had brought along two of his broad-shouldered lieutenants, strongmen from the operations department. One lieutenant sat on Voloshin's chest, while the other one set about lashing his genitals with a small whip.

Voloshin howled in the night.

His howl was heard by 518 prisoners hiding in their barracks and awaiting the verdict of the Moscow commission: they hadn't worked for a month at that point. This scared them.

The camp director had been drinking in his house for the last month.

"Tell us what you know, Voloshin, tell us everything," said Ivanov as he calmly worked on his well-groomed nails with a little file.

I sat with a piece of paper, ready to write down the testimony of the accused. Adr walked back and forth along the wall.

The pockmarked lieutenant took pleasure in whipping Voloshin on his fast-swelling groin, muttering, "Talk, you fucker…Talk, you fucker…"

Voloshin howled for about three hours. He lost consciousness a number of times and we brought him to by pouring water on him and rubbing him with snow. After that, he admitted that back in 1941, as a fifteen-year-old youth in a remote Siberian village, he was contacted and recruited by Japanese counterintelligence. When, choking on tears and mucus, he signed the "statement" compiled by Ivanov and transcribed by me, his hand shook and I could see his essence with my heart. His entire meat-machine being was filled with the image of his mother. He knew he was signing his own death sentence. At that moment, the meat machine in him was filled with the image of his mother—a simple Siberian peasant. His mother sat in his head, like a stone core, repeating the same thing over and over: "I borned you in torture, I borned you in torture…"

With that stone mama in his head, he would have signed anything.

The next morning a troika of horses wrapped in blankets drove a handcuffed Voloshin, two prison escorts, and a lanky field warden with a briefcase. The briefcase held the report of the investigating commission and the testimony of Lieutenant Voloshin.

We stayed on in the camp, awaiting the arrival of a comfortable automobile with a heater.

Ivanov and the lieutenants went on a drinking binge with the director of the camp, who was so elated that things had turned out well that he was ready to kiss their feet.

Adr and I ordered the sleigh to be readied, and we went "for a ride." In fact, it was clear WHERE we were drawn.

Leaving the gates of the camp, Adr directed the horse along the big road leading to the place where the ICE was mined. The road along which the columns of prisoners transported the mined Ice was covered in snow; no one had cleared it for a month. The camp director's well-fed horse had no trouble pulling the sleigh, and we rode along, covered with a bearskin. It was sunny and frosty.

Adr and I felt the ICE with our hearts even in the camp. But now the feeling grew with every step the horse took.

All around lay low mounds covered with sparse growth. The local forest had been destroyed by the blast in 1908 when the meteorite fell, and the new forest was growing in poorly, in clumps. The snow sparkled in the bright sunlight and squeaked under the sleigh runners.

From the camp to the site of the fall was seven versts.

We drove about three versts and my heart began to quiver. It sensed the ICE, like a compass senses iron ore.

"Faster!" I squeezed Adr's hand.

He lashed the horse. The horse took off and the sleigh whizzed along.

The big road forked around the mounds, crawling in a wide ribbon to another mound and then descending to the pit. We rushed along it.

I closed my eyes. I could already see the ICE with my heart. It loomed before me like a Continent of Light.

The sleigh stopped.

I opened my eyes.

We stood on the edge of the pit. Before us lay an enormous mass of Ice, powdered with snow. It sparkled in the sun, giving off a blue tint.

YES! The Ice was blue, like our eyes!

At the edges of the Ice mass various wood structures had been erected: poles, bridges, shacks for inventory, guard towers. All of this was pitiful, wretched, human—it dimmed and was lost to view next to the amazing POWER of the Ice.

It was OUR ICE! The ICE sent by the Light, the ICE that struck the breast of the sleeping earth and awoke it.

Our hearts quivered in ECSTASY.

We held hands and descended into the pit. We approached the Ice along a wooden bridge. With trembling hands I tore my clothes off until there was nothing on me.

I stepped onto the Ice.

A cry of rapture escaped my chest. Tears burst from my eyes. I fell onto the Ice and embraced it. My heart felt and understood this divine mass. A huge heart lay under me. It spoke with me.

Adr undressed as well. I jumped up and stepped toward him. Sobbing with delight, we embraced and fell onto the Ice.

Time stopped for us.

When we regained consciousness it was night.

We loosened our embrace.

A black sky bright with stars hung over us. The stars were so low that it seemed you could touch them. Two blurry half circles, tinged with yellow, shone around the huge bright moon. Somewhere far beyond the horizon, the northern lights blazed.

We lay in warm water. We weren't cold at all. Just the opposite— our bodies were burning. We had warmed a crater in the Ice that followed the contours of our entwined bodies. A cloud of steam stood over us.

A shot suddenly rang out nearby.

And then another.

Someone cried out: "Hey—ey-eyyyyye!"

I realized they were looking for us.

We stood up and left our "bath." We found our clothing and dressed. It was time to say farewell to the Ice, to return to the cruel world of the meat machines and to our brothers lost among them. We kissed the Ice.

Then we set off across the frozen bridges toward the shots and voices.

In Moscow everything worked out well: the results of the investigation satisfied the new minister of state security. Lieutenant Voloshin was shot as a Japanese spy, as were eight of Abakumov's people against whom he'd given evidence under torture. Another "nest of spies" had been liquidated in the system of rehabilitory labor camps.

Camp No. 312/500 began working again; the prisoners' picks rang, the brigadiers shouted, the guard dogs barked, and cubic meters of ICE were transported to the capital. From there they went to other countries where sleeping hearts waited for the awakening blows of the Ice hammer.

We worked precisely and with great focus.

In two years, ninety-eight brothers were found.

It was a huge victory for the Light.

But the ill-starred year of 1953 was at hand.

In March, Stalin died.

The next night, Kha convened us at our dacha. Six brothers and six sisters sat in the half dark of the spacious living room, next to the blazing fireplace. Kha sat in a rocking chair. He wore a lilac Chinese robe with silver dragons on it. He fingered rosary beads from Bukhara. Tongues of flame played across his stern, handsome face and burned in his blue eyes. Kha said, "A redivision of power is about to take place in the USSR. Enormous changes will follow. They will touch many of us. It is imperative to be prepared. We must take care of our brothers, and of the Ice. The majority of our people must be sent out of Moscow and Leningrad into the provinces. It will be less dangerous that way. We must begin this work without delay. Adr and I will take on the technical side of things. As far as the quarrying of Ice is concerned—it is difficult to predict what may happen. It isn't clear what will become of the camp and the project. They may survive, but they may be closed."

He was silent for a moment and turned his eyes toward me, "Khram, you are the only one of us who knows all the heart words and sees with your heart. What does your heart tell you?"

"Only one thing—something huge and threatening looms over us," I answered honestly.

"What does it resemble?" asked Adr.

"A red wave."

"Then we have to act now."

We were silent for a long time. Then Kha smiled and began to speak.

"This morning I received joyous news—the first shipment of Ice arrived in America. Soon we will find out the names of our American brothers!"

Everyone jumped up. We exulted. Throwing off our clothes, we stood in pairs, embraced, pressing chest to chest, we fell to our knees.

The fireplace went out. But our burning hearts quivered in the dark.

The spring and the early part of summer passed in intensive work. In order to send our people to different cities we needed money, a good deal of money. Kha advised us to rob a bank collection truck. It was easy for me to follow the vehicle and the people guarding the bag filled with those packets of paper that meat machines value so highly. My heart knew everything about the bank cashier collector—from his collarbone broken in childhood to his passion for playing the accordion. He also loved sniffing women's toes, talking about soccer, and reading books about the war. At just the right moment, when I signaled, Zu shot the vehicle guard, Shro cut the collector's throat, and Mir grabbed the bag of money from his hands.

Half a million rubles was more than enough for moving one hundred people.

This was our main task. At the same time, we accomplished many other things: an emergency store of Ice was placed in three refrigerator factories, and we infiltrated our people into a variety of up-and-coming organizations and destroyed the witnesses. In the last case I was absolutely irreplaceable. All I had to do was walk up to the door of an apartment to know who was home and what they were doing. Mir, Zu, and Shro took care of the rest. Almost every day their knives interrupted the meaningless existence of yet another meat machine whose memory could harm us.

We were merciless to the living dead.

And suddenly.

Like the thrust of an unseen sword: on June 26, Beria was arrested.

Heat blew from the Kremlin. The illusions of Beria's cohorts evaporated: some shot themselves, some went on a binge. Others hurriedly wrote denunciations of yesterday's friends.

But Kha remained calm.

"We have managed to do it," he repeated.

After the arrest of his patron, he, like many MGB generals, became vulnerable. We no longer had any rear guard, no support from above. I begged Kha and Adr to hide.

"We must fight here," Kha objected.

"We have gone through three purges with the help of the Light, and we can make it through this one as well," said Adr, smiling.

My heart was apprehensive. Something was creeping up on us. I raged at them about the coming disaster. But all my arguments shattered against the wall of their courage.

On the other hand, both of them constantly wanted my heart, foreseeing that we had very little time remaining. During the day we worked on business. At night we froze chest to chest, heart to heart.

Their hearts were inexhaustible.

My arms could barely untwine from their necks, my knees trembled, my body blazed.

Kha's wife poured water on me and slapped my pale cheeks.

I was happy.

During these close, sultry July nights, Kha and Adr learned all 23 heart words from my heart.

And they found the Light.

Forever.

On July 17 they were arrested.

It happened during the day. I was sleeping in the old, cluttered apartment belonging to Yus, whom we had sent to the Crimea with two young brothers. My heart woke me. It was in a bad way.

A sense of petrified horror overtook me. I rose, dressed, and went out. I walked through sun-drenched Moscow to Belorussky Station. It was the first time since my return to Russia that I felt a sucking emptiness in my heart.

I moved like a machine—without feelings or ideas.

Making my way to Belorussky, I stood on the noisy platform, looking at the trains. Then I went to the long-distance ticket window. I waited in line.

"Where are you going?" the cashier asked me.

"I'm going to . . ." It took enormous effort to force myself to think and I decided to go there, where the ICE was, OUR ICE. And where was our divine ICE? In endless Siberia.

"To Siberia," I said firmly, handing money over through the window.

"Now, now, Varvara Fedotovna, why should you pay money for that?" a sarcastic voice spoke into my ear from behind. "We'll send you to Siberia as a business expense."

Two men grabbed me forcefully under my arms.

"Citizen Korobova, you are under arrest," said another voice.

A couple of hours later I was already being interrogated at Lefortovo prison . . .

That day six associates of Beria were arrested, six high-placed generals of the MGB, one of whom was Kha. At the same time, lower-rank MGB employees, who were connected to Beria and his people, were also arrested.

"What tied you to general Vlodzimirsky?" was the first question that Investigator Fedotov asked me.

"Nothing tied me to the general," I answered honestly, seeing through Fedotov with my heart: a premature birth in the hay fields, orphaned, a difficult childhood, tears, fights, the navy; he liked water, cognac, having intercourse with fat women and making them repeat swear words, beach volleyball, and thinking about Saturn while defecating; he was afraid of spiders and scissors, of being late to work, of losing documents; he liked stew, remembering People's Commissar Yezhov, making little boats in the spring, the Black Sea port of Gagra, and beating people on the face and kidneys.

"And what is this?" he showed me a photograph.

I still could not see any images. In the middle of the glossy paper two shiny spots merged.

"What is this, I'm asking you?"

"I can't see it," I admitted.

"Are we going to play the fool?" Fedotov wheezed angrily.

"I really cannot see any images on photographs, not only on this one. Over there you have a portrait—I nodded toward a dark patch in a red frame. "I can't see who it is."

Fedotov looked at me angrily. His plump face slowly turned red with blood.

"That is Vladimir Ilich Lenin. Or haven't you heard of him?"

"I've heard of him."

"Is that so?" he clapped his strong hands and laughed nastily.

I said nothing.

"Vlodzimirsky and your husband, Korobov, are friends of Beria.

And Beria, just so you know, is an agent of foreign intelligence services. He has already given evidence. About Vlodzimirsky, among others. I'm offering to let you tell us honestly about the criminal activities of Vlodzimirsky and Korobov."

"I didn't know General Vlodzimirsky well."

"You didn't know Vlodzimirsky? But on this photo he's pawing you. Naked."

"I repeat, I wasn't close to General Vlodzimirsky, and didn't know him well. I knew his heart well."

"What?"

"And this photograph records a moment when our souls spoke in a secret language."

"That means you confess that you were his mistress?"

"By no means. I was his heart sister."

"And you never slept with him, even once?"

"I slept with him many times. But not like an earthly woman would. Rather, like a heart sister. A sister of the Eternal and Primordial Light."

"A sister of Light?" Fedotov laughed maliciously. "What kind of nonsense is this, you stinking cunt? A sister, shit! What holes did he hump you in, you regiment hooker?! You're all from the same goddamn gang, Beria's spies! You made your viper's nest in the MGB, you reptiles! Tell the fucking truth!"

He hit me on the face.

I said nothing. I looked at him.

He rolled up his sleeves, all business.

"You'll remember everything for me in a little while, you rotten cunt."

He came out from around the desk and grabbed me by the hair with his left hand. Then he began to beat me on the cheeks with a practiced right hand. He probably expected that I would cry out, like the majority of meat-machine women, and, covering my face, beg him for mercy.

But I didn't even raise my hands to my face.

I looked him straight in the eyes.

He swung his hand back and slapped me on the cheek even harder. His coarse palms smelled of tobacco, eau de cologne, and old furniture.

"Talk! Talk! Talk!" he said as he slapped.

My head went back and forth, and my ears rang.

But I kept looking straight into his small, piercing pupils.

He stopped slapping me and brought his reddening face right up to mine.

"So you're a bold one, are you? I'll turn you into mincemeat, salt and pepper you, and make you eat yourself! Why so quiet, you dried-up cunt?"

Inside he was absolutely happy. His heart sang, and in his bald head orange flares blazed and extinguished.

I said nothing.

During the first two interrogations he shouted and whipped me on the cheeks. Then a second investigator appeared—Revzin. At first he tried to play the "good cop," initiating intimate conversations with me, asking me to "help the organs of state security expose Beria's gang." I spoke only the truth: the brotherhood, Kha and Adr, 23 words.

I did this because my heart was absolutely certain that they would not need our secrets. The meat machines didn't see the truth—they looked right through it, they couldn't distinguish the Divine Light.

It was incredibly wonderful to speak the truth, to delight in it.

They swore and laughed.

Finally, they got sick of hearing about the singing of hearts. They undressed me, tied me to a bench, and began to flog me with a rubber plait. They were in no hurry, they took turns: one would flog, while the other shouted or quietly cajoled me to change my mind.

I felt the pain, of course.

But it wasn't like before, when I was a meat machine. Previously, there had been nowhere to escape from the pain, because the pain was the master of my body. Now my master was the heart. And the pain couldn't reach it. It lived separately. My heart felt the pain in the form of a red serpent. The serpent crawled over me. But my heart sang, mesmerizing the serpent. When it crawled for too long at a time, my heart shrank, flaring violet. Then I lost consciousness.

They poured water on me.
While I was coming around, they smoked.
Then their simple hands once again took up the plait.
Everything repeated itself.
I said nothing. My heart sang. The red serpent crawled.
The water rang.
Then the investigators grew tired.
They took me away to the cell. I fell asleep.

I awoke from a squeak. The door opened, and three people came in: Revzin, a doctor, and some kind of lieutenant colonel. The doctor examined my swollen thighs, blue from blows to the hips and buttocks, nodded professionally, and said, "Everything's fine."

Revzin called two escorts. They grabbed me under the arms and dragged me along the corridor, then up the staircase—way up high, to that very same office. It was light there—rays of sun beat at the window, the crystal inkstand shone, the copper door handle reflected the eyes and buttons of Revzin. And on the wall, in a red frame, an unseen Lenin swirled.

A small, angry Fedotov came in the room with plaits. They again tied me to the bench. They took two whips and began to whip me simultaneously along my swelling thighs.

Two red serpents began to slither over me. They became orange. Then blindingly yellow. The yellow sun sang in my head.

"Tell us the truth! Tell! Tell! Tell us!"

But I'd already told them the truth.

What on earth did they want from me?

The amber-colored serpents wound themselves into a wedding ring. They liked being on my body.

Sweat poured into my eyes.

My heart flared in a violet rainbow: it could feel that my body was being destroyed.

And my heart helped my body: my brain turned itself off, and I fainted.

I awoke on the floor.

Nastya Vlodzimirskaya was hanging over me. They were holding her under her arms and by her hair, so her head wouldn't slump down onto her chest. They'd done more than beat her. They'd torn her to shreds.

"Do you confirm it?" some fat major asked her, a man who loved cats, mashed potatoes, and gold watches.

From Nastya's broken mouth a screech sounded. And something dripped on my head.

"There you go!" The major exchanged a joyfully malicious glance with Revzin.

"And you talk about sisters!" Fedotov said, kicking me with a new boot.

"We're not a bunch of dumbbells sitting here, Korobova." Revzin looked down on me. "You forgot that we're professionals. We dig up everything."

"They only spoke English at home," the major told Fedotov confidentially. "Eye gow to sleap, mye swheat ledy!"

They jeered. And their waist belts squeaked.

I closed my eyes.

"Just what do you think you're pretending?" Fedotov kicked me again.

I opened my eyes. The fat major and Nastya were gone.

"Now then, Korobova, here is your evidence." Revzin brought me some papers covered with childish handwriting. "If you sign, you'll go to the hospital and then to the camp. If you don't sign—you'll go to the other world."

I closed my eyes and whispered, "The purpose of my life is to go to the other world. To Our World...Our Light..."

"Shut up, you bitch! Don't pretend to be crazy!" Fedotov snarled. "Read it to her, Yegor Petrovich."

Revzin mumbled: "I, Korobova Varvara Fedotovna, born in 1929, having established sexual relations with General Lieutenant Vlodzimirsky, L.E., was recruited by him in 1950 as a liaison between the military attaché of the American embassy, Irwin Pierce, and the former minister of the MGB, V. S. Abakumov. My first task was to meet with Pierce on March 8, 1950, at the boat station in Gorky Park, and to hand over plans to him—"

"That's not about me," I interrupted.

"It's about you! It's about you, cunt!" Fedotov growled.

"Sign it Korobova, don't play the fool!"

"I'm not Korobova. My true name is—Khram."

I closed my eyes.

And the amber serpents again crawled over me.

I came to on a gynecological chair. There was a terrible aroma of smelling salts in the air.

"She's a virgin," came a voice from between my legs.

The doctor straightened up, began tearing off his rubber gloves. He was large and wore glasses. He was afraid of his mother, of dogs, and of doorbells at night. He loved to tickle his wife until she got hiccups. He loved crabs, billiards, and Stalin.

"So, what do we do now?" muttered Fedotov just above my ear.

"I don't know." The doctor disappeared.

"I didn't ask you!" Fedotov snapped back angrily.

"Who then? Yourself?" The doctor laughed, clattering his instruments.

A needle pierced my shoulder. I shifted my eyes: the nurse was giving me a shot.

My spread legs were bluish-yellow in color. My abrasions were bleeding.

My eyes filled with moisture. And I felt like sleeping.

"Well, so?" The doctor let out a big yawn.

"To the hospital." Fedotov nodded thoughtfully.

I lay in the prison hospital for a week.

There were six other women in the ward. Two had been tortured, four had pneumonia. They talked constantly among themselves about their relatives, food, and medicine.

I was treated: a perfumed ointment was rubbed into my legs and buttocks.

The doctors and nurses said almost nothing to the prisoners.

I looked out the window and at the women. I knew everything about every one. They weren't interesting to me.

I remembered OUR PEOPLE.

And their HEARTS.

When I got better, they took me back to interrogation.

The office was the same, but the investigator was new. Sheredenko, Ivan Samsonovich. A slim, well-built thirty-five-year-old with a handsome face. More than anything on earth he feared dreaming of a white tower and dying at work from a heart attack. He loved hunting, fried eggs with lard, and his daughter, Annushka.

"Varvara Fedotovna, your former investigators were scoundrels. They have already been arrested," he informed me.

"That's not true," I answered. "Fedotov is having lunch right now in the Lubianka cafeteria, and Revzin's walking down the street."

He looked at me attentively.

"Varvara Fedotovna, let's talk as Chekhist to Chekhist."

"I never was a Chekhist. I simply wore your uniform."

"Don't be absurd. You worked with Lieutenant Colonel Korobov…"

"I worked not with him but with his heart. Now it knows all 23 words."

"You went on a business trip on the order of the minister of state security, and you visited Camp No. 312 / 500, where they extract—"

"The Ice sent to us from Space, to awake the living."

"The director of the camp, Major Semichastnykh, was arrested and gave evidence against Colonel Ivanov, you, and your husband. The three of you beat false testimony out of Lieutenant Voloshin in order to hide the true activities of Abakumov and Vlodzimirsky. This was necessary in order to—"

"So that the camp would continue to extract the Divine Ice, which thousands of our brothers and sisters all over the world await. Thousands of Ice hammers will be manufactured from this Ice, they will strike thousands of breasts, thousands of hearts will awaken and speak. And when there are 23,000 of us, our hearts will pronounce the twenty-three heart words 23 times and we will be transformed into Eternal and Primordial Rays of the Light. And your dead world will disintegrate. NOTHING AT ALL will be left of it."

He looked at me carefully. Then he pushed a button. An escort entered.

"Take her away," said Investigator Sheredenko.

I was examined by a psychiatrist—a small, round man, with a meaty nose and feminine hands. He was afraid of many things: children, cats, conversations about politics, icicles, his bosses, even old hats, which "stubbornly hint at something." The only things he truly loved were playing backgammon, sleeping, and writing denunciations.

In his soft, female voice he asked me to hold my hands out in front of me, to look at his little hammer, count to twenty, answer a bunch of silly questions. Then he tapped his little hammer on my knees and picked up the receiver of a black telephone.

"Comrade Sheredenko, this is Yurevich. She's absolutely healthy."

After this, Sheredenko spoke with me differently.

"Korobova, two questions: Why didn't you and your husband have sexual relations? And what were you and your husband doing so often at General Vlodzimirsky's dacha?"

"Adr and I didn't need sexual relations. We had heart relations. At Kha's dacha we would engage in conversations of the heart."

"Enough playing the madwoman!" he said, slapping his palm on the table. "When did Vlodzimirsky recruit you and your husband? What were you supposed to do?"

"To awaken brothers and sisters."

"Awaken?" he asked nastily. "I see, you don't want to do this the good way. All right then. We'll awaken you, too."

He picked up the telephone receiver.

"Savelev, bring the fruits and vegetables."

Escort guards appeared. I was taken out into the courtyard. Sheredenko walked after me.

Cars stood in the courtyard, and the sun warmed us.

I was taken to a dark green van with a sign reading FRESH FRUITS AND VEGETABLES. The escorts and I sat in the back of the van;

Sheredenko sat in the front seat with the driver. The van took off. Inside it was dark; light penetrated only through a few cracks.

We drove for a short time, then stopped. The doors opened and the guards took me out. They immediately led me downstairs into a cellar. Sheredenko followed.

We arrived at a metal door with a peephole; the guard knocked on it. The door opened. It smelled of cold. We were met by a mustached overseer wearing a floor-length sheepskin coat. He turned and walked off. We followed him. He opened yet another door. I was pushed into a small, square, empty room. The door slammed shut, the lock clanked. Sheredenko said through the door: "If you get smarter, give us a knock."

The cell was lit by a dim lightbulb. One of the walls of the cell was metallic. A coating of hoarfrost covered it in white.

I sat down in a corner.

In the metallic wall something hummed faintly. Barely audible, it gurgled.

I suddenly realized: a refrigerator.

I closed my eyes.

The cold grew slowly. I didn't resist it.

If the red serpents of my beating had crawled over the surface of my body, the cold made its way inside. It took away my body in parts: the legs, shoulder, back. The last to yield were my hands and fingertips.

All that remained was my heart. It beat more slowly.

I felt that it was the last bastion.

I really wanted to fall into a deep, long, white dream. But something was in the way. Something was bothering me. I couldn't go to sleep. And so I entered a waking reverie. My heart-sight became even sharper. I saw the corridors of the cellar with its guards. Another eight people were sitting in other refrigerators. They were in bad shape because they resisted the cold. Two of them wailed incessantly. Three others danced around on their last legs. The rest simply lay on the floor in an embryonic position.

Time ceased to exist.

There was only the cold. Around my heart.

Sometimes the door opened. And the mustached guard asked me something. I opened my eyes, looked at him. And closed them again.

One time he put a cup of boiling water next to me. He placed a piece of bread nearby. Steam rose from the cup. Then he stopped coming.

The prisoners in the cells changed: meat machines couldn't withstand the cold. They admitted to everything the investigator demanded from them. They were carried out of the cells like frozen chickens.

New ones were herded into the refrigerators. They jumped up and down and wailed.

My heart beat evenly. It existed. On its own. But in order to keep from stopping, it needed work.

And I helped it work.

I constantly surveyed the environs with my heart: I saw the frost, the iron wall, the hallway, the cells, the walls, the rats on the garbage heap, the trolleys, the meat machines going to and from work, the pickpocket stealing an old lady's wallet, a drunk falling on the sidewalk, troublemakers with guitars in doorways, a fire at a factory that manufactured irons, a meeting of the Party committee of the automobile-highway institute, sexual acts in a woman's dormitory, a dog run over by a tram, newlyweds leaving the marriage office, a line for noodles, a soccer game, young people strolling in the park, a surgeon sewing up warm skin, the robbery of a food kiosk, a flock of doves, a conductor chewing a sandwich of smoked sausage, invalids at the train station, the streets, the iron wall, the frost.

The city surrounded me on all sides.

The city of meat machines.

And in this dead mixture, like red embers, burn the hearts of OUR PEOPLE.

Kha.

Adr.

Shro.

Zu.

Mir.

Pa.

Umi.

All of those who remained in Moscow.

I saw them. And spoke with them. Of the Kingdom of Light.

Sheredenko came in.

He talked and shouted. He stamped his heels on the frozen floor. He shook some papers. Blew his nose. I looked at his dead heart. It worked like a pump. It pumped dead blood. Which moved the dead body of Investigator Sheredenko.

I closed my eyes. He disappeared.

Then I saw OUR PEOPLE again. Their hearts shone. And they swam around me. There were more and more of them. I reached out to more and more new ones, to ones that were far, far away. And finally, I saw the hearts of ALL OUR PEOPLE on this gloomy planet. My square refrigerator glided in space. Around it, their hearts swam like constellations. There were 459 in all. So few! Nevertheless, they shone for me and spoke to me in OUR language.

And I was happy.

My cheeks were painfully cauterized.

I woke up. I was in a hospital ward. The ceiling had six lights. A nurse was putting something on my face. A towel dipped in warm water. The smell of alcohol. The trace of a shot in the crook of my elbow.

Some colonel came in quietly. The nurse and the towel disappeared.

A chair squeaked. And boots.

"How do you feel?"

I closed my eyes. Seeing the world with my heart was so much more pleasant to me.

"Can you talk?"

"About what?" I said with great difficulty. "About the fact that you are afraid of drowning? You almost drowned twice, isn't that so?"

"How do you know?" he smiled awkwardly.

"The first time was in the Urals. You swam out with three boys, fell behind, and at the bridge you got caught in an undertow. Some soldier saved you. He pulled you by the hand and kept saying, 'Hold on, you horse's prick, hold on, you horse's prick...' The second time you almost drowned was in the Black Sea. You dove off the piers. Swam up to the shore, as usual. You never swam out to sea from the shore. But a homeless dog dove in after you, the beach favorite. She could feel that you were afraid of drowning, and she swam nearby, barking, trying to help. This caused you to panic. You thrashed your arms about in the water and rushed toward the shore. The dog barked and swam nearby. Fear paralyzed you. You were certain that she wanted to drown you. And you began to choke. You saw your family—your wife in a chaise lounge and your daughter with a ball. They were right nearby. You swallowed salt water, let out bubbles. And suddenly your feet touched bottom. You stood up. Breathing heavily and coughing, you screamed at the dog: 'Get the fuck out of here, you mutt!' You splashed water on her. She came ashore, shook herself off, and ran toward the stand where one-armed Ashot was grilling shish kebab. You stood waist-high in water and spat."

He stiffened. Horror filled his gray-green eyes. He swallowed. Inhaled. Exhaled.

"You need to—"

"What?"

"Eat."

And he left quickly.

For the first time I remembered about food. In the cell and the hospital they pushed bowls with something brown at me. But I didn't eat. I was used to eating only fruits and vegetables. I hadn't eaten bread since '43.

Bread—is a mockery of grain.

What could be worse than bread? Only meat.

Then, I think, for the first time in these two weeks I wanted to eat. I called the nurse.

"I can't eat kasha or bread. But I would eat some unground grain. Do you have any?"

She left without a word, to tell the colonel. Through the thickness of the brick walls I saw him, slouched over and gloomy, pick up the telephone receiver in his office.

"Grain? Well... give it to her if she asks. Only that? Give her oats."

They brought me oats.
I lay there and chewed.
Then I slept.

That night the colonel came to see me. He closed the door behind him and sat on the edge of the bed.

"I didn't introduce myself earlier," he said quietly.

"There's no need. You are Viktor Nikolaevich Lapitsky."

"I understand, I understand..." He waved his hand. "You know everything about me. And...about everyone, most likely."

I looked at him. He unbuttoned the collar of his tunic, sighed convulsively, and whispered, "Don't be afraid, there aren't any listening devices here. You...can you say whether they'll arrest me or not?"

"I don't know," I answered honestly.

He was silent a moment, then he glanced to the side and whispered hurriedly, "I haven't slept for eight days. Eight! I can't fall asleep. If I take barbital I fall asleep for an hour and then jump up like a madman. There are big changes going on. Arrests being made. They are sweeping away everyone who worked with Beria and Abakumov. But who didn't work with them? You also worked with them?"

"I worked for us."

"Two of my friends from the third section have been arrested. Maslennikov committed suicide. Maslennikov! You understand? Khrushchev's broom is sweeping clean...Hmm..."

I said nothing. My heart knew what he wanted. He broke into a sweat.

"I've lived through two purges—in '37 and in '48. It was a downright miracle that I didn't fall under the wheel. I just don't have the strength to live through another one. You know, I haven't slept for eight days. Eight!"

"You said that."

"That's right, yes."

"What do you want from me?"

"I...I want...I know—that you are a real spy. A real agent. For whom—I don't know. I think it must be the Americans. But—you're a real, genuine intelligence agent! Not like those fake ones that our strongmen are breaking by the hundreds in order to hand in their cases. I'm offering you a contract: I'll get you out of here, and you help me to go abroad."

"Agreed," I answered quickly.

He was surprised. Wiping the sweat from his brow, he whispered, "No, you have to understand, this isn't some cheap provocation and it's not…not the fantasy of some sleep-deprived Chekhist. I am really proposing this."

"I understand. I told you—I agree."

Lapitsky stared hard at me. Some reason appeared in his feverish eyes.

"I was sure!" he whispered with delight. "I don't know…I don't understand…why, but I was sure!"

I looked at the ceiling. "I was also certain that I would get out of here."

And it was true.

Colonel Lapitsky took me out of the investigatory isolation unit at Lefortovo on August 18, 1953.

A fine rain was falling. We drove to Kazan Station in the colonel's official car, which he abandoned there forever. Then we got on the commuter train and rode to the Moscow suburb of Bykovo. There, in a dacha belonging to relatives of Yus's sister, lived Shro and Zu.

They greeted me with excitement, but not as someone who had died and been reincarnated: their hearts knew that I was alive.

Having strangled Colonel Lapitsky, we spent two days in heart conversation. My pining heart was unquenchable. I drank and drank my brothers. To the point of exhaustion.

After burying Lapitsky's corpse at nighttime, the next morning we left Moscow.

Three days later at the station in Krasnoyarsk we were met by Aub, Nom, and Re. Adr and I had awakened all of them in the cellar of the Great House.

Thus, I ended up in Siberia.

One dark December morning my heart shuddered from pain twice: in far-off Moscow Kha and Adr were executed. The meat machines had stopped their strong, warm hearts forever.

And we were unable to prevent this.

Six years passed.

I returned to Moscow.

Three brothers had died of natural causes. The old lady Yus had died as well. The Primordial Light, shining in them, was reincarnated in other bodies that had only just appeared on earth. And we were faced with having to find them once again.

The camp that mined the Ice has been disbanded. The professors who substantiated the importance of studying the "Tungus ice phenomenon" were posthumously dubbed pseudoscientists, and the secret project "Ice" was liquidated. The *sharashka* where they prepared the Ice hammers was liquidated as well.

Nonetheless, the brotherhood strengthened and grew. The stores of Ice mined during Stalin's time were sufficient for all. In 1959 we were grateful to the prisoners of Camp No. 312/500. With their bricks they laid the foundations necessary for an ice base. Cubometers of Ice slept in refrigerators and underground storehouses, awaiting their hour. Part of the Ice was sent abroad through the old MGB channels. From the remainder of the Ice we made Ice hammers.

They were rarely used, since the search for OUR PEOPLE was narrowed. It became more local. Now, without the support of the MGB, we searched for others of us cautiously, meticulously preparing for the hammering. Train stations, movie theaters, restaurants, concert halls, and stores were the main places we searched. We followed people with fair hair and blue eyes, kidnapped them, and hammered them. But more than anywhere else, for some reason, we had luck in libraries. Thousands of meat machines were always sitting there, engaged in silent madness: they attentively leafed through sheets of paper covered with letters. This gave them particular pleasure, comparable to nothing else. These thick, worn books were written by long-dead meat machines whose portraits hung ceremoniously on the

walls of the libraries. There were millions of books. They were constantly increasing in number, supporting a collective madness that
made millions of corpses lean devoutly over sheets of dead paper. After
reading they became even deader. But amid these petrified figures
were some of us as well. In the huge Lenin Library we found eight. We
found three in the Library of Foreign Literature. And four in the History Library.

The brotherhood was growing.

By the winter of 1959 there were 118 of us in Russia.

The stormy 1960s arrived.

Time sped up.

New possibilities arose, new perspectives opened.

Our people began to move up in their jobs, to occupy important
positions. The brotherhood again infiltrated the Soviet elite, but this
time from below. We had three new brothers in the Council of Ministers and one in the Central Committee of the Communist Party.
Sister Chbe became the culture minister of Latvia, brothers Ent and
Bo held leadership positions in the Ministry of Foreign Trade, sister
Ug married the commander of PVO troops, brother Ne became director of the Malyi Theater.

And most important—brothers Aub, Nom, and Mir organized a
scientific society for the study of TMP: the Tungus Meteorite Phenomenon. It was supported by the Academy of Sciences and subsisted
on government money. Expeditions were sent out to the site of the
fall almost every year.

Chunks of Ice again flowed to Moscow.

We were working.

In the 1970s the brotherhood increased in strength.

Our newly acquired brother Lech became the director of Comecon. The most extraordinary thing was that his daughter turned out
to be one of us, as did his grandson. This was the first time that we had
a living family. Lech, Mart, and Bork became the bulwark of the
brotherhood in the Soviet nomenklatura. Comecon began to work

for us. Thanks to Lech we established close contacts with our people in Eastern Europe. We began to supply Ice to them directly, bypassing the complex, conspiratorial channels Kha created under Stalin.

I took a small management position in Comecon.

This allowed me to travel often to other Socialist countries. I saw the faces of our European brothers. I came to know their hearts. Speaking in different earthly languages, we understood one another perfectly.

We knew WHAT to do and HOW to do it.

The brotherhood grew.

In 1980 there were 718 of us in Russia.

And worldwide—there were 2,405.

The 1980s brought a great deal of fuss and difficulty.

Brezhnev died. Russia's traditional redistribution of power began. Four of our people lost important positions in the Central Committee and the Council of Ministers. Three from Gosplan were demoted. Brother Yot, a well-known functionary of the All-Union Central Soviet of Trade Unions, was kicked out of the Party for "protectionism" (he promoted our people into the leadership of the union too actively). Two brothers from Vneshtorg fell during the campaign against corruption and were given long sentences. Sisters Fed and Ku lost their jobs in the Central Committee of the Komsomol for "amoral behavior" (they were caught during a heart conversation). And Shro, my loyal and decisive follower, was sentenced for assault with physical injury (one of the people we hammered ran away and denounced him).

But Lech survived.

And two of us, Uy and Im, became colonels in the KGB.

Ice was extracted and exported to twenty-eight countries.

And the Ice hammers struck hearts once again.

Andropov and Chernenko died.

Gorbachev came to power.

The era of glasnost and perestroika began.

The USSR began to disintegrate. Comecon was disbanded. And Lech died almost immediately after that. This was a huge loss for us. Our hearts said ardent farewells to the great Lech. He had done so much for the brotherhood.

The Party lost more and more power in the country. Panic began to overtake the loyal echelons of power: the Soviet nomenklatura recognized a mortal danger in the impending democratization, but could do nothing.

Private enterprise appeared. The smartest representatives of the nomenklatura began to move into business. Using their old connections, they quickly made a lot of money.

OUR PEOPLE were also able to reorient themselves quickly. It was decided to establish commercial firms, banks, and stock companies.

In August 1991 the USSR fell apart.

By an irony of fate, one day three brothers and I found ourselves on Lubianskaya Square and observed the monument to Dzerzhinsky being dismantled. When it was tied with steel cables and lifted into the air, I remembered my arrest, my refrigerator cell, the interrogations, the amber serpent, the evil faces and dead hearts of the investigators.

The dismantling of the monument was directed by a blond fellow wearing a tank-division helmet. He had blue eyes. We got to know each other, and a few hours later, in a specially equipped cellar, we hammered Sergei. And his heart spoke his true name: Dor.

Thus, Dzerzhinsky helped us to find one of our brothers.

The rapid-fire 1990s took off.

The cheerful and frightening era of Yeltsin began.

For the brotherhood it was a golden time. We managed to do what we had dreamed of: we secured positions in the power structure, established mighty financial structures, and founded a number of joint ventures.

But the main success of the brotherhood was that our brothers infiltrated the highest echelons of power.

In two years, brother Uf, whom we acquired at the end of the 1970s in Leningrad, had managed a meteoric career: from being a docent of the Engineering Economics Institute he became a vice premier in the Russian government. He directed the economic reforms and privatization of state property. The sale of hundreds of plants and factories passed through Uf's hands. In the first half of the 1990s he was, for all intents and purposes, the owner of Russia's real estate.

It is impossible to overestimate his contribution to the brotherhood's quest. Thanks to the redheaded Uf we attained genuine economic freedom. The issue of money was solved for us forever. And on the planet of meat machines money moved everything.

I blessed him. Our strawberry-blond Uf.

His small but inexhaustible heart often spoke with mine.

Uf headed a radical wing of the brotherhood. The radicals tried to increase the number of brothers by any means possible in order to live to see the Great Transformation.

Unlike them, we in the mainstream were not so egotistical, and we worked for future generations.

But Uf, with his great economic burst, brought the future closer: by January 1, 2000, there were 18,610 of US in the entire world.

And for the first time I believed that I would LIVE TO SEE IT!

We celebrated the New Year in a small circle at Uf's country home. This was the only acceptable holiday for us of all the meat machine's holidays: after all, each new year brought the hour of the Great Transformation closer.

After a short heart conversation we sat on a rug around a mountain of fruits and ate in silence. For the most part, we tried not to speak in the language of the meat machines.

And suddenly Uf froze with a plum in his hand. His blue-gray eyes squinted, his small, stubborn mouth opened.

"One year and eight months from now, we will become Rays of Light!"

I froze. The others did too.

Uf looked around at us with a piercing gaze. He added decisively: "I know!"

Suddenly his eyes grew moist, his lips trembled, the plum fell from his fingers. Tears flowed down his cheeks.

I ran to him, and embraced him.

Drenched in tears, I began to kiss his freckled hands.

I awoke, as usual, in the morning.

From the gentle touch of sister Tbo. Her hands were stroking my face.

Suddenly I remembered: today was a special day. A day of Greeting.

I opened my eyes: I saw my spacious bedroom with tender blue walls and a golden ceiling, Tbo's blue-eyed face, her soft hands. Gentle music sounded. Tbo pulled the blanket off me. I turned on my stomach. The sister's hands began to massage my no-longer-young body. Brothers Mef and Por entered silently. Waiting until the massage was over, they lifted me and carried me to the bathroom. There they helped me to empty my intestines and bladder. Then they lowered me into a bath of frothing cow milk. After about ten minutes they took me out, washed off the milk, and rubbed my chest with sesame butter, placed a mask of sperm from young meat machines on my face. Sister Vikha arranged my hair and put on my makeup. I moved into the dressing room where Vikha helped me to choose a dress for today.

I always dress in blue for special days. I chose a dress of restrained blue crêpe de chine, a little pillbox hat of blue silk with a blue veil, blue patent-leather boots, and bracelets of turquoise.

They took me into the dining room.

It was a large half circle, decorated in the same golden-blue tones. White roses and lilies stood in four gold vases. Outside the wide windows was a green fir forest.

Presiding over the table set with a gold service, I reached out my hands. Mef and Por immediately wrapped them in warm, moist napkins. Brother Rak served a dish of tropical fruits. One of my six secretaries entered—brother Ga. He began reading the updates.

Listening to him, I ate leisurely.

He finished reading and left.

Having finished my meal, I stretched out my hands again. Once again, two moist napkins carefully wiped them.

They carried me into the hall for heart conversation. It was round, without windows. The walls of the hall were fashioned of blue jasper.

Three naked brothers kneeled in the center of the hall. I lowered myself to my knees next to them. Their arms embraced me.

Our hearts began to speak.

I taught them the words.

But not for long: our embrace ended with a sweet moan, and I was carried into the room of rest.

A quiet room, with soft, golden-blue furniture, it was imbued with Eastern aromas. While I lay in a soft armchair, my hands were massaged. Then I drank tea made of herbs from the Altai.

My secretary entered.

I understood: it was time.

They carried me out of the house. My dark blue bulletproof automobile and two guard vehicles waited in front of the marble porch. It was sunny and there was a springlike freshness in the air. The last bits of snow had retreated, green grass was pushing up on the lawns. A woodpecker tapped on a dry branch. The gardener Eb was restoring a pyramid in the stone garden. A guard with a machine gun strolled by the gates.

They put me in the car.

We drove into Moscow.

The heavy limousine traveled silently, rocking me softly. I looked out the window. I loved the environs of Moscow, that extraordinary combination of wild nature and wild habitation. Here earthly life seemed less horrid to me. The road ran through massive stretches of forest, and among the trees one glimpsed the silhouettes of dachas, the same as forty years earlier. In the Moscow suburbs nothing had changed since Stalin's time. The fences had simply grown higher and richer.

Moscow, on the other hand, was completely different. It had spread out. There was too much of it.

We drove along the Rublev Highway past white prefab buildings. Meat machines think them ugly, preferring houses built of brick. But what is a human house, in fact? A terrifyingly limited space. The incarnation in stone, iron, and glass of the desire to hide from the Cosmos. A coffin. Into which man falls, from his mother's womb.

They all begin their lives in coffins. For they are dead from birth.

I looked at the windows of the prefab building: thousands of identical little coffins.

And in each one a family of meat machines prepared for death.

What happiness that WE are different.

Driving along Mosfilmovskaya Street, the limousine turned toward Sparrow Hills. As always, it was empty and wide open. Only Moscow University rose as a monument to the Stalinist era.

After a few smooth turns, we drove up to our rehabilitation clinic. It was built five years ago. Newly acquired brothers and sisters lay in it. Here we healed their wounds from the Ice hammers.

Sister Kharo rolled a wheelchair up to my car. I was helped to sit in it and rolled into the clinic. In the hallways I was greeted by the experienced sisters Mair and Irey. I greeted their hearts with a flare.

"They are ready," Mair informed me.

They took me into the ward.

There, on a large white bed, lay three newly acquired hearts. They were exhausted by the crying that had shaken them for an entire week.

My heart began cautiously to pluck at these three awakened hearts.

In a half a minute I knew everything about them.

When they awoke, I spoke to them.

"Ural, Diar, Mokho. I am Khram. I welcome you. Your hearts wept for seven days. This weeping is in grief and shame for your previous dead life. Now your hearts are cleansed. They will no longer sob. They are ready to love and speak. Now my heart will speak the first word of the most important language to your hearts. The language of the heart."

The three newly acquired looked at me.

And my heart began to speak with them.

PART III

1. Unpack the box.

2. Remove the **video helmet**, **breast plate**, **mini freezer**, **computer**, and **connection cords** from the box.

3. Plug the mini freezer into an electrical outlet immediately in order to keep the **ICE** it contains from melting. Remember that the battery is capable of maintaining the necessary temperature in the mini freezer for **no more than** seventy-two hours!

4. Familiarize yourself with the **counter-indications**; when you are certain that the **ICE** Health Improvement System is not counter-indicated for you, find a quiet, secluded room and lock the door so that no one will disturb you during the session. Bare the upper part of your body, put on the breastplate, and fasten the belts on your back and shoulders. The mechanical striking arm should be positioned to strike exactly in the center of your breastbone. Open the mini freezer; remove one of the twenty-three **ICE** segments provided. Remove the **ICE** from the plastic packaging and place it in the striking-arm socket, securing it with the **socket latch**. Connect the cords to the **ICE** system. Insert the plug of the computer adapter into an electrical outlet. Sit down in a comfortable position. Relax. Try not to think of extraneous things. Hold the **directional controls** in your right hand.

Press the **ON** button. When you are certain that the mechanical arm is positioned so that the **ICE** will strike precisely **in the center** of your breastbone, put the video helmet on your head. The **ICE** Health Improvement System session lasts from two to three hours. If you experience any discomfort during the session, press the **OFF** button, which can be distinguished from the **ON** button by its rough surface.

5. When the session is over, remove the video helmet and the breastplate and disconnect the system from the electrical source. Assume a horizontal position; try to relax and think about eternity. After regaining your calm, get up, detach the **tear-aspirators** from the helmet, wash them in warm water, wipe them dry, and reinsert them into the video helmet.

Counter-Indications

The **ICE** Health Improvement System is **categorically** counter-indicated for individuals with cardiovascular disease, nervous system disorders, or psychiatric conditions; pregnant women, nursing mothers, alcoholics, drug addicts, war invalids, and children under the age of eighteen.

Warnings

1. We do not recommend more than two sessions in a twenty-four-hour period.

2. If you experience discomfort after the session, contact **ICE**. Our doctors and technicians will provide you with the necessary recommendations. Remember that the Health Improvement System is intended for **individual application only**.

3. If you interrupt the session, remove the unused **ICE** from the

striking arm **completely**. In order to continue the session you will have to insert a **new ICE** segment.

4. Do not expose the equipment to the effects of direct sunlight, humidity, and low temperatures.

Additional ICE to restock your mini freezer may be obtained from authorized ICE dealerships.

COMMENTS AND RECOMMENDATIONS
FROM THE FIRST USERS OF THE
ICE HEALTH IMPROVEMENT SYSTEM

Leonid Batov, 56, film director

Until recently I was a steadfast, principled enemy of progress and regarded the technological novelties of our century with suspicion. This was not a matter of my having "environmental" views, not at all. Rather, it stemmed from the very logic of my life and my art. I led a fairly secluded life, lived in the country, and socialized with a small circle of like-minded people. Once every four years I made a film. My films were termed "elite," "hermetic," and even "arrogantly marginal" by many film critics. They are right: I was always a supporter of elitism in art, of "films that are NOT for everyone." I believed my primary enemy to be Hollywood, that huge McDonald's which overran the world with cinematic "fast food" of dubious quality. My heroes and teachers were Eisenstein, Antonioni, and Hitchcock. Politically speaking, I was an anarchist, a devotee of Bakunin and Kropotkin, who struggled against the faceless machine of the state. I actively supported the Greens, even taking part in two of their actions. I was born and grew up in a totalitarian state and had always experienced a certain inner tension; I expected aggression from without. Why do I speak of my political convictions now? Because everything in man is interconnected. Ethics and aesthetics, food and attitudes toward animals. It was precisely such an inner tension that I experienced when the courier brought me the **ICE** system. Representatives of the manufacturer had called me on several occasions and spent a long time convincing me to accept this gift. At first, naturally, I refused. I was sick and tired of the ads for the system and the hullabaloo surrounding it which has convulsed our mass media in recent months. I repeat: I have never believed in "instant paradise," neither in life nor in art. On the other hand, the shouts of the mass media about the "collapse of the world-wide movie industry" since the system came out, the comparisons of the system to a torpedo capable of sinking Hollywood, elicited a certain professional curiosity. In short, on receiving the box with the system, I had my breakfast, drank my traditional cup of fruit tea, moved my old leather armchair to the middle of the room, sat down, and followed the instructions to the letter. I put on the helmet and pressed the ON button. At first it was pitch dark. But the little hammer with the ice began to strike my chest evenly. A minute passed, then another. I sat there, staring at the dark. The ice hammer pounded away at my chest. There was something touching and amusing about this. I remembered how, in my childhood, when I lived in the provinces, a huge woodpecker inhabited a grove near us. No one had ever seen such an enormous woodpecker—neither Father nor the neighbors. Big and black, with white fuzzy claws and a white head. Everyone went to the grove to look at the huge woodpecker. Finally someone said that it was a Canadian woodpecker, that it wasn't native to any part of Russia. Apparently the bird had flown out of the zoo or someone bought it and didn't take care of it. He worked like clockwork, tapping incessantly. And so loud, so resoundingly! I would wake up from his tapping. And I'd run out to watch him. He wasn't afraid of anyone, he was busy with his own affairs. We got so used to the black woodpecker that we started calling him Stakhanov. And then one of the delinquents from the next street over killed the woodpecker with a stone. And hung him upside down from a tree. I cried so hard. Perhaps it was that very day that I became "green"…And suddenly, remembering the dead woodpecker and staring into the dark, I began to cry. There was such a warm, sharp feeling in my heart, the sort you have only in childhood when you experience everything directly.

I felt terribly sorry for the woodpecker and for all living creatures. Tears poured from my eyes. The tear aspirator in the helmet began to work immediately. It was such a pleasant feeling; the tears were sucked up so tenderly. I was trembling all over from this attack of universal compassion. And the little hammer kept on tapping and tapping, and what I felt wasn't a blow but a sort of soft pressure in the middle of my chest. These attacks of compassion for the living rolled over me in waves, like a tide. Every wave ended in tears, which immediately disappeared in the tear aspirators. The little hammer began to strike more rapidly, and the waves came more quickly. An unending avalanche broke over me. A waterfall of compassion. I was utterly convulsed by sobs. It was phenomenal. The last time I cried like that was sixteen years ago, when Mama died. I don't remember how long it lasted—half an hour or perhaps an hour. But I felt no fear or discomfort. On the contrary, it was very pleasant to cry like this, it purified the soul. I gave myself over entirely to these attacks. The crying gradually ended and I calmed down. The hammer tapped so fast that it seemed there was an opening in my chest all the way to my very heart. The feeling of universal compassion was replaced by a feeling of extraordinary peace and bliss. I have NEVER felt so peaceful and well in my life! And at that moment on the inner screen of the helmet an image appeared. Rather, it didn't appear, it flared—bright, wide, and strong. I saw before me the cliffs of an island rising out of the ocean. It rose from the sea like a plateau, almost a perfect circle in form, and was several kilometers across. And I was standing on the edge of this island, holding hands with other naked people standing nearby. A girl held my left hand and an elderly man my right. They, in turn, held hands with other people. And we all formed a huge circle extending along the perimeter of the island. Somehow I understood that there were exactly twenty-three thousand of us in that circle. We stood there, very still. The ocean splashed below. The sun shone at its zenith. The blindingly blue sky spread out over us. We were all naked, blue-eyed, and fair-haired. We all awaited something with the GREATEST reverence. That moment of awaiting the greatest event continued and continued. It seemed that time had stopped. And suddenly something in my heart awoke. And my heart began to speak in a completely different language. It was amazing! My heart was speaking! For the first time in my life I felt my heart SEPARATELY, as an independent organ. It felt all the people standing in the ring, it felt each heart. And all the hearts, all our hearts, all TWENTY-THREE THOUSAND of them, began speaking in unison! They repeated some new words, although they weren't words in the sense of speech, but more like flares of energy. These flares grew, multiplied as if they were constructing an unseen pyramid. And when there were twenty-three of them, the most amazing thing happened. It is impossible to convey in any language. The entire visible world surrounding us suddenly began to melt and grow pale. But it wasn't at all like in the movies, when the frame pales because of a wide-open aperture. The world was actually MELTING, that is, falling apart into atoms and elemental particles. And our bodies along with it. It was INCREDIBLY pleasant: a great relief after decades of earthly life. They disappeared, disappeared, and suddenly a torrent of light

Galina Uvarova, 38, deputy of the State Duma

Yesterday I received an unexpected gift from the **ICE** Company—a system of the same name. The nine-month hubbub around this project resulted in a successful birth—a new child of advanced technology appeared in the world. In the presence of my husband, son, and friends I tried out this "miracle of the XXI century," by means of which its creators intend to "resolve the problem of human discord in our difficult world." Putting on the helmet and turning on the apparatus, I waited. The "miracle ice," loaded in the mechanical hammer, began to strike me in the chest. The first minutes passed in silence and darkness. In a state of expectation, in pitch dark, people usually begin to think about things past. For some reason I remembered how my father once took me to the countryside, to see his relatives. I was about ten. These relatives had slaughtered a calf specially for us. His name was Borka. And I saw his head in the larder. I was horrified and scared. I ran out of the larder. At dinner, my country aunt suddenly asked me, smiling, "Now, then, is Borka tasty?" I began to cry. Then I suddenly felt terribly sad. And wearing that damned helmet I began to weep. Apparently the nervous tension of the recent election campaign took its toll. My husband began to pull at my shoulder, but I pushed him away roughly, something I had never permitted myself. The tears flowed even harder, in a regular flood. I simply broke down. When it was all finished, a picture arose—we all stand in a circle, holding hands. Naked. And suddenly everything around begins to disappear. And we turn into rays of light

Sergei Krivosheev, 94, retired

I feel very happy and hopeful after receiving the **ICE** Health Improvement System free of charge. Thanks to it, I feel energetic and optimistic. I tried it on October 18. The details: At 14:30 I connected everything and sat down on a chair. I was assisted by: my son and his wife. At first nothing happened. So I waited. And then I felt a certain agitation, but it was pleasant. Most important, I remembered many things that I had completely forgotten. I remembered 1926, how I went hunting with my father when I was just a boy. It was near Vyshniy Volochek on the lakes. Father and three of his pals and fellow workers were duck hunting. That morning they had shot nearly a boatful of ducks. The boat was in the reeds by the shore. I sat in the boat. Our two dogs, Entente and Kolchak, would swim out to retrieve the ducks that had been hit if they fell in the water, or search for them in the reeds. Then the hunters called the dogs to them and I remained alone in the boat with the dead ducks. And who knows why, I began to feel very sorry for the ducks. They were so beautiful. But I understood the scariest thing back then: no one could ever bring them back to life. I cried so hard. I cried and fainted. Then I cried some more. I got very tired. But then I awoke on the shore of an enormous lake. I am standing with some people. And we all pass easily into a very pure light

Andrei Sokolov, 36, temporarily unemployed

All of you weasels should be hung up by your pricks so you don't shit on people. This stinking **ICE** is an invention of kike Freemasons who want to enslave mankind. Russia has already been humiliated, crucified, they want to cut her up and sell her off like bear meat, and now they're out to fuck her over in the mental sphere. They choose the "necessary" people and hand out this shit for free. But I'm not one to take to that immoral dishonesty. This fucking system is opium for the Russian people. They want to get us all hooked on it, and when we turn into retards they'll bring in fucking UN troops and aim their guns at the Kremlin. And we'll all be speaking English. It's a nasty fucking system: first I started crying my eyes out because I remembered how we buried my little sister when she got electrocuted on the farm, and then all kinds of bullshit started—I'm standing around with naked hookers and pederast perverts! And no one's ashamed of themselves. Most of all—even I'm not ashamed. And then—everything disappears and there's something like this kind of bright light

Anton Beliavsky, 18, student

On September 10 my sister told me that I was one of two hundred and thirty people to whom the company **ICE** was giving its super system for free. I didn't believe it at first, but my sister showed me the newspaper where it was written. That was cool! I'd heard so much about this system, they were always talking about it on TV, writing in the papers and magazines. I saw a report on the company, on its unusual story, on how they set up a huge plant to manufacture synthetic Tungus ice in Siberia, and how the company is very rich, but the Russian part is only twenty-five percent, and that they want to revolutionize the video and film industries, to destroy the old cinema and create something really awesome that will make everyone go bananas. They called me, and then delivered the box. My sister and I opened it; there was a computer, a helmet, and a breastplate. Also a kind of briefcase-size freezer with twenty-three pieces of ice. I took off my T-shirt, sat down on the sofa; my sister helped me put on the breastplate. I put a piece of ice in the hammer, connected the computer and the helmet, plugged everything in, put on the helmet, and flipped the system on. The helmet design is really cool, just like Darth Vader's. And it's comfortable inside, really soft. At first nothing happened. The hammer began to thump the ice against my chest, that's all. But it didn't hurt.

I relaxed, sat back; it was dark in the helmet, like in a tank. One minute, two, five. Nothing! I was already thinking, okay, it's just another bunch of bullshit. My sister was sitting next to me. I said, "Mashka, we've been had!" And then suddenly for some reason I remembered something. I was fourteen years old when I first got asthma. My very first attack was in the early morning. They were laying down some kind of pipes outside right under our windows and these jerks started drilling the asphalt at around five a.m. They had a compressor for the jackhammer; they turned it on and it began pounding away rhythmically—*trrr, trrr, trrr, trrr!* That morning I had a dream: it was like those jerks started up the compressor and connected the hose to our window. They were sucking the air out of our apartment. We had a one-room apartment; Mama and Mashka slept near the window and I slept on a fold-out cot near the sideboard. And it was like I woke up and saw that Mama and little Masha had almost suffocated. They were lying as though they were dead under that window. And I jump out of bed and then have to crawl over to them, because I can hardly breathe myself, and I start shaking them. But they die right before my eyes. What was so frightening was that I couldn't help them at all, and that damn compressor was sucking out the air and blasting away: *trrr, trrr, trrr!!* So I grab a chair and throw it at the window. But it doesn't break. I beat my fists against the glass as hard as I can, but I can't break it. Then suddenly I realize—that's it! They're both dead! And they will never be brought back to life. I began to weep—I wept so hard! Then I began to sob convulsively. So hard and so long that my sister even got scared. She told me later that my whole body was wracked by sobs. It went on and on, and then I kind of started to feel tired, and then completely exhausted. I felt so good and calm, it was like nothing bothered me, I didn't care about anything, and I felt totally high inside. And—*bam!* A picture lit up: I'm standing on this awesome island. It's so big, like a cliff. The sea is all around. Sun, a bright blue sky, incredible fresh air. And I'm standing in a huge circle with naked people, and we're all holding hands like children. And there are lots and lots of us. And then I suddenly realize: there are exactly twenty-three thousand of us. Exactly! And that really kind of hit me—*wham!* And in my heart there was this kind of sucking feeling, but in a good way, it was sweet. And there was this rush, as though my heart had a pipe in it, and whoosh, it was off with a whistle. Suddenly I could feel the hearts of all of those people. And it was this really strange but cool feeling that all of us are the only ones on earth. And we began to talk with our hearts. But it wasn't any kind of normal conversation, when you tell someone something, and they answer, like: "Who are you?" "I'm Anton." "I'm Volodya, hi." Not like that. It was more like a conversation without words, but really powerful. And then our hearts all began to kind of vibrate: one, two, three . . . It was so cool! And when it got up to twenty-three—then . . . I just can't explain it. . . ! Suddenly everything all around began to dissolve, sort of disappear forever, and us too—*whoosh!* And we melted in this gentle light

Max Alyoshin, 20, anarchist

When I received the **ICE** system, I immediately decided to test it in our commune. It's in this really awesome condemned building. They're going to restore it and then fill it with the bourgeoisie. There's nothing there, not even any electricity. But we solved the problem— at night we hook up to the neighboring kiosk. And so I got into the helmet, turned it on. At first—it was fucking dark and that ice hammer was humping away at my breastbone. It was a real bummer, no rush, no high. Then all this bullshit got into my head: really ancient memories. It was like I was still in Elektrostal, just a little guy; in the morning I run out into our yard and there's this incredible fucking winter, snowdrifts, all kinds of kids out with their mamas. And my mother's the groundskeeper. And right near the third entrance door, she's chopping ice with a pickax: *whack! whack! whack!* A nice sound. And I'm walking around the yard like a goddamn cosmonaut: my grandma put a bunch of clothes on me, so I look like a head of cabbage. I've got felt boots with galoshes on my feet, and the snow crunches under them like sugar. I have a shovel in my hand, and I walk over to a snowdrift and start making a spaceship out of it with my shovel—I dig and dig, and Mother keeps on chopping and chopping. And suddenly I need to piss really badly, because I didn't take a leak before going out, because I wanted to go out so bad. And I don't want to go home to piss—walk all the way up to the fourth floor, then Grandma will unpack me, take me to the john, it would all take way too long. So I keep on digging and digging, and Mother keeps on chopping and chopping. And then I start to piss into my felt boots, not even piss, but just let a little out at a time. And my boots are so warm. But then suddenly I feel like shit. I'm digging the deck, and I start whimpering from anger. But Mother chops and smiles at me. And suddenly I begin to cry, fuck, so hard that I can't see anything and I fall into the snowdrift and I cry and cry and cry. But my mother thinks I'm playing. And she keeps on chopping that fucking ice, and I'm wailing till I'm totally exhausted. And I get so tired that I lie there in that fucking snow like I'm in the grave. I can't move a finger. And then suddenly—fuckin' *whammo!* I'm on an island. An island in the fuckin' ocean. And I'm standing in a circle with twenty-three thousand people who are standing and holding hands, completely quiet. Me, I'm also holding some chick's hand with my left hand and some old guy's with my right. Fuckin' shit, man. Then—*whacko-fuckin-bam*—there's this jolt in my heart, like a rush—then a second, a third, and on and on to the twenty-third! And *whoosh*—we're all heading for fuckin' nirvana, we float away and the light

Vladimir Kokh, 38, businessman

In my opinion, the whole thing is very suspect. I experienced only:

1. Pity, yearning, sadness (when for some reason I remembered the time three schoolboys and I threw stones at a cat).

2. Weakness, deadly fatigue (when I stopped crying).

3. Euphoria (when I found myself in a huge circle of similar people, felt heart palpitations, and suddenly began to disappear, and everything all around too, becoming light

Oksana Tereshchenko, 27, manager

I really wanted to try out the **ICE** system. Not just because I'd heard a lot about it. Even a long time ago, I think it was about three years back, when the Japanese found the Tungus meteorite, or rather, what was left of it, and Russian and Swedish scientists discovered the "Tungus ice effect," I was very intrigued by this event. This discovery promised a revolution in sensory experience. And for that matter, I liked the whole story of the Tungus meteorite, the fact that it's a huge chunk of ice, ice with an unusual crystalline structure that doesn't exist in nature. Ice, fallen from the sky, a huge chunk, which no one could find, but it turns out that it had been found and quietly chipped away at. Where did that ice go? What happened with it? Who were these people? It's still a mystery. Now that scientists have synthesized this unusual ice, the whole thing is even more interesting. So when they informed me in our office that I was one of the two hundred and thirty initial testers, I was stunned! It was a huge surprise. Our commercial director included me in the list of two hundred and thirty without even asking me. He just saw how I was always surfing the Internet and following the "Tungus effect." And when fate willed that I was among the first testers, he said that I should try out the device here, in our office, in front of our coworkers. And everyone supported the idea! That was it—and so yesterday when I came to work as always at 9:30, I brought the box with me. Everyone was already waiting. In the packing room they moved the bundles over to the wall, placed the director's leather armchair in the middle. Two coworkers helped me put on the breastplate, load the piece of ice in the little hammer, and plug everything in. I connected the helmet, put it on, felt around for the start button with my finger, and pushed it. Right away the hammer began to peck at my chest with the ice. It was dark in the helmet. It was funny and a little ticklish: *tuk, tuk, tuk, tuk*, like a bird pecking and pecking at me between my breasts! It was funny because I imagined myself from the outside: the manager of the company sitting in a bathing suit and helmet, this thing pecking at her chest, everyone standing around and watching to see what will happen. But nothing happened—it was dark in the helmet. And I began to worry. I don't much like the darkness. And when I sleep alone, I always leave the light on. I've been that way since childhood, since I was about ten, I think. The thing is, my father would drink, and when he'd come home drunk, he'd be rough with my mother. We lived in a military settlement, in a two-room apartment; they slept in the little room, and I slept in the big room. And several times I heard my father raping my mother, that is, she didn't want to and he just took her by force, he was so drunk. And she would cry. One time I couldn't stand it; I got up and turned on the light in my room. And my father immediately quieted down. He didn't even get mad at me. And then I just started doing it a lot. And I began to be afraid to sleep in the dark. And when I thought about that, sitting in the dark helmet, I suddenly remembered really vividly an incident from my childhood. One time, it was in the summer, Mama put me down for a nap during the daytime, and went off to the store. I woke up—and there was no one home. The refrigerator was making a knocking noise. It was big and fat-bellied, made a lot of noise, and was always knocking and rocking: *knock, knock, knock*. I got dressed, went to the door, and it was closed. I went to the window and saw Mama in the yard. She was standing with our neighbor lady. They were talking about something happy, and they were both laughing. I began to beat on the glass and shout: "Mama, Mama!" But she couldn't hear me. And the refrigerator kept on knocking and knocking. And I was wailing and looking at Mama. And the most awful thing was that she couldn't hear me. I felt so sad from this vivid memory that I began to cry. And then I just started wailing out loud, like a little girl. But there was something really pleasant about this weeping, something intimate, a feeling of something you can never bring back. That's why I wasn't embarrassed at all; on the contrary, I cried as openly as I could. It went on for a long time, my heart would stop so sweetly, the tears rolled down and were sucked up somewhere so pleasantly. It was very very sad, but very sweet, too. I was only afraid of one thing: that one of the coworkers would be scared and pull the helmet off me! But they all turned out to be politically correct! So I cried to my heart's content, and the ice hammer kept on tapping away at my chest. And a kind of astonishing peace set in, really magical, as though my soul had flown above the earth and saw everything and understood that people have no reason to rush around. And it was so amazing that I completely froze still so as not to spoil it, so it wouldn't end. And the peace just floated and floated, and it was like flowers were blooming in my heart. And suddenly a bright, glistening image appeared on the inside screen of the helmet. It was the ocean and a bit of land in that endless blue ocean, and we stood on that land—twenty-three thousand wonderful people! We were all holding hands, forming a huge circle a few kilometers wide. We all felt fine and comfortable standing like that. We were waiting for some decisive moment, something important. I was entirely transformed into the expectation of something, as if God were supposed to come down from the sky to us. And suddenly our hearts seemed to wake up all at once. It was an incredible jolt! As though a huge organ began to play inside us. Our hearts began to sort of sing scales, rising ever higher and higher. This heart singing in unison was unlike anything else. My whole body grew numb and everything flew right out of my head. And the notes kept on going up and up, like a chromatic chord—higher, higher, higher! And when they'd come to the very top, a real miracle occurred. We began to lose our bodies. They just kind of dripped away somewhere, disappeared. And everything all around us as well—the shore, and the waves, the fresh salty sea air—everything was sort of sucked away, like a cloud. There was nothing scary about it, just the opposite, my whole soul welcomed this disappearance joyously. It was an unforgettable moment. I kept on dissolving and dissolving, like a piece of sugar. But not in water. There's light

Mikhail Zemlianoi, 31, journalist

There can no longer be any doubt that a new era has dawned: today we are living in the age of the **ICE** system. Yesterday we still lived in the age of the cinema. The moment when I stood in the circle and suddenly began to disappear, when there appeared a shining light

Anastasia Smirnova, 53, organic chemist, professor

The Tungus Ice Phenomenon (TIP) interested me immediately, as it did many scientists. My imagination was fired by the entirely new crystalline structure of this cosmic ice formation, which fell on Siberia nearly a hundred years ago. Our entire department made a model of this complex, multifaceted design out of cardboard, painted it the color of ice, and hung it from the chandelier. It spun and turned above our head, its facets sparkling, promising a scientific revolution. And it has come. The discovery made by Samsonova, Endkvist, and Kameyami means more than the Nobel Prize and international recognition put together. The discovery of SEK vibrations is the bridge into the future of new biotechnologies. The **ICE** system is merely the first sign. It is a trial balloon released by a human genius. I was not surprised that I ended up as one of the two hundred and thirty lucky ones. On receiving the system, the entire section tested it out every day. But I was the first. And I can honestly say: It is amazing! At first there were tears and extraordinarily intense childhood memories; then emptiness, peace, and flight! And what a flight it was! It was something like a collective orgasm, and I felt that the light

Nikolai Barybin, priest

Our world is truly tumbling straight into the Devil's jaws. This so-called **ICE** system is yet another hellish invention hastening the fall of contemporary urban civilization. On receiving this "Greek gift" from the company **ICE**, I initially wanted to turn it down, since my Russian Orthodox heart whispered to me, "This ice comes from the Evil One." As a pastor, however, I am obligated to know the enemy in person. I honestly tried this system on myself. At first I felt a terrible fear, which turned to grief. But what was the object of my grief? It is shameful to say—it was a broken bicycle. It happened when I was ten years old. This incident had completely vanished from my memory, but the Ice system reminded me of it painfully. Then a spell of absolute depravity ensued: I saw myself naked in an enormous circle of "the chosen," standing above the world and awaiting a miracle. But it was not the Lord's mercy they awaited, not repentance, not the absolution of sin, not the advent of the Kingdom of God. They simply yearned to be transformed into streams of light

Kazbek Achekoev, 82, retired

When the Soviet Union existed and our Republic was part of the

USSR, there was a movie theater in our regional center. I worked there almost thirty-four years as a film technician. I showed movies to the people. And I quite respected the cinema myself. I never understood and still don't understand the theater—what's it for? But I quite respected the cinema. My favorite films were—you couldn't count them all! There were lots. But my most favorite were genuine comedies. And my favorite comic movie actors were Charlie Chaplin, Mister Pitkin, Louis de Funès, Fernandel, Yuri Nikulin, Georgi Vitsin, Zhenia Morgunov, Dzhigarkhanian, Etush, and Arkady Raikin. This is our gold mine. But when the USSR died, and the Republic received its independence, the movies went downhill. There were hardly any new films. And then the war began. No one was up to movies. My wife and I took our sons and went into the mountains to our relatives. We lived there six years and eight months. But my son Rizvan died anyway. And my grandson Shamil disappeared. When we returned to the regional center, everything had been destroyed. The movie theater was a hospital. But life began to settle down. We got electricity again. They started getting things in order. And my grandson Bislan suddenly told me that I had won some new equipment through the newspaper. He had written us all down on the application and sent it to the offices. And six months later the answer came: Kazbek Achekoev. The company delivered the equipment right to our house. We all looked at it. And I said, "but what does it do?" Bislan said, "It's a new technological miracle. First of all, it shows you movies right in your eyes. Second, it makes you feel really good." I said, "You go and try it out on yourself." But Bislan replied, "Grandfather, you are the person who won it; you have to be the first to try it." I said, "I don't see so well, and I'm farsighted." He read the instructions and said, "Your farsightedness is within the norm. Everything will be fine." I said, "No, I'm too old for these experiments." My sons tried to persuade me. I kept on refusing. Then our neighbor Umar came over, and said, "Kazbek, you spent your whole life showing us movies, now it's your turn to watch." Well, I agreed. They sat me down in a chair, took off my shirt, put this thing on my chest, and put a piece of ice in it, like a bullet in a gun. And put a helmet on my head. Then that ice began to shoot me in the chest. But they didn't

show anything in the helmet. I asked, "Bislan, why aren't they showing anything here?" And he said, "Grandfather, be patient." Well, I
sat there quietly. That ice kept on shooting me and shooting me. I sat
there. There was nothing to do—so I started thinking about the movies, remembering things. How I showed the movies, what films I
showed, different bits of them. And then for some reason I remembered the Great Patriotic War. We were new recruits, we were first
sent to the Kharkov area and then to Viazma. This was in September
1941. The Germans had cut off the head of two of our foot-soldier
divisions, and we began to retreat. There were about two hundred guys
left from our regiment. And when the dawn broke, we began to escape
the encirclement through the swamps. And we ended up right under
their machine guns. The Germans were waiting for us. Right in front
of my eyes they killed everyone around who was walking. They just
cut them down like hay. And a bullet took a chip off my rifle butt and
I fell into the swamp. Everyone who remained alive also fell in the
swamp. And just lay there. The Germans watched to see if anyone
moved and they killed them right off. There were three machine guns
that shot dead-on and in short rounds—only five bullets: *bang! bang!*
bang! bang! bang! Not more. Then they'd wait, and again: *bang! bang!*
bang! bang! bang! Some of our guys began to quietly crawl through
the swamp, but the Germans killed them right away. Because they
could see everything in their binoculars. Everyone around me died.
Two guys who were wounded cried. I realized that I had to pretend to
be dead and lie there until nighttime—then crawl out. It was first
thing in the morning, about six o'clock. I closed my eyes and lay there.
The Germans shot at anyone who moved. They killed everyone off.
But I lay there and didn't even breathe. My face was halfway in the
swamp water, but the left side was above water. And so I'd breathe
this way: I'd suck a little bit of air in through my nose and let it out
into the water through my mouth. The Germans settled down. Then
suddenly: *bang! bang! bang! bang! bang!* And I'm still lying there.
And the sun began to bake. Somewhere over there the battle was going
on. Someone would rush through that swamp again, and they just cut
them down and cut them down with the machine guns. Well, then I
got good and scared. I wasn't even nineteen at the time. I was lying

there with corpses all around me. And suddenly a frog came of out of the water and jumped onto my hand. Right next to my face. And I could see that one of its feet was torn off. A bullet must have torn it off. And it sat there on my fist, breathing and looking at me. And I looked at it. And I felt so sorry for myself and for that frog that tears began to pour from my eyes. And I began to cry—like I'd never cried before. Stronger and stronger. And then suddenly—*whoosh!* I'm suddenly standing somewhere naked, bare naked, people are holding me by the hand, and it's so nice, and sort of free, and we're singing, and then everything begins to sort of flow, and that was it, and nothing, and only light

Viktor Evseev, 44, butcher

I heard before that they'd manufactured this artificial ice which, when you pound someone in the chest with it, awakes various cardiac centers. And then suddenly—I received this system for free, they had some advertising campaign. And I tried it. It's pretty interesting. Although it takes a long time. At the end, there's this great high, we all stand in a circle and suddenly—*whoosh!* And we disappear in light

Lia Mamonova, 22, saleswoman

This is really ... something. I don't know how to put it. At first it's all as dark as dark can be, quiet as the grave, just this mechanical arm banging at your chest like a jackhammer. Then there's a kind of compassion in your soul, you feel this sort of sucking sadness. And immediately there's all these pitiful thoughts that get into your head, like —everything sucks, people are shit, life is hard, and that kind of stuff. After that I saw a maternity ward where there's a whole room full of newborns abandoned by their mothers. And it was like, I went there at night and stood there. And they were all sleeping. And I felt so sorry for them that I just started blubbering buckets. And I'm like sobbing and sobbing, I can't stop. I saw their tiny little feet and hands and I just wept. And I cried so long and hard that I fell on the floor and fainted—*bam!* I couldn't stand it. And I really just lost consciousness there from helplessness, or I just fell asleep. And when I woke up—we were standing this uninhabited island and there were twenty-three thousand of us. And everyone was naked. But we weren't screwing, just standing and waiting. And suddenly God came down right from the sky and took us. That light

Anatoly Omo, 27, Web designer

This is a real cult thing. New. Radically new. This isn't any "Health Improvement System," but a new-generation simulator. Which the company **ICE** is pushing hard. Cool controls, awesome picture. Fucking amazing quest. Complete effect of being there. Plus the ice itself with its super qualities, which there's been so much buzz about in the media. The ice is fifty percent of the effect. The high makes you want more. Right away. But in sober daylight you realize—this is the start of an enormous new platform. Until now, we've just been floating, playing with our sweet little games: Quake, Myth, Sub Command, Aliens Versus Predator. Now we've arrived on the shore and stepped barefoot onto genuine ice. Ouch! I feel like saying, Fuckin' fantastic: we've arrived! We stand in a brotherly circle and transform into light

Anya Shengelaya, 33, poetess

It is divine in all senses! It prepares us for death, for the transition to other worlds. I haven't felt such excitement for a long time, haven't forgotten myself, haven't disconnected so completely from our squalid, gray reality. Our earthly life—is a preparation for death, for transformation, for great journeys. Like dolls, we are forced to doze in our earthly membranes until the Higher Powers awaken us in our graves and resurrect us. As Lao-tzu said, "He who cannot love death, does not love life." This marvelous apparatus teaches us to love death. And it actually does improve health. Because truly healthy people are those who are not afraid of death, who await it as deliverance, who yearn for awakening and the beginning of a new birth, in other worlds. In one instant we all shone with the light.

PART IV

A RAY OF sun crawled across the boy's bare shoulder.

A plastic clock with a laughing wolf ticked loudly on a stool. The breeze coming through a half-open window fluttered a semitransparent curtain. Down in the courtyard, a dog barked.

The boy slept, his mouth open. The green head of a plush dinosaur stuck out from under the edge of his blanket.

The sunbeam slipped over the boy's plump cheek. Illuminated the edge of his nose.

His lips twitched. The bridge of his nose wrinkled. He sneezed and opened his eyes. He closed them again. He yawned and stretched, pushing back the blanket with his feet. The dinosaur fell on the rug. The boy sat up. He scratched his shaggy head and called out, "Mom!"

No one answered.

He looked down. The dinosaur lay belly-up between a slipper and a water pistol. The boy dangled his legs off the bed. Yawned again. He slid off the bed and shuffled into the kitchen.

There was no one there. An orange lay on the table; there was a note under it. Rising on his tiptoes, the boy pulled the note out from under the orange. The orange rolled across the table, fell off, and rolled on across the floor.

Moving his lips and toes, the boy sounded out the syllables: "Bee . . . hoooome . . . ve . . . ry . . . soooooon."

He put the note back on the table. He squatted and looked around. The orange lay under the sideboard.

The boy farted. He stood up and shuffled into the bathroom. He pulled his underwear down and peed for a long time, moving his lips. He pulled up his underwear and walked to the sink. He pushed a wooden box over and climbed up on it. He rinsed his mouth out. Looked at his toothbrush and then held it under the water. The water began to wash the toothpaste off the brush.

"Cats and dogs…" muttered the boy and shook the brush.

The toothpaste fell in the sink. The boy splashed water on it.

"Catsndogs, catsndogs, catsndogs, sail away, begone!"

He washed the brush and put it in a glass. He jumped off the box. Ran to the kitchen. Looked under the cupboard and shook his fist at the orange.

"You scoundrel!"

He opened the refrigerator and took out a chocolate-covered cream-cheese roll and opened the wrapping. Bit off a piece. Chewing, he walked into Mama's room. Picked up the TV remote. Sat on the floor and turned on the television. Eating the cream-cheese roll, he flipped through the programs. He licked his fingers and wiped them off on his T-shirt.

"There." The boy crawled over to a shelf with videocassettes, and pulled one out. "Dinosaurs. Stop."

He began to put the cassette into the VCR, but suddenly noticed a new object. A blue cardboard box with the large white letters **ICE** stood in the corner. The box was open. The boy went over to look at it. There were some blue objects in it. The boy picked up the one on top. It was a helmet. He looked at it from all sides, and then put it on his head. It was dark in the helmet.

"*OOO-boom-boom-boom-boom-boom!*" The boy shot a machine-gun round with his two fingers.

He took off the helmet and put it on a chair. He pulled the breast-plate out of the box, turned it this way and that, and tossed it on the floor.

"Nuh-uh…"

He took a blue case out of the box. The cord on the case reached over to the wall outlet. A blue light burned on the side of the case. The boy put the case on the floor. He touched the button. He farted.

He pushed the lock button.

The case opened. Inside, in soft blue plastic cells, lay a single piece of ice. Twenty-two sections were empty.

"A 'frigerator…"

The boy picked up the piece.

"Cold."

The ice was packed in a frosty piece of cellophane. The boy picked at the blue strip, then pulled on it. The strip tore open the cellophane package. He pressed out the ice into his hand. Examined it. Licked it one or twice.

"Not ice cream."

The phone rang. The boy picked up the receiver.

"Hello. She's not home. I don't know."

He replaced the receiver. He tapped the ice on it.

"The ice froze stiff. It came over to warm up."

He tapped the ice against the glass of the sideboard.

"It's me, ice!"

Sucking on the ice, he went into his room. There in the corner, on a wooden stand for CDs, stood little plastic figures of Superman, an X-Man, and a Transformer. The boy put the ice between them.

"Hey, dudes, I'm ice, I came to see you!"

He picked up the Transformer, who held a laser spear in his hand. He jabbed the ice with the end of the spear.

"Ice, hey ice, who are you?"

He answered with the ice's voice: "I'm cold!"

He asked with the voice of the X-Man: "What do you need, cold ice?"

He answered with the voice of the ice: "Warm me up!"

Outside, dogs began barking.

The boy looked at the window. He scowled.

"Aha! Again!"

He ran out on the balcony. It was warm and sunny. Down below, three stray dogs were barking at a Doberman walking with his bespectacled owner. The Doberman ignored them.

"Catsndogs!" the boy exclaimed, raising his fist at the dogs.

He went back to his room. The ice was lying under a Transformer's spear.

"Get out of here, you fat ice!" the boy roared and stabbed the ice with the spear.

The ice skittered onto the rug. The boy sat down next to it. He whined in a high voice, "Be nice to me, I'm cold!"

He picked up the ice with two fingers and crawled across the rug with it, squeaking and whimpering. He bumped into the stuffed dinosaur.

"I'm cold!"

"Let's go, ice, I'll warm you up."

He helped the ice to get on the dinosaur's back. He crawled with the dinosaur over to the bed. He helped the dinosaur clamber onto the bed. He put the dinosaur on his pillow and placed the ice next to it. He covered them with his blanket and roared: "You'll be warm here, ice."

He remembered the orange. He ran into the kitchen.

The ice lay next to the dinosaur, jutting out from under the blanket. The sunlight shone on its wet surface.

23,000

The Meat Coagulates

THE ORANGE still lay under the sideboard.

The boy got down on the floor, stuck his hand under the sideboard, and stretched toward the orange. But his hand couldn't reach it. His fingers retrieved only dust and a dried-out cherry pit.

"Jiminicrickets!" the boy muttered angrily in the darkness under the sideboard.

He threw away the pit and threatened the orange with his fist. He rose up on his knees and sat for a while, picking his nose. Then he stood up and looked around. On the counter near the sugar bowl, a bottle of ketchup, and a jar of instant coffee lay a silvery-rose compact Mama had forgotten. The boy took it, turned it every which way, and opened it. Staring back at him from the mirror was a blond boy with protruding ears, somewhat bulging light-blue eyes, and a flat nose. He had the small, slightly drooling, perpetually open mouth of a retarded child.

"Good morning, Mickey Rourke," the boy said. He closed the compact and put it down. He opened a drawer below the counter. Eating utensils were in the drawer. The boy took out a spoon, got back down on the floor, and tried to roll the orange out with the spoon. It didn't work.

"I'll arrestetact you, you Chechen!" the boy snarled at the dusty linoleum, banging his spoon on the floor. "C'mon! C'mon, c'mon!" he added in English.

The unattainable orange lay there in the shadows.

The boy sat down. He looked at the spoon. He knocked on the

sideboard with it. He stood up and bumped his head on the open drawer. "Ow! Jiminicrickets!" he exclaimed, rubbing his head. He tossed the spoon back in the drawer.

He grabbed a table knife and compared its length to the spoon.

"No, just the same old jiminicrickets."

He tossed the knife back in the drawer. He closed the drawer. He walked over to the electric stove. On the wall above it hung a colander, a two-pronged fork, a slotted spoon, a ladle, and a rolling pin.

"Aha!"

He stood on tippy-toes, reaching for the rolling pin, and with great difficulty managed to touch its rough wooden tip. The rolling pin swayed. The boy studied it. Then he moved a chair over to the stove and climbed up. He stood up straight. He grabbed the rolling pin, but its string was still hung on the hook.

"Just a minute, jiminicrickets," said the boy, and, not letting go of the rolling pin, he lifted his bare left foot and placed it on one of the burners.

He tugged on the rolling pin. But the short loop of twine didn't want to come off the ancient hook. Grunting, the boy began to raise his right leg. This wasn't comfortable. He grabbed the rolling pin tightly.

"Upgrade, you fatty…"

He pushed his right foot off the chair, and stood up on the stove, swaying as he tried to keep his balance. He grabbed on to the rolling pin with both hands. The string slipped off the hook. The boy farted and started to fall backward with the rolling pin in his hands.

"Whoa, now…" Strong hands caught him softly and sat him down on the chair.

The boy turned his head around. A strange man stood there.

"Misha, Misha," the man said, shaking his head reproachfully. "Is that the way to do things?"

The man was tall, broad-shouldered, and had a kind, tan face. His emerald-blue eyes looked friendly. His strong hands held the boy carefully. His hands smelled good.

"Did you decide to become a rock climber?" The man smiled broadly, showing his strong white teeth.

"Nuh-uh," the boy gurgled, squeezing the rolling pin in his hands watchfully.

The man picked him up from the chair and set him on the floor. He squatted down nearby. The man's smiling face was right opposite the boy's face. He had a small scar on his head. His short, reddish hair stuck up like a hedgehog's.

"If you want to get an orange from under the sideboard, then it's better to use a mop, not a rolling pin. You know why?"

"Nuh-uh." The boy's large clear-blue eyes looked up at the stranger from under his brow.

"Because your grandmother rolls out dough for piroshki with a rolling pin. But Mama cleans the floor with a mop. Do you like piroshki with egg?"

"Uh-huh. And I like little meatballs."

"So let the rolling pin roll out piroshki."

The man pulled the rolling pin from the boy's hands and hung it in its place.

"And now we'll get your orange."

The stranger walked confidently out of the kitchen, opened the door to the toilet, took the mop, and returned to the kitchen with it. Leaning over right to the floor he easily rolled the orange from under the sideboard. He rinsed it off in the sink, dried it with a dish towel, and handed it to the boy.

"Eat, Misha. And get dressed. Mama's waiting for you."

"Where is she?" asked the boy.

"At Auntie Vera's. On Piatnitskaya Street. Do you remember Auntie Vera? The one who gave you the dinosaur?"

"Yes."

"Well, I bought that dinosaur. In the Children's World store."

"But...who are you?"

"I'm Auntie Vera's husband, Mikhail Palych." The man proffered his large palm. "Let's get acquainted, we're both Mikhails!"

The boy offered his hand. The strong tan fingers carefully formed a ring around the boy's hand.

Dogs barked outside. The man went and looked out the window, peeking through the curtains.

The boy began to peel the orange.

"Do you dress yourself or does Mama help you?" asked the man, still looking out the window.

"Myself."

"Atta boy," the man said, pulling the curtain closed. "When I was six I dressed myself too. And I already knew how to ride a bicycle. Do you have a bicycle?"

"Uh-huh. At Grandma's dacha. But that's where Tolik made the model eight. It's spitting," the boy said as he stuck his finger in the orange.

"Tolik?" asked the man.

"The bicycle. But Tolik doesn't spit. He squeezes through the fence to Mokhnacha and steals everything from them."

The man drew a deep breath and exhaled.

"You know what, Misha, why don't I peel the orange for you. And you go get dressed."

"Are we going to Auntie Vera's dacha?"

"That's right." The man took the orange from the boy. "So let's not lose any time. We want to go swimming. It's broiling hot today... And we don't want to sit in traffic jams. Come on, Misha, let's get going!"

The boy ran into the bedroom. In the entryway near the front door stood a large blue suitcase.

"Is that your suitcase?" the boy shouted.

"Mine," the man replied.

"What's in it?"

"Nothing!" The man laughed. "Get dressed, my little stuntman!"

The boy went into the bedroom.

He took his shorts off the back of a chair and started putting them on. But then he saw the soft, fuzzy dinosaur lying on the pillow, half covered by the blanket. Near the dinosaur lay a tiny piece of ice. A wet spot spread over the pillow from the melting ice.

"Hey you, you fat ice!" Getting his shorts tangled, the boy ran over to the bed and threw the ice on the floor. "You peed in your pants, ice! Upgrade, upgrade!"

The boy pulled on his shorts, then put on his shirt and sandals. He picked up the piece of ice and ran into the kitchen with it.

"The ice peed on himself!"

The man sat on a chair in the kitchen and smiled as the boy ran in. The orange was on the table next to him. The boy threw the ice in the sink. The man stood up.

"You're dressed? Good for you."

He took out his cell phone, punched in a number, and said, "Okay."

He put the cell phone back in his pocket.

"It's time, Misha."

"What about the orange?" the boy said, craning his neck to look at it.

"Later. Everything later . . ." The man quickly took a tiny spray can out of his pocket, pinched his nostrils with one hand, and sprayed gas at the boy.

The boy shook his head and frowned. He turned away, covering his face with his hands. He snorted and ran out of the kitchen. In the hall his legs gave way and he started to fall—into the hands of another man just entering the front door. The first man hurried in from the kitchen, still holding his nose. They leaned over the boy. The first man was taller. The Brothers of the Light called him Dor. The second, a blond man with luxuriant hair and a small, dark-blond beard, was called Yasto. Both of them had strong, muscular, tanned arms. These arms set to work deftly: they retrieved a small syringe filled with a brownish liquid, quickly gave the boy an injection in his upper arm, undressed him, and pulled a pair of disposable diapers on him.

Dor opened the blue suitcase. A camel-hair blanket lay inside. They wrapped the boy in the blanket carefully, leaving his face uncovered. Then they placed him in the suitcase. Yasto gently lifted one of the boy's eyelids. The blue eye, transparent around the perimeter, looked out at them, thoughtful and immobile.

"He's sleeping," Yasto muttered.

"Are those two downstairs?" whispered Dor.

"Yes."

"The elevator?"

"As it was."

"Then you'll carry it."

"All right."

They held the boy's helpless, pale hands for a moment, closing their eyes as though petrified. Then they came to life and closed the suitcase. Yasto softly picked up the suitcase and carried it to the door. They opened the door a crack and stood still, listening attentively. The stairs were quiet. Dor and Yasto looked into each other's emerald-blue and gray-blue eyes, and embraced headlong, pressing against each other's chests with passionate strength. Weak fetal sounds issued from their lips, their strong arms hugged each other tightly. Their bodies were tensed, frozen, and their heads trembled. Their hearts *spoke*.

"Dor," Yasto said hoarsely.

"Yasto," Dor exhaled.

They moaned and pushed away from each other abruptly.

They shook off their trance and calmed down. They inhaled deeply. And exhaled smoothly.

Dor stepped out the door and began to walk down the stairs: the elevator didn't work. Waiting a bit, Yasto followed him with the suitcase. Dor trotted down the stairs at a leisurely pace, his strong, supple body moving spryly.

A homeless man named Valera Sopleukh occasionally spent the night between the first and second floors of this sixteen-floor prefabricated concrete-panel apartment building. He had spent the previous night in the stairwell with his girlfriend Zulfia. She had just woken him up, demanding some beer. Kneeling and swearing hoarsely, Sopleukh was fumbling in his dirty pockets, digging out the change that remained from yesterday. Hearing someone coming down from above, Sopleukh lifted his head and pleaded as he usually did.

"Compatriots! Give a former diver something to help quench his thirst!"

Descending the stairs toward them, Dor stuck his hand in his pocket. The homeless couple saw him.

"Buddy, don't be a skinflint, I'm also—" Sopleukh began to speak, but he didn't finish the sentence: Dor struck him on the head with brass knuckles quickly and with incredible force. The feeble crack of his skull could be heard. Zulfia stepped back, opening her toothless mouth. Dor stepped toward her and struck her across the bridge of her nose. Her head was knocked against the graffiti-covered wall. Sopleukh collapsed on the stairs without a peep. Dor stepped over him, wrapped the brass knuckles in a handkerchief, put it back in his pocket, and continued down the stairs. Yasto wasn't walking as fast, since he carried the suitcase cautiously. Passing between the tramps lying on the floor, looking askance at Zulfia's convulsing legs and the puddle of urine forming near her, he instinctively lifted the blue suitcase higher, continued down to the first floor, passed by the elevator and announcement board, and, gripping the steel handle of the entrance door with his left hand, went out into the courtyard.

It was hot and sunny there. A dusty car, a Zhiguli, was parked right in front of the entrance. A balding, blue-eyed blond man in a gray T-shirt sat at the steering wheel, watching three stray dogs who were growling at him. As soon as the dogs saw Yasto, they growled even louder and backed away from the car. Yasto placed the suitcase on the backseat and got in next to the driver. The Zhiguli started up and began to drive out of the courtyard.

"That's it?" the driver asked.

"That's it," Yasto answered.

"Those dogs," the driver grumbled.

"They can sense us, can't they?" said Yasto with a nervous smile.

"I didn't know that before."

"Your heart is young, Mokho." Yasto brought his scratched hand to his lips and sucked on the drop of blood forming.

The Zhiguli turned onto Ostrovityanov Street and a massive, dark-blue Lincoln Navigator pulled in behind it immediately. A thin man named Irei sat at the wheel, and Dor sat next to him.

"Where to?" said Irei.

"They'll decide themselves." Dor held his masculine face in his palms from exhaustion.

The Zhiguli turned onto Profsoyuznaya Street, drove a bit farther, and stopped. The Navigator stopped nearby. Dor jumped out and opened the back door. Yasto, getting out of the Zhiguli, handed him the suitcase. Dor placed the suitcase on the Lincoln's backseat and sat next to it; Yasto closed the door of the Lincoln from the outside. The

Navigator took off, pulling out from behind the Zhiguli with a sharp turn. Immediately on its tail was a black Mercedes S500 with tinted windows and blue police plates. Inside the Mercedes were Obu, Tryv, and Merog, dressed in police officers' uniforms. Obu held a cell phone up to his ear.

"It's me."

"I'm coming," Irei answered, letting the Mercedes pass him. Dor opened the padlock on the blue suitcase and lifted the lid. The boy slept in the blanket. His face was slightly pink. Dor picked up the boy's hand. It was cool and helpless. He leaned over the boy, placed the child's hand to his chest, and closed his eyes for a moment.

Suddenly two cars in the right lane collided and one of them hit the Lincoln. The Lincoln jolted and swerved. Dor grabbed the suitcase and held it down on the seat.

"Arrr," Irei snarled, dropping his phone and grabbing the steering wheel tightly.

"Don't stop!" Dor said, glancing out the rear window.

"Who are they?"

"Meat, meat," Dor comforted him, looking at the stopped cars. "A regular accident."

The Lincoln sped on. Its damaged fender stuck out at an angle. At the traffic light it stopped next to the Mercedes. Dor opened the door and handed the suitcase to Merog, who placed it next to him on the backseat. The Mercedes raced off through the red light. Merog opened the suitcase and looked at the sleeping boy. He closed his dark blue eyes. His face seemed to turn to stone immediately.

The car swung onto the outer-loop highway, the MKAD.

Suddenly the Mercedes swayed and they could hear the weak knocking of a flat tire.

Obu pulled onto the shoulder. The Mercedes listed to the right.

They all looked back and forth tensely. Merog closed the suitcase and pulled out a pistol with a silencer from a sports bag. Tryv reached under the seat, picked up a short-barreled automatic, and released the safety.

Obu looked out the window.

"Both tires on the right. That's no coincidence."

"Are there two spares?" Merog asked.

"There are, thank the Light," Obu answered, taking the automatic from Tryv. "Change the tires."

He immediately got in touch with Dor.

"We've stopped. Two flats. It's no accident. We need brothers."

"I'm coming," Dor answered.

"No! It's dangerous. Your rear fender is bashed in."

"That doesn't matter."

"You'll attract the meat."

"I *believe the heart*, Obu. I'm coming to you."

"Dor, we need brothers! The meat machines are coagulating. I *know this*."

"I'll call Chit."

"It's dangerous! The meat senses them. We need regular brothers!"

"I'll call them."

Tryv got out and set about changing the first tire. A Lincoln Navigator with a bent fender passed by and stopped about ten meters ahead. Obu lowered the dark window. A white highway police Toyota with a blinking light and a siren drove up to the Mercedes. An overweight lieutenant with a puffy, disgruntled face and an unlit cigarette in his plump hand saluted them.

"How's the good life?"

Continuing to turn the jack, Tryv lifted his head.

"Hey."

"Two at the same time? Wow! As they say, shit happens, even to a Mercedes. Need some help?"

"If you're not in a hurry, he could use some," said Merog instead of Tryv, lowering the dark glass and holding a gun ready below the window. "I burned my hand badly yesterday, and the senior lieutenant here, Varennikov"—he nodded in Obu's direction—"has a herniated left ball from sexual strain!"

Obu, Merog, and Tryv laughed.

"In our demanding work even things like that can happen." The lieutenant grinned and yawned nervously, patting his pockets. "Just a sec, guys, we'll lend a hand. Helping our own is a sacred duty… Damn, where did I put my… like always, it's in the car …"

He turned around. "Alyosha, toss me the lighter!"

The door of the Toyota opened and a sergeant of the HP jumped out holding a Kalashnikov. Something clicked in the lieutenant's hand and a jackknife shot open.

"Here you go!" All red with excitement, the lieutenant took aim at Tryv's neck, but instead the blade plunged into his shoulder as he turned; at the same moment, Merog fired from the window of the Mercedes, and the well-aimed bullet lodged in the fat lieutenant's head. The sergeant opened fire. The bullets hit Tryv and ricocheted off the armored Mercedes. Dor threw open the Lincoln's rear door and fired a long series of rounds at the Toyota. The windshield shattered; riddled with bullets, the lieutenant collapsed. The barrel of a Kalashnikov emerged from a zigzagging silver Jeep and fired at the blue off-road. An explosion rocked the car, sending Dor flying to the ground as he ran off. Lowering the Mercedes's back-door window, Obu fired repeatedly at the Jeep. The Jeep crashed into a GAZelle, and someone began shooting from its shattered windows. Several cars in the left lane of the highway collided; one of them burst into flames. From the windows of the Mercedes, Obu and Merog continued to shoot at the Jeep, as did Dor from the road. A milk tanker driving at high speed began to brake, trying to bypass the burning car, but a stray bullet hit the driver in the throat. The tanker swerved to the right and slammed into the black Mercedes; the yellow tank with the blue sign MILK rolled over and cracked. Milk gushed into the cabin of the Mercedes through the open windows. Choking on the milk, Obu and Merog tried to pull the suitcase with the boy out of the car. Obu was wounded in the neck and losing strength rapidly. Milk filled the car; Merog felt for the handle of the back door, opened it, and fell out onto the road with the suitcase. Obu stayed in the car. Milk flooded onto the pavement through the open back door of the Mercedes. Merog grabbed the suitcase and sat on the ground, looking back. Traffic on the MKAD had come to a halt. Two cars and the demolished Lincoln off-road were burning. There was no sign of life in the silver Jeep. Staggering, Dor walked toward Merog from the burning Lincoln. The explosion had seriously wounded Dor, and he was taking his last steps on Earth, clutching an automatic in his right hand and with his left holding up his guts, which threatened to fall out of his torn stomach. His bloody, burned face was unrecognizable.

"Gather a Circle of Strength," he wheezed, and collapsed.

His blood mixed with the milk.

Merog's whole body shuddered; he ground his teeth, grabbed the automatic that fell from Dor's bloody hands, picked up the suitcase, jumped over the metal guardrail, and, spattering drops of milk, rolled into the roadside ditch and from there across the grass and into the bushes—toward the looming high-rises of Tyoply Stan.

People caught in the traffic jam leaned out the windows of their cars and boldly shouted, "There, he's over there!"

"Guys, catch him!"

"Where the fuck'r you going? Stop!"

"Oh my God!"

"Nikita, call the police!"

"But he's a cop himself—a goddamn Jekyll and Hyde."

"Catch that snake."

"Hey, there's a highway police station right up there!"

"They heard the shooting, they're probably on the way already!"

Lots of people made calls on their cell phones.

Merog ran through the bushes, bypassing the garages, and came out on General Tiulenev Street. On this Sunday the street was almost empty, there were only a few cars. There weren't many passersby, either. For the most part, people weren't walking but were standing, listening to what was happening on the outer-loop highway. Hiding behind a corrugated-tin car garage, Merog set the suitcase on the ground, wiped his face, which was wet with milk, and took a look around. Three women near the entrance to one building were talking excitedly, trying to see what was happening on the loop through the trees and bushes. A group of teenagers dashed out of another building and ran toward the road. A muffled explosion was heard from that direction—probably the gas tank of the burning car. A passing green Daewoo Nexia stopped. The driver, a stooped, gloomy, thin man with a cigarette in his mouth, got out and stood on tiptoe, looking toward the highway.

"What kind of shit is going on over there?" he loudly asked no one in particular.

"Terrorists," Merog answered, peeking out from behind the garage and aiming the automatic at the man. "Freeze," he said.

The man looked sullenly at Merog and the milk dripping from his police epaulettes.

Merog picked up the suitcase with his left hand and approached the car.

"Open the back door."

As he walked the milk squelched loudly in his boots.

The man looked anxiously at Merog.

"I'll count to one." The short muzzle poked the thin man in the stomach.

The man seemed to wake up. He opened the back door.

"Sit down in the driver's seat. But slowly."

The gun muzzle pushed against the skinny back. The man began to sit down in the driver's seat. From the direction of the MKAD the sirens of police cars could be heard. Merog placed the suitcase on the backseat, waiting for the man to sit down, then Merog sat next to the suitcase.

"Drive." Merog stuck the barrel of the automatic between the front seats.

The man grasped the gearshift. A drop of milk rolled out of the gun barrel and fell on the driver's bony hand. The hand put the car in first. The car began to move.

"Faster," Merog ordered.

The driver sped up.

Merog took the smoking cigarette from his mouth and threw it out the window. The car reached a fork in the road.

"Right," Merog commanded.

The Nexia turned onto Tyoply Stan Street. Merov opened the suitcase a crack: the boy was still sleeping in the blanket as before. Merog closed the suitcase and stuck his hand in the wet left pocket of his pants. The pocket was empty—his cell phone was still in the Mercedes.

"Hand me your cell," he ordered the driver.

The man took his cell phone out of the front pocket of his sweater vest and, without turning, handed it back. Merog took it and began to dial a number.

"I . . . I don't have any money on it," said the driver.

Merog flung the phone on the floor of the car. They came to a new fork.

"To the right," Merog ordered.

They drove along Academic Vinogradov Street. The whir of a helicopter could be heard overhead. Merog opened his window and looked up: the helicopter was hovering fairly close by. Poplar tufts caught on the lashes of Merog's dark bluish-brown eyes. He wiped off the fluff and looked around. The street was coming to a dead end. To the left were high-rises, to the right the green of a forest park.

"Turn left. Toward the building," Merog ordered.

The man turned.

"Park."

The Nexia drove up to the building and parked next to the other cars.

"Turn off the engine."

The driver turned off the engine. Merog closed his window.

"Close your window."

The man did it.

"Now take your clothes off."

"What?"

"Shirt, jeans. But make it slow, got it?"

The man took his shirt off. Underneath it there was a thin, pale body with an anchor tattooed on the shoulder. Merog took the shirt. Squirming on the seat, the man pulled off his shorts. Merog took them. The man looked back. Sweat broke out on his temples and his nose.

"Look straight ahead."

The stooped man looked ahead at the courtyard filled with cars and tin garages. Merog slugged him powerfully in the back of the neck with his fist. The head and its thin, badly cut hair jerked backward; the man's teeth clacked. His head fell against the seat next to him. Merog pulled off his wet shirt and pants, and put on the driver's shirt. It was small and very tight on Merog's muscular torso. The shorts were also tight. Merog found the button that opened the trunk, and opened it. He got out of the car, looked around in the trunk, and took out a large plastic bag. Back in the car, he put the automatic inside the plastic bag. He took the suitcase in one hand, the bag with the automatic in the other, and walked toward the buildings at a leisurely pace. Suddenly a passing pigeon struck him hard in the back of the neck. Merog sat down. The pigeon fell to the pavement, its wings flapping and sending clumps of poplar fluff flying. Looking back at the bird, Merog got up and quickened his pace. Rounding two highrises, he headed for the entrance to the third, and pressed the first button he saw.

"Who's there?" a voice asked.

"Let me in to hand out flyers."

The door began to beep; he entered and headed up the staircase. Passing three floors, he stopped. He set the suitcase down. He looked through a slightly open window on the landing: everything was calm down in the courtyard. From far off the howl of sirens and the whir of helicopters could be heard. Merog closed his eyes and pressed his forehead against the recently washed glass. His lips opened. He froze in concentration and stopped breathing. His heart began to *speak*.

Upstairs shuffling steps could be heard.

Merog opened his eyes. The door of the garbage chute banged shut. A female voice muttered angrily. Bottles clinked.

Merog inhaled. He grabbed the suitcase and ran quickly up the stairs. Between the fourth and fifth floors a heavy woman in a pink robe was trying to do something with the broken garbage-chute door.

"The pigs," she muttered, closing and opening the door.

The barrel of the automatic pushed against her side.

"Ay!" she shrieked, turning around angrily.

"Stay still."

The woman opened her mouth but, on seeing the automatic, fell silent and turned utterly pale. Her full, unpainted lips blanched.

"What's . . ." She moved back.

"Who's home?"

"Mama . . . and . . . uh . . . my daughter."

"Walk back."

"We don't have any money...only 1,500—"

"I don't need money," he said, pushing her.

"Uh, what...what do you need?"

"To hide for an hour. If you behave yourself, I won't touch anyone. Start yelling—I'll shoot all of you."

The woman walked over to the half-open door. She entered the one-bedroom apartment. Loud voices sounded from the television. Chicken was being fried in the kitchen. Merog set down the suitcase in the foyer and slammed the door. The woman went into the living room. She turned off the television. She whispered something. Merog glanced into the room: the woman stood with a ten-year-old girl, pressing her close.

"Everyone in the bathroom. Sit there until I leave."

The woman and the girl walked backward out of the room. The girl looked at Merog with curiosity.

"I'll tell Mama...she doesn't hear well," mumbled the woman.

"Tell her, but make it fast."

The woman and the girl went into the kitchen. Merog followed them. In the kitchen a short, fat old lady was frying chicken breasts in a pan. The woman went over and turned off the electric stove.

"What are you doing?" the old lady shouted in surprise.

"Mama, there's a man with a gun here!" the woman shouted in her ear.

The old lady turned around. Merog stood in the door with the automatic. The old lady stared at him.

"We'll sit in the bathroom until he leaves!" the woman shouted into the old woman's ear.

Holding a fork and a dirty kitchen towel in her hand, the old lady looked at Merog. He opened the bathroom door wide and turned on the light.

"Quick."

"Mama, go, quick!" the woman shouted, nudging the old lady.

A drop of chicken fat fell from the fork.

Without taking her eyes off the stranger or letting go of the fork and towel, the old lady entered the bathroom. The mother and daughter followed her.

"Are you from Chechnya?" asked the daughter.

"No," Merog answered. "Where are the tools?"

"What tools?" asked the woman.

"Carpenter's."

"We don't…have any…here, but in the wall cabinet there must be something left."

Merog closed the door on them, fished around in the cabinet, found a hammer and a couple of nails. Setting the automatic on the dirty, scratched parquet floor, he quickly nailed the door to the bathroom shut.

The girl began to cry. The mother comforted her. Then started crying herself.

"What does he want? What does he need? What are they going to do—blow something up?" The old woman asked in a loud voice.

Merog lifted the suitcase and carried it into the living room. He swept a vase with a bouquet of daisies off the table, along with a pile of women's magazines and a machine for measuring blood pressure. He put the suitcase on the table. He opened it. The boy slept facedown in the blanket. Merog carefully turned him on his back. Paying no attention to the sleeping boy's face, he carefully examined his chest. He ran his fingertips along the shoulder blades and touched his cheekbones. Merog's fingers froze. And trembled. His whole body shuddered, and he stepped back from the boy. He fell on his knees. He vomited on the floor.

He quickly wiped his mouth, inhaled and exhaled deeply. He got up. He found the phone, picked up the receiver, and dialed the number.

"I'm alone."

"Is he with you?" a voice asked.

"Yes. Academic Vinogradov Street. At the very end."

"Wait."

Merog replaced the receiver. He exhaled in relief, went over to the window, and looked about. In the courtyard and on the street everything was quiet and calm. The sun was warming things up, the poplar fluff floated in the air, a few people strolled by at a leisurely pace. A Volkswagen and two bicyclists passed by.

Merog yawned nervously, wiped his wet hair with the curtains. He returned to the suitcase. Once again he approached the boy but, clenching his teeth, moaned, stepped away, and punched the back of a chair. The chair cracked and flew into pieces. Rubbing his hand, Merog went into the kitchen. In the bathroom the women sobbed and whined quietly. Glancing at the pan of fried chicken with disgust, Merog took a basket of tomatoes and an apple from the table. Looking out the window he bit off pieces of each. Along Academic Vinogradov Street came a wide six-wheeler pulling a trailer that carried an orange Caterpillar excavator with a huge bucket. The vehicle moved with caution, barely avoiding scraping the parked cars. In the woodland park you could hear the growing roar of diesel engines. Two powerful bulldozers, breaking young trees and mutilating the older ones, crawled across from the wooded area to the street and headed toward the trailer. After them, skidding and crushing the bushes, came a crane with a boom. Merog stopped eating. He threw down the unfinished tomato and apple. Across the courtyard, moving backward toward the entrance, were two cement mixers. The mixers were on and turning. Another cement mixer rounded the corner of the neighboring building and began to turn onto the street, stopping in front of the slowly crawling bulldozers. One of the bulldozer drivers stuck out his head and shouted something at the driver of the third cement truck. That driver turned off his motor, got down, lit a cigarette, and smiled at the halted bulldozers. The bulldozer driver who had shouted also got out and approached the other man.

"Where'd you come from?"

"I'm from the sixth," the smiling fellow answered.

"Well?" the bulldozer driver said, squinting in confusion. "What did you get in the way for? How can I make the turn?"

"Don't get all steamed up, man. There's a shitload of other stuff still on the way!"

"So where are we supposed to go?"

"Khokhriakov will tell us everything. Let's have a smoke."

"What the hell do I want Khokhriakov for... I still have three trips to make!" the bulldozer driver complained irritably.

"The bosses know best," said the other guy with a grin, yawning.

"Think they're so fucking smart…" The bulldozer driver sighed, taking a cigarette.

A truck drove into the courtyard from around the corner of the next building. Workers in yellow overalls holding shovels stood in the back. The truck stopped.

"Come on, guys, quick, quick!" a voice shouted. Two of the workers jumped down immediately and began digging up the courtyard like maniacs. Two women pushing strollers stared at them in bewilderment. From the cabin of the truck a fat little man got out with a gas-powered saw; waddling along on his short legs, he started it up with a roar, rushed over to a linden tree, and the blade's serrated teeth bit into the trunk. Sawdust began to collect.

"So much for that, goddamnit," the short man cried out. "Bobrov, Egorych, chop 'em up! Cut down the rest."

"They're chopping down trees!" one of the women with a carriage said in horror.

"Hey, what are you doing?" said her friend.

The workers continued without answering. A window on the second floor opened and an old lady stuck her head out. After her a man, chewing and naked to the waist, also looked out.

"Why are they…?"

"Like I said—those bastards will stop at nothing to defend their garages!" the old lady grumbled with defiance.

Two trucks with covered trailers drove into the courtyard. From the cabins two Tajik guys with picks slowly emerged. Spitting on their hands and exchanging a few words, they reluctantly shouldered their picks and began to break up the pavement. Two asphalt crushers drove out of the forest onto the street; their steel tips grabbed the asphalt. In the building the tenants began to look out of open windows. The sawed linden tree swayed and tumbled, its crown demolishing the swings of the playground. The tenants shouted indignantly. The little fat man ran up to an old poplar with his whining saw and furiously set to it. The orange excavator rolled off its base, knocking over giant, overfilled dumpsters. The containers tipped over and the trash fell onto the street. A long-nosed and very unhappy old man in an old BMW drove up to the cement mixers and gave them orders: "Pour it there, where you're standing!"

Cursing, the drivers climbed into the cabins. The crane's boom began to turn in between two tin garages, snagging them as it moved; a GAZelle reversed and pushed its way in backward. The vehicle's cabin held a steel basket with ten Azerbaijanis in red hard hats and protective suits. The crane picked up the basket and began to raise it quickly. The basket swayed, the Azerbaijanis shouted at the crane operator. Concrete flowed from the churning mixers onto the square in front of the building. The crawling excavator hooked two cars, and their alarms rang out. The old poplar swayed, cracked loudly, and began to collapse slowly, its branches catching on telephone and electrical wires, trees and balconies. With tremendous force, its crown hit the glassed-in balcony of the apartment where Merog was hiding. The window frames cracked, the glass shattered. Shouts rang out from open windows.

Observing everything happening around the building, Merog grew pale. Dashing over to the suitcase, he closed it, grabbed it, and ran to the front door. He opened the door and immediately slammed it shut: indignant tenants were running down the staircase. Someone rang the doorbell. Merog froze. Then they knocked. And a woman's voice sounded: "Nina Vasilevna, they crashed into your balcony! Nina Vasilevna!"

The doorbell rang again.

On tiptoe, Merog went into the kitchen and with suitcase in hand cautiously looked out the window. Down below, immersed in the din of the asphalt crushers, a growing crowd of tenants followed the machine operators back and forth; someone tried to climb into the cabins with them; cement poured out of the mixers and crawled toward the building; human feet sludged through it; the Tajiks hammered away with their picks, the earth diggers dug, the short guy sawed through the next poplar, shouting angrily. Merog took a close look: the short guy's face was all red, his head shook, and he was frothing at the mouth. A woman in a dark-blue robe decorated with silver dragons ran up to him, grabbed his reddish, bristling hair, and pulled him off the poplar. Shorty dug his heels in, resisting; the saw in his hands was still roaring. He jerked away with his whole body, drew back, and slashed the woman across the face with the saw. She screamed, grabbed her face, and sat on the ground. The crowd gasped and screamed. The short guy, muttering and pulling his head into his shoulders, stared at the woman with a crazed look. He let out a sob. The men in the crowd rushed at him, shouting. And suddenly that very same long-nosed and extremely unhappy old man, who had arrived in the dusty BMW, stuck his fingers in his mouth and let out a whistle so unexpectedly loud that for a moment it cut through the roar of the machines and the cries of the crowd. The crowd shuddered and froze. As if by command, the machines stopped crunching the asphalt. Everyone stared at the old man. He had obviously not realized his strength: his extraordinarily strong whistle turned out to be too much for his skinny body. Blood spurted from the old man's large nose, his eyes rolled back; he raised his thin hand, clenched his bony fist, snorted, tottered, and fell flat on his back. Immediately, with furious cries, the people with shovels and the Tajiks attacked the building's tenants. Picks and shovels flashed above the crowd, the cries of the wounded could be heard. The excavator's bucket, after smashing a balcony on the second floor, crashed into the window and pushed farther into the apartment. With loud cracking and crunching it scooped household articles onto the lawn in front of the house. The asphalt crushers crawled over to the building, placed their steel tips against the walls, and with a crash began to destroy them. From the next courtyard a red fire engine approached, directing a stream of water at the windows of the building. Firemen in helmets nimbly unrolled the fire hoses. The Tajiks and people with shovels, scattering the crowd, burst into the entryway with their bloody picks and shovels. Simultaneously, the Azerbaijanis used the electric saw to rip the roof to pieces.

Merog's whole body shuddered; he licked his dry lips. The doorbell kept ringing and fists pounded on the door.

"Nina! Ninochka! Nina! Save us!" a woman's voice howled.

Merog grabbed the automatic and threw the door open wide. On the other side three women were crowded together. Screaming and wailing, they pushed in through the doorway. Merog fired straight at each of them in succession. Clumps of meat flew into the stairwell, the women fell one by one. Picking up the suitcase in his left hand, Merog ran across their dying bodies and flew up the stairs. Other neighbors were running down the stairs. Some of them were holding axes and knives. Merog began to shoot them, climbing higher and clearing the way. Crashes, cracks, and cries sounded through the building. Merog climbed several flights and saw four Azerbaijanis with pistols entering the building from the roof. They fired at him. Dodging out of the way, he fired his last round. The Azerbaijanis collapsed with cries and groans, but there were others coming in after them. Shots rang out and a bullet hit Merog in the neck. He tossed the empty automatic, held the wound, and rushed downstairs with the suitcase. Another bullet pierced his side. Moaning, he kept on going. The Azerbaijanis didn't give up. The lower floors of the building shook; cracks snaked across the walls; the firemen's water spray beat at the windows; the tenants who were still alive screamed. Merog looked down—a crowd of Tajiks with picks in hand was climbing up from the second floor.

"Catch him!" they shouted on seeing him. Holding on to the suitcase with both hands, he raced through the first open apartment door and froze: in front of him rose the bucket of a bulldozer, raking out the contents of the apartment. Merog held the suitcase tightly to his chest. The bucket moved forward with a grinding sound. It crumpled some low shelves loaded with dishes, bookshelves cracked, a leather sofa popped open, and a television exploded. The bulldozer's huge teeth came closer. Merog took a step and rushed back. But the sweaty dark-faced Tajiks were already very close.

They struck his head with a pick and Merog fell. Countless swarthy hands grabbed the blue suitcase. With his last bit of strength Merog fought them. Shrugging him off, the Tajiks opened the suitcase, shaking the boy onto the floor. Merog clutched, clutched, clutched with his bloody hands.

"That's him, the fucking bastard!" a woman's voice screamed in English, and through the Tajiks' filthy hands, a pretty hand with a gold-plated Browning stretched, stretched, and stuck the barrel to the pale, rosy, defenseless chest of the sleeping boy and pulled the trigger.

"Noooooo!!!" Merog screamed wildly, jerked forward, and sunk his teeth into someone's stinking foot in a worn-out sneaker.

"Filthy dog!" came a roar from above, and the sharp end of a pickax entered Merog's temple with a crunch.

Merog opened his eyes.

The Mercedes was still driving along the MKAD.

And the boy was still asleep next to Merog in the open suitcase. Merog exhaled with a heavy moan and shook himself. He leaned over and pressed his head to the boy's body.

"What is it?" said Tryv, looking back from the front seat. "*I can see*: your heart is uneasy."

"I'm losing the border between worlds," Merog answered. "Meat dreams are crawling in."

"That's only natural, brother Merog. Meat dreams crawl in when the meat begins to clot."

"The meat is pressing on all worlds," added Obu as he moved into the left lane. "Your heart is young, Merog. Place yourself on the Ice. Those meat dreams will fall away."

Suddenly the Mercedes swayed. A flat tire knocked softly.

Obu moved into the right lane and pulled onto the shoulder.

Everyone sitting in the car looked back and forth tensely. Merog closed the suitcase, pulled out a pistol with a silencer from a sports bag. Tryv reached under the seat, picked up a short-barreled automatic, and released the safety.

Obu looked out the window.

"Both tires on the right. That's no coincidence."

"Are there two spares?" Merog asked.

"There are, thank the Light," Obu answered, taking the automatic from Tryv. "Change the tires."

And immediately got in touch with Dor.

"We've stopped. Two flats. It's no accident. We need brothers."

"I'm coming," Dor answered.

"No! It's dangerous. Your rear fender is bashed in."

"That doesn't matter."

"You'll attract the meat."

"I believe the heart, Obu. I'm coming to you."

"Dor, we need brothers! The meat machines are coagulating. I *know this*."

"I'm calling the shield."

"It's dangerous! The meat senses them. We need regular brothers!"

"I'll call them."

Tryv got out and set about changing the first tire. A Lincoln Navigator with a damaged fender passed and stopped about ten meters ahead. Obu lowered the tinted window. A white highway police Toyota with a blinking light and a siren drove up to the Mercedes. An overweight lieutenant with a puffy, unhappy face and an unlit cigarette in his plump hand saluted them.

"Now that's the good life."

Continuing to turn the jack, Tryv lifted his head.

"Hello."

"Two at the same time? Wow! As they say, shit happens, even to a Mercedes. Need some help?"

"We'll manage on our own, Lieutenant," replied Merog instead of Tryv, lowering the dark window and holding his gun at the ready. "We have to deal with a shitload of this stuff nowadays!"

Obu, Merog, and Tryv laughed.

"You got that right." The lieutenant grinned; patting his pockets, he yawned nervously. "Damn, where did I put it ... in the car as usual ..."

He turned to shout to his partner, but Merog held a lighter out the window.

"Officer ..."

"Uh-huh." The lieutenant leaned over and lit his cigarette. "Thanks. Well then, good luck."

"You too."

The lieutenant, puffing on his cigarette, got into the Toyota and drove off.

Merog closed his eyes for a moment and exhaled with relief.

"I have to rely on the Ice."

"The Ice—is our altar. It provides balance. And the Light provides energy," Obu spoke out.

"The Light provides energy," Merog repeated, and closed his eyes again.

Tryv changed the tires.

The Mercedes drove on. Merog again opened the suitcase and carefully held the hand of the sleeping boy.

"The meat is strong. But there are limits to its strength. Meat is dangerous, brother Merog. But it doesn't have any altar," said Obu.

"Meat only craves and coagulates," Tryv added, wiping his hands with a damp cloth.

"Because it senses that the end is near."

"Because it feels that its end is near," added Merog, carefully squeezing the boy's senseless, cool fingers.

The Mercedes turned onto Kiev Highway toward Vnukovo Airport.

The Lesser Circle of Hope

MY HEART feels the presence of brothers.

And I leave my dream. Which I see constantly in recent years. A dream that helps me to sleep on the planet Earth. My *shining* dream. The dream that is always with me:

We are finally together, all, all, all of us down to the very last, we are nearing the Place, it's already quite close, I see it, it emerges from the fog, it's inevitable, it is so desired and unavoidable that I'm afraid I'll lose consciousness at the last moment, and I hold, hold, hold on to the brothers and sisters, my arms embrace them, I am among them, in their dear, intimate crowd, I press close to them, I touch their bodies, which will soon dissolve into the Light, very soon; which will dissolve together with me, dissolve forever. I look into their faces, dear, close faces that have surrounded me all these decades, helping us to keep moving toward our goal; I hear the beating of their hearts, the last blows of these meat motors hiding the Light, the Light intrinsic to us, the Light that we will all soon become, the Primordial Light. The Light that does not allow us to perish on the frightful planet Earth, the Light that is very, very, very close.

Brother Mokho's hand touches my face. I *recognize* and *recall*.

And my body wakes up. I open my eyes. Brother Mokho and sister Tbo are standing at the head of my bed. They are excited. And I immediately *understand* why. They don't have to speak any wretched, pitiful, Earth words: their hearts are shining *with joy*. My heart *quivers with the expectation of joy*. I listen to their hearts. My heart and I understand just what kind of joy. It is much older and stronger than the hearts of the brothers. But it hasn't lost its ability *to quiver innocently with expectation*. My heart *trembles*. Just as it did back then, in the Alps, when I was a young girl. My chest bled. The Ice hammer shook it and awakened my young heart. The old man Bro *touched* my heart. He touched it so that it *began to tremble with the sweet expectation of the Light*.

I move my fingers. And lift my thin arms. I stretch them out to the brothers. My hands shake. Leaning over, Mokho and Tbo clasp my palms. And place them on their chests.

My heart *greets* their hearts.

Mokho and Tbo take the blanket off my body. It is woven from mountain grasses that extend the life of the flesh. My old body meets the air of Earth. This air is bitter and destructive.

Brothers Mef and Por, who help me every morning, enter. Their bodies are young and muscular. They exude strength and calm. The brothers' strong hands lift my body. It is gaunt from earthly life. Withered from heart knowledge. Drained by the *absence* of the Gift of Search. A gift that only Bro and Fer possessed. A gift that allows *all to be found at once*. A gift that would not reveal itself to *just* me for these sixty years. Which I so *agonizingly* craved all my *true* life. For which my heart prayed *incessantly*. For which my brain raged. For which my blood boiled. For which my bones throbbed.

The brothers' hands carry me into a spacious stone room. A blue basin awaits me. The brothers carefully place my feeble body in the warm basin. It fills with fresh cow's milk. The milk gurgles and foams. It swallows my body. The brothers' voices sound in the room. Each of them says something quietly. And each of them *remembers* my heart. Dozens, hundreds of voices join in an invisible din under the marble cupola. They are always with me. I *listen* to them. The voices ring. Every morning begins with this music for me.

I close my eyes.

And hang in space.

And see all of *ours*.

At this moment there are 21,368.

Including me—21,369.

In the world of meat machines the remaining 1,631 are being found. Their voices can't be heard in the choir. I cannot *see* their hearts. They still await their awakening. They await their encounter with the Ice hammer. They wait for us.

Quickly giving me its warmth, the fresh milk leaves the basin. Mef and Por lift me. They wrap me in a sheet woven from choice linen. They sit down on two blue stones. The brothers' fingers help my weak body rid itself of the reprocessed food of Earth. Then they wash me under an icy stream of mountain water. The crystal stream wakes me up. It retains the memory of the calm mountains.

And I begin to live.

Mef and Por carry me to the wardrobe. I sit on warm marble. I choose the dress for the day. My dresses are in various shades: from pale sky blue to dark royal blue. But the dresses are all identical.

I know with my heart that today is a special day. I choose a silk dress of the purest sky blue. Sister Vikhe combs my completely gray, thinning hair with a turquoise comb. Sisters Niuz and Pe rub my body with sesame oil. Supported by the sisters' arms, I stand up. And the dress envelops me. The sisters hold me under the arms. They lead me to a small, spherical room. It was carved from purple mountain stone. Water drips here, and there is a chalice of tea made from the grasses of the taiga waiting for me. It gives strength to my old body. In the mornings I stay in this room for 23 minutes. Sipping tea slowly, *I release* my heart. And concentrate with my mind. The purple sphere has forced me to remember the merciless world of Earth. I remember the language of meat machines, their customs and desires. Their gloomy work rises in me. It prepares me for further struggle.

After the purple sphere I begin work.

But today is a very special day. And a *special* job is imminent. The world of meat machines does not interest me. I walk into the Dining Hall. It is spacious and white. The windows are open. The sound of the tide reaches the Hall from the shore. The ocean we created beats nearby. Its roar reminds us of the Great Mistake. In the middle of the Dining Hall is a large round table made of lilac-colored stone. The Middle Circle fits around this table: 230 brothers and sisters.

I sit down at the table. Fruits and vegetables lie on it. Each morning all the brothers and sisters living with me in the house on the island sit around this table. Today they are here as well. I *see* their hearts.

Ga, Noro, Ret, Mokho, Tbo, Mef, Por, Vikhe, Niuz, Pe, Shey, Forum, Das, Ruch, Bi, O, Vu, Stam, On, Ut, Ze, and Iugom sit with me. But not to begin the meal as usual. They want to tell me something very important. They know what my heart *sweetly* guesses. About which I have dreamed again these last years. Which has *grown* in premonition. Which beats in the heart like a wave of light. And which we all craved deeply.

In the Dining Hall we all usually speak only in earthly language. So that our hearts are calm during the consumption of food. But this morning we don't think about food. Brother Ga, my main assistant in this house, breaks the silence.

"Khram, he is already with the brothers."

"I *know* this," I answer, restraining my heart.

"The meat is coagulating." Sister Shey shudders. "The meat is resisting the Brotherhood."

"I *know*."

"The meat is creating difficulties." Forum looks *straight* at me.

"I *know*," I replied, coping with a heart *flash*.

"The Brotherhood is fighting for him," said Brother Vu. "He is on his way to us."

"I *know*."

"A shield protects him."

"I *know*."

"If the Light moves the meat aside, he will be with us here this evening," said sister Ze.

She isn't able to restrain herself. Her heart *flares*.

"I *know!*" I reply, blazing in response.

My powerful heart *flares*. It violates the strict order of the house.

We *speak* with our hearts. We have been waiting too long. And many times our anticipation has come to naught. But this time, too, the hearts of all the inhabitants of the house only *believe*. But I—*know*! Because I *wanted it to be so*! I wanted *desperately* to know that this time everything would come true, would fall into place, would be established, everything would come together, come together, be launched, would merge: that the meat curtain would open, that the remaining, the lost, would be acquired, that the Great Circle would be closed. And hearts would shine. And muscle fibers would disintegrate. And bones would crack. And the brain would crumble. The chain of suffering would snap. And the Light would disperse, spreading atomic dust across the Universe.

The heart *didn't know* anything else before.

The heart *doesn't know* anything else now.

The heart *speaks* of what is most important.

We grow still around the round table.

Our hearts *blaze*.

Secret words *radiate. They flow* with the Primordial Light. There are exactly 23 of us in the house now. The Lesser Circle. The smallest of all. There are the Middle (230) and the Great (2,300), convened by the brothers at fateful moments. These are Circles of Support. And Decision. But today, the day of *anticipation*, there is a Lesser Circle. This is a Circle of Hope. Eight times we have *waited*. And our hope was not meant to be. The frightful world of Earth took the Most Important Hope away from us eight times.

Today we *hope* for the ninth time. With the Lesser Circle of Hope. By assembling it, we *know* that another six Lesser Circles have been formed by the Brotherhood. They are far away from here. The ocean divides us. In different countries six Lesser Circles have joined together. The brothers *feel* us. Their hearts *burn* with hope. I *see* all these Circles with my heart. Each of them.

I *speak* with them.

Forty-eight Earth minutes.

Our hearts *calm down*. Our hands separate. I open my mouth and with a full chest I exhale the bitter air of the ocean. The air above the Great Mistake. Which demands correction.

The brothers and sisters watch me.
Their hearts *listen carefully*.
"We must be *prepared*," I whisper.
Their hearts *understand*.

Hearts of Three

AT THE eleventh kilometer of the Kiev Highway, a black Geländewagen with blue flashing lights, followed by a Jeep with bodyguards,
began to pass the Mercedes driven by Obu.

Obu, Tryv, and Merog cried out joyfully.

"It's Uf!" Merog shouted and *flared*. "Thank the Light! The shield
is with us!"

"The Light is with us!" declared Tryv and Obu.

"The Light is with us!" Obu repeated joyfully, falling in behind
the Jeep.

The cortege of three black cars sped on.

They turned off at Vnukovo, then proceeded toward the airport,
passing the main terminal and arriving at the one for private airplanes. Merog quickly got out of the Mercedes with the blue suitcase.
He relinquished it to two *eager* pairs of hands in the Geländewagen.
One of the pairs he couldn't help but recognize—decisive, white,
with golden hairs on wide wrists and small pinkish nails.

"Uf!" Merog sighed, and his heart *flared* with delight.

The suitcase disappeared into the depths of the Geländewagen,
the door with tinted glass closed, and the car drove up to the terminal
gate. Following the car with an excited gaze, Merog placed his hands
on his breast. His lips trembled and his legs felt weak. He fell on his
knees.

"Uf…"

Obu and Tryv jumped out of the Mercedes, ran over, and began to
lift Merog. A policeman strolling past the terminal spoke up.

"What happened?"

Obu and Tryv lifted Merog to his feet.

"It's his heart," Obu said to the policeman.

"Uf," said Merog, and with a moan he inhaled.

Obu and Tryv led him, swaying, to the car.

"There's a shitload of work, it got to him," Obu said, curling his lip and making a wry face, and going around the policeman, who was staring at them.

"Well, should I . . . you want me to call the airport doctor?" the policeman asked, pulling his walkie-talkie out of a pocket.

"Thanks, pal, but we've got everything we need," Tryv answered.

They sat Merog down in the Mercedes; Obu turned the car around and they drove off.

After a cursory examination of documents at the swing gate, the Geländewagen drove out toward the aerodrome. The security Jeep followed it. The vehicles pulled up to a small jet. The guards got out and surrounded the Geländewagen. Uf and Bork stepped out. Uf carried a briefcase, Bork the suitcase. One of the guards reached for the suitcase, but Bork shook his head.

"No, I'll carry it myself."

Uf shook hands with the head of the security guards, who in turn wished them a safe trip. The airplane's hatch opened and the stairs were lowered. A pretty blue-eyed stewardess in a blue uniform and blue gloves stood at the top of the hatch and smiled warmly. Uf climbed the steps first, shook the stewardess's hand, entered, and tossed the briefcase on a seat. Following him, Bork carried the suitcase and set it down in the cabin. Two pilots came out of the cabin, greeted Uf, and reported on flight preparations. Uf greeted them with a few formalities, and they went back into the cabin. The pilots weren't Brothers of the Light. The stewardess, sister No, locked the door to the cabin. Bork and Uf placed the suitcase on the table and opened it. The boy slept. Bork grew terribly pale, shuddered, and *flared*. His lips trembled, he went down on his knees near the suitcase, grabbed the rug with his hands, dug into it, and squeezed, breaking his nails. A deep moan escaped his lips. Sister No, on seeing the boy, covered her face with her elegant fingers.

Uf remained calm. His powerful heart, which had accomplished many great feats in the name of the Light, obeyed him. He carefully uncovered the boy, laid him down more comfortably, sat in a chair, and placed a hand on Bork's shuddering blond head. And quickly *helped* with his heart. Bork's cheeks grew rosier, his eyes shut partway, and his head hung powerlessly on his chest.

"The Light is with us," declared Uf, covering his small white eyelashes.

"The Light . . . Light . . . L-l-l-l-l . . ." Bork babbled almost inaudibly, and with a moan fell flat on his back.

Shaking off her stupor, No leaned over Bork.

"His heart is tired of waiting," said Uf.

"Help me," asked No. "I can't manage."

Uf came closer, took Bork by one arm; No took the other. Their hearts *helped* Bork's heart. He opened his eyes. They raised him and sat him in a chair.

"The Light will soon rid you of that body," said Uf, and he touched Bork's pale, perspiring face with his fingertips.

Bork kept staring at the boy. Pushing Uf's hand away, he wanted to get up. But Uf held him back.

"Rely on the Ice."

With a moan, Bork closed his eyes. His whole body shuddered. He took Uf's hand and held on to it as though it were an *anchor*, constantly glancing at the boy sleeping in the suitcase.

"Restrain yourself," Uf said.

And he felt *strong* hearts approaching and looked through the window: a black Mercedes 600 with government license plates accompanied by a police Audi was approaching the airplane.

"Brothers! Thank the Light!" No pressed Uf's hand to her chest, stood up, and rushed to the exit.

Soon brothers Odo and Efep entered the cabin. Odo—large, heavy, gray-haired, blue-eyed, and long-bearded—was arrayed in a dark-purple cassock. On his chest hung a cross and the encolpion of a metropolitan of the Orthodox church, while his plump white hand clutched a pastoral staff. Efep had grayish-blue eyes. He was short, sported a buzz cut of grayish hair, white mustache, and neatly trimmed beard. He was dressed in a light-gray suit with the three-color pin of a deputy of the Russian Federation State Duma on his lapel.

Closing the door of the cabin after them, No stood at the door.

On entering, the brothers halted. Their eyes fixed on the boy sleeping in the suitcase. Odo handed the staff to No and, without taking his eyes off the boy, slowly sat on the floor in front of the suitcase, his cassock rustling. Efep stood still; his wall eyes gazed without blinking.

Uf stepped toward them. He held out his hands.

Efep held out his. Odo slowly reached out with his own powerful hands. The three brothers joined hands and formed a circle over the sleeping boy. They closed their eyes.

Bork in the armchair and No, standing with the staff at the door, froze.

After a few minutes, a slight shiver ran across the brothers' shoulders. Their hands unclasped.

"Yes!" said Odo in his deep bass voice, opening his eyes.

"Yes," whispered Efep, exhaling with relief.

"Yes," said Uf clearly.

Bork sobbed and clenched his teeth, writhing from joy in his chair. Tossing aside the staff, sister No rushed to Bork and, trembling, embraced him.

Odo, Efep, and Uf paid no attention to them.

"I was certain. But not entirely," Uf said.

"Even Khram doesn't *see* sleeping hearts," muttered Efep, blinking rapidly.

"Khram *knows* but doesn't *see*," Odo murmured. "Only the Great Circle is capable of *seeing*."

"Only if the sleeping meat is in the center of the Great Circle," Efep objected.

"The Great Circle no longer has need of sleeping meat." Uf sighed sharply.

"The sleeping meat is here," Odo said in his deep voice, picking up the staff from the floor and rising from his knees, stroking his beard, as was his habit.

"The meat will awaken." Efep carefully brought his face close to the boy's face.

"The meat will become Light!" Odo cried, shaking his gray mane.

Bork and No sobbed.

"Rely on the Ice!" roared Odo, striking the floor with his staff.

Bork and No sniffled and grew quiet.

"Brother, our *hearts* envy you." Efep took Uf by the hand. "You are flying with him."

"You will see Khram. You will help with the *meeting*!" Odo continued.

"You will close the Great Circle!" Efep squeezed Uf's hand hard.

"You cannot fly with me," said Uf, *supporting* with his heart.

"We *know*," Odo answered.

"We *know*," Efep calmed himself and *calmed* Uf.

"I also *know* this," Uf said with a tortured smile, and his small, reddish eyelashes closed. "Your place is here. The meat is coagulating."

"We will *restrain it*!" Odo roared with certainty.

The boy moaned in his sleep. Everyone, except Uf, was on guard.

"He needs to sleep another four hours," said Uf. "It's time, brothers."

Odo and Efep *flared* briefly: "Uf! No! Bork!"

"Odo! Efep!" Those remaining *flared* in response.

Efep was the first to leave the cabin. Odo cast a grave look at the sleeping boy, *subdued* his heart flare, knocked his staff on the floor, and left, his cassock rustling.

Bork, Uf, and No took the diapers off the boy, dressed him in blue shorts and a blue T-shirt with a large crimson strawberry on it. They put him in a chair to sleep.

Uf pressed the button to call the pilot. There was a delicate knock on the door of the cabin. Sister No opened it. The thin, well-built, black-haired, brown-eyed pilot entered. Uf shook his hand. The pilot glanced at the sleeping boy, and quickly turned his eyes to Uf.

"Are we ready?"

"Yes," Uf nodded.

"I'll call the border guards," said the pilot, and left.

Soon a green border-guard Lada drove up to the airplane. A young lieutenant and a middle-aged captain came on board and began to check all the passports and baggage. The boy was written in Uf's passport as his son.

"Too much soccer, eh?" said the lieutenant, glancing at the sleeping boy, and stamping the passport with the word EXIT.

"If only!" Uf said, shaking his head sadly as he took his passport back. "Computer games. And it's impossible to get him away from them."

"At age six? Not bad!" said the lieutenant approvingly, nodding his head.

"And where are we going with all these computers?" the round-faced customs officer said ingratiatingly, looking Uf in the eyes.

"To the Other World," Uf answered seriously.

Bork's and No's hearts shuddered *sweetly*. The customs officer lingered a moment and felt sad; he nodded goodbye and headed for the exit.

"*Bon voyage*," smiled the lieutenant.

"*Bon rester*," Uf replied.

The officers left. The hatch closed. The engines began to hum and the plane moved out onto the runway.

"When he wakes up, we'll be flying," Uf said, fastening the boy's seat belt, sitting in a nearby seat and fastening his own. "Another small dose will be needed. But not deep sleep. There's a border there, too."

"I'll pick out what we need," said No.

The jet took off.

Uf looked out the window at the Country of Ice disappearing below and leaned his strong, strawberry-blond head against the clean white headrest of the chair.

"*Gloria Luci!*"

The Arsenal

ON JULY 7, at 4:57 a.m. local time, the freight train traveling the Ust–Ilimsk–St. Petersburg–Helsinki route crossed the border of Finland and began to brake for the customs house. The first slanting rays of the rising sun slipped along two blue locomotives coupled together and eighteen grayish-white refrigerator freight cars painted with huge blue signs saying ICE. As soon as the train stopped, a junior lieutenant of the customs service and two policemen with a German shepherd approached the locomotives. The blue door of the second one opened, and a tall, well-proportioned blond in a light-blue summer suit and white-and-blue tie, wearing a silverish ICE Corporation tie-pin, walked down the steel stairs. In his hand he held a blue briefcase.

"Good morning," the blond said cheerfully in Finnish, and smiled.

"Goot murning," the short, sharp-nosed customs officer with a thin mustache answered, not very cheerfully.

The blond handed him his passport and the customs officer quickly found the stamp with a mark denoting the border crossing; he returned the passport, turned around, and walked over to the white customs building. The blond walked vigorously along with him, while the policemen remained near the train.

"Judging by the burning smell, you're having a dry summer too?" the blond said in excellent Finnish.

"Yeah. But that's your peat swamps burning," the customs official answered in a grumpy voice.

They entered the building and walked up to the second floor. The Finn opened the door into a small office. The blond entered. The customs officer closed the door behind him and remained in the hallway. A corpulent, balding captain sat at the customs desk drinking coffee while he leafed through papers.

"Hello, Mr. Lapponen."

"Nikolai! Hello there!" The captain smiled, offering his plump, strong hand. "Long time no see!"

"The last two trains came through in the daytime. Mr. Tyrsa handled them," the blond said, shaking the outstretched hand.

"That's right, yes, yes." The captain looked at the blond man and smiled. "You're always in shape, full of energy. It's nice to see."

"Thank you." The blond clicked the lock of the briefcase, opened it, and handed over a package of documents.

Lapponen took them, put on his narrow, gold-framed glasses, and thumbed through the documents.

"Eighteen as usual?"

"Eighteen."

The blond took a small Ice hammer, as long as his fingers, with a piece of mountain crystal instead of a piece of Ice, and placed it on the documents.

"What's that?" said Lapponen, raising his eyebrows.

"The company ICE is turning ten this year."

"Ah!" Lapponen took the souvenir. "And here I was, thinking you were trying to bribe me."

They both laughed.

"Ten years!" Lapponen spun the tiny hammer. "Like Shumakher? Time flies, and we're just standing here blabbing away. All right then, let's take a look."

He stood and picked up the folder.

"Now they have to look at every car. And I'm required to be present. It's the times, you know."

"I know."

"The law is the law."

"The law makes us human," said the blond.

Lapponen grew serious, and sighed. "Well put, Nikolai. If only all Russians understood that."

They walked over to the train. The customs inspection began. In each refrigerator car the Ice was sawed into identical metrical cubes. The last car was only one-third full.

"Didn't have enough ice in Siberia, is that it?" Lapponen laughed and stamped the customs statement.

"They didn't make the loading date," the blond said, taking the documents and putting them in his briefcase.

Lapponen held out his hand. "Have a good trip, Nikolai."

"Have a good stay, Mr. Lapponen," said the blond, and shook his hand.

The customs officers went back into the building, the blond to the head of the train. He climbed the rungs of the locomotive and closed the door after him. A green light shone down the tracks; the train started up and began to crawl along slowly. The blond opened the door of the salon. The salon was delicately illuminated by a soft blue light; it was decorated in a high-tech style, with soft lilac-gray furniture, a transparent bar, and four small sleeping compartments. The second driver dozed in an armchair; behind him, dishes clinked in the hands of a strapping blond woman, the conductor.

"That's it," said the blond man as he sat down in an armchair and placed his briefcase on a glass shelf.

"It takes so long now," said the strawberry-haired engine driver, stretching as he woke up.

"Times have changed for the meat." The blond yawned, taking off his jacket and placing it on a hanger. "Mir, give me—"

"Some gray tea," the conductor finished his sentence, her dark-blue eyes glancing at him.

"That's right. And add four plums."

The attendant did as asked and brought him a tray. "You didn't sleep at all, Lavu."

"Sleep is with me," he answered and took a bite of plum.

The attendant sat down near him, put her head on his lap, and fell asleep immediately.

Lavu ate the plums and drank the grayish infusion. He closed his eyes. The second engineer followed his example.

The train gained speed and passed through the forest.

Forty-eight minutes later it slowed down, switched off the main tracks, and crawled slowly through a dense forest of fir trees. Soon the gentle slope of a hill and huge silver-colored gates with the blue sign ICE could be seen through the forest. The train moved up to the gates and gave a signal. The gates began to open.

The sleepers in the salon woke up.

"Thanks be to the Light," declared Lavu.

The attendant and the second engineer squeezed his hands.

The train passed through the gates and into a dark tunnel leading underground. But it wasn't dark for long. Not far ahead, light cut through the darkness and on both sides narrow platforms with smooth, shining blue-and-white walls were visible.

The train stopped.

A large group of guards in blue uniforms immediately appeared, and workers in white coveralls and helmets arrived on hydraulic loaders. Lavu, briefcase in hand, was the first to step out onto the platform;

ignoring everyone, he headed at a fast pace for a glass elevator in the middle of it. He took out an electronic key and placed it in a three-sided recess. The elevator doors opened soundlessly, and Lavu entered. The doors closed, and the elevator began its ascent. It stopped quickly. Lavu stepped out and found himself in front of a massive steel door monitored by a video camera. The door had another three-sided recess for an electronic key. He placed the key in it. The doors opened onto a large, bright, greenish-blue, completely empty hall with a huge mosaic of the ICE Corporation logo covering the entire floor: two crossed Ice hammers against a flaming crimson heart. On the heart stood a thin, gray-haired old man dressed in white, with a white, neatly trimmed beard. His yellowish-blue eyes regarded Lavu attentively. Lavu placed the briefcase on the marble floor.

"Shua!"

"Lavu!"

They embraced. The old man was far *wiser* in heart. Therefore, knowing what a long journey Lavu had had, he *restrained* his heart, allowing it only a short, gentle *flare*—a brotherly greeting.

Lavu froze in the old man's embrace with relief: Shua's heart always gave him an *unearthly* peace.

The old man was the first to break the embrace; his wrinkled but firm hand touched Lavu's face. In American-accented English he said, "The Light is with us."

"The Light is in your heart, brother Shua," said Lavu, regaining consciousness.

The old man looked straight at Lavu's young face as though seeing him for the first time. He had retained the ability to *rejoice* at meeting every brother as if for the first time, as though discovering a close and intimate heart once again. This gave the old man *enormous* strength. Shua's heart *could see* farther and deeper than many Brothers of the Light.

"You are tired after your trip," Shua continued, taking Lavu by the hand. "Let's go."

Lavu took a step, but turned around, looking at the blue briefcase he had left on the floor. It stood right on one of the huge mosaic Ice hammers, its color blending with the Ice and almost entirely disappearing.

"It's not necessary now," Shua smiled. "No one needs it anymore."

They left the hall and entered Shua's apartment right away. Here everything was simple and functional; all the rooms were made of stone in cold hues. Shua led Lavu into the room of Peace. Lavu was met by brothers Kdo and Ai, who greeted him with a heart embrace, undressed him, rubbed him with oils, placed him in a labradorite bathtub with herbal infusions, and then drew back. Shua gave him a bowl of berry tea.

Lavu took a swallow of the tea from the bowl, and lay back on the stone ledge. "I don't yet believe it," he said. "My heart *knows*, but my reason doesn't want to believe."

"Your reason is sometimes stronger than your heart," the old man replied.

"Yes. And it upsets me."

"Don't be upset. You brain has accomplished a great deal for the Brotherhood."

"Thank the Light."

"Thank the Light," the old man repeated.

Silence hung in the room. Lavu took another sip, and licked his lips. "What should I do now?"

"Today you will fly to Khram. She requires help. It will also help your heart."

Lavu didn't answer. He drank the tea slowly and silently. All the while the old man sat immobile, some distance away. Finally Lavu placed the empty bowl on the wide edge of the tub, stood up, and stepped out of the greenish water. The old man handed him a long robe and helped him to put it on. They went into the dining room. Here six large candles were burning, and there was a round table with fruits. Shua took a bunch of dark-blue grapes, Lavu chose a peach. They ate silently until they were full.

"Why is Khram calling me?" asked Lavu.

"She *is meeting* you," Shua answered.

Lavu's heart *throbbed*. And *understood*. He trembled.

"She needs a Circle." Lavu's lips moved, his voice barely audible.

"She needs a strong Circle," Shua echoed. "A Circle of those who *know* the Ice. Now you will be with her. Until the end."

"But you are stronger in heart than I am. Why aren't you with her?"

"I cannot leave the Arsenal. I am *holding it* with my heart."

Lavu *understood*.

Shua's yellowish-blue eyes watched attentively. His heart *helped* Lavu to recall Khram. He had seen her twice. But had only spoken with her heart once. Lavu was *shocked* by this heart. It *knew* without barriers.

"When do I fly out?" he asked.

"In four and a half hours."

Lavu controlled his shaking fingers, inhaled and exhaled.

"May I see the Arsenal for the last time?"

"Of course. We *are supposed to* go there."

"Now. Right this minute!"

"Not now, brother Lavu. Right this minute your heart needs some deep sleep in my bedroom. You are overwrought. And you're losing your balance. Only the strong in heart enter the Arsenal."

"I agree," said Lavu, calming down.

Two hours and ten minutes later they entered the elevator. Lavu had rested on Shua's spacious bed, covered with white moss, and he looked cheerful and calm. He was wearing the same light-blue summer suit and a fresh white shirt. The elevator went down. When it stopped, large Chinese guards—with automatics—appeared before the door. Passing by them, Shua placed his palm to a blinking square. The door slid to one side. They entered the large Sawing and Grinding Workshop. Here several dozen young Chinese were at work. Their strong hands placed a metric cube of Ice onto a slowly moving conveyor, sawed it into the necessary number of rectangles, ground them down, drilled a cavity in them, polished them, and sent the readymade Ice hammer heads on their way down the conveyor belt to the Assembly Shop. Shua and Lavu moved between the rows of workers. The Chinese, paying no attention to them, went about their work intently and deftly. Their swift hands flashed by in a blur, trying to work rapidly so the Ice had no time to melt: a strict penalty was meted out for each drop. Shua and Lavu made their way slowly through the entire workshop. Beyond it was the Hides Workshop, where more young Chinese cut narrow strips from the hides of animals who had died a natural death and placed them on the conveyor belt. Next was the Handle Workshop, where handles of the necessary width and length were planed from oak branches. The two Brothers of the Light passed through this workshop as well and entered the Assembly Shop. It was the largest of the four. Entering it, Lavu stopped and closed his eyes. Shua took him carefully by the shoulders, *helped* him to overcome his fear. Lavu opened his eyes.

In this workshop, fifty-four Chinese were assembling Ice hammers. It was cold and the Chinese worked in white gloves, hats with earflaps, and blue padded cotton coats. The walls and the ceiling were decorated with traditional Chinese landscape paintings. Cold air and soothing Chinese music poured from the ceiling. The finished Ice hammers were placed onto glass conveyor shelves that descended vertically. Lavu walked over to the conveyor and stopped. His eyes followed the hammers floating downward; his heart *greeted and bade them farewell*. Each of them. Shua *understood* Lavu's mood. The artificial light, indistinguishable from daylight, glinted off the polished hammers, sparkled on their curves, and flowed into their cavities. The Ice hammers slowly and implacably disappeared from sight.

"The power of the Ice . . ." Lavu's pale lips declared.

"Will be with us." Shua held his elbows from behind.

Lavu couldn't tear himself away from the mesmerizing spectacle of the hammers floating down. His heart *flared*.

But Shua *supported* him: the old man's strong hands held Lavu, his heart *directed* him, his lips whispered, "Downstairs!"

They walked to the doors of the elevator. It took them farther down. And once again they were met by guards with automatics: the Chinese guards' eyes met theirs with indifference. To open the lowest door, Shua had not only to use his palm, but a ray of light scanned the cornea of his eye and sensitive detectors listened as he said, "Brother Shua, keeper of the Arsenal."

Half-meter-thick steel doors opened silently. And right after them a new group of guards appeared, dressed completely in white, wearing gas masks, and carrying white automatics in white hands. They guarded the last door—a small round one made of extra-strength steel. The password of the day was the Chinese word for acorn: *"Xian xu go!"*

On hearing the password, the guards stepped aside and turned away. Shua unbuttoned the top button of his shirt, took out a platinum key that always hung around his neck, put it in an inconspicuous opening, and turned it. Invisible ice bells rang out, and the massive door moved inward and to the left. Shua and Lavu stepped through the opening. The ice sounded once again and the door shut back in place.

Before them the Arsenal of the Brotherhood of the Light was spread out.

An enormous underground cave, narrow but endlessly long, preserved hundreds of thousands of Ice hammers lying in even rows in glass cells lit from below. A low, arched ceiling hung over the sleeping Arsenal of the Brotherhood. The white marble floor tiles maintained an ideal cleanliness. Rows of glass cells were covered in hoarfrost: the constant cold preserved the precious Ice. There were no people here: only two robots, like indefatigable ants, shuttled across a monorail above the sleeping hammers, keeping track of and preserving their icy rest. A bit farther on, a glass conveyor silently filled the Arsenal with hammers newly manufactured by swift Chinese hands; the new hammers floated overhead in an endless, menacing, sparkling train, and merged into the rows of sleeping weapons.

Lavu took one step, a second, a third. Shua stood still, *letting go* of Lavu with his heart.

"The Ice . . ." Lavu's lips spoke.

His fingers touched the glass cells and quivered. Lavu's heart *quivered*. Shua came up behind him.

"There's no more Ice *there*," Lavu murmured. "Today I accompanied the last train."

"Now the only Ice is here," Shua answered calmly, *not helping* Lavu with his heart.

"Only here," said Lavu

"Only here," Shua repeated firmly.

Lavu's heart *struggled*. But Shua stubbornly continued *not to help*.

Lavu sank to the floor. He exhaled. And after a long pause he said, "It's hard for me."

Shua went over to him.

"It's difficult for you to believe. And *understand*."

"Yes."

"Rely on the Ice."

"I'm *trying*. Even though there's no more Ice *there*. It's hard for me." Lavu's voice trembled.

"The Ice is here"—Shua lowered his hands on Lavu's shoulders—"and it will be with us until the very end. And there is enough for everyone. I *know* this. And you, too, brother Lavu, *must* know this."

Lavu sat, immobile, staring at the marble tile of the floor.

"You *must* know this," Shua repeated, *without helping* with his heart.

And Lavu's heart *dealt with it* by itself. "I *know*."

He rose easily. His heart had *calmed down*.

"Who will make the last hammer?" he asked calmly.

"It has already been prepared."

"By whom?"

"By me. We came down here for it."

Lavu *understood*.

Shua pushed a blue button on one of the cells. The glass screen slid to the side. Shua picked up the Ice hammer, quickly touched it to his breast; his heart instantly *flared*, and he handed the hammer to Lavu.

"You know whom it must awaken."

Lavu took the hammer. He touched it to his breast, and *flared*.

"I know."

"You *not only* know," Shua said with certainty, *helping Lavu*.

"I... know..." Lavu said tensely. And suddenly he smiled joyously. "I *know and believe!*"

Shua embraced him forcefully. The Ice hammer touched Lavu's face. Lavu squeezed the wooden handle of the hammer. And cried out. His pale-blue eyes instantly filled with tears: his heart *knew and believed*.

"Let us go. I will *say farewell to you*," said Shua.

Gorn

KHRAM sat in her gold armchair on the pier and watched the ocean. That was the way she always *met*.

The northwest wind hadn't subsided as sunset approached, and the waves, breaking and spraying the dock, crawled along the rose-colored marble toward Khram's chair, licking at her bare, thin, weak feet. Khram's clear, large eyes, a pale blue that was almost washed out, gazed intently at the horizon, where the sun's disk, hidden behind straw-colored clouds, touched the ocean. Next to Khram sat brothers Mef and Por, offering up their muscular, bronzed bodies to the humid wind. The other brothers and sisters *waited* in the house, each in his or her place.

Khram's heart *jolted*.

"They're already here!" her lips whispered.

And, leaning her bony arms on the smooth golden armrests, she began to rise. Mef and Por jumped up and held her.

"Already!" she repeated, and, like a child, she smiled joyously, revealing her old, yellowed teeth.

Mef and Por stared at the ocean horizon: it was empty as before. But Khram's heart could not be mistaken: a minute passed, another, a third, and to the left of the lackluster, drowning solar disk, a point appeared.

It was immediately noticed from the house: joyous cries rang out.

"The meat did not prevail!" Khram's thin fingers squeezed the brothers' wide wrists.

Brothers and sisters ran down a stairway leading from the house to the piers.

The white craft drew nearer.

Khram moved toward it, but her bare, wet feet had reached the edge of the pier. The brothers held her back. Her body quivered; her heart *blazed*.

"Already here!" Khram gave a senile, demented screech and thrashed in the brothers' arms.

Her thin body twisted, foam frothed on her wrinkled lips. Brothers and sisters ran over, embraced her, fell to their knees.

"Rely on the Ice!" Ga *helped* with his heart.

Others began *to help* right away, restraining their own wails and sobs. But Khram's heart didn't *want* to rely on the Ice: her deformed fingers dug into the arms and faces of the brothers, her frail body thrashed and writhed, foamy spittle flew out of her mouth as she gave a hoarse howl: "Heee-eee-rrre! Hee-eee-rrre!"

For the first time in many long decades of constant, incessant expectation, the heart of the oldest and strongest member of the Brotherhood *could not handle* what had been achieved. Her heart *had lost its bearings*. Mighty and wise, it suddenly became young and inexperienced, as though the blow of the Ice hammer had awoken it only yesterday. Khram's heart *quivered* powerlessly.

The Brotherhood felt this.

They picked Khram up, surrounded her, pressed her to their bodies. The hearts surrounding her *flared*. Khram writhed. Dozens of hands lifted her to the sky, now sparkling with the first stars.

"Rely on the Ice!" they said with their lips and hearts.

Khram writhed.

And then, as though arriving from the approaching boat, a huge wave rolled over the edge of the dock and doused the crowd with white, salty foam as they fought for the *bewildered* heart. Khram grew quiet and fell into a deep faint. Por carefully took her in his powerful arms. Khram's heart relied on the Ice, finally giving her peace.

The craft grew closer.

Everyone watched it.

Its white, sharply tapered hull parted the waves effortlessly. It made a half circle and moored at the dock. Uf stood on the deck with the sleeping boy in his arms. Everyone standing on the pier shuddered, but held back their shouts and cries. The boat rocked on the waves. The rope was thrown out and secured; the gangway was lowered.

Uf walked down onto the pier with the boy in his arms. After him came Lavu carrying a metal trunk, and then Bork.

The brothers and sisters parted silently. Uf took several steps across the wet marble. His face was tense and immobile, like a mask.

But his gray-blue eyes shone. And he restrained his powerful heart *as best as he could*. Everyone *felt* this. And they also restrained their hearts. Uf saw Khram, unconscious, in Por's arms.

"What happened to her?" he asked.

"She *was waiting*," answered Por.

Uf *understood*.

"Let's go in the house," he said, and started up the stairway.

Por followed. The rest came after them. The ocean wind blew at their backs, ruffling their clothes, blowing the long white hair of the unconscious Khram.

Uf carried the boy into the house, passed by the small terrace and the agate hallway, and entered the Hall of Awakening. Round, full of light, greenish-blue, and spacious, it served as a place for heart conversation. In this hall the hearts of the Newly Acquired were awakened, the road to the Primordial Light was opened for them. The high, narrow windows were open, and the ceiling was a round, translucent cupola.

Uf carefully placed the boy in the center of a sky-blue mosaic circle. He stepped back and sank to the floor. The brothers and sisters sat down silently around the edge of the circle. Por laid Khram on the cool floor near Uf, who gently cradled the white-haired head of this wise heart in his arms.

Silence reigned in the hall.

The only sounds were the ocean waves and pelicans calling out sleepily to one another on the shore, preparing for the night.

"Open the sky," Uf ordered.

The cupola slid back noiselessly. Over the brothers' and sisters' heads, a new moon rose in the evening sky, which was still tinged with the orange-rose light in the west. The sun was setting. The stars twinkled ever stronger. A half-light filled the hall. Everyone sitting froze. Darkness descended from the deepening blue sky. And the faces of the brothers and sisters were plunged into it.

Night fell.

Khram began to move. Her feeble moan sounded in the hall. Uf carefully raised her head. Khram's lips opened in the dark: "He . . . is here. With us . . ."

"Yes," Uf answered softly, and *gently* repeated this to her with his heart.

Khram recovered consciousness. She was helped to sit up. Her long hair was pushed back from her face. And she *beheld* the sleeping boy.

"He'll wake up soon," said Uf.

"I *know*," Khram's lips whispered.

Everyone froze again.

A night bird flew over the open ceiling of the hall.

The boy moved.

A shiver ran through the bodies of all the figures sitting in the circle. But Khram already *possessed* her powerful heart. Her heart obeyed. She *knew* what to do. And she *understood* that it had to be done quickly.

The boy raised his head. Then he pushed himself up and sat on the marble floor. He swayed a bit. He turned his head and weakly called out, "Mama."

Everyone in the circle sat stock-still.

"Ma-a-a-m!" the boy called louder.

And he lay back down on the floor.

Khram squeezed Uf's hand. "Take him on your chest. *Shield him. Push against him.*"

Uf *understood*. He ripped off his shirt. He went over to the boy, took him under the arms from behind, lifted him, and pressed the boy's back to his chest.

"Mama, Mama!" the boy cried out and whimpered.

"The hammer!" Khram demanded in a loud voice, and stood up.

Lavu placed the case at her feet. It was the standard refrigerator case of the Brotherhood, which could hold seven Ice hammers. The lock clicked and Lavu opened it. A blue light illuminated the inside of the case and Khram's face. In the case, steaming frostily, lay a single hammer. Shua's hammer. And immediately three expert hammerers of the island house stepped forward: Das, Vu, and Ut. Their experienced arms and hands had shattered hundreds of Ice hammers, awakening dozens of hearts. But Khram shook her head.

"No. You will kill him. I *know* this."

The boy whimpered on Uf's chest. A murmur went around the circle: Who would strike him? The dark figures of the brothers shifted anxiously: If the experienced hammerers couldn't, then who could? In the darkness the sisters rallied.

"Khram, I can do it!"

"Khram, give me the hammer!"

"Khram, my hands will do it!"

But Khram shook her head. "No."

Everyone talked at once.

"Who will strike the blow?"

The boy whimpered. Uf stood silently.

Khram leaned over and picked up the hammer.

Everyone grew quiet.

Holding the hammer in her hands, she moved toward the center of the circle. Her bent, emaciated body obeyed her poorly. Swaying and dragging her bony legs with difficulty, she made it to Uf. On seeing her, illuminated by the blue light of the open case, the boy grew quiet. Standing before him, Khram straightened up. Hoarse breath burst from her mouth. She squeezed the handle of the hammer. The hammer shook in her hands, sparkling in the dark.

The boy stared, unblinking, at Khram. She looked him straight in the eyes. The hammer trembled in her hands. Slowly, she began to pull it back, getting ready for the swing. Everyone in the circle sat still, *directing* their hearts.

Uf closed his eyes, *in preparation*.

The hammer made a half circle and struck the boy in the chest. And it immediately flew from Khram's hands and fell on the stone floor, shattering into blue shards that glowed and sparkled in the darkness. Khram fell at Uf's feet with a moan. The boy cried out and lost consciousness. The sisters rushed to him. Uf held him and kept his eyes closed. The sisters' hands touched the boy's body.

"Speak with the heart!"

"Speak with the heart!"

"Speak with the heart!"

The boy's heart remained silent.

Uf opened his eyes. His strong heart, no longer an *anvil*, came to life. It *supported* the sisters' insistent hearts from the back.

"*Speak with the heart!*"

The boy's bare legs jerked. Everyone was still.

"Gorn! Gorn! Gorn!" said the awakened heart.

Uf cried out and, his heart growing faint, began to fall backward. He was caught and laid on the floor. The boy was picked up and carried swiftly down a bluish-gold staircase into the quiet, cozy resting place of the Newly Acquired. The brothers and sisters rushed there.

The Hall of Awakening emptied out.

Only Uf and Khram remained, lying on the mosaic floor. Blue light still issued from the open case. Khram awoke first. Pushing up on her arms, she *felt* Uf. Then *she saw* him. Crawling over, she lay next to him, embraced him with her thin hands, and softly *jolted* his heart. Lying on his back, Uf shuddered, stirred, and drew the humid night air into his lungs.

"Gorn ..." his lips exhaled.

"Gorn," Khram repeated.

Their heart *pronounced* the new name.

"I believed. But I did not *know*," said Uf.

"I didn't believe. But I *knew*," Khram replied.

A falling star flashed in the night sky above them.

Uf reached out and picked up a piece of the Ice lying nearby; he squeezed it and placed it on his breast. Khram's fingers opened his fist and touched the Ice. Their hands held the piece of Ice together.

"The Ice did *it*," Uf said.

"You were the one who *made it happen*," came Khram's reply. "You *were able*. You *forced* everyone to believe. Everyone except me ..."

"I believed because I *wanted to*. I wanted to so strongly."

"Your heart *knew*, knew that we would live to see it. That we would *see* it."

"It didn't *know*. But I believed the Light. The Light in my heart."

"In your wise heart."

"The Light helped us."

"The Light helped us," Khram repeated.

"Our Light."

"Our Light ..."

Their hearts *shone*.

The stars shone above them.

The Great Circle

MEROG was directing an iron machine. I sat next to him. Obu, Tryv, and Yasto sat in back. Merog drove the iron machine through the main city of the Country of Ice. The clocks of this city showed 18:35. The streets of the city were filled with large numbers of iron machines. Machines carrying meat machines. Which were heading from the center of the city after the end of the working day to their stone homes where the close friends and relatives of the meat machines awaited them. Where the happiness of the body waited.

We were driving from the center of the city on a street named in honor of a certain meat machine who was very well known in this country. Eighty-eight years ago this meat machine, with the help of his cohorts, had overturned a dynasty of meat machines that had ruled the Country of Ice for more than three hundred years. He had established his authority based on the equality of all meat machines before the new law. According to which all meat machines in the Country of Ice were supposed to live as one family. And work for the good of this family, for the happiness of the bodies of all the meat machines of the Country of Ice. For seventy-four years the meat machines of the Country of Ice lived by this law. And then they stopped living by it. Because there could be no brotherhood between meat machines. And they couldn't feel they were one family for very long and be glad for the happiness of other bodies. Each meat machine wanted happiness for his own body above all. In order to achieve happiness for their bodies, meat machines would deceive, steal, and kill. For that reason they could not live long in the world. Meat machines constantly competed, found enemies, crowded out and stole from one another. Countries attacked other countries. Meat machines were constantly arming themselves, preparing more and more perfect weapons. And they constantly killed each other to achieve the body's happiness. The body's happiness was the main purpose of meat machines. And the body's happiness occurred when it was pleasant and convenient for the meat machines' bodies to exist. To live for the happiness of their own bodies—this was the primary law of all meat machines on the planet Earth.

Moving slowly in the stream of iron machines, we arrived at a square named by the local meat machines in honor of one meat machine who flew into near-Earth space in an iron machine forty-three Earth years ago. In those years the Country of Ice was extremely proud of this flight. Because the meat machines of this country were able to manufacture an iron machine capable of such a flight. The rulers of this country wanted to show other countries the power of their country. So that the other countries would respect and fear the Country of Ice. On the square stood a metal sculpture of the meat machine who made that flight. It was made so that the local meat machines would remember the meat machines who had died a very long time ago.

From this square we turned right. And drove down a street named in honor of a meat machine who was one of the leaders of the Country of Ice several dozen Earth years ago. On this street there were fewer iron machines. They passed us; the meat machines sitting in them were hurrying to get home sooner and receive their long-awaited body happiness. We passed a stone building on top of which four gilded iron rods were joined together. The windows of the building were open. The singing of meat machines could be heard from it. They sang about the love of a celestial being who, in their view, created the Earth, themselves, and everything existing on Earth. Praying to this being and his son, who came to Earth in order to teach the meat machines to live in brotherhood, they hoped that after death they would be given another body and eternal happiness of this body. Through the window I saw their bowed heads. As they prayed they never suspected *who* was driving past them in an ordinary iron machine.

We turned left and found ourselves near a big building in which intelligent meat machines conveyed their knowledge to young meat machines. There were many such buildings in the Country of Ice, but this was the largest of them. It stood on a hill and rose above the main city of the Country of Ice. We drove by this building. Hundreds of young meat machines were coming out of its doors. They sat at tables all day long, listening to intelligent meat machines or reading thousands of letters on paper. These young meat machines were preparing for their future life. They were learning how to build iron machines and buildings, make calculations, manufacture combinations of substances, fire iron machines into near-Earth space, write letters on paper, find stones and metals in the Earth, conquer other countries, deceive and kill other meat machines.

Passing by that large building, we turned left and ended up on a square. There were many iron machines and meat machines walking around. In the middle of the square, meat machines were selling food. They sold fruits, vegetables, and corpses or pieces of corpses of various animals. The meat machines hurrying home bought their food. In order to prepare their complex food from it at home. Some meat machines stood in groups, drinking the fermented juice of grains and drawing the smoke of rotting leaves into themselves. This gave their bodies pleasure.

The crowd of meat machines moved toward a small building and entered its doors. This was the entrance into the underground. There hundreds of iron machines, moving along steel rails, carried the meat machines to different parts of the city. Leaving our iron machines nearby, we headed for the entrance to the underground. The crowd of meat machines surrounded us. We descended under the earth along with this crowd, paying money to enter. The crowd of meat machines coagulated with their desires. In the crowd were exhausted meat machines hurrying to their homes where the close friends and relatives of the meat machines awaited them, as well as warm and complex food, beds, and a glass box in which shadows of meat machines moved and spoke. There were meat machines who had drunk their fill of the fermented juice of fruits or grains, which made them more cheerful and lively than the others; they talked loudly and laughed, feeling a temporary happiness of the body. A crowd of meat machines, wearing the same color of fabric on their heads and tied around their necks, loudly shouted the same words over and over; these meat machines were going to a special place where tens of thousands of meat machines watched tensely while twenty meat machines on a grass field rolled and kicked a bouncy sphere; depending on the movement of this sphere the meat machines shouted joyously, cried, or fought with each other. A group of young meat machines, having drunk the fermented juice of grain, was heading for a special building where the shadows of meat machines were shown on a white wall in the darkness; the young meat machines discussed these shadows quite ardently, comparing them and debating which of the shadows was better; the young meat machines strove to resemble these shadows.

A long, wide iron machine drove up, and its doors opened. A crowd of meat machines rushed toward the doors. A crowd of meat machines inside began to exit. The meat machines pushed; some tried to exit, others to enter. We squeezed through the doors. They closed behind us. And the iron machine set off. Inside, meat machines stood and sat. Those entering tried to sit down on empty seats as quickly as possible, so that their bodies were more comfortable. The sitting meat machines dozed or looked through packets of paper covered with letters. Reading these letters, the meat machines put them together and made words that elicited various fantasies in their heads. These fantasies distracted the meat machines from their everyday concerns. Like the fermented juice of fruits or grains, the letters on papers gave the meat machines' bodies temporary pleasure. Pushing aside the crowd, a meat machine without one leg, leaning on two wooden sticks, moved through the iron machine. In a plaintive voice it asked for money to buy food. A few meat machines gave the legless meat machine some money, but most pretended that they didn't hear the plaintive voice.

Soon the iron machine stopped. We got out, squeezing through a crowd of meat machines. And we immediately felt *ours*. There were many of them in the crowd, moving in one direction. We followed them. *Ours* walked through the crowd that rushed to the exit. The meat machines pushed and shoved, trying to get ahead of one another. We walked against the crowd. At the opposite end of the underground space was a yellow door with a sign in the language of the Country of Ice. The sign warned that only meat machines who worked in the underground rooms were allowed to enter. *Ours* walked through this door from time to time. We also entered it. Right behind the door sat brother Tiz in the uniform of the meat machines who keep the order. He only let *ours* through. We entered and descended deeper underground with the help of a mechanism.

We reached an underground shelter. Meat machines had dug it in case of a big war. Tens of thousands of meat machines were supposed to fill this shelter and to live calmly underground for several months. Nine years ago the Brotherhood took over the shelter. The meat machine responsible for the shelter, who reported to the government of the Country of Ice, had been destroyed. Brother Ma took his placc.

Other iron machines took us to the center of the shelter. Here the Brotherhood had built a large, round hall. When I entered, my heart fluttered: many of *ours* were already gathered in the hall. They had gotten through in various ways: some, like us, through the underground of the meat machines, some from above. Brothers and sisters kept on entering and entering. My heart *shone* with anticipation. The brothers and sisters stood side by side in complete silence. We didn't need to speak in the language of meat machines: our hearts *waited* for another *conversation*. I looked at *ours*. *Powerful* hearts were gathered here: Uf, Odo, Stam, Efep, and Tse. There were young hearts too, who had been awoken by the Ice hammer recently. Our hearts *were preparing*. Finally a machine informed us that exactly 2,300 brothers and sisters had gathered in the hall. The rest of the brothers and sisters remained outside the doors. Sister Tse's strong heart *flared*: A signal! On the smooth floor of the hall, 2,300 blue circles luminesced. Each of us stood on our spot. We formed a Great Circle. We raised our hands. And joined them.

I *felt* the heart.

We were ready.

But suddenly one heart *fell away*. Immediately, the Great Circle wasn't closed! We let go of each other's hands. Brother Dlu collapsed on the floor. Something had happened to his body: he had fainted or died. He was carried out quickly. Sister Iuked entered the hall. And stood on the place of brother Dlu. The Great Circle closed. Our hands joined again. Our eyes closed. Our hearts *flared*.

We *saw* Brother Gorn.

He *shone* in the center of the Circle.

I awoke from the touch of brother Obu's and brother Yasto's hands and tongues. They stroked me and licked my face. Their hearts were *stronger*. I opened my eyes. There was movement in the hall:

brothers and sisters were leaving. We had to leave the same way. We left the hall, sat down in the iron machine. It carried us and other brothers and sisters to the exit from the underground. Passing brother Tiz, we walked through the yellow door and ended up in a crowd of meat machines. Their clocks showed 7:28. Meat machines hurried to work. The majority of them didn't want to go. They coagulated with gloomy displeasure. The crowd moved silently from the entrance to the iron machines that took them to their destinations. We moved through this crowd. The meat machines were rushing down, while we were moving upward. They pushed us silently. Passing through the crowd, we came out into the air. There were many meat machines here as well. They were walking toward the underground, which swallowed their bodies. Many of them greedily sucked the smoke of rotting leaves into their body as they walked.

Skirting the crowd, we walked down a street bearing the name of a meat machine who had tried to see meaning and harmony in the world of the Earth. Gradually we came to the square where we had left our iron machines yesterday. We bought fruit from the meat machines and ate it. We got into our iron machines.

And drove off in search of Brothers and Sisters of the Light.

Gorn's Morning

GORN AWOKE from gentle caresses. Soft hands stroked his body and face. He lay on a wide bed strewn with the petals of blue roses. Over his head a tropical garden of palms, magnolias, and tiger trees spread out. Birds called loudly to one another; large, multicolored butterflies fluttered by. The sun had already risen, and the unsteady shadows trembled on the white body of the boy, sleeping on his back, and on the tanned bodies of two girls lying on either side of him.

Gorn raised his head. The girls immediately sat up on the bed. These were the thirteen-year-old twins Ak and Skeye, acquired by the Brotherhood twenty-six months ago in the Crimea; they possessed hearts that were powerful, *intelligent*, and far from childish. During the night they had been brought here to the island, from Ceylon, where they *met and calmed* the Newly Acquired in the smaller southern house. The girls were wearing identical short pants of goldish blue beads; the nipples of their tanned breasts were hidden by large sapphires cut in the form of octagons. Each girl's hair was plaited in 23 long braids and covered with gold dust. Precious stones of all possible hues of dark and light blue shone in their braids. Their necks, wrists, and ankles were adorned with gold necklaces inset with diamonds and turquoise. The girls' dark, supple bodies were fragrant with cocoa butter.

Gorn turned over and groaned. The girls carefully helped him to sit up. The boy glanced at the colorful world surrounding him and stared at the girls.

"Good morning, brother," the twins said simultaneously.

The boy looked at them, opening his small, dim-witted mouth. He was wearing light underpants, woven from high mountain grasses. On his chest was a wide white bandage. The twins smiled at him, holding him by the shoulders. On Gorn's lower lip a drop of saliva appeared, detached itself, and stretched heavily down. Skeye wiped his mouth with her fingers.

"Don't you want to sleep some more?"

"Uh-huh," he said, looking at Skeye.

Then he moved his gaze to Ak.

"We are your sisters," the twins said simultaneously.

"Nuh-uh." Gorn looked at them, immobile.

"We are your sisters," the twins repeated once more.

"When?" said Gorn, licking his wet lips.

"Right now," Skeye answered.

"You have lots of brothers and sisters. It's just that before you didn't know about it." Ak took his hand. "My name is Ak."

"Mine is Skeye." Skeye took the boy's other hand.

"But you . . . where?"

"We are here. With you. Forever."

The boy turned his head, looking all around. A large black-and-yellow butterfly glided down and landed on the blue rose petals between the boy's legs. He stared at the butterfly. The butterfly sat there, fanning its wings.

"Striped," the boy muttered and licked his wet lips. "Big? Like that?"

The twins held him by the hands.

"Where is everybody?" Gorn asked, without taking his blue eyes off the flapping butterfly wings. "Where's Mama? And Auntie Vera? Will they come?"

"We'll tell you all about it now," said Ak. "You just have to hug us tighter."

"How?" Drooling, the boy stared, mesmerized, at the butterfly's wings.

"Like this." The twins took his arms, dove under them with their golden heads, and pressed against the boy.

Their arms entwined his white body, their tanned bodies pressed against the boy.

"*Hello*, brother Gorn!"

The twins' hearts throbbed. And smoothly *took* Gorn's heart.

The boy's face quivered and his eyebrows flinched. The short blond hair on his head stood up.

"Catsundogs," said his lips.

He farted. Four waves of a slight tremor passed through his body; his fixed eyes filled with moisture. Two birds, calling to each other in the branches of the cherry tree nearby, grew quiet.

The boy stopped trembling. He froze. Urine bubbled between his legs.

Pressed to him, the twins seemed to turn to stone. The boy shuddered without blinking or shifting position. And peed on himself again. The urine quietly streamed onto the white silk bed strewn with blue petals. The puddle between his legs grew, flowing across the fabric. The blue petals, floating on it, moved along. The urine reached the butterfly. The petal on which it sat rocked and floated away. And the butterfly flew off.

Ak, Gorn, and Skeye were locked together for forty-two minutes. Finally the twins' hearts *grew quiet*.

The twins shuddered, their lips opened, and greedily, with a moan and a sob, drew in the warm, humid, aromatic air of the tropics. The twins unwound their arms and fell back on the bed, knocking off some of the rose petals. The boy remained sitting, gazing straight ahead. Lying back on the rose petals, the twins greedily and joyfully breathed. The voices of the two birds awoke again in the branches.

Gorn blinked. And moved his right leg with his fingers. His wet lips quavered, his tongue moved in his mouth.

"A-m-m-m . . . a . . . m-m-m . . . but give . . ." Gorn said, and found the twins with his eyes.

They breathed, gazing at him rapturously. Tears flowed from their eyes.

"Give me, give . . ." Gorn bleated, and his arms stretched out to the twins.

Ak and Skeye took him by the hands.

"Give me, give me, give . . ." Gorn mumbled, grabbing them and drooling.

The twins rose with some difficulty and embraced Gorn. Now it was they, *tired* of heart, who leaned on the boy. He *wanted* their hearts powerfully.

"Give me, give me, give!" he whimpered, clutching at the shoulders and heads of the swaying twins.

They cried silently, entwining him in their exhausted arms. Their hearts had *grown faint* in meeting Gorn's heart: they had not yet met a heart of equal might. Even Khram's powerful heart was nothing compared to this still very small heart, which exuded such amazing strength.

"Give me, give, give!" Gorn roared, and his face was distorted by a tortured grimace.

The twins *began to speak* with him again.

Gorn grew still. His eyes turned glassy. Saliva ran freely from his open mouth.

Another thirty-eight minutes passed.

The twins shuddered and with a moan fell back on the bed.

Gorn stirred. His face was blazing. His arms quivered. From his open, dried-out mouth came intermittent puffs of hot breath.

"And . . . give me, and give, and give!" he whined.

The twins lay, barely breathing.

"And give me! Give! And give! And give!" Gorn roared.

Ak barely managed to wrest her gilded head from the bed. Skeye breathed in spurts, like a fish thrown on the shore. She didn't have the strength to rise.

"And give me! . . . Give! Give!"

The forest surrounding the bed rustled. All the brothers and sisters of the ocean house had been here from the beginning *of the support*. Hidden behind wide leaves and thick trunks, they followed the first *conversation*. Now their hearts were *worried*.

"They need *help*. Support them!" Uf said, approaching the bed.

"They *won't hold out*!" Shey yelped.

"He's *stronger*!" Das cried out.

"They are *collapsing*!" Bork growled.

"And give me! Give! Give! And gi-i-i-i-vvvve!!!" Gorn roared as loud as he could and tore at the hair of the unconscious Skeye.

The foliage of the surrounding forest began to move. Dozens of arms stretched out toward Gorn, who was roaring. But he didn't notice anything and continued to roar, shaking Skeye's head, spitting tears and saliva. His awakened heart *desired*.

"I'll *hold them up*." Uf stepped forward.

"No!" Khram screeched, *stopping* everyone. "He *desires* them! *The first ones! You'll extinguish it!* They must do it! We'll help them! We'll be their *support*! Everyone *stand behind* them!"

Dozens of arms lifted Ak and Skeye and pressed them to the boy. Gorn grabbed them greedily and grew still. Khram pressed against Ak's back, Uf pressed against Skeye's. Skeye opened her eyes.

"*Speak!*" ordered the hearts of those surrounding them.

And the twins again *began to speak* with Gorn.

The brothers and sisters *supported* them. Uf pressed Skeye to the boy; Khram, who didn't have the strength to do this with Ak with her weak arms, pressed herself against Ak's tanned back. Mef and Por supported Khram from behind. Shey, Bork, Niuz, and Pe held Uf. The rest surrounded the bed, stretching their arms in front of them and placing their heads on the bed. Their hearts *encompassed and supported*.

Another 23 minutes passed.

Ak's and Skeye's hearts *fell silent*. The twins were unconscious.

The brothers' arms lifted them and laid them down. Blood flowed from their ears and nostrils.

Gorn grew still and then shuddered. And everyone felt his heart *shine* for the first time. It had *been filled*. And acquired its *first* peace.

Gorn moved. And he saw everyone surrounding him. Everyone looked at him silently. He leaned his hands against the bed, rose up on his knees. Then he stood and straightened up. The look in his wide-open eyes had become more attentive and meaningful. His eyes seemed to have shed during the night, becoming more transparent. The blue in them had paled, drawn toward the pupils. His eyes slid over the surrounding world. Now the boy saw it differently: not yet as Gorn, but no longer as Misha Terekhov.

The world surrounded the boy. This world was new now. And still not fully understood. By itself it didn't attract him. But something in it was *highly* desired. Something attracted him and tormented him. It was *infused* in the world.

Gorn cast his eyes about. He could vaguely *distinguish*.

Between the leaves, sky, branches, butterflies, grasses, and the bed with blue petals were those who had frozen, looking at him. And *it* was in them. The greatly desired. That which was stronger than the world. Without which it was already *impossible* to live.

Gorn walked, swaying, to the edge of the bed. The brothers and sisters stayed still, looking at him and *listening* closely. Reaching them, Gorn stretched out his hand. And touched a face. It was sister Shey. He touched her face. Shey's heart *froze*. Ga, who had sat down near Shey and the bed, also froze. Gorn touched his face with his other hand.

None of the brothers or sisters made a sound.

The birds left the tiger tree that spread out over the bed.

Gorn's open lips moved: "Bi-ig? Like . . . tha-at?"

Everyone stayed still, contemplating the Newly Acquired heart. A powerful heart. The one that they had waited for for *so* long and *so* desperately. Gorn's every movement elicited *ecstasy* from the brothers and sisters. It was as though they were afraid to *scare off* the just-awakened heart.

Gorn touched Shey's and Ga's faces. He turned his gaze to Bi, Ut, and Forum, approached and began to touch them.

"A-a-a-lot? A-a-l-soo? The saaame?"

Khram was kneeling near Forum. Gorn stretched his hand to her. Their eyes met. But Gorn no longer looked with his eyes. He was *already* trying to *see* with his heart. Khram *felt* this.

"You, the same? Mi-i-ne?"

"*Yours! With the heart!*" Khram spoke, not only with her lips.

She took Gorn's hands and placed them on her old, thin breast.

"*Yours! With the heart!*"

Gorn grew still. His heart *flared* with premonition. It began to *know*. His hands twined around Khram's delicate, wrinkled neck. He pressed against her.

The still bodies of the brothers and sisters moved. They reached out toward Khram and Gorn. Their hearts *shone*.

"M-m-mi-mine. With the h-h-h-heart," said Gorn.

"*With the heart*," whispered Khram.

"With th-th-the h-heart," Gorn repeated.

And he *understood*.

His heart *froze stiff*. The *past* awoke in him. Now it was *separate*. And it *arose* before his awakened heart in all its horror.

A tremor ran through Gorn's body. He jerked violently and began to bend backward. His small mouth opened wide and a deep moan emerged.

Khram *understood* immediately what it was.

And they all *understood*.

The ring of Gorn's arms released, his head arched back. And he fell flat onto the waiting palms of the brothers and sisters. Sobs wracked him.

Khram closed her eyes in a sweet exhaustion.

The heart crying seized Gorn. He sobbed, his legs flailing in spasms, his fingers scratching his white chest. His head arched back, tears and saliva flew into the faces of everyone helping.

"Thank the Light!" said Khram, joyfully clasping her bony elbows.

Dozens of arms lifted the sobbing boy and carried him along the stone path to the house. His weeping resounded in the wild tropical forest. Birds and animals listened cautiously and called to one another in the foliage warmed by the noonday sun.

Only Khram and Uf remained by the empty bed: Khram sat on the stone square, holding herself by her elbows and placing her head on the silk corner of the bed. Uf sat stock-still near the corner diagonally opposite. They were divided by the bed, strewn with crushed blue rose petals and soaked with Gorn's urine.

Their hearts were silent in *exhaustion*. It was the very same *intoxicating* exhaustion of acquiring. And this time, *what* an acquisition! Khram and Uf *understood* what kind.

"He's stronger than I *expected*," said Khram, running her cheek over the cool silk.

"Much stronger," Uf replied.

"He will be the *strongest*."

"He *already* is the strongest."

A gust of ocean wind rocked the tops of the trees and wafted through Khram's long white hair.

The blue petals fell from the bed to the stone.

"We *held on*," said Uf.

"The Light helped," Khram whispered in a barely audible voice into the smooth corner of the bed.

From the tree a large blue-bronze beetle fell on the bed. He made a sort of lazy effort to turn over. His shiny black feet crumpled the roses.

"Now everything will fall on you," Uf said.

"I'm *ready*. I've been waiting for this my whole life*,"* said Khram, and lifted her head.

"He'll *lean* on you for support. Only on you. I won't be with you."

"I'll *manage*. And I'll *hold on*."

"We'll help with a Great Circle."

"First we need a Middle one. And more than one."

"They're already getting together."

"I have to have *support*."

"It's already there. We are supporting you."

Uf stood up.

"You're going back." Khram *understood*.

"I *must return*."

"I know you are *needed* there ... The meat is coagulating. You will *hold it back*."

"I'll restrain it. And I'll keep the Brotherhood together."

He turned away and walked down the stone path.

"*Keep it well*," said Khram's old lips.

Olga Drobot

THE TOASTER beeped and two pieces of toast jumped out. Filling half of a large glass of pineapple juice with ice, Olga went over to the toaster.

"Papa and Mama," she thought to herself instinctively, taking a sip from the glass and putting the toast on a plate.

But in a loud voice she immediately forbade herself to think those thoughts. With an English *imperative* she dismissed them: "Begone!"

The psychologist had been right: "A sword, slicing off a difficult past." At first Olga didn't believe in it. But six months after *that day* the "sword" began to work and help. It chopped off the ghosts of her parents that arose in virtual space in any pair of things or beings—in a pair of shoes, in cooing pigeons, in stone figures next to corporate gates, in Adam and Eve, in the president's two lifted fingers, in a pair of gold earrings, in the number 69, in a two-volume edition of Edgar Allan Poe, in copulating flies, and finally in the three-year absence of the twin towers, which had been standing *then* and had been visible to all *three* of them from the south window of the loft. Now Olga looked out of her sixth-floor Manhattan apartment alone. Not at the place where the World Trade Center towers had stood three years ago, but at the funny water towers on the roofs of the neighboring buildings, which always reminded her of Martians from the cover of Welles's *War of the Worlds*. A novel that her father had loved. And she had never read ...

"Olechka's a gooooood girl!" said the parrot in the cage next to the window.

She remembered him, old Fima, walked over and poured some

food into his cage, added water to his bottle, cut off a piece of apple and wedged it between the bars. Fima began to peck at the apple with his terrifying beak, while squinting at Olga.

"He remembers too," she thought.

And she immediately swung her invisible sword, cutting it all off: "Begone!"

Fima chewed away, showing his thick tongue, and said, "Don't worry!"

"Be happy!" Olga nodded and laughed.

It was time to begin the day.

Olga spread salty goat cheese on a piece of toast, put three circles of sliced cucumber on it, and covered them with two lettuce leaves. She slapped down a piece of turkey on the lettuce, circles of tomatoes on the turkey, then added another piece of toast to make a fat sandwich before biting into it. And then, grabbing her glass, she sat down at the computer. Washing down a piece of sandwich with the icy juice, she hit a key on the keyboard. The monitor came to life and a deep male singsong voice greeted her: "Hi, O-ol-g-a-a!"

"*Privet saliut*," she answered in Russian.

She glanced at her e-mail: four messages. One from work (a reminder that after vacation, on the sixteenth, Olga had to be in Philadelphia with a contract for the delivery of marble). Another was from Liza in Chicago (for the sixth time she swore that she would come "to eat, drink, and shoot the bull in Russian"). The third was from Peter, a colleague of her father's (he invited her to a barbecue this weekend).

"He always wants to introduce me to someone, the old geezer." Olga grinned, remembering openhearted, fat Peter, a fancier of German beer, free jazz, and picnics. "No, Peter, I'll already be far from here on Saturday…"

But the fourth…

"Yes!" Olga joyfully stamped the floor with her bare foot.

Hello, Olga.

Yesterday I sat on the site almost all night. There's some news. First of all, I finally wrote to the elusive Michael Laird. And he answered me! He has in fact been the coordinator of the Society for the last two years. I sent him your letter, with the story of your abduction, with photographs of you and your deceased parents. Now you and I are in the database of the site. Soon we'll have a lot of friends. The headquarters of the Society is located in Guangzhou (southern China). Michael advised us to fly over for a more substantive conversation, since he doesn't really trust e-mail. And he has something to show us in Guangzhou. The Society will help with visas, they have a standard invitation with a hotel as well. The invitee only has to buy the ticket. In connection with this I was thinking—why not combine our journey to Israel with a visit to Guangzhou? After all, China is closer to Israel than Göteborg and New York! That's for starters. Secondly, we'll kill two birds with one stone and save time. And honestly, I'm sick of all these months of living on conjecture and guesswork. I feel like getting a move on, doing something.

I await your reply eagerly,
Yours, Bjorn Vassberg

Olga gleefully clapped and, forgetting about her sandwich, began clattering on the keyboard.

Bjorn Vassberg, greetings!
    Your idea is wonderful and I like it a lot. I'm sure that the information that we'll get in Tel Aviv will be very important and explain a lot in our story. After that we can fly to China and meet with Laird. That would be fabulous! Especially since I'm on vacation at the moment. I await the invitation from you and then I'll go straight to the Chinese embassy. As far as Tel Aviv is concerned, everything is in order, I reserved two rooms in our names at the Prima Astor hotel. It's right on the seashore, I've stayed there before. As soon as you get your visa and buy a ticket, let me know. I would like to meet in the airport. My password for meeting is: *Odin v pole voin*. I await yours!

Till we meet!
Olga

That evening, when Olga returned from a bicycle ride in the park, Bjorn's answer was waiting for her. It included the invitation to Guangzhou and the password: "*Kräftskivan.*"

"Something in Swedish . . ." Olga laughed and rushed to look up the address of the Chinese consulate in New York.

"Tomorrow, tomorrow!" she thought as she printed out the invitation, found two photographs, and placed it all in her dark-blue American passport.

She made herself a large coffee with milk, sat down at the computer, and typed in the address: www.icehammervictims.org. A picture emerged on the monitor: a girl and a boy naked to the waist were pressing their palms to the wound in the center of each others' chests. Above the picture were the words "Official Site of the Society of Ice Hammer Victims." Below were the usual links: History of the Society, News, People, Photo Gallery, Personal Stories, Publications, Conjectures, Join Us! Olga clicked on Personal Stories. She skimmed over well-known text—she'd already read all of them a long time ago. At the end she found three new ones.

Stephanie Treglown, fourteen years old, Newcastle, Australia

A week before Christmas holiday two women came to our school, assistants to a director who said that they were looking for girls to play extras in a remake of Peter Weir's well-known film *Picnic at Hanging Rock*. Everyone in Australia knows this film—my parents always watched it, even when I was little, we have a VHS cassette and a DVD of it. My parents and I visited the cliffs of Massedon where those tragic events of February 14, 1900, took place, when the senior class of the Abelard Girls' School set off on St. Valentine's day for that very cliff to have a picnic, and three girls disappeared without a trace. All the girls in our class really wanted to be in the film. These director's assistants, Debora and Ellen, said that the director of the remake would be David Lynch, that the casting was taking place now, and that Lynch was choosing completely unknown schoolgirls for the parts of the girls, so that it was quite possible that one of us might get to play a real role in the film, with lines. They chose three girls from our class, including me, and another seven from the school. We were all blue-eyed and light-haired. I was so thrilled when they chose me! I especially liked one of the girls in Weir's film—Miranda. She's so pretty and gentle, like an angel! She has incredible blue eyes and lovely blond hair. And it was quite a shame that she didn't really become a Hollywood star, that she acted again only in *Mad Max*, and that was it. Ellen and Debora said that after Christmas we would have to go to Sidney where everyone chosen would get together, and Lynch himself would make the final choice among us. They would pay our way. And Mrs. Halle, Suzy Halle's mother, went with us. We arrived in Sidney around noon and went to the opera on the shore. It's an enormous building, I was there twice when I was a little girl—for the opera *Peer Gynt*, and the ballet *Giselle*. We were taken into one of the auditoriums, and the entire room, with 1,500 seats, was filled with schoolgirls! And all of them were blue-eyed and light-haired! I had never seen anything like it! And among them were lots that looked like Miranda. Of course I immediately realized that there was no way they would ever choose me—there were so many beautiful girls in the hall! We waited for Lynch. But instead of him, three people got up onstage—a kind of plump guy, an old woman, and a thin, bald man, very serious. The old woman told us that Lynch was very busy, and therefore his assistants would do the choosing. The woman introduced herself as the author of the film script. And these three sat in armchairs in front of the stage and asked the girls to come up to them in pairs, in turns. The girls began to do this. The three looked attentively at each pair, and then asked them to come over and the old woman placed her hand on each girl's chest. Right where your neck begins. It continued like that for almost four hours. And during this time, out of 1,500 only 36 were chosen. I was one of them. Then they wrote down my phone number and address and said they'd be in touch with me by e-mail. And I went home, terribly happy. I was in seventh heaven! Out of our entire school I was the only one chosen! I began to wait for news. But day after day passed and no one wrote to me. I had to wait. My parents and school friends tried to reassure me—films aren't made that fast, just wait. And so I waited. But a terrible accident prevented me from becoming an actress. When I was coming back from school and crossing Main Street, a car stopped and a woman sitting in the driver's seat asked about the road to Sesnok. I said to go straight and turn right at the light. She laughed, and pointed to her ears: "I can't hear!" I went over to her and repeated it. The last thing I remember was that the woman was holding a broach shaped like a little musketeer's gun. When I came to, I was already in the hospital. My neck and chest hurt terribly. My chest was bandaged up, I was wounded. Later they told me that I had been found on the highway. A car hit me when I was talking to that woman. And the woman had disappeared.

"That's right Stephanie, you didn't become an actress." Olga smiled sadly. "And David Lynch is unlikely to film that remake."

"Fimochka's a go-o-oo-d boy," the parrot cried.

"The best of all." Olga nodded.

And she began reading the second story.

Dzhamilya Sabitova, thirty-eight years old, Temirtau, Kazakhstan

I have been working at our municipal market for four years. My husband, Taimuraz Sabitov, and I had our own stand, Beshbarmak. We cooked hot meals for the traders at the market. We made beshbarmak, pilaf, baursaki, and lagman. The merchants were always pleased because my husband and I are good cooks. And the management of the market was happy with us. On April 4, 2005, I was working at the stand with my sister Tamara, since my husband had gone to Karaganda to buy kitchen supplies. Tamara is seven years younger than me and has always helped me when my husband is busy. That day, as usual, we cooked everything in the morning, and at about 1:00

p.m. we opened the stand and began serving. Merchants came to us, took the food, and went back to their places with it. Everyone really loved us at the market because Tamara and I are very pretty. Our mama is Russian, and our papa is Kazakh. Mama's blond and her eyes are dark blue, very beautiful. And the main thing is Tamara and I have the same eyes and the same light hair. From Papa we got our nose, lips, and black eyebrows. And everyone always joked that we were Mama's girls. In Kazakhstan there aren't many people with blue eyes, and there's not many blondes, either. Because of that the men always flirted with us when they bought their food, they'd say all sorts of silly things. That day a man came over to the stand. He wasn't local, I'd never seen him before. He was a tall, well-built blond with blue eyes, handsome and well dressed—you could tell he was rich. He asked if our pilaf was tasty or not. We said—try it, everyone says it's good. He took a cup of rice and tried a little. Then he said—it's delicious, probably because you two are so pretty. And he began talking about how we were such beauties and all. I asked what he bought at the market. He said he just came to take a look at his friend Tofik Khalilov's market. That was the owner of the market, a very rich man. And the man said that he liked the market, especially if beauties like us worked there. He was just having fun, joking around with us. Tamara asked what he did and he said he had a business in Alma-Ata, two restaurants, and that he came to Karaganda on business and dropped by Temirtau to visit his old friend Tofik. And he asked—what were we doing that evening? We answered that we were washing and putting away the dishes, and going home to our husbands and children. Then he asked us to go with him to Tofik's for pilaf. We turned him down, we said that our husbands wouldn't let us go out at night, and that we were really busy. Then he offered to take us to a restaurant right now. And he was in good spirits, joking around with us in a cheery sort of way. He made Tamara and me laugh, he was so funny. He said that sometimes you have to take a break from wives and husbands, so you'll love them even more. And he kept on trying to talk us into going with him. So we said—all right, but only for an hour. He said—all right, you choose the restaurant. Tamara says—Zhuldyz. That's the most expensive restaurant in Temirtau. He says—no problem. So we locked up the stand and went with him. And when we left the market, he walked over to his car, a really expensive one, brand new and gorgeous, and he opened the back door—have a seat, ladies. We sat down, he drove, and turned on the music. And then suddenly a partition went up, and we were behind glass . . . and there was something sour in the air, and I fainted. I came to on the ground. I raised my head—it was the middle of the night, my head was in the sand, and a dog was barking somewhere. As soon as I tried to sit up—my chest began to hurt terribly, like someone had hit me really hard. I looked around—I was somewhere in a wasteland outside of town. And I saw Tamara lying next to me. I touched her, but she didn't move. She was dead. So I sat next to her all night. I cried and sat. I didn't have the strength to go anywhere. In the morning some workers were driving along the highway from Sarani and noticed us, picked us up. They called my husband and took us to the hospital—my whole chest was beaten up, one big bruise. But on Tamara it was even worse—everything was broken, her breastbone was broken, her ribs were broken and stuck out through the skin, I couldn't look at the wound. I spent a month in the hospital while my chest healed. Then the police said—it was a maniac.

"Uh-huh . . . the usual story," said Olga. "He didn't take you and your sister out to Zhuldyz after all . . . Of course it's a maniac, Dzhamilya. A maniac. Who flies from New York to Sidney, from Sidney to Karaganda. And then . . . voilá! He's in Zürich again! This maniac sure lives the good life . . ."

Thomas Urban, fifty-two years old, Zürich, Switzerland

Three years ago I was in a car accident and for a time I completely lost all short-term memory. I forgot my wife's name, didn't believe that I had a daughter, didn't know that I was an architect, and so on. My long-term memory, on the contrary, became so vivid and strong that events from my early childhood and adolescence began to surface, memories that I had never recalled before. For example, I remembered in great detail how my fifth birthday was celebrated at home, who was there, what we ate, what we said, what presents I received. I also recalled many other things. During the six months I spent in the clinic, I remembered quite a lot. It was as though I were being shown a film about myself. Among the myriad episodes from childhood and youth one very strange one arose. I still can't find a sensible explanation for it. It was the summer of 1972, when I was fifteen years old. My older sister, Miriam, bought me a ticket to a Led Zeppelin concert in Zürich at the Hallenstadion. I didn't know this group very well at the time, but a lot had been written about it in young people's magazines, and it soon became a super band. My sister bought me an expensive ticket, and I turned out to be right in front of the stage. The concert was amazing, I was seeing these great musicians for the first time, I saw Robert Plant up close, I heard his incredible voice. The concert made a huge impression on me. Before that I had only been to see the Who and Chicago. But Led Zeppelin was a head above those bands. I especially liked Robert Plant—he was tall, slim, with a golden mop of hair, blue eyes, and a "golden" voice. When the concert was over, the audience went wild. We ran onto the area in front of the stadium stage and shouted, "Led Zepp! Led Zepp!" And then I saw two girls, very pretty, curly-headed blondes, holding a poster that said ROBERT PLANT FAN CLUB. Young people crowded around them. I went over too. Next to the poster there was a table where a third curly-headed blonde was sitting and signing up fans for Plant's club. I read the conditions for membership on the poster: long blond hair and blue eyes. I was eligible! My hair nearly reached my shoulders at the time—I was imitating George Harrison. The girls wrote down my address and telephone number, saying that they would call. And I set off happily for home. At home I broke open my piggy bank, went out and bought two Led Zeppelin albums. I listened to them constantly. And a few days later I got a call and they said that the Robert Plant Fan Club was holding its first meeting. I got right on my bicycle and by 4:00 p.m. I was at the address they'd given me, in a rich area of Zürich on Hadlaubstrasse. There was a big old villa, covered with wild grapevines, a poster saying LED ZEPPELIN on its gates, and a large portrait of Robert Plant. I left my bicycle at the fence, rang the bell at the gate, and stated my name. I was let in and I entered the villa. It was an old, richly furnished house. And the song "Whole Lotta Love" was playing nonstop! It was so strange in that old-fashioned setting, amid Victorian furniture—and then the music of Led Zeppelin! One of the curly-headed blondes met me in the foyer and guided me into a spacious living room. About thirty kids were already sitting there: light-haired, blue-eyed girls and guys. For the most part it was people my age, but there were some who were older. There was a table of nonalcoholic drinks, cigarettes, and chips. First we listened to the music. Then we started talking, getting to know each other. During this part other blond kids came in. The whole hall filled up gradually and then the music stopped. And a blindingly beautiful woman came out—tall, stately, with bronzed skin, goldish hair, a proper aristocratic face, and dark blue eyes. She was dressed all in blue, wore blue gloves, even her shoes and all the jewelry on her was deep blue. Standing in the middle of the room, she began talking to us. Not in the Swiss dialect but in pure German. She said that Robert Plant was an angel who fell from heaven and got lost among humans, that he sang in the language of the celestial spheres, that in listening to his voice we would become freer and kinder, that we would understand what heavenly love was, that today we would begin our fellowship, that the music of Led Zeppelin would help us to become beautiful both outwardly and inwardly. Her deep, calm voice was mesmerizing, and we couldn't take our eyes off her. She picked up a flat blue box with a picture of a falling golden angel on top, opened it, and offered it to us. In the box were small chocolate figures of this same angel in gold foil. "Commune with the music of the celestial spheres!" she said with a smile. And at the very same second Robert Plant's voice rang out, powerful and poignant: "Baby, I'm gonna leave you." We all began to take the chocolates from the box, unfold the foil, and eat. It was good Swiss chocolate. I ate my chocolate. A few minutes later I fainted. I woke up at night lying on some pavement somewhere. Two cops were shaking me. It was in the center of town, near the Odeon bar, where students drink. My mangled bicycle lay by my side. My head was spinning, I was nauseous. And my chest hurt horribly. It was completely crushed, and the police told me that most likely a car had hit me. They called my parents and I was taken to a clinic. They found alcohol in my blood. Then I fell into a feverish state, and my temperature soared. They bandaged my chest and gave me a shot to help me sleep. I spent two weeks in the clinic. A small dent remained in the middle of my breastbone. I still have it. No matter how I described the Robert Plant Fan Club to my parents, whatever proof I offered that I had actually been in the villa, they didn't believe me. They were certain that I had been drinking with friends in some bar, ridden off drunk on my bicycle, and got hit by a car. Then I went to Hadlaubstrasse and rang the bell of that very villa. A maid opened the door. Naturally, no club had ever existed in this villa, the maid had never heard of Plant. A family of Hassids lived in the house; many years later I learned that they were the biggest diamond dealers in Switzerland. My peers and friends didn't know anything about this club, either. Once in the tram I met a girl who had been at the villa that time. I recognized her. But she smiled and said that she had never been there. And so all this was forgotten, like some strange dream. Until I got in an accident and lost my short-term memory. And then I remembered, remembered everything that had happened after I ate that damn chocolate! I crawled from the chair onto the floor. But I didn't fall asleep, I just couldn't move. I couldn't move a finger. But I was conscious, I heard and saw the red-gray pattern of the rug

near my nose. And I heard what was happening to others—
they either froze stiff in their chairs or fell on the floor. Then I
heard several men come in. A kind of muffled hustle-bustle
could be heard. Then I was grabbed under the arms and
dragged down some steps. I ended up in a basement. I was
trussed up and chained to the wall. Next to me some guy and a
girl were in chains too. Someone's strong hands ripped my
shirt off, and I saw them open a sort of long case. There were
strange hammers in it; at first I thought their heads were made
of glass. Some muscular light-haired man took one of those
hammers, swung back, and slammed the guy next to me in the
chest with all his might. That same woman in blue went right
up to the fellow and pressed again his chest. Then she shrank
back. The man hit him again. She came up again, and then
said, "An empty nut." The guy was taken down from the wall
and dragged away. The man took another hammer and began
to strike the girl's chest in the same way. The lady in deep blue
pressed close to her, like she was listening. The man had struck
such a blow that the hammer had shattered and pieces flown
off. Again the woman said, "An empty nut." The girl was un-
chained, but when they dragged her away, I noticed that blood
was trickling out of her mouth, and her legs were thrashing
convulsively. At the same time they dragged in another two
and started attaching them to the wall. Then the man came up
to me with the hammer, swung back, and struck me in the
middle of the chest with all his strength. The blow was so powerful that slivers sprayed from the shattered head of the hammer. Everything swam before my eyes from the pain. But I still
couldn't move. The woman in blue pressed her ear against my
chest, listened, and shrank back. He hit me again. Everything
went blurry. The beautiful woman came up close again, wiped
shards of the hammer off my chest with a blue glove, and I realized that the hammerhead wasn't glass at all but ice! She
pressed her ear to my chest. I began to lose consciousness. The
last thing I heard was "An empty nut." Then everything was
just like it was—the Odeon bar, the police, alcohol in my

blood, a broken breastbone, a crushed chest…This affair surfaced in my memory a year ago. I wrote it all down immediately so I wouldn't forget anything. On leaving the hospital after the accident and thinking about the girl who had been beaten to death, I went straight to the library and dug out the newspaper files for the summer of 1972. And I discovered something striking! It turned out that that summer in Zürich four girls and two young men disappeared without a trace! Their photographs were published in the paper. All of them were blond and blue-eyed. In the very same summer, forty-eight people in a condition of alcoholic and narcotic inebriation had been hit by cars. All of them had serious wounds to their chests. The chief of the Zürich police in an interview in *Neue Zürcher Zeitung* declared that he had never seen such a mass series of young people being hit by cars during his entire twenty years of service. With great difficulty I found three of the forty-eight, all my age, who had suffered that summer. All of them had blondish hair (two had already gone gray) and blue eyes! And all of them had seriously scarred chests. One even showed me the scar in the center of his breastbone. And all of them had been at that Led Zeppelin concert! And later, as I did, had signed up for the Robert Plant Fan Club. But they hadn't been in any villa. And to my stories about the basement where we'd had the breath knocked out of us with an ice hammer, they reacted, to put it mildly, with skepticism. My attempts to contact the owners of the villa were also unsuccessful. My family basically thinks that I dreamed all this up when I lost my short-term memory. My doctor is certain that this is a temporary aberration caused by the memory loss. Let God be their judge…When I took to surfing the Internet, curious about abductions, and I finally came across your site, I shouted out for joy! I have read so many testimonies! So many people were kidnapped and beaten with an ice hammer, beaten till they died! So that means that I'm not insane! That means it all happened! Who did this? Why? Who are these vile beings? How I would like to find out!!

"Me too," said Olga. "I really would."

She stood up, stretched, glanced out the window. It was getting dark. A stifling July evening crawled across New York and lights went on. But here in NoHo, as always, it was great in any weather. Olga pulled a cigarette out of her pack, walked over to the north window, which looked out toward the East Village, and lit up. So today she had read three more stories. There were more than four hundred on the site. She remembered many of them, and her thoughts kept coming back to them. These stories had now become the main book of Olga's life, stakes sunk into the shaky, unreliable world that had taken her parents from her. She leaned on them for support. They wouldn't allow her to wring her hands or collapse into depression. She could recite the names of people who had suffered from the ice hammer as though they were the names of brothers and sisters: Marie Couldefille, Edward Feller, Kozima Ilishi, Barbara Stachinska, Nikolai and Natasha Zotov, Iozas Normanis, Sabina Bauermeister, Zlata Boyanova, Nick Solomon, Ruth Jones, Bjorn Vassberg. They had all experienced torture by ice. All had writhed, coughed up blood, and lost consciousness from the excruciating blows. All had painfully returned to life, crying in anguish, inhaling the air with their crushed chests. All had tried, in vain, to find sympathy from friends and family, to prove that everything that had happened was the truth. And they had all crashed into a wall of incomprehension, just as they had with the ice . . .

Now these three had been added to them.

"They give everybody a shot of something to destroy their memory," Olga thought to herself as she smoked, staring out the window. "But it doesn't work on everyone. Or maybe they don't have time to give everyone shots? Or . . . they think that the person is already dead? But I was alive. And Bjorn. And Barbara. And Sabina . . ."

The parrot coughed in his cage and ruffled his feathers. He spoke quietly: "Locomotive."

Olga put out her cigarette and walked over to Fima. Her late father had taught the parrot the word "locomotive."

"No, Fimochka, not a locomotive. An airplane. And, judging by everything, really soon." Olga stuck her finger in the cage and stroked the parrot's pink claw. "And you'll be staying with Amanda again. Will you miss me?"

"Locomotive!" answered the parrot.

Khram and Gorn

GORN CAME to on the second day.

His heart cried out the grief of six years of earthly life. His small body was exhausted. His face had grown thin and haggard. And he had matured. Now he was no longer a retarded boy, who had suffered a meaningless earthly life, but *Light-bearing* Gorn. Now he was prepared for great feats in the name of the Light. He was beginning his new path in life. A great path. All this time I was continuously near him. I *retreated* from his heart when it cried. I sat and *watched*. And *protected* him. Now that his heart had cleansed itself of the past, I could *draw closer*.

Gorn *was waiting*.

I placed my fingers on his eyelids. His eyes opened. And looked at me. They were the eyes of a brother. The most *important* brother of all. And I am the one who has to *initiate* him into the Brotherhood. His heart had calmed down. It was ready to *heed*.

And so, I began to *speak* with him.

Gorn's heart is *open*. It *desired*. Its strength amazed me. It is a new strength. The Strength we have all been waiting for. I could help him.

I *placed* my heart as a Light-bearing shield between Gorn and the world. My old body became a *shadow* of the *shining* shield. The shadow of my body shades him from the world: It isn't yet time! The world of the Earth lies beyond my stooped back. The round, inconstant, self-devouring, and dangerous world of the Earth drones behind my back. My back is a wide shadow. Gorn's pure heart should not *see* the world: It isn't time yet! It *isn't prepared* to touch the world of the Earth. The ruthless world. Which devours itself. Which coagulates with the rage of self-destruction. My trembling hands shade continents. My bony fingers spread out, hiding cities. The meat machines coagulate under my wrinkled palms. Villages and tiny settlements, roads and mechanisms crowd behind my flaccid thighs, which preserve the scars of torture. My shoulders hide the terrible order of earthly armies. My head shades the countries of the north where we found so many of *ours*. I cover the violent world of meat machines with the shadow of my torso, turning my *shining* heart toward the long-desired brother.

I *protect* Gorn.

I *protected* Gorn.

I *cherish* Gorn.

I *feed Gorn.*

Gorn's heart is *opening* in leaps and bounds. It *flows* with the radiance of desire. It *demands*. Its *growth* is swift. No one in the Brotherhood is so *swift* of heart as Gorn. No one *burgeons* with Light so rapidly. We are joyful. We *shine* and exult. Our hearts *girdle* the Newly Acquired one, shining with the joy of the Light. And the exultation of the Light fills the Brotherhood with ecstasy: We *believe!* Gorn forced us to *place our faith* in the Fulfillment. What our hearts *dreamed* of, *spoke* of in Great and Lesser Circles, moaned over in our sleep, whispered about on our deathbeds—had come closer! And Gorn brought *it* closer.

We will protect his heart and body.

Each morning my hands wake up Gorn's body. And my heart *wakens* his young, powerful heart. Sisters pick Gorn up and carry him into the room of Ablutions. The sisters wash his body with the purest water, infused with flowers and grasses. They dry him with silken fabrics. They anoint him with oils. They dress him in clothes woven of mountain plants. The sisters give Gorn tea to drink, made from grasses of the taiga, which give calm and strength. They offer him the fruits of tropical trees.

His body grows.

But his heart *grows* much faster.

His heart grows stronger. It *feeds* off the Light. He learns the first words of the heart language. He *sucks* in words from our hearts. In Gorn's heart the immeasurable power of the Light grows stronger. Even my strong and experienced heart restrains this *onslaught* with great *difficulty*. Gorn wants to *embrace* everything right away. But he cannot *contain* it all. He *craves* with ferocity. It is my lot to *quench* the thirst of his heart. And I do this with *extreme* caution, so as not to harm him. Or the Brotherhood. For I understand *who* Gorn is for us. Brothers and sisters on all the continents understand this. Their hearts are *shining*. Hands are joining. Lesser, Middle, and Great Circles are forming. They flare in the dark gloom of earthly life, sending us heart Light. We *accept* it. It strengthens our hearts. We *share* the Light with Gorn.

I *guard* Gorn.

I *preserve* Gorn.

I *fill Gorn*.

I *hold* Gorn.

And the Light in his heart *grows* and *expands*.

Gorn's heart gradually *fills* with Light. But knowledge of the world of Earth I *move aside* for Gorn: It is still early! It is not time! Only when his heart is strengthened may he *touch* the world. Which we created. In which we *went astray*. Only a *full* heart can *see* the world. And *understand* its essence.

I prepare Gorn's heart for the most important.

Bjorn and Olga

A VERY tall blond man wearing a lemon-yellow T-shirt and white shorts strode vigorously through the crowd, pulling a red suitcase rattling after him.

"There he is! What a beanpole!" Olga thought as she quickly finished her grapefruit juice and put six shekels down on the bar.

The blond man approached. He smiled cautiously. In the photograph he sent Olga by e-mail his chin seemed heavier and his neck less muscular. On the blond man's upturned nose drops of sweat mingled with freckles.

"*Odin v pole voin*," he painstakingly pronounced the passwords in a deep, chesty voice.

"*Kräftskivan*," Olga replied, sliding off the tall metal barstool. Her small heels touched the floor.

"Two and a half heads taller than me," she noted to herself, stretching out her small hand. "Hi, Bjorn."

"Hi, Olga!" He smiled even wider.

Olga firmly shook his huge, sweaty palm with her small hand.

"I didn't expect you to be so tall," she said in English. She noticed the word KRÄFTSKIVAN curving around a red crab on his yellow shirt.

"Six foot seven," he answered honestly. "And where's your red hair?"

"Sometimes you need to change something about yourself," Olga said, donning her dark glasses, heaving the strap of her bag onto her shoulder. "Well, let's go, shall we?"

The Swede spoke English with a typical Scandinavian accent; Olga with an acquired American one.

Not noticing her heavy bag, he turned his head. "And where is . . ."

"Follow me." Olga moved decisively to the exit. "What is *Kräftskivan*?"

"The holiday of the crabs," said Bjorn, catching up with her in two steps, his suitcase clattering behind him.

"You mean when they eat them?"

Bjorn nodded with a smile, and added, "I already translated your password from Russian. That is, someone helped me translate it: One soldier can win the war."

"Wonderful!" said Olga, tossing her head back. "Now you know the principle of my life."

They went out into the dry, hot July air. They got in a taxi. Olga slowly pronounced the address in Petah Tikva in Hebrew.

"Off we go," the driver answered in Russian, smiling at Olga in the mirror.

Not the least bit surprised, she took out a cigarette. "May I smoke in the car?"

"We're not in America, are we?" The driver grinned. "Smoke to your health, as much as you want, take deep breaths."

"Thank you." She lit up.

"He is from Russia?" Bjorn asked.

"Yes." Olga opened the window despite the air conditioner and turned her face to the warm breeze.

"Here there are many people from Russia." Bjorn shook the fair head on his long, sturdy neck.

"Yes." Olga flipped the ash into the air. "There are a lot of people from Russia here."

They rode in silence to Petah Tikva. Zipping past a hilly, sun-drenched landscape, the car entered dusty, scorching Tel Aviv. After winding through the streets, the driver stopped near an unusually long building.

Bjorn tried to pay, but Olga beat him to it, handing the driver a fifty-shekel bill.

"Are you a feminist?" Bjorn asked, extracting his large body from the car.

"Not anymore." Olga looked at the rosy-white three-story build-ing stretching half the block.

She went over to a small limestone stoop. Large brass numbers, 1-6-7, hung on the door. Olga rang the bell. After a moment, a pretty woman about fifty years old opened the door.

"Olga Drobot?" she asked in friendly voice, in Russian tinged with a Jewish accent.

"Yes, hello." Olga took off her dark glasses.

"I'm Dina. Come in."

"Hi, I'm Bjorn." The Swede nodded his head.

They entered a small foyer.

"Are you hungry?" the woman asked. "Honestly, now!"

"Thank you, Dina, we're full." Olga put her bag down on the ground. "We'd like to do what we came here for as quickly as we can. If it's possible, of course."

Dina sighed. "Just now it is possible. Until he falls asleep."

"Excellent."

"Follow me," Dina said as she climbed a staircase.

Olga and Bjorn followed her. It was cool in the house, and some-where up above a dog shut in a room whined. On the second floor Dina led them to a door, opened it, and looked into the room. Her beautiful hand gestured to them to enter. Olga and Bjorn went in. It was a small bedroom, for one person. The venetian blinds on the window were slightly closed. On a narrow bed under a quilted blanket lay a thin old man in lilac-colored pajamas. His hands rested on top of the blanket; an empty cup stood on his chest. His breathing was heavy and loud, and the cup moved in time with his breath. On seeing the guests he picked up the cup and moved it from his chest to a bedside table.

"Papa, these are the people," said Dina.

"I guessed," said the old man. "And I would really like it if a half hour will be enough for you. Or else I'll fall asleep again. This disease is so wonderful, it's actually a delightful disease. Permanent sleep. Well, it's not the worst illness, is it now, Dinochka?"

Dina nodded. "I already said it a million times: I'm jealous, Papa."

"Go be jealous"—the old man grinned, baring his beautiful false teeth—"and bring them our carrot juice, the best in the world."

"How would I manage without your suggestions, Papa!" said Dina, tossing her head and leaving.

"Sit down, we've already brought chairs for you." The old man turned, leaning against two folded pillows. "And let's get down to business."

The guests sat; Olga got out a small Dictaphone.

"David Leibovich, we won't trouble you too long, but believe me this is very—" Olga began to speak but the old man interrupted her.

"No superfluous words are necessary, I beg you. For the last sixty years I've told this story about three hundred and eighty-six times. If today is the three hundred and eighty-seventh time, it won't dislocate my tongue. Especially since close friends of Dina's are asking about it. So are you ready?"

"Yes," Olga replied.

Bjorn sat there, not understanding a word, his back straight and his tan fists on his white knees. Dina appeared with two tall glasses of fresh carrot juice wrapped in napkins and offered them to the guests.

"All right, *bikitser*," the old man said, holding on to the edge of the quilt like a railing. "How I got to the camps doesn't really matter. I was in two camps, in Belorussia and Poland, and then—over there.

In short, I ended up there in the spring of '44. I'd just turned seventeen. Well, you know what kind of place it was and what they did
there, I don't have to tell you. When our group arrived, we managed
to crawl out of the cars; they lined us up straightaway, looked us over,
and chose twenty-eight from the entire group. I was one of them.
And we all looked alike only in that, first of all, we were all Jews, like
everyone in the train cars, and second—all of us had light-colored or
reddish hair and blue eyes. Now I'm all gray, my eyes have gone
muddy, I'm lying here parallel to the horizon, but then I was a well-
built, handsome fellow, blondish and blue-eyed. Of course, I didn't
understand where we were going and why we were chosen. None of
the twenty-eight understood, and what was there to understand?
There was nothing to understand. It stank of burned people all the
time and ashes flew around everywhere, that's all you needed to understand. In short, we were deloused and then taken off to the barracks. And in this barracks I saw only blue-eyed and light-haired
Jews. There were two of those barracks: men's and women's. And everyone was blue-eyed and light-haired. There were a lot of redheads.
It was kind of strange, you even felt like laughing. And there was lots
of talk and guessing going on about this, a lot of people joked glumly
that they were going to make us real Aryans and send us off to the
eastern front to fight for the Führer. Some said that they were going
to do experiments on us. But they didn't do anything to us. The experiments were done on others. And it was others that went into the
crematoriums, from other barracks. So then, six months passed. We
weren't made into ashes, as it turned out. And over this time both
barracks were almost overflowing: with each train that arrived they
kept on adding and adding blue-eyed Jews—five, ten, or more. And
sometimes—not a single one. Then the front came nearer, the Germans started getting nervous, and the ovens worked full tilt. But still,
no one touched us. And then in October, it was the eleventh, exactly,
we got the command: 'Raus!' We left our barracks, and they looked
us over. They picked out some who had hidden with us who had black
eyes. Or brown eyes. Or green eyes. There were some of them too. We
hid them. They were separated from us. Then we were loaded into a
huge troop train and it left the camp, heading west. We didn't know

what to think, but still we were happy that we'd left that cursed place. It stank of death there. We were sure that we were being taken to Germany. But the train traveled only for about two hours and then stopped. We were ordered out of the train. So we got out. The train stood in a clear field. There was an enormous sandpit right nearby. It was this huge gully, a sandy ditch. The guards from the train took up their places along the edges of this pit. And we were ordered to go down into it. Well, we all realized that we weren't going to any Germany, but that they'd just finish us off here. In the camp we'd heard that the Russians were attacking hard. So the Germans were in a hurry to get rid of us. And we walked down into that pit. What else could we do? There was nowhere to run—there was just a big field around. There were about two thousand of us. No less. We went down into the pit. We were ordered to sit. We sat. And prayed. Because we understood that they would start shooting off their machine guns any minute. But no one shot at us. We sat there and waited. Guards with automatic weapons stood around the edges of the pit. And suddenly, up above, from where we'd come down, two SS officers appeared with two suitcases. They opened the suitcases and took two old people out of them. They weren't even exactly old people, but something totally strange, at first I thought that they were adolescents from our camp, emaciated, all skin and bones. But then I saw that it was an old man and an old woman. They were unbelievably thin, thinner than we were, and all sort of white, as if someone had been keeping them underground. Their hair was white as snow and very long. The SS officers carried them in their arms like children and brought them down to us. And this old couple, held in the arms of SS officers, stared at us. They had very strange faces, not evil and not good, but something bizarre, like they had already died long ago and didn't give a fig about anything. I've never seen faces like that. Even in camp the goners had different faces. These faces were still very unusual. These two also had blue eyes. They watched. But it was the same kind of thing, it was like they looked straight through us. You know, there are times when a person starts thinking and fixes his eyes on something without seeing it. That's the kind of eyes they had. They looked at us and muttered something we couldn't hear. And the

SS officers started picking out some of us: one here, another over there. This went on and on. And then they took a young guy who was sitting just by me. It was Moishe from Kraków. I met him in the camp and we even became friends a little. He was older than me. Before the war he worked as a salesman in a department store. Like me, his whole family had been killed. He was very religious and said that if God left him alive, he would become a rabbi. This Moishe from Kraków, he always carried a piece of paper with him, the waxed kind they used to wrap dried fish in before the war. He kept it with him all day long, crumpled up. And in the evening, when they called lights-out and locked the barracks, he lay down on his bunk and smoothed that paper out on his palm. It was given to him by a rabbi in the ghetto who said that this paper here, it is you yourself: during the day life crumples you up, turns you into a little ball, and in the evening you straighten yourself out, you forget about the world and again stand before God in all your truth. At night he always smoothed the paper out and placed it under his head. That piece of paper helped him. When they dragged him out of our crowd, this old man and woman got all worked up. They were actually writhing and shaking. And then I thought they had epilepsy. They only took about thirty of us. They took them to the train and put them in the car. And they took the epileptics away. The head guy gave an order to the guards and they went back to the train. All of us, we started praying because we were certain they were going to shoot us now. I put my head down, stared at an ant, because the ant was going to live, and they were going to shoot me any minute! And suddenly I heard the engine whistle and the train jerk. They up and left. The train wheels rolled and rolled and rolled. And that was it. The train was gone. No SS officers. We were sitting in the pit. And there was nothing but empty field all around. No one understood anything. So we stood up, climbed out of the pit, and walked off. No one had the strength to run. People wandered off in different directions. I made my way with three guys, they were all from Warsaw, and I was lucky because after all we were all blue-eyed and had light-colored hair, and the Poles, even though they're anti-Semites, they took us in, umm, they, it was ... *azokhen vei* ... there still were ... kind ones and scum ... that *pani* was named

Veslava, and her father had lost an arm . . . and they . . . and they . . . but . . . not only . . . as usual . . ."

The old man yawned and began to snore immediately.

"That's it," said Dina, standing at the door; she went over to the old man and straightened his blanket.

He snored very loud, his mouth wide open. His head shook on his pillow. The dog locked upstairs whined louder on hearing his snore.

Olga put the Dictaphone away and stood up. Bjorn, who didn't understand any Russian, also stood.

"Tell me, Dina, did any of the two thousand survive?"

"Yes." Dina took the empty cups from the guests. "In Israel he met two of them. About fifteen years ago. But where they are now, I don't know."

"But did he try to find out—what this was all about? Why they were put in those two barracks, taken away in the train, and then let go?"

"Yes, yes," Dina muttered, "of course he tried . . . Excuse me, I have to take the dog out."

She opened the door and ran up a narrow wooden staircase. Somewhere up above a door opened and a young female voice said angrily in Yiddish: "Your egoism knows no bounds!"

"Don't you see we have guests?" Dina answered in Hebrew, unlocking the door. "Let's go, Fifer."

The dog turned out to be a huge silky black mastiff. Dina led him downstairs by a thick leash. Olga and Bjorn also went downstairs.

"And what did your father find out?" Olga asked, lifting her bag.

"He found out—" Dina opened the door and the dog, pulling on the leash, literally jerked her out of the foyer onto the street.

"Stay! Heel!" Dina shouted in Hebrew, struggling with the dog.

Olga and Bjorn went out into the street with their things. The sun was scorching.

"And what did he find out?" Olga, squinting from the blinding sun, set her purse down on the white, hot sidewalk.

"That blue-eyed Jews were chosen on personal orders from the camp director."

"What for?"

"There was no written explanation." The dog pulled Dina farther down the street. "It seems it was just some kind of German madness..."

"Did anyone write about it?"

"What?"

The small window in the attic opened; a girl with curly hair stuck her head out and shouted loudly in Hebrew: "My mother is an egotist!"

And she slammed the window shut.

"Did anyone write about this? In the newspapers? Or anywhere?" Olga shouted to Dina.

"What?"

"Was this written about?"

"Yes, but no one understood...akh, you..."

"What?"

"No one ever understood—what it was...and...and...Heel! Heel! And why it was done!" Dina shouted, balancing, and then disappeared around a corner.

Olga looked back at the house. The old man's loud snoring could even be heard on the street.

"What did she say?" asked Bjorn.

Olga sighed and put on her dark glasses.

"What did she say?" Bjorn asked again.

"That life can't be turned back," Olga muttered in Russian, as she noticed a taxi up ahead. "All right, then, let's go to the hotel."

In the car, Olga felt cold from the air conditioner; Bjorn kept asking questions, she kept sighing, muttering, "Later, everything later."

The hotel Prima Astor that Olga had reserved over the Internet was located about a hundred meters from the sea. Olga noticed that the sea was smooth and calm. They were put on the same floor, in small one-person rooms. After taking a shower and changing into a linen blouse and striped shorts, Olga invited Bjorn into her room, sat him down in the sole chair, settled herself on the bed, and translated the old man's monologue for him from the Dictaphone recording. The Swede listened to it, silent and tense, his hands on his knees. Then he moved his large legs and long arms, stuck out his lower lip, and said thoughtfully, "It sounds like the truth. We should think about it very seriously."

"That's a profound observation!" Olga nodded ironically, taking a cigarette out of a pack and lighting it.

"You think that I'm too—" the Swede began, but Olga interrupted him.

"I don't think anything," she said rubbing the bridge of her nose. "You know, Bjorn, first of all, I don't like the heat, and second, I have jet lag."

"I have tablets. I already took some."

"Great. Then you can go to your room and think seriously for an hour and a half or so. And I'll take a nap. Okay?"

"Okay." He stood, smiled guiltily, and left.

Olga finished her cigarette, lowered the green blind, pulled back the covers, undressed completely, and lay down, covering herself with the sheet. The air conditioner rumbled quietly over the door.

"Sleeping sickness," Olga thought, running her palm over the cool, fresh sheet. "Well, it's certainly better than insomnia..."

Her hand touched her stomach. Her body was tired from the last few days.

"Two barracks. Two barracks..." Her fingers touched her navel and climbed higher. "Two barracks in an open field... no hope and no grief... Lord, why did I come here..."

Her fingers felt the scar on her chest, the small dent in her breastbone.

"A piece of paper. For wrapping herring. That's good. I should get one of those. And straighten it out for the night... Life crumples you..."

She fell asleep. She dreamed about Todd Belieu, the top manager of the elite kitchen department, naked and incredibly thin. He was walking around the room with an iron stick, muttering something in Hebrew, and banging on the kitchen sets to test their durability.

Olga woke up when the phone rang. She opened her eyes. Evening twilight filled the room. The phone on the table by the bed was ringing. She picked up the receiver.

"Yes."

"It's Bjorn. Olga, it's already 20:07."

"Oh my God . . . Okay, I'm getting up."

She took a shower and got ready. And knocked at Bjorn's door five minutes later. Soon they were sitting in a small restaurant not far from the hotel. Bjorn ordered the local beer and lamb chops. Olga ordered chicken on toast, water, and coffee. She wasn't very hungry.

"So have you thought about it seriously?" she asked, putting out her cigarette in a clay ashtray.

"Yes. Yes. I think it's the same people who kidnapped us and our families."

"So they existed before the war as well?"

"Yes."

"And who are these emaciated old people?"

"I don't know. Perhaps it was their leaders." He took a large swallow of beer.

Olga looked at the strip of foam remaining on his upper lip. He noticed, and wiped it off with a napkin.

"It was probably related somehow to Fascism."

"How?"

"I don't know. But those people back then, and us now—we've all got blue eyes and light-colored hair. And the Fascists had that idea of a Nordic race."

"The fair-haired devil?"

"Yes. The fair-haired devil."

"But there were Jews in the barracks. The Fascists hated us, destroyed us. And I'm a Jew. And my parents were also Jews."

Bjorn sighed. "It's strange. But all the same, Olga, I think that it's connected to Fascism in some way."

Olga lit another cigarette.

"I don't know . . . My parents and I were kidnapped by three blue-eyed guys. One was a blond, that's definite, and two of them, I think, had dyed hair. Then, when they beat me with that ice hammer, they kept on saying the same thing: 'Speak with the heart.' Until I fainted. What does Fascism have to do with that?"

"I don't know. It's just my intuition."

Olga laughed.

"It sounds funny, I understand," said Bjorn, "but so far intuition is all we have. There's nothing else."

"Intuition!" Olga scoffed angrily. "In broad daylight some sort of monsters kidnap people, beat them to death. They disappear. No one knows who they are! The police give annual numbers of people who've disappeared. Statistics! Is that normal?"

"It isn't normal. When I told everything to the police, they didn't believe me for a long time. A hammer made of ice! 'Speak with the heart . . .' They looked at each other for a long time and thought I was nuts."

"They didn't believe me, either. Then they did an expert analysis of the wounds. Mine and my," she stammered, "my papa's and mama's. Their breastbones were completely smashed. But all I had was a broken rib and some cracked bone. There was a puddle where they found me."

"The ice they beat us with had melted," Bjorn said. "I first thought that it was glass. He didn't hit me very hard the first time. Then, when the hammer cracked, I realized that it was ice. And there was a puddle, too. Not only of water."

He looked at his huge hand, clenched it in to a fist, and opened it. "There wasn't only water. Blood came out of my brother's throat. Blood . . . a lot of blood. And mine too."

They fell silent.

At that moment a plump waiter brought them a large dish with grilled lamb and placed it in front of Bjorn. Olga glanced at the sizzling, juicy meat. She raised her eyes to the waiter.

"Do you have Russian vodka?"

"Of course!" The waiter smiled. "Two orders?"

"Bring me"—Olga thought a minute—"a bottle."

The waiter nodded without surprise and returned with a sweating bottle of Stolichnaya and two glasses. Olga silently poured the vodka into the glasses. Bjorn stretched out his fingers and a glass disappeared in his palm.

Olga squinted at the neighboring table. Three dark-skinned elderly Jews sat there, eating slowly.

"Only four months have passed, and I . . . can't believe it," Olga said. "It's all . . . some kind of dream. Very disturbing. Very . . . very . . . I hate it!"

And she downed the vodka in one gulp.

Bjorn sighed. "I've come to believe already. When my brother was buried, I went into his room. There was a diary there, I'd never read it. I broke the lock and opened the diary. On that day he wrote: 'Today in Göteborg there's my favorite sky, the color of blue corundum. That means it will be a lucky day.' After that I believed that Tomas was no longer, that my younger brother was gone."

He sighed again and drank his vodka.

"Blue corundum . . . what is that? A stone?"

"Yes. My brother studied geology. He knew stones very well. He said that my eyes resembled alexandrite and his resembled aquamarine."

"My mother told me that my eyes were the color of Prussian blue plus a little bit of emerald green."

"Was she an artist?"

"No, just a restorer. But a long time ago. Before emigrating."

Olga filled the glasses. She looked at Bjorn's awkward hands and smiled for the first time that evening.

"You're really big. Was your brother like that too?"

"An inch taller. And he played basketball better than I did too. On the street they called us 'lampposts.'"

Olga looked at him with a smile. "How is it said in Swedish?"

"Lamppost? *Lyktstolpen.*"

"*Lyktstolpen.*"

Vodka on an empty stomach quickly inebriated Olga.

"Let's drink to them. For . . . ours. Only we mustn't clink glasses."

They drank. But Olga drank faster.

"Do all Russian girls drink so fast?" asked Bjorn, stopping to take a breath.

"Not all of them. Only the chosen. Eat while it's hot."

She took a lamb chop from his plate and bit into the juicy meat.

"How come you haven't asked me about my theory?"

"What is your theory?"

"I think that the ICE Corporation knows who beat us with the hammer."

"It doesn't know."

"Have you seen their device, Bjorn, have you tried it?"

"Of course I have. Who hasn't tried it . . ."

"But there's ice there too! There's an ice tip that hits you in the chest. And you feel some sort of sadness, then a group of people appears, and you feel really good with them."

"It's just a computer game for the new generation. There's no doubt that the ICE Corporation invented the sensor device, and spread the myth of the Tungus ice which supposedly elicits unusual sensations when it strikes people in the chest. They claim they went to great trouble to get this ice, transported it from the tundra, all the tips are made only from this ice . . . But that's a myth. Ice is ice. Whether falling out of the sky or freezing on the ground—it's the same. No matter what their 'experts' say, the myth of the Tungus meteorite ice is only a pretext so they can sell their product at a higher price. So much has been written about this. Serious scientists have ridiculed them. It's not even worth talking about. ICE has made billions on its device. Why would they need to kidnap people and clobber them with ice hammers?"

"Well, someone is using their idea!" Olga shouted so loud that the people sitting at the neighboring table looked over at them.

"Maybe it was the other way around."

"What do you mean, the other way around?"

"Maybe ICE is using someone else's methods?"

"Banging on people's chests until they die?"

"Yes."

"And what kind of method is that?"

"I don't know yet. Something from the ancient cults. Maybe the Celts, for example, or maybe the Yakuts had a rite like that. Maybe shamans did it, although I didn't find any ritual like that on the Internet or in our university library."

"Then who is it? Satanists?"

"Doesn't look like them. More likely—Fascists."

"And how is this connected to Fascism?"

"It's connected somehow. I'm certain. The German Fascists used ancient mythology. For that matter, they had their own theory of the universe. I found it on the Internet. As they saw it, the entire universe surrounding us consisted of ice. And only the hot willpower of human beings could melt space for life in the ice."

"Then why the hell are they whacking people on the chest with this ice?"

"I don't know. Maybe in order to test man's will? Whether he is capable of melting the ice?"

"Nonsense! And for this they're ready to murder?"

"Well, lots of secret societies easily murder people to forward their goals, even though those goals seem crazy to normal people."

Olga threw the remains of the lamb chop on her plate. "Who then, who are they?"

"We're here in order to answer that question."

"Who, who killed my parents?" Olga pounded the table with her fist, knocking over her glass, which fell on the floor and shattered. "Listen, I'm, I don't know…completely drunk." Her head rolled back. "Let's go back to the hotel."

"All right." Bjorn raised his basketball arm, calling the waiter.

In the hotel Olga collapsed on the bed. Bjorn stood near her, his head nearly touching the ceiling. He clearly didn't know what to do.

"Who killed my parents?" Olga asked once more.

"The same people who killed my brother," Bjorn answered.

Olga slapped herself on the cheeks, then grinned a drunken grin. "What do you know. I got drunk on two shots. I'm drunk as a skunk!"

"You're just tired from everything."

"That's right. I'm tired from everything. When is our plane?"

"At 5:20 in the morning."

"Oh my God…You'll wake me up?"

"Of course. Good night, Olga." He swayed a bit and took a step toward the door.

"Wait."

Bjorn stopped. Olga looked at him. He looked at her.

"You think that guy from Guangzhou knows something?"

"Why would he have gotten in touch with us otherwise?"

Olga nodded. She sat up on the bed.

"Show me your scar," she said.

He took off his yellow T-shirt with the red crab. Olga stood up and staggered over to him. On Bjorn's chest were two purple scars. Olga's inebriated eyes wobbled back and forth at eye level with the scars. Bjorn looked down at her. Olga took off her blouse.

"I just have one."

Between small breasts with large brown nipples were white scars in the form of brackets with a small indentation in the bone between them.

"They broke off a piece of my bone." Olga raised her head and looked Bjorn straight in the eyes. "Pretty, isn't it?"

"Yes," he answered quietly.

They stood silently facing each other.

"Remind me, what did they call you on the street?" Olga asked, swaying and grabbing her white belt with both hands.

"*Lyktstolpen.*"

"*Lyktstolpen!*" she laughed. "What do you want now, Lyktstolpen?"

Bjorn looked at her attentively. "I want...to wake you up at 4 a.m."

"Of course." She stepped away, letting him through and leaning against the wall, running her hand over it. "*Bonne nuit*, Lyktstolpen."

"*Bonne nuit*, Olga."

Leaning down, Bjorn left, carefully closing the door. Olga pushed away from the wall, went into the tiny bathroom, and turned on the water in the sink. She saw herself in the round mirror.

"Good night, orphan."

And splashed water on the mirror.

Above the World

I AWAKEN later than my heart. It sleeps very little. It keeps *vigil* while I sleep. For it *knows* that the Fulfillment is near.

My heart awakens my body.

I rise, wash my old body. And head for Gorn. He sleeps on his white bed. I wake his body. Then, when the sisters' hands have washed his body and rubbed it with oils, I wake Gorn's heart. It awakens. I *adore* this moment.

This morning his heart wakes up most sublimely. Power and clarity *shine* in it. Today, Gorn is ready *to see* the world.

Today I will *show* him the world.

The world of our Great Mistake. Which we will soon correct. Gorn sits in the Refectory. I feed him fruits. He devours them. He doesn't ask me about the tree on which the fruit grew. He is not interested in the form of these fruits. He simply eats them. The wisdom of the heart is with him. He is no longer a boy from a city of meat machines. He is our most *beloved brother.*

His lips are sticky from the fruits of the earth. I wipe his lips. I pour water for him. He drinks it. We leave the house together. He looks at the world surrounding us. He looks *through* that world. His heart already *knows how* to do this. He is prepared *to see* the essence of the world.

Today I will *show* Gorn what he must know. I take him by the hand. We walk to the shore. The ocean, created by us billions of years ago, splashes at our feet. Brothers and sisters stand behind us. They watch the sky. A point appears in it. It comes closer and grows. It is a white machine that knows how to fly in the sky and land on the water. It lands on the ocean. It waits for us. I lead Gorn onto a small machine that knows how to float on the surface of the water. This machine takes us over the water to the white flying machine. Gorn stands, holding on to my hand. He looks. And asks no questions. His heart has a *presentiment*. But I do not touch his heart with mine. I *prepare myself.*

Arriving at the flying machine, we sit down in it. The door closes. The machine flies up off the surface of the ocean. Gorn looks out the window. He sees our island, our Home. He sees the brothers and sisters standing on the shoreline. The brothers and sisters move away from us. Gorn's heart *flares*: for the first time brothers and sisters are moving away from him. His heart *trembles*. It doesn't want to part with the other hearts. It doesn't want *to lose*. I stand nearby and *watch*. But I don't *help*: Gorn must deal with it himself. He *can*.

His eyes fill with tears: He is losing brothers. They are growing smaller. They turn into dots. The most beloved in this world disappear. Gorn cries aloud. His hand lets go of my hand. He throws himself at the window. His face pushes against the glass. Tears fall from his eyes.

"I waaant . . . waaant . . . I waaaannt!" he shouts into the glass.

But his most beloved disappear: our island is already no more than a dot. It is barely visible on the surface of the ocean. It drowns in the ocean. The ocean we created. Which Gorn created.

I stand tensely by. And I don't *help*.

"I waaannnnt . . . I waannnt!" his body roars.

"I waannnt!" his brain roars.

But his heart is *silent* for the moment.

The island disappears into the ocean. Horror grips Gorn. His body is rigid. His face presses against the glass. He freezes. His brain comes to the realization that the ocean has swallowed his brothers and sisters.

I *freeze*.

And the brothers and sisters below *freeze*.

We wait.

We believe.

We *want*.

And Gorn's heart *flares!* It *stretches* to his beloved hearts! His near and dear. It *sees* them! They are alive. The ocean did not swallow them. Gorn *sees* everyone on the island! And I *see* that he *sees*!

I rush to him. I embrace him from behind. I *help* and *direct*.

He grows stiff from what he has just discovered: It turns out that the brothers and sisters are close by. The eyes don't see them, but the heart *sees*. Each and every one! Gorn *looks at* them.

And I *gently* help him.

And FOR THE FIRST TIME we *look* together. And I realize that *everything* will be done. That he and I will accomplish our Great Task. And I *watch* him with the heart, as if for the first time. And he *watches*, feeling me. And the brothers and sisters below *see* us.

The iron machine carries us through the air. Gorn and I fly over the ocean. I embrace Gorn. I *help* him. Since his heart awoke it has *learned* quickly. It can already do a great deal. But now it has discovered *something new*: It is possible to *see* great distances. And it's possible *to see* the brothers and sisters even beyond the horizon. And with my heart it's possible *to see THEM ALL AT THE SAME TIME!*

But one must prepare for this.

In order to see ALL OF OURS, one must know and understand the world in which they ended up. One has to know how to *place* the world on his hand. Like an apple that you, Gorn, eat every morning. For it is only when the world becomes no bigger than an apple to you that you will be able to accomplish the Great Task.

I *support* you, Gorn.

I will *show* you the world.

Gorn understands. He wants to *understand* the world. But he cannot ask me himself. With my heart I *move* toward him. My heart *takes* his heart. We *look* together. The world is below us. Seven times must I *look* at the world with Gorn. And that will be enough for him to *understand* what lies below us. Seven views of the world *are sufficient*. We *look*.

VIEW ONE: The immobile is more perfect than the mobile, ice is more perfect than water, petrified plants are more perfect than living plants, the absence of motion is more perfect than motion itself, silence is more perfect than sound, the absence of action is more perfect than action itself. Repose is the highest perfection.

VIEW TWO: At the foundation of the perfected world lie repose and wholeness, integrity, indivisibility, and uniformity; the perfected world must not change and develop, since any development violates integrity and wholeness, leads to losses and changes; repose and wholeness need no development, the absence of development defines eternity, and eternity is the most perfect of all worlds.

VIEW THREE: The simplicity of a world testifies to its perfection; the simpler the world, the less it is prone to changes, the closer it is to eternity; complexly structured worlds are inconstant and ephemeral, they self-destruct rapidly, violating world repose and the world harmony of immutability.

VIEW FOUR: Stones are more perfect than plants, plants are

more perfect than animals, animals are more perfect than humans, humans are the most imperfect creatures on the Earth we created.

VIEW FIVE: The imperfectness of humans engenders their anxiety, their anxiety facilitates instability, instability leads to the urge to reproduce, reproducing stimulates wars, wars force people to multiply; man is dependent on the continuation of the species, he is not free, he is not self-sufficient, he cannot be viewed outside the sequence of previous generations.

VIEW SIX: Man's instability spreads to animals and plants, forcing them to destroy one another and multiply, multiply and destroy, which intensifies the instability of the world of Earth.

VIEW SEVEN: The unstable world of Earth spreads pernicious waves of instability, begets the instability of the Universe, violates its primordial perfection; the Universe collapses because of tiny Earth, the center of the collapse.

Gorn *saw* the world.

He *sees* it.

And he *understands* it. Gorn's hands are pressed against the glass. I take his hand. The world lies like an apple in his palm. Now the world is *immobile*. It can be examined calmly. It can't get away from Gorn and Khram.

Gorn is happy. His heart breathes *strength*.

He understands that he *is capable*.

And I close my eyes in ecstasy.

Tsintsziu

THE BOEING 747 Jerusalem–Hong Kong flight landed at 9:30 a.m. At 11:36 a.m. Olga and Bjorn had crossed the border into mainland China and were on the train. At 12:40 p.m. they registered at the Hotel Guangzhou in the center of Guangzhou. And at 1:00 p.m. they met in the lobby of the hotel next to a two-meter-high sphere of smoky glass adorned with two golden dragons.

"For some reason they gave me a room for nonsmokers." Olga put her plastic key card in her wallet.

"You can change it," said Bjorn, turning sharply toward the white-and-gold counter where four young women in ivory-colored uniforms hovered.

"Forget it, later." Olga held on to Bjorn by the strap of his video camera. "Can you at least smoke down here? Ah, there's an ashtray…"

They walked over to a group of massive armchairs made of shiny, chocolate-colored leather and sat down. Olga lit a cigarette.

"Have you been in China? Oy, sorry. I asked you already…"

"In Beijing, nine years ago," Bjorn repeated with a smile.

"Hmmm…" She looked out at the street beyond the glass doors. "It looks dirtier here than in Hong Kong. Or not really?"

"I haven't noticed anything yet."

"Listen, has this guy been here a long time?"

"I haven't a clue. I only know that he's English and that it happened to him in Edinburgh seven months ago. And that he was clinically dead."

"Jeez… Although… I was out for a long time, too. I even had a dream: something about a fire. It was like my old childhood room was on fire, and my slippers and legs, too. And the nails on my feet began to melt… Probably because it was fairly cold in that basement."

The hotel's glass doors slid open silently and a blond man of medium height entered briskly. He was wearing light shorts and a light shirt with palm trees on it. Hanging on his back was a broad Panama hat.

"Bjorn Vassberg?" asked the blond, as he approached. "I'm Michael Laird. How are you?"

"Hello, Mr. Laird. Bjorn. And this is Olga Drobot."

"Hi, Michael." Olga held out her hand to the blond man first.

He seemed to be about forty, although quite youthful looking. His narrow face with its pointy chin, sunken cheeks, and slightly hooked nose was friendly and resolute. His dark-blue, almost black eyes were intelligent and open.

"You're just off the bus, are you? Tired? How do you handle humidity?" he asked quickly.

"July in New York isn't much better," Olga answered.

"You're American?"

"For the last fifteen years."

"Lovely. I've only been to America once. Quite a long time ago."

"Me too," Bjorn interjected.

"Comrades in misfortune." Olga summed up.

They laughed.

"Are you hungry?" asked Michael.

"I am!" said Olga, patting her stomach.

"Great. I know a marvelous restaurant," said Michael, putting on his hat. "Shall we go?"

They left the hotel and grabbed a taxi. Michael quickly gave the address in Chinese. And the very young, short-haired, nicely dressed taxi driver, separated from the passengers by a nickel-plated grate, drove them through the oppressively sun-drenched streets of Guangzhou.

"You know Chinese?" asked Olga.

"Conversational, a little. You can learn enough to get by in three months. But the characters are considerably more difficult," Michael answered.

The taxi passed a group of Chinese on beat-up mopeds and motorcycles who were racing away from some police cars. They were all wearing motorcycle helmets, faded overalls, and flip-flops. The taxi driver said a few sharp words and clicked his tongue. The moped riders accelerated and swerved into a side street, the police at their heels.

"What was that?" asked Olga.

"It happens all the time here." Michael glanced out the grimy window. "Private gypsy cabs. Competition for the taxis. It's forbidden, and they regularly set up raids."

"Is it cheaper?"

"Of course," Michael chuckled. "A funny thing happened with an English girl I know. She's studying Chinese at the local university. Late one night, after carousing with other students, she got on one of those *motos*, told the guy the address, and negotiated a price. And suddenly—boom, the police: 'Aha, a private taxi.' Well, this girl decided to help the *moto*: 'This isn't a private driver,' she said, 'he's my

Chinese boyfriend. We're going to Etsizunkhui.' The policemen roar with laughter. The Chinese boyfriend in the helmet turns his face toward her, and the police shine a flashlight on him: he's a toothless old peasant!"

Bjorn and Olga laughed. The corners of Michael's handsome lips curled in a smile.

They arrived at the restaurant, Bjorn paid the driver, and they got out of the cab. The huge glass building of the restaurant was decorated with red lanterns and multicolored paper garlands. In front of the entrance eight young women in red dresses stand in two rows. As soon as Olga, Bjorn, and Michael walked over, the young women sang out "Welcome" in Chinese and bowed.

In the front of the restaurant was a menagerie: in aquariums, nets, and cages, edible creatures wearing a doomed look swam, wriggled, and simply sat. There were fish, turtles, snakes, silkworms, chickens, rats, rabbits, cats of all sorts, and even a sad-looking dog with mangy fur and a frightened look on his face.

"What is this, it can all be eaten?" Olga asked. "Cats! How horrible!"

"They have a special dish called 'The Battle of the Tiger and the Dragon.' It's a combination of the fried cat and snake meat," Michael explained.

"Disgusting." Olga frowned. "No, I'm just going to have fish."

"I think I will too," said Bjorn, glancing to the sides.

A young woman with raspberry-colored lips, wearing a gray jacket, black skirt, white gloves, and holding a notebook, walked up to them. After a brief discussion, Michael ordered lobster sashimi and fried baby bamboo with ginger, wonton soup, and a fillet of carp. The waitress wrote down the order in her notebook and ran off to the kitchen. Her colleague, who had the same raspberry-colored lips, led the guests into the dining hall. It was the hour of the midday meal and the restaurant was full. This was where wealthy Chinese ate. In the center of the hall, surrounded by tall, powerful air conditioners, stood the red-and-gold character that meant "happiness."

"We need more privacy," Michael suggested, and Olga and Bjorn nodded.

Soon they were sitting in a small, separate room at a round table with a transparent lazy Susan. Two waitresses wiped their hands with warm cloths, then placed ice water, green tea, and little bowls with nuts and vegetable hors d'oeuvres in front of them. When the girls had gone, Michael spoke.

"Please show your chests."

Bjorn and Olga were not surprised by this request, and they pulled up their T-shirts. Michael looked at them, then unbuttoned his palm-tree-decorated silk shirt. In the center of his tanned chest three small purple-white scars showed.

"They struck you three times?" asked Bjorn.

"I remember two. Then I lost consciousness," Michael answered, separating his chopsticks and deftly picking up nuts with them.

"Where did this happen?" Olga asked.

"In Edinburgh."

"Did they kidnap you?"

"Yes. After work. Some woman asked me to help her open the trunk of her Jeep. As soon as I opened it, I was pulled inside, and they pressed a mask to my face. When I came to I was in a house, hung up on a wall as if crucified."

"Alone?" asked Olga.

"No, there was another guy and a girl too. Also blonds. They were beaten to death, I think. At least I don't see how they could have survived those blows."

"And then?"

"Then I work up in the middle of the night in the port. Despite my beaten chest I felt incredibly good. I lay in a puddle near a pub and looked at the stars. I didn't want anything but those stars . . . The police picked me up. And they found heroin in my blood. Needless to say my whole story about blue-eyed kidnappers with an ice hammer elicited nothing but a smile from the policemen. Then I felt really sick. The emergency rescue team had to do a bit of work."

"Heroin . . ." Olga picked up a nut distractedly. "They found plain old alcohol in my blood."

"My brother and I were simply thrown in the river. But he was already dead by that time," said Bjorn.

"You wrote me about that." Michael sighed.

The waitress brought them sashimi and soup.

"That was fast," Olga said in surprise.

"The Chinese style." Michael smiled, and suggested, "Maybe a little bit of cold sake?"

"They drink sake in China too?" Olga broke apart her chopsticks with a crack.

"Everything Japanese is fashionable here now. Since we ordered sashimi, we can drink sake."

"How do you say 'sake' in Chinese?"

"*Tsintsziu.*"

"*Tsintsziu*," Olga said.

"*Tsintsziu*," Bjorn repeated.

"*Tsintsziu!*" Michael told the waitresses, who nodded and left.

Olga looked at the tender pink lobster sashimi laid out in thin layers on a large plate, sighed, and tossed her chopsticks on the table.

"Somehow I can't eat anything. Listen, Michael, do you know who they are? Who are these monsters? Who hit us with ice? Who killed my parents and Bjorn's brother?"

Michael chewed on a nut, put down his chopsticks, wiped his lips with a napkin. And firmly answered, "Yes, I know."

"Who?" Olga almost cried out.

Michael sat and locked his hands together in front of him.

"Olga, we're dealing with a huge, powerful force."

"Does it have any relationship to the ICE Corporation?" Bjorn asked.

"A very direct one."

Olga and Bjorn glanced at each other.

"Why are they doing this?" Olga asked.

"They're looking for 'theirs.'"

"What does 'theirs' mean?"

"The Brothers of the Light."

"What are the Brothers of the Light?"

"It's 23,000 rays of the Primordial Light. They engendered the Universe with all the stars and planets and later they were mistakenly incarnated into living creatures on the planet Earth who eventually developed into human beings. There are 23,000 Brothers of the Light. They are scattered around the world. And they want very much to become rays of the Primordial Light once again. To accomplish this they need to find each other, join in a circle, and speak with their hearts. As soon as this happens, the Earth will disappear and they will again become rays of Light."

There was a long pause at the table.

"So this is just a sect?" Olga asked.

"You could call it that," Michael agreed, taking a sip of green tea.

"What does the ice have to do with it?" asked Bjorn.

"The ice of the Tungus meteorite awakens the sleeping hearts of the brothers. If they are hit in the chest, the Light, dozing in the heart, awakens."

"But ... the ICE device works the same way! It also strikes the chest with a small ice tip, and the user experiences a kind of high. And this is the very same ice of the Tungus meteorite, they say in their ads. But they don't say anything about some Brotherhood and Primordial Light."

"The ice used in the device has no connection with the Tungus meteorite. It's regular frozen water."

"But then why the device?"

"The device that the ICE Corporation developed has several purposes."

"What are they?"

"Well, first of all, there's a lot of money involved and the opportunity to acquire legal status. Second, if the police come across incidents of blue-eyed blonds being kidnapped and hit with ice hammers, they figure that it's just the ravings of some abnormal users of the device. The device is a screen for the Brothers of the Light. A lot of things can be hidden behind it."

The waiter entered with three pitchers of sake, poured them into three white cups, placed them in from of the diners, and left. Olga and Bjorn sat looking at Michael and trying to understand what they had just heard. Bjorn was the first to break the silence.

"On your site I became acquainted with about thirty stories of people who had been abducted by these bastards. How could it be that the police and the secret services haven't taken an interest in this yet? Do they just think we're all drug addicts or crazy computer-game fanatics?"

"It's not only blue-eyed blonds that disappear in the world. People disappearing is a totally normal sort of thing. Are the secret services interested in the ICE Corporation? Of course. But my friends and I are carrying on our own investigation. Now we have the wherewithal. When it happened to me, at first, like you I started banging on every door and searching for the individuals who carried it out. I didn't find them. But I did find other victims like myself. With the same scars on their chests. And they knew who was doing all of this."

"How did they find out?"

"That's a long story, Olga. The first private investigations began back in the sixties. Then people with the scars on their chests began to work together. And in tandem you can find out a lot. There are a hundred and eighty-nine of us now."

"One hundred eighty-nine!"

"Counting you." Michael smiled.

"And . . . where are they?"

"Here."

"All of them?"

"Yes."

"Why in Guangzhou?" Bjorn asked.

"Because this is the Brotherhood's turf. They are here. And that's why we have to be here too." Michael's face toughened and he pursed his lips sternly. "If we want to win, if we want revenge, we have to be here."

He picked up his cup of chilled sake. Silent for a moment, he gritted his teeth, emphasizing his thin, tough cheekbones, and said, "Olga and Bjorn. With your arrival there are more of us."

Bjorn picked up his cup. Olga picked up hers, slowly. She obviously liked Michael's unexpected sternness. He stretched his cup out to them.

"To us. And against them."

Bjorn and Olga clinked glasses. And drank.

Michael looked at them and placed his full glass back on the table.

Olga and Bjorn looked at him questioningly. He gave a sigh of relief and clasped his hands. And said, "Forgive me, I forgot to warn you: the Brothers of the Light don't use alcohol."

Olga looked into his blue-black eyes for a second, then cried out and pushed away from the table and headed for the door. But her legs gave way, her head flopped over helplessly, and her body collapsed on the floor. Bjorn stood up sharply to his full height, but a moment later he too swayed and began to fall. Michael grabbed Bjorn by the belt on his shorts, and to keep him from falling backward, jerked the Swede toward himself. Bjorn collapsed on the table, his face in the soup, his chest on the dish with the sashimi. His huge hand grabbed Michael by the wrist, but in vain—Michael brushed Bjorn's powerful but now powerless hand from his wrist, and pushed Bjorn in the shoulder. Bjorn slid off the table and onto the floor, smashing dishes along the way.

Michael took a red napkin off the pile and began cleaning the splashes of soup off his face and shirt.

The waiter who had brought the sake appeared in the doorway. He glanced at the two bodies lying there and asked Michael, "The usual?"

"The usual," answered Michael, taking a nut with his chopsticks.

Friends of Dead Bitches Society

OLGA OPENED her eyes. She lay on the lower level of a plastic bunk bed in a two-person room without windows. A matte overhead light on the ceiling burned like daylight. A peephole glimmered in the steel door. Cool air poured through the ribs of an air-conditioning vent over the door.

Olga moved. Her body felt limp and groggy, almost as if it weren't hers. She brought a hand to her eyes. Opened and closed her fist. She noticed that she wasn't wearing her own clothes: instead, she was dressed in striped pants and a jacket of the same material. There were white socks on her feet. Olga sat up on the bunk. Her feet in the new white socks touched a smooth concrete floor. She saw a pair of black slippers next to the bunks. She stood up. She glanced at the upper bunk: no one. She licked her dry lips. She was very, very thirsty. And then she suddenly remembered: Bjorn, the restaurant, lobster sashimi. And those decisive blue-black eyes.

"Lai . . . Laird," she croaked and again licked her lips.

She shook her heavy, disobedient head.

"Laird, Michael . . . the sake."

The door opened. A Chinese man wearing a blue uniform and carrying a white stick entered. Moving aside, he made a sign with his head: Go.

Olga frowned sullenly at him and at the light green hallway behind the door.

"I'm thirsty," she said.

The Chinese man repeated the gesture. And he slapped his stick in his hand. Olga put on the slippers and went out of the cell. And immediately in front of her there was a second Chinese man, a copy of the first.

"Are they brothers or what?" Olga thought gloomily.

The door behind Olga was closed and locked with a key. The second man gestured for her to follow him. Olga went, making her rubbery, poorly coordinated legs take step after difficult step. The slippers shuffled across the floor. The hall wasn't long. It ran into a door with a code lock. The Chinese man punched in a code. The door opened. Olga didn't have time to take it all in before the twin guards pushed her into the spacious room. The door slammed shut.

For the first moment Olga thought that she was in a meat-processing plant: dozens of people in gray coveralls and aprons were working with some sort of small carcasses resembling sheep, taking them off the hooks of a moving conveyor, skinning them, cutting and splitting them. Some were working in gas masks. The space was light, although there were no windows, as in the room. Light music played softly. And despite powerful ventilation, it smelled of dead flesh.

Olga stepped forward.

A few people glanced at her. They were all Europeans. All fair-haired. She approached the slowly moving conveyor belt. Dead dogs hung on the steel hooks. Dogs that she'd at first taken for sheep.

A short, hunched blond man with glasses, a grizzled beard, and ears that stuck straight out, came over to her. His lackluster blue eyes gazed at her calmly through thick round lenses.

"Are you new?" he asked.

"Where am I?" asked Olga, noticing a small white number on the shoulder of his gray coveralls: 77.

Her eyes squinted at her own left shoulder. There was a number there, too. She hadn't noticed this in the room.

"One hundred eighty-nine," read the old man in the glasses, and his gnarled finger pointed toward the far end of the room. "You with that tall fellow over there? Are you American?"

Olga saw Bjorn removing a dead dog from a hook. He waved to her, his huge hand in a rubber glove, put aside his instrument, and made his way along the line toward her. The short, heavy canvas apron was obviously too small for him. Bjorn looked ridiculous in it. And it was specifically the short apron, tossed about as Bjorn's enormous knees moved, that woke Olga up for real. Her eyes filled with tears, and she threw herself at Bjorn's chest, sobbing. Bjorn embraced her awkwardly, trying not to touch her with the rubber gloves, which were covered in dog blood.

"All right, all right, we'll talk later." The man in glasses gently patted Olga's quivering back and glanced at the large clock on the wall. "It will be lunch soon. Let her stay with you for the time being."

Bjorn nodded. The old man in glasses pointed in a calming gesture to the observation camera, and moved away. Olga sobbed, her face pressed into Bjorn's solar plexus. His work clothes smelled of sweat and carrion. The workers glanced sympathetically as the two embraced.

Calming down a bit, Olga rubbed her eyes with the sleeve of her uniform.

"You slept two whole days," said Bjorn, looking down at her.

He had a small bruise on his cheekbone.

"Did they beat you?" Olga said, touching the bruise.

"No. That was the table. When I fell. Are you all right?"

"Just fine!" Olga looked angrily around her. "What is this?"

"Come on, I'll tell you everything."

"What are they all doing?" she said, seeing the blood on his gloves. "How disgusting...What is this—a dog-meat plant?"

"Just about. I've been here since yesterday evening."

"Why?"

"I woke up earlier. Insomnia, you know..." He tried to joke and squinted at the observation camera. "Let's go over to where I work. There are extremely painful penalties for idling."

He led Olga to his work station. The corpse of a dog lay on his metal table—a reddish-black mutt, with sharpened, old, yellowed canines, sagging tits, and glassy, half-closed eyes. Judging by the frost coming out on her matted fur and claws, she had been slightly frozen. She emitted a weak smell of dog and dead flesh. The dog's skin had been slit on her paws and stomach. This was done by a stocky, tow-headed fellow. He cut open every corpse this way. Bjorn took up a special electric knife and began to carefully and not very skillfully peel the hide away. The stench of carrion grew stronger.

"Ugh..." Olga turned away.

"There's a mask." Bjorn pointed.

Olga took the gas mask off a hook and put it on.

"How about you?"

"So far I don't need it." Bjorn shook his head. "It's easier to talk without it."

"Where are we?" Olga mumbled through the new Chinese gas mask.

"I don't know. They say under the iceberg."

"Under the ICE?"

"Yes."

"Who says so?"

"The others who are here."

"And who are they?"

"They're the same like us."

"They were hammered too?"

"Yes. And at some point they also found the site of that Michael guy. And then—just what happened to us. They came here to fight against evil. In short, you and I weren't the only idiots..."

"But why..." Olga looked at the dog skin, which peeled off the corpse's leg with a crack. "You . . . that is . . . they . . . why, why, why all this?"

"What do you mean? Why are we here? I am not the one to ask this question."

"Why all this? Why all this nasty stuff?"

"Why are we skinning these dogs? Because at that end of the workshop the women cut the skin into strips. Which are then used somewhere to tie the ice to the handle. Then they have an ice hammer."

"How do you know this?"

"Well, I spent a whole night among our comrades in misfortune."

"But . . . but why did I sleep so long?" Olga took off the gas mask, which got in the way of talking.

Bjorn spoke seriously, "Here you go, put on these gloves and help me."

"I'm not going to do this shit!"

"They give electric shocks. And don't let you eat. Or drink."

"That's right," she remembered, "I'm really thirsty."

"There's a drinking station over there in the corner."

Olga looked at the observation camera.

"And what now?" she asked indignantly. "Bastards! The day after tomorrow I have to be in Philadelphia with a contract! They'll fire me!"

Bjorn laughed bitterly. "I think we've already been fired. From the living."

Olga looked at him attentively.

"What should we do?" she asked.

"Skin dogs," he answered seriously. "And not make any sudden movements."

"What?" She squinted furiously. "Sudden movements? I'll obliterate them, the scum!"

She shook her fist at the moving observation camera and cried out loud, "Fuck you!"

The camera focused on Olga immediately. The workers froze. Up above, on a small balcony jutting out from the wall, a door opened silently. A Chinese man in a uniform emerged from it. Two side doors also opened and guards appeared in them as well.

Olga's lips trembled from anger. But Bjorn, his hands in gloves covered with dog blood, grabbed her wrists.

"Olga!"

The dead, cold blood turned her to stone.

"Olga."

She turned to look at Bjorn. But her lips were still distorted with hatred.

"They'll kill us at the drop of a hat," Bjorn said. "You've got to understand."

Her gaze drilled straight through Bjorn.

"And you've got to understand: this is completely serious."

She looked at the Chinese. They stared at her, immobile. Bjorn gently wiped her wrists with a paper towel. And began putting new gloves on her hands.

"Go get a drink. And come back over here to me."

A stocky fellow, who sliced the corpses open, winked at Olga and Bjorn sympathetically. He took another corpse off the hook and dropped it with a thud on the table in front of Olga. It was a bitch with matted gray-brown fur. Olga looked at the dog's frosty tits. She turned her gaze to the conveyor. Only bitches hung from the hooks.

"But why... are they all females?" she asked distractedly.

"No one knows," said the stocky guy, taking off his gas mask and wiping the sweat from his freckled forehead, looking at Olga with a half smile. "Not even the old-timers."

It was clear that he liked Olga. Softening, she looked at the frozen dog tits, while Bjorn pulled the gloves on her helpless hands.

"You know what we call each other?" The stocky guy grinned.

"No," Olga mumbled.

"Friends of Dead Bitches."

Seeing All

THE GREAT night has arrived.

The Earth has fallen asleep. The meat machines are immobile

until dawn. They sleep and dream their meat dreams. But the Brotherhood of the Light isn't sleeping. The Brotherhood has waited a long time for this night. It has traveled a long path to this hour—an entire Earth century. The Brothers and Sisters of the Light moved toward this. They brought the Great Hour nearer. They struggled and were tormented. They perished and were reborn. They suffered and prevailed. They labored and overcame. They tore brothers and sisters away from the world of the meat. They protected the Newly Acquired.

Iron birds take off into the night air. They serve the Brotherhood. They lift Khram and Gorn into the night air. In the main iron machine Khram and Gorn are lifted into the air. This machine will help them. It was created for this night. It was created for this night alone. For the first and last flight. In order to help Khram and Gorn. The flying machine rises higher and higher. The Earth is farther and farther away. From the flying machine one can see farther and farther. The other flying machines fly close by, guarding them.

Khram and Gorn sit, embracing, in a glass sphere. Their bodies are naked. Their eyes are closed. Their chests are together. Their hands are intertwined. Their hearts are *prepared*.

The glass sphere flies above the sleeping Earth.

Khram and Gorn are strong. They are *capable*.

The Brotherhood is also prepared. All across the Earth, Circles of the Light have formed. Great and Lesser Circles. In different countries. Thousands of brothers and sisters are frozen and still. Their eyes are closed. Their hearts are *prepared*. They are *waiting*.

Khram and Gorn soar over the Earth.

The night helps them. For it is only at night that the meat machines are immobile. They are all in *their own* places. They are all *visible*.

The Earth lies in the palms of Khram's and Gorn's hands. They *hold* it like an apple. They are *prepared*.

The flying machine rises to the heights. This is its limit. The moment of Beginning has arrived.

Khram's and Gorn's hearts shine cautiously.

All the Circles of the Light on the Earth below instantly shine in *response*. They give *strength* to Khram and Gorn. They offer them *support*. They guard and *hold them*.

The hearts of Khram and of Gorn shine ever *stronger*. They gather the *power* of the Light. They prepare themselves. The iron machine soars over the world of meat machines. Its mechanisms are prepared to be of use to the Brotherhood one last time. They are on alert. They depend on Khram and Gorn. The iron head of the flying machine awaits its *commands*. To remember those whom Khram and Gorn *will see*. In order to help find them. The Brotherhood controls the complex mechanisms of the flying machine. The brothers grow stock-still.

The Brotherhood of the Primordial Light *grows still*.

Everything is now in the *hearts* of Khram and of Gorn.

Everything depends on them.

Everything *rests* on them.

One second passes.

Another...

A third...

THEIR HEARTS HAVE FLARED!

It has come to pass!

Khram and Gorn *have seen*.

Their hearts *see* EVERYONE.

All 23,000. Including Khram and Gorn, 23,000 brothers and sisters on the planet Earth.

All the brothers and sisters, Khram and Gorn see *all* of them, down to the very last one. Gorn *sees*: 22,437 are on Earth; 563 are now in the air.

Khram's and Gorn's hearts *shine*. Their bodies tremble in the glass sphere. It is hard for bodies to *withstand* the power of the Light. It will tear the meat bodies into 23,000 pieces, they will fall apart on account of the Primordial Power. They won't be able withstand the Force of Unearthly Light. But the Circles of Light on the Earth shine in reply. The brothers and sisters *stand*. *They hold them* like a shield. They *help* with support. *They contain them*.

The complex mechanisms of the flying machine have come to life. Its iron head begins to work. It receives commands from Khram and Gorn. They issue from the embracing bodies of Khram and Gorn. They flow into the head of the flying machine. The machine sees along with Khram and Gorn. But not with heart *vision*, with its own iron vision. It sees everyone that Khram and Gorn *see*. It determines the place, commits it to memory, finds through the machines of the Earth the names of the sleeping brothers and sisters. New names flow into the iron machine. They join with glittering flares. They are collected in order. They are conveyed to hundreds of other irons machines that serve the Brotherhood. The machines remember the new names, they find out their new addresses, they find earthly ways of acquiring these brothers and sisters.

The iron machine flies across the night sky, chasing the night. It flies west. During the night it must circle the entire planet Earth, manage to do it in one night. All the brothers and sisters are sleeping now. While they are immobile. While they are *visible*. While millions of meat machines are asleep. While millions of meat machines are immobilized. While they can be picked out.

Shining are two hearts above; *shining* are thousands below.

Khram and Gorn *see*.

They *see* EVERYONE.

They *recognize* each one.

The head of the flying machine works. It remembers. The machine flies west. The countries of meat machines float under it. And the hearts of sleeping brothers and sisters flare like points of fire. Those who have remained in the violent and ruthless world of the Earth. Whose hearts are sleeping. Who must still be saved, torn out of the meat of earthly life. Returned to the world of Eternal Light. Acquired for the Great Transformation. For the Great Victory. For the Great Return to the Primordial Light.

The iron machine flies through the night sky. It flies around the entire Earth from east to west. It hurries after the night. It carries a glass sphere across the sky. The Earth of meat machines sleeps. And knows not what awaits it.

Work Day Done

OLGA'S workmate cut the 1,128th strap from dog hide with crude iron scissors. It slid across the metal table and Olga caught it, used her left hand to press the rib spur down, and began to clean off the black fur stuck to the skin. Her co-worker, a blue-eyed, broad-shouldered Norwegian named Kristina, stole a glance at the clock.

"It's already five of."

Olga didn't want to look at the clock: after a week of work in the Friends of Dead Bitches Society, she had lost any sense of time. In her head time either stretched out and crawled like a snail along the stone banister of Mama's house in Newark, or raced ahead like the train from Newark to New York, where Olga had first gotten her degree in economics, then an MBA, then lived in NoHo in a small loft near the university, a cozy loft with two windows facing south and two facing north, a loft on the sixth floor, a loft where there were books, little statues, knickknacks, Papa's Arab and European pictures, Mama's music collection, a large stuffed tiger she slept with, and the parrot Fima who could say "lo-co-mo-tive," and whom she would never, ever hear again . . .

"Begone!"

Having cleaned the strap, she swept the fur into a garbage bag and placed the finished strips in a transparent box. Each box like this could hold five hundred strips. In one day she and her co-worker were supposed to fill two of these boxes. For two days now Olga and Kristina had exceeded the quota, for which they were to receive a bonus. Having finished cutting the strips, Kristina placed the dog hide in a special bag and set about wiping the scissors, which were crusty with dog blood, with a rag. Olga sealed the transparent box of strips, walked over to the wall, and pressed a button; a white niche opened up. Olga put the box in it and pressed the button again. The niche closed. Returning to her work station, Olga took off the canvas apron and hung it on a hook. She sprayed disinfectant on the metal table and began wiping it clean with a paper towel.

The bell signaling the end of the working day sounded.

Olga glanced over at the other end of the shop: Bjorn was wiping his table and talking to his neighbor. Both were smiling.

"He has the energy for humor." Olga sighed, and tossed the paper towel into the trash.

Kristina put the scissors and knife away in the table's metal drawer, rose, and, taking off her gloves, stretched and groaned with relief.

"Blessed Virgin . . . that's it!"

"The end of a rotten business," Olga muttered, throwing her gloves into the bin.

"The day is over, thank God," a plump Danish peasant girl with a fabulous blond braid who worked at the next table said to them with a tired smile.

"Yeah, yeah," yawned her co-worker, a rough, masculine Polish woman. "If only all their damned ice would melt tomorrow . . . melt!"

"Do you mean the company or the ice?" Olga asked, as she rubbed her neck.

"The one the other!" the Polish woman answered in her awkward English.

They all laughed in exhaustion and strolled toward the women's showers, while the men, talking to one another, wandered off to shower too. The guards let them all stream out into the hallway, opened the doors to the showers, admitted them, and locked the doors behind them. One hundred and eighty-nine people worked in the Friends of Dead Bitches Society. There were more women—a hundred and four. As an old-timer of the bunker, the Australian, Sally, explained to Olga, this was because after the blows from the ice hammers women survived more often than men. Sally was number 8. She had spent four years in the bunker and was the senior female. The head of the men was the stooped Horst, who wore glasses and had been abducted by the Brotherhood back in East Berlin. He had been brought to the bunker six years ago. According to him, nine people worked there at the time.

Olga found her hook with the number 189, the last in the long dressing room, took off her clothes, which smelled of dog, pulled off her socks and underwear, and walked across the warm tiles to enter the showers with the crowd of naked women. A light steam filled the room, and ten lines formed around ten showers. Everyone took a turn under the shower. Olga got in line behind a small, plain girl with dark-blond, tousled hair. The girl stood, her lackluster, slightly bulging blue eyes vacantly staring at the nape of the woman ahead of her who was laughing, telling a joke to two other women in an unknown language.

"Albanian? Moldavian?" Olga thought without energy. "Are there really three of them? There aren't any Russian women here at all. Nine Americans. Fourteen Germans. Ten French, it seemed. Swedes —twenty-five in all. I'm the only Jew. Russians and Jews the weakest women? Forgotten how to survive? It's strange . . ."

On the other hand, in the men's section, there were seven Russians. And they were all fairly nice guys. One of them was a former athlete, another a chef, the third a professional thief, the fourth some kind of bureaucrat. And all of them cheerful. Olga thought of them with warmth: she liked to sit with these guys after her shower and talk in the forgotten language of her childhood.

"*Dozhdik dozhdik, kap, kap, kap.*" Rain, rain, drip drop, drip drop, she muttered in Russian, and licked her lips nervously: she really wanted to smoke. But that was possible only in the bunker.

"Are you American?" the woman standing behind her asked in an unusually muffled voice.

"Why, do I look like one?" Olga turned around and saw a swarthy, svelte woman of about forty-five with a terribly deformed chest.

An intricate purple-white cavity yawned in the area of her breastbone; the right breast was missing; the collarbone, broken in two place, had grown back bent into a half circle. Nevertheless, the woman was truly beautiful: a well-proportioned, stately figure, Indian cheekbones, light-chestnut hair with gold highlights, and dark-blue, deep-set eyes.

"Wow! They really gave it to you." Olga stared at the cavity.

"Nineteen blows," the woman said in a flat voice.

Her breathing was fast and shallow, and her narrow nostrils flared. The cavity moved in time with her breath, as though she were breathing in the humid steam of the shower room.

"Liz Cunnigan, Memphis," said the woman, holding out her dark hand.

"Olga Drobot, New York." Olga shook her hand.

"Olga? Are you Polish?"

"A Russian Jew."

"Are you brand new?"

"Well, not entirely. I've been here a week. And you?"

"My sixth month."

"Yikes. Are you used to it?" Olga kept glancing at the moving cavity, the edge of which was covered in drops of sweat.

"People get used to everything." Liz's eyes looked at her calmly. "Do you play with anyone?"

"Yes. And you?"

"I'm with the Swedes." Liz smiled slightly. "Come over to our Swedish corner. It's nice there."

"The Americans aren't bad, either." Olga stood under an available shower, remembering that she had never seen Liz at the American corner. "I'll come over sometime. Thanks."

The hot water embraced her body pleasantly. Olga moaned with pleasure, leaning back her head and putting her face under the stream of water. But she had to wash up quickly. Letting the water flow over her, she bent her head under a plastic faucet, and pulled down on a small handle. A silvery drop of shampoo dripped on her head like snot. She squeezed out a second on her palm, rubbing the shampoo between her legs, under her arms, and over her breasts. Then, turning to face the queue, she let the stream run down her back and washed her hair. For the first few days, she always looked at the wall when she showered, turning away from the line, not wanting to share this short-lived pleasure, not even a glance, with anyone. Now she liked to look at the naked women waiting their turn. They were all waiting. And in this waiting there was something helpless and inexpressibly intimate and dear. They all had marks on their chests, they had all tasted the ice hammer, they had all survived, they had all been lured here, under the ICE, and they were all like her. The estrangement of the first days had passed. Olga stopped feeling shy and wild. She had already grown accustomed to it.

Olga put her soapy head under the shower and washed the foam off her hair. She put her thigh under the water and began to wash it with her hands.

"Any dog fur grown in yet?" Liz asked and the Norwegians standing in the nearby line laughed.

"It's more likely bitch tits will grow in." Olga grinned, washing her crotch and glancing at Liz's one neat nipple. "The only problem is who to nurse?"

"What do you mean who? The Chinese!" said a Norwegian, laughing.

"There's not enough milk for all of them," Liz objected calmly.

Everyone roared with laughter. There was a certain comfort and freedom in this laughter. A certain oblivion. Olga liked standing under the streams of warm water and listening to the laughter. It allowed her to forget about everything for a moment. She closed her eyes.

"Sweetie, speed up!" others in line shouted.

Olga came to. It was time to hand over her place of *natural* oblivion. She left the water, shook herself off, and headed for the exit. A Czech girl slapped her rear end and whistled at her. Kristina winked and poked a finger at her wet stomach. Olga, laughing, shook a fist at them as she walked by. Leaving the showers for the changing room, she took a thin but clean towel from her hook, rubbed her hair, then her body. Leaving her gray working clothes on the upper hook, she took down the "inside" outfit, a sand-colored pair of pajamas with the number 189 on the shoulders, and put it on. She took a short brush from the breast pocket and brushed her dyed hair while looking in a round mirror attached to the wall between the hooks. She observed that her natural reddish hair was already quite noticeable at the roots. Sticking her socks and underwear in a pocket, she put on her slippers and went into the cafeteria through an adjoining door.

The spacious, calm, light-green cafeteria contained all of the prisoners in the bunkers. It smelled like boiled vegetables, and the same light classical music played. Men and women, coming out of the showers, lined up together for food. Olga looked for Bjorn in the crowd but couldn't find him: he was probably still washing. However, she immediately noticed the Russians, who had a lively conversation going. She walked over to them.

"Ah, here's our Stakhanovite!" said Sergei, a tall guy with a white-toothed smile and a shock of smoky-blond hair.

"What's a Stakhanovite?" asked Olga.

"It's a worker who massively exceeds quotas," explained Lyosha, a chubby fellow with a round child's face and lively, dark-blue eyes.

"Forgotten Russian in that America of yours, have you?" grinned Boris, a homely, thin man. "Go on, get in ahead of us."

"I don't remember all the words," said Olga, getting in line in front of them.

"Well, that's as it should be," said the unsmiling Igor, gloomily scratching his unshaved cheek. "There's all kinds of bullshit in Russian . . ."

"Now, you blockhead, don't go insulting Russia," said the earthy, fiery-red-haired Pyotr, poking him in the stomach. "I'll friggin' lay you flat, don't you worry!" he said in a comically threatening voice.

"Get lost, Azazello," said Igor, shoving him in reply.

"Gentlemen, don't quarrel. We're on enemy territory," said Sergei in a pretend official voice, and they all laughed tiredly.

Olga looked at them with a smile. The Russians here in the bunker reminded her of her childhood on the outskirts of Moscow. Along with their words and jokes, the world of her earliest memories surfaced: gray prefab buildings, filthy snowdrifts at the entrance, kindergarten with a potted palm and songs about the little creature Cheburashka and Lenin, her hurried, frantic mother, her stubborn, incredibly talented, and very loud father, her sick grandfather, the "Red October" upright piano, strep throat and the customary Russian New Year's tree, the neighbor's cat Bayun, the first grade of Soviet school, the second, the third, the game of rubber bands at recess. And emigration.

After that—it was only memory.

For some reason, here in the bunker, Olga cherished first memories more than other memories. Distant and lost in the twilight as they were, it was more pleasant and comforting to fall asleep to these memories of snowdrifts, cats, and strep throat.

Their turn in line had come. Two Chinese in white coats furnished her tray with the usual food: vegetable soup, a boiled egg with mayonnaise, rice, cabbage salad, two pieces of cold fish in tomato sauce, Jell-O with whipped cream, and a glass of orange juice. Picking up the tray, Olga moved to the third Chinese standing between two pans with the main course. On the left was fish, on the right chicken fingers. Olga chose the fish, and tray in hand, walked toward the Russian table. Three people sat there. But then someone from the American table called her name. A tall, golden-haired fellow, slightly resembling Bjorn, stood and gestured for her to come over. The Russian table was also actively waving at her... Olga halted indecisively, not knowing which to prefer—the forgotten, dimly familiar, but touching Russian world or the well-known, comprehensible, and reliable American.

"Miss, would you deign to share this modest meal with me?" An old voice with a strange accent sounded next to her.

Olga lowered her eyes and saw an old man sitting alone at a table. All of the tables here were for two, but most of them were pushed together to form national groups. Virtually no loners remained. She hadn't noticed this old man earlier.

"Believe me, I wouldn't dare to insist. If you have other preferences, do not hesitate to follow them. But I would be extraordinarily touched even by your brief presence at this miserable little table."

He spoke perfect, terribly old-fashioned English. But the accent indicated that the old man wasn't English. Olga placed her tray on his table and sat down across from him.

"Marvelous. I thank you." The old man stood, his shaking hands raising his napkin to his narrow, colorless lips and wiping them. "Let me introduce myself—Ernst Wolf."

"Olga Drobot," she said, reaching over the food to shake his hand.

The old man touched his lips to her hand. His bald head trembled slightly.

"You betrayed us with the Jerries." The Russian table laughed caustically.

"Are you German?" Olga asked.

"Yes."

"Why don't you sit at the German table? There are so many of you here."

"There are two reasons, my dear Miss Drobot. First, in the course of fifty-eight years of imprisonment, I have come to understand that solitude is a gift from on high. Second, I simply have nothing to talk about with my current compatriots. We have no common themes."

"And you think that they will emerge with me?" Olga broke off a piece of her roll.

"You reminded me of a certain lady who was very dear to me. A very long time ago."

"And it was only for this that you . . ." Olga lifted her fork to put a piece of fish in her mouth but suddenly realized exactly what he had told her. "What? Fifty-eight years? You've been here fifty-eight years?"

"Well, not exactly here." He smiled, baring his old dentures. "But with them. With the Brothers of the Light."

The fork slipped out of Olga's hand. "Fifty-eight?"

"Fifty-eight, my dear Miss Drobot."

She stared at him. The old man's face was calm and otherworldly. His pale-blue eyes were attentive. The whites around them were extremely yellow. Judging by the even features of his wrinkled face, now unhealthily yellow and liver-spotted, in his youth he had been a handsome man.

"When did it happen?"

"In 1946, October 21. At the villa of my father, Sebastian Wolf."

"They hammered you?"

"Yes. And decided that I was *ein taube Nuss*. An empty nut."

"And then what?"

"And then I successfully became a slave of the Brotherhood. Although, in fact, I had been one before the hammering as well."

"They used you before as well? In what way?"

"The most direct. It is quite easy to use children, honorable Miss Drobot."

"I don't understand."

"My father, Sebastian Wolf, was one of the better-known members of the Brotherhood. And we lived with him. One fine day he decided to hammer me. And my sister as well. She perished, and I survived. Before this he had used us as obligatory decorations. And Mama as well. But she died earlier."

"But . . . how old were you when you were hammered?"

"Seventeen."

Olga stared at the piece of fish on her fork. She picked it up and lifted it to her mouth. And once again dropped it on her tray. "I don't feel like eating."

The old man nodded his yellow head with understanding. "Nor do I. After the final bell everyone has a poor appetite. But then in the morning everyone's hungry as a horse! The reasons are entirely objective!"

He laughed.

There was a childlike helplessness in his laughter.

"Solitude—is a gift from on high . . ." Olga recalled.

"What happened to your father?" she asked, looking at the old man's trembling hands.

"The last time I saw my father was when he crushed my ribs. My sister, I admit, had tired him out. And he wasn't very precise with me: the rib broke in and hit my liver. But I survived. Although since that time my face is yellow, like the Chinese. Believe me, Miss Drobot, in the first days after my arrival here they took me for one of them! I'm friends with the Chinese."

He pinched off a piece of chicken and put it in his mouth. His dentures clacked softly. He chewed as though performing hard labor. His thin white hair shook on his yellow head.

"Tell me, why didn't they just kill you . . . us? It would have been so simple. Keeping you and hiding you for fifty-eight years! What for? And us as well . . ."

Wolf finished chewing and wiped his lips with the napkin.

"You see, Miss Drobot, when a person is killed and then burned, something of him still remains. The ashes, for example. And not only that. Something more essential than ashes. When he leaves this world against his will, a man forms a kind of hole in it. Because he is torn from this place forcibly, like a tooth. This is the law of life's metaphysics. And a hole is a noticeable thing, my esteemed Miss Drobot. It's visible. It takes a long time to heal. And other people feel it. If the man continues to live, he leaves no holes. Thus, to hide a person is much simpler and more advantageous. From the metaphysical point of view, that is."

Olga grew thoughtful. And understood.

"They killed 'empties,' as they call us, only in Russia. Under Stalin, when the Great Terror was on, and later, when the 'small terror' took place. The Brotherhood wasn't worried about metaphysical holes created after the death of individual beings."

"Why not?"

"Because Russia itself was one large metaphysical hole."

"Really? When I lived there I didn't notice it."

"Thank God!"

"Why?"

"If you had noticed it, Miss Drobot, you would have an entirely different expression on your face. And believe me, I wouldn't have invited you to sit at my table."

Olga looked at him attentively. She laughed and clapped her hands. The old man giggled in satisfaction.

"Eat, eat, Miss Drobot. There's a long night ahead."

Olga set about eating. The old man took his portion of Jell-O and put it on Olga's tray.

"And don't argue with me!"

His hand and the Jell-O trembled in time.

"*Danke*, Herr Wolf," said Olga.

"*Pazhaluusta*," the old man said in Russian and laughed, his dentures clacking.

Olga slowly ate half of her dinner. She wiped her lips with a paper napkin and dropped it in her soup.

"I will take the liberty of asking, Miss Drobot, what is your profession?"

"Manager. And you? Oh, that's right . . . forgive me."

"Your question is utterly appropriate. During my prison affair with the Brotherhood, I have done time in seven places. Four of them had rather good libraries. Thanks to them I managed to master three professions: translator from the English (I translated three of Dickens's novels for myself), cartography, and—you'll find it difficult to believe, Miss Drobot—an ocean navigator, that is, a pilot."

"Cool!"

"Cool! I love that American word."

The old man also finished his meal.

"Tell me, is there any way they might let us out of here? Sometime?" Olga asked.

"What for?" The old man's colorless eyebrows arched, and yellow wrinkles ran across his large forehead.

"They won't . . . let us out?"

"Miss Drobot, you are too young. That's why you're asking such questions."

Dejected, Olga fell silent.

"Stay calm. And stop comforting yourself with illusions. Our life is now divided into two parts: the first and the second. And we can't get away from that. Therefore we have to try to make the second part more interesting than the first. It is difficult. But it is quite possible. I, to give one example, have managed to do this. And you have to agree that the Brotherhood provides a great deal of help in this regard. Local conditions are incomparable to those in normal prisons. Despite all their ruthlessness, the Brothers of the Light have been extremely humanistic toward us empty shells. They know our weaknesses quite well, and the needs of the meat machines."

"Meat machines? Who's that?"

"It's you and me," said the old man, rising and picking up his tray. "So keep your chin up, Miss Drobot."

Smiling, he wandered over to the dish-washing window. The tray shook terribly in his hand. Olga remained at the table. The old man's words had struck a deep chord in her, making her blood run cold.

"Two lives. Before and after," Olga thought, turning the empty glass dripping with orange juice. "So what now? Scrape hides forever? And wait for the lights-out bell to ring? Learn to be a pilot . . . Ridiculous! No, it's not possible! No way! I'd rather hang myself in the toilet stall. So what then, after the bell? I won't go to the windows. They murdered my parents, David turned out to be an asshole . . . What do

I have to lose? I couldn't have children. Twice…What am I living for? For whom? For Fima? Here, or anywhere, what's holding me back? I have nothing to lose. Pilot, pilot, now what shore should we head for…'Baby can you twice find the way to fuckin' paradise?' I can't find it, either…I'll hang myself. Today. Tonight. For sure, as Pyotr says…"

She closed her eyes.

A large, familiar hand touched her back.

"Bjorn!" she said, without opening her eyes.

"Why do Russians wash and eat so fast?" Bjorn hung over Olga like a bell tower, smelling of cheap shampoo and clean clothes.

"You know, I'm actually Jewish." Olga opened her eyes.

Bjorn's face was content. His cheeks were flushed from the shower.

"What a positive personality," Olga thought enviously as she looked up at him. "A regular walking security complex. Healthy food throughout childhood…and they have good dairy products in Sweden…"

"I just wanted to eat with you," he admitted honestly.

"Tell me, do you ever get depressed?" Olga stood, picking up the tray with the remains of her food.

"It happens sometimes," he said, taking her tray. "But I know how to fight it off."

"Teach me."

"There's no basketball court here. Only a hockey rink!" Smiling at her, Bjorn took a few sweeping steps with her tray.

Olga followed him.

"I wonder, are there rebellions here?"

"You already asked. No, there haven't been any group ones."

"You already told me." She yawned nervously. "Well, so, should we go?"

"I have to eat."

She clenched and unclenched her fists.

"Do you want to hang out together today?"

"I wouldn't mind…Which corner?"

"We could go to ours, the Swedish table."

"They invited me over there today, too!"

"We've got a tight group." He set the tray in the return window.

"Let's try…" Olga yawned nervously again, and shivered. "Am I pale?"

He leaned over.

"A little. Do you feel like getting together?"

"No! Not at all."

"What are you going to do now?"

"I don't know…I'll go and read something."

"I'll come to the library."

"Okay."

Olga walked out of the cafeteria into the hallway and went into a large, clean bathroom. After urinating into a Japanese toilet with a disgustingly warm seat, she washed her hands, looking at herself in the mirror. Next to her a Romanian girl, a tall, beautiful model, was brushing her teeth.

"The chicken has a strange aftertaste today." The Romanian spit out water. "They're obviously mixing something into it for us."

"I had the fish." Olga touched and smoothed out the wrinkles around her eyes.

"A sort of metallic aftertaste," said the Romanian, looking at her teeth. "What is it? Lead? What if it's mercury? And my teeth are getting discolored. Some kind of metal…Haven't you felt it?"

"I ate fish," Olga repeated, and left the restroom.

Walking down the hallway, she reached the living quarters. It was very spacious, and fresh from the air-conditioning. Dim lighting illuminated rows of double bunks, stools, and shelves with personal items. The male and female sections were divided by a small passage with no doors. The walls and ceiling of the male half were a grayish green, while the women's were pinkish gray. The men's half was called the Garage; the women's, the Ham. In the Garage and the Ham, dozens of empty beds awaited new owners.

Olga went over to her bed, took a pack of super-light Chinese cigarettes and a tube of hand cream from her night table, lit up, squeezed out some cream, and, rubbing it in, threw herself on her bed with pleasure.

"Oh my God…"

From above, the golden-curled head of the Irish girl Meryl hung down. "Olga, do you have any pads?"

"Yes."

"I forgot to order them. Would you give me a couple?"

"They're in the night table."

"I'm too lazy to get down." The Irish girl grinned.

"And I'm too lazy to get up," said Olga, blowing a stream of smoke at her.

Meryl got down, opened the drawer, and took a few.

"I saw you eating with that yellow German guy."

"That's right. He asked me to."

"So he's got a thing for you."

"Probably... He's an interesting old guy."

"They say he's their old stool pigeon."

"So what? Do we have anything to hide?"

"Well"—Meryl shrugged her shoulders, pulling down her pants and putting on the pad—"a lot of people want to get out of here."

"Somehow it's not really noticeable," said Olga, smoking with pleasure, staring at the plastic bottom of the upper bed where she'd scratched "Fuck off, Ice!" the first night she'd been there.

"You're new. That's why you think everyone here is content. Everyone just dreams about waiting for the bell and standing up at the gates."

Smoking, Olga grabbed her foot and held her smooth heel with pleasure.

"Meryl, I have neither the energy nor the desire to argue with you."

"So I'm right!" Meryl whacked Olga on the sole of her foot.

The Ham gradually filled up. Conversations hummed, and it smelled of cheap Chinese perfume. Some of the women slept, some played cards, and others went over to the Garage. Men dropped by "to have a cup of water." It was the only drink allowed in the living quarters; each section had automatic water fountains marked with the characters that meant "water," which filled plastic cups with ice-cold or hot water. They drank water endlessly in the bunker, in large and small groups, in pairs and alone. The prisoners of the ICE respected water and the characters that stood for it. They invited one another to drink it, they marked birthdays and holidays with it, and with it they remembered the dead.

After smoking two cigarettes in a row, Olga dozed for about forty minutes to the sound of women's conversations and the clack of scissors; nearby one Lithuanian was cutting another's hair. As soon as the click-clack ended, Olga opened her eyes and looked at the wall clock: it was 6:30. Stretching, she stood up, drank a cup of ice-cold water, and headed for the library. There was no television and not even a simple screen with a video machine in the bunker. They never brought magazines and newspapers here, either. Still, the library was quite respectable. Olga walked through the hallway, opened a door with a picture of an open book on it, and found herself in a long, light room with shelves and dozens of tables. The books were on shelves. About fifteen people were sitting and reading. It was forbidden to remove books from the library.

Olga walked over to the bookshelves.

Most of the books were in English. There were a few in German, French, and Italian as well. Trying to find something in her almost completely forgotten written Russian, just for the hell of it, the only thing Olga noticed was the collected works of Leo Tolstoy. After spending several hours in the library, Olga had understood its strict principle: Only fiction was to be found on the shelves. There were no books at all on technology, medicine, philosophy, history, culture, geography, or the exact and applied sciences. Likewise there were no newspapers, magazines, or other periodicals. Reference books were entirely missing. There wasn't any poetry. On the other hand there were quite a number of dictionaries. The largest share of the underground library was occupied by world classics in English translation and a great number of collected works. The authors of detective and pulp-fiction novels were similarly represented in multiple volumes, and the books were at least thirteen years old. Contemporary literature was completely absent. There were very few individual works.

Olga moved along the shelves slowly. Yesterday she had begun to read Nabokov's *The Gift*, but quickly grew bored and picked up Agatha Christie's *Murder on the Orient Express*. Reading about the charming Poirot was comforting, but when she was on page 62, lights-out sounded in the bunker. For some reason she didn't want to return to the *Orient Express* now. She stopped at the shelf marked "F." Flaubert? She'd read *Madame Bovary* in college. It was at the beginning of May when everything was blooming. The image of the decisive and passionate woman, eating arsenic by the handful, had merged with the aroma of blooming narcissus. A strange aftertaste remained in her memory, one which she didn't care for at all right now. Faulkner? *The Bear*, which her parents loved, she had never read to the end. Feuchtwanger woke memories of something boring and German. Anatole France? She wasn't familiar with the author. Fielding? Once again, probably an Englishman. Fitzgerald! *Tender Is the Night* had been one of her favorite novels when she was younger. She randomly pulled out the third volume of Fitzgerald's collected works, opened it in the middle. The story was called "The Diamond as Big as the Ritz." Olga didn't know it. She sat down at the nearest table and plunged into the story. Olga read quickly. In the charming language she'd loved since her youth, Fitzgerald described the diamond mountain, overgrown with thick forest, which a stingy, powerful man stumbled on by chance one day. He settled on its slopes. The fantastic treasure turned him into a monster. He imagined that he was equal to God, and built a marvelous castle on the mountain. With him in the fantastic castle lived his two enchanting daughters—Jasmine and Kismine—and his obedient wife, mute as a plant. Olga imagined the diamond mountain, covered with forest.

"Diamonds look like ice," she thought. "But diamonds don't melt . . . The ice mountain. And we live under it . . ."

She raised her head and looked at the ceiling. Little lamps were burning there.

"Fitzgerald? Boring!" said a woman sitting behind her, who had unceremoniously looked at her book. "Syrup with shit!"

Olga looked around.

The woman was plain, with tangled red hair. Her fading, pale-blue eyes looked at Olga with malice and tenaciousness. Her thin lips shook nervously. A whitish mustache grew over those lips. Olga hadn't seen her before.

"This is what you should read." The woman showed Olga a book with comic depictions of a soldier on the cover.

"*The Good Soldier Švejk*," Olga read.

"Do you know it?" the woman asked aggressively.

"I don't like army humor," said Olga, and turned away.

"Idiot! It's the healthiest humor there is!" the woman shouted fiercely.

"Doris, leave her alone," advised a fat, rosy-cheeked Italian sitting next to the redhead.

"Idiots! What do they read!" The redhead shook with anger.

Olga continued reading, not paying attention. The redhead bickered lamely with the Italian. And suddenly, shouting out "Fuck you!," she spat at her. The Italian slapped her in the face. The redhead began to beat the Italian with a book. They grabbed each other. The redhead's cry turned into a hysterical, anguished shriek. People moved away; people sitting behind jumped up and tried to separate them. The rest of the library visitors hooted and whistled. Two Chinese guards rushed in the door, grabbed the fighting redhead, and dragged her out of the library while everyone else hooted and howled.

Everything happened so fast that Olga only shook her head and laughed. "What a bunch of nonsense!"

"That redhead's a witch," the Italian muttered, looking over her scratched hand.

"Is she out of her mind?" Olga asked. "Who is she? I haven't seen her before."

"She's from South Africa. They let her out once in a while," the Italian woman said, sighing. "Her and two other psychos. Why do they keep them here? They should just send them up there, to a normal psychiatric ward..."

"A Chinese one?" joked a French guy with a buzz cut. "Maybe you'd like to go there?"

"Ladies and gentlemen, don't forget what's written on the walls," a gray-headed old Icelander spat out.

On the wall hung a black sign: QUIET!

Everyone who was reading grew quiet. Again Olga immersed herself in the bitterly touching work of Fitzgerald. When the government planes bombed the castle belonging to the owner of the diamond mountain, when he himself grew quiet forever under the shards of diamonds and his lovely daughters became poverty-stricken orphans, Olga's eyes filled with tears. She read ...

> "I love washing," Jasmine said quietly. "I have always washed my own handkerchiefs. I'll take in laundry and support you both." ...
>
> "What a dream it was," Kismine sighed, gazing up at the stars. "How strange it seems to be here with one dress and a penniless fiancé!
>
> "Under the stars," she repeated. "I never noticed the stars before. I always thought of them as great big diamonds that belonged to someone. Now they frighten me. They make me feel that it was all a dream, all my youth."
>
> "It *was* a dream," said John quietly. "Everybody's youth is a dream, a form of chemical madness."

Olga shuddered, holding back sobs, and covered her face with her hands. Tears leaked through her fingers, and then burst out like a child's.

"Just hold on, honey, there's only forty-two minutes left." A tattooed fellow slapped *The Spy Who Loved Me* down on the table. "Bastards, they couldn't have made the bedtime bell at eight!"

"Quiet, Shtamp." A strapping Serb tore himself away from Chase and glanced sideways at the observation camera. "Everything is just fine here. We're happy with everything."

"I want to go-o-o ho-o-o-mmme." Olga sobbed. "I have a p-p-par-ro-rot there ..."

It felt terribly sweet and bitter to feel tiny and helpless under this mountain of ice.

A small, pretty American, Kelly, sat down next to Olga, hugged her shoulders, and said, "Sweetie, just hold on. It'll be soon now."

"No, it's even worse to wait in the library." A gloomy, light-bearded German spoke up as he got up and put a volume of Simenon back in its place on the shelf. "Sally, let's go have some water."

Sally, the senior inhabitant of the Ham who resembled Martina Navratilova, waved him on without looking up from *Fiesta*. The tattooed guy followed the German. And so did the quiet, sickly Estonian who had been reading Thomas Mann.

"The men's nerves break down." Kelly took out a handkerchief and wiped away Olga's tears. "Calm down, sweetie. Your home is here now. And we all love you. We ... are your family ..."

"Your brothers and sisters," muttered an Italian girl, leafing through the copy of *Švejk* that the redhead had abandoned. "Is this really funny?"

"It's a great book," a Hungarian in glasses answered.

Olga sobbed quietly.

Bjorn entered the library.

"What happened?" He went straight over to Olga, who was still crying. "Did someone hit you?"

"No, she just got sad." Kelly stroked Olga.

"They beat me!" The Italian laughed and suddenly began to sing loudly and deliberately in a man's bass voice.

Kelly laughed and applauded. Sally whistled, without lifting her eyes from *Fiesta*. An old man with cornflower-blue eyes plugged his ears with his fingers. Bjorn sat down next to Olga.

"Are you all right?"

"It's too ..." Olga slammed the book, wet from her tears, closed.

"Fitzgerald," Bjorn read the author's name. "I've heard of him. Is he the one who was an alcoholic?"

"Yes."

"A lot of American writers are alcoholics."

"Yes, yes," Olga muttered feebly.

Bjorn stared at Olga. She sat, remote, in Kelly's embrace.

"Do you have a bonus today?" Bjorn asked softly.

"I guess so ..."

"I do too."

Kelly's ears perked up.

"So you'll come to us?" Bjorn asked, examining Olga's ear.

"Probably ..."

"Hey, big boy, you're not the only one with a bonus." Kelly's yellowish-blue eyes stabbed Bjorn with a glance from behind Olga's head. "Olga, you were already with us. Our corner is really tight. Really powerful guys. Did you like it yesterday?"

"Olga," Bjorn spoke up, "ours is cooler. The Swedish corner is the coolest."

"Don't talk that nonsense in front of me!" exclaimed the Italian girl. "The Swedish corner! You'll waste your bonus. Come to us. We've already merged with the French. And the Albanians are with us, the Romanian, and three Macedonians. The Greeks want to join too. It'll be the coolest corner of all!"

"Don't listen to her, Olga. You know you're one of us; Americans are the coolest of the lot! And not just up there."

"Our group is cooler. Much cooler." The Italian wouldn't give up.

"Olga, you know you were invited to the Swedish corner—" Bjorn smiled nervously.

"Don't go, you'll waste your bonus for nothing!" Kelly didn't let up.

"Shut up!" Sally clapped her book shut and swung it down on the table. "You want to end up in solitary?"

"There are rules about waiting for the lights-out bell, ladies and gentlemen!" The old man shook from indignation.

"We're all equal here, for God's sake!" exclaimed a pockmarked Swede with bristling white hair.

"Olga, make the right decision!"

"Think, Olga!"

"Quiet, all of you!" Sally clapped her hands. "Read."

She opened *Fiesta* again.

Kelly stood up, put *The Hobbit* back on the shelf, and left, cursing. Bjorn sighed deeply, glancing at the camera. Olga turned to him.

"It's unbearable," he whispered, wiping the sweat off his pale face.

"Twelve minutes."

"Sometimes time is elastic," he muttered. "It stretches and stretches..."

"And then—snaps."

"Right. And then it snaps."

Olga sighed and stood up. "All right. I'll go and drink some water."

"Great idea!" Bjorn grinned nervously.

Olga put Fitzgerald on the shelf and went into the Ham. Bjorn hurried after her. Inside you could feel the tension: women were sitting on the beds, gathered in groups; the conversation got quieter when Bjorn entered. All of the women held cups of water. The French girls sat near the water dispenser. They were embracing, entwining their arms, pressing their towheads together. Olga walked up, stepping over someone's legs, pulled out a plastic cup, and pressed the blue button on the automatic water dispenser. Cold water flowed. A French woman with a luxurious mane of tight gold curls lifted her homely, pimpled, long-nosed face, and fastened her large gray-blue eyes on Olga. Olga took the full cup, lifted it to her lips, and sipped a bit. Cold water calmed her.

"Can't you come with us?" the French woman asked.

Olga shook her head. And went to her bed.

"I just shouldn't look at the clock," she persuaded herself.

She sat down on the blanket. Drank a bit. And looked at the clock: four minutes till. Sally, the Italian, and two Ukrainians came in. Olga drank water in small sips.

"Youth—is always a dream…" she recalled, looking at the plastic cup.

"One minute!" Sally called out.

Immediately everyone came to life and moved around. Dropping their things, taking their cups of water, the women went into the hallway.

"Here we are. The eighth time," Olga thought, mixing with the crowd and trying not to splash her water.

In the hallway everyone got all mixed up—men and women. The crowd approached large doors of opaque glass. The doors glowed blue. Conversations and muttering quieted down, the crowd grew still. All the prisoners of the bunker stood next to the door holding plastic cups filled with water. A siren sounded and the door opened. The crowd slowly and tensely began to push into a passageway, which was illuminated by a blue light. In the wall opposite were five windows. Near the windows were two guards with clubs. The prisoners stood, packed tightly against one another, but tried not to push so as not to spill their water. Pressed against the back of a limping Ukrainian, Olga carefully held her cup to her chest, covering the top with her hand. Her heart beat rapidly. Its heavy beats cleared her head of chaotic thoughts. Olga only looked ahead, moving toward the bluish window. Someone cried out briefly, someone else pushed. But the calmness of the crowd controlled the nerves of its individual members. The crowd of prisoners dragged itself to the windows. Each received his own and immediately left the blue room.

Finally it was Olga's turn. Leaning over toward the window she placed her dogtag against the electronic reader. A signal beeped and two transparent tablets with ICE stamped on them rolled out. Olga grabbed them and swallowed them immediately, washing them down with the water. She threw the cup into the trash and left the gateway, as the blue space was called. Her heart beat ever more strongly.

"I'll go to the Swedes right away," she thought.

Behind her she heard noise, yelps, and shouts: someone was trying to take someone's tablet.

"There they go . . ." Olga walked along the hallway and turned into the Ham. Some groups had already formed, sitting close in preparation for their voyage. But the Swedes weren't there.

"The Swedes are in the Garage today!" Olga guessed.

The French, Greek, Romanian, and Ukrainian girls began to reach for her hands, muttering, trying to convince her. An albino Icelander threw himself at her feet, grabbed her knees, and whispered in Icelandic, butting his forehead, sweaty with desire, against her. From his hysterical whisper only one comprehensible word issued: "Bonus!"

Plugging her ears, Olga ran into the Garage. She immediately noticed the Swedish corner: about ten people were already sitting on the floor, getting ready. She walked over, murmured something, reached out with a shaking hand, collapsed on her knees, and began to touch the others sitting there. They were expecting her, they welcomed her joyfully, touching her in turn with shaking hands, moving aside and letting her in. Eyes, light- and dark-blue, pale-sky colored and deep-sea colored, stared at her, shining and sparkling, promising joy shared among all. Trembling, she squeezed in, merged with them, held hands that were moist with excitement, feeling how the heart wave grew, how the chest brimmed over with joy, how the head spun, how the blood beat in the temple. The strength of the Swedish corner amazed her.

"Here it comes...already!" she thought, closing her eyes with pleasure.

New people who had just swallowed their portions of happiness came; they sat down, pressing in close, holding each other's hands tight, in an unbroken chain of pleasurable anticipation. Liz appeared, touched them, and by virtue of her presence found her place among them. Strengthening the joy, her red lips trembling. Silver curled. Greeks and fiery-red Israelis turned up; then a broad-shouldered Swede with sky-blue eyes and the pink cheeks of his disfigured face shaved bare. American woman were also present. They all had bonuses. They all craved happiness.

"The best are all here!" Olga's blood pulsed joyfully.

And—the moment of flight had arrived. Holding tight to her comrades in joy, she closed her eyes. But they wouldn't let her lose herself in the precious and joyous.

"Criminal! She ate the ice!"

Strong hands pulled, dragged her along the hallway. She felt with every cell how the two pieces of ice were melting, melting, melting in her stomach, the two divine, inimitable pieces that provided an unearthly joy. Oh, if only they would have time to melt. Just another few seconds! Melt, melt, melt, faster, my sweethearts, my body wants you, my body is crying out with desire, my body is sucking you and moaning...

"Open her mouth!"

Merciless faces, cold eyes, rough hands in rubber gloves. They separate her teeth with a stick, and a steel instrument spreads her mouth open painfully, against her will.

"The probe!" A plastic snake slips into her throat, crawls along her esophagus, spreads it open, and doesn't let her breathe.

Her body thrashes, writhes in their hands, but they hold her tight, tight, tight, and there, in the stomach, the nimble snake sucks out the exquisite, sweet, beloved, desired bits of ice, preventing them from dissolving, and already there is nothing, absolutely nothing to breathe, breathe, breathe . . .

Olga cried out.

And woke up.

"What's wrong?" Liz, lying near her, placed her hand on Olga's chest. "You're covered with sweat . . ."

Olga threw off the thin cotton blanket, lifted her head, sat up, and hung her legs over the bed. "Yuck, what rubbish I dreamed . . ."

It was dim in the Ham. The electric clock showed 3:47 a.m. The women were sleeping. Olga wiped her sweaty face with her hand. "Nonsense . . ."

"What is it, honeybunch?" Liz embraced her from behind. "Want me to bring you some water?"

Olga laughed sleepily and shook her head.

"I dreamed that they were feeding us some kind of ice narcotic . . . clear tablets of some sort . . . and I wanted them so badly, I craved them . . . and they took them away from me . . ."

"There are a lot of *ice* dreams here. It's normal." Liz stroked her. "At the beginning I dreamed that I was little, like a bug, and that I was frozen in ice. Forever. Forever and ever in that ice . . ."

"Oh, yeah . . . and there was a . . . library, too!"

"What library?"

"In the dream we had a library here."

"Fabulous. I want into your dream."

"And some kind of collective trips with those tablets . . . the Swedish corner . . ."

"The Swedish corner beat us in foosball this evening."

"Jeez, there's a gym here, not a library . . ." Olga shook her head. "And the men live separately . . . how absurd!"

"We can get by without men." Liz kissed Olga between her shoulder blades, and slipped down from the bed.

Walking over to the water fountain, she filled a cup with water, drank some, returned, and handed it to Olga. "Drink."

Olga drank the icy water.

"Strange . . . I've never once dreamed of home here."

"Neither have I." Liz embraced her.

"But that's ... really strange!"

"No, sweetheart, it's not strange."

"Why?"

"Because our home is here now. And there won't be another one." Liz yawned and pressed against Olga.

As she fell asleep, remembering her strange dream, Olga's shoulder could feel the cavity in Liz's chest.

"Bonus ... bonus ... icy ... rubbish ... bonus—just a bar of Swiss milk chocolate. Chocolate ... chocolate ... shaped like a bird, shaped like Fima. Fimochka's a gooooood bird. Fimochka's the best ..."

The Last Ones

THE BROTHERS' hands wake my body. They awaken Gorn's body. We are on our island. In our house. On our bed. We lie next to each other. Now, after the Great Night, our bodies look the same. They gave a great deal of energy to the Last Search. They are very old. So old that they can no longer move. The brothers' hands open our eyes, lift our eyelids. They carry us from the bed, wash us, feed us, and cherish us. So that the Light doesn't abandon us. But not only our bodies: Our bodies must be *taken care of* by all the Brothers and Sisters of the Light. All 23,000. Now each body is *especially* dear. For the Transformation is near. There is not long to wait.

Having fed us with nourishing liquids, the brothers lower our bodies into a marble bath. It is filled with fresh buffalo milk. It helps to maintain strength in our bodies. Our faces are close. I see Gorn's face close up. He is a little boy according to the laws of the meat world. But his face has grown very old this night. Gorn's body has aged as well. Now he is the same as I am.

Gorn looks at me.

We don't have the strength to speak in the language of the Earth— our lips cannot move.

But our hearts *speak*.

Today the Brotherhood should have acquired the last three of the

23,000. But these last three are *difficult*. They will be difficult to ac-quire, to tear from the meat world. They are mobile. One of them moves about the Earth, killing particular meat machines, and hides from others. Another lives in the Earth; he worked in a place where meat machines made fierce poisons, and he was poisoned by them, and his body changed and he began to dig into the earth and hide from meat machines. The third simply loves to jump and run wher-ever she wants.

Noadunop

AFTER living in Japan for six months and thirteen days, I finally realized what a bird's eye view of Tokyo looks like: New York after a nuclear attack.

I whisper this into a glass of Lychee, in my native Dutch, grinning at the discovery. Then I look down on the twilit city of sushi and *kogyaru*. How cool to sit on the sixty-first floor, sip my favorite cock-tail, stare at the Eastern Capital through two-inch-thick glass, and stir the ice in my glass with my finger.

A minute later I make a correction:

A failed nuclear attack.

It's true: there's a mass of identical skyscraper stumps that look like the leftovers of an atomic explosion, and here and there a hundred-story tower sticks up. It makes me think of Godzilla roaring and smashing the Eastern Capital in the old Japanese blockbuster. Proud loners—just my kind. I raise my glass and tap it against the window-pane—here's to their resilience as they wait for one more mega-earthquake, like Tokyo has been for the last seventy years. I can't tear my eyes away from the city. I like to take my time looking at things—ever since I was a child. And thank God. That's helped out a lot in my *complex profession*. After that Greek in London I've become even more careful. I *live* through my eyes. Now the sun's going down—it always sets quickly here. The street lamps are on already. And in the west—the rosy-orange haze of the disappearing sun. In five minutes it'll be dark—more than enough time to think about who you are and why. I'm satisfied with myself. I'm satisfied with where I am. Everything's coming up roses—so far. Here in this megalopolis I fit in. At least for another six months. In Europe and America they're looking for me. But for the last two years I've had Asian eyes, a totally altered nose, and my lips look a little different too. I shave my head like a monk. My old colleagues in the Corps would never recognize me. My regiment comrades from the Balkans wouldn't either. Only the tattoos. It's so fabulous that there's a place like Asia, where you can crawl off and disappear. I'm the spitting image of a Mongol— three people have told me so. Awesome. I'm a Mongol. I make the occasional raid. A descendant of Genghis Khan. That Greek was a breeze—two bullets in the gut and one in the head to finish him off, just like the movies. And the bodyguard couldn't do a thing. But preparing for it—a whole month of constant training—that was exhausting. Not being able to get a good night's sleep when I'm on a case really gets me down. It's totally exhausting. I'm skinny but I'm built, and those Japanese masseuses did a pretty good job working me over. And after three nights with two *kogyaru* from Shibuya I'm back to my old self. Yeah, I'm not a man of steel, like Bruce Willis in *Diehard*, but so what? I have my own little god to thank . . .

Now Tokyo's turned on the lights. Beautiful, no doubt about it. I always go to this bar before a job. This is the third time. It's become a tradition—a *new* one. Or half a tradition. The other half's down there by the bronze dog. Time to pay up and go. To Shinjuku. Misato-san is waiting. She's the new one. I need to buy her something . . .

I pay the bill and head for the elevator. A steel cabin, dropping me smoothly from heaven to earth. For some reason it always smells like melon. Grab a cab to Shinjuku. There's a traffic jam—rush hour. It's not far though. By the time I get there it's night. Shinjuku's all lit up like a Christmas tree. Seven minutes left. The girl'll wait, I know, but I hurry anyway. I'm a responsible guy, no matter what I'm doing. In the Isetan store I pick up my standard *kogyaru* kit: a Shiina Ringo CD, a *Titanic* DVD, a Pokemon with safety pins stuck in its spiky tail, and a box of Swiss chocolates. It gets them every time. Like a Glock 18 with a silencer.

There's Misato standing right by the bronze dog Hachiko, still waiting for its owner who keeled over after a heart attack. The Japanese put up a monument to a *dog*! How sentimental. Infantile. Thank God I've never had a Japanese client. Or a Chinese one. Two Arabs. One Greek. An Australian. The rest—Europeans. Though—there were two Russians in '98. Where do you put the Russians—in Europe or in Asia? They're just Russians. Those Russians turned out to be real trouble. They cost *blood*—a *lot* of blood. I got hung out to dry like never before. I had to make some serious changes. Change myself. Change my situation.

Misato's all dolled up like yesterday—in pink down to her exposed belly button, with a blue leather miniskirt, white fishnet stockings, and white platform shoes with yellow Pokemon buckles. There's another Pokemon attached to her wide patent leather belt and a tiny yellow one dangling from her mother-of-pearl cell phone. She's got red and yellow highlights in her hair, snowflakes and stars on her huge fake fingernails, pearl gloss on her eyelids, and she's wearing glittery, bright red lipstick. Not a trace of expression on her face, but her body's excellent. And compared to the locals, so's her height: 5' 6". A typical *kogyaru*: *ko*—young, *gyaru*—girl. The tropical girl style—that's what it's called—popped up a few years ago. Now it's being crowded out by acid-style, with shapeless robes and wool caps like the ones the blacks used to wear. But Misato copies her older sister, a first-wave *kogyaru*. Their motto's "Get wild and be sexy." Fine by me.

"Hi, John, how are you?" Misato bares her crooked young teeth with braces.

"*Kombova, Misato-san*," I smile in reply.

She speaks English (very badly) and I speak Japanese (even worse). I take her by her moist hand. Pushing through the crowd, we come out on Shinjuku Dori. We wander, talk. Misato's platforms clomp as we go. Japanese women have a weird way of walking. Most of them are pigeon-toed. A whore in Sapporo told me it comes from thousands of years of sitting on their knees.

Misato's navel doesn't have any piercings, but that's no surprise:

she's only in tenth grade, and it's still against the rules. The families and the schools here really put the pressure on. So the kids dress up in these bright, crazy outfits to compensate. In the evening, Misato's a *kogyaru*; in the morning—a schoolgirl in a dark blue uniform and white kneesocks. She walks briskly and cheerfully on her clopping platforms. I name a place where we can settle in. It's OK with her. Everything's OK. It's cool to go out with a European. Though of course I'm half Mongol. But I'm a *specialist* in cargo transportation. I even have a business card.

I take her to a place I know. Fifty dollars, all you can eat and drink for two hours. An hour'll be enough for Misato and me. I order a beer and a rice vodka cocktail for her—the *kogyaru's* favorite drink. We stack up sushi, sashimi, chicken barbecue, crab claws, and marbled beef. The waiter lights the gas burner under a wok full of water: you get to make your own personal soup. We toss crab claws into the boiling water, eat sushi, and drink. Misato's in a good mood. She giggles and leans back. I squeeze her knee. Misato slaps me on the forehead with a napkin wrapped in cellophane. We drink to our meeting in Shibuya. That's the *kogyaru* Mecca. Their hive. There are thousands and thousands of them there.

"Why you did choose me?" Misato asks.

"You're not like the other *kogyaru*," I lie.

She laughs, sips some more of her cloudy cocktail. She likes the prestige of being with a foreigner. Gulping down sushi, she tells me about her class's summer trip to Italy. She saw the Pope and ate tiramisu that was "better than in Tokyo." She liked the Italians. I tell her about soccer, about when I studied in England (I tell *everyone* I went to school in England) and rooted for Manchester United and how I got into a fight with some Italians and ended up in jail for a month. She laughs. The sushi and sashimi are all gone; now we're waiting for the crabs to boil. Pause. That's when I take the stuff from Isetan out of my backpack.

"For you."

She immediately changes from a *kogyaru* into a schoolgirl, slumped down, her movements angular, as she rifles open-mouthed through the bag; her silvery lips are practically slobbering.

"*Kavai! Sugoi!*—Sweet! Cool!" she sings out. She covers her mouth with her palm and bleats in surprise. "Wow! Wooo! Wheee!"

I sip my weak Japanese beer and let her enjoy the presents. When she gets like that, I want her. A sweet kid. Japanese women aren't for everyone. Alex can't stand them, Gregory isn't very interested either. Only Serezha Labocki likes them, though he likes the Chinese better. Japanese women are eternal schoolgirls. Awkward and shy. It can be a downer for Europeans. But for me it's a turn on. I like Japanese schoolgirls. Even when they're forty. Plus, to go out with a white woman would be curtains here. I have to be totally free, able to lose a tail at any second. Not to mention my skin.

The crabs are ready. Misato, excited by the presents and the rice vodka, pulls them out of the wok with chopsticks. I put the beef in the wok together with meatballs and mushrooms on skewers. We break open the crab claws with scissors, dipping the snow-white meat in sauce. Misato prattles on about America, where she's never been but really wants to go. After all, I'm an *American*. I really do have a decent American accent. I tell her about the Grand Canyon, about Los Angeles and Miami. The restaurant fills up with white-collar workers carrying briefcases and cell phones. They're noisy, in a rush to relax after another day's *selfless* labor. And tomorrow they'll get up again at six, schlep their way into town on the train for an hour and a half, and lay down their lives for a company that manufactures air conditioners. For me—this would be hell. Better to kill someone every couple of months than that . . .

Misato's drunk. She can't take another bite of the boiled meat. It's time. I've sobered up a little. Filled up on all sorts of delicacies. And I want to stick it to the tenth-grader. I take her by the side and lead her out. I pay at the exit. She giggles, stumbles over her own feet, and loses a platform shoe. Finds it. Giggles again. We stumble out of the restaurant. As usual, it's stifling and noisy outside. September. But the humidity's still way up there. The Love Hotel, that's what they call it, is only a stone's throw away. I'd never take a chick to my own room—not even if Gregory paid me the going rate of twenty thousand for once . . .

I pay and get the keys. We take the elevator to the third floor, walk down the hallway. I'm already hard. Good food and decent liquor always make me hard. In broken English, Misato asks if my wife is jealous. After all, I'm a *worker, a family man*. I tell her that we have an open marriage.

"How does she like Japan?" Misato asks.

"She likes it. But she misses New York."

"Ahhh," she nods sincerely.

I open the door, turn on the light: small room with a large bed. As always. And never anything else. I turn on the nightlight, turn off the overhead light. I give Misato a push. Like a doll, she collapses on the bed, laughing. While she lies on her back, giggling, I undress. She stares at me like an elephant in a zoo. I pull her platform shoes off, pull down the fishnet stockings. Under the silk panties is a black, slightly shaved pussy. Fresh as an oyster. Japanese pussy always smells like the sea. I spread her legs and lick her. She whimpers weakly. I stick my tongue in, pushing her knees up at the same time. Her knees have the usual bruises from the tatami mat. She whimpers. I guess she doesn't like it. It's not up to her though. Uncle wants to. It goes on for a few more minute, before Uncle pulls on a condom, spits on his hand, rubs the spit on his dick, and settles in.

I enter her slowly, in smooth thrusts. She's still whimpering. I shove it all the way in. She sobs and looks away. Her face is a distorted grimace. I screw her. She moans and whimpers. Japanese girls are helpless in bed. Not like the Chinese. Or the Thais.

"*Sugoi . . . Sugoi . . .*" Misato whimpers.

She sucks on a fake nail. I turn her sideways and lie down next to her, pressing against her pimpled bottom, squeezing her small breasts. Her pussy's young and tight. That's making things go too fast. I put on the brakes. I think about work. About tomorrow's departure. About an old hiding place in Bosnia where two drawers of bullets and three Glocks, two Berettas, and a Kalashnikov, all nicely oiled, are lying ready to go. I think about the dead Greek. About the house I'll buy when I retire to Goa.

Japanese girls don't know how to give head. It's a national trait. They don't like it. Misato tries, just like yesterday. No good.

"Get rid of the teeth," I tell her.

She does. And gags. So I flip her on her stomach. I ram my cock all the way into her little womb. It's like it wanted to get back in. She moans and cries into the flat pillow. Her back's soft and white. You'll never find white skin like this in Europe. Not to mention America.

I'm coming. It's time. I pull out of her, tear off the condom. Grab her by the hair, push her head against the bed. I grab my dick. A few convulsive movements of my hand—and I come in Misato's ear. She freezes, not understanding. Her ear fills with sperm. A modest little star earring sparkles through it. I hold Misato's head down, and take a good long look at her ear, full of *me*. Then I lean over, give her a kiss on the temple.

"Ooo, oh, oh." She's scared.

But she recovers quickly. She smiles.

"Oh my god . . . Ha ha ha . . ."

You can see that no one's ever fucked her like that. Her ear's lost its virginity. Good. Life'll be that much easier. So she was shocked. For me it's a *new* tradition. To come into a *kogyaru*'s ear before a job. Otherwise it won't come off.

VIENNA. 8:35

The target exits. Gregory and I are in the car. Gregory switches on the ignition, we move off. We take Gertnergasse to intersect with the target on the corner of Ungargasse. The Glock 18 with silencer is ready in my hand. The street's almost empty. A bicyclist goes by. Another. We pass flower sellers. A bakery. Viennese éclairs—delicious. In a beige raincoat and a beige hat, the target rounds the corner. He's carrying an apricot-colored leather portfolio. Always walks to his office. I press the button. The dark glass lowers. I stick the gun through window, and one, two, three, all in the head. I hear his glasses shatter on the pavement. He falls, dropping his folder and his hat, not to mention the will to live. I close the window. Gregory turns on Ungargasse. Hits the gas.

MUNICH. 10:56.

Serge got me out of Vienna in his Jaguar. A real pro. Unlike me. We say goodbye silently and I enter the airport terminal. Huge and empty. Has to be the day of the week. I look for my flight. Stockholm. 11:40. Great. Time for a mug of Munich beer. I love those unfiltered wheat beers. I pick up my ticket and boarding pass, go through security, and head straight for the bar.

"*Ein Weissbier, bitte.*"

A buff, tanned barman draws my beer and puts it on the counter. I take a barstool. Next to me's a handsome old guy wearing a hat with a feather. Bavarian. I light a cigarette. Everything went well. My hand didn't fail me; the Glock 18 was perfect. And Gregory drove *just right*: he's really got a feel for how I work. We've been together for six years, and so far there've only been two screw-ups: the Swiss guy and those Russians. Doesn't matter. Things could have turned out *much* worse. The beer's in front of me. I take a first gulp through foam. Excellent. This stuff doesn't change. It's just like it was in 1984, when I first went to Munich from quiet Rotterdam, a pimply young man. Ayaks vs. Bavaria. 2 to 1. The battle of the Titans. I almost got my nose broken that time in the Hofbräuhaus. We rushed over there after the game to have a beer, like idiots. Before the army I was a crazy fan. And now—I don't care. I've got my own game. My own penalty shots to make. And so far I've scored ...

The old man asks for a light. I hand over my lighter. He drops it on the floor. I pick it up and help him light his cigarette. His hands shake. A gray-haired, blue-eyed Aryan type. Must have fought in the war and yelled "*Sieg heil!*" Old people are helpless like children. That's what's in store for me, too. The guy probably has a big family. Maybe I will someday. I can't go on coming into a *kogyaru*'s ear forever. I drink up and board the plane. Everything's fine. The cabin isn't crowded. I guess Bavarians aren't dying to fly to Sweden on Mondays. Swedish beer is truly awful. I'll pick up the dough, knock back a few Czech Prazdrojs. I fasten my seat belt. From the net pocket I pull out a worn German car magazine, leaf through it. Curious: they rate the Mini Cooper the best car of the year. That's a woman's car. Not serious. Not powerful. Like the Germans after war. The best ones, our colonel used to say, stayed in the ground ... he was probably right. Better not to say anything about the best Dutch. Better to keep your mouth shut ... I'm the best of the Dutch. The Flying Dutchman ...

And what's this? A Cooper S, 165 horsepower. Not bad. Definitely more interesting. Let's see. That'll do. Headlights. Six air bags. Six? One for the balls? A parking sensor. Rain sensor. Rain...That means the windshield wipers turn on automatically...and the rain...the rain can pour...or shower...like in Goa...when they've already hung out the nets...and the girl with the boom box has already gone...gone to get the daiquiris, waggling her butt...and the teak bench...is wet...wet, the idiot, she spilled...spilled my glass...

The magazine falls from my hands. My body lists to the right, toward the aisle. The green carpet path on the floor swims before my eyes. The legs and red shoes of the stewardess.

"What's wrong? Are you ill?"

My arms are heavy as cast iron. I can't move them. I try to open my mouth. I'm drooling. Spit drips on the red shoes. From the right, in my ear—an old person's voice, in German: "Mark! What's wrong? Oh my God, he's sick again. I told him—better to stay at home... Fräulein, we need to get off..."

"Are you flying together?"

"Yes, yes! He's losing consciousness again. Help me..."

The old man's hand unfastens my seatbelt. And it doesn't shake at all.

I open my eyes. I'm in a large room. The windows are shuttered. The ceiling's high. I'm naked, strung up on the wall. My arms are bound with steel and rubber. My legs are tied. Two people sit across from me. One of them is the old man from the bar. The other is young, muscular. There's a long metal case in front of them. What's inside? I can imagine. A chain saw? I'm in for it. Seriously in for it. My head's empty. I'm calm. I can recall the details. They nabbed me, like a rube. That old goat slipped something in my beer when I was leaning over to pick up the lighter. Very simple. I tense my muscles. Test my strength. The old man stands and approaches. He comes up close. I see his face in front of me. Brave, wrinkled, slightly tanned. His dark blue eyes study me from under swollen eyelids. There's not a trace of expression on his face.

"How are you, Hugo?" he asks in English.

Whoa! He knows my real name. For everyone else Hugo van Baar died in Croatia and was immediately buried near Vukovar. What else does he know?

"Everything," the old man said. "We know everything about you. You're a hit man and you just killed a man in Vienna; then you were going to fly to Stockholm to pick up your money. Twenty thousand Euros. That's you in the present. We know your past as well. We know, for example, that as a boy you hated your stepfather and once poured sugar into the gas tank of his motorcycle so that he'd crash. Your stepfather didn't crash, instead he flogged you with a flyswatter. A flyswatter made of gray plastic. We know that you were afraid of hedgehogs. We know the name of your first girl—Elise. It took place in the forest, near the gulf. You were in too much of a hurry. At fifteen, that happens."

The old man stopped talking and walked away. Who are these people? How do they know all of this? My mother? She died of cancer in 1994, and she didn't know about Elise. Only Elise and I knew about Elise. Who told them? Elise? She's been in America for a hundred years. What about my stepfather? Mother couldn't have told him. Who are they?

"We are your brothers, Hugo," the old man said. "Soon we will awaken you. And you will become entirely different. Your life will begin again. To make it easier for you to awaken, remember the dream you had as a boy on the Zaelmans' farm. The dream about the dark blue apple. About the dark bl-lu-luuue apple. Remember, Hugo van Baar."

And suddenly I remembered. That dream! I'd completely forgotten. For eternity! An incredibly powerful dream—it shook me through and through. I was seven. My mother was still living with my father. One time we went to the Zaelmans' farm. They had cows and sheep, two dogs—Rex and Whiskey—and two kids named Maria and Hans. We played with the children and dogs all day long. And I was so caught up in one of the games that I got flung chest forward into an old seeding machine that had been left to rust in the burdock and weeds. I fell against it so hard that I almost fainted. The metal slashed my chest and I was bleeding. It was a serious wound, and

Zaelman drove Mama and me into Assen so they could bandage it up right. In the clinic they put me on a table, gave me a shot of anesthetic, stitched me up, and bandaged the wound. I dozed off on the way back. And I dreamed that we were returning from the clinic to the Zaelmans', riding in their old red jeep. Everything was so realistic, so tangible, like I was awake: Zaelman was driving the car, Mama was sitting in the back with me, I put my head on her lap, the wind blew through the windows, and I could smell all the smells. The car suddenly braked—I raised my head and saw that Mama and Zaelman were sleeping a deep sleep. I got out of the car, saw the Zaelmans' house, went inside, and realized that everyone in the house was asleep, the people and the dogs, and outside the cows and sheep were sleeping, too. Everyone and everything around me was sleeping, sleeping, sleeping. It was dead silent all around and only I was awake, I could walk and look and touch everything; I entered the living room, Maria and Hans were sleeping in the armchairs. Suddenly I saw a blue apple on the table; I walked over, picked it up, and realized that it was ice cold, but it felt *very* good to hold it in my hand, and I held it to my chest, which ached and burned, and it felt *so* good, everything felt so fresh and open that I began to sob in ecstasy, because sometimes things could be *so good*, *so terribly good*, and I realized that as long as I had the blue apple I would feel good, but I also understood that it was made of ice and it was melting, and that when it melted I would *never* feel so good again. I held the apple, but it was melting and dripping, and with every drop I was losing *the good*, losing it forever, and I sobbed like I'd never sobbed in my life, and I woke up because Mama was afraid I'd make myself sick sobbing in my sleep like that, but I was sobbing because that *marvelous* dream was fading and it would NEVER come again.

"There now, you've remembered!" the old man grinned and nodded to the strong fellow. "Go ahead."

The guy opened the long case. It contained a piece of frost-covered wood that had been fastened to a chunk of ice. An ice hammer. Roaring, I jerked forward with all my might, but the bonds held. The young man picked the hammer up, swung back, and hit me in the chest with all his strength. It hurt. I couldn't breathe. I stiffened from the terrible pain in my chest. He hit me again and again. Then I lost consciousness. And awoke because my heart *spoke*:

"Noadunop!"

Mi

IF YE ASK, Mother Earth will sweat secret, 'course she will. She's kind and good when ye pray right, hush-hush. Ask on the sly: Mama Damp Earth, spread out, open up yer damp. Kiss her like ye was her son, on the Face, on the Chest, on the Shoulders, on the Womb where the essence damp runs. Waitin'll be needful, snuff up the secret sap. Touch yer forehead to the ground and pray all the way: Mama Earth, open yerself ever and anon. That'll be yit. And then she'll start sweatin' and swellin' all soft. And that'll be yit. When the Earth sweat comes seepin', seepin', seepin', seepin' out middlin' and fluider, then say yer thanks: Mama Earth, thanks be to ye now and forevermore, on account of ye are, were, and will be till the end of days. That's whatcha gotta do, 'course ye do. And then slide yer hands into her gentle, don't go scaring her, don't force yit, no tricks now, take yer time, don't press any filthy hurrish, don't shove that damned upsider smutter. Mother Earth don't respect that putrid damned hurrish. No she don't. Just take yit sap slow, peaceful like, and do yit all proper, just right. So that Earth's hush-hush sweat don't droll off, the shrivel dry don't come back. Yer hands is in, then a little pressure, keep yit up so's yit feels good. And do the first parting teensy little by little, orphanish, like a chillun without a mama. Sorta awkward, seesaw, seesaw, sweaty, timid, that's what. So her feelings don't get hurt. So she don't belch none. So she lets ye in and takes pity on ye, that's what. So she does yit in secret. Finish the first parting to all the way, good and true. So she can feel yer fresh, soft nature. So she accepts yit with her damp. As soon as she lets ye in—then ye make the second parting, that's what. Real strong this time, like a grown-up, a thristow. So she c'n size up yer power. Then she'll letcha in and yit'll all be finely. Ye can live inside her flybe-like, homelike, in a good warmly big bosom, that's what. Yit's better than any house 'cause yit's a sight warmer and honester, yep. And here ye don't need nothin' from upside above even in yer thoughts. The soul's got peace and the body can rest, yit ain't hanging up in the air. An' if ye finish the second opening real good— then dive into the Earth and swim wherever ye need, just swim, like a slippery, greasy sliver of soap. Mama Earth will rub ye down with her inside oils, and off ye go. Down deep if ye want, where there's nuthin' but Earth. Upside above if ye like, where there's big ole roots and stones, when ye need 'em. Or iffen ye fancy—into the empty spaces, into the leftover cracks. When I managed to go far into the Earth, flybe away from the damned, shifty, the liars upside, firstly I respected the deep and did like I should oughta, that's what. Yit's easy, whoop and hide from the damned world with the Earth's fat. The deep shields and protects ye from everthing; yit'll cover and warm ye, yit'll give yer soul a good scrubbing, and make yer body so strong yit'll have peace for the ages and all time to come. The deep is good for most anything: dreams and prayers and them obscene lardious mechanics. But the deep won't keep yer belly full, no body-food down there. That's right. So ye cain't stay in the deep too long, that's what. The body wants food. And the soul—prayer. Mother Earth gives good food and feeds ye well. But the food is up above, under the rootstocks and grasses and sweet trees, oh so sweet. The food is up there, near that putrid world of filth, the surface. Lie long as ye like and rest up in the deep, gather yer peace and calm—and slither on up there like a flybe just right, that's what. There's sweet roots, bulbs, and there's live critters abiding their time in the Earth. At first I liked to catch blind mice and take my time sucking their blood, sure 'nuf. Them blind mice moles blood's got power for parting the Earth the way ye ought should. But only if yit's sucked out sap-slow, hush-hush, just right. Mole blood is powerful. On account of the blind mouse clan's been swimming just so in the Earth for ages, makin' little flybes along all the ways. I strangled moles in their burrows, dug up their passages and nurseries. I ruined their secret dens so's I'd be strong. So's I could flybe the Earth. So's I'd know how to behave myself and be right way in the Earth. I pulled worms outta the tilled land upside there, what feeds all the whores. I dug up wood lice and snails outta the forest rot, sidled up and caught 'em, bugs and beetles, that's what. Yanked the roots of sweet grasses down, gnawed on 'em. No hurry, I chewed them roots and bulbs cud slow, praying and thanking the Earth good and well for my food. Grass roots have energy and important juices, mighty, pure-bred, skin-tight. Yit's energy for the parting, for the breach, the swim-through sailing slice, the ice breaking, and the grass roots have whoa, that much and more. Just the right strength. Roots are friends with them worms and blind mice, they give 'em their strength with milk and blood, that's their willful, why not. They feed 'em in secret, peeling off the layers. And me, I'm friends with all of 'em, strong friends, good friends, with all of 'em that feed my flesh in secret, steep and popping, who make my armbones hard and strong as rock, who keep the goddamn above upside away from me so the vermin of the bright light cain't find me. Everone who helps me flybe burily is my friend. And everone who boulders is my enemy. Right away the Earth's deep togged me real good, no let up, needy. I dived right down into the deep for an age, snorted and sniffed, dug my heels in yit. I snuffled about hush secret, from the innards side. I did the spreading coredeep. The earth there is strong, lardy, thick. At first I scrambled together the power in the deep to keep yit, I sucked with my nose, I shuddered, drew in the Earth's juice, strengthened the might of my spirit and flesh all out. I rested in the deep, and Mother Earth's lard scrappled all the disgusting blasted mold the brightlight vermin left on me, cleaned me off squeaky. I cursed the bloody world upperside, that's what. I understood the essence of the World cowlly, by the eternal graten need. The essence of the Earth that holds the Sky and Stars and the Upper World, and the two-legged, four-legged, six-legged, and the multi-legged. And that's how yit oughta be, an eternal support, a cubic. Mother Earth supports and holds. I recognized growinged, and my guts learned the good rules of life in Mother Earth, the powerful, the stronged. But I didn't ken right off that not just to dive into the sweet Earth but to think long and gravenlyish about the good Secret. Ye need to search for a resting shelter. An onlyed lone one. Broke off from everthing else. I crawled and slithered, snifflying under the plowed fields and the forests. I flybered into places where the ground is crumbly, and that's how I skirted those bloody cities, stone upfaces, secret boulderal deepths. I strengthened my flesh-might with the worm, the mole, in the furrow grooves, taking my time. I did the breaches and the inrushes in ferocious cloutings, with the right moan, the fatty one. Then I moved the under stones, raked the roots earthfast, with a thrust not a grab. I excreted the digested gifts of the Earth with gratitude, with hush-hush, with innard prayer, and then I flybered farther, farther, farther, that's what. Not down the deep, but just under the roots, upwardly. Juicy and simple, the lardly way! Sometimes I heard the noise of the bloody world, filthy and brightlight. And the steps of two-legged vipers disturbed and troubled my spirit, wombed yit inside. Their voices, their vexations and knocks drilled into my body. From upperside fear and spirit rot yowled and descended, drippled furious from the nastified upper cities, then flowed down to the bottom dwellers in a wide fan of perdition, that's what. And there the two-leggerds writhed, strained, dangerously and brightly. They controlled false, dubious worlds for evil, pecked, grouged, and chiseled. The bright foul pests worked themselves bone naked and seduced their others endlessly, tirelessly, and juicily with lies. They shook clattered and built in preessing, destroyed in stench and devoured greedily. They sucked the strength from one another through generations, detachingly, with brutal mercilessness, hurrily, that's what. And a bloody damn tremor seeped outta the breached cities. Under the roots my nonmetallic body trembled, so there ye have yit. I could just feel the herding masses of two-leggerds bright bloody, they scattered the Countenance of Mother Earth with their foul hooved legs. I felt how they tortured her in scamper, tore at her with their sickly, hammered into her, and how she shuddered secretly and openly. How they wailed with rage of their damn entrails. How they built the bloody upside world. I skirted the cities. Swam around the villages. Laid a path down around the filthy nastily multitudes. I flybered furrowed just a little at a time, under the roots. In tears I entreated Mother Earth and prayed to her for the supple yielding. And she parted for me, sweating secret, for me alone, her beloved, her hush-hush. She let me pass through the underground marshes and between stones. My arms strengthened with this. My arms acquired eternal might. There were no hindrances, no hurdles. The oak roots cracked, the stones slid from their places, natural springs collapsed, the Earth slid yits stress. Mother Earth helped me acquire solitary, find a secret place for peace and prayer, that's right. She sweated and her flesh parted, letting me through without obstacles, rushing me through, me her grousling. I felt the fertile flesh of Mother Earth. I licked her secret underground sweat with a trembling tongue, sobbed from the languor of destroying hindrances, I scribbled and morrumbled, bled the underground lard. With a wombish moan I thanked her for her suppleness, wailed inside her from joyous belonging. I inhaled through my nostrils. Bellowed wombly without wicked words. I believed Mother Earth. Loved her stronger than myself. Relied on her fiercity. I directed the parting sweaty. I steamed on the underground of the filthy uppersiderds. Where they live and make their secret works, terrifying works to a quiet, solitary nature. I skirted those underish places, kept to the side, turned back. I flybered farther and farther around the Earth. I swam in deep and shallow. I flybered into the place where the filthy ones bury their dead. I made a parting and flybered between the bodies lying in the Earth's Flesh. Their bodies exhaled foul decay. Putrefaction and stench poured out of 'em, foul pus drippled. Mother Earth she withstood everthing, swallowed everthing humbly, lying down, what else? Fear turned me from touching the bloody remains. Foul upsider life slept in these bodies, burbled and ailed, remembered the horror of abominable affairs and the creations of the upsiders. I howled a howl, too, kissed my beloved clods, squiggled 'n' squirmed deeper down, salted myself cautiously and sniffed morcably. I looked for my own. I steamed in the bloody underground depths where they carried out their secret orrites. Where they manufactured and bulldrilled their killing machines to kill each other. Fear and trembling goosebumped me, I had to salter down and sweat, what else? I only rubbeled myself down with Mother Earth's lard, very careful, yes I did! The foul ditches breathed pain, rumbawled, desired. But I round-flybered the loathsome wanting, swam to my own, to the good. I swam and swam across the Earth. And sweatingly flybered a proper path. And came to the enormous, empty edgels. That's where the filthy upsider crawlers pulled what they needed out of Mother Earth. They broke and bruised and gouged for a long time, and took away and rottled, and tore Mother Earth to pieces in a hurry, foully. They pulled out Mother's cover, sucked out her prosperous entrails, an' did everthing foully, glumily. Then they left and left the emptinesses. I entered those Mothery hollows, stood up straight, that's what I knew was needed and what wasn't. And I found myself a secret place, an earned place. I set myself a quiet shelter there. I figured those hollow emptinesses that filth suckled out I'd fill with prayer to Mother Earth, that's what. In the hollows yit's easier for me to make the Great Prayer, and in earthly flesh, a Lesser Prayer, that's what. Because if ye want a Great Prayer ye hafta separate yerself from the earth, but a Lesser can be sternally and steenly make do with a snovel, straight off. I didn't flybe in the emptinesses, I just prayed and leaned motionless, cumbersome. I knew what I was doing. I understood the ambush, the salimnity. I rolled up in a little ring flybe so's I could feel and touch the Earth's body, so to pray with all my meat, yellatedly, that's what. I took the Earth in to the very end. And I was happy innardly and flybely. I could have lived like that in the forevermore ages to the very edge of Mother Damp, but the Earth parted. The upside whores penetrated. They crashed the calm. Blinded with upper light. Caught with a net. They tied and hauled, sucratly, furiously. I fought with 'em, with my arms, powerful from flybering. I wounded the whores and teared the nets. But they swathe me in foul metal. They bustled stubbornly, stickyly. They jump on me dense. I roared and teared at 'em. I prayed to Mother Earth. But no help came—they torn me away from the under lard, took me away from the innards, from the damp. They stretched me out with cruel steel to still me. They stole my moving craftily, foul. They speak among themselves in a verminous language I don't understand anymore. They shatter the edges of the Earth with disgusting sounds. They surround with the cunning of force, that's what. They ready tricky, terrible, unintelligible deeds. I pray and tense with all my strength. They take a hammer a tiny little iceslick out of a steel box whorishly made. They beat me with the iceslick in the chest and I'm stretched out and popping. They beat me hard and winnding. They beat me hard and swift. And my heart *speaks* to 'em.

"Mi."

Rikuosh

It's fun to jump . . . better than anything in the world . . . jump and forget everything . . . I jumped over the bench and forgot . . . there's no bench anymore . . . dum dee dum . . . I jumped over the ditch and there's no ditch anymore . . . I jumped over Erika's leg and then Erika left for Masterton and married a mechanic . . . I jumped over a rabbit and Anna cooked it in white wine . . . jump jump jump . . . *pink hills pink hills* dum dee dum . . . A square man has been hanging out in the bar since this morning . . . he goes and goes and goes around the world the square man . . . it's hard to jump over the square man . . . because he only drinks bourbon . . . jump jump jump and jump dee dum . . . I'm the Great Jumper of *pink pink hills* . . . when I was born there was a twister in the *pink hills* . . . I would have jumped over the twister, but it wasn't near us it was in Terriaqua and Masterton . . . we only had wind and the rain gutter bent and smashed the doghouse against the bar . . . jump jump jump *pink hills* . . . but Masterton got hit good . . . it's fun to jump and very good for you . . . when you jump you fly and forget . . . dum dee dum . . . but when you land you stand and remember what you jumped over . . . I'll jump over the *pink hills* tomorrow . . . but I won't jump over the square man from the bar . . . he walks walks walks about the world that square man . . . Erika Norma Joseph dum dee dum dee . . . and who else . . . the dog Fidel likes raw bones . . . when he gnaws a bone I jump over him . . . oh how he scampers about . . . the wind crawls into my dress . . . it's fun to fly and fly . . . when you fly you love yourself . . . and dum dee dum . . . *pink hills* didn't destroy . . . Kate tried to convince Mama to go to town . . . dum dee dum and dum dee dee . . . Sem Kuan the Korean bred chicks for *fried chicken* . . . I jumped over him . . . when you fly it feels good to

throw your head back dum dee dee dum...so your neck cracks...
when you fly it's fun to fart...but when you land you don't fart, no
one will understand how come...dee dum...and you can blow your
nose when you jump...and sneeze...dum dee dum...and you can
fart, blow your nose, and sneeze and sweat all at the same time...but
the most dangerous is to sneeze because you have to close your eyes
and dum dee dee dum dum...but I never jump with my eyes closed...
it's boring...and the square man walks and walks about the world...
dum dee dum and dum dee dum...that's my favorite song about the
square man from the bar...jump farther and more and shake your
head and dum dee dum...each time try not to break anything...
Fidel liked to drag handkerchiefs out of pockets and dum dee dum...
there are different jumps...I'm the Greatest Jumper of all countries
and continents...dum dee dum...horses are better than dogs...
and dogs are better than cats...it's fun to jump over dogs...they
don't see you...you fly over a dog and whistle and dum dee dum...
Fidel Fidel Fidel...but he doesn't see you...he looks all around...
jump jump jump...*pink hills pink hills*...dum dee dum...I don't
like spiders...it's scary to jump over a spider...but you have to...
you fly over spiders for a long long time...you fly fly and dum dee
dum...but you jump fast over a snake...because snakes are better
than spiders...and rats are better than snakes...flying over a rat is
fast...dum dee dum...it sniffs and can't figure out where you are...
jumping over cats is even better...the cat can't figure out where you
are either...but once you jump over the cat it understands everything...dum dee dum...but dogs never figure out you jumped over
them...I jumped through the *pink hills* today...and I have to jump
farther...farther...over the highway to the gulf...where the ships
are...and the cape where there's a monument to lost ships...there's
dum dee dum and dum dee dee...it's fun to jump over stones because they don't talk...it's hard to jump over the gas station where
Erika works, Erika with her hair in rollers...it's just that dum dee
dum...when I jump over the gas station it doesn't smell like gasoline
but like shit...it isn't Erika's shit or Erika's husband Stephen's shit...
jump over the Collinses' farm and forget...over the cows' trough...
and over the tractor and forget...dum dee dum and dum dee dee

...and the best is to jump over dumb old John and Sigurd...I jumped and forgot...dum dee dum...landed and remembered...dee dum running jumps are fun...a running jump just right so the square man doesn't see...he just walks and walks about the world, that square man...I jumped over the school and shouted and spat... dum dee dee dum...school is a bad place...they only jump in gym there...and they don't jump well because they don't like jumping and don't know...don't realize that jumping is great...it's dum dee dum...I jumped over the teachers...I jumped over the pupils... jumped over the school desk on the left side...I jumped over math and physics...jumped over drawing...dee dee dum...I jumped over 186...but I didn't jump over singing because singing is like the wind...and you mustn't jump over the wind...I'm the Greatest Jumper of all countries and continents...dee dee dum dum...I jumped straight over the square man and I'm not scared of him anymore...when I jump over something I'm not scared of it anymore... it's fun to jump just like that without a running start...then dum dee dum...you have to hold the air in so it doesn't burst your chest... you hold hold the air while you fly...you land and dum dee dum... you exhale the air and it already smells different...it's already dum dee dum...it's already after-jump air and no one needs it...breathe out the after-jumping air quick as you can and run around and about and up and down...so dum dee dum...you always have to choose right quick who to jump over...right now I dee dee dum...I'm jumping over the cleaners and there it's always dum dee dum...warm and damp...when I land I sweat like dum dee dum...I like to sweat like dum dee dum...not when I fly but when I land...but when I fly I like to yawn and swallow the wind and dum dee dum dee dum... after I jumped over him the square man was small like a square on the bathroom floor...and because dum dee dum...the green square smells like bourbon vomit...and I jumped over 45% on the supermarket glass...and dum dee dum...I jumped over 45%...and it doesn't smell at all anymore and I don't want to yawn...when you jump over something everything starts to smell dee dee dum...you smell yourself...or not yourself but someone else...when I jump over the streetlamp it smells like *cheeseburger*...but when I jump over McDonald's in Masterton it smells like Martin's motorcycle . . . and dum dee dum I haven't jumped over Martin's motorcycle yet . . . but I jumped over a liquor factory in Terriaqua . . . and it smelled dum dee dum . . . like grass like spit and the chair in the bar dee dum . . . and I farted over the factory and giggled . . . and now I'm running up down all around about dee dum . . . and I jump over a train station and dum dee . . . and it smells like the barn lock and grandma who's been lying in the ground near the old stone fence for ages . . . I'm the Greatest Jumper of all countries and continents . . . I dum dee dum . . . jump and jump . . . but you can't always jump . . . you have to wait while you eat . . . because it's hard to jump with food . . . food dum dum dee dee . . . wants to jump over the plate into your mouth and down your guts and then jump over your guts into caca into the toilet . . . and in the toilet dum dee dum . . . but the square man isn't jumping anymore and won't ever jump into the toilet . . . because the square dum dee dum . . . they don't jump but sleep and watch . . . I jumped into the town dum dee dum . . . I'd never been there . . . the city looked like the bar in Masterton dum dee dum . . . it's simple to jump over people in town . . . they're all together they don't move like dum dum dee dee dum . . . you don't have to take a running jump and look before you leap . . . I'm the Greatest Jumper of all countries and continents . . . I jump dum dee dum over cars . . . they smell like people . . . like people's sweat and like words . . . cars are fast but I'm even dum dee dum . . . I can jump over fast things too . . . if I jumped over Martin's motorcycle then I can jump over cars too . . . in flight I like to smell what's under me . . . dum dee dee dum . . . it's fun to spit and shout . . . when you jump you're not scared of anything . . . just jump far and high . . . then everyone will be happy . . . I jump over a newsstand . . . over cigarette butts . . . over dog shit . . . I jump over a movie theater showing *Shrek 2* . . . I jump over a tram . . . jump dee dum . . . over a cash machine . . . over a café . . . and suddenly a woman in sky blue says jump over me Sophie . . . I stop . . . you know me dum dee dum . . . she says everybody knows you you're the Greatest Jumper of all countries and continents . . . jump jump over me . . . and she bends down like in school . . . I take a running leap I jump dee dee dum . . . and my palms stick to her back . . . and then dum dee dum someone does something to me...and I can't jump anymore...I can only be in a basement on the wall...and call for mama...and then dee dee dum...they hit me in the chest with something cold...and dum dum dee dee I hear my heart *speak*.

"Rikuosh."

The Transformation Program

14:57. Guangzhou. The ICE Corporation office.

The huge, bluish-white office of the corporation's director. At the table, leaning back in a light-blue leather chair, sat the skinny, bald Rim. His tanned, dried-out face was immobile. His blue-green eyes were glued to the piece of Ice floating in a glass sphere suspended from the ceiling—all that remained from the huge block that fell to Earth. Rim *was waiting*, holding his breath. His heart was *preparing itself.*

Three long minutes passed.

The milky-white bulletproof glass door slid open silently. Shua, Uf, Atrii, and Tsefog entered the office. Rim stood up, shook off his stupor, and moved to greet them. The brothers who had entered stopped two steps away from Rim: They were *protecting* their hearts. Rim *understood* this. They had to conserve their hearts' energy and not expend it on brotherly greetings. Rim stood *stock-still*. Before him stood four of the Mighty. Each of them was responsible for the brothers in his part of the world. Each was a shield for his continent. Shua, the former keeper of the Arsenal, was now, after Dopob's death, protecting the brothers and sisters of America; Uf—of Russia; Atrii —of Europe; Tsefog—of Australia and Oceania.

The brothers who had just entered *understood* that everything was ready.

Rim walked over to the elevator and pressed the button. They all entered the elevator. It moved upward. There, under the very roof of the silvery-blue skyscrapers, a *secret* room awaited the brothers. One that none of them had ever entered before.

The elevator stopped. The door opened. The brothers entered a small, vaulted room clad in lilac marble. In the middle of the room stood a round table of sky-blue spar. In the center of the table a small circle shone gold.

The brothers sat down at the table in silence.

For a few minutes they sat, *preparing* their hearts. Then Shua spoke.

"You *know* that the Brotherhood has acquired the last three. The search is complete."

A slight tremor passed through everyone at the table. Of course they *knew*. But they had *restrained* themselves, not permitting any *joy* to disturb the balance of their hearts.

"The time for the Last Achievement has arrived. We must *decide* everything. And eliminate whatever hinders us."

"The meat is the only thing in our way," uttered Uf. "It's *coagulating*, sensing that the end is approaching."

"The Brotherhood must defend itself," Rim responded. "We *are able*."

"We are *ABLE*!" they all declared.

"The meat is counting on *a rift*," Atrii said. "*We shall move* the shields!"

"*We shall move* the shields!" they all declared, and *confirmed* with the might of their hearts.

"The ships have left their moorings," said Tsefog. "They will be in transit for six days."

"During this time the last acquired will *cleanse themselves* through heart crying," Shua concluded.

"There are eighteen *weak ones*," said Uf. "I *know* this."

"They may *grow in number*," declared Uf. "I *know* this. The meat *in each of them* will begin to resist. But their fear must be *removed*. Four of the *weak* are *flickering*," Uf continued. "They could *leave*. Then we would have to wait until they reincarnate."

"We need the *support* of the Mighty," said Atrii. "Khram and Gorn are not with us, they are on the island."

"Their hearts *are tired*," Uf summed up.

"They have *given* so much to the Last Search," Shua responded.

"They will *support* as well as they can," Rim declared.

"The Circle of the Mighty is needed," concluded Tsefog.

"The Circle of the Mighty is needed!" they all *cried out*.

Their hearts *spoke*. Hundreds of the Mighty across the entire Earth *responded*. The hearts of Khram and Gorn *responded* as well.

Forty-four minutes passed.

The Circle of the Mighty *shone*: WE ARE READY!

Distant hearts *were quenched*.

When everyone at the table had *calmed down*, Rim spoke.

"It's time!"

All five removed delicate gold chains from around their necks. On each chain hung a tiny gold pin. Each took his pin. Five hands holding these pins stretched toward the gold circle in the center of the table. Inside the circle five barely perceptible apertures could be made out. The brothers' hands fit the pins into the openings, and froze.

An intermittent signal beeped.

1, 2, 3, 4, 5.

The brothers pressed on the pins. The pins became embedded in the circle. The circle began to move smoothly out of the table. A gold cylinder rose over the table. It stopped. A hologram flashed above it, the emblem of the ICE Corporation: a shining heart flanked by two Ice hammers. The Ice hammers disappeared, the shining heart alone remained. A woman's voice spoke.

"The Search program is complete. The Transformation program has been launched."

Everyone around the table cried out. They grabbed one anothers' hands. Their hearts *flared*. Each of the five knew what the Transformation was. All had participated in its development, each *knew* the role he had played in it, each had contributed his *light* and earthly intelligence to it. They had all been waiting for it, moving toward it, and *craving* it, and their hearts had been *patient* in anticipation of it. They had all *tried* to live until it came to pass. But now each of them simply *felt* it with his heart. The hearts of Rim, Shua, Uf, Atrii, and Tsefog *felt* the signal issuing from the silvery-blue skyscraper to all four corners of the Earth: "Transformation!"

Each of the 23,000 had to receive this signal. He had to go and find each brother, each sister. He had to touch all of them. In thousands of cell phones, in dozens of languages, the word "Transformation" appeared; thousands of faxes printed the word on paper, it lit up on thousands of monitors, the young lips of brothers whispered it to thousands of helpless old people and infants whose hearts were already *prepared*: "Transformation!"

Ten hands interlaced, five hearts *flaming* with the Joy of Anticipating the Main Event of the Brotherhood. The hearts above the gold cylinder shone. The signal was flying to all corners of the Earth: "Transformation!"

Hundred of kilometers away, in the house on the island, Khram's and Gorn's eyes opened slowly: their *tired* hearts rejoiced, with a *quiet* joy…

The Key

ON WEDNESDAY morning, cutting out her 121st strip, Olga hurt her finger, and Horst, the brigade leader, transferred her to the old people. Settling at the table in a corner of the workshop, she began to sort the cut-out strips, placing them in plastic boxes. An older Rumanian woman who didn't speak English sat next to her; across from her, a gray-haired, trembling Icelander; and next to him, that German, Ernst Wolf. Olga had had lunch and dinner with him several times; he was interesting to her. When Olga ended up in the geriatric corner with a bandaged finger, Wolf smiled and winked at her like an old friend. It seemed to her that over the last month his face had grown even more yellow and withered, but he remained unfailingly cheerful, composed, and collected. He constantly joked with her in his old-fashioned English, learned in confinement. Olga liked the old man for some reason, although she, like her deceased parents, didn't have much love for Germans. But a kind of enchanting, charming calm radiated from Wolf. His unflappableness reassured Olga, infected her with confidence, which was so missing here in the bunker. Over their meals Wolf had told her a great deal. She knew everything about him and almost everything about the Brotherhood of the

Light. And the most surprising thing for Olga was that Wolf believed in the Brotherhood's mission, he believed in the 23,000, believed that once they gathered, the Brothers of the Light would bring the history of the Earth and humankind to an end. At first Olga laughed at the old man condescendingly, then she argued with him until she was hoarse. But then she began thinking seriously.

"You don't understand, my dear, to what extent our planet is unique," Wolf told her. "Believe me, there is and has never been anything like it. All those arguments about brothers in intelligence, about new forms of life on other planets, are utter nonsense. On a billion billion planets there is no life and can be none. The Earth is alone in the Universe, she's totally unique. And *Homo sapiens*—is twice, thrice unique. And if this is so, then the Earth must be seen as an anomaly, as a strange plant, as a lacuna in the body of the Universe."

"But perhaps—as a miracle?" Olga objected.

"Miracles are anomalies, Olga. And any anomaly in the Universe is a violation of its equilibrium, the destruction of order. A straight line can be drawn between two points, through three, through thirty-three. But there's no sense in drawing a straight line through a single point. Because one point is just a point. It's not a path. It's not a pattern consistent with natural laws. Therefore you and I, like our entire planet, are a mistake of the Universe. And we have no future."

"So that means you want the Earth to disappear?"

"I'm not against it, given my age and my present situation."

"And so you're on the side of the Brotherhood?"

"Oh, no, Olga, not at all. I am not on the side of the Brotherhood."

"But why? After all, in your opinion they are striving to correct the Universe's mistake."

"And they will try hard to do this, believe me. But I'm not on their side."

"Why?"

"Because I don't know how to speak with the heart. That's the first thing. The second is that they are physiologically repulsive to me. All in all," he said, "put it this way—Old Man Wolf is simply jealous of them!"

It was after this conversation that Olga began to think seriously about certain things. Lying on her bunk at night, her thoughts went on, accompanied by the quiet murmur of the air conditioner and the women's heavy breathing and snoring.

"What if it's actually true? What do we really know about our world? That the Earth is round? That spring will always follow winter? That humans evolved from the apes? That we're smarter than animals? In school and at college they told me that the Universe was infinite, that everything derived from the Big Bang, from a spark ... something flashed, and the stars and planets were formed. Everyone believes this. And what was before that? A void? Why? And who created the void? Where did it come from? It just appeared all by itself? People believe in what they can agree on ... A thousand years ago they believed that the Earth was the center of the Universe. And before that—that the Earth stood on the backs of four elephants ... If this Brotherhood really believes—if they are spending huge amounts of money based on what they believe in, committing crimes, kidnapping and killing people, if such a powerful corporation is seriously engaged in this—then perhaps it isn't the ravings of a sordid bunch of sect members, but the pure truth. And people are in fact divided into the chosen, who are able to speak with the heart, and the rest, who are trash. And the chosen ones will become rays of light at some point, and the Earth will disappear. And we will all die, like idiots ..."

Olga tried to share her thoughts with her neighbors in that cursed bunker. Bjorn listened to her attentively, then in his customary tedious manner refuted Olga's concerns regarding the Earth's destruction. He was certain that the kidnappings, the video games with the ice, and all the rest—was only the tip of the iceberg of the ICE Corporation, which was headed by a powerful group of international criminals who were trying to take power in China. Bjorn claimed that ICE was involved in secret experiments with genetic engineering. The goal of these experiments was the creation of a new race founded on entirely new moral principles, an elite that was capable of ruling a powerful country like China, and of achieving world dominance.

"Given its rapid technological progress, China needs only one thing to rule the world—a new ideology," Bjorn said with conviction. "A new ideology not only for China but for humankind in general."

Olga listened to this six-foot-seven graduate of his university's physics and mathematics department, who had grown up in a family of Swedish mathematicians who worshipped theoretical physics, who kept portraits of Bohr, Heisenberg, and Einstein at home, who trusted only formulas and technology; she listened to this giant who dreamed of a career as a great scientist, but who, because of an event that didn't depend on formulas, had ended up here, in a bunker where he skinned dead dogs, and . . . she didn't believe him. Bjorn's logic was too linear, his arguments were *too* correct. Whereas everything that had happened to him was totally illogical, was *anomalous*, and eluded logical analysis.

But Bjorn held stubbornly to his views.

He immediately swept aside any arguments about the Brotherhood of the Light, without letting Olga finish her thought.

"Olga, since childhood I have believed only in things that are subject to the laws of physics. Light is a directed stream of photons. Do you want me to write down the formula?"

Olga grew tired of arguing with him. She felt like she kept hitting a wall that wouldn't budge an inch.

"I was taught to believe only in what can be touched or understood logically. What I don't understand doesn't exist for me!" he said.

Bjorn's parents had been confirmed atheists, part of the left-leaning Swedish scientific elite. In the turmoil of '68 his father had joined with the Swedish Maoists, going to university lectures wearing a yellow armband with the Chinese character that meant "self-criticism" on it and carrying the little red book of the Great Helmsman.

Olga's parents had also been atheists. And they likewise taught Olga to believe only in what can be understood and touched.

"Whatever doesn't participate in the exchange of commodities simply doesn't exist," the professor of macroeconomics at the university Olga attended like to say.

Olga never believed in God, or in the supernatural. But as a Jew she believed in fate. Although fate wasn't so simple, either.

"Fate takes its own path," her mother would say. "You have to feel your own fate, believe in it, and not scare it off."

Her father would also mutter something about the "power of destiny." But for the most part the question remained murky.

"The millions of Jews who died in the concentration camps also believed in fate, believed in God," Olga thought. "So what? Fate turned away from them, God didn't help. So that means you have to believe only in your own powers and rely only on yourself."

Now, having become the victim of a mysterious Brotherhood, having lost her parents, and having ended up in this sinister bunker, Olga had lost belief in herself. Over the last two months she had realized there was something greater than herself, more powerful than her own will.

But what? Fate?

Bjorn didn't help Olga answer the question.

With a wry smile, the old man Wolf said horrible things she didn't want to believe. Wolf's calm arguments emitted a feeling of inescapable death and nonbeing. Olga tried to discuss all of this with other inhabitants of the bunker. Liz, who sometimes gave Olga a bit of affection at night, was convinced that the people who had kidnapped her and maimed her with the ice hammer and the people who now kept her in the bunker weren't connected. The infamous Michael Laird, who had lured them all to Guangzhou, had simply used information from police sources and organized a site for victims of this unknown cult in order to sell them all into slavery.

"But who needs straps from the hides of dead dogs?" Olga objected.

"Sweetie, in today's world everything's for sale," Liz replied. "I'm sure the Chinese use these strips for medicinal purposes. And they probably sell them for a lot of money to wealthy Europeans."

"But why can't they openly skin the corpses? There's a ton of cheap labor in China! To kidnap foreigners, support them, feed them, hide them—and force them to skin dogs! Nonsense!" Olga answered indignantly.

"Olga, it may very well be that these dogs . . . aren't quite so simple . . ." Liz intoned significantly.

"What are they—talking dogs?" Olga suggested sarcastically.

"A lot of us here are convinced that the dogs are infected with something. Or irradiated."

"Liz, some people have been locked up here for years. Why haven't they gotten sick?"

"Maybe all of us already have leukemia. The teeth of two of the Rumanian women have blackened. A lot of us have problems with menstruation, with digestion . . . The men are quietly going mad . . ."

"That's all from isolation! From a lack of vitamins! Leukemia has very definite symptoms."

"They aren't just regular dogs, believe me," Liz insisted.

Olga felt that Liz was dragging her into her own mania. But the other Friends of Dead Bitches weren't any better. Their opinions split them into three groups. The first group claimed that this was all the madness of a powerful corporation that was trying to unite ancient cults with the newest technologies in its quest for power over people; the second believed that it was somehow connected with forbidden experiments in cloning people; and the third believed that new psychotropic weapons were being tried out on the inhabitants of the bunker. The Russians had their own ideas, and, as always, they "knew absolutely everything."

"It's just one of the oligarchs who's lost his marbles," the gruff fellow Pyotr told Olga. "He watched too many films, read all kinds of shit. There's a lot of goons out there in the world, just turn on MTV— they show all kinds of mutants there! But there aren't that many of them with money: You've got bin Laden, and who else? So another one's turned up. I tell you Olga, I'd bet my life on it—this asshole is one of us, a Russian! I'm dead sure. He's getting off on it! Nothing else! And there ain't no secrets. Or maybe it's a group of mutants!"

"The shits've sniffed their noses right off and now they're just enjoying the high," Lyosha seconded Pyotr.

"Besides, China's close by, it's easy to make arrangements." Igor, the quiet one, shook his head.

"But the ICE Corporation doesn't belong to Russians," Olga objected.

"Everything can be bought!" Pyotr shook his red head. "Every sign, every brandy."

"The world went stark raving mad a long time ago, don't you get it?" Boris asked her.

Olga did get it. On September 11, at home in New York, in NoHo, it had truly seemed to her that the world had gone mad. During the catastrophe, she stood at her south-facing window and watched the twin towers burning. When they collapsed, and lower Manhattan was engulfed in an impenetrable cloud of smoke and cement dust, the earth shook underfoot. Also shaken was Olga's certainty that there was *something* fixed, unshakable, constant, *positive* in life, something which people had calmly relied on—a family, career, love, children, creative work, even money for that matter. For centuries people had stood fast on all of this. Now, though, everything had somehow cracked, collapsed, crept underfoot. Her parents had died. And even that wasn't enough. Now this bunker with its dead dogs! A real horror film . . .

Looking at Pyotr's cheerfully spiteful face, caught up in his stories about "international" gangsters, Olga could barely hold back tears: The horror of it was that *this* could quite well be true! After September 11, after the blows with the ice hammer to the chest, after the death of her closest relatives, after the site www.icehammervictims.org, after the kidnapping, after the bunker, after the smell of carrion and thousands of dog-skin straps—anything, anything at all, everything could be true!

"The world has changed quite dramatically, Olga," Wolf said to her after a meal. "An agonistic quality has appeared, don't you think?"

"Do you think that it's . . . because of the Brotherhood?"

"Absolutely." The old man smiled. "Experiencing a premonition of its death, our world is producing discordant movements. It is jittery. There was nothing of the like in the nineteenth century. And the twentieth? Two world wars, the atom bomb, Auschwitz, Communism, the division of the world into Reds and Westerners . . . Humankind somehow got the jitters in the twentieth century, don't you think? Take any field, science or art: the cloning of sheep, contemporary art, the cinema, contemporary pop music—these are convulsions. The world is going mad before its demise."

"How do you know about . . . contemporary pop music, living here?"

"From above, Olga, everything comes from above!" The old man stretched his yellow smile even wider. "Each person who ends up here has something new to recount. My picture of the world is quite adequate. The human tendency toward insanity is quite evident. Tomorrow some blue-eyed youth with a fractured chest will arrive here telling us that up above people are already eating nursing infants for breakfast, and presidents are chosen by the size of their genitals. And I won't be surprised. New manners and new morals emerge, Miss Drobot, on the threshold of the end!"

Filling the plastic box with strips, Olga sealed it with sticky tape, placed it on the cart, raised her eyes, and met Wolf's gaze. Smiling, he winked at her, as though he had read her thoughts.

"You are preoccupied with something, Miss Drobot?" the old man asked, smoothing a strip on the table with his yellowed, slightly trembling hands.

"You know what it is."

"Cease racking your brains. Everything will be as it should be. Wait just a bit—and everything will end. And how—you know. Patience, my child."

The old man's calmly derisive tone had begun to irritate Olga.

"The sages teach us patience / gray old men, already patients / it's easy when it won't be long / before you finally pass on . . ."

Wolf laughed. "Wonderful! Who is that?"

"It's Papa's parody of Omar Khayyám. My father translated Arabic poetry."

"I'm in full agreement with your late papa." Wolf slowly placed a strip into the box. "Truly, it won't be long . . . But patience, Olga, is what makes us rational people. You can cease being a rational individual and attack the guards. Or stab me with a knife for skinning our dear dogs. Or simply open a carotid artery with those scissors over there. There is always a choice between judiciousness and lunacy."

"So, in your opinion, suicide is lunacy?"

"Not exactly lunacy but a forbidden move. As in chess, you can't move the king beyond the edge of the board. The king has to play on the board. And man must live."

"And if living is unbearable?"

"Living is unbearable in any event. And therefore necessary!"

"And if life is . . . meaningless?"

"Much of life is meaningless."

"And illness…pain, suffering? Cancer, for instance?"

"Do you have cancer, Miss Drobot?"

"Not yet!" Olga answered and grinned bitterly.

"But I—do. Congratulate me!" The old man smiled.

Olga stared at him silently.

"I found out yesterday. At the medical checkup. Cancer of the liver, as was to be expected." The old man nodded.

Yesterday there had been an obligatory monthly medical checkup, the goal of which was to detect the seriously ill. As a rule, their fate was decided quickly—a few days later the guards would lead them away forever. In the bunker slang this was called "the ascension." Olga had witnessed three such "ascensions": an Irishman who had gone mad, a Hungarian woman who had slashed her veins open, and a Canadian with a serious form of asthma.

"Actually, Miss Drobot, I suspected that something of the sort would happen," Wolf continued, with unruffled calm, smoothing out yet another strip. "Half a century ago my papa missed, and the ice hammer hit me in the middle of my back. I must admit, the blow was powerful."

"And they…they already informed you for sure?"

"The diagnosis is obvious. It's time to ascend."

"But…when?" Olga asked and then caught herself. "Forgive my stupidity, Mr. Wolf…"

"Not at all. It was an entirely proper question." The old man smiled ironically. "Today, before the lights-out bell. As an old-timer they offered me a reprieve of two weeks. But I turned it down."

Olga nodded her head in understanding. Suddenly she felt how very much she would miss old Mr. Wolf.

"In connection with my 'ascension' today, would you allow me to invite you to a farewell dinner? The last supper, so to speak…"

"Of course."

"That's marvelous. We'll talk over dinner."

Wolf lowered his eyes and returned to his work.

"Cancer," Olga thought, glancing at his hands in their rubber gloves. "Tomorrow he won't exist anymore. But I'll still be here. Rotting alive…"

Wolf said nothing new to Olga over dinner. She talked a great deal and asked him a lot of questions, trying as before to understand and process what had happened to her. Wolf spoke little, repeating what he had said long ago, not responding, chewing the simple food for a long time, savoring pieces of fish and vegetables as though saying farewell to them. When he finished his dinner, he drank his luke-warm green tea quietly. Then he began to speak.

"Olga, last night I remembered something. To tell you the truth, I hadn't ever forgotten it. But I haven't told you this yet. You will re-member that I said I grew up in the villa of my father, a high-ranking member of the Brotherhood. The brothers often gathered at this villa. And one time when they gathered, I spied on them. Actually, they weren't really hiding...That evening there were quite a number of them, about fifty people. In the main parlor of the house they un-dressed to their waists, sat in a circle, and held hands. And then they froze stock-still. In fact, my father and some of the brothers had done this before, they'd embraced naked and stayed absolutely still for a long time. I even think they stopped breathing. For me, a boy, it was rather frightening to see this. But then I became accustomed to it. And when they made this circle, held hands, closed their eyes, and froze, I stood on the stairs of the second floor and watched. The ser-vants were also *their own*; the cook, the gardener, three guards, and both governesses were sitting in the circle. In the entire house there was only me and my sister, who was asleep in her room. Previously, spying on someone embracing my father, I would hide. That time I suddenly realized that there was no one to hide from—no one would notice me! So I descended from the second floor. The door to the room was locked from the inside. But I went around to the porch, opened a narrow window, and climbed into the room. The curtains were drawn. Only the fire was lit; the chandelier was extinguished. And so I went in and stood in the room. Fifty men and women, naked to the waist, sat with closed eyes, holding hands. They were completely immobile, as though they were petrified. The flames in the fireplace illuminated their bodies. I stood there awhile, then walked around them, examining each of them. It was so strange! I knew that my fa-ther lived a strange life, that something very strange was happening

654 · ICE TRILOGY

around my sister and me, even something frightening. Father was cold with me, we almost never talked about anything except my responsibilities. I socialized more with the tutors, but they too were rather strange, as if they were thinking about something else all the time, and pretending, even when they joked and laughed. School was the only release for me. There I had fun, had friends, played, it was interesting, even the mathematics lessons that everyone found boring made me happy. But at home I was almost alone. After the strange death of my mother, who was hit by a car in Berlin, the only person in my life I was close to was my sister. But Renata was still a little girl, I could only play with her. So that is how I lived. In short, when I walked around that circle of immobile people, at first I felt scared. It was as if these people had died. But I knew that they were alive! And my fear was unexpectedly replaced by anger. What they were doing made me feel so bitter, so sick to my stomach, so unpleasant! I realized that they were *violating* something, something very important! But I didn't understand…what, exactly. I simply began to shake with anger and I burst into tears from a feeling of helplessness. An unexpected feeling! Crying, I ran around the circle and began to hit and slap these people on their backs to make them come to, to wake them up. But they kept on sitting there immobile. I ran around the entire circle. I was *very* scared. Fear literally choked, squeezed, and threw me down on the floor. I started sobbing out loud. My crying filled the room. I sobbed and heard my own voice. Next to me sat the living dead. Finally I cried myself out. I lay on the rug, whimpering. I had never felt such loneliness as I did in those minutes. That is something I will never forget. And then, lying on the rug, I suddenly noticed through my drying tears that a poker was lying in the fireplace. The bent end of it lay in the coals, glowing red. And suddenly, unexpectedly for myself, I stood up and took this poker, approached my father, and touched his back with the red-hot end of the poker. The skin on his back hissed. There was a smell of burning and a bluish-gray smoke rose. But my father didn't even flinch. That smoke, that smell of burned flesh, that hissing in the absolute silence somehow calmed me down. I *understood* something. I realized that these people in the circle…were not people. I, my sister, the pupils in my school, passersby in the street—these were humans. This discovery calmed me deeply. I hung the poker in its usual location, next to the fireplace. Then I crawled through the window again, walked up the stairs to my room, and fell asleep. I slept deeply and calmly. And in the morning, as usual, my sister and I had breakfast with our father. Father was a vegetarian and ate only fruits, vegetables, and germinating seeds. I realized that he hadn't even noticed the burn on his back. And everything in our family continued as before. For a while … So that is the story, Miss Drobot."

Wolf fell silent and slowly, smacking his lips, drank the rest of his cold tea.

Olga sat quietly, struck by what she had heard. The crying boy with the red-hot poker stood right before her eyes. The old man rose from the chair, and stretched out his yellow hand.

"Dear Miss Drobot, I wish you good luck."

Olga realized that he was saying goodbye. After such a long, intimate story, this was rather sudden. She reached her hand out to Wolf, meaning to say that he shouldn't hurry to say goodbye, but she suddenly felt something in the old man's hand. He put a piece of paper in her palm.

"Mister Wolf—" Olga said, but he interrupted her.

"The very best to you, Miss Drobot."

The old man turned and walked into the Garage. But he hadn't yet entered the hall leading to the male half when the white door marked SECURITY opened and two Chinese in uniforms stood in front of him. One pointed at the door with his club. The old man walked obediently toward the bright opening. He stopped. Looked back. His eyes found Olga. He looked at her. He wasn't smiling as usual, he didn't wink. His face was calm and serious. Olga jumped up, raised her hand, and waved to him.

The guards grabbed the old man under the arms and dragged him inside. The white door closed.

Tears welled up in Olga's eyes. Squeezing the piece of paper in her hand, she went to the Ham, laid down on her bed, and sobbed into her pillow. People tried to console her but she waved them away. Crying her fill, she fell asleep quickly. And awoke from a gentle touch:

Liz was cautiously kissing her on the neck. Olga opened her eyes. It was dark in the Ham. The electronic clock showed 23:12.

"What's wrong?" Liz asked. "You're sleeping in your clothes. Are you tired?"

"Yes," Olga muttered as she sat up on the bed.

"Do you want some water?"

"I do." Olga wanted to run her palm down her face, but she felt the piece of paper in her fist.

She remembered Wolf, his story, the white door... She squeezed the paper in her fist more tightly. Liz returned with a plastic cup and handed it to her. Olga drank. The ice-cold water was pleasantly refreshing.

"Want to come to my bed?" Liz proposed in a whisper. "Rosemary went to her Scottish girl, and now you and I have a spacious bed..."

"You know, Liz, I'm kind of tired," Olga answered, placing the cup on the shelf and sliding off the bed.

"Well, I'll give you some energy, sweetie pie." Liz gently held Olga's breasts from behind. "You hurt your little finger? Sweetie pie's finger hurts? Let me kiss that little finger."

"Liz, not today, all right?"

"What, do you have your period?"

"No, I'm just really tired and want to sleep."

"You sure?" Liz embraced Olga's waist.

"Absolutely!" Olga grinned and yawned.

"Well, all right then. Go ahead and sleep, honey." Liz kissed Olga on the cheek, turned, and went back to her bed.

As she undressed, Olga watched Liz go. There was nothing between Liz and Olga but gentleness. It happened somehow naturally, though Liz had taken the initiative. She'd had women before Olga. Before Liz, Olga had been deeply in love with Leonora, her contemporary-history teacher, a tall, portly, kind, very calm woman. Olga fell in love quickly and deeply. Before that there had been the guy who made a woman of her; the affair lasted almost a year and then they drifted apart without hard feelings. Then there was another guy, for a very short time. But Olga had fallen hard for Leonora. It ended in disaster—Leonora didn't understand or accept it. Olga stopped going to her lectures, but passed history just the same...Olga didn't meet anyone else while she was in college. Then over six years she'd had two affairs. The last had been with a man whom she liked a great deal, but he was married and decided to stick with his family. And after that...after that there was only the ice hammer.

Waiting for Liz to settle down, Olga went to the bathroom. After the lights-out bell it was the only place that remained illuminated. She entered, washed her face, and glanced at the observation cameras: one in the left corner, another in the right. Six stalls open at the top so that everything could be seen. Which should she choose? Where could she hide from the cameras? Rinsing out her mouth, she realized—in the fourth stall from the entrance. The bottom of the stall couldn't possibly be seen...

Olga entered the fourth stall, pulled down her underpants, and sat on the toilet. She exerted herself and squeezed out a stream of urine. And slowly opened her fist. On her palm lay a thin, almost transparent piece of tracing paper, covered with minute handwriting. Olga unfolded it carefully and began to decode Wolf's microscopic handwriting.

I won't address you by name for safety reasons.

From our lengthy conversations, you, as a sincere and impulsive person, have most likely already come to a premature conclusion about my misanthropic cynicism and apostasy. I assure you, my child, that it is not so. Happily, even after everything that has occurred, I have not become a misanthrope. Even now, at the edge of death, I still feel that I am that very same boy with the red-hot poker in his hand, trying in vain to revive half-people. But they cannot be revived, for they are the enemies of everything living. I have hated my father and his Brotherhood my entire life. And I continue to hate them now, as I await a forced death at the hands of the Brothers of the Light. Alas, my child, they won't let me die of cancer! I am a patient man and I look on death stoically. But I do not at all desire that you should die by the will of 23,000 living dead. And with you, the entire Earth and her inhabitants. I confess that I am fond of you—as a thinking reed, and a woman. For that reason I am giving you the opportunity to defend your life and that of five billion *Homo sapiens*. The chance is extremely small, but theoretically possible. It was no accident that I told you the story about the poker. As an observant person, you should understand my idea. The end of the Earth will be the Prime Circle, in which the entire Brotherhood, all 23,000, will gather. I don't know where the preparations for this event are being made, in what corner of our planet the launchpad for the Children of the Light is situated, but I am certain of one thing—no simple mortals will be there when it takes off. There will only be brothers and sisters of my now departed father, who never gave my sister and me any paternal warmth. When the last Circle gathers, when they grasp one another's hands, begin talking in their language in anticipation of the beginning, they will cease hearing or feeling anything, just as those in the parlor of our house did back then. At this time you will be free to do with them whatever you like. The main thing is to find the launchpad. This is strategy. Now about tactics. I am certain that you are reading my farewell missive in the toilet. I am more than certain that you, a person with a quick Jewish mind, easily found the only safe stall for reading—the fourth from the entrance. If you will now lower your right hand and feel the edge of the toilet, you will find a key there. This is the key to the door in the hallway between the Ham and the Garage, from which, as you recall, the cleaning man and woman emerge once a week, in order to clean up our—forgive me, now it's your—temporary dwelling. Behind that door are auxiliary premises, more simply put, the altar of the underground guards of cleanliness. This space, as far as I know, is connected with the guards' room, where two guards are constantly on duty. At night, as far as I know, these two are the only guards in the bunker. Four others, on duty during the day upstairs in the workshop, leave the bunker at nighttime.

I wish you luck!

I am not signing this for the same reasons of safety.

P.S. Forgive me that for the possible salvation of the Earth it was necessary to sit on your toilet. By the way, do not forget to flush this letter down.

Olga folded the note and lowered her right hand, feeling around the edge of the toilet. The key had been stuck there with chewing gum. She took the key and clutched it in her fist. Her heart thumped: Aha! With the letter in her left hand and the key in her right, Olga froze. The possibility of escaping overwhelmed her.

"It's possible! So—it's possible. It's possible to try!" thudded in her head.

"I must," she whispered.

Life had acquired meaning again. Instantly her body filled with energy.

Everything must be thought through. But whom should I escape with? It would be impossible alone…With whom? Who can be trusted? Think, think, my orphan!

She shuddered. She carefully opened her hand and looked at the key. It was homemade, cut out of a narrow steel plate.

It was time to return to the Ham. The only thing left was to flush Wolf's letter down the toilet. She really didn't want to. She remembered the old man, pretending until the very last to be a cheerful cynic, remembered his story about the boy with the poker, trying in vain to return his father to life, and tears filled her eyes. Old man Wolf had been a *terribly* lonely man. Since childhood.

"A father's…warmth," she said, and sobbed.

Crumpling up the letter, she dropped it in the toilet. She stood and pushed the button to flush it down.

Farewell, Country of Ice!

WE ARRIVED that evening in a large bulletproof car at a building where prominent meat machines of the main city of the Country of Ice were gathered. Brother Obu sat behind the wheel of our car. I sat next to him. Brother Uf sat in the back. Another bulletproof car with the guards stopped behind our car. Brothers Merog, Tryv, Dor, and Bork sat in it with weapons in their pockets. I got out of the car and opened the back door. Brother Uf got out of the car. Brothers Merog, Tryv, Dor, and Bork quickly got out of their car and surrounded brother Uf. Brother Uf entered the building. Merog and I followed him. The other brothers remained outside. In the entryway of the building there were guards; pictures valued by the meat machines hung on the walls: a furry animal who liked to sleep in the winter depicted against the outline of the Country of Ice; a bald meat machine with a mustache and a beard, who carried out a coup in the Country of Ice eighty-eight years ago; an iron hammer crossed with an iron instrument for cutting ripe ears of grain; ripe fruits against the flag of the Country of Ice; a bird of prey with two heads. We passed the guards and walked up the staircase. Meat machines with devices allowing them to capture and multiply images of faces stood on the side of the staircase. They immediately pointed these devices at Uf's face and furiously began to capture and multiply his image. Several other meat machines began to ask Uf various question connected to the gathering of meat machines and the future of the Country of Ice. Uf shook his head no, and Merog and I pushed away the loud, clamoring meat machines. When he reached the top of the staircase, Uf entered a large room filled with meat machines. At the opposite end of the hall stood a raised wooden platform for meat machines to talk from, and over the raised platform on the wall hung the large word RECONCILIATION and under it, in slightly smaller words, WE'LL SING TOGETHER!

When we entered the hall, a small, middle-aged, but wide and powerful meat machine stood on the platform saying that it was long overdue for all meat machines living in the main city of the Country of Ice to reconcile with one another and not be enemies, since hostility only damaged the Country of Ice, which had so many difficulties anyway. This meat machine reminded them that meat machines with different desires and interests had gathered here, but today was a day of reconciliation, and this reconciliation should occur through songs that the meat machines of the Country of Ice like to sing. According to the meat machine speaking, these songs helped the meat machines of the Country of Ice to live; the grandfathers and great-grandfathers of those standing here were helped by these songs in the difficult years when the meat machines of the Country of Ice fought against the meat machines of the Country of Order and were victorious. To conclude the talk, the stocky meat machine began to sing about the main city of the Country of Ice, about the light in the windows of buildings, about the domestic comfort of meat machines, about the ringing of metal objects that the meat machines have hung in tall buildings in all ages, in order to ring them when everyone needed to gather and pray. Uf walked around the room. Merog and I followed him. Meat machines turned and looked at Uf. Some said hello, but some turned away angrily. Uf found brother Efep in the crowd. He was standing with seventeen of our brothers and sisters, who had been working all the time with Efep in meetings of meat machines responsible for the laws by which the meat machines live. Efep and the rest of the brothers were prepared to abandon today's meeting of meat machines on Uf's command. We walked over to him. Uf was restrained. He could not allow himself to *show his joy*. Walking over to Efep, he made the sign: It's time! Efep's heart *flared*. But he *understood* that all of them could not leave at one time. He gave the command to the brothers. And they began to leave the hall gradually. Others stood and pretended that they were singing or listening to the speakers. A strapping meat machine with an angry, decisive face climbed the raised platform and began to talk about how it was time for reconciliation, that they had to do away with the internal enemies of the meat machines who are keeping the meat machines of this country from becoming happy. Then this meat machine sang a song from the time of the war between the Country of Ice and the Country of Order; about how the meat machines of the Country of Ice were at war with the Country of Order, and how the meat machines of the Country of Ice wouldn't waver in the struggle for their country. Most of the meat machines standing in the hall sang along; a few whistled as a sign of protest. Our brothers quietly left the hall. Uf stood and chatted with various meat machines that approached him. When the song was over, the meat machine with the mustache said that today the song should reconcile them all, and in a delicate voice sang about a fuzzy insect flying to a flower, and about the daughter of meat machines who do not have a permanent home, and about the daughter hurrying at nighttime to another meat machine so that they can do pleasant things to each other in the dark. Most of the meat machines in the hall began to sing along with the mustachioed meat machine; a few even began to dance around, but the mustachioed meat machine sang and cried. As soon as the song finished, a large, well-fed meat machine got up on the elevated platform and said loudly that it would be a crime to bury the skin of the bald meat machine in the ground, that for decades the meat machines of the Country of Ice had loved this bald meat machine, who carried out a coup and did so many good things for the Country of Ice; that the skin of the bald meat machine should lie on the main square of the Country of Ice for eternity, so that little meat machines could come to the building and decorate it with flowers. Then this well-fed meat machine began to sing about the meat machine who once traveled far from its home on a four-legged animal, couldn't find the road back, and slowly froze to death. At this moment Uf gave the sign to leave. And all of us, including brother Efep, headed for the exit. When we walked through the crowd of singing meat machines, some of them spoke angrily to brother Uf, saying that they did not like the songs of the Country of Ice. But Uf walked silently through the crowd. And his heart *rejoiced*. And I realized that we would *never* see these meat machines again, that we would never hear their strange songs again. We went outside and got into our iron machines. Brother Efep and other brothers and sisters got into their iron machines. Our iron machines traveled away from the center of the main city of the Country of Ice. A while later we arrived at the place where iron machines capable of flying land and take off. A large white flying machine was waiting for us. This was the last, eleventh flying machine exporting the remaining brothers from the Country of Ice. Ten such machines had already flown off, filled with our brothers and sisters. We entered this machine by a staircase, and Uf was the last to go up. He decided to be the last to leave the Country of Ice. His powerful heart *completed* everything that had happened to the Brothers and Sisters of the Light in this country. He stopped at the door, and his heart *flared*. Everyone sitting in the flying machine *felt* the reason that Uf's heart flared. His mighty heart *was rejoicing and saying farewell*. It was rejoicing because all the Brothers and Sisters of the Light down to the very last one had left the Country of Ice, that he, Uf, had lived to see this moment, that the Great Transformation was close at hand. But Uf's heart was also saying *farewell* to the Ice that had been destined to fall in this particular large country, farewell to the Ice that had allowed the dispersed Brotherhood to gather again, to the Ice that no longer was. Tens of thousands of Ice hammers had been shattered against the chests of meat machines in this country, many brothers and sisters had died trying to gather the Brotherhood, many of them reincarnated as those now sitting in this white flying machine. Uf's heart *rejoiced and said farewell*. And our hearts *rejoiced and said farewell* along with his. Casting a last glance at the earth of the Country of Ice, Uf turned away from it and entered the machine. We closed the door after him. Inside the flying machine were the brothers and sisters with the most powerful hearts in the Country of Ice. Their assistants were with them, like myself and Merog, like Tryv and Bork. The hearts of everyone sitting in the flying machine were glad, greeting Uf's mighty heart. We all knew how much Uf had done for the Brotherhood; we *felt* his shield, *preserved and cared* for his mighty heart. The coagulating meat tried constantly to destroy Uf, swallow him, crush and demolish him. But Uf was *wise* of heart—he slipped away from bullets and from the fury of the meat, deftly going head to head with influential meat machines, deflecting their blind rage so they would direct it against each other to the advantage of the Brotherhood. Uf helped the Brotherhood to acquire colossal wealth in the Country of Ice, arranged things so that millions of meat machines continually and for practically nothing worked for the Brotherhood, bringing the hour of the Great Transformation closer. The flying machine roared and began to take off. It was flown by our brothers as well, there were no meat machines here. Dozens of hands stretched out toward Uf, dozens of hearts *shone* for him. He walked past and touched everyone, touched us with his hand and his strong heart. The flying machine tore away from the earth. Our hearts *flared*. Everyone understood that the Great Exodus from the Country of Ice was completed. Everyone *knew* that dozens of such flying machines would carry the Brothers and Sisters of the Light from dozens of other countries. So that everyone WOULD meet in the Great Last Circle.

Upward!

A VAGUE noise woke Olga up early: people were making a racket, but she really didn't want to get out of bed. She opened her eyes with difficulty. In the Ham everyone was bustling about, jumping out of bed, running into the hallway. Way down the hall, a dull shot rang out, then another. Then—a shout was abruptly cut off. In underpants and T-shirt, Olga jumped out of bed, glancing at the clock: 4:16. She opened her fist: the key! The key wasn't there. Then she remembered: over dinner she'd given it to the Russians, told them everything, hoping that they'd help with the escape. She'd trusted those hotheaded Russian guys . . .

"What happened?" Meryl asked, hanging over the top bunk.

"They offed someone!" Sally shouted, hurrying into the hall half naked.

"They tricked me! They left without me!" Olga realized. Furious, she punched the bed.

She ran out into the hall with other women: almost the entire population of the bunker was crowded around the open door of the storage room. Everyone was pushing and shoving and swearing. The men were armed with whatever they could find—unscrewed chair legs, pieces of drawers and shelves. Clearly the Russians had spread word of the escape, and the Garage was ready. The Ham wasn't far behind. Women shouted as they tried to jam their way through the door; Olga noticed that some of them were carrying manicure scissors.

"It's like shouting 'fire' in a theater," she thought.

There were young people and middle-aged people in the crowd, and even an old Ukrainian woman with unbrushed hair elbowing furiously as she clutched a twisted wet towel and shouted, "Outta my way, pushers and shovers!"

Olga rushed forward in confusion, worming her way through the crowd. She pushed into the dimly lit storeroom, filled with other Friends of Dead Bitches. Hurrying forward, she glimpsed a door into the well-lit guard room on the left. Two uniformed Chinese guards lay on the floor, their heads bashed in. Nearby, the bare legs of one of the Russians could also be seen, apparently the fat guy Lyosha; one smooth, hairless leg in a white unwashed sock jerked convulsively. The smell of blood cut through the smell of people just roused from sleep.

"It's begun!" Olga thought, both excited and afraid.

The storeroom was a meat grinder: people wailed, others swore, others pressed with all their might against the pale blue walls; someone's nightclothes split and tore, brooms cracked underfoot, a harrowing cry came from a woman who had fallen on the floor.

"Oh my God . . ." a male voice sobbed desperately; Olga realized that she would soon be crushed. Close by she could hear curses and prayers in different languages.

"Oh Mama," Olga implored, her face pushed against the sweaty nape of a cheery, freckled Swede.

The Swede's head shook with strain; something in his body cracked and he farted; behind, people shouted and pushed and shoved. Olga found herself hurled abruptly into a wide corridor, where she landed on the floor with the Swede, a beaky French woman, and a long-haired German. A young man fell on top of her, yelped, and tried to scramble over her like a tree trunk. Shrieking and scratching, Olga clambered across the muscular Swede.

The French woman was half crushed. She swore, "*Oh . . . salauds, putain!*"

"A-a-a-a No! NO!!!!" someone squealed.

Beneath Olga, the Swede was groaning, and the young man on her back began to yowl. She braced her legs, bellowed, and with all her might pushed up and freed herself from the jumble of bodies. Stumbling, she ran down the corridor with the crowd. The hall was long, well lit, and fairly wide, wider than the one in the bunker. Here and there were doors: on one, a red cross, on another, a picture of a dog's head, on a third, the number 7.

Down the hallway Olga ran, her bare feet slapping against the warm linoleum. Others ran alongside, bumping each other and cursing. Just ahead the hall forked: people huddled in confusion, feverishly trying to make up their minds which way to go. Someone muttered "Elevator" and waved to the right; a group ran off in that direction. Suddenly Olga noticed drops of blood on the floor. They led to the left.

"The Russians!" she thought. "The wounded one! The guards shot him..."

For some reason she felt sure that the Russians knew the way out, and she rushed to the left. This hall was just like the last, but without doors, and it stretched on before forking again. There was someone running behind Olga and someone just ahead. Again, the red drops led left. Olga followed them and ran smack into a group of escapees who were beating two Chinese women in white coats. The women didn't even try to resist. Nearby, on the floor, lay an overturned cart with cups, thermoses, and plastic jars.

"Here are the elevators!" Sergei's shout sounded ahead. "This way!"

Through a muddle of backs, hands, and faces, Olga saw the three stainless steel elevator doors, each decorated with an image of a red heart flanked by two Ice hammers. Abandoning the lifeless Chinese women, everyone ran to the elevators. Sergei, limping and holding a captured gun, was one of the first. Olga rushed toward him. Suddenly the doors opened, revealing two rows of guards with automatics, one standing, one kneeling. There was a shout in Chinese, and the guns roared into action. Olga froze in her tracks as the bullets literally cut the people ahead of her into pieces. Light-haired, blue-eyed people, riddled with bullets, fell to the floor. Bullets whizzed everywhere, ricocheting off the walls, scattering blood and shredded flesh. Still, Olga hadn't been hit.

"That's it..." she thought. "Now it's my turn."

Cold with fear, Olga turned wildly to the right, her whole body braced in expectation of being shot. She saw the open door from which the two unlucky Chinese women had probably emerged with their cart. Exhausted, stumbling, falling, certain that she wouldn't make it—the air was so thick with bullets—Olga grabbed the door-jamb with one hand while her feet struggled for traction on the floor. Then someone kneed her in the back, hurtling her through the door, before slamming into her and knocking her flat.

Olga rolled across the smooth floor.

The door slammed shut. The room was almost quiet. The only thing to be heard was black-haired, brown-eyed people killing blue-eyed, light-haired ones. Olga rose onto her hands and knees and looked around. By the door, in all his heroic height, stood Bjorn. Pale, his mouth hanging open with terror, he leaned back against the door.

"Lyktstolpen!" Olga laughed hysterically, jumping up. "Mamochka, oh my God . . ."

Bjorn looked all around:

"An elevator! Another elevator!"

Olga turned. As far as she could tell they were in a large room adjacent to the workshop where they'd cut the strips of dog hide: long metal tables, low metal cabinets, a large glass cabinet, and on top of it a plastic dog head, a full meter high, the dog's crimson tongue hanging out happily. There were stickers on the cabinet beneath that featured red-and-gold Chinese characters followed by exclamation marks. The square door of a large freight elevator was inset in the wall.

"That way!" Olga shouted, rushing toward the lift.

As if on automatic pilot, Bjorn pushed himself away from the door and ran behind Olga, overtaking her in two leaps. His huge palms, spattered with blood, slammed against the elevator's black call button. The thick doors opened immediately, as if awaiting his touch. The inside of the elevator was spacious.

"Amazing!" Olga gasped, jumping in front of Bjorn.

Muttering in Swedish, he followed. On the left was a panel with a red button on top and a black one below. On the right, covering the entire wall, was a poster displaying the same happy dog with lolling tongue. Next to the dog were the same exclamatory Chinese characters they'd just seen, as well as a small picture of a very happy Chinese family whose smiling pater familias held out a flask.

Olga pressed the red button.

The elevator moved smoothly upward.

Bjorn's and Olga's eyes met.

"Lyktstolpen..." Olga said again, covering her mouth with the palm of her hand and shaking her head with abandon.

Tears shone in her eyes.

Bjorn held her awkwardly by the shoulders.

"You knew?" she asked.

"Not exactly..." he mumbled. "The Russians only told the Americans and the Germans."

"Those pigs!" sobbed Olga. "I was the one who gave them the key. And they didn't even tell me..."

"Russian anarchism... *The Brothers*... what is it... *Karmanazov*, right?" Bjorn tried to joke.

"Karamazov, Lyktstolpen..." Olga muttered, looking around the elevator.

The lift soon stopped. The doors opened. Before Bjorn and Olga spread a dimly lit space reminiscent of the laboratory of a pharmaceutical factory. There were rows of tables and chairs, shelves and metallic cabinets along the walls, a huge portrait of the same dog, now accompanied by two excited families with flasks, and... Olga saw a window with a pre-dawn sky and a pale full moon. The sky was real, the moon behind was too. Tears welled up in Olga's eyes again.

"Bjorn! We're above ground."

Bjorn paid no attention to her, but entered the workshop. It was empty. He approached a large steel case with wide doors and opened it: it was a refrigerator stuffed with dog legs, all of them skinned. Olga hurried over. They stared silently at the piles of dog legs. It must be here in this workshop that they manufactured the product that made all those Chinese families so happy.

"Bitch's paw." Olga suddenly remembered a forgotten Russian curse.

Bjorn slammed the refrigerator shut. Olga rushed to the door of the workshop and tried the handle: locked. She ran to the window again: the third floor. Not so high, but the glass was too thick to break.

"How do we get out of here?" she said, thumping the glass. The moon was melting, giving way to the sun.

Bjorn slid open the door of a tall cabinet. Inside were stacks of cardboard boxes bearing the image of the dog. One box wasn't sealed. It contained the familiar flasks.

"The elevator only goes down. But where's the toilet?" Bjorn looked around.

"You need to go?" Olga grinned nervously.

Bjorn saw four narrow doors in the corner. He opened them and peeked inside. Behind two of the doors were toilets. The third was a small cabinet stuffed with packs of labels for the flasks. The fourth contained mops, a stepladder, and plastic buckets.

"Nothing!" Bjorn slammed the door angrily. Then he looked up, and suddenly stopped. There was a large air duct on the ceiling above the door. The wide silver-gray pipe branched in the middle, ending in two intake vents.

"Wait a second…" Bjorn grabbed the stepladder. He opened it, climbed up, and hit the pipe hard with his massive fist.

The silvery metal bent under the impact.

"Wow!" said Olga. "I get it! I see!"

She grabbed one of the mops, unscrewed the handle, and tossed it to Bjorn.

"Here!"

Bjorn pounded on the pipe and brought it down to his level; then he worked the long mop handle into the gap between the sections and yanked as hard as he could. The pipe sections came apart easily. Metal crashed down.

"You don't get claustrophobic, do you?" Bjorn asked, jumping off the stepladder.

"I don't know… I used to be afraid of heights…"

"This… isn't very high."

He picked Olga up, lifted her like a feather onto the ladder, gave her a push—and she crawled into the duct.

"How is it in there?" he asked, glancing at the window.

"Dark," Olga replied from the duct. "Come on up!"

She crawled ahead cautiously.

Bjorn climbed the ladder and slid into the duct after Olga. The support bracket holding the duct shook under their weight but held fast. Olga crawled ahead. The vent was wide and warm. There was no air moving in it—most likely it was used only during work hours to ventilate the workshop. It was stuffy. So far, there was only darkness ahead. Olga crawled carefully forward. Bjorn crawled after her.

"Darkness...but we should, should..." Olga muttered in fright, trying to calm herself. "Lyktstolpen...you should have gone in first...I mean, you're Lyktstolpen, so...you've...you've...got a light bulb in your head..."

"What?" Bjorn asked in a loud whisper.

"Nothing—so far!" she replied.

He squeezed her ankle encouragingly.

Olga had crawled about fifteen meters when the duct veered left and came to a small grate though which a dim light entered. She cautiously brought her face closer to the grate. She could see a large room, crammed with tall wooden crates prepared for shipping. All of them were stamped with the dog's head logo. In the middle of the room were two forklifts.

"Crates, and inside—boxes, and in them—little bottles..." Olga thought automatically, looking around the room, "and in the bottles—juice...juice from bitches' paws...how wonderful..."

Bjorn crawled up from behind, his hand touching Olga's legs.

"What's there?" he whispered.

"A warehouse of some kind."

"Any people?"

"No. We've got to break the grate."

"Then we'll have to switch places," he said, beginning to turn around.

Olga wiggled backward. Bjorn tried to crawl over her. They were squeezed tight, surrounded by warm metal. Bjorn's massive chin poked Olga's chest. He tried to wriggle his large body free.

"We're getting stuck!" Olga panicked and squirmed against Bjorn. "Come on, Lyktstolpen...come on!"

Bjorn twisted and struggled, his weight making the duct shake. Olga groaned and, writhing like a worm, slithered back. Bjorn stretched toward the grate, grabbing it with his hands, straining all his muscles.

Suddenly Bjorn froze. He heard people speaking Chinese. Olga heard them too. She stopped dead between Bjorn's legs. Bjorn saw two Chinese workers in orange uniforms. Chatting together, they strolled across the room and stopped near the forklifts. They went on talking, and then one of them left. The other made a tour of the room while he inspected the crates.

"He's looking for us," Bjorn thought. "Or maybe—he's just looking?"

The man examined the entire room, climbed into a forklift, and turned it on. He drove over to a crate, loaded and lifted it, and carried it out of the room. Just then the duct began to buzz silently. Air poured through the grate onto Bjorn's face: the air intake had started up.

"Jeez...They start their work day early..." Olga whispered.

The air flowed through the duct, blowing on their overheated bodies. The forklift returned empty, picked up another crate, and left again.

"When he's taken out seven more crates he'll be right under me," thought Bjorn. "Wait till then, break the grate, jump down, and attack..."

Olga touched Bjorn's hand. He squeezed back and lifted a finger: hold on! She nodded, and squeezed his wrist in reply. With his face pressed to the grate, Bjorn followed the forklift's progress. It moved at a snail's pace, removing crate after crate. The first. Second. Third. Fourth. "Dislodging a thin grate held by four screws isn't hard," Bjorn thought..."You just have to wait." The fifth crate. The sixth. Bjorn readied himself, pressing his palms again the grate. Sensing what he was about to do, Olga tensed, carefully raising her knees. Preparing for the last second, Bjorn closed his eyes.

Suddenly, voices could be heard: Chinese spoken very fast. He opened his eyes: guards dressed in blue with machine guns ran into the room. They were followed by the same worker in orange and a blond European wearing a light suit. He issued a command in Chinese, and Bjorn recognized him. It was Michael Laird.

"Oh, damnit..." Bjorn whispered.

"What is it?" Olga whispered.

"It's bad, very bad..." Bjorn answered in barely audible Swedish, his lips pressed against the grate. "Very, very bad..."

"What?" Olga tugged on his leg.

Laird lifted his attentive face. His cold gaze fastened on the grating. A nasty grin stretched across his handsome lips. He pointed at the duct.

Bjorn shrank back, but it was too late. He began to retreat, turning over on his back and pushing Olga with his huge feet.

"Back! Back!"

"What? Where?"

Olga rolled around in the duct.

"Back, back!" His feet shoved hard.

Olga wriggled backward. Below, something clanked a couple of times, apparently settling in place. Bjorn kept on moving away from the grate, pushing Olga. His movement made the duct sway.

"Faster, faster!"

A roar came from below, followed by a buzz. Four thick, long drills, piercing the metal like paper, drilled into Bjorn and Olga's bodies. Olga screamed wildly. One of the drills entered her knee, another passed easily through her palm. The third entered Bjorn's stomach, the fourth slipped along his hips, slicing through them. Bjorn bellowed in pain, trying to get away from the drills. Olga couldn't stop screaming. Their bodies jerked in the air duct. The fifth drill went into Bjorn's chest, the sixth into his leg, the seventh and eighth entered Olga's shoulder and chin. Olga's cries turned to choking sounds, and the drills whined, digging deep into their flesh. Blood sprayed from their twitching bodies, filling the air duct.

"The Brothers of the Light don't drink sake!!!" Michael Laird's voice thundered down the duct.

Bjorn shuddered.

And opened his eyes.

Below, the forklift was approaching the eighth crate. Bjorn flattened himself against the grate. The screws cracked. The forklift picked up the crate. Bjorn rammed the grate down. Three screws flew out of their holes; the grating hung on a single screw. Bjorn pushed off of Olga with his feet and tumbled out of the duct, falling chest-first on the roof of the forklift. Roaring with pain, he grabbed the roof by its edge and swung himself down to the floor. The Chinese driver gaped at the white-haired giant who had fallen from the ceiling. He let go of the controls to reach for the can of Mace attached to his belt, but he wasn't fast enough: a pale fist as big as his head punched out his squinty eyes, propelling him from the driver's cabin. Bjorn limped as quickly as he could over to the fallen driver, lifted his arm, but didn't hit him. The driver lay motionless with an expression of surprise on his slack lips. Bjorn straightened up.

"Olga!"

She stuck her head out of the duct.

"Jump!"

Olga tumbled awkwardly over the edge of the air duct and fell shrieking into Bjorn's arms. He caught her like a doll and gently set her on her feet. She glanced at the driver lying on the floor. Blood trickled from his nose.

"...You did that?"

Bjorn nodded and limped toward the door.

"What's wrong?" said Olga, running after him.

"I bumped my knee...It's nothing."

"You know how to fight?"

"No. My brother knew how..."

The door out was next to the warehouse entry, and they looked in. In the distance, near the crates, Chinese workers were pottering about. The morning radio could be heard. Olga cautiously opened the other door: only an empty hallway.

"We need to get to the first floor." Bjorn stepped into the hallway. "There's got to be a staircase somewhere."

"Or an elevator..." Olga muttered.

They moved along the hallway, which turned to the right, then forked. At the fork they stopped. Red characters and an arrow pointed right.

"This way!" Olga decided, running ahead.

Bjorn limped along behind. Voices approached. They rushed back and took the left turn. Thankfully the hallway turned left again—and led right back into the very same warehouse with the open gates. Around the corner, though, close to the gates, Olga noticed a small elevator door and indicated it to Bjorn with her eyes. He gave her a thumbs-up.

When the workers turned back toward their crates Bjorn and Olga rushed to the elevator. They pressed the button. The car was on the fourteenth floor, coming down. An outcry arose in the warehouse. Olga and Bjorn heard the workers chattering loudly in Chinese. They must have discovered their unconscious comrade.

"Damn . . ." Bjorn muttered.

Olga pressed her cheek against the elevator's steel door.

"Come on, come on sweetie . . ."

8, 7, 6 . . .

The workers' voices came nearer. They were headed for the entry. Bjorn and Olga froze.

5, 4, 3, 2 . . .

Around the corner they could see two worried workers talking in Chinese.

The elevator stopped, and the doors opened on a narrow car containing two Chinese in white rather than orange uniforms. With a shout, the workers from the warehouse suddenly caught sight of Bjorn and Olga. The men in white stared, uncomprehending. Bjorn barged into the elevator, brandishing his fists. Olga squeezed in behind and fumbled for the buttons. Men in orange ran shouting after them. Olga pressed a button and the doors began to close. Bjorn slugged away at the white-uniformed Chinese, while the ones in orange raced up and grabbed Olga's T-shirt. Screaming, Olga elbowed them; her T-shirt ripped, she kicked, the shirt tore, the doors shut, and the elevator moved upward. Bjorn was hammering the guards in white so hard that the elevator shook. Thrusting her fist past Bjorn's, Olga struck them too, making contact a couple of times. Bjorn roared and the Chinese fought back silently.

"King Kong!" flashed through Olga's head.

A blow sounded, another, a third. Both Chinese sank to the floor.

Breathing heavily, Bjorn examined the elevator buttons. His expression was completely wild, not at all normal. His cheek was scratched, and a drop of blood was quivering on it.

"Where? Which way?" he muttered, trying to understand the direction the elevator was heading in.

"Up." With a trembling finger Olga wiped the drop of blood from his cheek.

A nervous shiver ran the length of Olga's spine. Her teeth chattered.

"Fifth, sixth . . . damn it! Where's it going?" Bjorn pushed a button. The elevator continued upward.

Olga was shaking. Standing in her torn T-shirt, she held herself tightly by the elbows.

"What is it?" Bjorn was upset, looking at her.

"N-n-nothing . . ." her teeth clacked. "Goosebumps . . ."

Bjorn pressed the button again. The elevator kept on going up.

9, 10, 11, 12 . . .

The Chinese sitting in the corner hiccoughed and stirred weakly.

13, 14. The elevator stopped. The door opened. A spacious hall with several elevator doors spread before them, lit by a wide window through which Guangzhou could be seen awakening beneath the rising sun. Bjorn and Olga leapt out of the elevator. Bjorn pressed the lowest button to send the unconscious guys in white uniforms down to the ones in orange, and the elevator doors slid shut. There were five elevators in the hall—four small ones, including the one they'd arrived on, and a large one bearing an emblem on its silvery-blue doors: two Ice hammers flanking a crimson heart. There was no other way in or out.

"Down, down!" Olga dashed to one of the smaller elevators. It began to hum quietly. 1, 2, then 3 lit up.

The elevator was coming up.

Bjorn went to another one. It too started upward. The third also. Three elevators were quickly rising.

"They're coming after us," Bjorn realized, looking at the floor numbers.

Olga pressed the wide button of the large elevator. It opened: it was spacious, super contemporary, clad in silvery light-blue mirrors. The two of them entered. There were only two buttons on the panel: one blue and one red. Bjorn pushed the red button—the elevator didn't move. He pushed the blue one—the doors closed and the car rose smoothly.

"Up? Why are we going up again?!" Olga angrily slammed her fist against the button panel.

Shrugging his powerful shoulders hopelessly, Bjorn stood staring vacantly at the buttons. There was no floor indicator in the cabin. The elevator kept going up and up. Finally it stopped. The doors opened. Olga and Bjorn froze: right in front of the elevator stood Michael Laird with a trim gray-haired older man. They were surrounded by four brawny blonds.

"Thank the Light!" said Laird with a smile. "I knew you'd make it."

Olga and Bjorn stared at him, nonplussed. Bjorn came to first. He hit the red button. But the elevator didn't budge.

"There's no way back!" Laird's impassive smile spread.

One of the strong blond men lifted a long-barreled gun. Quickly and silently, he shot twice. Clutching their chests, Bjorn and Olga fell back onto the silvery floor of the elevator cabin. The blonds pulled them out and placed them on a greenish-blue rug at the feet of Laird and the old man.

"Two," Laird spoke. "You *knew*, Shua."

"No, Ev, I didn't *know*. It's just that the Brotherhood needs two part-hammereds *now*."

"Only two." Laird nodded in agreement and shuddered. "The power of the Light tames the meat."

"The power of the Light moves the meat aside and brings Eternity nearer, Brother Ev," the old man said quietly.

Laird began to tremble. His face took on a helpless expression.

"Eternity!" His lips grew pale as he spoke the word. "The Eternity of the Light!"

The old man took him by the hand and squeezed.

"Rely on the Ice," he ordered in a voice that was stern and yet at peace.

A Third of a Meat Day

ON OCTOBER 16, 2005, at 18:35, an enormous twelve-deck, blue-and-white cruise ship with a picture of a flaming heart on its massive deckhouse left the port of Hong Kong. Aboard the ship were 2,490 Brothers and Sisters of the Light. They had all been acquired by the Brotherhood in the Country of Ice and over the course of two days had gathered on the vessel. Eight identical ships were already on their way. But not because the brothers and sisters from the Country of Ice turned out to be the most disorganized—simply because Hong Kong was only 160 miles from the site of the Transformation. Other vessels with brothers from other countries were sailing to the secret location by their own routes.

The weather favored the Brotherhood: in Hong Kong it was a gentle, warm autumn, the evening sun illuminated high fluffy clouds; the breeze, which changed directions in the evening, blew softly over the sea. The ship gave four farewell signals and sailed out of the bay on a southwest course. The Brothers and Sisters of the Light preserved their calm on this enormous vessel. The entire crew of the ship consisted of Brothers and Sisters of the Light.

In a spacious stateroom twenty-nine of the Mighty gathered, those who had been protecting the Brotherhood in the Country of Ice. Among them were Uf, Odo, Stam, Efep, Tse, Ma, Bork, No, Amii, and others. All of them sat in comfortable armchairs arranged in squares. The formation of Circles and conversations of the heart were strictly forbidden on the ship: the Brotherhood was preserving heart energy for the Great Transformation. And only two of the twenty-nine—Khram and Gorn—did not sit in chairs but rested in baths made of thick glass. Their weakened, aged bodies were immersed in the milk of high-mountain yaks, mixed with the sperm of young meat machines. Only their faces, emaciated from their Great Labor and lined with countless wrinkles, could be seen above the white surface.

Absolute silence reigned in the stateroom. Each of those present *was preparing* himself, understanding that less than nine hours remained until the Great Transformation.

When the ship reached the open sea and the shore lights disappeared, Khram's eyelids twitched. Immediately two of Khram's devoted assistants—Tbo and Mef—went to her and carefully raised her eyelids. Khram's eyes opened. Tbo pressed a button at the head of the bath—and a tiny, semitransparent microphone slid out. Khram's pale-blue eyes looked around the gathering. Her lips began to move with difficulty, but they parted. Khram sighed deeply. Air came out of her lips. And she said, "Thanks to the Light."

Her weak, barely audible whisper, amplified by the speakers, floated around the stateroom.

"Thanks to the Light!" everyone replied.

No one dared *answer* the great sister with his heart. Each *understood* the importance of what was happening. Each was *sparing* himself and her. Khram was also preserving her powerful heart for the Last Conversation. For that reason the brothers now spoke in the language of meat machines.

"Is everyone here?"

"Everyone, Khram," Tse confirmed.

"I forbid you *to know* yourselves, therefore I am asking you in an alien language."

"We understand you, Khram," Odo answered.

"I want to live until it happens," Khram whispered.

"You will live until then," Uf said with certainty. "And we will all live until then."

"How much longer do we have to wait?"

"A third of the meat's day," answered Genyakhno, who commanded the ship.

"Are there many weak ones?"

"One hundred and forty-six," Bork answered. "On our ship—sixteen."

"Are there any extremely weak ones?"

"There are, Khram. Brothers Oriip, Dlu, and Yuts, and sister San."

"Has everything been done to support them?"

"Everything, Khram."

Khram fell silent, moving her lips. Her eyes were half open. A few long minutes passed. Khram again drew air into her body, and whispered, "How many very young ones?"

"Two."

"Who are they? "

"Brother Khozheti—two months old; brother Moohn—four weeks."

"They need outside support."

"We've taken care of that."

"Who will hold them in the Circle?"

"Two of the part-hammered."

Khram grew thoughtful. She licked her lips carefully.

"Where are they?" she asked in a whistling whisper.

"Here, on the ship," Uf answered.

"I want to see them."

Uf nodded to four of the brothers, who entered the elevator, went down, and after a little while returned, carrying the sleeping bodies of Bjorn and Olga. They were placed on the rug in the center of the stateroom.

Khram set her gaze on them.

"When will they wake up?"

"In four hours," Brother Ev replied.

"Are you certain that they will help us?"

"We are certain, Khram," Uf answered for all of them.

"Will there be others in the Circle besides these?"

"No, only these two."

Khram grew pensive. Then she spoke: "Wake Gorn. We want to *look at* these two."

Tbo and Mef placed their hands on Gorn's head. And soon he opened his eyes. Khram waited for Gorn to wake completely and come to himself. And she cautiously *touched* his heart. Gorn's heart replied. His small body, submerged in the bath, shuddered. His slightly bulging eyes stared at the two sleeping bodies.

Khram and Gorn *began to speak* with the heart.

They *watched* Bjorn and Olga sleeping on the floor. This continued for twenty-seven minutes. Then their hearts *grew silent*. Gorn yawned and shuddered, rippling on the milky surface around his head, and again fell into a deep sleep.

Khram exhaled and inhaled carefully.

"Some water!" she requested.

Tbo held a porcelain drinking vessel with warm spring water, sweetened with the honey of wild Altai bees. Khram took two small sips, then breathed deeply. She swallowed some more. Tbo carefully wet her ancient lips.

"We *saw* these two," Khram declared. "They will help the Circle. Leave them here."

Everyone stirred in relief.

"Brother Ev didn't collect the part-hammered in vain," Stam spoke up. "He *knew*."

"They are a layer between us and the meat machines," sounded Khram's whisper, amplified by the speakers. "Only they are capable of providing the last *outside* assistance."

"Because there is a *longing* for the Light in them," Tse nodded.

"Even though they don't know it!" Odo shook his thick beard.

"That's right, they don't know it," Khram said. "Therefore they will help us."

"These two were the best of all the part-hammered that brother Ev gathered," Uf told them. "When they were given the opportunity to escape, they themselves came upward, to the Throne."

"I *know*," Khram whispered quietly, and closed her eyes.

Toward the Light

OLGA CAME to from someone's awkward touch. Only one person could caress her face and head so clumsily. She opened her eyes. Bjorn, leaning over her, was stroking her with his enormous hands. Because of Bjorn's wide, shovel-like palms, she could barely see the ceiling of light wood with its opaque light fixtures.

"How are you?" Bjorn asked.

She moved a bit, pulled up her legs, sat up, and said, "Okay…"

Bjorn held her by her shoulders. Olga looked around: she was in a wide room with a low ceiling and round dark windows. Blond men and women sat in armchairs all around. There were two transparent bathtubs, filled with something white. Milk? Above the milk the faces of two people who were sleeping—or dead—could be seen: an old woman and some kind of Lilliputian. The blonds looked silently at Olga. She remembered everything. And understood.

"Brothers of the Light," her lips spoke.

"Brothers of the Light." Bjorn nodded.

"Brothers of the Light!" Sister Tse spoke up.

"I thought they killed us," Olga muttered.

Bjorn was tense and silent as he looked around.

Suddenly sister Tse stood up, walked over, kneeled, and took Bjorn's and Olga's hands into her small but powerful hands.

"Don't be afraid of us," she said calmly.

Olga and Bjorn stared straight at Tse.

"We are with you. And you are with us," Tse said.

Her eyes, dark blue with a barely noticeable dark brown halo, shone in anticipation of something very important, something that would *not fit* inside her. Bjorn was the first to *feel* this. He grew uncomfortable.

"Where are we?" Olga asked.

"On a ship."

"Which … one?" said Bjorn, losing his composure.

"The one sailing to Happiness."

Olga had already come to: she remembered the Ham, the dead bitches, the escape, and the trap set at the top of the skyscraper. Freeing her hand, she returned Tse's gaze, planning to say something lamely ironic, but in the same *instant* she suddenly felt that Tse was telling the *truth*. And stopped, surprised at herself.

"To what … happiness?" Bjorn muttered tensely.

"To yours?" Olga managed to squeeze out the question as she began to shake.

"There is no such thing as 'ours' and 'yours': Happiness is always one! One for everyone."

And suddenly all the people sitting in the armchairs rose, approached, kneeled, stretched out their arms, and touched Bjorn and Olga.

"Happiness is always one!" Tse repeated and added: "Happiness—is the Light!"

"Happiness—is the Light!" they all said at once.

Bjorn and Olga began to tremble.

"We were all moving toward the Light," Tse continued. "We, and you. But we knew where and toward what we were heading; you didn't know this. But you felt it. Unconsciously, you reached for the Light for thousands of years. You wanted it. You invented gods for yourselves. Prayed to the Creator. Hoped that he would resurrect you from the dead. But you didn't know that the Creator was close by you. You didn't know the Way. We show you the Way. And now we—and you—are on the Way. There is no road back. And only a very small bit remains . . ."

Tse pronounced the last words with a tremor, *restraining* her heart. Everyone else gathered there also shuddered. An attack of trembling seized Bjorn and Olga. They began to shake so strongly that their teeth clattered. The arms of the Brothers and Sisters of the Light embraced their bodies.

"You will be with us at the Last Hour," said Tse, squeezing Bjorn's and Olga's fingers.

"You will help us. So that Happiness will arrive!" the others said.

Tears flowed from Bjorn's and Olga's eyes. They began to sob. And for the first time during the ordeal of these months they suddenly felt *very* good. *So* good, the kind of good that happens only in childhood, when your family, who loves, protects, and cares for you, is nearby. Soaked with tears, they began to kiss the hands of the Brother and Sisters of the Light, forgetting their past, forgetting their torment and fears, forgetting the suffering and waiting, forgetting the horrifying life of the last months. The brothers' and sisters' hands were nearby. The brothers and sisters who led them to Happiness, to the Light.

"We are with you," Tse repeated. "You are with us . . ."

Olga and Bjorn cried: The brothers and sisters were with them! Loneliness was over. Over once and for all! And it all turned out to be *so* simple! Simple, like the Light. After all, it shines for all! And nothing else is needed. Only to make it together with everyone to Happiness. To the Light . . .

An hour passed.

Bjorn and Olga sat in the center of the stateroom surrounded by Brothers and Sisters of the Light. Their tears gradually diminished, and the trembling left their bodies. Calm settled in. A feeling of kinship and belonging to the Great EVENT came over them. Bjorn and Olga felt *so* good and peaceful that they were afraid to scare off the new feeling that had suddenly descended on them like a star.

They *waited* along with everyone.

Soon everyone felt the vessel shudder slightly. The huge ship had slowed down, and after a number of smooth maneuvers, it stopped.

"It's time!" said Uf.

And everyone began to stir. And the Great Event toward which the Brotherhood had striven all these seventy-seven years, from the moment when brother Bro found the Ice, resounded in each of the Brothers and Sisters of the Light. Khram and Gorn came to and stirred in their baths. They were taken out, dried off, wrapped in warm blankets, and carried. The Mighty of heart began to leave the stateroom. Khram and Gorn were sent below on the elevator; the rest began to descend the staircase. Bjorn and Olga followed them. The lower deck was filled to the brim. Brothers and sisters stood in expectation, letting the old and young go first. Olga and Bjorn were in the crowd. But sister Tse was nearby, and her hands touched Bjorn's and Olga's bodies encouragingly.

The exodus from the ship onto the shore took nearly an hour and a half. The time had come, and Olga's and Bjorn's bare feet walked across a wide gangway and stepped onto a concrete pier. It stretched from the island into the sea, a long strip illuminated by spotlights. Eight identical piers branched off like concrete rays from the circle-shaped island that the Brotherhood had purchased eight years earlier and outfitted for the Great Transformation. Holding hands, Bjorn and Olga walked in the stream of Brothers and Sisters of the Light, maintaining absolute silence. The only noise was the rustling of clothes and the gentle slapping of the night tide against the piers. The sparkling stars of the night sky spread out above them. A warm night breeze blew around them. Olga glanced to the left—there, in the distance, an identical large, illuminated white ship was moored to an identical pier. Illuminated by spotlights, an unending flow of Brothers and Sisters of the Light also proceeded along that pier. They were moving toward the island. Bjorn glanced to the right—there, in the distance, another white ship was moored; there was also a pier and also a stream of brothers and sisters. A *sweet* shiver passed through Bjorn's and Olga's bodies. They *felt* that very soon the most Secret, Great, and Joyous Event would occur. And that they would have to wait only a *very* short time. A shiver of anticipation possessed them. And as though sensing this, sister Tse, who walked behind them, placed her palms on their backs. Peace radiated from these palms. Her palms calmed and directed them.

"There is no longer any hurry!" Tse whispered.

Bjorn and Olga *understood*.

The pier stretched toward the island. The night island swam up, came closer. The pier gradually turned into a bridge that slowly rose and widened. The nearly ten-kilometer-round island had been a small mountain rising from the sea. The Brotherhood had cut off the mountain peak, leaving only its base. A sturdy bridge, supported by concrete piers, led to the leveled base. Nine such bridges led the Brotherhood to the island, to the Last Mooring. The 23,000 silently walked toward the last goal. Searchlights illuminated the bridges. But the island itself lay in darkness ahead of them. Olga and Bjorn moved along with the crowd, counting the steps to themselves. Adults and children, old people and adolescents, men and women walked nearby. They pushed carriages with the very old and the sick, they carried small children. Everyone walked in silence. The rustling of clothes and the noise of the steps merged in a single unbroken sound that intoxicated Bjorn and Olga. As before, they felt *very* good. They were walking with their kin. And they had so many kinsmen!

Finally the bridge touched the island. Bjorn and Olga set foot on the earth of the island, which was covered in white marble. The entire island was a perfectly even plaza, covered with the whitest, finest marble on Earth. As soon as the Brothers and Sisters of the Light stepped onto this marble, sensors hidden in it came to life, and around the giant Circle 23,000 small marble lamps lit up in a dim blue light. Each lamp was a place in the Circle. There were 23,000 places in the Last, Most Important Circle of the Brotherhood. A stir went through the crowd of arrivals from the Country of Ice; everyone began undressing, throwing aside the unnecessary clothes of meat machines. Having undressed to their bare skin, each of them walked to the Circle and stood on the spot shown by the lamp. Bjorn and Olga began to undress. They felt so good and calm that they didn't want to speak at all: words were powerless to express what had filled their hearts over the last few hours. They had hardly finished undressing when familiar small palms touched their backs. They turned. Tse stood nearby, naked; with her, also naked, were the twin sisters Ak and Skeye. Each of them pressed an infant to her breast. These were the smallest brothers of the 23,000—two-month-old Khozheti and four-week-old Moohn. Wordlessly, the sisters handed the infants to Olga and Bjorn. And without a single word they took the defenseless and helpless bodies of the brothers. The infants' chests had been hammered; the Brotherhood had acquired them very recently—the Light of old brothers and sisters had resettled in them: ninety-year-old brother Ezhor and eighty-three-year-old sister Mart. The infants slept, breathing heavily, wheezing in their sleep.

"You must hold them in the Circle," Tse whispered. "None of *ours* can do this, because each must be in his place. This will be your Great Assistance to the Brotherhood."

"We'll do everything!" Olga's lips whispered.

"We will help!" Bjorn whispered, tenderly holding Khozheti on his chest.

Tse turned and vanished into the crowd, each searching for the right place. Although no one had any numbers or personal places, in the Last Circle each stood wherever his bare feet took him. Across nine bridges from nine ships arriving from nine ports of the world, Brothers and Sisters of the Light hurried to the Circle. The crowd of naked bodies swelled, spreading out around the Circle. More and more brothers and sisters took their places. Each one who stood on a lamp was instantly illuminated by its dim bluish light. More and more of these glowing figures appeared in the dark of the Circle. And the Great Circle gradually took shape.

Bjorn and Olga moved toward the Circle, holding the heavily breathing infants to their chests. The honor of the Great Assistance had fallen to them. They understood this with each cell of their bodies. They had to help the Brotherhood, support the tiniest brothers in the Great Circle, not let them leave life until the Circle began to speak in the language of the Light. With the greatest caution, Bjorn and Olga moved among the sea of undressed bodies. The warm infants snuffled, breathing with difficulty in their arms. The Circle was being built.

Under the southern night sky faint stars and a slim sickle moon appeared; the glowing, naked figures arose and united, assuming the shape, forming the Great Last Circle of the Brotherhood. The old sat down or kneeled, stretching their trembling arms to those standing nearby. The young and strong immediately held their hands, giving them strength and hope. Naked young children stood, illuminated by the bluish light, stretching their slim hands to the adults standing nearby. Khram was placed between Uf and Shua; Gorn between Stam and Atrii. The hands of the Mighty took the emaciated, flaccid skin of the hands of those who had once seen the entire Brotherhood and helped to gather it together. Strong, gray-bearded Odo squeezed the hand of five-year-old Samsp and Fow, wise Stsefog held twelve-year-old Bti and eighty-year-old Shma, thundering Lavu took the hands of the twins Ak and Skeye, Merog stood next to Obu, Bork with Rim, Mokho with Ural, Diar with Irei and Rom, Mir with Kharo and Ip, Eko with Ar.

Bjorn and Olga walked around the Circle carefully, avoiding the sitting and standing.

"He's so little and defenseless—his heart beats in such a fragile, wounded chest, his breathing is so heavy…I've got to carry him, carry him to his place…warm him against my chest with my warmth…defend him with my breath." The words throbbed in Olga's head.

"Help, help everyone with anything I can…be peaceful, my tiny little brother…I will help you…my body, my heat, my will shall help you. I'll hold you and protect you ... I'm strong, I'll be able to ... my blood, my muscles, my bones will serve as a support, lean on them ... lean on them ..." Thoughts flared in Bjorn's brain.

They walked and walked around the Circle.

And suddenly in front of them hands rose up: This way! They were being called. Bjorn and Olga went. Sister Tse stood near two empty spaces. Nearby in the Circle stood Ev and Aub. The three of them had kept places for Bjorn and Olga.

"Stand with us," whispered Tse.

She trembled slightly.

Bjorn took his place on the left side of Tse, Olga on the right. The bluish light shone from below on Bjorn's and Olga's naked bodies. They froze in place, holding the infants.

The words "good and peaceful ... right and inevitable ... true and irreversible" were pounding in Olga's temples.

"Help and defend ... carry out and withstand ... begin and complete" pounded in Bjorn's temples.

The Circle was gathering. The naked, semi-illuminated crowd was dispersing, disappearing and being absorbed by the Circle. The harmonious, perfect Circle swallowed the chaotic crowd. The chaos of searching bodies was replaced by the calm of places found: the figures lit with blue stood still, becoming immobile. Fewer and fewer searchers remained.

Bjorn and Olga stood in their places, holding the smallest to their chests and staring in a trance at the bluish Circle that extended far out on the island, stretching to the night horizon in a scarcely discernable blue thread and smoothly returning, standing next to them again in the immobile figures of brothers and sisters.

Time seemed to be compressed: each moment could become the last.

There were no more searchers near them. On the right everything was smooth and clean. It was only on the left that a few lone bodies ran about, searching for their place. But then everyone on the left settled down as well, distributed themselves, and calmed down. Some people's spines sparkled in the distance; shadows flickered on the marble. And everything grew quiet, motionless.

Bjorn and Olga stayed completely still.

Terribly long minutes passed . . .

Everything grew COMPLETELY quiet.

The Circle closed.

Absolute silence hung over the island. Even the tide couldn't be heard here. The warm night breeze died down.

Bjorn and Olga were still. Their bodies seemed to have turned to stone in the bluish light. They stopped breathing. For they *heard* the Earth. It stopped in anticipation. The Circle had gathered. The Earth lay on all sides of the Circle. The stars shone over the Circle.

Everything was ready.

And suddenly Sister Tse's broken whisper sounded.

"Turn them. Heart to the center . . . of the Circle . . ."

Bjorn and Olga shuddered and came to. They understood what was wanted of them. In the Circle everyone stood and sat facing the center. Only the two tiny ones slept, pressing their faces to Bjorn and Olga, turning away from the Circle. Olga and Bjorn gently turned them, holding the infants' delicate backs to their chests.

And suddenly arms stretched out, from the left and the right. But not to hold hands with Bjorn and Olga. The hands of Tse, Ev, and Aub carefully held the tiny fingers of the infants. Bjorn's and Olga's hands were needed to hold the tiny ones.

The Great Last Circle was ready.

And an invisible, powerful, irreversible wave coursed along it: 23,000 hearts, which had been restraining, resigning themselves all these last days and nights, let themselves *go*.

And the Great Last Circle began to speak.

And 23,000 began to speak for the last time.

Bjorn and Olga froze again. A rapturous terror embraced them. They felt that the Circle *had begun to speak*.

The hearts of Khram and Gorn, Uf and Odo, Shua and Efep, Stam and Atrii *spoke*. For the last time the hearts of Ak, Dke, Bork, Rim, Mokho, Ural, Ikos, and Ar *spoke*. And the tiny, entirely inexperienced hearts of Khozheti and Moohn also *spoke*. Their little bodies quivered in the hands of Bjorn and Olga as the invisible wave passed through them.

And the Circle filled with Words of the Light.
And the secret Words flowed through the Circle.
And the Words passed their judgment.
And they corrected the Great Mistake of the Light.
And the brothers and sisters *spoke* in the language of the Light.
And 23 times they *spoke*.
And the last, 23rd Word was *uttered*.
And the Earth shuddered.

God

THE LIGHT blinded Olga.

She squinted. And opened her eyes again: the rising sun shone on the horizon.

Olga lifted her head with great difficulty: she was lying on her back. She stirred. Each movement—hard, excruciating, as though after long years of hard labor. Her head felt heavy and empty inside . . . she pressed her palms against the cool stone. Squinting from the sun in her eyes, she began to rise. Suddenly she froze: on her chest lay an infant. He was dead. Olga stared at him, confused. The infant lay between her breasts. The rising sun illuminated his small, blue body. On his tiny chest was a dark spot of dried blood and a large bruise. Olga looked at the infant. He was cold. And recalled a wax doll. On the infant's head were thin, fair hairs. The morning breeze stirred it.

Olga tore her gaze away from the dead child and looked around. She lay naked on white marble that stretched all the way to the horizon of the rising sun. And close by . . . lay the Brothers and Sisters of the Light. They lay flat on their backs, motionless.

Olga took the child off her chest and placed it on the marble. Moving was incredibly hard; her entire body hurt. She rose up on her knees, braced her legs, and stood up.

The entire huge Circle in which the Brotherhood had stood during the night now lay on the marble. Fair-haired men and women lay flat on their backs, their arms stretched out at their sides. The row moved smoothly along a parabola into the distance, toward the horizon of the rising sun, and, describing an enormous circle, returned again to Olga. The first in this circle of bodies was a young man and a middle-aged woman with short reddish hair. The very one who had directed them yesterday, told them where to stand and what to do... now she lay in motionless repose on the marble. The woman's mouth was open; her face was frozen in a convulsion of suffering; her eyes were half open. Swaying, Olga leaned over and took the woman's hand. Her hand was cold. Olga placed her fingers on the woman's neck. Her fingers touched lifeless, cool flesh. The woman was dead. Her half-open eyes stared at the clear blue sky.

Olga turned her gaze to the right. There lay a young man. She recognized him: Michael Laird. The very one who had met them in Guangzhou, who had spoken about the Brotherhood, who had given them drugged sake to drink. The one who had met them at the elevator at the top of the skyscraper.

Now he lay naked on the marble, his arms flung out. His dark-blue eyes were half open. Olga touched Laird's hand: it was cold, lifeless. The expression on his face was pitiful.

Olga straightened up with a moan. She took one step, then another, then a third.

Next to Laird lay a stout blond woman. Her fingers were squeezing Laird's hand. Olga walked over, touched her next: dead. The woman's other hand held the hand of an old man. His head was arched back, his sharp Adam's apple stuck out under his flaccid skin, his toothless mouth was slightly open, his faded blue eyes stared tensely at the sky. The old man was also dead. And his neighbor, a teenage girl, was also dead and also looked at the blue sky.

Stepping back and swaying, Olga moved along the Circle.

All the brothers and sisters lay on their backs, arms spread out on both their sides, most still squeezing the hand of their neighbor.

Olga walked over and touched their bodies. Her fingers found only dead, cooling flesh. After a few dozen steps, Olga stopped. And she understood that in this enormous circle, no one was alive.

Her memory finally returned: Being shot with a tranquilizer, the ship, the brothers, the exodus, the naked crowd, the rapture and the spell, the anticipation of a great miracle, the blue circle, the infant on her chest, Bjorn.

Bjorn!

She looked around. The dead lay all around her. Olga opened her mouth, moved her dry, mute tongue. Her tongue could barely move.

"B...b...jorn," she said with the very greatest difficulty, and went back to her place in the circle.

It was immediately recognizable—a gap in the even row of corpses, the only violation of order. Bjorn lay next to the same red-headed woman: large, naked, with long, strong legs. His left hand was raised up, his right covered the small body of the dead child who rested on his chest. Bjorn's eyes were closed. But the blue eyes of the infant were staring up, the tiny mouth was half open in a questioning look.

"You...ou..." Olga kneeled down and crawled over to Bjorn, taking his hand in hers.

His hand was cool.

"You...ou...ou..." she said in a wheezy stutter. "You...ou... ou, you..."

He lay immobile, like a throne for the dead infant who looked questioningly at the sky.

"It-i-i-i-t-t-s," Olga whispered. "You...ou...ou...ou..."

With a limp, unwilling hand she beat him on the shoulder.

The Swede didn't move.

"You..."

Bjorn continued to lie there motionless.

Sniffling and shaking, she lifted his eyelid. The familiar blue eye lay under it. And that eye jerked. The eyelid slipped from under the finger and closed. Opened. Bjorn blinked.

Moaning weakly, Olga embraced him. But something cold hindered the embrace. She had a difficult time pushing the corpse of the child from under Bjorn's arm. The hard little body fell helplessly face-down on the marble, hitting its lifeless little head.

Olga wheezed and shook on Bjorn's awakening chest, touching his body with weak hands. He moved, moaned, and stretched his legs. Finally he saw her. His dried lips tried to open, in an attempt to say something. But all that came out from his lips was a weak hiss.

"Kh...h...h...a?" he whispered, and tried to lift himself.

But Olga shook, embracing him and pressing him to the marble.

"Whaaaat?" He turned under her.

Pulling herself away with incredible difficulty, she took his head and tried to raise it.

He sat up.

"This..." With a trembling hand she pointed to the bodies lying near them.

He turned his gaze to the circle of dead. He looked at it for a long time, trying to understand. His head shuddered and shook back and forth. Then he stood up cautiously. The rising sun illuminated his large, stooped figure. Swaying a bit, he took a step. Olga embraced him. They stood still, supporting each other. Bjorn took another step. He stopped. He took another step. And slowly walked along the circle of the dead. Olga moved behind him. Bjorn walked, swaying, looking intently at the bodies lying there. He passed by several, stopped, went over to a woman. He leaned over. Her face, distorted in a grimace of bewilderment, stared at the sky. The glassy gaze of the departed woman reproached the sky for her death and for the death of the Great Brotherhood. Bjorn stood there, swaying back and forth, without the strength to tear himself away from the gaze of those glassy light-blue eyes, and their eternal heart injured. Olga came up to him, embraced him, pressed against him. Together they looked at the dead Brothers and Sisters of the Light.

"Th...th...they..." Bjorn wheezed.

"They..." Olga whispered.

He moved to the side and lowered himself onto the marble. Olga sat down next to him. They sat in silence for a long time, their heads bowed.

The sun rose, gained strength, and blazed.

The white marble plateau of the island sparkled under its rays.

Bjorn stirred, raised his head, and kneeled.

"This..." said Bjorn, shaking and stuttering. "This..."

"What?" Olga whispered.

"Everything."

"What?"

"I mean…all this…" He slapped the palm of his hand on the marble, on Olga's shoulder, on his leg. "All of this here…was done. It was created. Strong. Very. And they…crashed against it. They all crashed."

He suddenly stopped, shaking with emotion. Olga also froze, and stopped breathing.

"But this. This was all…done"—he took a deep breath—"for us."

Olga, leaning on the marble, didn't breathe.

"For us," Bjorn said more resolutely.

And suddenly he smiled feebly.

"For us!" he repeated.

"For us," Olga repeated.

Bjorn stared straight into her eyes.

"And this was all done by God," he declared.

"By God?" Olga asked cautiously.

"By God," he declared.

"By God," Olga answered.

"By God!" he said with certainty.

"By God." Olga exhaled, shaking.

"By God!" he said in a loud voice.

"By God!" Olga gave a nod.

"By God!" he said even louder.

"By God!" Olga nodded again.

"By God!" he shouted out.

"By God," she whispered.

They stopped still, looking into each other's eyes.

"I want to talk to God," Bjorn said.

"So do I," Olga declared.

"I need…need to tell God. A lot of things. I have to talk to Him." Bjorn thought hard. "But how do I do it?"

Olga said nothing.

"How to do it?" Bjorn asked.

"We have to return to people. And ask them."

"What?"

"How to speak with God. Then you can tell Him everything. And I can too."

They grew silent.

A weak sea breeze slipped over their naked bodies.

Bjorn rose from his knees, glanced at the wide bridge piled with clothes and at the enormous light-blue ship, rising above the pier like an iceberg. A flaming crimson heart adorned its deckhouse. But it reminded Bjorn not of the Brotherhood of the Light but of the World of People. Bjorn held out his hand to Olga.

"Let us go!"

Olga stood up and gave him her hand. And they went off, their bare feet stepping across the sun-warmed marble.

OTHER NEW YORK REVIEW CLASSICS*

* For a complete list of titles, visit www.nyrb.com or write to:
Catalog Requests, NYRB, 435 Hudson Street, New York, NY 10014